## "I'M CONVINCED A MAN NAMED AARON PARDELL IS HERE, ON THROMBERG. . . .

"You know your people. Will he come forward of his own accord?" Gail asked.

"No, I'm sure he won't." Forester remained standing, a position aimed not at the anxious troops but at her—as if defending one of his own. *So*, Gail told herself. *He wasn't completely motivated by self-interest.* Such an individual would have been more—straightforward—to work with, if less than trustworthy in a pinch.

"Why?" she asked, truly curious.

"You're Earthers," Forester said, his tone making it clear her question surprised him. "If the welfare of all of us hasn't mattered to you before now—why should the welfare of one?"

"Had you considered that the welfare of this one might have an impact on everyone else on the station?" she suggested carefully, wary of what she might be revealing.

She'd misjudged Forester's intelligence, or maybe life under Thromberg's harsh conditions had honed his instincts. His response was instantaneous. "You're after the Survivor. . . ."

# IN THE COMPANY OF OTHERS

Julie E. Czerneda

**DAW BOOKS, INC.**
DONALD A. WOLLHEIM, FOUNDER
375 Hudson Street, New York, NY 10014
ELIZABETH R. WOLLHEIM
SHEILA E. GILBERT
PUBLISHERS
www.dawbooks.com

First Printing, June, 2001

6  7  8  9

DAW TRADEMARK REGISTERED
U.S. PAT OFF AND FOREIGN COUNTRIES
—MARCA REGISTRADA.
HECHO EN USA

PRINTED IN THE U.S.A.

# ACKNOWLEDGMENTS

Book five. Many endured my anxiety as I ventured into new territory. (Hey, third person can be scary!) I want to thank all of you, especially my tireless, brilliant alpha, Roxanne BB Hubbard. Thank you, Tanya Huff, for help with the First Defense Unit, as well as your "wow!" Thank you, Luis Royo, for leaping into space with me. A wonderful cover! Thank you, Eric Choi, for doing your best to keep that leap accurate. Any errors or flagrant artistic license with physical laws are mine alone. And thanks, Ruth Stuart, for the work your so-called prize entailed.

Thank you, Sheila Gilbert, for letting me run with this. I appreciate your confidence more than I can say, not to mention your keen eye. And, though sadly late, my deepest gratitude to Michael Gilbert, for not only lifting me from the slush, but gracing me with his warmth and humor. I'll always treasure the image of that Canuck Cardboard Box, dented, of course.

Several people trusted me to treat their names well. I've tried. My thanks to the real Susan P. Witts, Raymond Alexander, Josh Malley, Aya Tobo, Nalo (Aisha) Hopkinson, Dianne Peitsch, John (Temujin) Picray, Michael Picray, Chris Taggart, and Isaac Szpindel, as well as Ms. Nicoll's students: Les Baier, Mike Barber, Matt Miller, Neil Johnson, and Jana Miller. For the record, your fictional characters have nothing to do with the real you (except any nice bits).

I've also been overwhelmed by generosity this year, from good wishes to smoked albacore. You know who you are! And thank you, Jihane Billacois, Torbjørn Pettersen, Marcel de

Graaff, Liz Holliday, and David D.U. Brims, for crossing oceans as well as time zones to become friends.

My best wishes and congratulations to two special readers, Ryan Hubbard and Colin Czerneda. The world awaits, gentlemen.

To Jennifer and Scott, who listened seriously to such odd comments from their mother as: "I don't want to stay on the station!" "They made me!" "I'm still on the planet!" Understanding like that is priceless. Thanks!

And Roger? Better than anyone, I know how much you've given of yourself this year. As always, you amaze me.

**Titan University Archives**
**Excerpts from the personal recordings of**
**Chief Terraform Engineer Susan Witts**
**Access Restricted to Clearance AA2 or Higher**

. . . The first seeds arrived today, Raymond. I couldn't resist the urge to touch them. Dry little flecks of nothing that will change a world. The Stage One engineers can keep their comet-shifting launchers. The Stage Twos are welcome to their landform machines and atmosphere purifiers. I'll accomplish as much or more with these. One day, you'll see.

What a relief to be off the transit station! I don't care how big they are, or how modern, they still make me feel like I'm breathing yesterday's air. They're building more all the time. Eventually, there'll be enough stations to handle the passenger and freight traffic to all the systems with terraformed worlds. Glorified bus stops, crammed with customs officials and other bureaucrats. I suppose the stations have their use. But you won't catch me staying in one any longer than I must.

While I'm away, you're going to hear things on the news about me and this project. Don't worry. They'll be good things. We have a lot of support back home. Sol System is more than ready for this—Earth herself is bursting at the seams with people eager to start new lives someplace that isn't a mining dome or station. We're making those places. I'm making those places, Raymond.

I hope you'll be proud of me. I hope you know how hard it was to take you back to Earth and leave you with Grandpa and Grandma. We'll be together again. We both have to be patient.

I know that's hard, too. Back home, some people don't understand why they have to wait for Stage Three, my stage. They want these beautiful worlds now, seeing only that sixteen planets have gained blue skies and flowing water. But they have to wait, just like you and I. Right now, the land is barren. The cycling of nutrients through water, soil, and air hasn't even begun. They'll wait and be glad, Raymond, because I'm going to bring life to these worlds, life that will welcome and nourish the people who come here.

What a dream we're living! Humanity—prosperous, at peace, and ready for adventure—about to expand as never before. Within the next fifty years, the first worlds will receive their immigrants—maybe your children, Raymond—while terraformers like me will have already moved on to the next set of planets ready for Stage Three, then to the next. We'll be like waves sweeping outward until human beings are living on every suitable world we've discovered. Until we own this entire sector of space.

Not that everyone is happy about the terraforming project. You'll hear complaints, I'm sure. Not too loud or too many—it isn't fashionable to question humanity's Great Dream. But you'll read in your history books how this is a relatively new dream for us, and some people still hold to an older one. *Is anybody out there?* We all had it, you know, in one form or another. Since well before I was born, Earth and the system Universities were sending deep-space expeditions in all directions, searching for others like ourselves. True, they found life almost everywhere, but nothing with intelligence.

We're alone, Raymond.

By the time I was old enough to join such an expedition, our mission had changed. If we wanted company, we were going to have to provide our own. We were to locate worlds with the right kind of sun, the right elements, and no indigenous life. Stage One engineers were pelting planets with ice even before we'd finished cataloging all the possibilities. It was . . .

Drat. McNab's on the comm. Sorry, Raymond. I'll add to this later.

Be well, my son.

And think of me out here, making you a brand-new world.

# Prologue

"WHAT about the next world, Jer?" Gabby asked with a careful lack of interest. Her hands were sore, having been clenched together too long under her sweater.

Her companion—business partner, captain of the *Merry Mate II*, and husband—keyed her request into the boards, his stubby fingers sure and quick. From where she sat, Gabby could see the red band staining the readout. "Posted," the man said, the word merely echoing what they both expected. "They're everywhere, Gabby. We'll have to move on."

Gabby opened her throbbing fingers, pressing them over the roundness they guarded. The ship was no place to give birth, not if they wanted a future for their child. She'd known the risks in this search, but they'd all seemed so distant in the beginning, the possibilities so endless. Time had a way of narrowing options. She gazed at her husband, seeing past the shadows of beard and fatigue to his gentle, round-cheeked face, and sighed softly, letting some of her tension out with her breath. "We could try a station—just for a little while."

Jer Pardell winced, then covered the motion with a cough. *As though she wouldn't notice.* But of course she had. They'd been together too long, were so closely linked as a working team that one was forever finishing the sentences the other had begun. "There's no such thing as a 'little while,' stationside," he said almost harshly, but it was his fear for her. "Stations here would strip off our cargo and then make us pay for air rights—might even impound the ship. You know that, Gabby. They're as hard up as the rest of us, since the Quill." He scowled at the red-stained screen, clearing it with a stab. "Stations don't need more people. You heard Raner, last stopover. Earth's clamped down—put holds on all travel vouchers and transports. Who knows how long that will last? And if you try to stay onstation? Head tax, sterilization for permanent residents, dowries to keep immigrant status . . ." he took a deep breath. "We can't live like that. Our child won't live like that. Our baby will be born a citizen, under a sky."

Despite her concern, Gabby's spirits rose a little. *A sky.* The ship, now home and livelihood, was supposed to have been temporary, merely their passage to a glorious new world. They were the lucky ones, to still have this much freedom when most had none. *Jer's doing.* He'd seen the way things were moving and kept independent, protecting them from the increasingly desperate hordes clinging to the stations and fading hopes.

*If you were planet-born,* she reminded herself, as she had so many times in the past months, *you already had a home.* A citizenship no one could strip away.

Gabby rubbed her thumb in little circles against a protuberance firmer than the rest, smiling to herself as the push became harder and then disappeared with a tremble like a laugh. "What are they like?"

"The dreaded Quill?" Jer leaned back in his slingchair, relaxing himself, perhaps recognizing her familiar preoccupation. "Probably three-meter tall giants with googly eyes and long tentacles."

Gabby raised one eyebrow. "That's not what you said yesterday."

He chuckled. "I'll have a new one tomorrow, guaranteed correct, and just as wrong." Speculation was a familiar game; the wilder the better. Not that anyone out here would dare claim to have really met a Quill, face-to-whatever—the mere suspicion of such contact guaranteed a ride out the nearest air lock.

Everyone knew what mattered: the sudden, fragmented reports . . . the stunning news that a non-Terran life-form—the Quill—had accidentally been released on the terraformed worlds . . . the way those reports had ceased almost immediately. Then, worse, the terrible discovery that rescue teams sent to those worlds died as well. Everyone did, whether they landed or hovered at low altitudes.

But what turned a reasonable fear of an unknown danger into outright hysteria was that no one, learned or otherwise, could determine the cause of death. Any bodies recovered by remotes appeared to be perfectly healthy, unblemished by attack or contagion.

It was as if their lives had simply been stopped by the Quill.

Gabby shuddered. "I didn't believe they'd been spread so far. Not to the unfinished worlds. But it must be true—Earth's posted this world! Does this mean the Quill can survive where we can't? What hope's left then, Jer?"

Jer reached across the distance between them and laid his hand on her shoulder. Gabby pressed her cheek against its warmth for a moment. "They can't spread on their own," Jer reminded her. "All the xenos say so, Gabby. They're harmless now."

"Harmless?" she echoed, unable to keep a rare bitterness from her voice. "How can anything be harmless that's ripped the very ground from under us? This was to be a human sector, Jer. More than a hundred new worlds being made ready for us—for our babies—not for those mindless things!"

Jer withdrew his hand, an unhappy look on his face. Gabby understood. They were a team, but, until now, she'd been the one always able to see through a tangled problem to its roots. Her loss of control obviously flustered him as much as it surprised her. Jer didn't know what to say or do to comfort her. *Neither did she*, she sighed to herself.

"There are other worlds," he offered finally. "No one would transport a Quill now. They aren't going to spread any farther, Gabby. Earth was wrong to pull in the deep exploration fleet—everyone says so. There are other worlds out here," he repeated, as if stating it made it so.

She eased herself from the slingchair with a practiced roll; Jer had tried to lighten the gravity in the ship from Earth-normal for her, but Gabby had detected his tampering and insisted her husband restore it. *He trusted her judgment*, Gabby thought, though it was her first child. Not his first, not technically. He'd contributed to three offspring according to his biospecs, born of women who opted for his sperm, probably drawn by his ship-suited smallness and childhood resistance to lar fever. Women were practical that way. *She'd be practical, too.*

"I'll leave you to it, then," she said calmly, stooping for a quick kiss. "Call me if something comes up."

Jer Pardell watched Gabby waddle out the doorway to the passage with a mixture of pride, concern, and a hope he wouldn't let go. *It was different when you saw it happening,* he thought, *when the signs of new life were inextricably wrapped in the one life more important than your own.*

When she was gone, Jer turned back to the console. He called up the nav-tapes, grunting as he reviewed the painstaking course they had followed over the past weeks, threading their way through space that was supposed to belong to humanity and now seemed exclusively the property of something else. He asked for alternatives, checking and rejecting courses based not on trade prospects or fuel, but on the timing of an event beyond their control.

*Nothing.* Jer thought glumly of the stations, built to service the expansion of humanity and now bursting with homeless settlers. He shook his head once, hard. Then he unlocked a set of tapes older than the others—junk really, family records of no interest to anyone else. He began to read.

"There it is." Jer stared at the readout on the system. For once, the numbers added up to Terran norm without the warning slash of red. But the little shiver that ran down Jer's spine did not escape Gabby's sharp eyes, despite the distraction of a birth more impending than either of them had thought. "What's wrong?" she asked.

Jer started at her voice. "It's possible nothing is," he said, eyes still fixed on the numbers which measured atmosphere, moisture, and climate, his voice filled with wonder. "The readout's good—damn good. We don't have to be down long anyway. It's uninhabited."

"Are you sure?"

"The terraform station is empty; vegetation's well in place. This had to be one of the first terraform experiments—it's way off the main lanes. We'll have to let Thromberg Station know as soon as we head back. Instant heroes, Gabby. That'll be us."

Something in Jer's voice lacked conviction. Gabby froze and asked, "What about the Quill? I thought they'd contaminated every terraforming project. That's what Earth claims."

"Guess not, Gabby." His eyes flickered to hers and back. "This world's not posted. No warn-off beacons. Looks to be nothing on it at all beyond the standard. And," this as she uttered a small involuntary sound, "I daresay we're past being fussy, if this impatient child of ours is to be born downworld."

Gabby smiled at him as she eased herself into another position, her smile becoming fixed as another contraction rippled across her abdomen. "Impatient is the word, husband-mine." She studied the readout, then snorted. "What's this? You've named it Pardell? Fool," she said fondly. "We can't afford to apply for naming disposition. If every spacer's brat ended up with a world named for them—"

"I didn't name it." Jer reddened. He didn't seem able to take his eyes from the readout, as though still finding their luck hard to believe. "I went through some old tapes. Family tapes. This *is* Pardell."

"Oh." Gabby eyed her husband with some alarm. He was neither a secretive nor a cunning man, traits she'd always appreciated. "Your grandparents must have had more credits once, then."

"No." Jer wiped his palms on his thighs before looking at her sideways. "Naming privilege."

*After five years*, Gabby thought, *he finally surprises me.* "You've been holding out on me, Jer. You didn't tell me your family was famous."

"My grandmother was a terraform engineer. She was first to live on Pardell—that gave her naming privilege. My father was born here."

Gabby felt a deep glow of rightness. With the exception of Earth, family members were almost never born on the same world. It made all their searching worthwhile. Then a worry trickled through her mind, an inconsistency. "Why didn't we come here first? Why didn't you tell me?"

"My family doesn't talk about my grandmother." Jer didn't met her eyes. "And I didn't know about this world until I looked in the old records. I thought my dad had wiped her tapes, but they were in the database. I don't know if he missed these or somehow wanted me to find them one day."

"I'd think your father would have been proud of her. Terraforming—"

"Gabby . . ." Jer looked at his wife with a confused sadness.

"They fought before I was born. He refused to see her again—even changed our family name. Easy enough, since by then we were living on the *'Mate* and hauling freight to whatever station was being built. So I never met her or knew she was alive back then. Mom told me about her, after my dad passed away. Turned out Grandma was about as big a celebrity as they come. Really famous. Mom didn't want me to find out from a stranger."

All her instincts said to let him stop there, that she really didn't want to know, but Gabby prodded: "Who was she, Jer?"

"Susan Witts. My dad was born Raymond Alexander Witts-Pardell."

"*The* Susan Witts . . . ?" Gabby felt her face harden into fierce lines, but couldn't help that or the way her voice rose. "Susan Witts infected the terraformed worlds with the Quill! All those people, hundreds of thousands trapped on the stations—it's *her* fault we've no place to go! It's *her* fault old Mother Earth won't take any of us back. Do you know how many curse her name every night?"

"They can curse her all they want—she's hardly going to notice. Using her shuttle to give Titan a new crater wasn't exactly an inconspicuous suicide, was it?" He paused. "Susan Witts was never part of my life, Gabby. I didn't see any reason to make her part of ours. Maybe I'd have told you, once we'd started living on a world she'd helped prepare for us. But then the Quill changed all that. She couldn't have known what they'd do, what would happen to all of us, out here. It didn't matter—I couldn't tell you whose grandson I was after that." His defense seemed oddly automatic, as if used to himself so often he no longer heard the words.

An abrupt shift by the baby under her ribs made Gabby swallow what she would have said. It gave her time to look at Jer, to see the new misery aging a face already drawn with stress. A face she knew better than her own by now. "Damn you, Jer," she said, but more kindly. "This is a great time to bring skeletons out of stowage. Anything else I should know before I give birth to your baby? A sister prone to mass murder? Or maybe a great-uncle who believes the universe is carried on the back of a shellfish?"

Jer leaned over to her, burrowing his face past the collar of her coveralls into the warm softness of her neck. His nose was cold. Muffled, he said, "We'll be all right, Gabrielle. I promise."

Gabby rubbed his close-cropped hair fondly with one hand, her other stretched to the controls to replay the information on the world below them. All of a sudden, she needed all the reassurance she could get, unable to believe the work of the woman who had brought them to the brink of disaster could be their salvation now.

Pardell turned out to be pleasant enough, Terran-norm of course, with deep blue seas cut into thirds by narrow, ribbonlike continents. If those continents looked a bit regular, well, everyone knew terraformers had budgets, too. Only one continent showed significant amounts of green; these were patchy areas, as though the terraformers hadn't bothered to finish their work, or as if they'd tried a variety of seeds and only some had survived.

They'd not had time for more than a glance during approach before clouds obscured the view. Gabby sat, silent, licking beads of sweat from her upper lip, She checked the shuttle's fuel as surreptitiously as possible. Jer wouldn't be the first expectant father to have forgotten to top up the tanks. She didn't intend to stay downworld any longer than it would take for the recorders to prove her baby's citizenship. Her eyes glistened with anticipation and her thoughts focused inward again.

They landed without incident. Jer was a careful pilot under any circumstances, and now, with his anxiety for his wife and unborn child, the craft touched the grass-coated ground with a master's gentleness. He grabbed the equipment they'd packed weeks before, eyeing Gabby's pale, determined face with a decidedly suspicious look. "Can you make it?" he asked. "Do you want the grav belt?"

Gabby didn't think this deserved any of the air she was drawing in lightly through her nose, carefully opposing the rhythm of her contractions. She stood and held Jer's arm in an ironlike grip. He helped her to the air lock, managing somehow not to bang her legs with any of the bags he carried. *Not that she'd notice.*

The air was warm, heady with the smell of earth and life. Triumphant, Gabby allowed herself a deep breath and doubled over in pain. Jer dropped everything, put his arm around her shoulders to keep her from falling to her knees. A liquid warmth gushed be-

tween her legs, almost immediately turning into a chill dampness.
"Timing . . . was never better, Jer . . ." she managed to say past
the smile the urgent pain couldn't erase. *At last, at last. . . .*

Jer wiped his hands dry, contented to his bones. His shoulders
ached. His wrist throbbed, especially where Gabby's nails had
broken through the skin. What strength she had! Everything had
happened so quickly. He'd have to watch this on the shuttle's vid
recording when they were back on the ship.

The seed-heavy tips of the grass rustled together with every
breeze, as if to remind them where they were. He drew the fra-
grant air in through his nostrils, trying to remember the last time
he'd been to Earth and if it had smelled this wonderful.

*Welcome to your world*, Jer thought to himself as he sat beside
Gabby, watching her sleep. The tiny life curled between her
breasts squirmed slowly, as if delighted to find no obstructions to
the stretching of his limbs. Jer stroked his son's fist, then was
amazed that such a tight wrapping of fingers could uncurl so
quickly, like a flower opening. He felt love welling up from his
heart, love such as he'd never known before in all his life. Tears
slid unnoticed down his cheeks.

*LOVE.* Jer sobbed, his heart near to breaking with the emotion.
Deep, warm, rich, the future, the past, his eternity, Gabby's
fulfillment—all of this beat through him, against him. The baby's
head teetered and flopped. Jer saw his son's eyes, not quite focused, darkly blue. Another surge of love crushed him. *LOVE.*

Gabby moaned in her sleep. Her eyes flashed opened, stared at
him, pits of terror. *FEAR.* Sharp, ice, futility, ending—her arms
tightened convulsively over the baby. Somehow Jer managed to
free himself from the paralysis locking his muscles long enough
to fling himself over them both. The fear faded back.

There was time for Gabby to meet his eyes, for the knowledge
in hers to break his heart. He drew in the sweetness of her breath,
the wet newness of the baby. Then *LOVE* came again, and
crushed them utterly.

The Quill were on Pardell after all.

# Chapter 1

SAMMIE'S Tavern had been several meters of access corridor in the days before the Quill—before Thromberg Station welded shut every second bulkhead to make more rooms throughout its Outward Five levels, moving the crush of homeless into space formerly intended for industrial use and warehousing. Across the hole approximating a doorway in one wall, its cut, jagged edges hammered into a safer smoothness, Sammie's boasted a fabric curtain to keep in the fragrance of stale beer and staler patrons, a token separation accomplishing very little at this time of station-day, when odd-cycle work crews were stumbling off-shift and even-cycle were staggering on. Still, visual barriers gave the illusion of privacy, luxury in a place where there was almost none.

The tavern, as always, was packed so full it was difficult to see if there were chairs and tables, let alone find them. The press of flesh to flesh eased in only two places. One marked the narrow aisle behind the bar, necessary allowance so the bartenders could attempt to keep up with the demand with about as much success as someone bailing an ocean with cupped hands. The other opening, less immediately obvious but as well defined, was the room given one man, presently leaning against the counter like the rest.

It was an unconscious distancing, a habit familiar enough to be unnoticed by all, including the dark-haired man at its core. At first glance, he might have been any immie or stationer seeking a moment's oblivion. His clothes were regular-issue tunic and pants, well-patched, with neater repair work than some and cleaner than most. Unusual in this crowd, though not unique, he wore snug-fitting gloves. His spare frame was slightly less than standard height, and lean to the point of almost gaunt—but then again, so were the majority of his companions. Few fattened or grew full height on station-rations. The unremarkable man slouched comfortably over his drink, deep in conversation with the bartender. It was only the instinctive way others avoided touching him, even when it required significant effort, that set him apart: a nonmalicious avoidance, as though he formed a natural hazard, like the edge of a cliff.

"Six dibs?" the man was asking, the words rising with disbelief, his hazel eyes squinted half-closed as though that was all he wanted to view of Sammie's thick girth, mismatched teeth, and amply-stained apron. "When d'you start importing Earth lager, Sammie? Four's pushing hard enough for the watery swill you're pouring down our throats."

There were cheerful comments and nods of agreement from the men and women crushed elbow-to-elbow along the thin, tarnished metal bar, as well as those leaning companionably on their shoulders. The bartender shrugged irritably. "Prices' up for ever'thin' Pardell. If'n you'd show up more of'n, you'd be aware—"

Pardell flashed a sudden grin, crinkling the skin around his eyes while stripping years from his thin features. "If I showed up more often, Sammie, I'd be even more destitute than the miserable stationer scum you let in here—"

"Keep 'r up, Pardell—" Sammie growled warningly. Stationers were not only outnumbered everywhere on Thromberg by immigrants, or immies—the very people they'd been originally been brought here to assist—there was no longer any obvious way to distinguish the two unless you accessed an individual's registration data by retinal scan. Or asked, which would likely earn you a bloodied nose.

The blending had been deliberate, reconciliation and survival in one. The first, and deadliest, Ration Riot had surged throughout the station two weeks after the partial collapse of the still-new hydroponics system. As blame flew down every possible corridor on wings of fear, everyone's face grew pinched with hunger; it only added fuel when stationers were accused of hoarding. The match was lit when rumor—the only way news traveled through the station—spread that only those immies willing to be sterilized and become stationers would continue to be fed. The uprising was mercifully brief and contained to the Outward Five levels. It was mercilessly violent and consumed too many innocent lives.

In the anguished aftermath, enough truth was found behind both rumors that stationers throughout Thromberg gathered in quiet, somber groups, unable to meet the eyes of passing immies, talking in hushed tones about how the real enemies were the Quill and the blindness of Earth. Station insignia started disappearing: from a tunic on this man, from the coats of all the meds in the infirmary on night shift, suddenly gone from every stationer working in Outward Five and elsewhere. Unorganized, unsanctioned, and oddly healing—no one commented out loud, but the tensions between stationer and immigrant slowly eased. Eventually, only the original station records remained, kept to make sure everyone received their fair share of work and food.

Good intentions aside, each knew the other—for better and worse—and the final generation of immie and stationer kids grew up knowing precisely how to start each other's tempers flying.

"Aw, Aaron . . . don't you try and pick a fight again," this loudly insincere complaint came from Pardell's right-hand neighbor, a stationer named Hugh Malley.

They'd been friends even before being orphaned by the third and most recent of the Ration Riots, nine years earlier, a friendship presently belied by the bigger man's fierce scowl. Work in the recycling depot had laid its characteristic curve of muscle over already massive shoulders and barrel chest, making Malley's share of the bar surface necessarily greater than most. He took advantage of that space to thump down one huge, scarred fist with sufficient emphasis to spill the frothy heads from most of the containers foolishly left sitting in front of their owners. Grumbles about this waste were conspicuously absent. "No fights," Malley repeated. "We owe Sammie here dibs for the last ruckus. You know I hate cleaning up this place."

Pardell blinked innocently. "You hate cleaning up anywhere," he replied, raising his own voice to be heard over the growing din as those behind began murmuring in anticipation. Sure enough, an instant later the bar's bell sounded and, automatically, all of those presently leaning on the bar, including Malley and Pardell, snatched up their drinks and straightened to let others squeeze by them. Sammie and his coworkers went into a frenzy, collecting dib chits from those moving out of immediate reach as well as from those newly arrived and impatient.

Malley settled his heavy forearms companionably on the shoulders of the two men now in his former place, neither arguing beyond a strangled grunt. Pardell toasted the nervous-looking immie in front of him, relieving any concern he might be drunk enough to try for the same service. The tavern settled back into its comforting babble of voices and laughter as smoothly as if nothing had happened at all.

*Smooth, because it had to be*, Pardell told himself, helplessly sliding into one of those detached, intense moments of thought that consumed him every so often, no matter what he was doing, or where he was. He usually tried to turn the feeling from aloof to amused; he usually failed, settling—as now—for a mild sense of dislocation.

While it lasted, it was as if the tavern suddenly expanded along each axis; the people crammed inside faceless and strange, any movement slowed, every sound stilled. *This bar*, Pardell observed, with no choice but to accept perception—*was a monument to human adaptability*. There was no doubt the overcrowding on this and the other stations had produced its share of nightmares—*he'd lived some*—but it had also produced ways of coping. Queuing was a lifestyle, manners an essential skill. There was a seething, reasonably efficient economy based on barter and turnabout. In fact, the entire station operated that way, half keeping the reverse daylight/night cycle from the rest, allowing the available space and equipment to be used around the clock. It had become the stuff of romance as well as convenience, given there was someone in every bed no matter the time. *It did make it awkward keeping track of anyone on reverse hours—*

"Rejoining us any time soon, Aaron?" Malley's rumble interrupted Pardell's thoughts, startling him back to a noisy, companionable reality. The big man suggestively held up his own container, a piece of pipe of generous depth, one end welded shut. Intricate etchings covered its surface, extraordinarily fine work considering the size of the hands responsible. But then Malley's appearance was the last thing to judge him by, as most in their section knew. A ferocious intellect that absorbed anything and everything in reach, off-shift Malley earned half again as many dibs teaching as he did as a laborer. There hadn't been a subject yet which he didn't know—or couldn't learn—well enough to keep ahead of his students. Rumor had it, those joining Malley's work shift had to pass an exam. *It was more accurate*, Pardell smiled to himself as he considered his friend fondly, *to say only those willing to debate anything from astrophysics to poetry while heaving scrap metal managed to keep sane.*

Pardell obediently raised his container, a white plastic cup, to Malley's. In another place and time, it would have been disposable. Here and now, despite its plain appearance, the cup was a prized possession; its ship markings, *Merry Mate II*, proof of a heritage few could claim and none could replace. "I was just thinking, my friend," Pardell protested mildly after sipping his beer. "There's no law against it."

Malley wasn't letting it go, turning to look Pardell in the eyes. His own, dark brown beneath a broad forehead and straight-line brows, were clouded. "There's no law against butting in line, but the last person we saw do it ended up in pieces. Messy, little pieces. You know better than to make people nervous, Aaron. Going all spacey in a crowded room is one of those nervous-making things. Okay?"

*Nervous.* Pardell looked down at his gloved hands, trying to think if there had been an instant of his life when he didn't have to listen to warnings, make the effort to blend with others. Suddenly, the boisterous crowd, the heat and smells, the sounds—*everything*—became overwhelmingly real. Pardell inhaled slowly and carefully through his nostrils, fighting the irrational urge to gasp for air, recognizing the signs with helpless frustration and more than a little disappointment. *He'd overstayed his tolerance.* "Time I headed home, anyway," he announced, pouring the rest of his beer into Malley's as nonchalantly as possible. The reminder hadn't offended him; Malley was right. Odd behavior wasn't tolerated, not here, where getting along meant being safely predictable and following the unspoken rules.

Those rules definitely included not pushing one's way in through the doorway so people trying to leave were shoved back against others. Pardell and Malley turned at the commotion with everyone else, the growl of outrage vibrating in a wave from the door to the bar. The following, ominous hush let Sammie's roar through clearly: "Enter onna *right*, morons! Where're you raised, huh—?"

The rest of what the usually vocal Sammie might have said died away. "Malley! What's going on?" Pardell hissed. Malley, taller by a head than most, was staring in the direction of the tavern entrance. "Who—?"

"Strangers," Malley said, astonishment clear in his hushed voice.

"How many beers have you had?" Pardell muttered, straining to see for himself. The station might be bursting at the seams with humanity, but people kept to their own sections. Thromberg had sacrificed a significant amount of its interconnectivity through the emergency modifications to house the immigrant population trapped here, and, unstated, Station Admin was nothing loath to keep its inhabitants in isolated communities. Especially since the riots.

No doubt Sammie's regular clientele knew each other on sight, all too well. "Thought you knew everybody," Pardell teased his friend.

"Shut up," Malley said almost absently. "They're Uniforms. Earth Uniforms."

"Earthers? On-station. In Sammie's." Pardell wasn't sure which was more ludicrous: the idea an Earth ship could dock at the station without the news spreading translight, or that such troops would simply walk in here first. Outward Five was nowhere near the stem docking ring, by any measure. "In Sammie's," he repeated numbly.

"Shhsh. I'm trying to hear what's going on." Despite this, Malley gave a low growl of his own when bodies suddenly pressed closer on all sides, everyone facing the door with the quivering attention of a crowd unsure whether to bolt or cheer.

His strong arm made a wall between Pardell and the nearest set of shoulders. "Watch where you're going, Denery!"

Syd Denery's back rammed into Malley's elbow before the smaller immie could help himself. He craned his head around to face Pardell, an anxious look on his wizened features. "Sorry, Aaron. Can't help it. They're shoving us back to make room for the Earthers. Maybe you should head out before it gets worse." With another contortion, Denery managed to twist minutely farther away, as he did so, informing his immediate neighbors in an urgent, cheery whisper: "Hey, Aaron's back here, y'know. Careful, you louts!"

"I'm all right," Pardell said to the world in general, feeling the familiar humiliating heat of an angry blush on his face.

"No," Malley countered. "I don't like this. You should get out of here—"

Pardell sputtered: "How—?" just as the unthinkable happened and a mass of people fell backward toward him as though knocked flying in some game. Amid the cursing and apologies, he felt contact on all sides.

*Confusion. Anger.* FEAR!

. . . Time stopped. All Pardell could hear was his own heart, hammering like some frantic bird caged within his ribs. There must have been dozens of people touching him, connecting with him, bombarding him with their emotions until he knew he couldn't stand another feeling . . .

PITY.

. . . It drowned him even as his body was wrenched free. Suddenly, all of the connections were broken at once as Pardell felt himself launched through the air. He had an instant to be amazed at the pile of struggling, intertwined bodies beneath him before Malley's toss landed him on the floor behind the bar.

*Anything broken?* Pardell asked himself cautiously, unwilling to move and find out. He remained curled where he'd dropped, ignoring the spilled liquid and crumpled containers under shoulders and hip, working on controlling the natural impulses of his stomach and waiting for his heart to resume something closer to a normal beat. Breathing took a fair amount of concentration.

"You okay, Aaron?" Sammie leaned over him, warily distant. "Malley's go'n nuts out there."

Pardell jerked his head in what he hoped looked like a nod and not the prelude to convulsion. He'd had plenty of those as a child, learning to cope with his reaction to the inadvertent touch of others. Adolescence had been worse, far worse; adulthood had moderated his body's confusion to a tendency to vomit and a blinding headache. *Like the one presently building behind his temples.* He swallowed carefully, feeling his stomach subside, at least.

His friends would be upset to have done this to him. They'd grown up together; very likely, he wouldn't have survived the process without their help in keeping a safe distance. Mutual gain, since anyone touching him received a low-level shock, like a static discharge, but that had never diminished their sense of responsibility for him. *Always the weakest. "Look out for Pardell."* If he'd heard it once. . . .

Pardell felt his hands clenching into fists. "I'll be fine, Sammie," he ground out, easing to his feet. He glanced down at the mess on the floor. "Let me know the dibs on this—"

"Not your fault," Sammie mumbled surprisingly. "Get that lump of a Malley outta here 'fore he tosses someone bigger in my face."

Pardell didn't bother nodding, although his headache had started to fade. He was more intent on the scene on the other side. Things were, to put it mildly, rather interesting.

Like the parting of a flood, the tavern patrons had somehow been dammed up on either side, many jumping on tables to gain a better view as well as breathing space. It didn't appear as though any had left. *Novelty was as rare as privacy*, Pardell thought, as intrigued as the rest. The curtain hung limply across the door, unmoving for perhaps the first time in a decade. There was an unprecedented amount of filthy floor showing in front of the bar, a glimpse Pardell could have done without, having recently been pressed to it.

In the now-becalmed center stood the mannerless fourteen who'd caused such an uproar. *Earthers for sure*, Pardell thought with wonder, almost forgetting his sore head and battered body parts. He'd never seen one before, but there was no mistaking either the flawless uniforms or the well-fed faces. Seven men and seven women, lined up in two tidy rows, similar to the point of caricature. *Someone*, he decided, *liked jutting jaws, black hair, and high cheekbones.* The troops, for they were patently military of some kind, looked jittery, standing at a very uneasy attention with their eyes rolling as if attempting to track everyone in the room at once. Pardell wasn't sure if this was because they were dismayed by the closeness of the crowd or by being weaponless. *Had they tried boarding Thromberg with weapons,* he reminded himself, *they wouldn't have made it this far.* Stationers and immies might not always get along, but neither tolerated Earther arrogance—not when Earth's idea of helping the desperate meant the occasional supply ship and suggestions of patience.

Malley was standing closer to the bar than most, still part of the crowd. Although his jacket had split open along its right shoulder mend again, there was no sign Sammie's fear of more flying bodies was about to come true. Pardell caught Malley's meaningful look his way and shrugged slightly in reassurance. He was bent, but nothing worse, thanks to his friend's quick thinking. Several others, the less drunk, mouthed "sorry" at him or otherwise looked embarrassed.

Then the curtain opened to allow someone else in and every local face assumed the same expression, as though a riper odor than usual had permeated the room. Sammie rubbed his hands marginally cleaner on his stained apron before coming around to the other side of his bar, a move that raised more than a few eyebrows. *It settled several outstanding bets on what Sammie wore on his feet,* Pardell chuckled to himself, watching a few of the gamblers in question glumly examining the splayed toes in their quite serviceable, if homemade, thongs. "What's the meaning of this, Forester?" Sammie demanded without a trace of his customary lowerdeck accent, inspiring the collection of other wagers. "I expect compensation for this interference with my trade and customers—"

*Sector Administrator Garfield Forester.* No need for the name—everyone in Outward Five would recognize the receding double chin and mottled skin, those odd washed-pale eyes under shaggy brows. The man used every possible opportunity to stick his face in front of them on the vid screen and complain about something or other; let alone his popularity as a subject on washroom walls.

*Why was* he *here?* Pardell wondered. Everyone knew Forester as a straightforward bastard: efficient and ruthless, but not inclined to visit those in his care. He'd gone from running the station's main cargo bays to being in charge of ten thousand homeless. Needless to say, the change hadn't been appreciated by either side.

Odd to see Forester without his usual trio of security from Inward Four, though Pardell was sure the man had been delighted to exchange his scruffy escort for the spit-and-polish Earthers. After all, station security was distinguishable from their fellow stationers only by the crossed belts they wore on duty, the belts holding vital equipment such as comm equipment, a force rod or two, and, most importantly, a day's rations in case duty meant missing their scheduled turn in line at the dispensers. Until those had been added, escorts had tended to be unreliable around the supper hour.

Outward Five supplied security personnel for Inward Four, and so forth up the length of the station—a policy that reduced the risk of having to hit a member of your own family over the head when maintaining order. Of course, on Thromberg, the definition of order had evolved to suit the times. Station Admin used to have volumes of picky little rules and regulations, with keen-eyed officers watching for crime and mischief. Now, what mattered was containing trouble to one location, whether it was a malfunctioning air vent or the start of a riot. Thromberg's surviving security was very good at spotting trouble and locking it down until trouble died away or killed itself.

Anything else was handled locally. Each section had become like a small town, with those who assumed responsibility and those who happily avoided it. Both types understood that stability depended on the whole more than any individual. Station Admin ignored the tendency of persistent troublemakers to simply disappear. And, usually, Station Admin could be ignored—except when they conducted sweeps. Those annoying searches were ostensibly to look for hoarders, but everyone knew they were really hunting station equipment that had been "relocated." Kept people on their toes.

*So why was Forester down here, with Earthers?* It wasn't routine.

Pardell's own eyes narrowed thoughtfully as he took an easy, slow step back. Tanya, Sammie's oldest granddaughter and seniormost of his bar staff, mirrored his movement, slipping forward with convincing casualness to scrub at a ring marring the bar's metal surface that likely predated her birth, in the process almost completely blocking him from view. He could just see Sammie's back each time she leaned forward.

*Not that Station Admin knew any reason to single* him *out*, Pardell assured himself, but it was always safer to avoid notice. He wasn't the only one quietly fading into the background. Sammie's was a haven for many unwelcome elsewhere.

"We'll be out of your way in a moment, Mr. Leland," promised Forester, his real voice a thready echo of those rich tones heard daily on the interstation comms—if any still paid attention to those announcements. Pardell couldn't recall the last time he'd listened. "We're looking for a non-reg'd individual named Pardell."

Pardell closed his eyes briefly, wishing he'd placed his own bet. *What were the odds?* While he couldn't for the life of him imagine why Forester came after him with Earth troops, there were some—minor—infractions he could imagine might be of interest to Station Admin. *Not that most in the room couldn't say the same.* Creative housekeeping had become an honored skill on Thromberg.

"Non-registered? By your people?" Sammie repeated, putting a distinctly ironic twist to the words. "How could that possibly be, Administrator Forester?"

By the sound, Forester had gritted his teeth. "Non-reg as in not a stationer or immigrant. You know the type I mean. The kind of refuse that keeps you in business."

"I'll take your slur under advisement for litigation, Administrator." Sammie stepped forward, his stained apron jutting ahead of him, thick, capable hands curling almost into fists. "What do you—or these Earthers—want with this Pardell?"

Forester didn't retreat, but his erect stance developed something of a backward tilt. "That's none of your concern, is it? As you've noticed, our guests have come quite a distance—let's not keep them waiting while you and I debate." Forester coughed, as though the well-shared air of the tavern was not to his taste, or it could have been his proximity to Sammie. "I want Aaron Luis Pardell. Now. I understand he frequents this level—has acquaintances here . . ." His voice trailed away suggestively. Then, loudly: "Anyone know this man? Step forward if you do."

Even Forester had to sense the rising tension in the room. *Give one of their own to Admin?* Pardell asked himself. Barely likely—and there'd have to be a reward or a serious grudge involved.

*Give one to Earthers?*

There'd be blood first, even from those who might otherwise consider Pardell himself a waste of air.

"As usual, your informants have lied to you, Administrator," Sammie said with some of that tension edging his voice. "Look elsewhere."

"Hey!" came a voice from the crowd. "Not so fast. I know the guy you're after—tall, heavyset fellow? Pardell. Yeah, I know him. Hangs around the ration line a lot, looking for handouts."

*In a falsetto, yet.* Pardell bit his lip to contain a grin. Trust Denery. He'd owe the man major dibs for this one. There were a few equally unhelpful descriptions shouted out at random. Given the level of alcohol consumed in the room earlier, he was surprised no one burst out laughing.

*Though Forester won't believe a word of it*, he warned himself, losing that impulse himself, *but he won't risk looking a fool in front of the Earthers either.* Pardell wished he dared lean farther to one side or that Tanya's grandfather had thought to polish the metal sheathing behind the bar to make some sort of mirror.

Fourteen pairs of fresh-from-a-box mag boots clanged in unison as the Earthers acknowledged a new arrival. Pardell's curiosity got the best of him and he sidled as close as he dared to Tanya to catch a better look past her ample shoulder.

Forester was tall for a stationer, closer to Malley's height than Pardell's, but without his mass; the matched set of Earthers were tall and lanky as well. The figure now holding the curtain to one side, as though uncertain of welcome or justifiably offended by the atmosphere in Sammie's, was dwarfed by comparison.

It didn't matter.

She, or he, wore a floor-sweeping, metallic green cloak, complete with hood and goggled respirator. It resembled the gear used by the meds and their assistants during outbreaks of infectious disease, but made of layers of such fine, gauzelike material it could have been mistaken for some flight of fashion. One gloved hand kept the heavy, well-patched curtain open; the other held a notepad, curled protectively within the crook of an arm. The figure took a step into the room, letting the curtain fall, then fumbled abruptly at the respirator, finally pulling it down under her chin with an impatient yank.

For the face was female. Pardell released the breath he hadn't realized he'd been holding.

*Not a pretty face*, he decided. *Not one to easily forget either.* It might have been the combination of impatience and disapproval drawing her lips into a thin line—or the glitter of absolute determination in those bright blue eyes. Her cheeks were indented with the reddish pinch marks left by an ill-adjusted respirator. Rather painful-looking marks at that. *Not a happy lady.*

They were her troops, all right, having frozen into a rigid attentiveness the moment she'd opened the curtain. Two more had followed her in, essentially filling the cleared part of the room. Forester was practically groveling. Pardell noticed everyone else, including Malley, seemed suddenly more entertained than wary, as though the arrival of this mystery woman was part of a free vidshow. *Maybe*, he thought with disgust, *they expected her to take off the cloak next and dance on the bar.*

What she did do was take one more step to confront Forester. Given her expression and obvious discomfort, the controlled, pleasant tone of her voice surprised Pardell almost as much as her clipped accent—unfamiliar to an ear used to station drawls. "Is there a problem, Administrator?"

"I'm not getting the cooperation I expected, Professor Smith."

*Hard to imagine a less exotic name, which strangely added*

*to the mystique.* Pardell found himself leaning forward expectantly with the rest, still keeping behind Tanya. Malley sent him a warning scowl. Professor Smith arched one slim, dark eyebrow, then looked away from Forester to survey the room. "I'm not surprised. What did you do?" she asked calmly. "Threaten to close the place? I wouldn't cooperate either."

Sammie almost smiled, then apparently remembered it wasn't an expression that sat well on his square face and compromised with a nod. "Completely unnecessary, Madame," he said briskly. "This is a peaceful—inn. The Administrator here, he comes in and disrupts my business. My patrons and I have been subjected to indignities." He deepened his voice for emphasis: "And there's been a distinct loss of dibs. I can tell you that without checking my tills."

Her other eyebrow rose. "'Dibs?'"

Pardell was amused by the contortions of Forester's face as the stationer heroically managed to keep his mouth shut while Sammie went on to explain, at some length and with considerable gusto, the barter system allowing patrons to make their purchases based on recorded work exchanges. The crowd, growing bored and likely thirsty, became involved by way of throwing out examples, many of them totally incomprehensible and a couple profanely hopeful. The Earther woman appeared fascinated. "But we don't call them in—the work, that is—very often anymore, Madame," Sammie finished. "It's coin of the realm these days."

"I see. Mr. Leland—"

"Call me Sammie. Please."

Pardell was sure he spotted the ghost of a dimple at the corner of her mouth; it could have been the poor lighting. "Thank you. Sammie. I believe there may have been a misunderstanding. I'm here to offer Mr. Pardell a job—a job for which I would pay him in other than 'dibs,' as you've ably explained them. I assure you I mean him no harm and that it has nothing to do with Administrator Forester or any other station personnel. So," Smith raised her voice, although she had everyone's rapt attention, turning in a slow circle to address the entire crowd. Her gaze passed over the bar as if it wasn't there. Pardell fought the urge to duck. "Please relay this message to Mr. Pardell for me: if he's interested, he should come to the docking ring, and introduce himself to any member of my crew. There's a once-in-a-lifetime opportunity waiting for him. In the meantime," this as she faced Sammie again, "my sincere apologies for disturbing you and for any losses you've incurred." Forester began to sputter. The professor bent down and picked up the broken remains of a cup to wave under his nose. She silenced him completely by adding: "Send the bill for the next three rounds to the *ERC* Deep Space Vessel *Seeker*."

Professor Smith swept up her Earther troops, Administrator Forester, and her cloak, heading to the curtained door with a suddenness that suggested she either knew very well to get out of the way of the imminent stampede to the bar—or she'd accomplished what she wanted here and was in a hurry to do the same elsewhere.

*Or both*, Pardell thought uneasily, distracted as the bar's bell rang automatically, its message to patrons lost in happy confusion.

# Chapter 2

THE cup had been washed so many times, the letters walking around its base were faded and broken. *Clear enough.* Gail's finger followed the "*Merry Mate II*" pensively, avoiding the razor-sharp edge where the cup had shattered, aware the three men in front of her traded puzzled looks.

*They don't appreciate the irony of it*, she reminded herself, forcing down triumph and impatience with the ease of tedious practice. To be fair, they didn't have the information to do so; she had no intention of providing it. She raised her eyes when she was ready and not an instant before.

"Have you briefed the guards you've posted on the dock?" she asked.

Commander Daniel R. Grant of the Sol System First Defense Unit 518—presently assigned to the *Seeker*—pressed his lips together in utter disapproval, an all-too familiar expression. *Unlikely to change any time soon*, she thought. The twenty-four FD troops and their leader disapproved of many things she required of them. "As you ordered, Dr. Smith," Grant said in a tone so neutral it grated. "They are to wait for Pardell to arrive, then immediately bring him on board to you."

At this, the man beside the commander, Captain Tomoki Tobo, gave another theatrically-dismayed sigh. For once, he seemed to have found common ground with his military counterpart. Neither of them approved of bringing a stationer—any stationer—on the *Seeker*. Their novel alliance had nothing to do with her and everything to do with the thousands of angry would-be immigrants on the other side of the air lock.

*She didn't*, Gail thought with sudden revulsion, *need to be reminded*. As if anyone from Earth could forget what had happened in those first months after the Quill: the swarming and overloading of unguarded ships, the pathetic broadcasts for help still traveling through the space that had swallowed their senders whole, the riots and near anarchy.

As if any from a station could forget—or forgive—Earth's panicked response to the desperate flood of returning immigrants, brought on by terror that they carried the Quill and would contaminate humanity's center. The Patrol had been ordered to turn back any station-origin ship trying to enter Sol System, to fire on and destroy those who refused to believe they couldn't go home. To defend against their own.

*Stationers try to take an Earth ship to Sol today? Only if they had a death wish*, Gail decided. *And any of that particular bent would have readily found their desire satisfied long before the* Seeker *docked*.

On the surface, twenty years later, things were more civilized. There was an assumption of some responsibility for the stranded immigrants by Earth, motivated by guilt as well as self-interest, the latter an awareness that casting aside the stations entirely could come back to haunt the home system. Not that the stations looked to Earth any longer for help or hope of a future. Like Thromberg, twelve of the thirty-three original stations had been stable for a decade or more. Some were close to sustaining themselves, if not of growth.

The others? Well, no one spoke of those.

Gail looked from Grant to Tobo, finding it ironic that the survival of humanity under such desperate conditions had become a source of fear; sufficient at least to bind these two together against her for the first time.

Until now, the two officers had maintained a relationship comprised of equal parts disdain and respect: Tobo's disdain and Grant's respect. Tobo—short to Grant's regulation height, chubby to Grant's regulation fitness, and of pure Kanshu lineage to Grant's peculiar blend of who knew how many ethnicities comprised the military's ideal soldier these days—spent much of his time inventing ways to demonstrate how little the troops understood about life on a starship. Grant, Gail had noticed, appeared torn between his awareness that, onboard the *Seeker*, Tobo was a superior officer, and an obsessive need to prove he and his people could handle anything. The *Seeker*'s journey from Sol System had been punctuated by the results—inconvenient at best and often messy. Gail had managed to convince Grant that Tobo's idea of randomly shutting down lowerdecks' gravity in the middle of shipnight wasn't essential to his troops' training for space. Convincing the vastly entertained Tobo, whom she suspected of hiding a vid in the troops' quarters, had taken a fair amount of outright yelling.

Her inner smile faded as the third man spoke, his voice high-pitched and scornful. "At the risk of repeating myself, this is ridiculous. With that plan, you'll end up with a hundred 'Pardells' in your lap by shipnight." Manuel Reinsez, like Gail, sat at his ease while Grant and Tobo stood almost at attention. The semi-retired Chilean xenopathologist was old even by the standards of Earth, which granted the risky rejuv treatments sparingly, based on an arcane formula combining health factors and projected contributions to society. Gail suspected Reinsez had had more than one, or had qualified unfortunately late in life for his first. The man's face wasn't merely wrinkled—his sallow skin was so limp it draped free from brow, cheek, and jawbones. When he felt in the mood—or had had too much sherry—Reinsez would pull the loose skin of his jowls back to hide his ears, pursing his lips to imitate a fish. A dead fish.

*A shark, more like it*, Gail reminded herself, careful not to show any response beyond polite attention. She could handle Grant's anxious efficiency. The man was patently a superb officer, simply out of his depth in their current situation. The stats and vids of the station he had to rely on for information were so dated as to be laughable and Tobo's campaign hadn't exactly boosted Grant's self-confidence.

She'd probably been wrong to turn a blind eye to Tobo's peculiar sense of humor, but he was the closest thing to a friend and confidant she'd had on this trip; a closeness which didn't mean he knew everything about what she was doing here.

Professor Reinsez thought he did. His presence was Titan University's latest grip on her project and its tightest. Without Reinsez on the *Seeker*, they'd still be in synchronous orbit over the campus, battling endless red tape and obstructions, her already minimal funding sucked dry by bribes to faceless individuals and shapeless organizations to keep fuel in the ship's belly, let alone gain support to move her project up the waiting list.

*Dibs*, Gail thought wryly. *The stationers had no idea how much* cleaner *that concept sounded.*

"I'm well aware we may have to screen a multitude of impostors, Dr. Reinsez," she said out loud. "But unless you have a better suggestion . . . ?"

Reinsez waved both hands in denial, slouching more comfortably into his chair. "Not I, Dr. Smith. Not I. This is your show. I'm along for the entertainment value."

"And to report our findings to Titan's Directors," Gail added gently, a reminder intended for Grant's ears. *It never hurt to keep the cards in view*, she thought. *Theirs, if not hers.*

"But of course, Dr. Smith," Reinsez agreed, eyes glistening within their deeply creased lids. "That goes without saying."

"Then we're done here." Gail put the cup shard on top of the pile of studies she planned to read later this shipnight, after pulling free the topmost, withdrawing her attention from the others in the certain expectation they each had their own tasks to pursue and knew better than to waste her time.

Sure enough, Tobo and Reinsez left without another word, but Grant closed the door behind them, turning back to stand in front of her again. Gail glanced up, lifting one brow interrogatively. "What is it, Commander?"

"Have you heard from Thromberg about the remotes, Dr. Smith?"

Gail leaned back in her chair, a tactic she'd developed to avoid craning her head at a bad angle in order to look attentively at anyone whose own head endangered doorways. *Maybe*, Gail hoped, *he'd think she was relaxing.* Not for the first time, Gail pondered the rumors about cloning in the military—Grant's deeply chiseled features, long-limbed form, and stiff bearing resembled his troops so closely they might have been younger versions of the man before her now—then dismissed them. It was simply that the military had long ago adopted a policy of physically coordinating its units to produce the desired look for a specific political event, like a matched team of horses to draw a ceremonial coach. These days, Earth had little other need for her soldiers: police forces dealt with on-planet issues, and Sol

System had its patrol to handle off-planet ones. Most citizens only knew there was still a planetary military during parades or state funerals.

A few, such as herself, bothered to notice Earth's military continued to zealously train its men and women for a new role: to protect humanity against what might be out there. First Defense.

A mandate they'd failed with the faceless Quill, dying or retreating to safety with everyone else. Now, for some unknown reason, Earth's military might, represented here and now by these twenty-five cookie-cutter soldiers, guarded her. Gail tried not to scowl. *A little overzealously, too, considering humanity remained quite alone in the intelligent life department.*

"I haven't heard, Commander," she told him. "If you still feel it's necessary to deploy your satellites outside the station, I can press the issue with Administrator Forester. But I don't hold out much chance of success. They're—prickly—about surveillance here."

Vids, familiar from every street corner and hallway on Earth and her system companions, were conspicuous by their absence on Thromberg. They'd all noticed it and, when she'd asked, Forester had almost refused to help them further, spouting what amounted to a rant about the right to privacy. The Earthers, herself included, settled for feeling mystified and, in Grant's case, more vulnerable. The remotes he was so passionately set on using were his answer—independent bundles of cameras and other devices which could be set to watch the station from a distance, giving them advance warning of ship movements.

"Yes, completely essential," the commander insisted. "You know I objected strenuously to docking the *Seeker* in the first place. You could have sent us on a shuttle, stayed in safety—and kept our only weapon free."

"They wouldn't have let a shuttle dock under those circumstances," Gail reminded him. "You know that. And as for keeping me safe . . . ?" she left the sentence hanging between them like a challenge, daring him to pick it up. She'd made it clear from the moment the military approached with its offer of protection that she'd accept it for her work, not her person. Less publicly, but just as adamantly, Gail had insisted Grant's unit be under her direct authority, not Reinsez's. They'd surprised her by complying. *Anything to get the troops a little practice*, she told herself, not for the first time.

Perhaps Grant felt the same way. "Understood, Dr. Smith," he said, lips twitching as though about to smile. It was the closest to an outright expression she'd caught on his face. "But perhaps I can suggest a compromise. Let me send out one probe—" before she could utter her immediate objection, he raised a hand to ask her silence, continuing quickly "—if they object, we can say it was a maintenance 'bot out to check the ship that went astray. It would make one spiral orbit of the main station cylinder, sending us the image, then drift off into space."

"And if they haul it in? I need their cooperation, Commander. I can't afford to alienate these people in any way."

"If they haul it in, it will be an ordinary 'bot, like the ones their own facilities would use. The transmitter's a bit more powerful, that's all, but they'd need an expert in current Earth tech to know." Grant paused as if for emphasis. "I think we're pretty safe in that regard, since Earth doesn't let her experts migrate outsystem."

Gail sat forward, chin on the heel of one hand, and studied Grant's face more closely than she ever had before. He bore her scrutiny solemnly, his wide-set, brown eyes almost pleading. There was a pulse visible in one temple, beating strongly beneath the faint whiteness of a puckered, oddly circular scar. Otherwise, his smooth, olive-toned skin was unmarked, and unrevealing. "If they haul it in," she said at last, "and have any complaints about it whatsoever, I'd have to claim no knowledge or approval of your actions. For whatever that might count with them—" Gail began to shake her head. "It's too risky, Commander. What are you expecting to find out there to make it worthwhile?"

Commander Grant reached out and lifted the cup shard from its place on her pile of studies. A thrill of alarm fingered Gail's spine as he turned the shard in his hands, but all he said was: "You're a scientist, Dr. Smith; I'm a soldier. Our jobs aren't all that different, you know. Like you, to do mine I need to observe what's around me. Right now, that's a station without external or internal vid feed for my people to tap; it's a population that, if not actively hostile, is as close as I'd ever want to come to it; and it's an environment we can't hope to explore in person. We're no use to you—to your project—if we can't see what's out there. Let me do this. For all our sakes."

Gail tried not to look relieved as Grant put down the cup shard, then she slowly nodded, just once. "We didn't have this conversation, Commander," she advised him coolly. "And I didn't ask you to work with Captain Tobo to have a maintenance 'bot do a routine check on the *Seeker* while we're in dock. Are we clear?"

*Gods, an actual smile*, Gail told herself, though the expression strangely increased Grant's resemblance to a hunting cat rather than diminished it. A definite smile accompanied by a snappier-than-usual salute. "I didn't hear a thing, Dr. Smith," he assured her. "And thank you." He rushed out, obviously eager to be at his spying.

Gail picked up the cup shard and idly followed its lettering with her finger.

No need for Grant to know she was every bit as eager as he was to see what else might be docked to Thromberg Station.

*No need at all.*

# Chapter 3

*It wasn't fair!*

Pardell rammed his foot into its boot. Despite an anger sending spots before his eyes and shortening his breath, he took care nothing was folded or pinched in the process. Next, he tightened the straps that kept the overly-large mags attached to the soles; unlike the Earthers' new gear, his was cobbled together from a sequence of other space suits, and the mags to hold him safely to the station's outer plates were cut from ones originally three sizes too big. From Aaron Raner's suit.

*He may have grown since, but he'd never fill them.*

Thinking about the dead was unlucky, especially here, where so many of the dead had been stored for identification. *The only place inside cold enough.* Pardell could see his breath when it passed through the thin cone of light from his wrist lamp.

Thromberg itself had bled that day, ripped along a fragile seam during the frantic exodus of too many people, in too few ships. There had been repairs and reclamation efforts in the years since, but none in this section of the aft docking ring, not yet anyway. Here remained only freezing air, darkness, and those ruined, twisted structures no one was desperate enough to salvage. Yet.

Pardell closed his eyes and let the emptiness seep into his bones, resting his head against the frigid, damp wall until the part of his scalp in contact grew numb and ached with cold. The isolation soothed him; a shame he couldn't savor it long. Others used this passageway, always hurrying, usually in pairs or groups. Pardell didn't need to remember Malley's warnings to know: *blend into the mass, stay inconspicuous.*

He finished suiting up, *maybe slow by Earther standards*, he told himself, *but one of* them *would never get this suit to hold air.* One by one, Pardell snapped an assortment of small bags to their rings, having retrieved them from their hiding places. He tested each with a sharp tug. A loose fastener had cost him an irreplaceable set of readers once, the bag floating out of reach to join the other such orphans forming a tenuous band in the vicinity of Thromberg Station. Station Admin routinely sent out barges to sweep clear the approach lanes to the stern ring. No one bothered back here.

Check done, Pardell switched off his light, listening to his own breathing, feeling the soft press of the frigid darkness on his lips and eyelids. He tapped his helmet gently against his right leg, a child's habit, counting out the seconds . . . *five* . . . *fifteen* . . . *one hundred and one* . . . still no lights, no other sounds. He was alone. The habit answered to caution as well as courtesy: caution, in case he was this even-cycle day's target for menaces ranging from the authorities sending down an engineer to a crazy after a 'tastic fix; courtesy, because manually cycling the 'lock was hard enough for one, so most of the older 'siders needed someone with stronger arms to help them through. If you saw or heard them struggling to catch up, you waited.

Anger rushed back, making Pardell's hands fumble at the helmet fastener, anger at the Earthers whose elderly didn't suit up in the dark, but, even more, anger at one Earther in particular: the woman who had walked into Sammie's and stolen his peace.

Pardell cued on the helmet's reddish interior illumination with his chin in order to see the gauges lined up below his jaw; all that remained of the suit's fancy remote display pads were sealed-over stitch marks on each wrist. Only low-maintenance gear had endured decades of use—that, or what new devices clever, desperate hands could cobble together. He made himself continue the checks, fighting the emotional overload. *Malley'd talked some sense*, he had to admit it now, if he couldn't to Malley's face—not right away, at least. No one would give him up; he had the choice of tailing it and keeping out of sight until the Earther ship left, or of attempting that long, impossible walk to the docks.

Smith hadn't realized what she'd asked of him, or if she had, she played some game he was safer clear of—Malley had the truth of that as well. How'd she think a 'sider could make it to the stern docking ring—the living, breathing heaven to the hell he crouched in now? Was she Earther-blind to the difference when she'd been escorted down to Sammie's? Surely she'd noticed how the press of people in the corridors increased with every level. Hadn't she seen for herself the change to a population whose reflex was to crouch to one side to allow others through, and whose eyes never met in more than a courteous slide past, granting one another the only room they could?

*Not the Earther*, Pardell thought bitterly. Not with her troops and her Station puppet to clear the way down.

*And without that kind of escort, no way up.* No way for him to cross the checkpoints without being counted and discovered. No hidden shortcuts or byways that hadn't been found and welded shut by now. Station Admin tolerated his kind only as long as they stayed invisible.

He didn't have the air to waste debating the extent of Smith's craziness with himself, Pardell judged, tipping his head to view the display within his helmet. Turning his wrist light back on, he followed its thin wispy beam, playing it over iced black walls until it reflected from faded lettering. Air lock S17. Pardell gave the inner door a gentle pull to test for vacuum. When it shifted grudgingly in his hands, he swung it wide with a practiced heave. There had been an entire series of 'locks in this section, a set for each docked ship: passenger hookups, emerg 'locks, service gates, the huge cargo passages. Since the destruction, they were all supposedly inoperable, either damaged so they couldn't open—as children, Pardell and his friends used to scare one another with made-up stories about ghosts, trapped inside— or sealed when the ring was abandoned, to protect station integrity.

Air lock S17 showed traces of its seal: shiny, congealed lumps the cutting torch had failed to melt free clung to the doorframe here and there, looking like some blighted growth on the metal. It was, naturally enough, a capital crime to be caught breaking a station engineer's seal. Naturally enough, no one bothered to check down here as long as the ring stayed airtight and powered down. S17 had been an emerg 'lock; as such, it was barely large enough to hold three in suits. Cramped quarters, but with a bonus: emerg 'locks had dual systems designed to keep them functional in power failures.

*Or in a failure to provide power*, Pardell grumbled to himself, stepping over the sill and reaching back for the inner door. From this side, the door's scars and blisters were ample evidence entry had been forced from outside the station, not in. *Before his time.* The mechanism hadn't been harmed, and he braced both feet against the sill to use his body's mass to haul the door shut. The oversized mags didn't help. It took three tries this time, and Pardell felt himself heating up, a maddening bead of moisture winding its slow path down the side of his face. The suit's faltering conditioning system had the contrary habit of allowing his toes to approach frostbite when he needed warmth, then, without warning, kicking in to hoard every iota of his body heat so sweat floated around in his helmet, beads stinging when they collided with his eyes.

He dogged closed the inner door and wasted no more time, sliding the panel over the station air vent, then cranking the hydraulic-assisted hand pump to evacuate the chamber until the sensors would allow the outer door to be opened manually. It took fifty-three full pumps.

Pardell shone his light over the outer door. It glinted from a misshapen ring of steel clipped to a chain, in turn spot-welded to the doorframe. The assembly was crude, but strong. A similar one hung outside, in vacuum.

He slipped his gloved hand inside the ring, drawing it close to his side. Jase Cohn claimed the ring was from the neck seal of a 'suit worn by a stationer who'd tried to keep out his family. It wasn't the right size or shape, but the notion pleased some. Ring in hand, Pardell leaned his helmet against the outer door and listened. *Nothing.* He brought the steel ring up and thumped it, five times, in a specific rhythm. The vibration reverberated through his helmet, like some muted bell. He listened again. *Nothing.*

*Habit again*, Pardell thought, but he wouldn't volunteer to be the first to break this one. Not so long ago, there'd been an armed guard leaning outside at all times, ready to slice the suit of anyone exiting the air lock without the code. Or the code would be answered by another, perhaps a warning to be weapons-ready, or demanding information. There hadn't been a guard since Rashid had died at the post, victim of either old age or a too-old suit—or both. *It didn't mean*, Pardell reminded himself, *there might not be one this time.* It would only take a change in the situation to restore the self-preserving instincts of the 'siders. A change like Earthers on-station, naming names.

Safe for the moment from defenders and their ghosts, Pardell stepped out of air lock S17 and into a scene of brilliant confusion, squinting at metal fired by the noonday sun.

The builders of Thromberg Station had perhaps fancied it a planet, setting it in close enough orbit to a white dwarf to make daytime on the station's surface a contrast between blinding glare and utterly black shadow, its light a rich feast at any hour for the mammoth collectors isolated from the station's spin. The sky was starkly black as well, except sunward, where the station's orbit paralleled a sparkling belt of ice-rich cometary debris, raw material for its industry and the sole reason life lingered in Thromberg's giant belly.

The station had been built to process a steady stream of immigrants on their way to the six terraformed worlds within its reach, capable of comfortably—albeit temporarily—housing thousands; providing air, water, and food; complete with immense luggage and freight handling capability; and hosting the bureaucracy, human and machine, to speed people to their futures. There had been lounges to entertain those waiting their turn on the transports, and customs stations aplenty to catch those planning to take advantage of their futures in ways Earth didn't condone.

Today, the luggage and freight areas still echoed with work crews, but their arms loaded and harvested transparent pipes packed with fungus and other simple organisms, the stuff of life rather than personal belongings or mail. If the exodus and riots hadn't killed so many, even that harvest might not have been enough. The customs stations were rumored to be jails. The lounges, Pardell had heard, were hospitals now, places where those who'd lost all hope could quietly apply for sterilization and so qualify for permanent station citizenship. Their rations, despite all talk of equality with immies, were supposedly somewhat better. *Maybe on the inward levels*, Pardell thought wryly. His stationer friends seemed to eat what he did. They drank the same swill, for sure.

If only by coincidence, the builders of Thromberg had planned well for the crisis caused by the Quill. But they could never have imagined what would happen to their station's smooth, polished exterior.

Pardell shut the air lock's outer door, relieved to find himself alone, and surveyed the part of Thromberg Station that no one acknowledged and no one dared touch.

Closest to him in the glittering metal forest was the *Endeavour*, her asteroid grapples biting deep into the multilayered skin of Thromberg like the jaws of a bloodsucking insect. Welds, some old and some fresher, made sure those grapples wouldn't come free again. There were welds and repairs on her hull as well. *Endeavor* had been a battle zone, once, and bore her scars of melted metal proudly.

*It was still a battle, merely frozen in time*, Pardell thought. He could count—and name—dozens of other starships from here; they continued beyond the long curve of the station, a crust thinning only where too close to the inhabited sections within. Shuttle or transport, freighter or private yacht: each was locked in its death's grip with the station, driving in pipes to siphon off air and water, many tapping station power lines. All had sacrificed moving among the stars so those they carried could live, forming a city out of their now-lifeless shells.

A city stretching in all directions, bordered by vacuum and held intact by a bloody determination to survive. Station Admin had tried to stop them, rejecting any responsibility for the ships who'd ripped Thromberg apart in their flight to Earth, only to be forced back by Sol System's killing zone. The ships had ignored all warnings, knowing the station had no warships or weapons, that it was a terminal designed to welcome voyagers, not protect itself. So the authorities had turned turtle, closing the docking rings and sealing air locks, refusing to expose themselves even to service the dying ships.

Pardell's lips pulled back over his teeth as he looked for, and found, the *Haida V*. She was an old freighter, a piece of junk that should have been out of service and scrapped, but the kind of ship a bit of coaxing and a lot of luck kept running. She'd arrived at Thromberg with the rest, her holds jammed with survivors from another ship crippled when her Captain hadn't believed Earth would fire on her own. The *Haida* had been almost out of fuel and her Captain well out of patience with panic-stricken fools. After a standoff lasting three days and two deaths, she'd ignored both hysterical warnings and normal docking protocols, ramming the dust-pocked nose of her ancient ship into the station with force enough to fuse them together. Then she sent two groups of space-suited volunteers outside. One group stood armed and ready, while the other drilled into the station and connected the ship's systems to Thromberg's own lifelines.

Station Admin hesitated—stunned perhaps by the audacity of the attack, despite it doing little more than lodging the nose of the *Haida* deep into Thromberg's whipple shield, that layer of metal and composites ready to be sacrificed as it absorbed energy from the unavoidable rain of micrometeors and other debris. Or perhaps there had been agonized debates on how to help or who to blame. *Maybe*, Pardell sometimes thought wistfully, *someone had pleaded*, "Look the other way."

Meanwhile, other ships, many as close to failing as the *Haida V*, made their own decisions. Like a drift of pollen landing on the mirrored surface of a lake, they matched velocity with the slower aft ring and touched down as if by plan, choosing their times by when the station's spin shadowed her wounded side, as if that kept what they were doing a secret.

It wasn't a secret, of course, nor was it truly meant to be. By crippling their ships and welding them to the station's plates, those returning from their attempt to reach Earth threw themselves on Thromberg's mercy instead, waiting to see if the air lock doors would finally open and grant them the only home humanity had left.

Pardell's eyes followed the feathered melt-lines along the *Endeavour*'s hull. *It could have happened like that*, he sighed to himself, straightening up and testing the hold of his mags on the station's pitted shield plates before letting go of the door handle. But the stationers had been caught reeling from the damage caused by the exodus; parts of the station were uninhabitable;

and calm reason still couldn't refute the dread of the deadly
Quill somehow arriving here next. Rumors burned through the
station like so many wildfires: maybe the Quill had contaminated the ships limpeted to the station like so many parasites;
maybe that was why Sol System had fired on their own instead
of letting them come home.

That had to be the reason.

Fear spread, and what could have been the brightest day in
Thromberg's history turned into its darkest. Desperate spacers
burned their way through the station's 'locks and waged war in
a maze of darkened corridors; equally desperate stationers
suited up and attacked the ships on the surface, many dying simply from underestimating the passionless constraints of vacuum
and gravity.

Too many died in places and ways they'd never imagined.

It was hard to say, later, if they fought each other or, on some
deep, terrified level both sides thought they were striking back
at the Quill. Regardless, it might have continued until all were
trapped or dead, but abruptly all hostilities ceased. A deal had
been struck, though neither side ever admitted it. Instead, the
spacers retreated to their ships, posting guards on key air locks
to watch the stationers retreat in turn. Station Admin quietly
ceased any restoration of the sections directly below the ships,
except those repairs necessary to keep air and water flowing
through the systems.

Soon, faces once familiar, now haggard and drawn into those
of strangers, began showing up in the ration lines, sometimes
doing occasional work that didn't require an immigrant registration number or station ident. They didn't have quarters or assignments; it seemed poor manners to ask about either, when it
was common enough knowledge where they lived. It was a tenuous tolerance from the beginning. During the Ration Riots, the
Outsiders, as they came to be known, were the first and easiest
targets. Most learned to stay away from large gatherings.

*Old news*, Pardell reminded himself, tilting back to judge the
angle of the cable he wanted, almost unconsciously listening for
the reassuring whine of the suit's conditioning system as it
dumped heat. Today, 'siders had more in common with the virtually imprisoned immigrants who'd never fled the station, and

some immies frankly admired what appeared to be 'sider free-dom. *As if these ships could ever fly again.* To Pardell's knowledge, few could boast real crews anymore, those with skills finding work inside the station. The ships themselves? Most had been gutted for any parts worth trading. The station looked the other way when 'siders lined up for rations, but it took something solid in hand to gain medical care, clothing, or simply a pocketful of negotiable dibs for beer.

The haphazard arrangement of ships, combined with their tangled roots into heaved and buckled station plates, made moving around on the surface tedious at best. Pardell glanced up, checking for traffic on the cable system. Clear. *One break today,* he told himself, inclined to feel morose.

The cables tethering the largest ships to one another had originally provided private comm feed between their Captains but, as ship systems failed and died—or were scavenged—the cables had become playgrounds and passageways for 'sider children. When those children grew up, they threaded more cable from ship to ship until the black sky loomed behind a web of glittering steel. Along that web, one could slide from one end of the docking ring to the other.

It wasn't for the faint of heart. Pardell switched off the mag under his left boot, careful not to disturb the placement of that foot against the plate beneath him. There were two large homemade clips on his belt, each attached by its own coil of fine wire to a reinforced loop. Taking one clip in his gloved hand, Pardell opened it so he held a hook, before reaching down to very gently switch off the mag under his right foot. His position had to be just so, his body perfectly symmetrical—

He pushed off gently but firmly, arms outstretched, hook in his left hand, aiming for the uppermost of the set of three cables catching sunlight in fiery streaks overhead. Passed the first. Missed the next by a slim margin; like most of his generation, he was prone to showing off even when alone. *There!* The hook snapped closed around the third cable.

Pardell's body kept heading out into the void until stopped by his grip. He used the change in momentum to start his spiraling slide along the cable, heading away from the air lock. The tops of starships swept by beneath him, like the jagged rocks of a dry river. *Plenty of ways to die out here without snagging your suit fabric on a rust bucket*, Pardell remembered Raner's lectures, but his awareness of the hazard posed by the ships was at best subconscious; he was too busy watching for the glint of anyone else sliding in his path. Right-of-way mattered, when you were using inertia for propulsion. There were several other space-suited figures in sight, but all were specks beading distant threads.

Pardell readied the second clip on his belt to snag an opposing cable as it rushed toward him, a move he made with the unconscious grace of practice and the necessity of risk. Time the spin and release right, and you flew in a new direction with hardly any loss of speed. Time it wrong—well, it would be a dark, three-hour trip, depending on whether you waited for your air to run out or spent it screaming for help that couldn't possibly arrive soon enough. The only mobile ships were owned by Thromberg or Earth, and they were snugged to the stern docking ring at the opposite end of the station.

*Assuming either heard, or either cared.*

There were a couple of kickoffs along Pardell's usual route home, spots where the cables passed close enough to a hull to allow a well-timed push in the desired direction. Otherwise, he whirled along with deceptive slowness, eyes almost closed against the station's glare despite the autodark of his helmet, until he got a glimpse of something where nothing belonged.

Pardell, currently sliding along using his right clip, brought up the left one in time to snag a cross-cable, pulling himself to a halt.

The instant he stopped moving, he knew he'd made a mistake, for the *something*, which with any respect for physics should have continued in its trajectory, stopped as well. It hovered alongside where he hung, looking for all the world like a forlorn and misdirected work 'bot—except that, instead of the lurid yellow of a station 'bot, this tiny satellite was a dishonest black, as though to prevent it from standing out in the sunlight.

*Not that there were any station 'bots*, Pardell reminded himself. Everyone knew the last one had been brought down by 'sider fire in the same conflict that slagged the *Endeavour*'s hull, adding a lengthy list of dangerous work assignments to those now done by living beings.

Pardell's mouth went dry as he pumped his legs to start sliding down the cable that led away from his home, daring the spy to follow him deeper into the network of metal that could snag it in the blink of an eye. He was disappointed when the operator refused his bait, but the 'bot wouldn't last long anyway. Spies weren't tolerated.

*One thing was certain*, Pardell decided with a chill for once having nothing to do with his suit. *The Earther wasn't trouble.*

She was disaster.

# Chapter 4

"IT'S simply asking for disaster!" Forester said, hands waving wildly enough to bring Grant's omnipresent guards to semi-alertness. "What could have possessed you to breach our rules like that? What gave you the right to risk everything we've managed to achieve?"

"It was a mechanical failure—a mistake—and we have apologized," Captain Tobo replied, with possibly a shade too much emphasis, *but then*, Gail thought, *by her count it was the sixth time he'd made the same point.*

She schooled her face into something pleasantly neutral, having needed to make her point only once: the Earth Research Council vessel was hers and, while on board the *Seeker*, Administrator Forester was her guest. He'd minded his manners—at least made no overt threats—and, despite his passionate outrage, appeared inclined to believe their protestations that the 'bot hadn't carried recording equipment, only a short-range visual feed meant to show the exterior of their ship. Nothing that could transmit the length of the station.

They'd seen nothing.

Gail was convinced this was a belief the stationer preferred, rather than held. In her case, it happened to be the truth, but only because the uproar from the station had been too immediate to give her time to view what kept Grant tight-lipped and Tobo apologizing. *Tobo*, Gail thought curiously, *never apologized.*

Forester had shown up outside the *Seeker*'s air lock before the 'bot had completed half its planned passage over Thromberg Station, a passage terminated by a station-run barge with a net—that much they'd told her. Strident official protests from almost every imaginable station bureaucrat had arrived almost simultaneously, clogging the comm system. *So much for stealth.* They might as well have batted a wasp nest from a tree and expected its inhabitants to ignore the event. Gail hooded her eyes, looking at Grant. Among the many questions she'd reserved for later was how the station had detected the military's little spy within minutes of its launch. *Something wasn't adding up*, Gail decided, but she didn't have time for new puzzles.

*Time.* It had always been her enemy. Hers was a mind that raced through problems, grasping concepts in a flash of insight before moving hungrily to new ideas. So few processed at her speed that she'd long ago learned to break her dissertations into palatable chunks for academic reviewers; learned to accommodate, if never to understand, why it always took them longer to see the obvious connections.

It was a hard-learned patience, a skill she practiced even now, having needed it lately more than ever.

Her parents, while appreciating Gail's gift, had known she would need such tools to survive it. She'd spent her summer vacations with a series of private tutors, receiving training in deportment and speech more suited to someone planning to run for public office than a seven-year-old missing her front teeth; lessons, as she grew older, ranging from meditation to manners, based in as broad a range of ethnicities as possible. She'd shown a flare for diplomacy, for understanding cultural patterns and how forces shaped societies.

A flare, but no desire. For as long as she could remember, Gail had known exactly what she wanted. She wanted a problem to solve—a problem no one else could overcome. Something that would make all of Earth sit up and take notice.

The Quill.

In her teens, Gail abandoned the social sciences and became a biologist. A brilliant one. But the Earth had thousands of brilliant biologists. She switched universities, studied xenobiology and terraforming. The Earth had hundreds of experts in those fields, most out of work. Even the never-inhabited Stage One and Two terraform worlds had been posted with warn offs. In case.

Finally, she became an analytical historian, specializing in recent events, pouring through manifests and records, publishing astonishing works detailing for the first time the most probable course taken by the Quill, postulating the direction of their origin—the first solid evidence as to the home of the deadly pests.

But no one cared.

The new worlds, confirmed or potentially contaminated, were abandoned; the stations were left to deal with their populations; and the Quill were merely *something* out there—something convenient to blame for the quiet, steady reduction in Earther exploration funding, for the drawing inward and consolidation of Earth's once-vast ambitions to endless renovations of the domed colonies on Sol System's immediate neighbors.

They'd cared once. When Gail was born, there were research facilities being established throughout Sol System, all devoted to finding a way to destroy Quill tissue without harming the tender Terran ecosystems built at such cost and with such hopes. They floundered on the same rock—there was no Quill tissue to test. Every known specimen had been destroyed in the frenzy to protect humanity. The contaminated worlds? The pests were there—the Quill Effect killed every human foolish enough to land—but the most sophisticated remotes and robot probes failed to retrieve a scrap of Quill tissue. It couldn't be found.

Earth had given up years ago. *She hadn't.*

"Dr. Smith?"

Surprised her attention had wandered, Gail shook her head slightly, gambling she would probably disagree with anything the stationer proposed, heard or not. Tobo's lips quirked, as though he knew perfectly well she'd lost track of what was going on, before he said helpfully: "I have no objections to letting the station techs keep the 'bot and give it a once-over. Maybe they can find out why it cut loose from its protocols and went roaming."

"Commander?" Gail raised her brow to get Grant's reaction. It was the FD's toy, after all.

There was nothing to read from his composed features. "I've no objection, Doctor," Grant offered smoothly. "Ship's equipment has nothing to do with me."

Administrator Forester didn't bother hiding his relief. *Why? What was going on here?* Gail wondered again, intrigued in spite of herself. "Thank you. I'm sure that will go a long way toward alleviating any—" he appeared to struggle for a word, then settled on a lame: "—any questions about what happened."

"You take your privacy very much to heart here," Gail observed dryly. "Rest assured, I have no interest in Thromberg Station or its population, with the exception of obtaining the assistance of Aaron Pardell. Have you made any progress in locating him for me?"

Forester's face tried to work into a smile but failed. "Surely there's someone else who can help you, Dr. Smith," he ventured, with an almost desperate air. "I can't imagine what possible use this man could be, even if we find him. I have to tell you in all honesty: this Aaron Pardell may not even exist."

"That's not the message you sent to Titan U, Administrator," Gail reminded him, chilling her voice several degrees. "In that, you claimed to have his birth record. I trust you aren't about to tell us that was a lie."

"No! No. Well, not a lie . . ." Forester, who'd been standing during his tirade against the *Seeker*'s deployment of a potential spy, chose that moment to sink into the seat he'd been offered and earlier refused. Out of the corner of her eye, Gail noticed Grant's two guards weren't relaxing. *Probably enjoyed having something to do*, she told herself, making a private vow to keep them very busy if Forester was about to tell her they'd come to Thromberg for nothing. "There's no proof this Aaron Pardell was actually born here," Forester continued. "What's on file is an application for stationer birth registration from an Aaron Raner—on behalf of a child he claimed to have found abandoned. It doesn't say if the application was granted, but I doubt it was. There aren't any other records for the name."

Gail glanced down at her notepad, tapping a key once, twice, until a very short list of names came up. *There.* "Who is this Raner?" she inquired, keeping her voice matter-of-fact with an effort.

"Raner was a stationer."

"Was?" Commander Grant prompted when Forester didn't volunteer anything more.

"Was," repeated Forester firmly, as if that were that. Gail wondered if she'd be forced to have one of Grant's experts tap into the station's record system. They'd refrained until now, hoping for cooperation. *This*, she decided, *didn't sound as though much more would be forthcoming.*

*Meanwhile* . . . Gail opened her eyes exactly the amount to show her innocent attention. "If we believe the application was for a real baby, Administrator, then Aaron Pardell was born shortly after the stations imposed absolute birth control on their populations. Surely there aren't many individuals his age—"

Forester leaped to his feet, his cheeks suffused with red. "Get your history straight, Dr. Smith," he grated. "The stations didn't impose birth control. Earth ordered the sterilization of permanent station residents and controls on immigrant fertility as a condition for food shipments. It was obey or starve—but we had children when this all started. And plenty were orphans."

Gail lifted two fingers to hold Grant and his people, waiting until they'd definitely eased back before saying softly, and quite sincerely, to the outraged stationer: "I'm deeply sorry, Administrator. I meant no offense, nor to bring back difficult times and terrible choices. But, despite your lack of records, I'm convinced a man named Aaron Pardell is here, on Thromberg. So, if his age can't help narrow our search, what can? You know your people. Will he come forward of his own accord?"

"No. I'm sure he won't." Forester remained standing, a posture aimed, not at the anxious troops, but at her—as if defending one of his own. *So*, Gail told herself. *He wasn't completely motivated by self-interest.* Such an individual would have been more—straightforward—to work with, if less than trustworthy in a pinch.

"Why?" she asked, truly curious.

"You're Earthers," Forester said, his tone making it clear her question surprised him. "If the welfare of all of us hasn't mattered to you before now—why should the welfare of one?"

"Had you considered that the welfare of this one might have an impact on everyone else on the station?" she suggested carefully, wary of what she might be revealing to Tobo and Grant, let alone Forester and the vids she knew full well Reinsez regularly tried to plant in her office.

She'd misjudged Forester's intelligence as well, or maybe life under Thromberg's harsh conditions had honed his instincts.

"You're after the Survivor," the stationer breathed as if thoroughly impressed, then burst into laughter with an almost hysterical edge to it, his thin shoulders shaking. "Gods, if that doesn't beat all. You and this fancy Earther ship, these troops in their me-only uniforms—falling for that tired nonsense."

Gail was spared having to answer by Tobo's quick: "You aren't making sense yourself, Administrator. What are you talking about?"

"This place breeds a lot of stories, Captain," Forester gasped, almost wheezing as he attempted to regain something of his dignity. "Hang around long enough and you'll hear even wilder ones. Maybe you'll find one more to your liking!"

Gail steepled her fingers on her desk. "Administrator, I'm many things, but I am not a fool. The Survivor Legends are just as widespread in Sol System as here." *A minor exaggeration.* For Tobo, she added, "The details vary, but all revolve around a brave hero who lands on one of the contaminated worlds and returns with the secret of how to withstand the Quill Effect. Some versions include the establishment of a hidden colony. Some have the Survivor forgetting the secret and wandering from station to station trying to find it again, only to fail. Others have him—or her—becoming the savior of humanity." She raised an eyebrow. "Do I have the essence of it correct, Administrator Forester?"

Mirth forgotten, Forester nodded, tight-lipped.

Gail hardened her voice slightly, tapping her fingers on the desk in emphasis. "So, perhaps you can accept that we are here for something other than chasing myths, that Earth might have financed this state-of-the-art ship and my considerable expertise for something other than daydreams, and that if I require this individual, Aaron Pardell, perhaps—just perhaps, Administrator—" this with sudden sharpness, "you and your station should bend every resource to my aid instead of offering obstructions."

Her attack drove the red from Forester's face, but he didn't back down. *This was,* Gail reminded herself, *an individual who kept order among thousands of rightfully frustrated people.* "Perhaps, Dr. Smith," he countered almost smoothly, "you and your—scientific—staff should share your reasons with us, if you expect our help."

*If?* Gail repeated to herself. She'd come a little too far to tolerate an "if" from a man like Forester. "I expect you to obey orders," she snapped. "Or have you forgotten who runs this station?"

"Orders?" He snorted derisively. "Oh, you mean TerraCor Limited? Or Earth? If you think either of them has any authority left here, you've been badly misled, Dr. Smith. Thromberg's independent—"

"Is that so?" Gail put her hands flat on the desktop and pushed herself up so that she leaned forward, straight-armed, and stared right at Forester. "Since we are being so frank with one another, let me be totally clear with you, Administrator. I have all the 'authority' I need to give any orders here I choose. With one comm signal from me, the food supplements ready to unload from the dozen or so Earth transports docked alongside us stay in their holds. A word to that man beside you," a nod at the ominous Grant, "your station comes apart at the seams. If you have any doubts I'd do the one—or am capable of the other—try me now."

Gail waited for Forester's reply, carefully not looking at Grant—who in all likelihood could do what she said, given the crates locked in the *Seeker*'s hold, but wouldn't—or at Tobo, who was likely completely surprised by all this, but would keep a straight face. *If you want something*, Gail told herself, *claim it first and loudest.*

"None of that will be necessary, Professor," Forester said heavily, first to break their mutual glare. "I don't doubt your authority or willingness to exercise it." He met her eyes again, no defiance left, only a strange wistfulness. "We've been abandoned to fend for ourselves, you understand. Having Earthers assume we'll merely smile and ask how high to jump after all this time—well that's not going to sit easily with some, that's for sure."

Gail seated herself and nodded graciously. "I have no intention of demanding the impossible, Administrator. My needs remain very simple."

"Pardell," Forester said, shaking his head in total disbelief.

"Pardell," Gail agreed.

*        *        *

"You were lucky."

Gail leaned her head back against a luxuriously embroidered cushion, her lips twisting into a grin. "Luck, my dear Captain, had nothing to do with it. Forester was testing me. My guess? Anything other than a strong response from me would have opened the doors to tedious rounds of bargaining, and I have no intention of being blackmailed to get what I'm after. They must have thought they had an edge with that 'bot of Grant's—" She let her smile fade. "You did record a transmission, didn't you?"

Grant and Tobo were the only ones left with her in the office. The three of them sat at their ease in the broad, welcoming chairs in one corner, sipping on the faintly bitter tea Tobo insisted be served. Gail was faintly surprised Reinsez hadn't already stormed in, demanding explanations or, at the very least, annoying her with his analysis of what he would have done.

*Had he been the one in charge*, she told herself firmly. *Which he wasn't.*

Nor was Reinsez immune to the aftereffects of his own favorite sherry, something Tobo ensured was in plentiful supply in the ship's galley, hence rare moments of peace such as this in which to contemplate what might happen next. After he slept it off, the university's watchdog would doubtless skim through all the vid recordings he could find. Gail was reasonably sure her office and bedroom were clear of the devices—she'd had Grant's people sweep both very quietly, five times now—but, as at home, she undressed with the lights off to be sure. *There was something*, she thought, *about never knowing who might be watching.*

"Deployment Specialist Peitsch is very capable. Here." Grant tossed her the viewer, a disk already set to play. His face turned inexplicably grim. "It's—well, it's not what I expected."

Tobo gave a short, humorless bark. "Who would?" he said, then waved impatiently at Gail, urging her to see for herself.

She cued the viewer with one hand, raising her teacup with the other as she started watching the dizzying perspective provided by the 'bot as it spun away from the underbelly of the *Seeker* and headed out along the seemingly limitless arc of Thromberg's white flanks. The image quality was as exceptional as the subject was dull.

Gail took an idle sip then froze, the cup barely touching her lips, as the 'bot began passing over what was not in the least dull or ordinary.

"Good gods," she whispered involuntarily. "What—? They have a fleet out here?"

"Once, maybe," Grant corrected, his voice rough and low. "Watch. The 'bot's going in closer. See?"

She did, indeed. Plainly, the ships were derelicts, attached to the station's hull by a bewildering variety of wires and conduits, grapples and beams. "What a mess . . ." Gail muttered to herself, finding herself offended at the sight, as if some parasitic fungus grew on the station's side. "What are they doing? Storing scrap?"

"Surviving," was Tobo's low growl. Gail spared a moment to put down her cup and look at him. For the first time since they'd met on Titan, Tobo's face was completely serious; if she didn't know him better, she'd say he looked as though he'd love to strangle someone.

Gail gazed back into the viewer. The 'bot had moved on, but the blight of dead ships continued—*it must coat the entire aft ring of the station*, she realized with sick wonder. No questions now why Forester was so anxious about external surveillance— or why the *Seeker* had to choose between such a limited selection of approved docking approaches. They kept this part of their artificial world well out of sight of visitors.

*The question was why?*

Then, Gail saw it. "What?" she exclaimed before she could stop herself, her fingers hurrying to pause the display and back it up a few heartbeats.

She watched a second time as the 'bot slowed to follow a space-suited figure careening along one of the cables slung between the ships. Just as Gail was sure the figure was out of control, one of its arms swung outward, somehow latching onto another cable and so coming to an abrupt halt. The 'bot went up close, so close, it reflected itself in the blackened curve of a helmet.

A helmet that belonged in some museum. Gail felt as though she'd stepped back in time. *Who would use such antiques these days?* And the rest of the suit was a mess, crisscrossed with tape and mends until the original silver blue was almost obscured.

The figure moved in an odd fashion that nonetheless effectively propelled it away. Gail almost protested when the 'bot swung in another direction, forgetting this wasn't live feed. Then she subsided, seeing that the space suit wasn't alone out here. Once she knew what to look for, the barnacle crust of ships swarmed with life, sliding down cables, moving in and out of air locks, working in small groups.

"Survival," she echoed Tobo's judgment, and shuddered. "They're—living?—outside the station?" The visual turned black and shut down. It must have been when the station discovered the 'bot. Which meant that Forester and the rest knew perfectly well what was out there.

"I'd heard talk from freighter captains," Tobo said. "I hadn't believed it—you hear all sorts of junk—"

"This is real," Grant objected.

Tobo took the viewer and ejected the disk, turning it over in his hand thoughtfully. "Yes."

Gail was pleased her hands didn't shake as she picked up her teacup and refilled it. "What did these captains say?"

"That Thromberg was damaged when so many immigrants tried to run for Earth at once—to go home," Tobo said in a slow, careful voice, as if listening to his own words. "The stationers were just as afraid of the Quill, but they had nowhere to run, no ships of their own. When the immigrants were—turned back—at Sol, those that survived tried to return here. But the stationers believed their ships had been contaminated by Quill."

"That's ridiculous—" Gail began.

"By what we know now. Then, it was believed Earth fired on the ships and drove them back to prevent the spread of the Quill."

Grant's voice slid into the following pause: "A station can't defend itself. The rings were designed to expedite the movement of large numbers of ships. All they could do was refuse to help—they must have sealed up the docking rings, locked the ports and air locks. The station left them outside to die," He spoke as though making a tactical observation, until the last, when the words dropped a startling, menacing octave.

"Life finds a way," Gail observed, watching the disk harbored in Tobo's hands. "Life survives however it can, wherever it can. Like these people—by staying on their ships all these years."

Tobo pocketed the disk and leaned forward, his elbows on his knees. "According to what I was told, that's not quite true. The Outsiders, as they're called, are supposed to have secret ways on and off the station. The stationers look the other way, too busy dealing with the immigrants who didn't leave."

Gail and Grant traded glances—his was decidedly gloomy. "Why don't I like where this is going?" he asked neither of them in particular.

"Because," Gail answered, "it may mean we've been looking in the wrong place for Aaron Pardell."

# Chapter 5

LIKE her young owner, the *Merry Mate II* was skin over bones, more patchwork than whole, and worth little more than her mass in materials by most standards.

Pardell felt uncommonly aware of the similarity after the day's events. "As if I care what any of them think," he muttered under his breath as he hung his suit over the line in the gap between his second- and third-best socks. There weren't fourths, but he'd never needed them anyway. He pinched the fabric of the nearest. Still damp. It took forever to dry things anywhere except in the warmth of the galley, but Raner had brought him up to know food and laundry shouldn't mix.

The suit was sweat-damp inside and, to be honest, gave off an aroma that didn't belong in a galley either. His boots were worse; he'd had to pour liquid out of both and the linings shed irreplaceable bits of themselves in the process. Encountering the Earther's spy 'bot hadn't helped the old gear's function, nor had his unusually long, circumspect route home afterward. At least the station's clean-up barge had come hunting—a forgivable intrusion, since it scooped up the 'bot—but by then Pardell hadn't felt like taking any more chances.

*Smith had been hunting* him. He knew it as surely as he knew the entry codes for the *'Mate*.

Pardell gave his empty suit an unnecessary whack as he ducked under it. "Why? Why me?" he asked the universe in an aggrieved tone, despite knowing he'd get no answer, despite a mouth-drying suspicion he knew the answer already.

Other years, earlier years, there would have been a chorus of responding voices, ranging from cheery to profane. The *'Mate*'s three cabins, galley, and private washroom might technically be his legacy from his foster father, but her space was a luxury not to be wasted. Aaron Raner had left their port open to anyone willing to put up with what he vaguely termed his son's allergy. Some stayed only until witnessing young Pardell's convulsions, especially those who inadvertently touched him and caused one. Others had stayed for years, becoming family until accident, old age, or station temptations took them.

Raner had never explained what debt or obligation turned him from stationer to Outsider, even when Pardell was old enough to understand the difference and young enough to ask. He did know it had something to do with him, that for some reason Raner couldn't keep him on the station and had chosen to stay here with him. As a child, he'd suffered confused pangs of guilt; as he matured, he grew to understand how very lucky he'd been to have the stationer care for him. Raner, a quiet, peaceful man, had been killed before Pardell could express either feeling, cut down with so many others in an aisle slippery with wasted blood.

Since then, Pardell had hoped for company, having been raised to share his living space and unhappy alone. But there were no longer enough 'siders to fill the ships and most stationers were unwilling to venture outside even if they'd been welcome.

Immies were welcome. A handful had ventured outside in the early years, seeking missing family or friends, trying to comprehend the finality of the new distinction between in and outside. Most had reentered Thromberg, afraid to trust their lives to aging equipment for the sake of a little more room and privacy; very few, in fact, risked any of what little security station registration, address, and work ident granted them. They'd lost enough already.

Unspoken was the burden of choices made by either side, and consequences to be borne, however unfair.

Pardell busied himself in the galley. He brought out the bags he'd carried on his suit, opening a couple to dump his share of the daily ration on the table: an odd assortment of bars, jellies, and some quasi-mauve globules Yves McTavish, the immie working the dispenser this shift, had proudly announced looked just like grapes—a fruit grown on Earth. *Give them credit,*

Pardell grinned to himself, *for putting the same thing in our hands every day and making it look like something new.* As for the grapes—Pardell held them up to the light and shook his head. Familiar with the station's idea of how best to keep everyone fed, he knew food could come in different shapes and textures, some warm, some cold. It made life more interesting. But mimicking Earth plant material? It seemed pointless and a little obscene. Perhaps it comforted the older ones.

*Doubtless the Earthers had brought their own supplies.*

For a moment, as Pardell nibbled a "grape," curiosity consumed him. What would a real grape be like? Were there any on her ship? What else might be different?

Pardell's thoughts unfolded, freezing the moment, expanding the galley of the *'Mate* outward until he lost every sense of himself and saw only events, consequences, possibilities. He saw *forward* to a time when, unless checked, the differences between humanity's sundered parts would become so pronounced there could be no commonalities, to a potential future when Earther would name a distinct species as well as culture. *They would meet the alien, no longer knowing themselves.*

"Assuming," Pardell told the grapes, forcing himself free of abstraction, "they ever let us breed." That was the crux of it; the fertility inhibiters were in the "grapes"—in all the rations so no one could escape them, even if anyone was crazy enough to want to disrupt Thromberg's precarious balance. Of course, he knew better than to express any opinion on that subject near the hard-eyed immie women. It took little these days to launch the calmest, most rational female into an uncomfortably detailed and direct commentary on the passing of time and its effects on a woman's body—especially since the latest Earther stupidity.

*Not that anyone blamed them,* he thought. Some charitable group or other in Sol System had raised funds to send a transport to Thromberg, a transport loaded with embryo storage equipment and cases. Noticeably lacking was the equipment to thaw the embryos, the explanation being that the group would care for the unborn, making sure the immigrants had a lasting legacy, a living posterity which would live safely on Earth.

The ship had been sent back empty, except for a short, somewhat unlikely suggestion on where to send it next. *What good's a legacy I'll never hold in my arms*, Pardell could hear Amy Denery now . . . *We came out here to make families and a new world, not to be harvested.*

Filled with these and other restless thoughts, Pardell toyed with his rations. Usually he'd pull out a reader if he had to eat alone. Today, he knew he couldn't concentrate and tried for a novel arrangement of food on his plate instead. He created one, but it required the annoying grapes be squashed between two fingers and lined up in a spiral from the middle. Their interiors were a very ordinary and disappointing pink.

Abruptly, the result reminded Pardell of the way Malley's mother's insides had spilled over the floor as she pushed both him and her son ahead to the safety of the air lock, strange whorls and cloudy, translucent sheets steaming as their warmth spent itself on the icy, dark surface.

He grabbed the plate and flung it, and its contents, against the wall.

"Wasteful, young Aaron."

Pardell started violently, fearing that the Earthers had followed him home and somehow knew the precious codes to his ship, even as he recognized the voice and relaxed again with a shudder. "Damn it, Rosalind," he said unsteadily. "It's not polite to sneak up on people."

Rosalind Fournier, forty years his senior and once senior systems engineer on a freighter which had failed to hold its crew or air, tsked-tsked at something. *His lack of respect or the fake grapes?* Pardell wondered nonsensically, his heart still pounding as he watched her enter the galley. Rosalind was naturally elegant, though dressed in bits and pieces of other people's clothing, a tall, willowy woman whose age showed only in the salt and pepper of her hair and the fine lines edging her mouth and eyes. She even moved the clumsy artificial hands her crewmates had fashioned for her with a terrible grace, her own hands having refused to release the white-hot handle keeping the emergency lock open until everyone else had escaped the inferno behind her.

It was said she shot her own captain for trying to push his way out before the wounded.

All Pardell knew for sure was Rosalind and Aaron Raner had

been close—close enough that she had the *'Mate*'s codes, and lived here with them more often than not. Until Raner died. *Then again*, he reminded himself, *nothing had been the same after that*.

"How have you been, Rosalind?" Pardell asked, having re-captured something of his breath. He intercepted her attempt to salvage the food he'd thrown at the wall. "I'll do that." It wasn't the wasted grapes—he was all too familiar with her spacer's fastidious horror of loose objects, despite the *'Mate*'s current condition.

"I heard what happened in Sammie's," she said, taking a seat at the galley's long table and spreading the contents of her ration bag alongside his. Exactly the same, save her pseudo-grapes were intact, but that was to be expected. The point was to show one wasn't planning to freeload. As a visitor, you chipped in everything you had, if you wanted a real welcome and not directions to the nearest air lock. Of course, Rosalind was family—there was no question of her right to sit here any time she chose. But she always observed the courtesies, particularly those she and Raner had established for the Outside in the first place.

Pardell eyed his guest, well aware there was also no question of Rosalind Fournier's ability to take what she felt she was owed—from anyone. "The Earthers," he returned shortly. "News travels fast."

"Hardly news," she said offhandedly. "Nothing calls in for docking rights without my hearing about it first. You know that." He did. There were those 'siders, Rosalind prime among them, who had never ended their vigilance where it concerned either ship movements or new regs from the station. *For some*, Pardell thought half-resentfully, *the old habits would rule until they died*.

"Then what brings you here?"

Rosalind's eyes narrowed. *Disapproval.* "I heard about your little accident."

The blush heated his cheeks again. "It was nothing—"

Rosalind gestured to the water container in the middle of the table, producing a metal cup from her pocket. Pardell filled it, then poured one for himself. They sipped in unison, once, then again.

The small ritual soothed him, as she'd doubtless intended it should. "It really was nothing, Rosalind," he repeated more calmly. "You needn't worry. Hugh Malley was right there and got me out of it—a bit uncomfortably, mind you. I was fine."

Her lips twitched. "The man thinks fast. A good friend, young Aaron."

"The best," Pardell concurred, then fell silent.

Neither spoke for a long moment: Pardell no longer interested in conversation, given the uncomfortable nature of the likeliest topic, and Rosalind apparently deep in her own thoughts.

In the quiet, the *Merry Mate II* hummed, her machine voice at the edge of detection, her systems purifying and warming the air, recycling waste, lighting the darkness. As a child and, to be honest, even now when alone or escaping uneasy dreams, Pardell imagined the ship herself was aware and able to think; silent not by choice but because her machine thoughts were simply too different from his own to share. Knowing himself already too different, he kept such fancies to himself.

Still, Pardell viewed the past, not as Raner or others had told it to him, but as if he could see it through the *'Mate*'s sensors, for this ship had borne mute witness to the events that brought Rosalind to sit in silence across from him at this table and led to so much blood and fear.

Pardell could see it all now, as though reflected in the water of his cup . . .

. . . Adrift, derelict, abandoned. The approaching freighter looming out of the utter dark, her grapples slipping forward to gather in the lost one. The code to open her ports delivered by the only one who now could, stationer Aaron Raner, his face streaming with tears as he races through empty corridors calling the names of the missing, reigniting ship systems with his voice, since all but the emergency beacon have fallen to standby levels to conserve power.

In the last place he looks, the man finds a cold speck of life, life that whimpers and shrieks at his touch.

Crewed again, strangers fumbling, then sure at her controls, retracing a familiar taped course, the approach to Thromberg locked in and accepted. All systems nominal.

Docked time, drive systems dormant, a pause like peace. Communication links to the station activated; traffic along the link is steady, unremarkable.

Suddenly, proximity alarms shrill through every plate and joint. *Danger! Damage! Thieves!* The stationer, Aaron Raner, is back, keying in codes to mute the ship's response to what is happening at her locks. Burning, voices, power fluctuations, the scream of evacuating air. Agreeable, sensible orders to seal up tight. Then all fail safes are turned off and the *Merry Mate II* finds herself ripping away from the station. *Danger! Damage! Thieves!* Her machine cries are silenced again, this time with a lock, this time for good.

A tape grants stability and purpose. She accepts it, switching system drives to translight, aiming for the origin of her living cargo, if not her own. Origin for the *'Mate* was the Callisto shipyards, in orbit around Jupiter. Perhaps, if machines had longings, she feels one for the safety of home.

There is no safety here. This isn't a convoy; she's one of a crowd, a torrent, a streaming irregular mass of translight drives corrupting the very space she rides until some tumble off course, losing themselves in nothing. Their final signals pass through what's still real and travel ever away, becoming ghosts for the future.

Meanwhile, voices argue throughout her corridors, unfamiliar voices debating topics of no concern to a ship; Raner's voice urges caution, reason. The stationer does not touch her controls but holds the codes for their use. When not calming others, he stays with the tiny speck of life, speaking words repetitive in their softness, adapting tools to touch without pain.

A restful time for a machine, given direction and asked only for speed. Does she dream then or hum in chords of power?

Plummet from translight. Sol System.

Raner has muffled her alarms; she can't shout *Danger! Damage! Thieves!* But warn offs streak red across all her boards. The strange crew and Raner curse and shout to no avail. They use her sensors to see for themselves.

Vast distances are made conquerable by convention; so the patrol ships knew to wait here for incomers. This is the lane swept clear of hazards for those bound to Earth. Now it is filled with them.

How absurd to simply stop, hanging Solward of Neptune. How much more absurd to stop as one of this company of vagabonds, this fleet come together for no more organized rationale than fear has its time and any movement can seem to safety.

Incoming transmission: *Turn back. Sol System is under quarantine to protect humanity from the Quill contagion. No one from the stations will be permitted to enter until this ban is lifted.*

*Turn back or be destroyed.*

The *'Mate's* chronometers keep track of time passing; her crew are frozen in place.

A broadcast from one of their companions: garbled, incoherent pleading. It ends abruptly.

*Danger! Damage! Thieves!* The *'Mate's* alarms are mute, but her views show for those waiting how the leading ships are being targeted two at a time, five, now ten.

Raner shouts a command; the tape is ejected, reversed, reinserted. The ship hits translight breaking all the rules; space shatters around her as others do the same, space that splinters into light as those who hesitate become small suns instead.

Do ships mourn? Humans do.

Do ships comprehend governments and laws? Humans must. The Patrol who killed the ships enforce the laws set by Earth for all of Sol System. Earth is the heart and mind of humanity, an overburdened heart and overcrowded mind perhaps, but nonetheless the seat of all policy. What Earth fears, everyone fears.

Oh, there are other voices. The great system universities— Titan, Luna, Phobos, and, the oldest, Antarctica—come closest to independence and pride themselves on being opinionated. Their mandate is to look outward, to pave the way for humanity to expand beyond Sol, to seed a future beyond Earth. But the Quill had struck them first and hardest, stealing away the terraforming projects they'd designed, at the same time crippling the huge corporations who'd invested everything in humanity's next stage of growth. The universities and corporations had learned the lesson of fear well.

*Danger! Damage! Thieves!* Not quick enough. A blast catches up as translight engages; the *'Mate* screams without sound. Autorepairs initiate, cut speed, necessitate deviation, alter the panicked flight.

Other ships are hobbled, some crippled, some die. Their combined flight is a halting one as suited crews work to exhaustion helping passengers, bundled within freight canisters because there are no more suits, make the dangerous transit to healthier ships.

The tiny speck of life in the *'Mate*'s cabin sleeps; perhaps ships do as well, given a course and repaired systems.

Plummet from translight. Thromberg Station.

The *Merry Mate II* is already late; Raner utters a command to stop them before approach is locked. Suspicion or caution; both are improvements over blind risk. Perhaps the ship approves.

Her screens capture the crew. They stare out at the spectacle of the vast cylinder of the station besieged by hundreds of ships, large and small, fully intact to barely holding air.

Raner cries out at something he sees. A ship careens past them, too close, out of control, bleeding her air as flame. *Danger! Damage! Thieves!* the *'Mate* cries silently. Specks tumble from the ship: pieces of debris, suited survivors. The station is forgotten in the urgency of dealing with what can be done.

Codes allow the unlawful—gravity off, both of the *'Mate*'s freight locks open to space, her holds scoured to vacuum, her interior protected only by bulkheads and access door locks. A silent cacophony as both mag boots and scrap thump home on her outer surface, a confusion of what should be saved and what her sensors scream to avoid. It continues, spreads into her holds as some move within while others reach her hull.

The proper place of things is restored: relief to systems designed to prevent risk. The holds warm, fill with air as well as moans and molecules of scorched flesh. There is a woman Raner cares for, ignoring urgent demands about courses and futures. She left her hands in the other ship, it seems; not the most sorely wounded, since her voice lifts to be heard with Raner's, discussing courses and futures after all.

A ship can see all ways at once; inside, outside makes no difference. The *'Mate*'s forward views fill with Thromberg's white curve, emergency patches like fingernail scratches of dull gray metal scoring its perfection, every intact docking port inhospitably closed.

Communication links overload repeatedly, kicking off-line as too many voices demand to be heard. Perhaps the ship is overwhelmed with human passions and cannot bear to listen. One voice gets through, calling for Raner by name. Perhaps the man is overwhelmed and cannot bear to answer.

Do ships grow impatient? Boards flash demands as resources run low—perhaps that is one and the same.

Do humans? Never doubt they consider time an enemy. As the hours accumulate, the voices sputter and fade to ominous, waiting silence. Many on the *'Mate* sleep. Raner does not. He divides his time with mechanical precision between the baby, the woman—Rosalind—and the *'Mate*'s view of the station.

Sensors, like a sleeping dog's ears, react first to change. One of the dozens of ships hovering in line with the *'Mate* powers up without warning, unforgivably close to others—*Danger! Damage! Thieves!* the *'Mate* would wail if she could. No need for her alarms—Raner stands at the view screen, statue-still, watching the ship as she moves deceptively slowly from the line, acceleration disguised by perspective, heading for Thromberg.

The *Haida V* sends out her ship-protest as proximity alarms and emergency ident codes, machine cries humans can ignore at will. Thromberg's horrified echoes fill the monitors with flashes of red. The collision fools the eye but not sensors set to calculate the tangents of debris. The *Haida* is pockmarked by shards of the station's metal as they ricochet off her hull; the *'Mate* braces herself to be next.

*Haida* stays in place, her nose fused within the mass of buckled plates by either luck or desperate planning. Suited figures leap from her air locks, drifting down to the larger mass of the station, some with cabling stringing out behind them that catch the last flare of sunlight over Thromberg's long belly.

Wrongness. Perversion. Are these concepts to a starship?

Perhaps the 'Mate rationalizes the attachments as being like those in a shipyard; where hoses and other lines are temporary, messy things; where humans work together to aid and repair ships. There's no doubt the *Haida* needs aid and repair.

There's no doubt others do as well. As the light from the star Thromberg orbits as home is lost behind her rim, the waiting turns into something else. One by one, then by the dozen, other ships power up and approach the station—ever so slowly, as if fearing to be chased away again, as if lacking the bold courage—or insanity—of the *Haida*. They hurry to touch down in the shadows, crews scrambling outside in the utter cold to gnaw their way into the station's promise of warmth and safety.

The docking area rolls back into dawn, waiting ships synchronized to its spin, strange silence from all concerned. Below, the station's surface looks oddly normal, like the landing field on some airless moon. This is where ships should be, this is where they were welcomed once. The 'Mate listens, but where there should be the reassuring overlap of codes and instructions comes only silence. Saving grace for all—those landing understand they must touch only here, on the docking ring itself, or risk wobbling the seemingly invulnerable station from her orbit.

Nightfall. There are new stars nearby as ships turn on their docking lights to avoid ramming one another as wave after wave descends to join the others on the station. The 'Mate is soon alone.

Do machines face conflicts within their programming? Humans must. Rosalind arrives on the bridge, given room by the rest. She stands by Raner, the stationer, for a moment, both look at the scene in the 'Mate's screens, then she whispers in his ear. He shakes his head violently, utters incoherent words. Others grab his arms, they are rough, the 'Mate is alarmed by violence near her controls. *Danger! Damage! Thieves!* but her silenced voice counts for naught.

There is sudden stillness. Raner shakes an arm free, stares at Rosalind, then reaches forward to input the codes for manual control. The 'Mate drifts down and away from herself, an inner distancing that perhaps brings a certain resigned peace. Raner pulls his other arm from a now-loose grip and leaves the bridge to care for the tiny speck of life.

Does the *'Mate* know this is her final journey? Perhaps there is comfort in that as well.

Pardell knew there was no point rushing Rosalind. She'd seen the worst his peculiar nature could do, had sat with him while Raner tried drug after drug to control the convulsions. She'd made sure someone would stay with him after Raner's death, although making it clear she couldn't bear to remain. Since then, her habit was to drop in, like this, unannounced but usually for reasons that showed she kept track of him. It had been comforting, until today.

*Today*, Pardell thought suddenly, *he'd had too much of being watched, even by those who cared about him.*

Rosalind's right hand was thick and paddlelike, incapable of fine movement. Her left hand was more elaborate. Under its three-fingered glove was a small yet powerful servo mechanism her crewmates had liberated from an internal repair 'bot with no further need for it. At the moment, Rosalind was using it to turn her cup in delicate circles on the tabletop, alternately gripping, twisting, and releasing. She could as easily squeeze its metal flat, but Rosalind loathed waste. She seemed to find her own movements fascinating, and didn't look up at him when she asked suddenly: "Why do you risk it, young Aaron?"

He knew what she meant and considered pretending he didn't, then shrugged. "Sammie's? It's not a risk. I'm with my friends, Rosalind."

Her eyes lifted. They were a pale gray, with flecks of oily black; cold, penetrating eyes that missed little and forgave nothing. "Your friends hurt you today."

"It was an accident!" Pardell snapped. "My friends look out for me—they always have. With them, I can be myself and not some—" the word died on his tongue.

"Freak?"

*It shouldn't hurt from her*, Pardell told himself fiercely, *not when he thought it all the time himself.*

But it did.

Rosalind reached for his hand. He put his fingers into her gloved prosthesis carefully, slowly—*forgiveness*—remembering all the times she'd been the one to bandage his knee or some other scrape, or help fit a new-to-him suit as he grew out of the old pieces. Her loss had given her the ability to touch him, and he would never forget that comfort. "I don't want to upset you, young Aaron," she told him, her voice softer than usual, almost gentle. "But sometimes you need reminding. You slide a cable so fine it scares me—it scares all of your friends."

Pardell took back his hand. "What do you want me to do, Rosalind? Lock myself on board the *'Mate*? Use the comm as my only way to interact with others? Don't you think this—" he held up his hand and stripped off its glove, feeling the cold touch of air; beneath, his skin was pale and clean, veined under its surface in faint gold, like the imperfections in marble "—is punishment enough, without making it completely impossible for me to have a normal life?" He sighed and looked at her. "There's such a thing as being too safe."

"There's such a thing as being not safe at all, young Aaron," Rosalind turned his words back on him, her eyes full of foreboding.

"The Earthers," Pardell sighed again as he pulled on the glove, feeling exposed without the covering even though it did nothing to protect him from touch. "I'm not a fool. While it would be nice if the Aaron Luis Pardell they hunt has inherited controlling shares in a major Earth conglomerate, maybe Terra-Cor itself, everyone knows there's nothing about me worth anyone's attention but my—condition. Unless you're planning to tell me it's my wealth." His wave extended to include the galley around them and, by that, the dead ship herself.

Rosalind merely looked pensive, as if he'd given her something new to consider. "Don't undervalue the old girl," was all she said.

"And don't underestimate the curiosity value of a mutation," he said sharply, refusing to be distracted. "What else could it be? They've always been after the station to report any deformities or sickness—we all know it's to justify how Earth treats us here—now somehow they've heard about me. Sure, they'll pay me. Anything to have a freak to show off."

"Obvious," Rosalind agreed, then added deliberately: "Is the obvious always valid?"

Pardell's thoughts fractured and re-formed, as she'd intended, and he squinted at her. "You know something about these Earthers," he said suspiciously. "What?"

Servo fingers stroked their paddle counterpart. "Not as much as either of us would like," Rosalind began by admitting. "I know their ship, the *Seeker*. She was shown off last year by Titan University's Works Department as some sort of marvel— a prototype research vessel, crammed full of the latest scanning gear and who knows what else. This is her first recorded departure from Sol System, although her captain and crew have deep-space experience. And I know Professor Gail Veronika Ashton Smith, of more disciplines than are worth mentioning—if only by reputation."

"And—" Pardell prompted, his mind's eye flashing on a small, round face with determined blue eyes and a hint of dimples.

"Smith is said to be exceptionally brilliant, to have alienated or left behind most of Earth's academic community, and apparently has one mission in life—to destroy the Quill."

"The Quill?" Pardell made a grimace and tilted his home-made chair back to consider this. The *'Mate* had long ago succumbed to the practicalities of furnishings that could come and go with the people using them. Rosalind had hated it when Raner ripped out the retractable stools and traded their mechanisms for medicines; Pardell remembered the day as one of their more memorable arguments. *He'd hidden in the abandoned bridge.* "Then—why me?" he asked her, now thoroughly puzzled. "I don't know anything about the Quill beyond what comes through station scuttlebutt. They're giants with googly eyes and long tentacles, last I heard."

"Or they were never a threat at all."

"Pardon?"

"You heard me." Rosalind made a sharp metallic sound by tapping a finger against the tabletop, demanding his attention. "There are those who believe Earth deliberately planted rumors about contamination to cover up their own failure—that the terraforming engineers couldn't do what they promised and the worlds weren't ready. No alien invasion, no fatal Quill Effect. Simple incompetence. And if it were true—how long do you think any of us would stand for what's happened as a result?"

*The Quill, a hoax?* Pardell stared at her, then sniffed, then finally broke out in a laugh he could no more help than he could fly. "You've been Outside too long, Rosalind. You can't have it both ways—if there are no Quill, why would Earth send Smith to destroy them? And what about all those who never returned from the contaminated worlds? Are you saying they were ambushed—or kidnapped—by embarrassed engineers?" He managed not to laugh again—her expression having gone from tolerant to that icy glare those pale eyes delivered so well. "Well, think about it, Rosalind," he said persuasively. "How could a cover story that caused mass panic and hysteria, that cost all those lives, possibly hold together? People, Earthers or not, aren't that stupid."

"In large groups, people are far worse, young Aaron. I'm sure you remember."

He clung to what mattered, willing to grant Rosalind whatever fantasy held her. The older ones were often stuck in their own preferred view of things. "So you think this Smith doesn't know about my condition—that she's here because, for whatever reason, she thinks I can help her with the Quill." A flood of something new coursed through Pardell's thoughts. *So that's what hope feels like*, he told himself, trying to keep it from his face. "Her job offer might be the real goods, after all."

"Are you listening to anything I'm saying, young Aaron?" Rosalind demanded, her voice cold and even. "Nothing good comes from Earth. Nothing. Whether you believe in the Quill or entertain other possibilities, there hasn't been a ship dock with supplies that didn't have a price, or a transport arrive that didn't bring some new restriction or other trouble with it. What matters here is all bets are off. I don't know—and you can't know—what Smith wants. The only thing certain is that an Earther is desperate to find you . . . and that better warn you, young Aaron. That better keep you out of public view until her ship leaves dock and then some."

A chill of excitement, not fear, raced down his spine even as he nodded obediently. *Anything*, Pardell told himself, *had to be an improvement over being sought as a freak.* He'd find a way to hide his true nature; it could be done. It had to be.

"Wipe that notion," Rosalind Fournier told him bluntly, too used to reading his expressions. "Now."

Pardell blinked at her. "What notion?"

She snatched his hand before he could move it out of her reach, clamping shut her servo fingers until he winced with pain and stared at her, quite astonished. *She was hurting him deliberately. Why?*

"Do you think you are the only one so desperate for a future you'd try breathing vacuum if it looked promising?" Rosalind asked slowly and clearly, as if it was necessary for each word to sink into his mind separately, like hot rivets. Her fingers didn't relent their pressure; instead, they squeezed tighter. "This isn't some fantasy from one of your readers, young Aaron. Those people want something. You don't know what it is; you can't begin to guess the price."

He'd had enough. *Of her. Of everything.* "Let go of my hand," Pardell ordered, in a voice that burned passing up his throat. "Now."

Rosalind looked down at their hands; hers opened and Pardell pulled his back to safety. The fingers throbbed. "You know you can't trust them," she persisted. "At least tell me that."

"I don't know anything—that's the problem, Rosalind. And I won't find out here, will I?" Pardell subsided, feeling a sudden despair as unsettling as the hope had been. "It's pointless arguing. I couldn't reach the *Seeker* and this Professor Smith even if I wanted to."

Her look was the same one she used to give him when he protested his innocence as a child, caught with the evidence of a late night raid on the ration cupboard ringing his mouth. "It would be difficult," she conceded almost cautiously.

"Impossible's more like it," he nodded, then it struck him. "But you could go, Rosalind."

"Me?" she arched a hairless eyebrow.

"Sure," Pardell spoke faster, warming to his idea. *It could work!* "Station Admin has you registered with full stationer status. You've been in the stern docking ring a dozen times this year alone. More, I bet."

Rosalind nodded reluctantly, as if suspecting being truthful might not be her wisest course. "I don't keep count. You know none of these semi-automated Earther ships have engineers on crew, so station calls me to help with emergency repairs on the odd stuff. Pay's respectable, if the company's not. Why should I go this time?"

*Ah*, he was sure he spotted a glimmer of interest in her eyes. "You could check things out," Pardell continued, trying not to sound too eager. "Maybe have a good look at this marvelous prototype starship while you're there. Do a little fact-finding. In the interests of learning more about the Earthers and their plans."

The glimmer had grown to an almost sparkle, though Rosalind's expression remained doubtful. "This is extortion, young Aaron," she accused. "You know I'd love to get a peek inside that ship."

This time he reached for her hand. "Not extortion, Rosalind—helping me. Help me find out what I might be missing. I don't want that ship to leave and never know."

"And if it is the obvious, after all?" she asked him.

Pardell could almost hear Raner's voice. *"You can trust Rosalind; she'll never avoid the painful places in the name of kindness."*

"If they are after a freak," he told her evenly, "they can try another station."

# Chapter 6

*T*HERE *had to be another way to hide the thing*, Gail grumbled to herself as she looked into the mirror and used a micro scalpel to make a small, precise incision in her scalp, just beneath the hairline and above her right eye. She'd numbed the area with ointment, but there was no way to numb her revulsion about slicing her own skin.

Gail pressed her finger behind the bloodless cut, her other hand at the ready. Got it. She surveyed the long, thin shard captured in a crease of her palm, less than pleased to have to rely on black-market tech. But the device had passed her tests on Earth.

*Time to see if it had done the job she'd asked of it out here.*

She slipped the tiny object into an almost invisible slot in a disk that otherwise looked perfectly normal. When done, Gail slid the disk into a pocket. Before leaving the washroom, she took a second to run a bead of skin sealant along the incision, surveying the result critically before nodding to herself with satisfaction.

Gail's quarters were larger than standard, although standard on the *Seeker* would have been generous enough. There were fancier staterooms, but they were reserved for visiting dignitaries or sponsors—potential or present. Gail's meticulous habits in her office and lab were here, in precious privacy, tossed quite literally aside. The floor was buried under clothes and overflow paper. Her bed was blanketed in reports and note-covered scraps. Carpet showed in a serpentine path from the door to her bedside and to the washroom—Gail's concession to the needs of the cleaning stewards.

Gail found a reasonably clear space on her bed to sit cross-legged, viewer in hand. In case the FD's latest sweep had missed one of Reinsez's little spy-toys, she made a point of holding up a disk with an easily-read label as if considering it—something fact heavy she might be expected to review before sleeping. Dozens such hung in the storage bags suspended from her ceiling. Then, she palmed the one and inserted the other from her pocket, bending forward so even someone standing beside her couldn't see past her shoulder and hair to the screen.

*It had worked.* While image quality varied from remarkable to adequate, depending on the lighting and her proximity to taller others, Gail held in her hands a visual record of her trip through the station, including the time wasted in meetings and meals. She sped past the latter, then slowed the playback to a crawl beginning with her first look inside Mr. Leland's dim, smelly bar, easily marked by the change in brightness as she'd removed her veil to assist the vid.

*How could so many fit inside?* Gail asked herself again. The washroom of the campus faculty club offered more floor space. She remembered the smooth feel of the bar in the club's main lounge, all sculpted wood, designed to give every patron a choice between total privacy or the subtle hint of others nearby. The maximum that spacious room had ever held was probably half of those crowded into Sammie's. *Nothing like this—overwhelming physicality.* Gail shuddered.

Those on Thromberg Station didn't seem to mind. Despite the fact that several of Sammie's customers were definitely the worse for the local brew, they'd all seemed healthy and happy enough, given most were at the extreme lower end of the normal range for body mass. Forester had boasted about the success of their ration distribution system. Gail supposed the line between preventing starvation and providing adequate nutrition had blurred for all of them years ago.

There was no audio, but Gail didn't require it, confident of her ability to recall anything said that mattered. It was her eyes she didn't trust, knowing the tricks they played on memory: the way the brain stored images that were like averages of what was really there; the way fleeting glimpses were lost before you could notice what you'd seen; even the way one eye was maddeningly blind to what the other saw at any moment in time.

She adjusted a control. Too close a view of Sammie's mismatched teeth panned outward to the crowd behind. Gail halted the image.

*That man.* Huge, long-armed, the face of a god, and a standing shock of red hair that must cause trouble in a 'suit helmet. He'd be striking in any group on Earth; here his massive frame was so out of place she remembered him vividly. What she hadn't remembered seeing was this.

He wasn't looking at her.

She'd had the rapt attention of everyone from the moment she'd lifted the curtain. The proof was in this recording. Yet, as Gail advanced the playback second by second, she saw this one man had glanced away from her and back toward the bar.

It was a quick, furtive glance. Gail would never have caught it without the vid. *So,* she asked herself, *what or who were you looking at, my giant friend?*

Half an hour later, Gail removed the disk, surreptitiously sliding in the one she'd pretended to watch into the viewer before tossing it aside. She dropped back on her piles of reports and blankets, legs still crossed, feeling the stretch burn pleasantly along her lower spine and outer thighs.

She'd found him. The direction of the big man's glance had helped, but once she'd known where to look, it had been easy. His clothing betrayed him. The figure ever-so-briefly glimpsed from behind one of the aproned bartenders didn't belong there, despite being dressed like every other customer in shabby stationer gray.

Gail had stared at his face—what the image revealed of it—so long that now, when she closed her eyes, she could still see it. *Intense,* she judged it. A little scared, but too curious to stay hidden, like a young fox she'd encountered during a camping trip. Not handsome by Earth standards—there was something not right about the cheekbones, close under the skin, an unusual angle to his oddly large eyes, or maybe the chin was too firm for the rest of the jaw. *Not an ugly face,* Gail decided, *but different. If he were smiling,* her tired mind went further than she planned, *it might be quite a nice face.*

*Which was irrelevant,* Gail told herself firmly, pushing out her legs to clear some sleeping space. She was willing to bet she'd now seen Aaron Luis Pardell in the flesh and equally sure traditional methods weren't going to find him in person.

*A good thing*, she yawned, *Pardell had such an easy-to-find friend.*

While Gail had no intention of sharing her vid or its method of concealment with anyone else, the description she supplied was more than enough for Forester. "In Sammie's?" he interrupted before she was half done. "That's got to be Malley—Hugh Malley. Second-generation stationer. Works in metal recycling. We don't have many his size here."

"I can believe that," Grant said almost fervently. Gail wasn't surprised Grant remembered Malley. She was willing to bet Grant and his people had automatically calculated how much more force it would require to subdue a man of Malley's size— or how much of the tranquilizer they'd all carried concealed in their sleeves would be necessary to put him down hard, should he be a threat.

*They'd agreed to appear weaponless*, she reminded herself, the entire debate ringing completely clear in memory, but not to being that way.

"So now you want Malley instead of Pardell?" Forester looked as though he wanted to comment, then met her eyes. For some reason, he changed his mind, saying simply: "Good. Malley I can find for you. He doesn't use his room share much, but he's got a hideyhole in the same section as the recycling plant. Most of the workers sleep close."

"Why?" Gail asked curiously.

"It's close," the stationer repeated. His tone seemed to expect her to share some inside joke. When she didn't respond, Forester continued almost impatiently: "The incoming loads wake them up. They move fast enough, they get to sort the scrap first—usually nothing, but enough tech and hardware slip by the inspectors to make it worthwhile having quick eyes and quicker fingers on both shifts.'"

"You allow people to steal from the scrap metal?"

Gail answered Grant's question when Forester looked offended. "It's to the station's benefit to be sure nothing's wasted," she said calmly. "I imagine there are similarly independent operations throughout Thromberg, aren't there?" She didn't wait for an answer. "How soon can you contact Malley?"

"Man's gone to bed," Forester said after a glance at his wristchrono.

"It's the middle of the afternoon," Grant protested mildly, as aware as Gail that the station kept Sol Standard time, as did every ship.

"Even-cycle, yes," Forester agreed. "Judging by when we found him in Sammie's, Malley runs odd-cycle. Now's his dead of night."

"Then wake him," Gail said. "We don't have the time to waste, Administrator."

The stationer shook his head, then rubbed one hand over his chin as though to emphasize the grizzled whiskers beginning to sprout here and there. "Look, it's bad enough you folks have me running double cycle. It's not done to interrupt someone's sleep, okay? You can't make it up later—someone else needs the bed."

Now that Gail paid attention, Forester did look exhausted. Unhealthy-looking at best, now dark shadows stained the skin under his eyes and his skin was distinctly paler. "Your bed, too?" she asked skeptically.

"Of course," he informed her, looking surprised by the question. "Your people keep asking for me by name, rather than consulting my office. I haven't made it back to my quarters for my assigned night since you arrived." Forester smiled somewhat wanly. "I sincerely hope you'll be able to do without my services soon, Professor Smith, or I'll be of very little use to anyone."

*As if you'd willingly leave dealing with us to anyone else*, Gail decided, but said only: "My apologies, Administrator. We were not aware your staff would keep you from your bed simply to answer routine requests. Let my comm officer know whom to contact during your night cycle and we'll be sure to leave you in peace."

"Don't worry. I wouldn't have missed all this," he confirmed unnecessarily, tired eyes gleaming. "I'll catch a few winks, then get hold of Malley for you. My office?" Forester paused suggestively.

"Here," Grant countered, before Gail could utter a word. His look to her wasn't asking permission. She nodded anyway.

After the station administrator left, Gail turned to the commander, anticipating his curiosity. "You want to know why I've asked to see this Malley."

Grant, his posture subtly relaxed once the stationer was gone, tilted his head to one side, regarding her with a bland expression. "I trust you'll tell me what I need to know, Professor, when I need to know it."

*They'd learned a fair bit about each other on the trip here*, Gail said to herself, inclined to be amused. "Walk with me to the lab, Commander," she said impulsively.

His agreement meant dismissing one of the two FDs standing guard outside her office. Normally, one would stay by the locked door while the other followed her. Gail had grown so accustomed to their unobtrusive presence, she still didn't know the names of more than a handful of the specialists in Grant's unit.

She still didn't know why she put up with their shadowing in the first place—especially on the *Seeker*—but the FD higherups had been quite clear. She was key to this mission's success, so she would be guarded even in a total lack of apparent threat.

Grant matched his longer strides to her impatient ones, their feet in syncopated rhythm as they headed down the main corridor. *Waste of precious time.* Gail begrudged the distance from her office to the lab—her quarters were midway, at least—but Tobo had insisted she keep herself close to the bridge. His reasons were sound enough, she had to admit, but the design of the *Seeker* hadn't been meant to accommodate a scientist who was also essentially in command.

*No*, she thought, *her kind was supposed to keep aloof from the day-to-day running of the ship and in their place, aboard the science sphere*. The *Seeker* had been designed for a specific purpose: to conduct potentially hazardous research in space, most particularly, research into alien biologies and technologies, should such ever be found. From the outside, her structure was deceptively simple, a pair of asymmetrical spheres connected by a slender cylinder. Her translight drive protruded from the underside of the smaller, aft sphere, almost an afterthought jarring its graceful curve to an atmosphere-capable snout. This was the command sphere, containing the bridge, crews' quarters, cargo holds, and her office—in other words, the half of the *Seeker* responsible for getting them place to place. *And now perhaps more*, Gail thought, sliding her eyes sideways and up. From this perspective, Grant was a column of blue-gray uniform topped by the straight line of a firm jaw and black hair that was beginning to show a bit of curl as it grew out of whatever regulation length his former duty had required. Others in his unit were also letting their hair grow, which wasn't helping her tell them apart at any distance.

Gail didn't know them and she didn't know—yet—what they'd done to the *Seeker* during her orbits of Titan, beyond the fact that modifications had been made. Titan University had been grimly silent during the entire process and neither she nor Tobo asked for details. Gail had been reasonably sure any questions would have stopped not just the military's preparations but her mission itself.

After walking in mutual silence for several minutes, more because Gail wasn't going to start a conversation in any hallway filled with passing crew, they arrived at the first of two interior lockouts. One of Grant's people stood stone-faced by the doorway, but Gail ignored her as she entered the day's code then waited the interminable seconds as the door's sensor net compared its stored version of Gail Smith with the one trying to pass. The door talked to itself for a few seconds, then swung open.

*The others believed they had equal access*, Gail thought with satisfaction, knowing better. One of her first tests of her military supporters had been the establishment of a new, hidden, level of clearance. She could now lock them all out, should the need arise. Especially Reinsez. Gail wasn't fool enough to think Grant's people hadn't done the same to her, but in this, she was willing to gain what leverage she could.

Past the door, they entered the automated walkway. Each took hold of a support bar along the wall as the floor shifted into motion, taking them through the *Seeker*'s wasplike waist to the core of the larger stern sphere. That sphere held the research facility itself, currently home to the over sixty scientists and technicians working in the *Seeker*'s maze of laboratories. Most of the space remained unassigned, waiting a purpose. They could build almost any device or tool they might need within it, then dismantle the parts when done to be ready for the next experiment.

*The waist itself*, Gail thought as she and Grant stood still, yet sped along as the conveyor moved them, *could be much more than it seemed as well.* The semitransparent walls and ceiling were deeply corrugated, the only hint that this corridor differed in any way but length from others on board. The corrugation allowed the waist to be extended in stages. The first changed its interior into a gravity-free chute for emergency travel between the spheres. A further extension turned the chute into a narrow tether, little more than a housing for power and communications cabling, as well as holding the two parts of the ship together. The publicized reason for this feature was so the science sphere could be dragged through the upper limits of an atmosphere to conduct its research. The unstated reason was to contain any alien biohazard released within the sphere.

Last, and not least, the science sphere could completely detach. This option had two purposes: first, the sphere could be left in orbit around an interesting world for prolonged research, while the mobile command sphere went for supplies or to gather other data at a distance. The other?

If a deadly alien pest, such as the Quill, contaminated the science sphere, it could be destroyed.

Gail was fully aware that Titan U expected her to keep their precious new ship in one piece. She had a tiresome pile of memos reminding her that retracting the tether and reconnecting the spheres was prohibitively expensive and risky. Of course it was—since reattachment required crew working from outside, let alone the downtime before the *Seeker* could move safely.

She was also aware that the waist, because of its versatility, was the only area of the ship guaranteed to be free of vids. Robotic sweepers automatically scoured every foreign molecule from its interior following any use. A most convenient cleanliness.

"Holding," Gail warned Grant as she twisted her hand on the bar to pause the walkway.

They were approximately midway, the waist stretching to almost points in both directions, the opaque surface of walkway and hand bars exaggerating the effect. The transparent walls and ceiling formed a black arch overhead, presently shaded against Thromberg's tiny sun. Gail always found it strangely claustrophobic, unsure if her discomfort was because she knew her hand on the wall was mere centimeters from vacuum or because of the small red switch on the bridge that could instantly negate even that protection.

*So the place made her queasy—it remained ideal for her purpose.* "I've reason to believe this stationer, Malley, can get a message to Pardell."

Grant raised one eyebrow. "Progress, then."

"I hope so," Gail said, perhaps more fervently than she'd intended. "We'll see if Forester's cooperation extends far enough to be useful. In case it doesn't, I want your people to be ready to do some digging . . . now that we finally have a name which appears in their database."

Grant's eyes brightened. *No doubt he had to listen to complaints from his missionless and bored experts*, Gail thought with some sympathy. "A name makes a difference," he admitted. "A big one. Are you sure you want us to wait, Professor?"

She frowned, but not at Grant. "We both agree this is a volatile situation. They were faster picking up your probe than expected—and their reaction wasn't pleasant. I daresay the same could hold true for any type of intrusion."

A nod. "A reasonable conclusion. When—if—you want us to proceed, be assured we'll take extraordinary precautions."

What those might be, Gail didn't want to know. What she did need was extraordinary cooperation. "I'll be blunt with you, Commander," she warned, seeing his eyes narrow ever so slightly in anticipation that here was likely the real reason for her invitation. *Good.* She liked working with people who tried to predict her. It made so many things easier. "There's no if. Before we undock, I want you to grab as much information as you can from Thromberg's systems about Malley, about Pardell— because I don't trust Forester's explanations—and two other names. Aaron Raner." She paused.

Grant didn't hesitate. "The man who requested the adoption papers for Pardell. No problem. The other?"

Gail reached across the narrow corridor of the waist to tap Grant ungently on his broad, hard chest. "This information comes to me, and me alone, Commander Grant. Are we clear?"

He didn't salute, but there was something of the intention in his eyes. "Yes, Professor. My people and I are fully aware of the chain of command."

Satisfied, Gail let herself smile. "The last name—for the moment, at least—belongs to a Royce/Douglas freighter, Pica-class, originally registered out of Earth and transferred to Thromberg twenty-three years ago. The *Merry Mate II.* Her reg code was AJST 866 C1066."

There was nothing subservient in the look this gained her. "So," a shade too polite, "despite all the protests, you wanted the probe out there. To look for this ship."

She *did* like working with Grant. Gail arched one brow, then twisted the handle to start the conveyor moving again. "What I want is a shorter distance to my lab, Commander, but we each have to deal with what we have, don't we?"

# Chapter 7

*NOT smart.*

Pardell didn't need to imagine Rosalind's dry voice in his helmet to know her opinion. Part of him shared it.

But what was he supposed to do? Sit alone in the *'Mate*? Wonder what was happening on-station? Worry that his only chance for a better life was preparing to undock?

After Rosalind had left—without promising more than to *consider* heading up to the docking ring—he'd thought it over from every side until his brain ached. If the *'Mate* still had a comm system, he could have contacted the *Seeker* himself. A joke suited to his mood. Oh, there was a panel marked "comm ops" on the ship's bridge—with nothing left behind it but the ends of connectors. Currency, long spent.

But there were other comm systems.

Pardell slowed his descent along the cable by twisting the hook to add friction, reaching the station plate with virtually no force left to send him back up again. He flipped on the mags to lock down the soles of his boots before releasing his hold. *Habits.* There were none to guide him in dealing with strangers.

This air lock was in poor shape. Hardly anyone used it these days, preferring to walk the longer route through Thromberg's air-filled corridors. Truth was, Pardell told himself, there was little need anymore to avoid moving through the station. Rosalind and her cohorts might deny it, but he could see a time coming when, if nothing changed, the station would quietly accept all who were left outside—if only to replace those lost within. How long after that Thromberg's population could continue to survive, he'd no idea. They shouldn't have lasted this long, but people were stubborn that way.

Pardell's lips twitched in what was close to a grin. He probably had a little too much of that stubbornness himself.

The warped outer door still held tight, but Pardell waited until he was through the inner one and it locked behind him, before removing his helmet and looking around. No one in sight—not that this far corner of the abandoned ring was ever popular. Too much debris blocked line of sight and there was too little in the way of alternatives if one was trapped here. He was one of the few who routinely used this air lock, something only he and Malley knew. They had a secret place nearby—one of those things kids did who played together without the complete approval of adults.

Not much of a place, even for a hideyhole, but it sufficed. The innermost layer of the whipple shield overhead had been rammed through the interior wall plates and down into the floor, coming heartstoppingly close to opening up this part of the station to vacuum. Engineers and techs had stabilized it with sprayed cement and left well enough alone. People didn't like the look of it. *Fine by him.* Pardell listened to his heartbeat and nothing else for a count of one hundred and one, then heaved aside what looked like a twisted mass of worthless plastic but was a panel woven from the least appealing scraps they could find.

He paused, using his wrist lamp to survey the interior of the cavelike space. Malley'd surprised a trio of 'tastic heads in here once. Unfortunately for the trespassers, it had been after the stationer had reached his full growth and temper. Pardell preferred a more cautious, limb-preserving approach and kept himself ready to retreat if necessary.

The thin beam of light slid down the ominously tilted slab of metal forming the roof and two walls of the shelter—some of it melted and re-formed—then briefly investigated any pile of scraps large enough to hide an unwelcome guest.

Or a welcome one. Pardell's face burned unexpectedly at the all too clear memory of surprising Malley with a lady friend. The faint light had seemed a welcome and Pardell had hurried inside, only to confront a bewildering tangle of slow moving limbs and far more exposed flesh than was sensible out here where skin would freeze to metal. Aghast that his friend would bring anyone else to their hidden place, he'd hesitated a moment too long. No, in honesty, he'd been mesmerized by the sight of gentle touching, fascinated by their soft sounds of pleasure.

Malley's outraged roar when he'd realized they were being watched had not been one of those. Pardell had slammed on his helmet and run back to the air lock, cycling through it faster than was at all safe, knowing full well Malley would never follow him into vacuum.

They'd never spoken of the incident, but ever since, as now, Pardell made sure to check every corner of the room before committing himself to stepping inside.

Pardell shook himself. He was well aware of his own limitations and, while sometimes desperately envious, it was only right his closest friend should enjoy what normal people did with one another.

*Maybe the Earthers had a cure for what isolated him like one of those monks he'd read about.*

Pardell tore off his suit glove, rubbing that hand over his face as if to rub away the entire notion. It didn't help that his heart began to pound and his breath came treacherously faster. *I'm an adult*, he told himself furiously, embarrassed at this lapse into adolescence even alone and unwatched. *I have greater concerns than wanting to know how it feels to touch a woman's flesh, to be touched, to* . . .

Not to mention those were the very last thoughts he needed in his mind when negotiating with the Earther. He winced, then focused on the here and now, deliberately removing his suit one piece at a time, rolling up any still-sticky pieces of tape—discarding those now-useless strips whose adhesive had finished outgassing to vacuum—and putting each into a suit glove for later.

They'd put in hooks and made structures that were faintly chairlike—the place was quite homey, if you didn't mind decorating with what even Thromberg considered disposable. Most of the material against the walls and coating the floor was insulation. The cold could kill you, the moment you forgot about it.

Malley's suit hung, limp and musty, to the left of where Pardell hung his own. Although he was in a hurry, Pardell gave it a quick check. Malley hated wearing the thing with a passion, even though a suit had saved his life once. Pardell expelled a frosty breath in exasperation. The battery was low again. No need to wonder why—Malley had a tendency to plug an extra heater into it, especially when he came down here to worry away at some equation or problem at all hours of his night cycle.

Pardell gave it a quick recharge from his own suit battery. It was a dark, never-mentioned truth that there weren't enough suits for everyone on the station. Not even close. Although he'd chosen to live Outside, Raner had done what he could to make sure his family and friends had suits for their children. Malley's still had the leg fabric from that original gift. He and Pardell had used it to extend the arms on this one. Good thing Malley had finally stopped growing.

Pardell's hands dropped away from their fussing over the other suit. He was wasting time. It was morning for those running odd-cycle. Malley would be on the recycling floor, heaving metal fragments and engaging his coworkers in debates on the nature of consciousness between loads. If he wanted to catch him—and get Malley's help accessing the comm system in the factory—he'd have to hurry before the morning shift broke for rations. Depending on whether Malley had students, he could head off in any direction, leaving Pardell waiting for him in the corridor where he'd doubtless have to endure everyone's questions and apologies about last night at Sammie's. *No thanks.*

Pardell pulled the mags from his boots, tucking them neatly beneath his hanging suit, then stood up straight, looking down at himself until he was almost cross-eyed, making sure his coveralls were as tidy as possible. There was nothing he could do about the wrinkles at each joint and around his waist—those came with being a 'sider and spending most of your time crammed inside space gear.

After making sure the panel was across the opening, and pausing to listen for any sign he wasn't alone, Pardell left. As always, he did so with the smallest twinge of worry. Their cave wasn't a complete secret, as were his other hiding places. Leaving his suit here felt dangerous, despite Malley's assurances of its safety. Those assurances rang somewhat hollow at best, since Pardell knew perfectly well his friend hoped one day he'd forget about the *'Mate* and stay inside Thromberg for good.

Not likely. The *'Mate* was home and security. Leave her? Not unless Pardell had a new future and a new ship.

"'Bout an hour ago, wouldn't you say, Denery?" Lang looked up from the cards in his hand, frowning a bit in concentration.

"Less," Syd Denery replied quickly. His face, usually cheerful, was presently drawn in worried lines that had nothing to do with his chances at beating Tommy Lang at rummy.

Pardell looked from one man to the other, trying to grasp what they were saying. "Station Admin came down here, midshift, and just took Malley with them?"

Both nodded. "Didn't bother explaining," Denery said, anticipating Pardell's question. "Then again, when do they?"

"Who was it?" The lights flickered, once, and all along the narrow space, workers began getting to their feet, ready to return to their shift. He hadn't been quick enough to make it before the break. If only he had—Pardell eased out of the way, pressing his back against the wall beside Denery's chair. *Habit as well as courtesy.* It was easier for him to avoid the moving mass of people than expect all of them to avoid him.

Lang folded his cards and tossed them into the pile on the table. "I take it there's no time to win my dibs back this round, Syd," he grumbled as he stood. "'Bye, Aaron. You coming?"

"Be right there, Tommy. Cover for me if I'm slow—right?" Denery waited until the other left with a nod before saying: "There were four of them. Faces I didn't know. Anzetti said he'd seen a couple of them before—wasn't sure where."

"Did they say anything? Why they wanted Malley in particular?"

The off-shift was trickling into the corridor, claiming their turn at rations and chairs. Denery slid to his feet, coming to lean beside Pardell and speaking in a quiet voice that nonetheless sent shivers down Pardell's spine. "Spouted some nonsense about having him talk to Station Admin over improvements to the line down here. As if that would happen. But you know Malley. He'll grab any chance to blow off steam about how things are done."

"So they—or whoever sent them—knew exactly how to get

him to leave without kicking a fuss or calling over the floor boss."

A flicker of something grim in Denery's eyes. "That's my guess. I don't like it, Aaron. It's not routine."

*Not routine.* Stationer code for dangerous, since anything unexpected in Thromberg was considered a threat. It usually was. Pardell nodded, feeling sick to his stomach. "Earthers," he breathed the word, rather than say it out loud, with all these ears in range. Denery paled but didn't argue.

Instead, he looked up at Pardell and said urgently: "You get home, Aaron. Hear me? There's nothing you can do. You wait and I'll—I'll get word to you somehow when Malley's back."

Pardell had to smile. "Syd, you don't have the slightest idea how to get a message Outside and we both know it."

"I know when my friends are in sewage up to their eye sockets, that's what I know," the little immie said firmly. "Just you listen to me, Aaron. Please. And stay out of Sammie's—at least for now. Forester's left his people there."

"Sammie must love that."

Syd Denery snorted. "No doubt. Heard he's charging them rent for their table. You listen to me," he repeated, lifting one hand as though to put it on Pardell's shoulder, then stopping just in time. "You get home and stay there. This is probably nothing anyway. We should be feeling sorry for whoever has to listen to Malley ranting about alpha sorting protocols and bin sizes."

"I will, Syd," Pardell said earnestly, though not specifying which suggestion he planned to follow. "And—thanks."

When you grew up in a place, you knew that place. Pardell might not have spent every waking moment on the station, but he and Malley had been determined wanderers as children—too full of energy to stay close to either's home and too full of themselves to stay where it was safe. He'd had the Outside as an extra playground, true, but it was the tunnellike Inside that had fascinated them both. They'd explored every nook and cranny within their section of Thromberg. Since many of those had been add-ons following the riots, or subdivisions built without consulting the station's engineers, it was entirely likely the youngsters knew it better than anyone else.

So Pardell hardly needed to glance at level numbers or corridor codes to find his way from the recycling floors to the back entrance to Sammie's. Once there, he hesitated, automatically easing to one side to let staff and others pass him with a generous margin, and considered what Denery had told him.

Station Admin had taken Malley someplace. If the Earther was involved—Pardell couldn't help but focus his ire on one Earther in particular—then Malley might even be on the *Seeker* by now. His ship.

Pardell was consumed with sudden jealousy. The *Seeker* was his opportunity. His big chance. But the feeling faded just as quickly. He knew, beyond doubt, that Malley had been taken to get to him, not as a substitute. Someone knew them both, well enough to know Malley was the key. The why of it was easy. If they thought Pardell would refuse to step forward, if they were in too much of a hurry to hunt for him, then this was the logical ploy. What it said about their ruthlessness—about her ruthlessness—left Pardell cold.

It definitely changed his plans.

"Aaron Pardell?" the voice went from welcoming to scolding in the space of the two words. "What are you thinking—get in here!"

Pardell followed Tanya inside. The back of Sammie's was a combination of living quarters and storeroom. Sammie kept his remaining family close. He'd been one of the first businessmen to come on-station and, during the glory years, had sponsored more and more of his kin to join him. Since the Quill, he'd lost fourteen all told, including Tanya's father and grandmother to pneumonia during a lockdown that left the medical supplies on the wrong side of the sealed bulkheads.

The rest slept here on beds made from crates of beer. Since Thromberg's one and only brew had a life expectancy of about a week, those beds were in constant flux, frequently being dismantled at the most inconvenient times, according to Tanya and her sibs. The room itself followed the original curve of what had been a freight-capable hallway. Curtains darkened the half set aside for those on the opposing cycle. The entrance to the bar itself was locked from this side. Sammie preferred deliveries to come in the same way as customers.

There was the smell of something cooking from one corner. The tavern received a bit extra in the way of rations to sell at the bar—the balance sheet meant most of that extra came out of the family's allotment, so Sammie rarely let it leave the storeroom. Pardell politely declined an offer to share, after putting his own bag of rations on the nearest table. It would either be there for him later, or replaced with another. Those inside Thromberg observed the courtesies as well as any 'sider.

As he'd hoped, Sammie was home, sitting behind the sheet of metal that served as a desk. On seeing who followed his granddaughter inside, the bartender waved him over impatiently. "Pardell, you're just ten kinds of fool lately, aren't you?"

"Nice seeing you, too, Sammie," Pardell said, sitting on the nearest bed and pretending not to notice how quickly Tanya pulled the door closed despite the cloying warmth and smells inside. "Hear you have regular customers now."

The bartender exposed several misplaced teeth in a hungry grin. "Payin' ones at that. I could use more o' them types." Then he put his hands flat on the desk and stared at Pardell consideringly. "You'd be better elsewhere, Pardell."

"So people are telling me." Pardell didn't try to keep the emotion from his voice. "Means a lot, Sammie."

"Not enough, obviously. Or you wouldn't be here."

Odd how Sammie's speech patterns changed at whim. Pardell drew his mind back from its tentative leap into distraction, fiercely determined to keep to the here and the now. "I'm here because I need more than warnings, Sammie," he told the bartender. "It's no good for me to hide where I'm deaf and blind. I don't know what's happening. I can't find out what the Earthers want." He paused, then went on in a voice that surprised him by shaking with anger: "And now it's more than me—they've taken Hugh Malley."

Sammie blinked once. Pardell felt more than saw Tanya and a couple of others move closer. "You know for a fact Malley's with the Earthers?" Sammie asked, reasonably enough, "Man's been in trouble before without your help, Aaron."

"Syd Denery was there. Said four from Station Admin came for Malley—took him right out of his shift—made up some story about Malley's opinion being important in a redesign of the factory."

Tanya laughed once. "That would do it."

Pardell kept his eyes on Sammie, whose face was gradually twisting into a scowl. The bartender was unofficially the most influential person in this section of Thromberg. Nothing happened here Sammie didn't know about—nothing was decided by the residents without consulting with Sammie first. "Not routine," that worthy spat after due consideration.

Pardell nodded, "That's what Denery said."

The scowl deepened. "Didn't think Forester would make the connection between you two—it's not as though he's ever down here. Or would have noticed."

"Someone did." Before that sounded like an accusation, Pardell added: "Who doesn't matter. And if Admin's taken Malley inward or stern to ask about me, we can pity the fools who have to talk to him. But if it's the Earther . . ." He let his voice trail away.

"Seems to me they don't need to ask Malley a thing." This interruption came from Tanya, who stepped forward until she stood against her grandfather's desk, a vantage point allowing her to glare down at them both. "If they want you that bad—well, it's working just fine, isn't it? You aren't playing it smart."

He didn't quite smile. Tanya should have been a mother by now; she had all the fire and no one to protect. It didn't pay to cross her in this mood, but he had no choice. "We don't know what they want," Pardell stated, his voice flat and level. "All we know is they're changing things." He hesitated. There was nothing to be gained by talking about Rosalind's reaction—'sider business would only make them uneasy.

Sammie's look sharpened, as though he knew Pardell could have added more but chose not to; he only said: "You said you wanted help. What kind?"

Something tight inside Pardell eased, and he took a deeper breath to cover it. "I need to find out what's really going on: where Malley is; what the Earthers want; how far Forester will go to back them."

An unexpectedly eloquent wave of a thick-fingered hand. "I can ask some questions. No guarantees they'll be answered—or how fast. No matter what the Earthers are really after, they've sent people running for sealed sections. There's talk of stockpiling, Aaron Pardell. That's serious trouble, true or not."

Pardell closed his eyes for an instant. Worse and worse. *Damn her.* This place that worked so well on the surface depended on the most fragile balance of trust and mutual self-interests. Any push—any at all—could destroy it. He looked at Sammie, putting all his determination into his voice, saying: "We have to know the truth about them. If it's only me on their list, that's going to help—but the longer it takes to be sure, the less people will believe anything but their fears. I have to talk to the Earther—Dr. Smith."

A stern look from her grandfather quelled Tanya's outburst before it was more than an indrawn breath. "It can be arranged," Sammie told him bluntly, an unusual admission of the power he could exert if he chose.

"Thank—"

"But," Sammie continued, interrupting Pardell's gratitude, his own tone heavy, "it's not your decision or mine to make."

Pardell searched the other's face, reading nothing in those suddenly worn-looking features but grim sincerity. "Whose is it, then?" he asked, honestly curious.

"There'll be a meeting. That's all I can say."

"To decide when I can talk to the Earther."

Sammie waved a finger at Pardell, looking irritated. "Not when. *If.*"

Pardell swallowed hard, a physical action that helped to keep down the questions he desperately wanted to ask. No point pushing Sammie—not if he wanted help. But he couldn't help one slipping out: "Whoever they are . . . why would they care? How could what I do possibly matter to anyone else?"

He didn't really expect an answer, but Sammie drummed his fingers on the metal, a soft counterpoint to his words: "You know how it's been, Aaron. Immie, stationer—or 'sider—we've survived by taking care of our own without Earth interference or help." Sammie paused until Pardell nodded impatiently. "What you don't know is there's another side to it. It's nothing to be proud of, but it's the way things are. Haven't you ever wondered why folks here never call their families in Sol System and ask for handouts? We have families, you know. Some of them well-off and even powerful. But no one here goes begging to Earth for personal gain."

"Thromberg Admin controls the comms—" Pardell ventured, flashing to his conversation with Rosalind and her paranoia about Earth, hoping he wasn't meeting its partner here of all places.

"Admin? They have nothing to do with this. Listen, Aaron. There are rules here. We all obey them, 'siders as well as everyone else. You enter on the right. You share. You don't butt ahead in line. And you don't contact anyone off-station without permission. No deals on your own." He lifted his hand and slammed it down, making Pardell jump.

"You try," Sammie continued in almost a whisper, although it hardly seemed anyone else so much as breathed in the storeroom. "You die."

# Chapter 8

"WE have a—small problem, Dr. Smith."

Gail cocked her head, although there wasn't a vid pickup on her desk comm. "Did you not notify me that Mr. Malley was on his way to my office, Tau?" Second on this shift to Commander Grant, Comm Specialist Tau was one of the few in the First Defense Unit Gail had come to know—but not because of his obvious competence. No, poor Tau was a man so utterly reliable and practical, Tobo had managed to trick him more often than any of the others on the trip here. Eventually, Grant had had to ask her to intercede.

There were some strange, unidentifiable sounds through the speaker, then Tau's voice came again, somewhat breathless. "To be precise, Doctor, I notified you that Mr. Malley had—arrived—at the air lock, with his escort."

"Don't keep either of us waiting, then. Bring him up here."

"That's our problem, Dr. Smith. He—ah—doesn't want to come on board."

A corner of Gail's mouth twitched as she imagined what might be happening outside her ship. So much for Grant's insistence on having this meeting take place in her office. "Stay put," she ordered, then shut off the comm and grabbed her cloak. Thromberg kept its interior too chill for her taste.

*If they'd tried any harder to make the man welcome, someone would be in the hospital*, Gail decided a few moments later. From the way everyone stared at her, she'd surprised them all by walking out the air lock—a happy circumstance directly related to there being only one guard at her door at that moment, and that one seemingly traumatized by the choice of following her quick exit or staying behind to call in a warning.

No, if they'd set out to make a spectacle out of what should have been a discreet visit, they couldn't have been more successful. Malley was standing to one side, dressed in what had to be protective gear from his workplace. The broad belt, worn and ripped overalls, and heavy shoulder padding did nothing to diminish his startling resemblance to a gladiator. *The man was beyond massive*, Gail decided admiringly. And beyond annoyed.

Her own eyes narrowed as she ignored the station personnel, busy helping two of their members up from the floor plates, and four of Grant's people, arrayed between the entrance to the air lock and the ship. Instead, Gail studied Malley's face. He'd noticed her arrival as well, standing motionless except for perhaps a slight heaving of his chest. One of the tears on his left sleeve looked fresh.

It was the sweat that cued her. He'd hardly exerted himself enough, in this cold air, to have beads glistening on forehead and cheekbones, a runnel passing in front of one ear to slide under a jaw that was, literally, clenched to the point of pain. His eyes kept darting past her to the open air lock. Their pupils were dilated despite the bright lighting.

*So.* Gail heard the pound of footsteps behind her and could see for herself the ring of curious onlookers gathered at a discreet distance—for Thromberg—which meant at least two hundred people could hear anything said. "Welcome, Mr. Malley," she said calmly, stepping completely away from the air lock. "Let's not bother going inside, if you don't mind. I feel like taking a walk. Would you join me?"

She wondered if anyone else saw and understood the flash of surprised gratitude—and shame—that swept across Malley's face. Before Grant, who doubtless was either behind her or listening in, could argue, Gail walked right up to Malley and slipped her hand under his arm. It felt more like a steel girder than flesh, yet there was a feather-soft trembling perceptible under its surface. She'd been right: more than anxiety or distrust—possibly a full-fledged phobia. The cause didn't matter. They'd never get this man into the ship of his own free will.

Malley nodded stiffly, accepting the direction she indicated. Gail had the distinct impression that not only would any direction away from the air lock have been acceptable, but that only her hand on his arm kept him from bolting.

"My apologies, Mr. Malley," she said quietly, steadily, as though she dealt with distraught men three times her mass on a daily basis. "I'd no idea the Administrator would be so zealous in interpreting my request to meet you."

Unlike Grant, Malley matched her shorter strides without obvious effort, perhaps a consequence of life in the crowded Outward Levels, she thought, where he must rarely be able to stretch his legs. They were hardly inconspicuous—Grant's people had quickly moved to enclose the two of them within a box of blue-gray, matching them step for step—but it felt private enough.

"You should be flattered, Dr. Smith," Malley replied, his deep, low-timbred voice running through her bones like a distant rumble of thunder—a sound she realized he'd likely never heard. "Forester isn't prone to being zealous about anything— let alone requests."

An educated voice, at that, now seemingly free of discomfort. Gail tilted her head to look up at him and promptly discarded all preconceptions she'd had about this conversation and this man. "Mr. Malley, I'll not waste your time or mine," she said bluntly. "I know you're friends with Aaron Pardell. I need you to convince him to talk to me. It's vital."

"Vital? Aaron?" Malley repeated, not bothering to deny her knowledge. "Nice enough guy," he went on, deepening his already low voice an improbable octave. "But a pretty lady like you could do so much better." He pressed his arm against his side to gently imprison her fingers, and smiled down at her as if they were strolling alone under moonlight, instead of on a cold deck in the middle of a throng of nosy strangers.

Gail yanked her hand free, hearing a choked-off cough from behind. Grant. Malley's flirting had been a deliberate attempt to put her off-balance—she couldn't believe she'd let him startle that much response from her. When she checked Malley's face, there was nothing warmer in its expression than a mild satisfaction. "This isn't a joking matter, Mr. Malley," she said evenly. "Do you want me to get into issues such as why Mr. Pardell isn't registered on-station? We know what's outside—"

Malley startled her again, this time by the speed with which he stopped, took her arm in one hand and put the other across her mouth to silence her. Gail met his eyes; the urgent message in them made her wave back her alarmed guards without hesitation. The big stationer bent down until his breath warmed the skin of her ear. "If you'll talk like that—here, in the open—you don't know enough."

He released her, then stood back as though equally prepared for her guards to attack him or for her to resume their walking conversation. Involuntarily, Gail licked her lips and tasted the salt from his hand. "Understood," she said finally. "Let's go somewhere private. You pick the place," she added immediately, seeing him swallow and reasonably sure it was the thought of the ship, not her offer.

"My sort doesn't get up here much," Malley pointed out.

"The Docking Administration Office isn't far." This from Grant, who'd obviously had more than enough of being a spectator. His lips were now pressed into a hard line and the look he threw Malley was one of clear threat. Malley grinned in acknowledgment. *Not a man who backed down*, Gail concluded, adding another piece to the puzzle.

Grant had been right. The office was attached to the outward curving wall of the docking ring, between two sets of ship-sized air locks. It was little more than a roofless box housing some station staff, a countertop, and the seemingly inevitable line of people waiting their turn. Gail let Grant sweep everyone out of the room, willing—this time—to stand back and let her troops perform a little intimidation. It worked on the office staff, who protested only weakly; it seemed to amuse Malley.

When the small, cluttered space was emptied except for themselves, she claimed the only chair behind a desk and gestured Malley to take the one opposite. As he sat, the chair groaning in protest, Gail gestured to the rest to leave them.

Predictably, after nodding an okay to his people and watching them file out, Grant didn't budge. Gail waited. Malley looked from one to the other, definitely amused now. Finally, Grant took a quick step forward, bringing something from his pocket to place firmly on the desk in front of her. Then he turned to

Malley and said: "I'm on the other side of the only exit, Stationer. Don't forget that."

Instead of a sneer, which Grant probably expected—*and deserved, the melodramatic oaf*—Malley's face turned quite serious. "She's safer here, with me, than anywhere on this station," he told the obviously angry officer. "A conversation—that's all."

Grant wasn't buying it. "Just mind yourself, Malley—that's all I care about." He saluted Gail in a way that left no doubt of his disapproval, then spun and marched out of the room.

"Is he always like that?"

Gail gazed at the device lying in front of her on the stained desktop, making no move to touch it. Any contact with it would doubtless trigger both an ear-splitting alarm and most regrettable action from those waiting outside. "He feels I take unnecessary risks," she explained, unsure why she didn't want Grant misjudged by this man.

"Do you?"

"No," Gail said frankly. "I only take the necessary ones."

"Such as coming here, looking for Aaron." Malley leaned back, stretching out legs with thighs each broader than her waist. The chair gave one last protest then was silent. Malley was probably used to furniture complaining. "Do you mind?" he asked her, tapping one of his shoulder pads.

Gail steepled her fingers and rested her chin on their tips. "By all means, make yourself comfortable, Mr. Malley."

He unclipped the straps crossing his chest and upper body, then lifted the entire mass over his head. For an instant, Gail thought he planned to toss it into a corner, then he grinned at her and put it down on the floor with only a muted ring of metal to metal. "Mustn't get your soldiers imagining I'm throwing things at you."

Taking off the pads, Malley shed years as well—his shoulders still unusually broad and overmuscled to Gail's eyes, but now more in proportion to the rest of his body. Where the fabric covering his upper arms had worn through, the skin showed overlapping patterns of bruising, some brownish yellow, the latest an angry purple, as though he routinely hoisted heavy objects up on his shoulders without care. Coupled with the strong, fiercely intelligent lines of his face, he was a paradox Gail found inconveniently fascinating. She put it down to the rarity of sweaty manual laborers in her life and schooled her expression carefully.

After all, here was a source of information potentially more useful than anything Grant's experts could scavenge from Thromberg itself. She started with the practical. "You didn't want me to talk about those ships outside the station. Why?"

Malley kept his easy smile, but she thought his brown eyes hardened. "No," he rumbled. "That's not how this is going to work, Dr. Smith."

She blinked. "Pardon . . . ?"

"First, you owe me the dibs I'm losing being here and not on my shift." He waited for Gail to nod, then went on in determined voice: "Second, I want you to arrange a meeting between me and your pet, Sector Administrator Forester."

Gail blinked. "Why?"

"I was hauled up here on the pretense I'd get a chance to express my opinions on how things are being done on my floor. Well, I want that chance."

She kept from smiling at this, merely nodding again.

"Good." Malley brought his big hands up and locked them behind his neck. "Then there's only one more item to clear up, Dr. Smith."

"And that is?"

"What the hell makes you think I'll talk to an Earther about my friend, my home, or anything else, for that matter?"

*Not an outright refusal*, Gail decided. *A challenge.* There were stakes involved here she didn't know, but at least Malley wasn't leaving—yet. There had to be something he either wanted, or needed. She thought it highly unlikely he'd simply tell her what that something was.

"I appreciate your candor, Mr. Malley," she began, more cautious than she'd ever been with Reinsez—or Grant, for that matter—suspecting Malley of a different level of intellect, as well as being fully aware his was a personality forged under circumstances completely alien to her own. She dared not underestimate him. "While I've many questions, they can keep. It's only my curiosity, after all." Gail smiled, just enough to deprecate her own words. "If you're uncomfortable talking to me, I can give you a message for Mr. Pardell. You can go back to your work immediately."

Malley closed his eyes almost to slits, as though this helped him read her face—or as though he was daydreaming. "Oh, I'm a curious man, myself. Curious why Dr. Gail Smith, Head of the Department of Xenoecology and formerly lead researcher in xenobiological warfare—both at Titan University, Sol System—wants so badly to find one man. Badly enough to risk her neck and ship—not to mention potentially ignite a riot on Thromberg Station."

"You know my work?" Hearing the surprise in her own voice, Gail could have bitten her tongue. He'd thrown her off-balance again. *Damn him.*

"Information gets out here, if little else," Malley announced as if he hadn't noticed. "I've read your last eight papers—of those Titan allowed to go public, anyway. Some of your findings were interesting."

Gail wasn't sure if she was appalled or offended. "Some?"

He opened his eyes again, his expression one of guileless innocence. She wasn't fooled, being an expert in that expression herself. "While I'd enjoy discussing the finer points with you someday, let's leave it that I don't see any possible connection between your legitimate research on the Quill and Aaron Pardell. Which leaves me wondering what line of inquiry you aren't publishing—and how much risk to Aaron, and this station, you'd consider *necessary* to further it."

Gail almost slammed her hand down on the alarm, more than ready to have Grant and his troops grab this complacent, obstinate, overstuffed lump of a man and drag him on board the *Seeker* where they had the means to get answers to any question they wished. She wasn't sure which stopped her: imagining the triumphant "I told you so" on Grant's face, or the potential for violence from the hundreds of stationers milling between this office and the air lock.

"You could try telling me the truth, Dr. Smith," Malley suggested, the corners of eyes wrinkling good humoredly, as if he knew and relished her frustration.

"Trust you, Mr. Malley, with my life's work—just like that?"

Gail was so far from self-control she barely managed to get the words out. "You have no idea—"

"And neither do you, Dr. Smith," he countered, suddenly revealing the extent of his own emotion, feet thudding to the floor plates as he sat upright, massive arms swinging down with his hands tightened into fists. "You dock as though you own the place. You expect us to jump at your whim. And you have the gall to think I'd betray my friend for a day's dibs and a chance to shout at Forester. Think again!"

"I could have you hauled on my ship—"

Before Gail could finish her sentence, Malley was on his feet with that speed she found so unlikely in such a huge man, looming over the desk. He pushed the alarm within reach of her fingers as he put his face within a handbreadth of hers. His voice was incredibly low and utterly cold: "And I could snap your neck before your precious Earther grunts came through that door."

Gail believed him—*he'd only need one hand*—but she matched his glare with one of her own, refusing to retreat despite the hairs rising on the back of her neck. "That comes under necessary risk, doesn't it?" she said coolly.

She caught him off-balance, for once. Malley's teeth flashed in another of his mercurial grins and he straightened, then pretended to bow to her. "You don't lack for spine, Dr. Smith."

Since hers currently felt remarkably like a liquid, Gail fixed her expression into something approximately pleasant. "Nor do you. You know they'd kill you."

Malley shrugged. "They'd try," he corrected gently, with the sublime confidence of someone who probably hadn't lost a battle on his own turf in years. Gail didn't bother explaining that Grant and his people wouldn't fight fair—he probably knew.

*And this wasn't a man to have as an enemy*, she realized abruptly. As an ally, he'd be indispensable. There was only one way and, once Gail saw it clearly, she didn't hesitate. "You say you want the truth, Mr. Malley. Fine. But know this: that truth's more dangerous to the stability of your station than any conflict between us could be."

"I'm the best judge of that, Dr. Smith." His lips were still tight, but she had his interest. She was sure of it. "And I won't promise to keep your secrets. Not if they'll harm anyone on or off Thromberg."

"If you're the man I think you are," Gail said bluntly, "once you know why I'm here, what I'm hoping to accomplish, you'll keep it to yourself. I've no worries there." She paused, then went on with an urge to honesty she was usually able to resist: "But I have to warn you," she went on. "What I'm going to tell you will put a burden on you and on your friendship with Aaron Pardell—"

What he might have answered, Gail didn't find out. As she drew a breath to continue speaking, there was a commotion at the door to the office. A flustered-looking Grant burst in, managing to stay ahead, barely, of what appeared to be an angry delegation of stationers led by Administrator Forester himself. Behind, they could see the four other Earthers surrounded by stationer gray.

Malley sat back down and stretched out his legs once more. "Dr. Smith," he told her, "welcome to Thromberg Station."

# Chapter 9

HUGH Malley hadn't returned to his work, his hideyhole, or his assigned quarters by night, odd-cycle. Pardell ignored the changing rhythms in the corridors—and coming through the walls of Sammie's Tavern—that marked the swing from day to night for some, night to day for the rest. It was no longer fifty/fifty, as in the beginning. There were always deaths, some years more than others. There weren't replacements. Fate had taken more from odd-cycle, so its night was a little less peaceful, a little more intruded on, year by year, by those whose clocks woke them and sent them to work instead. One day, if nothing changed, they'd blend back to one clock and watch for time to end in synchrony.

Pardell shook off the reverie. Malley wasn't back. No need to expose himself hunting the news—it arrived on the feet of odd-cycle folks coming in for a last drink and left with those even-cycle folks who liked starting their day as they ended it. It'd take no more than an hour to spread throughout Outward Five.

Speculation? Ah, that ran more than walked. Didn't help there was scuttlebutt from the third cousin of someone's aunt who happened to be on the stern docking ring and who saw Malley with the Earthers. *No*, thought Pardell, rubbing his eyes and stifling a yawn, *that hadn't helped at all*.

Hard to sort the many versions into possible or nots. Anything could be true, with that woman and her ship leeched to Thromberg. Stories so far had ranged from Malley being shot, to his entering the Earther ship and not leaving it. Those two, at least, Pardell didn't believe for an instant. The dock would have exploded at the least violence to one of their own—and Malley enter an air lock?

Pardell rolled over in the bed Tanya'd lent him, pulling a blanket over a shoulder, feeling suddenly as cold as any time he'd been Outside. Malley'd been in an air lock exactly once. The time his dying mother tossed the two of them in one for safety. Pardell closed his eyes, remembering in spite of himself . . .

. . . It had been like some game or a reader story at first— something new happening, a change in routine. The boys had taken it that way; children do. The corridor main lights had been kicked out by Admin, hoping to stop people moving to and fro, but that only added to their trembling excitement. Mrs. Malley had made them put on their suits—a chance for Aaron to show off his skills, giving his friend lots of unasked-for advice. He and Hugh—she was the only one who called her son by his given name—had jousted with their boots, until Mrs. Malley hushed them, made them finish suiting up, and took them to hide in the abandoned aft docking ring.

Where did the riot start? Who died first? No one lived to explain it to those who survived. The thread of violence that reached the Malleys wasn't even part of the main struggle, just a pack of would-be looters being chased by the more righteous and better-fed. The boys and Malley's mother had been caught in a vicious crossfire probably neither side later remembered. Neither accepted the blame, for sure.

Mrs. Malley had pushed them into the nearest air lock. Pardell could still feel the pain of her emotions through him when he recalled that day, as though her hands had burned through his suit, driving him to do anything to save her son and himself, feelings intensifying even as her hands slipped down his back and away.

She'd loved them both.

And he'd done it, sealing the air lock, ignoring Malley's screams and pleas to let him out, to let him go back to her. Both of them being in suits, at least he'd been safe from feeling Malley's wild grief as well as his own.

He'd done it, rapping out the code, opening the outer door, grateful to the quick-thinking 'sider guard who'd grabbed his hysterical friend and hauled him to the safety of vacuum. They'd been saved. Pardell had lain back on Thromberg's white outer plates, soothed by the infinite darkness in almost every direction, shuddering as much with relief as grief. Malley had clung to the guard in absolute, blind terror, losing in one instant not only his mother, but everything that defined his universe.

Malley had never, ever, been able to go near an air lock since. . . .

*No*, Pardell thought, tasting the nightmare again, *his friend wasn't on the Earther ship*. Not unless they'd drugged or overpowered him somehow.

She was capable of that, he didn't doubt it, but there was no reason. What possible gain could having Malley on her ship provide? To wring the truth from him—another popular rumor? Easier to take him to the Admin offices and let Forester try to bore Malley into confession.

"Psst. Aaron. You awake?"

"Yes," he whispered, mindful of the others sleeping in this side of the storeroom. He rolled to his feet, dropping the blanket and squinting in the dim light. It was Silvie, Sammie's daughter and Tanya's mother. "There's news? Real news?"

She chuckled softly at his qualification. "Not about Malley—although I do like the latest, the one saying he planted a big kiss on the Earther right in front of all and she didn't look too worried about it."

Pardell stifled a laugh. "That sounds like something Malley'd pull. But I don't see the Earther taking it so well."

He followed Silvie's silhouette to the slit in the curtain and out into the lit section of the long room. There were people he knew gathered there, a couple of faces less familiar than the others. Most were older, the type that were easier to peg as immie or stationer if you knew the signs. No 'siders, other than himself. No surprise there.

No room to spare either. They'd pushed aside the beer crates to make a half circle where the oldest sat shoulder to shoulder. He must have slept after all to have missed these preparations, although moving things quietly was something you learned about the same time as learning to walk. Others waited cross-legged on the floor. A few stood, making a shadowed back row beyond the lights.

Room for him, of course. Pardell stepped forward, nodding thanks as they moved completely out of his way when for one of their own they'd simply turn a bit and make a joke of not stepping on toes. He knew where they wanted him. They'd left one crate waiting in the middle, under the brightest light. He sat on it, keeping his back straight as he'd been taught, resting his hands in plain sight on his thighs.

Sammie still wore his apron—it was a busy time in his tavern and doubtless he was planning to be back there as soon as business was done here. *Whatever business that might be*, Pardell told himself, wishing he'd thought to at least run his fingers through his hair first and blinking grit from his eyes.

"You all know Aaron Raner's son," Sammie introduced him briskly. "I've told you what went on last night, with the Earther Smith and Administrator Forester."

"Half of us were there, y'old fool!" came from the back row.

"Surprised you remembered, Warren," retorted another voice. There was a rill of laughter, quickly muted.

Sammie chose to ignore the byplay. "This meeting's been called to hear Aaron Pardell's request to contact these Earthers himself. He knows he needs your permission," this slightly louder to be heard over a murmur of low voices—an unhappy murmur. "Tell them your reasons, Aaron," he told Pardell. "Tell them what you want to do."

Their sudden attentive silence wasn't comforting. Pardell was used to trying to fade into crowds, not being the center of all eyes. He struggled to find his voice, coughed once, then finally got to his feet. "Thank you, Sammie. Everyone. I didn't think so many would—" *care*, was the word trembling on his lips. He changed it to "—take the time to hear my request.

"What I'm asking is permission to find out why this Earther came looking for me, what she wants. A comm link would be enough. I've no need to meet her face-to-face."

Someone in the back called out: "Didn't you see those dimples, Pardell?" and was shushed. But the comment broke some of the tension.

Pardell couldn't quite smile, but he felt a little more at ease.

These were family, in the sense that most were Raner's friends, even if they'd likely come more in curiosity about the Earther than interest in a lone 'sider. "I saw them, thanks. I'm more concerned with what she's done with Hugh Malley."

There were, surprisingly enough, no ribald suggestions following that. Perhaps they shared his worry. Or had some respect for Roy Malley, Hugh's uncle and sole blood relation away from Sol System. Pardell could see Roy out of the corner of his left eye, seated, as usual, closest to the door. The eldest Malley was a sour, silent man, prone to either dismiss or criticize anyone younger or who hadn't stepped on dirt sometime in their past. Seeing Roy here—well, that meant Malley's absence was something at least one other took seriously.

"So it's Malley you're worrying about, is it? Here I thought you were planning to ask for a ticket home."

Pardell squinted but couldn't see who'd asked the question. Didn't matter—they all waited for his answer. His hopes? They wouldn't serve him well here. Or Malley. He shrugged. "You know where my home is," he said flatly, a bitter taste on his tongue. "Think this Earther plans to fix up the *'Mate*?" Pardell paused and looked around at as many of them as he could see, finally resting his eyes on Sammie. "Sure, she talked about a job for me. We all know it was an Earther lie to draw me out. But why? Why me?"

A snort from Fy Wilheim. "We all know why, Mr. Touch-Me-Not," the former welder growled, his hand waving toward the sound of Pardell's voice. Wilheim had lost his sight using inferior equipment and now worked even-cycle in recycling, opposite Malley's crew. Pardell knew him well enough. Not fond of 'siders—there was history, a terrible one, behind those clouded eyes. Otherwise, a fair man and one the others respected. That didn't keep the blood from Pardell's cheeks as the others nodded in agreement with the old, hated nickname. "What bothers me is how they knew you existed—and how to find you. Someone's been talking out of turn."

*Out of turn.* A death sentence in times past. Pardell spoke up before it got worse. "I can ask her," he offered. "She won't know how we feel about that. She won't care. I can find out. The more we can learn about this, the better. It's the not knowing that's dangerous."

"To a youngster." This, from Silvie, produced another round of nods. "There's times it's best to keep heads down and doors locked."

*They weren't going to agree*, Pardell realized with a numb shock. They'd rather he hide down here until the Earthers gave up. They'd prefer anything to taking a risk. "What about Hugh Malley?" he asked desperately.

"We look after our own, 'sider." There was a shuffling of feet and restless movement, as though those words out of the darkness were all they'd waited to hear said.

Pardell looked into each face, "That's it?" he demanded, no longer keeping the heat from his voice. "I can't contact the Earther—and you won't let me help Malley? It's because of me he's up there!"

Sammie moved close to him, but didn't put a comforting hand on his shoulder, as he might have with anyone else. "Hush, boy. There's nothing you can do that won't make things worse. Think it through. Here, in Outward Five, we know you both—we have a fair idea what the Earther's play is with getting Malley to the docking ring. We all understand they're hunting you, not dealing with him. But the rest of the station? They're wondering what's up. They see a stationer—one of our own—getting cozy with Earthers. They see rules being broken and don't know why."

"What are you saying?" Pardell asked, feeling as though his lips were numb.

Wilheim answered for Sammie: "The Earther isn't Malley's trouble. She finds out he isn't her ticket to you, she's done and sends him back down. But if she doesn't do it fast enough, Malley's going to be up against the rest of the station. Only we can fix that, Pardell. No offense, but there's no good bringing 'siders into this mess." He paused, blinking though his eyes looked at nothing, or as if somehow they saw more than he wanted. "There's no good spreading more about you either," Wilheim went on. "Station's on edge. They'll be suspicious of anything—unusual—now."

Roy Malley nodded, as did most of the others. Pardell sank

back down to his seat. First Rosalind and now this. He didn't know if he was grateful to have others take charge, or terrified.

It didn't matter. Even as he nodded a mute good-bye to each of his seniors, Pardell could feel his own resolve hardening. The Earther was his problem and Malley was his friend.

He wouldn't abandon either.

# Chapter 10

ON the surface, it was a peaceful meeting of open-minded souls. A lie. Gail had endured its like enough times during her academic career to know when sharks cruised beneath the polite smiles and offers of refreshments, waiting for the careless or exhausted swimmer to make that one mistake.

Oh, she'd been here before. The setting didn't matter. On her own, Gail was confident she could talk her way out of what appeared to have once been a banquet hall and was now the seat for Thromberg Station's governing council.

Unfortunately, Commander Grant sat to her left, literally quivering with tension. The stationer, Hugh Malley, sat to her right, his too-casual posture just as clearly an indication of how he judged their risk.

*Was it a necessary one?* she asked herself, surveying those filling the room. It appalled her still, how many individuals the station would cram into any space. The air quality had to be suffering. She found herself involuntarily taking shallow breaths, through her nose, until she realized Malley was amused.

*Risk?—Not as though they'd had a choice*, Gail thought, taking a deliberately deep breath as she reached for a glass of water. They hadn't been offered anything more sustaining—she was long past regretting skipping breakfast. The stationers had moved quickly to overwhelm her guards and bring them here. They'd been made to wait for hours, apparently to face—*who were these people, anyway?* Less than a government. More than a rabble. Most were older. It was their number and determination, not their individual strength, that had brought the Earthers here. But they had something else in common. Gail struggled to put her finger on the notion. They all had the look of people who had survived and intended to keep on surviving; there was a certain hardness to their faces, a thriftiness to their movements and speech. Ordinarily, this would have been reassuring, but Gail thought again of sharks and waited for the gleam of teeth.

Sometimes, a frontal assault worked best. Besides, Gail told herself, at this rate her stomach would start complaining for her. She picked out Administrator Forester, presently standing in the row encompassing those privileged to sit at the long L-shaped table. "Since I am being treated as a prisoner, Administrator Forester, am I to assume I've committed some crime?" Gail demanded, making sure she projected her voice over the indistinct noise of so many breathing and shuffling about. "If so, I expect to be notified of any charges immediately—with the Captain of the *Seeker* linked by comm as witness."

Any shuffling died away. Forester looked decidedly uncomfortable to have been singled out. *Good.* But he didn't answer. Instead, a woman directly across from Gail spoke. "I am Leah Nateba, Dr. Smith. Chief Administrator for Thromberg Station, You haven't committed any crime we are aware of—unless it is of stupidity."

When sharks strike, Gail remembered, it's usually from below and fast. They go for a taste, not a hold; to test a potential prey, rather than risk the unknown. "Being uninformed can lead to several misconceptions, Chief Administrator," Gail replied calmly. "Enlighten me."

Nateba, as several here, had ivory-white hair in stark contrast to her dark skin. Her eyes were darker still, and not the least warm. "You have entered into private negotiations with this stationer—"

"Hugh Malley, Outward Five," that worthy piped up. "In case Forester hasn't enlightened you."

Gail resisted the urge to glare to her right. Nateba was doing an admirable job of attempting to impale Malley with a look anyway, for all the good it would do. Grant made an almost subliminal growling noise.

"—private negotiations, as I said," the Chief Administrator continued past the interruption. "Explain yourself. Dr. Smith," she added quickly, before Malley could take a breath to answer.

*Something wasn't tracking*, Gail recognized suddenly. There was hostility toward Earthers here—that wasn't new. But there seemed even more hostility being directed at Malley, who she would have sworn was a person who made more friends than enemies. He was one of their own, after all. She suspected a prohibition against direct contact between the regular station dwellers and such as herself. Forester should have warned her. Instead—she glanced at him speculatively—he'd deliberately encouraged her to meet with Malley. A trap, of sorts. Had Malley been in on it? She'd guess not, given his aversion to the air lock and his passionate refusal to contact Pardell.

But Malley must have known how his people would react to their private meeting—yet he'd been the one to insist. He'd been willing to risk it. *Why?* Gail shook her head at her own thoughts. "Explain myself? There's nothing to explain beyond what I've already told Administrator Forester," Gail enjoyed the man's flinch at being named. "I'm looking for someone on Thromberg. Hugh Malley knows him. That's all there is to it."

"So you have been—or are—seeking private negotiations with yet another on the station," Nateba leaned her head toward the man beside her, who promptly whispered something into her ear. "A person not registered. One Aaron Pardell."

Gail could feel Malley stiffen through his arm against hers—a necessarily tight fit given how many shared the table. *So.* There was a danger to his friend in this woman's questions. *No,* Gail thought, *not her questions*—in her learning of Pardell's very existence. If Pardell was in some danger on the station, she could use that to convince Malley to bring his friend to her, given she could ever arrange another private conversation with him. The odds of that happening appeared about nil.

"I have no problem with any and all of my discussions being public, Chief Administration," Gail said smoothly. "As I've said, I'm authorized to be here in order to further my research. I've no interest in your internal business, nor do I intend any disruption—"

"It's a bit late for lies, Earther." The teeth were showing plainly now, and others in the room leaned forward as if scenting blood themselves. Gail tried to ignore the hot breath stirring her hair as those behind moved too close for comfort. "Or did it surprise you when we detected your spy satellite? Would you be equally surprised to know your clumsy digging into our data banks was just as obvious to us?" There was a muttering from the gathered crowd—around two hundred, Gail fatalistically estimated—after each of these announcements. Gail did take the time to turn and glare at Grant, whose face bore no expression at all. It was his "against hopeless odds" face—she'd bet on it. If it was meant to express his expectation of surviving her ire about his so-called experts' lack of stealth, it was appropriate.

Gail not only planned to survive this meeting, she intended to profit from it. "You haven't brought us here to talk about whatever the *Seeker* might—or might not—have done," she said as much to the crowd as Nateba. "What do you want, Chief Administrator? An apology? Fine. I'll write one up for whatever you deem necessary. You want me to leave? I'd love to—but not without finding Aaron Pardell. Since this man," she jerked her head toward Malley, "can help me and you obviously cannot, I suggest you let us get to it."

Nateba sat up a little straighter, perhaps startled to find prey that flashed teeth in response. "Malley?" she used his name as the sum of her questions.

"The Earther's nuts," Malley rumbled from beside Gail. She could feel his deep voice through her arm against his. "I don't know a Pardell. If I did, I'd never turn him over to her. For any reason." This last a message aimed at her, no doubt.

"So." Nateba considered this, again leaning to one side, then the other, listening to whispered comments from her companions. She collected opinions from those behind her as well. "Thromberg's a big place, Dr. Smith," she said finally. "No one's denying there are those here who aren't registered with Station Admin—some always slip by. Criminals, mostly. Now, if your Pardell is one of those, I'd say he's hardly worth your time or ours. And if Malley's no help . . . seems to me you don't have much reason to stay."

Grant moved unnecessarily in his seat, not about to rise, just letting her know he agreed with everything the stationer was saying and wanted nothing more than a peaceful exit from this crowded place. What his people and Tobo might be doing on the *Seeker* at the moment, Gail really didn't want to think about— she was aware there were FD contingency plans, particularly as related to her insistence on visiting the station in person. None of them were likely to produce the resolution she needed: Pardell—and this Malley—both in her grasp and cooperative.

"Do you think much about the Quill, Chief Administrator?" Gail asked, arching one brow. She took a sip of water, giving them all time to do exactly that. "They are an enemy we share—"

"If they exist!" This shout from the crowd wasn't worth a glance in acknowledgment. Gail knew from the settling around the table that she had their attention. The name of their mutual enemy still had that power.

"Maybe you choose to ignore the Quill. You can, tucked here on your station." Gail smiled thinly. "I, on the other hand, think a great deal about the Quill—but you know that, of course. You've checked my credentials. I'm humanity's expert on the Quill." Gail sharpened her tone and leaned forward. "I am not here to waste my time or yours. Thromberg isn't my destination. I've stopped here because I'm collecting human genome markers, markers crucially important in testing retrieval equipment. Pardell, who does exist, is the sole surviving descendant of a family line I need. And that retrieval equipment?" She paused for effect, but it was hardly necessary—she had them all. "It's to collect samples of living Quill tissue, tissue we must have in order to develop a way to wipe them off the terraformed worlds. Worlds, I believe, that belong to your people."

The silence was palpable, as though everyone crowded into the room had turned to stone. Gail's initial feeling of triumph began fading. It faded further as the silence erupted into two hundred voices at once, and a huge hand around her calf yanked her painfully from her chair to land on her rump under the table. Grant was underneath almost the same instant, the three of them—for it had been Malley's painful grip pulling her down—huddling together. It would have been ridiculous, except for the look on both men's faces. For once, they seemed to be in perfect harmony, both glaring at her.

Almost immediately, Grant began leading the way to the nearest end of the table, crawling swiftly. Chair legs became obstacles as everyone around the table surged to their feet, their chairs falling to the floor and rolling this way and that. The shouts and other sounds were confusing without seeing what was happening. There didn't seem to be anyone searching for the missing "guests."

They reached the end of the table, and Grant lifted one hand to hold her back as he cautiously climbed out. Malley, perhaps assuming she was a fool, reinforced that caution by wrapping his hand around her ankle. Gail didn't waste the breath it would take to hiss disapproval. Grant quickly leaned down to signal them out.

They—and Grant's four guards who had been held off to one side and were now silently gathered around their commander— were the only people left in the room. Three huge exit doors remained ajar.

Gail was whirled around as Malley snatched her shoulder and pulled her to face him. "Now you've done it, haven't you!" he snarled at her.

Grant, perhaps sharing that opinion, didn't intervene. Instead, as Gail stood paralyzed, he asked the stationer: "Where have they gone?"

"Where do you think?" Malley growled, giving her a shake before letting go. Perversely, Gail reached out and fastened both hands on his arm.

"Where have they gone?" she demanded. "Tell us! What's happening?"

If ever there was doom written on a man's face, she saw it in Malley's. "What's happening, Dr. Smith?" he repeated in a tightly controlled voice. "You've given very frightened people a choice of targets. Most of them are going to help destroy your ship before any living or dead Quill contaminates their only home."

"We don't have any—!"

"And the rest?" Malley said as if he didn't hear her frantic protest—or as if it was irrelevant, which, Gail had the sickening realization, it most assuredly was. "The rest are now hunting Aaron Pardell. Thanks to you, Dr. Smith."

# Chapter 11

UNDER the circumstances, Pardell couldn't afford the risk of traveling where others did. It didn't matter much—there were no free-run corridors leading from the Outward Five to the stern docking ring anyway. Of course, that's not where he was supposed to be going. He'd suited back up and made his way to the air lock to satisfy Sammie, who'd sent Tanya as a reluctant escort to be sure Pardell had heeded good advice and headed home. Pardell didn't think Malley would mind Tanya seeing their hideyhole. From her careful lack of curiosity, he imagined she'd visited already.

He checked his slide, taking his time despite the urgency he felt. The stationers who met in the back of Sammie's knew their kind. *There were no old fools on Thromberg*, Pardell reminded himself. He'd had to believe their warnings of the danger to Malley.

Pardell felt trapped even out here, despite the endless distances to every side but one. He carried Malley's suit strapped to his back, as if carrying the man. It had meant waiting in the air lock until he was sure Tanya had left, then sneaking back on-station to retrieve the gear.

Getting the massive stationer *into* the suit was a problem Pardell left to the unimaginable future.

He watched for others of his kind out here, aware Rosalind and others wouldn't approve, hoping to spot them first. It was almost impossible to identify one another outside. Everyone's suit bore patches and replacement parts gleaned from the same sources. Only style stood out, and there wasn't much Pardell could do to disguise his own. Few were as fast or graceful on the cables, and, though he delayed where necessary to be careful, he had to move at his best pace. He chose routes through abandoned ships, a spreading graveyard where the cable system was no longer maintained. Risky, but less likely to be observed. As for explaining why he carried an extra suit? That would take some doing. He'd rather not.

The brief rest at Sammie's had helped. He'd eaten a bit as well. Still, Pardell fought to keep his hands from shaking, blinking sweat from his eyes. This side of Thromberg was in daylight again and his suit struggled to maintain his core temperature within anything resembling safe levels.

He dropped more than slid down the last stretch of cabling, coming to rest in the shadow of a Nautilus-class private yacht. A fancy toy, brought out here during the first wave of optimism and wealth, abandoned when her holds ran empty and her crew sought sturdier quarters. 'Sider kids used to play on it. Pardell ran his glove over the sleek curve of a hull destined to swim in atmosphere as well as vacuum, distracted by thoughts of lift, drag, thrust—teased by imaginings of dropping through a cloud to come out again in sunlight.

Sunlight without an atmosphere was a far less friendly thing. Pardell wrenched his foolish, wandering mind back to the present, angry at himself again, and again tired of that anger. One day, he'd learn to focus on a task and simply do it.

Such as what lay ahead. Resolutely, Pardell leaned down and activated his mags, feeling the thump through his lower legs as his boots flattened to the station's outer plate. Thromberg's stern horizon made a paired arc before his eyes, not as smooth as the aft section had been before the 'siders attached their ships. No, the stern ring had originally been intended to receive only freighters and automated cargo barges. It was festooned with servo handling arms and other gear—now almost half nonfunctional, according to Rosalind. Still, a rare glimpse of Thromberg's grand design before the Quill.

It would take him about an hour to walk to the nearest air lock. More importantly, it would take one-quarter of a tank of air if he paced it right. Pardell hit the chin switch and read his gauges. He still had three-quarters of a tank, the difference from full being what had brought him along the cables to here.

Pardell carried one extra air tank—all he owned. It was an

old emerg unit, about one-half the capacity of the one on his back, but he'd tested it before. He'd made sure the tank on Malley's suit was full, not that he'd touch it. If they couldn't both make it back, what was the point?

He took one last look at the comforting confusion of ships and cables that was home and safety, then began his march. The joke would be on him, if the air locks of the stern ring had been sealed from inside.

Thunk. Lift the heel to release. Swing the foot forward and down. Thunk. Lift the heel to release the back foot. Swing it forward . . . Pardell lost himself in the sensation of effort without struggle, satisfied to be moving in a direction that might help Malley without arguments and confusion. Everyone told him what to do. No one listened. Thunk . . . Lift . . . *Young Aaron, don't trust them* . . . Swing . . . Thunk . . . *Young Pardell, we don't want your help* . . . *Mr. Touch-Me-Not* . . . Lift . . .

*Freak.*

Thunk . . . At least now, here, it was his choice to be a fool or hero, precisely which depending on several factors beyond his control.

As the slice of station making up the stern ring came closer, Pardell realized he'd forgotten one of those factors.

There were tiny suited figures ahead. Not many, and none between him and his chosen air lock, but there could be more hidden in the intense black shadows cast by the servo booms and other equipment. So far, they all seemed busy with their own tasks. There wasn't much he could do beyond hoping they were also focused on their upcoming shift change, timed, for convenience out here, to the approaching terminator as the station rolled from sunlight to darkness.

Some of those workers were at the bases of what Pardell didn't at first credit to be starships. His feet kept moving as he stared at what the *Merry Mate II* and her sister ships had been. Perhaps some of these were just as old or as ready to be scrapped in favor of newer models, but to his eyes, they were all whole and beautiful, free of the haphazard cables and piping, ready to fly.

One in particular caught his fancy, an odd-looking thing set apart from the rest. It must be docked as far to this side of the ring as possible. Since that docking placed it closest to his air lock, he was relieved to see the ship didn't have any suited figures bustling around its exterior. In fact, there was nothing near it at all, a lack of comparison that kept him from judging its true size until he was much closer.

When he did comprehend the scale of the ship, Pardell gasped. It was a monster of its kind, made up of two globes, one much larger than the other, the smaller nestled properly into a real docking port rather than rammed down onto a buckled plate and held by welds and scraps. The globes were lit both inside and out, sparkling like the decorations Silvie used to hang in Sammie's for special days, until so many were "borrowed" she'd given up. The starship's globes were linked by a strange, dark tubelike structure, visible mainly in silhouette, though it, too, possessed a fine line of red lights, as though the ship's builders had insisted on fanciful touches everywhere.

Pardell didn't need the extravagant lighting to know it was an Earther ship. Most were, except for some freighters, barges, and tows the station had managed to keep operational. Not to mention only an Earther ship would be so distinctly new in its design.

There was a precise moment in his approach when he became convinced this wasn't just any Earther ship—but her ship.

The *Seeker*.

That was the moment Pardell almost panicked and turned back. Then calm reason reasserted itself. Why would they be looking out over the empty curve of the station? Even if they did, what could he appear but another of the workers—albeit one in a suit less maintained than most. Given Earther snobbery, they likely wouldn't notice that much. They probably had proximity alarms—the *'Mate* did, until Raner sold those parts as well—so he'd be cautious not to get too close. That was all. Just keep it casual and head for the air lock.

And hope it was still functioning. The unguarded part, he'd take on faith.

For the rest of his march . . . Thunk . . . Lift . . . Swing . . . Pardell studied the glittering technological wonder that was the *Seeker*, memorizing every detail in view. He'd share them with

Rosalind later—once she got over her pique that he was the one to see this beauty first. And recovered from her justifiable rage over his willfulness. Hmmm. Thunk . . . Lift . . .

Then again, Pardell nodded to himself, maybe he'd savor this particular experience on his own.

# Chapter 12

THEY'D been searched, enthusiastically, by stationers who likely knew all about concealed knives but who, it seemed, had no conception of the talents of the Earth military when it came to concealing anything else.

Grant and his four were still pulling toys out of various parts of their uniforms, as Gail and Malley watched in fascination. Grant's four? Gail struggled to dredge their names from memory, aware the two men and two women were preparing to risk their lives to return her to the *Seeker*. Ah, yes. George Tau, of course, but also Combat Specialists Art Mitchener and Natasha Loran, and Deployment Specialist Dianne Peitsch. Amazing how letting their hair grow was starting to transform them into individuals. Tau's was jet-black and straight, glossy in the station's lighting. Mitchener and Loran both sported curls, his tightly spiraled, hers beginning to fan out along the line of her chin. Peitsch's might try to be straight, but she had a pair of widow's peaks driving her locks in every direction but down.

They'd traveled together all these months, these four among the twelve rotating as her personal guard, a guard until now Gail had deliberately ignored and would have happily been without. As she stood beside the oddly comforting bulk of Hugh Malley, watching the FDs assemble various devices from the parts they'd carried hidden, she found herself wishing for no more than another irritating walk from her office to the lab with these people following behind, their greatest daily risk being caught dozing outside her door by Grant.

As if hearing her thought, Grant lifted his eyes from what he held even as his fingers made the last connections to what was suddenly a miniature transmitter. "They didn't seem overly concerned with us, Dr. Smith," he said, perhaps mistaking her silence.

"Yet," Malley offered, leaning one hip on the table.

Gail waved away both comments. "We must contact Tobo. He's—"

"The Captain and our people back on the *Seeker* have been kept informed," Grant said, flashing a grimly satisfied smile. He—and the others—reached up to the topmost buttons on their uniforms.

"No vids?" Gail snorted. Well, if ever there was a time to be grateful for her orders being ignored, this was one. She held out her hand and Grant dropped the transmitter into it without hesitation. "It's autosynched," was all he said.

Gail walked a few steps away, not for privacy, but because she couldn't stand still when so much could be happening outside her control. She thumbed on the device. "Receiving," chirped Tobo's voice.

"What's your status, Captain?" she asked.

"We seem to have inherited your meeting, Dr. Smith," Tobo answered in a reassuringly dry tone. "So far, they're milling around the main air lock. Shouting. Nothing terribly interesting. However, there's a sizable number here already and more are arriving as we speak." He paused, then reported: "Grant's people want me to prep the ship to undock without station cooperation but—"

"Do it. I don't how much you could pick up from their remotes—or what the troopers told you—but the situation is serious."

Another short pause. When he spoke again, Tobo's voice was grim. "Dr. Smith, if we undock on our own, are you aware it will rupture the wall in this section? Are you ordering me to murder these people because they are afraid of the Quill? I'm afraid of the Quill!"

"I'm ordering you to make it clear to Thromberg Station that I won't have my ship and mission threatened. Power up and disengage from your end, but hold position. I hope that's all it will take," Gail said measuredly. "If they force matters, give them as much warning to evacuate as you can, but don't hesitate to blow the couplings and get the *Seeker* out of here. Am I understood, Captain?"

"Yes, Dr. Smith. But we're not leaving without you."

Gail almost smiled. "Good. Because I'm not planning on staying here. Smith out."

"Hold it!" This stern command wasn't for her. Gail whirled to see Malley halfway to the nearest exit. The stationer could move quietly when he chose. She already knew he was fast. Grant's level voice stopped Malley in his tracks. He shrugged and walked back to them. A small, sharp gesture from Grant sent Tau, Loran, and Mitchener to each of the still-open doorways.

"I thought you were done with me, Earther," Malley said mildly. "Seems to me you have red lights to spare on your console as it is. Not going to be easy getting your boss here back on her ship—if there's a ship to get back to, that is."

"The *Seeker* can take care of herself," Gail disagreed sharply. "You and I still have business to discuss."

"You don't quit, do you?" Malley raised his huge hands in exasperation, letting them drop as a pair of snub-nosed weapons took aim at his midsection. He glanced at them and curled a lip in scorn—perhaps unimpressed by tranks. "Any business of yours has to wait," he snapped, all pretense at charm wiped away. "I need to warn Aaron. Now. You can't do that. No one else can. Let me out of here."

Gail stared up at him. "I've a better idea," she said. "Bring Pardell to us. We'll protect him . . . I give you my word. He'll be safe from the mob on the *Seeker*."

The stationer took a deep breath that shuddered near its end, as if he imagined facing the air lock again, then shook his head. "Even if I believed that—even if I thought Aaron would be safe from *you* once on board—there's no way to get him from Outward Five to here. He'd be picked off at the first reg checkpoint. And that's assuming the checkpoints are still open. If this escalates to a riot, every corridor will locked down to try and contain it. Thromberg's survived riots before, Earther."

"So how do you intend to warn Pardell?" Grant asked reasonably. "If he can't come here, how can you go there?"

"I don't," Malley growled back, his expression clearly showing his opinion of Grant's assumption. "We do have comm systems, Earther—and not all are controlled by Station Admin. Aaron has friends in Outward Five. Good ones. They'll help—get him out of the way once they know what's coming down-corridor at them. I just have to get word to them."

Gail tossed the miniature transmitter to Malley, who snatched it from the air with a surprised grunt. "Let me set it up for you . . ." Grant's offer trailed away as Malley made quick work of keying in a new frequency, then began tapping the pickup in a rapid code rather than speaking into it.

"What about us?" Gail asked Grant. "We can't risk the ship or any more personnel."

Grant accepted the transmitter back from Malley, whose tight-lipped look of relief seemed all the thanks they'd get. Gail wasn't offended. How could she be, when her ill-chosen words had put his friend in danger? She couldn't change that, but she didn't plan to leave this station without Pardell either.

"Malley? Any ideas?" Gail could see Malley was startled by the commander's question. She wasn't, having expected Grant to use every advantage he could find. A local expert could make all the difference.

Malley grabbed a chair from the floor, righted it, and sat himself down, stretching out his long legs. "On how to get you to your ship? None. Sorry."

"Could you get us stationer clothing?" this from Peitsch.

He didn't quite laugh, but the skin around his eyes crinkled. "Clothing wouldn't be enough. I mean, just how you stand would give you away." When Gail and the others exchanged puzzled looks, Malley did laugh, if without humor. "The distance you put between yourselves. No one here would waste that much space—it's rude. And your posture? Well, there's no other word for it, you look too damn arrogant. You couldn't pass yourselves off for an instant as anything but what you are. That's not taking into account how you smell."

"Smell?" Gail asked involuntarily. "We don't—"

Malley laughed again. "Yes, you do. New fabric. Expensive scents. And you wash in water, I expect? Often?" He made it sound like a sinful waste.

"Point taken. No disguise," Grant concurred. "Will they let us back to the ship without a fight?"

The stationer drew in his feet, leaning forward to rest his elbows on his knees. Even in this position, he could meet Gail's eyes without looking up. "They don't like or trust you, Earther. Now you've gone and started the notion that Quill could be near the station. So you're talking about terrified people—who don't like or trust you. A fight? There wouldn't be one. The first shove, the first swing, above all, any hint you've brought those on-station—" Malley pointed at the weapons still loosely held in Grant's and Peitsch's hands "—and you'll be dead. Any one of these people would never harm you. But get a riot started?" Malley shivered, his voice trailing away.

"No gain in delay, then," Gail made herself say briskly, trying not to swallow hard as the bile rose in her throat at the suddenly too-clear image of being torn limb-from-limb by a mob.

Grant looked thoughtful. "From what you're telling us, there could be. Let them mill around. Keep them focused on the *Seeker*'s air lock. The station shunted us away from the other ships, remember? That means there are 'locks not in use nearby."

"You're thinking of having your people on the *Seeker* meet us with suits at one of those," Gail guessed. "Then we could exit the station away from the mob and simply walk to the ship."

"Might work." This from Malley in a voice so calm it sounded unnatural. "Stationers and immies don't tend to think about—Outside—if they can help it. They'll assume you're the same way." He pressed his lips together, then added as though the mere thought was difficult to express: "Best warn your people to be on their guard. I've—heard—there may be others outside that don't take well to strangers."

"Thanks," Grant said, then raised a brow interrogatively. "We could use your help, stationer."

"Their thinking I'm helping you is what got me into this mess," Malley retorted, rising to his feet and dusting off imaginary soil. "I'm better clear. They see me with you, I'll be the first one turned into floor paste."

Gail shook her head slightly, stopping what she knew would be Grant's offer of another suit, and asylum for Malley on the *Seeker*. The stationer would refuse—she knew it. Instead, Gail gestured to the transmitter and Grant dropped it into her hand.

"Do we have another?" she asked. At his nod, she stepped close to Malley, again surprised by how much Malley there was, and held out the transmitter. "Take it," she urged him, pressing it into his hand when he hesitated. "Call me if you need help—for yourself or Pardell."

His fingers trapped hers around the transmitter. Instead of leaving, Malley looked down at her with a frown. "Was it true? About Aaron and your retrieval device? There's a chance to capture living Quill?" He spoke almost reluctantly, as if part of him feared the answer.

Gail didn't move. "Yes." She could hear Grant's low voice but not make out the words. Presumably he was making arrangements with the *Seeker*. Right now, all that was irrelevant. Malley was her chance—perhaps her only chance—to get to Aaron Pardell. And, she reminded herself, his ship.

"How certain—?" Malley began, then stopped himself with a head shake. "Nothing's certain."

"It's certain enough to bring me here," Gail told him quietly, earnestly, trying to project all of her own belief into her voice and expression. "We won't know until we try—but I swear to you this is the best chance we've had since the Quill arrived. It might be the only chance in time for the people on this and the other stations. It's that important."

Malley released her hand but stayed. His voice deepened—a sign he was troubled, Gail now suspected. His eyes were haunted. "That's what you meant—when you said knowing why you needed Aaron would change everything."

"Yes."

"Not everything," Malley disagreed. "He is my best friend. My brother."

Gail didn't flinch, aware Grant had gathered his people again, aware time was growing short and nothing guaranteed any of them would live once they left this room. "You know him better than anyone, then. Would Aaron Pardell want to help the people on this station?" she asked very softly. "Is he like you?"

"He's better than I am," Malley said, almost to himself. "We kid around, but when push comes to grab, Aaron's the kind who'll do without before seeing anyone else go hungry. Always been that way. Everyone who knows him is happy to give him room, no question."

"So if he knew why I needed him, he'd want to help."

"Dr. Smith—"

Gail ignored Grant. "Am I right, Mr. Malley?"

The stationer nodded very slowly, then his eyes narrowed as he stared down at her. "It doesn't matter. Aaron's a soft touch— I'm not. I've lost track of the number of times I've kept him from starving himself in a good cause, which doesn't mean I don't still do it. I'm not prepared to believe you that this project of yours is safe for him. I do believe you haven't told me anything close to the entire truth."

Grant interrupted again, but kept his distance. "Dr. Smith— they've left the *Seeker*. We must go to whatever air lock we can reach and start signaling our location."

"Talk to Pardell," Gail continued pressing Malley, trusting Grant to physically haul her away if things became truly urgent. "Keep the transmitter and contact me when you can—I'll send you more information, if that's what it's going to take. Just talk to him about it."

Malley looked almost convinced, then looked past her to Grant. "Your man's right. You have to get moving."

"Mr. Malley. Hugh."

"I'll come with you as far as I dare," Malley said instead of answering her directly, taking her arm and shoving her in Grant's direction. Gail didn't bother objecting—the man seemed incapable of noticing how much she disliked being pushed hither and yon. *Besides*, Gail admitted honestly, following Grant as they hurried toward the leftmost door, *stationer manners were legitimately the least of her worries now.*

# Chapter 13

*IT wasn't fair*, Pardell grumbled to himself. Oh, the air lock hadn't been sealed, but he'd foolishly expected anything to do with the stern docking ring to be in pristine condition. He should have known better—Thromberg showed her stress marks everywhere.

He secured Malley's suit and tugged a hammer from his waist belt. The outer door appeared to have not been opened— or lubricated—during his lifetime. With a careful air of "I'm busy working" for any observers, he began smacking the 'lock's emergency manual release, his other hand holding tight during each blow so the force didn't knock his mags free of the station plate. He'd automatically clipped a line from his suit to a ring designed for that purpose, but it would look pretty embarrassing to have to haul himself back into contact, through an Insider mistake.

Three smacks and the handle budged a quarter turn. He wrestled it the remaining distance, then waited impatiently for the interior clamps to disengage. The air lock should evacuate itself automatically to receive him, a quick process that for some reason was now taking an eternity. Pardell dared a quick look around.

There were suited figures emerging from the smaller globe of the Earther's ship.

*Nothing to do with him*, Pardell told himself. He turned back to the 'lock. The indicator was red; clamps were still in place. Choosing a spot at random, Pardell struck the door again with his hammer. Maybe the Earthers would assume this was a malfunctioning air lock and choose one of the others within an easy walk. Maybe they were out doing pointless maintenance on a ship obviously perfect. Maybe they'd never used suits before and wanted to go for a stroll in vacuum.

Pardell told himself the sweat burning one eye was due to his suit protesting its longest use in years and tried to keep from looking around again.

But he couldn't help it. The indicator flashed green just as he turned around—almost certain he'd see a row of figures closing in on him, figures in new suits with only one owner and full tanks of air, maybe even propellant rigs that worked.

He was wrong—they'd moved away from him. Pardell froze in disbelief, so ready for confrontation or worse he found himself gripping the hammer as if somehow it could be a weapon. How could they be ignoring him? After all, the Earther spy 'bot had practically touched his helmet.

But they were moving away. In fact, the first pair were now passing within the terminator, suit lights flaring as the station's own shadow caught them in its darkness, the rest following.

Like him, each of the figures carried an extra suit.

Pardell swallowed what saliva he could find in his mouth. *Not routine,* an alarm hammered in his mind. Something was wrong. Something major. These Earthers weren't an attack force—all they carried of any size were the suits.

They were a rescue.

And who would be with any Earther in trouble inside Thromberg?

*Damn. Damn. Damn.* Pardell used the word as well as his hammer to reset the stubborn air lock release back into its closed position—safety for anyone trying to exit as well as covering his tracks.

Then he grabbed Malley's suit and headed after the Earthers, quite sure this time he was being a fool and not a hero, but seeing no alternative.

# Chapter 14

A GHOST station, peopled by discarded things. Gail watched where she stepped, trying to avoid the litter of paper, trampled boxes, and, more rarely, food—all items presumably dropped as their owners answered their passions and ran to join their neighbors. Surely some must have run in the other direction, she thought uncomfortably, worried about family or friends. Perhaps not. There were no children here: a suddenly ominous difference.

As long as they were alone and unobserved, Malley appeared willing to stay with them. A good thing—he'd remembered enough of his own trip to the Admin offices and then to the *Seeker* to guide them on a route different than the one they'd been brought along, claiming it was faster. Gail kept to herself the obvious: that speed made it the likeliest route for the mob as well. She found herself straining to see ahead, worrying about catching up to stragglers.

"Feels like the damn aft ring up here," Malley said after a long silence, punctuated only by the rapid thud of their boots. Their pace was short of a run, but quick enough.

Gail thought she was the only one to hear, being beside the stationer—Grant and Tau were in front, with Loran way ahead and the other two a comfort behind. "What do you mean?" she asked, willing to be distracted.

Malley glanced at her, then shrugged. "Deserted. Empty. No one lives in the aft ring—it was too damaged. There's air, but no heat. We don't have many places like that. So this feels very— strange. To me. I guess you're used to it. Being alone in a place."

Listening to the sounds of six pairs of boots marching in

quick time, Gail was inclined to grin at this, but answered him seriously. "It depends on where you live, Mr. Malley. On Titan, everything's orbital or under domes. Space is still at a premium. Not so much as here—" a masterful understatement, Gail thought, "but most share accommodations, eating areas, hallways. You have to go to Earth or Mars to find enough room to be alone. Even there, people seem to enjoy being crowded into cities."

"But you've been in the open?" Malley asked, maybe a little too nonchalantly. Gail looked up out the corner of her eyes and saw his jaw clench once, spasmodically.

"It's not necessary," she said quickly, trying to imagine a life spent entirely within walls. "And a sky—well, it's like a roof, really."

"Really," he repeated, from his tone not in the least fooled by her efforts, but perhaps appreciating the attempt. "I'll take your word for it, Dr. Smith.'"

"Gail," she corrected, for no particular reason, unless it was that her title, from Malley, felt more like a challenge than an acknowledgment of rank.

"Left corridor," Malley called out softly. Loran, hearing this, checked back over her shoulder for confirmation, then went left at Grant's nod. They carried their weapons hidden in pockets, ready for use but not in plain sight. More of Malley's advice. Gail hoped it would be enough.

"Slow up!" The warning came suddenly from Malley. "There's a junction ahead with the main corridor to the Outward Five levels. It's where I came up. The stern docking ring and 'locks begin just past that point."

"What do we watch for?" Grant asked, signaling his people ahead with caution. Malley hung back and Gail stayed with him.

"You'll know trouble if you see it. Could be no one's there. They could have locked it down already."

"Or?" Gail whispered, as they all fell silent, eyes fixed on Loran as she eased to the wall's end.

"Or there could be some ruckus underway down-corridor— if stationers from up here tried to storm past our folks to get Pardell. There's not much good will between the levels." From the apparently unconscious way Malley's hands kept forming fists as he spoke, Gail was reasonably sure he would have vastly preferred an active role in whatever might be happening.

Loran's hand moved in an all-clear motion, sweeping them forward. Grant didn't let them hesitate in the opening, although Gail took a quick look as she ran past. Opening? There was none. A few steps in, the corridor ended at a massive steel plate that must have been swung out from the walls, then spot-welded in place. It wasn't airtight; just people-proof.

"Well, that's a relief," Mitchener said from behind Malley.

The stationer muttered something under his breath, then said louder: "Sure. If you like your riots made official and your friends locked on the other side."

Gail knew what Malley didn't bother adding: that had been his way home.

A strange vibration in the floor plates began shuddering up through Gail's feet. She started to reach out to halt Grant, to ask him what it was, then she heard a sound—like the ocean crashing against the rocks outside her family's oceanfront home in the south of France. There were gull-like noises as well. It was almost soothing . . .

Until Gail put the vibration and sound into context. Ahead of them were large numbers of moving people, shouting, smashing things. They were about to catch up to the inhabitants of this place.

Then she did reach out for Grant, but he stopped before she could touch him, motioning them against the far side of the hall. Loran came back at a breathless run, panting out the unnecessary. "Around the corner, where it opens up to the ring proper. We can't go any farther, sir, without being seen. There must be thousands—" She sucked in air, then said more calmly: "There's an air lock closer to us. Best we have troops coming from it, than stand outside knocking in plain sight, sir. In my opinion."

Grant gave a short laugh. "My preference, exactly. With your permission, Dr. Smith?" He held up a transmitter.

Gail glared at him and waved impatiently. Thinking about a mob and being close enough to feel and hear the power of hundreds of enraged people were completely different things.

"That's my cue to head elsewhere, Gail," Malley said into her ear.

Startled, Gail turned her head before Malley drew away, and found herself nose-to-nose with him. Before she could so much as blink, the big stationer grinned and planted a quick, light kiss on her cheek. Then he was off, running back the way they'd came.

"I take it we let Malley leave?" Grant commented, one corner of his mouth deepening.

Gail narrowed her eyes. "Think you could have stopped him?"

The commander's mouth spread into the beginnings of a real smile. "Probably not quietly."

"Sir?" Tau came forward with the transmitter. "They're at the outer door now. Sasha's predicting three minutes to get it open—equipment's not in AA shape. Then they'll be through, with our suits. It's a passenger egress, designed for hand luggage as well. We're in luck."

"Why?" Gail asked.

"It could have been one of the emerg locks," Grant explained almost absently. "Those fit a max of two, maybe three, suiting up inside at a time. We'd have to defend the air lock through three complete cycles minimum to get everyone suited and out. Lots of time for mistakes." He checked his wristchrono. "As it is, we should all be able to enter, lock up, and suit without undue risk."

"You didn't mention this potential problem when you brought up this plan, Commander," Gail said icily.

"It wasn't a problem, Dr. Smith. The FD's orders are to get you to safety. Any air lock would have done that. This is just—more convenient—for the rest of us." His brown eyes were frank and his matter-of-fact tone dared her to argue.

She didn't. His orders dealt with the continuation of her project, not an evaluation that the life of Gail Smith was worth more than any of the others now leaning against the wall, waiting through a very long three minutes.

*Had this been an unnecessary risk?* Gail asked herself, thinking over the past hours as critically and dispassionately as possible. Without Pardell and his ship, was the project already a failure? Yes, she was sure of it. The others didn't realize how key this individual was to her plans—if they had, knowing how difficult and unlikely it was to find one person on one of these stations, Titan U would never have let her have its flagship.

*Was the project worth dying for?* Gail listened to the steady, patient breathing of the others, trying to ignore the sounds of violence from the near distance. *Her life?* She knew herself too well, flaws as well as strengths. Death hardly seemed a high price for vindication of her work and ideas. Gail understood, without any pride, that the reason her mouth was so dry and her heart pounded inside her chest as if trying to run away itself was her dread that dying here, now, meant losing everything she'd done. Of being forgotten or, worse, being remembered as a fool.

*Their lives?* She turned her head, keeping it against the wall, to look at her guards—her companions. They could care less about the place in history of Dr. Gail Veronika Ashton Smith. *They were better than she was,* Gail thought, echoing Malley's judgment of his friend. They were prepared to spend themselves in order to free humanity—ironically, the very ones threatening to rip them apart—from the Quill.

She rolled her head straight, staring at the opposite wall. In the end, Gail decided with abrupt clarity, it didn't matter what motivated any of them. That prize was worth this risk and more.

Tau's voice was steady: "They're in, Commander. Air's up to pressure. Ready to open the inner door on your mark. Wait—"

"What's wrong?" Grant demanded, using hand signals to bring Peitsch and Mitchener forward, keeping Loran near Gail.

"They aren't alone in the air lock," Tau reported. "A station worker was coming in at the same time—indicated some problem with his gear—Sasha takes responsibility, sir."

"Sasha can take latrine duty, when we're home," Grant muttered darkly. "Okay, give the word—and make sure they keep the civilian out of the way. This has to be fast and smooth, people. Keep weapons out of view. Dr. Smith—will you need assistance with your suit?"

Gail translated that as: *do I need to waste anyone?* and almost smiled. "I'm capable, Commander. Deploy your people the best you can."

A curt nod.

Then, it was happening. Grant moved them at a brisk walk and Loran stayed with Gail. Just as well, because as they came around the final bend in the hallway the scene ahead would have made Gail run back the other way if she'd been alone.

The docking ring expanded in front of them, its floor and lofty roof curving away in the distance, one wall seeming to disappear into shadows and gantries to Gail's left. To her right, the various air lock doors began, the nearest of those a heart-stopping distance still to cover.

No one stood between them and that safety.

An irrelevant detail, since more people than Gail had ever seen in one place before stood just on the other side of the air lock.

They'd never make it.

# Chapter 15

HE'D made it. Easy as rations. Pardell stood inside the 'lock, waiting for the air to cycle, studiously ignoring the six in those achingly perfect suits.

There'd been the risk they'd recognize him from the surveillance tape the 'bot must have made—but minimal. Why would everyone on the ship be privy to such information? No, he'd marched right up behind them, switching on his wrist and helmet lamps as Thromberg's comforting, chill shadow caught up with him as well, then waited patiently as the Earthers fumbled to open the outer door. He'd almost offered to help.

He'd startled them, all right. When an Earther finally spotted him waiting patiently behind the group, there'd been a great deal of gesturing, likely a bowel function or two, and doubtless frantic chatter on whatever comm link they used among themselves. He'd heard their questions to him on the open frequency, of course, but tapped the side of his helmet with one gloved hand and shrugged, mouthing silent words they could see by the light under his chin. They'd seemed to have no problem believing his suit was malfunctioning. Likely, they'd looked at its patches and cobbled together parts and wonder how it worked at all, compared to theirs.

Pardell came close to forgetting his situation in his envy, running his eyes over what was to his suit what the *Seeker* was to the *'Mate*. He held Malley's behind him and as low as possible, likely out of their field of view.

Not that these were people interested in him. Quite the contrary, they were every bit as focused and tense as Pardell could imagine a team about to enter hostile territory would be. He'd debated whether to move right to the inner door, so they'd let him out first and he could scamper out of the way, or whether to hang back. They'd decided for him, lining up in pairs and leaving him in the rear, the suits they'd brought lying on the two side shelves inside the 'lock, the ones once used to keep luggage and parcels from underfoot as passengers waited to disembark.

However, they appeared to be planning to keep their own suits on, even their helmets.

Pardell wasn't about to tell the Earthers what to do, but he disapproved. Stationers had learned long ago how easily suits could be cut, hoses ripped apart. If the Earthers anticipated trouble inside the station, they'd be better off to leave their gear in the air lock, with a guard.

While fervently hoping for no such problem, Pardell knew he'd attract far too much attention—of the wrong sort—if he waltzed in looking like a lost 'sider. As soon as the air was halfway cycled, Pardell began stripping out of his suit, fingers fumbling as he rolled up and stored his pieces of tape, clamping on his emerg tank so its supply would be accessible immediately. He didn't expect to have time to spare on his exit. He shook out as many wrinkles as he could from his best fifthhand coveralls and ran fingers through his hair, finding it soaking wet with sweat. Some of the ends were still frozen. Pardell sighed wistfully, looking at the racks now filled with suits—he really could use a new one.

The Earthers looked even taller once Pardell took off his mags and straightened to his full height. Probably as tall as Malley. Their suits had some play to sleeves and girth as well. Not that the Earthers were likely to want to replace Malley's suit with one of their own, Pardell admitted to himself. But he could use their help getting the reluctant stationer into either. All of them.

*Something to worry about later.* Pardell braced himself as the inner door unlocked, the air cycle done, feeling cold drops sliding down his neck as the rest of his hair thawed out, and shivers that had nothing to do with cold at all.

# Chapter 16

ON some level, Gail felt numb, as if her limbs were chilled but unable to shiver for warmth. She waited for Grant, putting her trust in him because she had no other choice. By some quirk of mob psychology, no one of the multitude filling the floor ahead of them was looking their way. It appeared they were struggling to get past one another, to join in whatever was occurring farther down the ring.

Where the *Seeker* was docked.

"Grant," she said quickly. "What if Tobo threatens to cut the ship loose? That should clear the ring."

He kept his eyes on their destination, but answered: "If they believe him, they'd have to evacuate this way. We'd be trampled."

Gail pressed her lips tightly together, keeping back other suggestions, likely as useless. The man knew his job. She hated others interjecting their notions into her work—*you'd think she'd know better.*

Grant turned and faced them all. His olive skin didn't reveal much, whether a pallor or flush, but that was made up for by the deep lines stretching from nose to mouth. His voice was confident, with a harsh undertone. "We get Dr. Smith inside that air lock. The stationer was right to say it only takes one thing to turn the beast against us—make no mistake, that many people together can't think, can't reason, only react. We keep it calm. We keep it normal. No eye contact—no talking. If it gets ugly, use whatever force is necessary. Clear?"

Loran and Tau echoed the word. Mitchener merely nodded. Peitsch turned her dark eyes on Gail and said gently: "We'll get you there, Dr. Smith."

"Get us all there, Grant," Gail said, trying to keep her voice steady. "That's an order."

He sketched a salute. "We'll do our best, Professor."

They walked out into the open, hugging the right wall, Gail tucked within a fragile shell of blue-uniformed flesh moving with the nice, easy pace Grant had stipulated. Between Loran's elbow and Mitchener's waist, Gail could see the edge of the mob growing closer, backs to her still. The sound they made rebounded in the huge expanse of the ring, turning what might have been a chant into a loud, inchoate roar. Grant's analogy of a beast was a little too accurate. Gail fixed her thoughts on a niggling statistical problem she'd been dealing with on the trip to Thromberg.

The air lock door was opening, slowly, slowly.

Still the beast seemed unaware what was happening.

Five more steps. Gail lost her concentration as her tiny group reached the spot where they were as close to the air lock as the nearest part of the mob. They gained five steps. Ten more. A pair of faceless suited figures stood in the open doorway; one waved to them to hurry; she could see others behind.

A shout, clearer than the rest, yet wordless. They'd been seen!

Grant refused to hurry, keeping them to a walk.

Another shout, a chorus.

Gail kept her eyes on the air lock, now so temptingly close. They might make it.

It began in slow motion, like a vid she was replaying for details. A group sprouted from the mass ahead, coming as if to intercept them—the suited figures erupted from the air lock. The two groups blended into confusion, helmets rising well over the heads of the stationers. One by one, the helmets disappeared as more and more stationers realized what was happening and sought an available target.

No more walking. Even as the battle was joined, Gail was grabbed by both arms and lifted as her guards raced for the still-open air lock.

One man stood in their way, raising his arms and moving quickly to one side as three Earther weapons aimed at him. The unfortunate stationer who'd been in the air lock, Gail remembered, feeling a rush of sympathy even as her own arms felt as though they were being torn from their sockets. Then she was tossed inside the air lock, scrambling on hands and knees to reach the nearest suit. She tried to ignore what might be happening behind her.

She couldn't, when all sound outside the air lock abruptly ceased.

Gail turned, still crouched on the metal floor, suit half pulled up one leg, and looked out.

Grant, Loran, one of the suited Earthers—that suit sliced open and useless, as well as leaking blood—and Tau stood with their backs to her, weapons out and ready. There was a motionless, perfectly symmetrical arc of mob only paces beyond a line of crumpled shapes. Bodies. Too many. Gail didn't look at them closely, knowing she'd recognize two and should know more.

*Why the standoff?* she thought almost hysterically. The mob could overwhelm them in a heartbeat. Gail spotted Grant's hand making a push-behind gesture. He wanted her to close the hatch. She couldn't. Her mind told her it was necessary, but she was frozen in place—terrified any movement would restart the killing. She was capable of abandoning them, not of murdering them.

The mob's lips began moving. Not loud, this time, but one word, softly, as though it named something they feared and had to rouse themselves to attack. Gail strained to hear it, then didn't need to as she realized no one in the mob was looking at the Earthers—they were looking at the lone stationer still standing beside the air lock. Gail leaned forward slowly until she could see him clearly.

Aaron Pardell.

# Chapter 17

*A*N *oddly useful time for his mind to disengage*, Pardell told himself with approval, feeling his thoughts spiraling wider and deeper with every pulse of his name on the lips of strangers. If he wasn't contemplating the patterns of energy within a cohesive mob—seeing the edges as weak, volatile things, the core as helpless inertia, the front as the line of directed force—he would likely be gibbering with terror and curled up in a fetal position on the floor. Since that would be an embarrassing way to face death, and doubtless Malley would tease him for eternity in whatever afterlife friends shared, Pardell clung to this analytical frame of mind with all his might.

The Earthers. He felt no pity. They'd done this—turned reasonable, courteous individuals into this raving monster—and earned the consequences. Anguish for the stationers and immies motionless on the floor, yes. He could feel that. And for those who would wake from madness and find blood on their hands. There'd been suicides after each of the Ration Riots; there would be more tomorrow.

He was curious how they knew to name him. If it was possible to pick faces from the mass, were any those he'd recognize in return? Had the Earthers labeled him, somehow, or was it as simple as his walking out that air lock, in that company? Pardell turned the alternatives over, examining each, seeing how the results varied based on preconceptions.

A blast of fear laced with hate slammed against his detachment, ripping it to shreds. Pardell gasped and found himself back against the wall. No one had touched him. He could only assume it was so many experiencing the same emotions at once.

What were they waiting for! Did they want him to run for the air lock and his suit? Was that it? To prove he was dealing with the Earthers before tearing him apart? Would the Earthers turn their weapons on the crowd again, on his behalf?

Pardell seriously considered pretending to attack the nearest Earther guard so she'd shoot him and end the suspense.

"Pardell . . . Pardell . . . Pardell . . . "

He might want a name change after this as well. He closed his eyes, deciding this was all a nightmare and he was passing out from carbon dioxide poisoning in his suit, like the time . . .

"Aaron!"

Pardell's eyes flashed open and he looked around frantically. There was only one set of lungs on Thromberg that could shout and be heard over the growl of the mob. What was Malley—?

There was a broad hallway leading from the stern docking ring to Pardell's left. The thinnest part of the mob lay between it and the tableau in front of the air lock. The hallway mirrored a similar one, half-blocked by debris, in the aft ring. Pardell blinked away the urge to start comparing other features, staring with disbelief at a new mass of people rushing toward him.

Malley was in front—*no problem spotting the mammoth idiot*, Pardell thought wildly, nor identifying others similarly impaired. There was Denery, and more familiar faces from Sammie's. Worse and worse. Even if all of Outward Five had opted for a change of scene and a chance to bloody noses, they were still outnumbered a hundred times over and by a mob who'd already killed and been killed.

"This way!" Pardell turned his head right just enough to confirm the urgent command came from the air lock. Dr. Smith—looking a great deal less imposing with her hair mussed, one leg in a suit, and tears pouring apparently unnoticed down her cheeks—was holding on to one edge of the inner door frame. "Please, Pardell. They'll kill you. Hurry."

He was suddenly, gloriously angry. "This is all your fault," he accused, disregarding the mob, their chant, and the onrush of his friends. "Look what you've done!"

Smith seemed oblivious to common sense as well, stepping right out of the air lock and starting to move toward him, dragging the suit, only to be blocked by one of her guards. She looked over the arm holding her and shouted: "They've died for nothing if you don't come with me! Grant—let go of me—That's Pardell!"

Pardell turned away deliberately, then wished he hadn't. The press of new bodies from the left, led by Malley, had not so much met the outer edge of the mob as been absorbed. Friend and stranger milled around one another, not fighting—yet—but pushing with angry cries. At least it was diminishing the number of people chanting his name, which was a relief.

There was an instant in which he somehow found and met Malley's eyes, an instant in which Pardell felt an unreasonable hope the sudden arrival of calmer minds might prevail and they'd all talk about this later over Sammie's truly awful beer.

Then, warned by the sudden dismay on Malley's face, Pardell whirled to find dozens of hands reaching for him. He tried to run, but lost all control of his legs at the first deceptively gentle brush of fingers against his arms and back.

*Anger.* FEAR!

. . . He forgot how to breathe as the daggers of emotion penetrated every part of his flesh, the number of contacts changing as others grabbed for him, then were shocked loose . . . but more replaced those . . . and more . . .

RAGE!

. . . It had never been like this . . . At its worst, he'd always known he'd survive, that there'd be an end . . . His heart faltered, fought, faltered again . . . He convulsed in agony, heaving up under the hands . . .

HATE!

. . . What was Aaron Pardell crumpled into itself . . .

Then was lost.

# Chapter 18

"AARON!"

Gail thought the walls must have amplified Malley's horrified cry—she did know she'd never heard anything approaching that sound from a human throat until Pardell vanished beneath a surging mass of attackers in front of their eyes. She struggled against Grant's arm. "Help him!" she shouted. "You have to help him! He's the one this is for!"

Grant literally threw her back into the air lock—Loran following at his barked command to immediately start forcing Gail into the suit—but her words had penetrated. Grant and Tau holstered their weapons and started pulling people off the tower of moving flesh marking where Pardell had stood.

Their interference should have incited the mob against the Earthers again, but didn't. Loran, once sure Gail was suiting up on her own, hurried to the inner door with her weapon ready, her face set and grim. Gail, pulling on her gloves, looked past the guard's shoulder. Each person Grant or Tau grabbed and pushed aside seemed confused, disoriented, as if they'd been stunned. Most wandered away, while others stood in place for a few seconds, rubbing their hands over their faces or arms. As the mob saw the dull-witted faces of these compatriots, it faded back, edges dissolving, except where Malley and company continued to shove their way forward.

Once they succeeded, Malley let out a roar and launched himself at the remaining bodies, clearing them off through the simple expedient of latching his big hands around any body part available and heaving with all his strength. Oddly, those so mishandled didn't complain, merely picked themselves up from the floor to hobble or crawl away.

Grant and Tau were edged back as well. Several of those who'd come with Malley, most with black eyes or bloody noses marking their efforts to negotiate their way through to this spot, quietly but definitely placed themselves between the Earthers and their besieged friend.

Loran didn't prevent Gail coming out where she could see— perhaps the guard was angry enough at the death of her fellows to believe Gail deserved to see the corpse of the man she'd tried to find.

What Gail saw, she didn't at first believe. There were still between five and eight bodies lying in a haphazard mass, none of them moving. It was impossible to tell which was Pardell—they all wore the same stationer gray.

And all these people were dead.

There was no mistaking it. Those faces she could see bore a dreadful rictus, as though every muscle had convulsed at the moment of death.

"Did you shoot them?" she asked Grant in a low-pitched voice, unsure how she could have missed that and puzzled how they would have died anyway—the FDs' weapons were loaded with heavy tranks. Their shots into the mob hadn't killed anyone, merely knocked them cold and guaranteed a pounding headache to follow in an hour or so.

"No—" Grant's voice was equally perplexed.

Malley wrapped his fingers around another ankle, then uttered a curse and released his grip as if burned.

The mob found its voice again, this time in panic-stricken flight. Gail heard screams of "Quill!" and "Monster!" over the general mayhem of thudding feet. In only minutes, they were alone, except for those from Outward Five—and Malley.

He'd ignored the mob, instead taking two men with him to methodically tear apart what had been a freight trolley before the mob turned it upside down. Mechanically, Gail finished fastening her suit's gloves, coming to stand beside a motionless Grant. Loran and Tau, along with the surviving suited rescuer from the *Seeker*, had gone to check on their fallen.

In seconds, Malley was back. He didn't acknowledge Gail or the others by so much as a glance, going straight to work. He and another man used a grappling arm and its chain to snag the leg belonging to one of the bodies over Pardell—that grip allowing them to drag the body aside. They repeated the process on the next.

"What?" Gail took a step forward and the nearest stationer took notice and held up his hand to stop her. "Stay back, Earther," he warned. "It's not safe to touch him in this state. Let Malley deal with it."

"Deal with what?" she demanded. *Had the big stationer lost his mind, and the rest were humoring him?* She stared at Malley, only now noticing how his hands bled as he worked and his shirt hung from his lower arms in bloodstained strips.

Grant spoke from beside her. "He must have forced open the metal sheet blocking the corridor . . . let his friends up here."

Gail tapped the shoulder of the little stationer who'd warned her. "Did you know Pardell was here? Is that why you came?"

The man turned to look at her and shook his head. His wizened face held a terrible grief that silenced whatever else Gail thought to say. "We didn't know you had him," he told her, shrugging. "Malley sent down a warning about Aaron, but we all thought he'd headed Outside and home. Safe."

"Then why did you come?" Grant asked when Gail didn't.

"Outward Five doesn't care much for being locked down. And Malley seemed to think you Earthers might be in a spot— he owed you, for the warning to Aaron." The stationer—or immie, Gail realized, since she couldn't tell them apart— scowled and spat at her feet. "We'd have come sooner if we'd known you lied—that you had Aaron here."

Grant took up her defense. "Dr. Smith didn't lie. If you look in the air lock, you'll find two suits: Pardell's and one in his size," he nodded at Malley. "Pardell came after his friend on his own."

"He must have walked the length of the station," Gail added almost to herself, aghast at the thought of trusting that ancient, taped-together suit. "Then followed our people. He was trying to find Malley."

The stationer let out a heavy sigh. "Always playing hero," he said gruffly, but offered no apology for his accusation. "There," with grim satisfaction as the last body was pulled free and they could see Pardell.

There were no marks on his pale face. It looked just as she'd memorized it from her vid recording. Gail later remembered that was the most remarkable thing, how Pardell had seemed untouched by those who had tried to destroy him. He looked— peaceful.

She almost missed the shallow rise and fall of his chest.

Malley, still holding the grappling hook in a hand that dripped blood in mindless little spirals on the floor, didn't. She saw him close his eyes once, tightly, as if his relief was too much to bear, then open them and stare at her.

"Your ship," Malley began in a hoarse whisper, as if that warning shout had scraped his throat raw. "It has the latest Earther med tech? Real doctors?"

Gail nodded. "The best," she assured him quickly, startled how her own voice came out thin and liable to break.

"Malley—?" This protest from the stationer near Gail. "You can't—"

"What choice is there?" Malley answered roughly. "Do you think he's going to sleep this one off without help, Syd? If he does, think their families—" his wave included all the fallen, but lingered over the circle of corpses near Pardell, "—could bear him to stay?"

There was a low murmur of voices from the fifty or so who'd remained. One came louder than the rest: "Wasn't Aaron's fault."

"When did that matter?" Malley coughed to clear his throat. His next words, "I'm going with him," brought a sudden silence.

The stationer he'd called Syd was the first to speak up. "Malley. Makes some sense to let them take Aaron—help him, if they're willing—but it makes none to have you tangled up with Earthers. People will talk—"

"Talk," Malley repeated, his tone one of utter scorn and his raw voice breaking with passion as he went on: "You think I'm worried about talk! Those who know me won't believe it— those who don't? Guess who locked Outward Five down! So you worry about talk. I'm going to make sure the Earthers treat Aaron right."

Here and there, Gail saw heads nodding slowly, grudgingly,

then more. Then most. In spite of giving their approval, expressions ranged from grim to grief-stricken.

"I'll watch your stuff, Malley," Syd offered, giving yet another of his heavy sighs.

"Uh-uh," Malley disagreed. "Your *wife* can watch it." This prompted a smattering of laughter as Syd blushed. "Have Amy settle my tab and Aaron's at Sammie's—don't any of you try to claim what's not yours."

No one seemed to be fooled by this last warning. Gail watched, hardly sure what she felt as one by one, the stationers thumped, patted, or hugged Malley in farewell.

Afterward, each took a turn to gaze down at Pardell, some brushing tears from their cheeks. Many crouched at a distance, or went to a knee to whisper something. No one touched him.

"We'll see you to the ship, then." This wasn't so much an offer as an order from the stationer named Syd. It brought another, quicker, round of nods.

Gail looked at Grant, recognized his "not-on-my-watch" look, and spoke before he could open his mouth.

"Whatever—or whomever—it takes to get Pardell on the *Seeker*," she ordered, pitching her voice to his ears alone. "That's what matters now."

# Chapter 19

SO they retraced their steps through the strangely vacant docking ring surrounded by another escort in stationer gray. Gail was still flanked by guards—Loran and Grant, Tau and their surviving rescuer, who turned out to be Ops Specialist Allyn—and Malley was with them.

Malley and some of the others had righted the trolley and scavenged a metal slab, used as a countertop in a nearby office. Without offering an explanation of why they wouldn't touch Pardell or accept help, they'd employed other scraps of metal to push and pull his body on to the rectangular slab. It was then lifted on the trolley, making a reasonable gurney. Now, ahead of them, Malley pushed it alone, moving as quickly as the rickety structure would allow. He'd also refused any first aid for his hands or lower arms. He, like Grant, seemed to think their solitude could end without warning.

Grant, unwilling to gamble on what might happen if either the authorities or the mob returned, had asked the stationers to carry the bodies of the fallen FDs so he and the rest could keep their weapons ready. Others brought the suits from the air lock. Gail had suggested leaving them behind, an idea the stationers seemed to find incomprehensibly wasteful. She didn't waste her breath arguing.

Despite an air of urgency, it was a funeral procession, not a rescue, Gail thought, hoping she had more than deaths to bring back to the *Seeker*. Her eyes kept flicking to the limp form on the trolley, questions she didn't bother asking—yet—filling her mind so she was honestly startled by how soon they reached the *Seeker*'s 'locks. They'd been that close.

The mob had done its best to get at the ship, with bare hands and, from the look of it, some portable cutters and welders. The main and freight 'locks were inoperable; Gail didn't need to be an engineer to see that for herself. The inner door of the emerg 'lock was damaged, but intact, being designed to stay functional through worse.

However, that entrance into the *Seeker* was guarded.

A lone figure stood statue-still in front of the inner door, an older woman with graying hair wearing a space suit remarkably like Pardell's. She dangled her helmet from one hand, watching them approach. Another Outsider, Gail concluded.

Malley stopped the trolley with Pardell's body several paces before reaching the air lock, ignoring Grant's immediate protest, then moved to stand to one side of it. The other stationers halted as well; the Earthers doing the same as Gail fiercely ordered them to hold still.

Gail heard a name whispered somewhere behind her: "Rosalind."

"Dr. Smith," Malley called without taking his eyes from the woman. Gail shook Grant's hand from her arm impatiently and went to stand on the other side of Pardell, careful not to touch even the edge of the slab supporting him—much as she would have enjoyed something to lean against. She could feel Grant moving up behind her shoulder.

"Is he dead, young Hugh?" the woman asked, her voice toneless and flat. Her face reminded Gail of a painting she'd seen of a saint—ascetic, proud, intelligent. The 'sider must have been stunningly beautiful before events carved themselves into her skin. Even now, she was remarkable.

"No, ma'am," Malley said. "It's one of his fits. Too many— too many touched him before I—there was no way—" Another might have taken pity on the man as he struggled to speak through his emotions, offered comfort. This Rosalind merely waited while Malley steeled himself to go on. *So*, Gail thought. *No friend of yours, stationer.*

Gail spoke first. "I've offered the medical facilities on my ship to help Mr. Pardell. Are you a relative? Do you want to come with him?"

Those cold eyes released Malley and turned on her. With an effort, Gail kept from flinching; there was that much latent power in the woman's gaze. "Offer me your ship, Professor," Rosalind said, "and I'd consider it." The woman's empty hand lifted in an odd tossing-away gesture. "Otherwise, I prefer my freedom."

Gail nodded gravely. *More than another Outsider*, she decided. A former spacer, that was certain. A leader here? Definitely. "My invitation remains," she said calmly.

The woman came forward, ignoring them as she looked down at the unconscious Pardell. Without warning, she reached out to grip his jaw. Gail wondered why Malley didn't object, since he'd prevented all other contacts, then she saw that the woman's left hand was robotic, clumsy and ugly, but capable of gently turning Pardell's head from side to side as if she tried to read something from his slack features and closed eyes.

There was nothing to read on her face at all.

The woman named Rosalind let go, then backed away to leave the path to the emerg 'lock open. "He's beyond what we can do," she said to Gail. "If you are willing to try, do so. But don't think this puts young Aaron—or any of us—under obligation to you. Those scales are not in your favor, Earther."

"I understand—" Gail started to say.

"Do you?" Rosalind challenged, but instead of elaborating, she crooked one steel "finger" at Malley. "Young Hugh. Make sure he comes home again. Alive—or dead."

Malley nodded, lips tight. Accepting his vow, for Gail judged it no less than that, the 'sider woman lifted her helmet and lowered it in place on her head, her face vanishing behind its reflective visor. Gail realized with a shock both her hands were artificial—what she'd taken for a clamp held in a gloved hand was the woman's right hand. The arms of Rosalind's suit ended in cuffs locking over her wrists.

"Hold, there! Earthers! Don't move!" Gail, like the others, turned her head at the distant shouts. There were figures walking, not running, their way. She looked back quickly, only to find Rosalind was nowhere to be seen.

"Interesting woman," Grant said with distinct admiration. "Who is she?"

Malley shook himself, like a man rousing from a trance. "That, Commander, was Rosalind Fournier." He looked at Gail as though tempted to say more, then shrugged and said: "We don't have time to waste out here. Let's get him inside."

"There's a stretcher on the way," Grant assured them. It was obvious the impromptu trolley wouldn't fit through the hatch.

Then there was the question of getting Malley himself in— Gail eyed the huge, exhausted-looking stationer, wondering if one trank would be enough.

As if he'd read her mind, Malley pullIed his lips back from his teeth in what didn't remotely resemble a smile. "If you can keep both doors open, Dr. Smith, I'll get Aaron—and myself— inside."

Gail nodded and looked pointedly at Grant, who shook his head but pulled out his transmitter to consult rapidly with the *Seeker* on how to override the air lock's protocols. Leaving Tau to keep watch, he sent Loran and Allyn hurrying through the 'lock. Between them they carried Peitsch's body.

Meanwhile, Malley went over and collected his space suit from the stationer who'd carried it this far. Taking one leg of the suit in each hand, Malley grunted with effort then pulled. The fabric resisted then gave along old seams and new ones. He kept ripping at it, his expression surprisingly peaceful considering the effort he was exerting, and the speed with which the authorities—for Gail could now recognize Forester among those in the lead—were approaching. There was a bustle around the air lock as horrified crew members came out to retrieve the remaining bodies.

The suit tanks fell loose and rolled away. Then a battery pack. A stationer picked those up. Those nearest looked more amused than surprised. Syd, again close to Gail, confided: "Malley'd never put it on anyway."

When he was done, Malley kicked aside most of the suit pieces but held what now were two long strips.

"Malley—you Stationers! Keep the Earthers away from their ship!" This order was a little too clear for comfort, although its effect on their escort was to provoke some loud, and cheerfully obscene, countersuggestions. Malley's friends moved out in a ring, making it clear they planned to block or delay any interference.

Malley himself was moving with feverish haste—Gail wondered how much of that speed was his fear of the authorities and how much was covering his terror of the air lock. She resisted Grant's effort to push her toward the now-open inner hatch, but took a quick look to be sure she could see through the interior of the air lock to the open outer door. Yes, the *Seeker*'s bright welcoming interior was in plain view. There was a stretcher waiting, with FDs starting to bring it through.

There wasn't time. The first group of Forester's people had arrived and, from the angry shouts, were trying to bully their way through. They were outnumbered by Malley's cohorts—temporary situation in light of the reinforcements heading their way.

But Malley was ready. He'd already tossed the two straps he'd made over Pardell's body at chest and hips, bringing the ends around under the rectangular metal slab, and tying them tight. He then bent at the knees beside the trolley, massive thigh muscles straining his coveralls, and reached one long arm underneath to hook his wounded fingers over the slab's far edge, gripping the nearer one in his right hand. He tucked his left shoulder under the metal.

Gail thought no one watching believed what Malley was intending. She'd seen the bruises on his shoulders from lifting and carrying, but this was beyond reason. Just as she started to call for them to abandon the stretcher and help the stationer—bedlam behind letting her know the struggle was growing physical—Malley expelled a quick breath and simply stood up.

It didn't matter that he immediately lurched sideways under his awkward burden—he turned that movement into a staggering lunge toward the opening to the *Seeker*. Gail expected both men to land on the floor plates, but somehow Malley kept upright and moving, even as his whole body shuddered in reaction to passing inside the 'lock. The crew with the stretcher scrambled out of his way.

Grant pulled her along behind Malley. "Don't touch the body!" she shouted desperately, then saw Loran among the group waiting for them. She'd know to warn those inside.

Scattered cheers spilled around her before all sound from the docking ring was muffled by the inner door. Grant threw the lever to lock it.

Somehow, Malley'd made it all the way into the *Seeker*'s umbilical corridor—a temporary, though solid, link to this air lock they could retract or abandon, depending on the situation.

Gail suspected he couldn't have stopped inside the air lock itself.

The stationer was on his hands and knees, taking huge, rapid gulps of air. He'd dropped the slab to the floor, one end of it having caught the lower rim of the outer doorframe so the whole sloped. The makeshift straps held, keeping Pardell in place. The rough handling hadn't touched his slack expressionless features.

One of Pardell's arms sprawled limply over the side—gloved fingers so close to Malley's, Gail rushed forward in alarm. "Get back," she ordered a curious crewman. "Malley," she began more gently. "Watch your hand—"

His bent head moved in what she took for a nod of understanding, then he drew his hand away from Pardell's, leaving a bloody streak on the floor. Another deep breath, then Malley pushed himself up to sit back on his heels. His eyes were bloodshot but alert enough.

"How do we handle Pardell?" she asked bluntly. He looked up at her and nodded, rising to his feet. Around them, the confusion was developing order as fresh faces in FD blue-gray and crew white took over, a steward rushing to help Gail out of the space suit she didn't realize she still wore, two more with med staff bars on their shoulders standing hesitantly near their supposed patient. Either the dead guards or something said by the living ones made those two look very nervous. Gail, looking down at that pale, thin, somehow deadly face, couldn't help but agree.

"He has a—condition," Malley said, relaxing enough—or exhausted enough—to lean on the nearest wall. "It hurts him to be touched. Always has. Makes him sick. Sometimes, it sends him into fits like this, where he's unconscious for a few minutes."

"There's more," this grim accusation from Grant, who hadn't left Gail's side. "Something happens to people who touch him."

Malley shook his head—not denial, Gail thought, but regret.

"A nasty shock, usually, like the kind you get from a static buildup."

"That wouldn't kill anyone," Grant pressed, staring down curiously at what appeared to be a harmless young man. Perhaps he was assessing a new lethal weapon. Gail understood that side of the military mind-set—it was useful, even if she didn't care much for it.

"Aaron's never killed anyone," Malley started to protest, then sighed. "Okay. The worse it is for him, the worse the shock you get if you touch him. See? Until now, nothing like this— he's knocked out a couple of people. It isn't pleasant." Despite his words, Malley's tone lightened momentarily, as if remembering an incident from their childhood. Then his lips tightened. "What happened out there—it was bad. I'm amazed he survived—"

"Those who touched him didn't," Gail finished. "How long does this—reciprocal charge—last?"

"It doesn't matter. You can't touch him. Ever. Not even with gloves. Understand?" Malley's voice was under iron control, but still had a desperate edge. "It hurts him."

Gail looked down at Pardell's skintight gloves, noticing they were newer than the rest of his clothing as if recently replaced. *If they weren't protection*, she wondered abstractly, *why did he wear them?* "That's the drill, then," she told the med staff. "Use surface contamination protocols and remote handling arms only. Make sure everyone's informed and the affected corridors are cleared ahead of time. I don't want accidents."

Malley sagged, as if he hadn't been sure she'd take his word. Gail saved any further questions—they had time on their side now—and stepped out of her mag boots when the steward nudged her legs in reminder. It actually hurt to be free of the extra weight. Gail knew herself close to the end of the energy adrenaline and necessity had given her—just like Malley.

Grant, on the other hand, appeared disgustingly fresh, as if the day's events had been a training exercise. Gail used this as her reason to glare at him and order: "I want Mr. Pardell taken to the science sphere's medical facilities, not to the *Seeker*'s hospital bay. Understood?"

"Yes, Dr. Smith." Smoothly. Gail supposed the professional

paranoid in Grant was satisfied by the tighter security possible there. Fine. She wanted the widest scope of testing equipment available—and her scientists, not a crew doctor, conducting those tests. If there was anyone else she could have delegated to command—or it had been any other situation—she pushed away the desire to head to the lab. Curiosity was a luxury she couldn't indulge.

Malley straightened from his slouch. He didn't say a word as he watched the med staff and two of the FDs carefully lift the slab, and so Pardell, to the waiting stretcher. He didn't need to.

"Mr. Malley will be staying with Mr. Pardell," Gail added. At least then it sounded like her idea. "Make sure he's comfortable and those wounds are treated." She let her eyes travel over all of them. "Commander, report to my office when you're done in the science sphere."

Then Gail walked away briskly, her footsteps immediately picking up echoes as Grant sent her ever-present shadows in her wake. Maybe there was more she needed to do or say, but Gail knew full well that if she didn't leave now, she'd be the one leaning on a wall.

And weakness was something she didn't—for all their sakes—dare show.

# Chapter 20

GAIL should have known she couldn't escape so easily. A delegation was waiting for her at the end of the umbilical corridor—an angry one at that.

She would have stalked past the sputtering, flushed Reinsez in an instant, relying on Grant's people to deflect any foolish intention to chase her down the passageway to her office, but Tobo was with him. The *Seeker*'s Captain, Gail sighed to herself, deserved better—especially in light of what she'd ordered him to be ready to do.

Still, she wasn't prepared to lose her valuable momentum. "Walk with me, gentlemen," Gail ordered quietly, fixing her eye on Reinsez who, wondrously, shut his mouth and moved out of her way. "Commander Grant and I will give you a complete briefing in—" Gail winced inwardly but continued without missing a beat "—thirty minutes. He's tidying up a few details. I can, however, apprise you of our immediate situation."

"It's worse than I thought?" Tobo asked, his eyes somber but keeping it general. He understood, as always, there were things she wouldn't say, not in front of Reinsez.

"It's better," Gail retorted. "We've succeeded in finding and bringing aboard Aaron Pardell without having to bribe or coerce station personnel—" *That* for Reinsez. "Unfortunately, as you are aware, we've suffered unacceptable casualties. I don't want anyone leaving the ship." This with force. "Thromberg is not stable. And no one is expendable." *Today*, Gail qualified to herself, quite sure that was all she could promise.

"We can undock at your order, Professor," Tobo assured her.

Gail gave him a quizzical look, not sure she'd heard correctly.

Tobo smiled tightly. "Your—diversion—pulled the stationers away from us long enough for my crew to do a manual disengage from all of Thromberg's systems. We're floating free, Dr. Smith, and can move out—without damaging the station—when you're ready."

"Now. Let's leave now!" Reinsez blurted. "We must. You aren't to take risks with this ship, Smith—"

"Or with you, Dr. Reinsez?" Gail snapped, coming to an abrupt halt and forcing them all to do the same—or walk through her. "I remind you, you're here as an observer for Titan U, not to give orders." She relented, seeing how his skin had grayed beneath its surface. The last thing she needed was to send Titan's representative to join Pardell in the hospital. Minimum, they'd insist on her running back to Sol System for a replacement. "I have no intention of risking the *Seeker*, or our mission," Gail promised, sure of the latter and hopeful of the former. She starting moving again. "Are we safe to stay as is, Captain Tobo? I've some remaining business with Thromberg. It won't take long—but it is critical. I wouldn't ask otherwise."

He nodded, but was quick to qualify the decision with: "I recommend we vent the umbilical corridor and seal the outer hull. Commander Grant's people sent three of their 'bots to watch for attempts from the outside."

Reasonable. All quite reasonable and exactly what she didn't want. So much for resting. "My office—twenty minutes," was all Gail said, grateful beyond words to see the lift ahead. "In the interim, nothing moves; no further decisions without calling me. Are we clear, Captain?"

Tobo gave her a hard, suspicious look, but didn't argue. Gail entered the lift and, with an eyebrow, made sure she and her guards were its only occupants.

The door closed, and the lift began to descend. Gail gripped the handrail, using it to counter the floor's disturbing tendency to float under her feet. She snapped out: "Inform Commander Grant he's got fifteen minutes."

"Yes, Dr. Smith."

Gail allowed herself to drift in her own thoughts—mostly comparing the value of a shower to grabbing a meal, and whether it would be better to skip both for a boost shot, much as she hated relying on stimulants—when something else entirely made her flush and look up again. "I didn't get to tell them, before they died," she said suddenly.

The two, both men and of the same body type and coloring as Grant, appeared nonplussed. "Professor?" asked one, his voice uncertain.

"I'd planned to apologize. For resenting you, when what I resented was having this—this shepherding—forced on me by your superiors. I've taken it out on you, all of you.

They exchanged uncomfortable looks. One was younger than Gail herself, she realized. "We haven't noticed, Dr. Smith," he said.

Her emotions too complex to sort out, Gail found she could still be amused. "Trust me. It's not my custom to ignore people I—" suitable words eluded her. How did you refer to people who'd die for you? "What are your names?" she asked, instead. "Your whole names."

"Tech Specialist Chris Taggart, Dr. Smith. And this is Weapons and Code Specialist Michael Picray."

Picray ducked his head at the introduction. "Dr. Smith."

The lift stopped, but Gail found herself too unsteady to let go of the railing as the door opened. "Well met, then, Taggart and Picray," she said, to cover the moment. "I have to be ready for a briefing." Gail wasn't sure if she was reminding them or herself.

She must have looked about as capable as she felt. "Would you—like some assistance, Dr. Smith?" Picray asked.

Gail considered this, then shook her head and pushed herself forward. "Thank you, but as long as you keep the way clear, I can make it."

If Malley could enter an air lock—her new benchmark for raw, personal courage—she could stay on her feet and cross a hallway under her own power.

# Chapter 21

MALLEY followed a boot through his nightmare. Aaron's right boot, specifically, which conveniently protruded a worn heel from beneath the immaculate and likely new blanket an Earther had tossed over his friend. He fixed his eyes on it and ignored the barrage of *strange* threatening him from every side.

Harder to ignore the air. Malley took in the lightest possible breaths, despite his aching muscles and lungs, wary of the unfamiliar thickness of it. Humid, warm, and perfumed, possibly by real florals—the combination was something immies would probably kill to draw into their nostrils and a stationer like him wanted scrubbed. It carried no reassuring back-of-the-tongue taste of metal; the only human scent seemed to be his and Grant's dried sweat. Those lacks seemed worse than the shadowless lighting or the less-than-firm floor beneath his feet.

Aaron's boot traveled left, then right, then straight. He kept pace with it. Beside him, if he glanced down, Malley knew he'd see the no-longer gleaming boots of Commander Grant matching him step for step. *Likely couldn't take him now*, he thought without shame, fully aware he'd passed the limits of his body. Just as well Syd had slipped a weapon from one of the dead Earthers into his pocket during the confusion. Someone else had passed him a knife, now secured in the top of his boot. He sincerely hoped neither would be necessary before he knew his way around this—

*Ship*. Use the word, he admonished himself. It wasn't what sent that nauseating fear through his body. Malley understood precisely where that weakness lay. Until today, he hadn't cared, since he hadn't imagined ever wanting to go through—

*An air lock*. He made himself think the words, remember

every step. It hadn't been pretty, but he'd done it. The next
time—

There, he stopped. Obviously he'd have to leave the ship
eventually, but for now there were other things to deal with,
starting with here and now.

He raised his eyes from Aaron's boot at last, deliberately
looking around at what was, after all, no more threatening than
a corridor wider and taller than you'd expect on something
smaller than a station, with skin-smooth, pink-white walls. He'd
assumed they'd gone directly into the ship, but their first turn
had taken them from hard flooring to this cushioned stuff. Over
it, the stretcher's wheels rolled noiselessly. Synth-rubber, he'd
bet, for both flooring and tires—a source of complex carbohy-
drates Thromberg had recycled through biologicals well before
Malley had been old enough to realize he was eating his old toys
and mattress. Even today, the packaging protecting shipments
from Sol System wound up in the digestion tubes. There were
always jokes about how Sammie's beer improved after a
freighter arrived.

The floor was resilient compared to bare metal, but not lux-
urious. Malley decided some of the wilder stories about the inside of Earther ships were untrue. For one thing, he didn't see
plants hanging from the ceiling and running water used for decoration. And he could still hear footfalls. His, Grant's, the two
guiding the stretcher, the three uniformed guards leading and the
pair behind—they refused to fall into rhythm, echoing along a
hall Malley thought unlikely to be this empty. Smith's orders, no
doubt.

He didn't trust her at all.

*He'd had no other choice*, Malley told Aaron's boot.

Malley studied Grant with quick, sidelong glances as they
continued, understanding the grim weariness marking a strongly
featured, otherwise well-controlled face, but more interested in
assessing the easy way the man moved despite a posture suggesting significant stiffness in his spine. They all moved that
way, the stationer noticed. *Shared training.*

He was harder pressed to explain why they looked so much
the same, when the crew appeared to be, like the station, a het-
erogeneous mix. "Are you clone-sibs?" he asked finally. Mal-

ley'd read about this and similar techniques—seemingly commonplace means for increasing the number of similar organisms back on Earth. If so, this meant Grant had lost more than a few underlings.

Grant tugged a loose lock of his straight black hair and pointed ahead. The guard he indicated had black hair, all right, but it was starting to kink as it lengthened. "No. Our units are formed by appearance—looks better on parade."

*Parade?* He didn't see this man—or his people—doing much of that. Malley snorted. *Did the Earther think he was totally naïve?* "Wouldn't be anything to do with how matching troops could make it harder for an enemy to identify key individuals?" he asked. "Such as yourself, Commander? Or how they might underestimate your number? Should we discuss infiltration?"

Grant's eyes showed a little more interest. "These are aspects most people don't trouble themselves to consider, Mr. Malley. I find your grasp of them remarkabe—in a metal recycler."

"Oh, I grasp many things that might surprise you, Earther," Malley answered.

They came to a major junction, with this corridor splitting into three as well as a set of lifts along one wall. The guards leading the way entered the centermost corridor without hesitation, but one of the med staff turned to Grant and protested. "Commander. The hospital bay is just around the corner. Are you sure—?"

"Quite sure, crewman," Grant said, with an impatient jerk of his head. His hand was occupied steadying Pardell's space suit over one shoulder. When Grant saw that Malley had noticed, he shrugged. "We all grabbed something."

The suit looked like so much refuse against the Earther's one-owner uniform and probably smelled as ripe as its age. *Still.* "He'd be sorry to lose it," Malley acknowledged gruffly, nodding at the unconscious Pardell.

Grant looked dubious but didn't argue or pass the heavy suit to anyone else.

"Of course, you wouldn't have known that. Which means you brought it for the professor," Malley continued. "In the interests of her project."

It was as though shutters slid behind Grant's eyes, the way his expression went from tired professional to full caution.

Malley grabbed the stretcher with both hands to stop it. The white-clad meds jumped away in shock and the uniforms trained weapons on him. "Which is why she wouldn't want Aaron going to the nearest doctor," he told Grant, ignoring all the others. "I do."

This time Grant did slide the suit from his shoulder, passing it to the nearer of his guards, but his hand signal put away their weapons. He then spread his arms and showed the palms of his hands, as if he thought Malley'd be fooled into thinking them harmless. Or as if he thought the stationer had snapped—a judgment Malley wasn't quite ready to pass on himself yet.

"You told us about your friend's condition, Malley," Grant said in a reasoning tone. "The hospital bay in the science sphere is the only choice—it's equipped to handle anything the research team could imagine, including quarantine facilities and those remote handling arms. That's what we need, right?"

*Until he knew more*— Malley lifted his hands from the stretcher in surrender, sure the Earther knew it was a temporary one. Blood dripped to the floor from the deepest of several metal gashes on his left palm, and, self-consciously, Malley pressed that hand against the fabric of his coveralls.

"Here, sir," one of the med staff tugged at his elbow, holding out a sheet of what looked like clear plastic. "For your hand." Before Malley could argue, the Earther took his wrist and turned his palm to face up. He quickly applied the plastic sheet, simply laying it over Malley's hand. It seemed to melt into a pliable gel on contact, perhaps responding to warmth, oozing into the lines and creases—and wounds—on any skin it touched. Equally startling, the material immediately stopped the throbbing pain Malley honestly hadn't noticed until now.

Wordlessly, he held out his other hand, This time he saw how the Earther pulled the plastic clear of a protective layer, careful not to let it touch any surface before the stationer's skin. When the man pointed to Malley's shoulder, Malley shook his head. "That can wait. But this—" he held up his hands, now encased in what felt like transparent gloves, "—this is amazing. Thank you."

"My pleasure, Mr. Malley," the med answered with a smile. "We'll seal the cuts permanently for you later. And please don't worry. Commander Grant's right about the equipment on board. Your friend will get the best care outside of Sol System."

*Young*, Malley realized abruptly. The med, now back to pushing the stretcher with his partner, couldn't be any older than the man lying on it. He was likely younger. Thromberg didn't have any residents this—new. It was a sobering thought.

"About the care. He's right," Grant said quietly.

Malley raised his shoulders in a shrug, hiding the wince moving his left shoulder caused him. He was stiffening up already, even in this warmth. From the feel of the nerve spasming behind his shoulder blade, he'd likely pulled a muscle or two. *Nothing new.* Aaron always accused him of treating machinery better than his body. "I've no doubts you have all the technology you claim, Earther," Malley said. He wriggled his plastic-wrapped fingers in front of Grant's nose. "My only problem is what you plan to do with it." He put his lips together and let out an irritated noise. "No, that's not true. I have another problem." Grant raised an eyebrow in invitation. "How big is this damned ship?" Malley grumbled.

That heartfelt complaint surprised a chuckle from Grant and two of the others. "We're almost there," Grant promised.

*Almost?* The Earther's promise translated into an improbable distance along a curved hallway and a lift ride up, down, or sideways—no way to tell—to an equally featureless, and peopleless, curved hallway. For all indications otherwise, they'd gone in a circle. Malley would have suspected Grant of trying to confuse him, but the man looked too tired and in too much of a hurry to bother. Malley gave up his first plan of remembering how to retrace his steps through the ship, and thought glumly of the odds of finding maps or a willing guide when, not if, he and Aaron made their exit.

Another obstacle to be overcome was their destination, which turned out to be an unusually large, guarded door that reminded Malley of one of the ration vaults on Thromberg. Once there, Grant dismissed the med staff, changed the guards on the door for two of those who'd accompanied them, then stood to be identified by the lock. Malley leaned on a wall beside Aaron's stretcher and watched.

The door seemed pleased and hummed to itself as it opened. Grant's lip twitched up in a half smile as he looked back at Malley: "Saw how it worked?"

Malley grinned wolfishly back. "There's more than one way through a door," he assured the Earther, although he had no idea—yet—what that could be. The damned thing looked able to withstand an explosion. *What was on the other side, so worth protecting?*

He took a curious step forward to see for himself, and froze.

It wasn't just another air lock. That would have been bad enough.

*This was infinitely worse.*

You couldn't see space from inside Thromberg. Or from the inside of an air lock. You only guessed it waited outside, ready to rip the life from you.

*Here?*

They'd removed the walls and let the utter worst of his nightmares take their place. If his muscles hadn't locked in terror, Malley would have been running. There was no question that's what his mind was ordering: Run! in any direction away from that roadway to the void.

After a second, Malley heard a mindless whimpering and knew the sound. *Someone had broken.*

He found a small, thinking part of his mind could feel pity.

Then he realized the sound came from his own mouth.

# Chapter 22

THE boost shot *and* a shower—once Gail saw her reflection she'd made the time—might have helped erase the wear and tear of the last few hours, but it was pure and simple triumph that let her sit upright in her chair and calmly survey the others.

*So this was what it felt like to be the eye of a hurricane.* Grant, who'd arrived late to give a bald report, "things were settled," with no explanation, perhaps knowing she wouldn't want details in this company, was doing his best impression of a snarling cat; Tobo was pacing, with frequent stops to throw up his hands in exasperation; and she suspected Reinsez's rambling, disjointed arguments were the result of his having prepared himself for unpleasant topics with too many nips of sherry.

On the surface, her command threesome was arguing her decision to stay attached to the station. They were really venting their frustration at not knowing why.

Gail saw no reason to enlighten them, given she sincerely doubted the knowledge would help matters.

"If you are quite done?" she ventured in the next mutual pause for breath. "If you are, there are some constructive things to—"

"No, Dr. Smith," Grant was actually gritting his teeth over the words. She'd never seen anyone do that before and was inclined to be impressed. "If we cannot persuade you to take the safer, more rational course of action and pull the *Seeker* out to orbit distance, I will not call in the 'bots. In fact—Captain Tobo agrees with me—I want to put out armed patrols. We are vulnerable to sabotage—"

"—sabotage?" Reinsez's eyelids pried open further than Gail

had ever seen before. The extra expanse of yellowed eyeball did nothing to improve the man's appearance, which today included clothing even more rumpled than his skin. "That's the kind of risk we can't allow, you know. The man's right!"

Her lips curved in a deliberate smile. Without a mirror, Gail wasn't sure if it looked more like a threat than courtesy. She didn't particularly care. "You've vids scanning every square centimeter of our hull as well as all approaches to the ship," she reminded Grant. "You've guards watching the vids. You've guards watching the guards watching the vids. The only thing the 'bots are accomplishing beyond that is to inflame Thromberg even more—if that's possible." She paused, then turned her attention to Tobo. "Are you getting anything coherent from the comms yet, Captain?"

Tobo started to throw up his hands, then realized what he was doing and clasped them behind his back instead. "Coherent? If you count receiving dozens of invoices for damages."

"Ah," said Gail, genuinely pleased. "That didn't take long. Good."

Reinsez's face folded into a perplexed maze of wrinkles. "And how could you possibly conclude anything good about that, Dr. Smith?"

She steepled her fingers and gazed from one to the other. "Because it means Station Admin is back in control—partially or better. It also means they want to talk. Think about it. No matter how emotional their population, those in charge have to be readying themselves for the potential repercussions. They'll know this mob attack will play against them in Sol System should I choose to publicize it. I haven't—yet. They know that, too. Guaranteed translight communications are being monitored here. So, an attack from their accountants? A bluff, my dear Dr. Reinsez, to save face. Let them fling paperwork at us. Captain Tobo? I suggest you have your chief steward tabulate a few bills of our own. Make them big."

Grant had fallen silent. Gail pursed her lips, then added sincerely: "If you want me to press for murder charges, Commander, I'll do it. But do you really believe we'll ever know who was responsible?"

His eyes flashed at her, then dulled as if she'd given him an opening he'd give anything to use, but wouldn't. "Wrong place, wrong time," was all he said. "They knew the risks."

*They had to talk*, Gail realized, understanding perfectly who Grant held responsible. He'd need to get that out of his system before he would stop second-guessing her decisions.

And before she could rest, she wanted the names of those who'd died for decisions she'd already made.

*Later.*

"As a gesture to diminish tensions," Gail said firmly and very clearly, "I want those 'bots of yours back in their boxes, Commander Grant. And there will be no exterior patrols. I consider the situation as stable as it's going to get, gentlemen, and we will avoid any actions with potential to change things for the worse." She hesitated, then looked at the vastly unhappy Tobo. "While I don't condone sabotage under most circumstances, it might be prudent to make sure Thromberg can't restore the *Seeker*'s docking connections from inside. I'm sure the First Defense Unit can provide the necessary—expertise."

"Tech Specialist Aleksander is my Second, this shift, Captain," Grant said immediately. "She can set up the appropriate team for you."

"Thank you, Commander. Consider it done, Dr. Smith," the Captain replied with a distinct lightening of his expression.

When the others left, Tobo taking Reinsez's arm and literally hauling the protesting man out after Gail's meaningful look, Grant dropped into the nearest chair as if his spine had melted. He waited until the door closed before speaking, the guards outside under strict orders not to let anyone back inside during their private conversations without permission—even Tobo. One of these days, Gail feared the Captain would try and find this out. He was unlikely to be pleased.

"They're in the science sphere," Grant reported. "Dr. Temujin took charge. I assume that's acceptable—you hadn't specified."

Gail clicked her tongue against her teeth thoughtfully. Temujin must have been the seniormost on duty. A superb scientist—all her people were—but she'd have preferred Lynn or Sazaad, both having a more careful, methodical approach to novel situations. "As long as he agreed to the quarantine."

The commander shrugged. "Didn't like it being spherewide, but not inclined to argue. There were—circumstances."

"Circumstances?" Gail repeated, putting an edge to the word. "You went along to make sure there weren't any."

One dark eyebrow rose. "Tell your big friend—once he sleeps off a double-trank dose."

Gail understood immediately. "The waist," she said numbly. "He had a panic attack when the door opened and he looked inside, didn't he? I should have anticipated that—" The last was said with real bitterness. She'd given in to her own weakness instead of taking the time to personally ensure Malley and Pardell made it safely into the science sphere.

"If you were aware of the extent of Malley's feelings concerning air locks and space, Dr. Smith," Grant said mildly, "it might have been helpful to warn me about it. Fortunately, he was too terrified to put up the fight he was capable of—" He leaned forward, stretching one long arm to her desk, his hand opening to drop a small knife made from a shard of metal and one of the hand weapons he and the others had used on Thromberg. "I found these on our new guest." He leaned back again, regarding her with a deceptively casual air. "No sign of the transmitter you gave him, by the way." A significant pause, then: "Malley *could* have dropped it."

Like Grant, Gail was under no illusion the stationer had been careless with such a valuable device. He'd no doubt given the transmitter to someone else—or hidden it on the station.

"Where is he now?"

"Science sphere, as ordered. He's snoring—very loudly, I might add—on a cot near Pardell. Dr. Temujin wasn't very happy about that. Mind you, he was even less pleased by the guards I left behind."

Gail pushed at the knife with one finger, then made a decision. "Have these put back where you found them. Before Malley wakes up, if possible."

Grant's look became appraising. "He's no fool, Dr. Smith. He'll expect us to have searched him. Finding these—the stationer will assume he has permission to carry arms on the ship."

"He's used to alliances, Commander," Gail countered. "We win his trust, or we lock him in the brig, because I'm sure you'll agree we don't need a man of his abilities loose and looking for trouble on board."

"No argument there. But winning his trust? That'll take some doing." He chewed on a bottom lip then said bluntly: "Why bother? He's already shown he'll help us with his friend."

Gail shook her head. "Not good enough. Not for someone of Malley's potential. He's—" she shrugged. "I have a feeling about him."

"An authority-hating metal worker who grew up on a station," Grant said, as if making sure they were talking about the same person. He raised one eyebrow. "I'll have to look more closely at him myself, then—including, if you don't mind, keeping this new ally watched at all times."

"Fine. Now—" Gail found herself hesitating, unsure where best to begin. *She* wasn't, she admitted in frustration, *particularly good at taking others into her confidence.*

"Now, Dr. Smith," Grant filled in helpfully, stretching the words. A man merely content not to move, Gail judged, until she met his eyes and saw the lingering shadows of grief and exhaustion there. "You have your 'sider—and our new friend. I must assume we're still here because you want something else. Planning to tell me? Or is this another of those details to be revealed when I least expect it?"

*Gods*, Gail thought admiringly, *humor.* The man was either more tired than he looked, or they were actually making headway in understanding one another. "You're right. I want something else here." She held up the cup shard. "This," she told him, tapping the words along the base.

Grant's dark eyes narrowed and she could see his body tensing automatically from its inadvertent moment of relaxation. "The *Merry Mate II*. But you knew she was here well before finding that in the bar." A nod at the shard. *So*, Gail thought with satisfaction, *he had noticed.* Such a pleasure dealing with the observant. "Why that ship?" Grant gave a short laugh. "Let me guess, Dr. Smith. It's where our unconscious friend hangs that suit of his—making it one of those derelicts outside the station. Am I close?"

"On the money, Commander."

"And now we need the ship as well as the man?"

She gazed at him for a moment, then corrected: "I wanted the man in order to find the ship."

The FD commander's face bore a sudden, striking resemblance to granite. *Or was it ice?* Gail wondered. "You could have told me."

It was Gail's turn to be amused. "You didn't need to know. Then. Now you do."

"This old freighter is important enough to bring the *Seeker* all the way here."

"Yes," Gail insisted, her voice level but her hands tending to grip the edge of her desk. "As Pardell is in no condition to help—and I've no reason to believe Malley's ever been Outside—we'll have to find her ourselves."

Grant inhaled slowly, then let the air out again in an almost soundless whistle. "I'm open to suggestions, Dr. Smith. Most of the ships the 'bot caught on vid didn't have visible idents. They've been deliberately obscured in some cases, scoured away by dust in others."

"I don't know how. But we can't leave without the *'Mate.*"

*He could read her by now*, Gail sensed. Instead of arguing as Tobo might have, Grant nodded. "As you wish, Professor. But let the Captain put us at a distance. The station may not be armed, but you don't need a pulse cannon when your victim's sitting on the doorstep. A hammer works just fine."

"The station is no longer a threat," Gail disagreed. "We both know why."

His lips twisted. "Because by now the tranks have worn off? You think that's going to improve the relationship?"

"These people live by balancing debt," Gail said, keeping it blunt. "It's in our favor right now, Commander. Any blood is on their side of the scale, not ours."

Grant's nostrils flared. He was breathing hard, suddenly, as if everything that had happened since they arrived on Thromberg was hitting him at once. "They were under my command when they died," he snapped at her. "Following my orders—"

"*My* orders," Gail corrected. "And I'd give them again, based on the information we had at the time. Do you want to know why, Commander Grant? Do you want to know what they bought with their lives?" She curled her hands around the cup shard, as though cradling something precious. "Maybe—just maybe—the only ship to visit a Quill-infested planet and return with life on board."

That shocked the anguish from his face. "The Survivor?" he jeered. "You really believe in those tales—those legends about a Survivor of the Quill? My people died for this—this—nonsense?"

"Of course not." Gail was again grateful for the closed door. "As I told Forester, I don't chase legends—I deal in facts."

"What facts?" Grant immediately answered his own question. "Facts you have and I don't."

Gail looked at him for a long moment, weighing many things, then nodded. "Is the room clean?" she asked.

"Of course." Slight offense. This was one of the FD's responsibilities. She had to admit that so far, they'd been able to keep ahead of Reinsez and his toys—although Titan's representative had come on board with a seemingly unending supply.

*She had to take Grant's word for it.* Gail opened the lower left drawer of her desk and pulled out a rectangular box. It looked ordinary enough, except for the warning symbol on the top indicating its contents would be immediately turned to ash if any hands but hers tried to unlock it. More expensive, but also more secure than a simple gene key, which, though highly specific, could be stolen and used by anyone. Gail preferred not to take chances.

Inside were an assortment of old-style data disks as well as several sheets of paper—not ordinary paper, but privacy sheets which could be encoded to show their contents only after contact with a specified genome. They'd been "opened" already.

She plucked one sheet to hand to the commander. "Read this," Gail ordered. "My authorization," she added as his eyebrows rose at the warning stamped across the top of the page and the way origin and destination were blacked out.

**Titan University Archives**
**Excerpts from the personal recordings of Chief**
**Terraform Engineer Susan Witts**
**Access Restricted to Clearance AA2 or Higher**

. . . I received the request to cosign your loan for the freighter from Callisto shipyards, Raymond. I've done it, of course. You only had to ask. It didn't have to come through Titan. I would have bought you the ship—there must be enough accumulated salary in my account after all these years. I've no need for money out here.

A freighter, is it? The *Merry Mate II*? And a wife, I'm told. I suppose this means you've abandoned graduate studies. I can understand why. Sol System can feel pretty cramped when you've all of space calling. I met your father on a starship. Did I ever tell you that? For all anyone knows his ship is still out there, somewhere, exploring. I prefer to think so. It's better than imagining other reasons why they never came back. Space doesn't suffer fools.

I hear I'm already a grandmother. Where has the time gone? Jeremy Norman Pardell. A fine name, Raymond. I do understand why you changed yours before enrolling at Phobos University. They tell me I've become something of a celebrity back on Earth. That can't be easy on the family, but there was nothing I could do about it. People are starting to sign up for immigration. It's finally here, Raymond, and our name—my name—happened to be the one swept up in the excitement . . .

Grant stopped reading midway. "Pardell . . . Aaron Pardell . . . *Witts'* great-grandson?" he breathed. "I knew you were hunting one of the terraformers' descendants, but hers?" She waved at the sheet to keep him reading.

. . . one day the record will be set straight. It's not as though I'm the only terraformer. There's a team of us. Most have been with me since we started Stage Three, some since we began testing seeding procedures—where you were born, Raymond. I've been there lately, you know. It's becoming so beautiful, so very peaceful. The trees I planted for you are almost full size. Did I tell you

I'd thought about asking Titan's approval to open it for settlement, too? I wouldn't have minded retiring there myself, when that time comes. But the others convinced me not to try. They're worried we didn't follow Terraforming Protocols, which is ridiculous—the protocols didn't even exist back then. We were on our own, being told to develop this amazing technology. Everything was so— possible, then. If you ask me, they're just afraid Titan will take away their pensions if the secretary finds out we did something without petitioning the department for approval.

I suppose it doesn't matter anyway. We won't need another world, with sixteen official new homes waiting. Can anyone on Earth or under the domes of Sol System conceive how much room that is? How many people could live under these open skies? That's not considering the next set of worlds—which will be ready long before there are enough people for them. You've probably heard the sociologists predicting humans will become so used to wide, empty places, we won't tolerate being crowded anymore and that will drive us outward even faster. They could be right. There are five of us on World XI at the moment and we sometimes don't talk for days. Yesterday, I found myself begrudging poor Millie her share of the lab space. I can't enjoy the sunset if I can see someone else walking in the distance. The others tease me I should go back to Earth for a while and get used to people again.

What do you think, Raymond? If I came . . . would you let me in the door this time? Would you let me see little Jeremy? Meet your wife? Or does it keep going like this, with messages routing through Titan, with you locking me out of your life?

I don't want to argue anymore. Would it help if I admit I was a poor excuse for a mother? I will. But how could you ask me to choose between you and providing for the future of our species? Did you honestly believe I could simply pick up and leave the most significant and fragile project imaginable whenever you scraped a knee or lost a pet? You're a grown man, Raymond, and if you don't understand the importance of my work by now, well, there's certainly nothing I can say to convince you. History will have to do that.

I don't think I'll be coming to Earth soon after all. I wish you luck with your ship and congratulations on your family. If you need anything, anytime—you only have to ask. Remember that. I'm your mother and I love you, Raymond. Always.

When Grant looked up with a wealth of questions in his eyes, she answered what was likely to be his first. "Where did I get this? Her son returned her letters—they made it as far as a drawer on Titan. Seems someone in the terraforming department thought it could upset Susan Witts to know her mail wasn't being accepted by her family. After her death—and the Quill— every piece of documentation remotely connected to her was studied and then sealed. But these couldn't be read. Raymond Pardell had died in an accident, his body given a spacer's burial. Neither he nor Susan Witts had left their genomes on file."

"That didn't stop you," Grant concluded, leaning back and studying her.

Gail nodded. "I was interested. And I'd already begun recreating Susan Witts' genome as part of this project. As you know."

Grant had been briefed—he'd had to be, as his people were the ones who would conduct the planetside trials and, hopefully, find the Quill at last. *Risking their lives on her logic*, Gail thought with an inner chill, but didn't dare doubt herself now.

The Quill weren't the mysterious monsters the public at large believed. At least, they hadn't been. While no one claimed to understand how they'd become a threat on the terraformed worlds or how they killed, the reason Quill couldn't be found and captured by remotes was simple enough.

They were perfect biochemical mimics—so perfect, current methods constantly and utterly failed to distinguish what was Quill from anything else alive.

The Quill, according to admittedly sketchy observations, were little more than fungallike filaments with an alien, but not inexplicable, biochemistry. Some of that biochemistry resulted in an attractively fluid play of color on their surface, making the filaments into living jewelry—supposedly the reason some deep-space explorers had kept the filaments in the first place. Gail had her own ideas about that, controversial and not publicized.

Those ideas hadn't gained her funding for this project and control of the *Seeker*. What had was something much more acceptable, based on the finding that the Quill's biochemistry was also designed to produce a camouflage of genetic markers on the organism's exterior. Where an Earth animal might detect, then reproduce the color of its background in order to hide, the Quill seemed to detect, then reproduce the genome of its living background, perhaps for the same reason.

It hadn't been a scientist who'd made this discovery about the Quill. Spacers who wore Quill bracelets found they couldn't give their bracelets to anyone else. A filament was so attuned to its biological background that, once it touched one person's skin, an individual Quill wouldn't be worn against the skin of any other—reputed to drop to the ground and die rather than linger on a stranger. There were unconfirmed rumors that a Quill might move from a parent to a young child. The original match was precise enough, some stories had spacers using their Quills as substitutes for their gene keys.

This talent of the harmless, pretty Quill might have remained one curiosity among the millions recorded from the myriad life-forms found outside of Sol System, but the Quill became killers—killers with the ability to blend into their preferred biological background, completely hidden among the plant life on the terraformed worlds.

Until Gail Smith had her inspiration. Humans could find Quill—they had originally. So what was needed was a way to put humans on the surface to do the hunting. No technology had provided protection against the lethal Quill Effect. So Gail decided on a different approach.

She would use the Quill's camouflage technique against them.

They knew the original Quill had been brought to the terraformed worlds by the leaders of the various Stage Three teams—rare, previously untouched Quill that had been gifts from Susan Witts to celebrate their project. So Gail painstakingly identified and obtained the genomes of each terraformer, making the assumption that these would be the "human" patterns recognized by the alien life-forms.

Ironically, that of Susan Witts had been the hardest to obtain. Opening these letters had been the reward.

"What you were told about this mission—my project—was the truth," she told Grant. "I am collecting certain genetic markers and Pardell's, because of his heritage from Susan Witts, will be a useful piece of that puzzle. But I needed more—and I found it in this letter. A place." Gail paused triumphantly.

"A place," Grant repeated, looking puzzled. "What sort of place?"

"Somewhere new and untouched to conduct our trials," Gail put all her determination into her voice. *He had to be convinced.* "Titan University insists we use World IV. Nonsense! They've used it for all their failed experiments. The place is a minefield of mistakes—the last and worse when they sprayed one continent with herbicide then sent down three techs—who all died."

"Before our time, Dr. Smith," Grant commented. "Am I to take it you don't plan to follow Titan's directives?"

*Dangerous question, from a man who could stop her with a word in the wrong ears.* Gail met the commander's challenging look with one of her own. "We all want this to work, with no more lives lost, but if it's to work, we need to do it properly." Gail flattened her hands on her desktop. "I've spent years analyzing their mistakes; I don't plan to repeat them. First and foremost, we aren't going to a world where we'll hardly find room to land among the litter of dead shuttles and dessicated corpses."

Grant paused a heartbeat longer than comfortable before he said: "You're the boss." There was an unspoken "*for now*" in the sentence. "But how do we find this pristine playground? If Witts didn't inform Titan—I assume her colleagues were equally secretive . . . ?"

Gail nodded acknowledgment. "Those that survived weren't about to admit to anything—they were struggling to avoid lynch mobs, let alone Titan's review board or the ERC's Tribunal. I wouldn't have known without these letters." She smiled. "And these." She waved at the handful of disks in the box. "From a stationer named Aaron Raner."

"I was wondering when he'd come up. The station records we've pulled so far just give his name, some sparse details about his work on-station, then the man disappears. So, how does Raner tie in with this world you want—and the ship?" Grant nodded encouragingly, as if he was afraid she was regretting sharing this many secrets. Despite this, Gail couldn't be sure how much she told him actually was a surprise.

*It didn't matter*, she told herself. *As long as he went along.* "I'd been tracking Susan Witts' descendants; her son's ship, this letter, were all part of the trail I followed. But then I lost the *'Mate*. She'd been inherited by Jeremy Pardell, who'd applied for immigration for himself and his wife. But they weren't assigned to any station, since he was still running his freight business. One day, they just vanished from any records. I'd almost given up, when, lo and behold," Gail paused, reliving that dead-of-night moment when her board had lit up with a Christmas tree of cross-referencing hits and she'd *known* this was it, "up pops the *Merry Mate II* again—in Titan University archives. A letter from Thromberg Station, written by a stationer named Aaron Raner, to his uncle at a Titan-affiliated hospital.

"One of several letters, in fact. Raner had adopted a baby right after the blockade went up, a seriously ill baby whose symptoms suggested extreme dysesthesia, an impairment of the sense of touch in which light contact of the skin is misread by the nervous system as pain. Needless to say, Thromberg wasn't in a position to offer that level of care. Raner's uncle did his best to conceal his efforts to help—the climate of the times was not in favor of private communication with anyone outside of Sol System—but he needed data for those colleagues he consulted. As far as I can tell, they believed they worked on a hypothetical case study, but the uncle kept Raner's letters for reference. Those letters ended up—I'm sure unintentionally—in the university's data banks when the uncle died in retirement. Where I found them."

"Aaron Pardell." Grant's eyes became slits. "You knew about his condition before we arrived . . ."

Gail shook her head. "Not that it was anything like we've

seen. That was as much a surprise to me as to you. And I wasn't interested in his medical history. You can imagine I am now."

"So what brought you after Pardell if not that—or to finish the genome profile for Witts?" *Dangerous and suspicious*, Gail saw both in his eyes.

She took Susan Witts' letter from his hand, keeping it in her own. "This. The planet she mentions here and nowhere else. It's where Witts started her work, Grant. I'm convinced it's the first place where the Quill ran wild. Untouched, all this time, because no one knew this place existed. Lost, really, until Jeremy Pardell took his ship there."

"He—what?"

Gail leaned forward, looking intently at Grant as if it were possible to will him into understanding. *He was quick enough*, she thought. "Raner had to tell his uncle where the baby came from—that he'd found him, half-frozen, on a shuttle that had made an emergency return to an abandoned ship—the *Merry Mate II*. He left out Jeremy Pardell's name, saying only that the *'Mate* had been left in orbit around an unnamed planet. I asked myself—where would a man take his family, when the stations were bursting at the seams and Sol System was about to lock its door?"

"There are catalogs filled with planets—"

"Gas giants, balls of ice or molten rock, or with poisonous atmospheres," Gail rejoined. "The *'Mate* was a freighter—a temporary home—not a deep explorer. Pardell picked this world for a reason, Grant. He expected it to welcome his family. Raymond must have read his mother's letters after all, probably copied them. For all I know, he saved all of Susan Witts' documentation on that world and her early work. I believe Jeremy Pardell found his grandmother's world—"

Gail lost her train of thought for an instant, distracted by the feel of the letter in her hand and the terrible irony it represented. *Had Susan ever met her grandson?* The only surety was that she had died first, spared that added grief. Gail shook away the thoughts. *The past was the past.* "That's what's in the *Merry Mate II*'s records," she continued brusquely. "The location of that world—and probably the answer to many other questions, Grant. We can't leave here without them."

"Why? Why would he do it?"

"Save her letters?" she asked, surprised this bothered the commander. "How should I know?"

"No. Jeremy Pardell. Why would he risk landing? Why risk the Quill? Surely the warn offs—"

"Warn offs?" Gail carefully replaced the letter and closed her box. "That's the point, Grant. There wouldn't have been any around this world—no one but Susan and her most trusted team leaders even knew it existed." She stood up in her excitement, pacing back and forth behind her desk, firing words him. "Maybe the 'Mate was damaged or they had some emergency. Pardell must have believed the planet was safe. Who cares? That world is what matters. It's perfect."

Grant continued to look doubtful. "So you're saying Raner went after Jeremy Pardell—for whatever reason—and saved his ship and son. That he raised that son as his own. All without telling anyone about this, this mystery planet—maybe not even Aaron Pardell. Why?"

"Raner couldn't take the chance. Everyone feared the Quill. No matter how welcoming that world may have looked to him, he had to know *something* took his friends. *Something* triggered the 'Mate's distress beacon. And when Raner arrived back at the station—everything was going to hell here. He and whoever was with him couldn't risk any rumors about that ship, the baby—and the Quill."

"What if Raner was wrong?" Grant asked in a low voice. "What if this world is free of Quill? After all, the baby lived."

Gail understood the hope in his eyes, but raised her hand to stop him. "The baby lived," she echoed. "The only fact within their Survivor Legend—adding several dozen questions about our new guest to my list for the research team," Gail said dryly. "Unfortunately for Thromberg and the other stations, I've no doubt the Quill have beaten us to this world, as well as all the others. In fact, I'm convinced it will prove to be the first planet they contaminated. And they've been left alone since that time.

"Making it the perfect testing ground—and our legend, Aaron Pardell, the ideal subject."

# Chapter 23

HE must have ignored Aaron's warning and succumbed to temptation again. He knew better than to add some of Syd's special joy juice to Sammie's beer. *The last time . . .* Malley groaned to test that he still had a voice . . . the last time had felt pretty much like this, when he'd finally come to. Which, come to think about it, had been a day and a half odd-cycle after Sammie had insisted Malley had broken three tables and two noses—accomplishments he couldn't remember to this day.

*What day was this?*

Malley cracked open an eye and tried to focus, squinting against the onslaught of light. *Light?* Bad sign. Meant he was late for work. Of course, dark would be a bad sign as well. Could mean he'd missed an entire day of work. Problem with no longer having an even-cycle roommate—someone wanting his turn in the sheets made a great alarm clock. He'd missed rations. Maybe more than one set. Malley wasn't a big fan of sleep; he did like eating.

*Not at the moment,* he discovered, as the mere thought sent him heaving over the side of his bed, automatically aiming for where his boots shouldn't be.

Cool fingers supported his forehead. Malley froze in an agony of self-consciousness. He didn't usually forget bringing a friend home. To the best of his knowledge, he'd never subjected such a friend to watching him retch out his guts.

Mind you, he couldn't remember a headache as vile as this one before and found himself leaning gratefully against the hand now holding a cold compress to his forehead, imagining how Syd would look hanging by his ankles.

"Mr. Malley."

It was a such nice image—Syd's face all puckered up and red. Malley refused to budge or open his eyes. He had the sudden feeling this wasn't a hangover, but something far worse.

"Sir. Your head's rather heavy."

Nice voice. Soft, with an unusual lilt to the words as if the unseen woman almost sang them. Malley wanted to ask her a question, just to hear more of that voice, but realized he'd prefer to stay ignorant, with his eyes shut. He did roll back, freeing the hand of responsibility for keeping his face off the floor. As his head hit the pillow, he had a second of vertigo as he realized this wasn't his pillow, or his bed, or the orientation within the room he expected . . . but all that faded as he let himself spin back into sleep.

"Mr. Malley. Hugh! Wake up."

"Go 'way," he mumbled, then yelped in protest as someone rudely poked two fingers into the lower section of his rib cage. His eyes shot open, and Malley blinked several times as he processed where he was . . .

And what had happened . . .

The fingers left him alone during this discovery, their owner, Gail Smith, looking down at him instead. *There were worse things to wake up to*, Malley decided. The hair escaping from behind one ear had red streaks in its gold. Quite pretty. Seen this close, her blue eyes had intriguing dark rings around their irises, like the faceted edge of crystal. She hadn't slept—her lower eyelids were smudged with purple and her cheeks were pale. He smiled at her and caught a quick smile in return—complete with dimples.

A shame he'd love to wring her elegant little neck.

He sat up quickly, startling her back, and regretted the action as his head pounded—violently—twice. "This will help, sir," came the lilting voice again, followed by a slim dark hand holding out a cup of some obnoxiously thick liquid.

Malley took it, grimly ordering his stomach to behave—not that it felt as though there was anything in it, but having past experience as a warning. Over the rim, he scanned the room.

No sign of Aaron.

There were walls—real ones, without gaping holes to nothingness ready to swallow them all—

*Steady*, he told himself, taking a reluctant gulp of the liquid. Anything to get back his strength; anything to keep them guessing. Falling on his face in this company wouldn't just be embarrassing.

The cool mouthful was a pleasant shock. Malley took another hastily, then a third, letting that one linger over his tongue. "What is this stuff?" he asked in wonder.

"Orange juice—with a few additions to get rid of the trank aftereffects," Smith answered, pulling up a rolling stool and perching herself nearby with the obvious intention of waiting for him.

"It should help immediately."—This time Malley looked for the voice.

"Dr. Aisha Lynn," Smith introduced the woman who came to stand beside her and bow in his direction. "Mr. Hugh Malley. Dr. Lynn is one of our senior biologists as well as a medical specialist." The dimples showed again. "And she makes remarkable orange juice."

"Aisha, please," the doctor said with another quick half bow, hands tucked inside the pockets of a blindingly bright yellow-and-red coat, especially striking against the rich brown of her skin. The coat was worked with some kind of thread. Malley made the effort and focused his eyes. Yes, he hadn't been mistaken. Every possible bit of fabric had been embroidered with little six-legged creatures conducting what appeared to be very busy lives. It was almost an anticlimax to look up at her face and meet a wide, friendly smile under warm brown eyes. Her black hair was tightly braided to her head, stuck through at seeming random with more of the little six-legged figures, these in a gold-toned metal.

"Malley. Thanks." They didn't have cups of their own, so Malley regretfully shelved the idea of asking for more in his. Doubtless a medicinal beverage in short supply. His headache was fading anyway.

And he had more important needs. "Where's Aaron?"

"There." Smith pointed to a long, coffinlike box a few meters away. "He's—I'm told nothing's changed."

Malley stood, surprised to be able to do so without reeling. Remarkable juice indeed. He should introduce Aisha to Syd. Wonder what they could whip up together.

*Had to be better than Sammie's beer.*

Deliberately inane thoughts, keeping him from too close attention to surroundings more reminiscent of the tube and vat chambers on Thromberg than the cozy, crowded med wards in Outward Five.

No one interfered with him as he walked toward the long, white box. There were at least three guards and a handful of techs or maybe scientists, he couldn't tell which by looking, but none so much as moved. He'd seen Smith's hand signal and supposed he was grateful.

A flash of apprehension dried his mouth, leaving only the lingering, unfamiliar taste of the juice. What had they done to Aaron? Another step, and he could answer his own question.

*They'd put him in a bath.* There were a few, pay-as-you-go bathing rooms in Outward Five—more, if you believed it, in the other levels. Joke was, Station Admin needed more washing.

Aaron's bath had being submerged in common with those places. That was it. His friend seemed to be floating—his head and neck supported from beneath—in a glowing blue liquid Malley couldn't be sure was water. The liquid frothed white along the edges of the box, rising up in the corners. Aaron's clothes had been stripped from him, even his gloves. Tiny bubbles beaded every hair and crease in his skin, reflecting light. They formed chains outlining thin clear tubes penetrating that skin at neck, elbows, and abdomen.

Broader, almost sheetlike tubing covered Aaron's groin—incidental modesty—but nothing concealed the paired cuffs locking down both arms, and those clamped around Aaron's thighs and ankles.

Malley shook with the effort it took to stand there, looking at what they'd done. He couldn't begin to guess which would be worse: to have Aaron stay unconscious or to have his friend wake up and find himself imprisoned like this.

He did know he wasn't going to wait for the answer.

Plunging both hands into the warm liquid, he grabbed the supports for the nearest cuff and pulled. The device resisted.

Malley braced himself—only to be yanked away by rough hands on his upper arms. He didn't struggle, letting himself be turned and held for inspection, tossing back his head so he could glare down at his enemy from his full height.

*At Aaron's enemy.*

"What do you think you're doing?" the Earther demanded, angry red spots on each cheek. "I thought you wanted your friend cared for!"

Malley was glad the guards kept hold of him. "You call this 'care'?" he spat. "I'm no doctor, but this isn't how you look after someone."

He didn't expect the Earther to give him a startled look then rush to the side of the box. She had to step up on the narrow platform encircling the entire apparatus to see inside.

He was even more surprised when Gail Smith turned around, still on the platform, and ordered in the coldest voice he'd ever heard: "Get these cuffs off—now. And bring Dr. Temujin to me."

# Chapter 24

GAIL loathed fools. They were time-wasting at best, deadly at worst. She stood on the platform, her arms wrapped around herself, overseeing Aisha and her techs using the remote arms to detach restraints a fool had put on a helpless man, aware of the rage that same fool's actions had instilled in the man whose trust she desperately needed. If Temujin had done irreparable harm to this patient or that trust, she'd leave *him* behind on the station. *Naked and cuffed.*

She'd been a fool, too, blithely assuming she could leave Pardell to the care of others, more interested in the stationer she hoped to argue and coax into helping her. Gail made herself glance at Malley, seeing how the man's face had become gaunt with strain, the eyes which had sparkled with challenge now sullen and suspicious. The FDs had released him at her nod, but stood within reach. He might look too defeated to be a threat; none of them believed that.

No doubt Grant had told his people Malley was armed.

*Her own state was the more legitimate worry*, Gail judged. She had a great deal to accomplish here and now, but she could feel the boost shot's expensive energy fading. Her mouth was drying. Already, her skin was goosefleshed under her clothing. Soon—too soon—her body would demand the full price for cheating the exhaustion and stress of the day's events. There were good reasons sensible people avoided the drug. *Sensible didn't cover today.* Gail tried to summon up righteous anger at everyone and anything. Unfortunately, all she could muster was guilt, as though Malley's unhappiness was her fault, like so much else gone wrong in the past hours.

*Perhaps*, Gail admitted in a moment of rare honesty, *she'd*

*been a fool there as well*, allowing herself to be charmed by
Malley's intellect and boldness, fascinated by someone so physical and yet so much more complex. Perhaps. In her present
state, about five minutes from collapse, Gail doubted she could
muster the proper detachment to judge herself. She only knew
his opinion of her mattered beyond her ability to rationalize.

Right now, that opinion couldn't be worse. There was only
one way to improve it, if it wasn't already too late. Gail returned
to her study of Aaron Pardell.

The reason Pardell chose to wear gloves was now obvious.
To be fair, she might have reacted like Temujin, had she been the
one to discover the unusual appearance of Pardell's bare hands.
Blue-toned as seen through the steri-gel, the veinlike network
beneath his skin was nonetheless striking. Dense from fingers to
wrist, it gradually thinned to a few, thicker strands over his
arms, like lacework, disappearing at the top of his shoulders. A
similar patterning covered his legs and spread like a fan across
his flat belly.

Her first impression, of an elaborate tattoo or body paint,
changed when she observed that the network wasn't constant. A
subtle pulsation traveled along the largest branches. The smaller
vessels, if that's what they were, weren't always distinct, fading
at seeming random, then being restored.

*Maybe she shouldn't be quite so hard on Dr. Temujin*, Gail
told herself, seriously considering revoking the order letting
those hands float free. One breached the surface even as the
thought crossed her mind. Momentarily free of the gel, the hand
showed its true colors: the network gold under the white of
Pardell's skin, a filigree not quite paralleling the blue traces
marking his true veins. The contrast made his hand resemble
sculpted stone, not flesh.

Other than this, Aaron Pardell looked ordinary enough. Gail
ran her eyes over his body clinically, looking for signs of mal-
nutrition or other abnormalities. Nothing obvious. In fact, his
slight build had been misleading. Stripped, Pardell's body was
lean, but muscled like a gymnast. Gail recalled how easily he'd
flipped himself along the cables to avoid the spy 'bot, in spite of
wearing a suit and its tanks. His face . . . she looked away, discomfited by features totally lacking even the inner concentra-

tion of sound sleep, especially when she'd seen how expressive Pardell's face could be.

They'd better run a cognitive function assessment before getting Malley's hopes too high. *Or hers.*

"Come here please, Mr. Malley," she asked him without turning, one hand indicating her left. She knew the instant he was there—not only did he block the light, it was like having a pillar generating heat beside her. "Did you know he looked like this?"

"What of it?" the voice had dropped an ominous octave. "People don't come out of a mold—except your soldier clones."

Gail ignored the last. "Trust me, Mr. Malley. No one else has this type of—secondary veining. Has he always had it?"

"Yes. And before you ask, yes, Aaron's going to be very uncomfortable if he wakes up naked." Malley paused, then added in a thoughtful voice: "It might be more than being self-conscious. He's never come out and admitted it, but I think his skin reacts to intense light—maybe, to some extent, to any light. I've seen him cover up in a hurry when we've been working under norm and some Admin lout turned on the big spots to catch dust bunnies."

Gail glanced at Aisha, who nodded and dimmed the light levels within the med tank by half.

Maybe Malley took this as encouragement. One huge hand gripped the side of the tank near Gail as he asked: "What about those things you've stuck into him?"

"These are nutrient feeds," Aisha answered from the opposite side of the tank. She pointed to the tubes entering Pardell's neck and arms. "Because the patient is unconscious, there are also—arrangements—to handle his bodily functions."

A large finger stabbed at Pardell's abdomen. "And that one?" Malley demanded, from his tone ever-so-lightly mollified by Aisha's explanations, but still suspicious.

Aisha looked for permission, and Gail shook her head. The tube in question entered Pardell's skin exactly over one of the larger network vessels and probably punctured it. Doubtless a little of Temujin's creative curiosity. "Pancreatic sampler," she said glibly, curious herself. "We have to assess your friend's overall health before we try any potentially stressful treatments.

Anything you can tell us—any history—would improve our chances of success."

"What sort of history?" he asked her bluntly. That deeper voice again. Malley wasn't buying her explanation.

"Has he ever been exposed to radiation, mutagenics, nerve toxins, generator emissions—that sort of thing?" This rapid-fire questioning came from a new voice, as a plump, pajama-clad Dr. Stan Temujin came dashing into the room ahead of the tech sent to summon him. He looked wildly excited—a not unusual expression, since the man was capable of passion over slime mold—and Gail had a difficult time keeping her expression properly stern and displeased. Malley's looming presence helped.

"So you're the one—" Gail laid two fingers on Malley's wrist and he stopped.

"Allow me," she said, scowling fiercely at Temujin, at least until the man's delight at finding her with his new oddity faded into a puzzled comprehension that he was in trouble. Again. Gail sighed to herself. So many otherwise brilliant people had no control over their reactions.

"Dr. Temujin, this is Hugh Malley. A stationer from Thromberg and a friend of our patient, Mr. Aaron Pardell."

Temujin, at a considerable disadvantage staring up at Malley, pulled his robe together over his pajamas. He had the look of a mouse noticed by a lion, which might have had something to do with his being present when Grant had had a tranked Malley carried in and put under guard. Temujin bravely offered his hand, then dropped it when Malley ignored the gesture. Gail thought that just as well, considering the grip the stationer likely possessed when in a good mood.

"Good question," Gail said in a noncommittal voice. "Has he ever been exposed to such hazards, Mr. Malley?"

"On the station? No. Of course not. We're brought up to be careful. Outside?" *Did anyone else hear how his voice flinched past the word?* "Who knows? He's never said. There's Sammie's beer, of course."

"You can't possibly be implying there's anything wrong with that nice man's beer," she scolded with a deliberately straight face.

"Nice!" A snort, then a slightly easier tone. "It's not environment—not as far as Aaron knows. His skin's always been like this. Other than his sensitivity to touch, he's never been sick or broken more than one bone at a time. Bruises and frostbite. He's tone-deaf—that help?" The finishing touch of sarcasm Gail chose to take as another sign Malley was finding his balance again.

"Who knows what will be the key?" she told him honestly. "We're all playing detective here."

Malley looked back over his shoulder at Pardell. "He's never stayed under this long. Ever. You didn't give him anything—?" This alarming growl was directed at poor Temujin, who literally jumped back in shock.

"No! Nothing except nutrients," Temujin said quickly. Gail started to relax at this rare sign of intelligent discretion, then tensed as the man babbled on: "And an assortment of metabolic tags. you know, Gail, the 95-S series is ideal for experimenting with liver function—and I injected a marked ion trace to test—"

"Malley!!"

He'd moved quickly, but, for once, Gail found herself moving faster still, getting in front of the stationer's charge from the platform. She had no idea what Malley'd intended, but his expression didn't promise Temujin would enjoy the experience. She stood her ground, feeling ridiculous but completely determined this wouldn't deteriorate into another double shot of tranks for Malley or a flattened, if well-meaning, fool.

Malley stopped short of running her down, catching himself on the balls of his feet. The guards stopped, too, understanding her look but none too happy about it. "He—" words failed but his fists were white-knuckled. "He—"

"Yes. Dr. Temujin exceeded normal medical protocols by running some tests without permission on Mr. Pardell," Gail finished for him. "He shouldn't have—but I assure you they weren't harmful."

"How the hell would you know what's safe for Aaron?" Malley transferred his anger back to her. *Good*, Gail decided. She was better equipped for it.

*And he had a point.* "You're right," Gail agreed. "We don't know. But we'll have to run these and more tests in order to find out how to help him. Unless there's someone who knows more about him than you do—or information back on his ship . . . ?"

"What ship?"

Gail stepped so close to Malley she had to tilt her head back to keep meeting his eyes, a proximity probably giving her guards fits, but she had a feeling the stationer was accustomed to people who stood near enough to touch if they had something important to say. There was something wild and angry in Malley's eyes, but he was listening. She had his attention. *Barely.* "Your friend's an Outsider," she said quietly, earnestly. "We know that means he lives in one of the ships attached to the station. There could be recordings, logs—who knows what—on his ship that could help us treat him."

"I wouldn't know," Malley growled down at her. This close, the deep timbre of his voice sent those distracting vibrations along her bones again. "Even if I did—anything off-station is 'sider business, not mine. Aaron—we're friends, but 'siders are jumpy folks. Paranoid about some things, including their homes. I couldn't tell you which end of Thromberg he lives on, let alone guide you there."

Gail shut her eyes for an instant, sure they'd betray her disappointment otherwise. Malley being able to take her directly to the *Merry Mate II* had been a gamble at best, but she'd hoped—

It felt far too good to close out the light. Gail drew in a slow breath, feeling the floor tempted to spin. *Time's almost up*, she thought, oddly detached. Five minutes had been too generous an estimate.

Hands on her upper arms . . . Gail opened her eyes to find Malley studying her face. "Damn. You're riding a boost," he accused very quietly, so quietly perhaps only she heard. "Ordinarily, I'd be happy to see you crash and burn when it wears off, Gail Smith, but you're the only person making sense on this ship. Not to mention the only person who can get Aaron and me back where we belong."

Gail frowned and tried to twist free without making it obvious to those doubtless watching with interest—including the plentiful vids. "I'm fine," she hissed, regretting ever thinking Malley could be helpful in any way whatsoever.

"And I'm your man for a space walk. Tell it to someone else, lady. I've enough friends who live on the stuff. Mouth dry? Room spinning? You need ten hours plus—now—or the *Seeker* is going to be without a boss for a lot longer." His grip wasn't tight, Gail noticed, his hands were merely warm rings around her arms, one above each elbow. *Points of stability.*

"There's no time—" she protested, at a loss to know when or how she'd lost control of this interrogation. She was even more at a loss how to regain it.

"Order your mad scientist away from Aaron and make it clear I'm staying here," Malley insisted. "Anything else can wait. There won't be any nonsense from the station until something riles them again—if you're resting, it won't be you, will it?" His eyes bored into hers, his fingers suddenly digging into her flesh until Gail knew they'd leave bruises. Any harder and the bones might give. Given the spectators, she didn't dare protest and suspected he knew it. "You know I'm right," he whispered in a strangely urgent voice. "You can feel it wearing off already. Want to drop flat on your face in the middle of an order? I'd call that an unnecessary risk, wouldn't you?"

"Let go of my arms, Mr. Malley," Gail told him very quietly, meaning every word, "or I'll have yours removed."

Gail staggered slightly as Malley obeyed, spreading his arms mockingly wide and stepping back to bow as he did so. She quickly turned to put the stationer behind her and face those waiting. As she'd feared, she surprised amused looks on most faces, rapidly reassembled into serious attention or something approximating it. *Bah.*

She hated fools.

*But she wasn't one.*

Gail took a steadying breath, then said calmly, happy not to be watching Malley's face: "Stan, I want you to stick around and brief Aisha on the procedures you've got underway—and disengage any not related to Mr. Pardell's immediate comfort. Aisha, I'm told this comalike state has been temporary and self-terminating until now, so please get Mr. Pardell dressed in case he pleasantly surprises us." She paused, then added firmly. "Mr. Malley will stay here to help monitor our patient. Someone arrange a meal and change of clothing for him. And a shower. I'll be in my quarters."

"Sweet dreams, Dr. Smith." A whisper against her hair. *Funny how it sounded like a threat.*

Gail ignored it—and him. Instead, she stalked out of the room before any one could so much as imagine arguing or questioning her, picking up her current escort at the door.

Pretending, she admitted to herself, she wasn't running away from a confrontation she was in no shape to win.

*Sweet dreams indeed.*

# Chapter 25

*S*HIP'S *night—but at least they didn't expect him to sleep.* Not when it was odd-cycle day to Malley's brain and he'd spent more than enough time unconscious as it was.

He'd been told lights throughout the ship were dimmed, as they were in the lab, with only essential personnel tending experiments—and Aaron. Even the ship's crew was similarly reduced. So there had to be enough quarters for most of the ship to rest at once. *No wonder they couldn't understand one another*, Malley concluded, reaching for the topmost of a pile of white, soft sheets he supposed had no other function but to dry water from skin and hair. Living like this, with everything new or in abundance, had to create a mindset incapable of grasping the reality of the station.

*That didn't excuse her.*

He did like the shower. It hadn't taken much to convince him he didn't need to conserve water—or the lather—although he'd inhaled a lungful of both at first and choked so loudly it had brought an anxious steward to the door. He'd reassured the man and been more careful.

Aisha had apologized for what she called spartan accommodations. Malley knew the reference, but couldn't see why she'd use it for a private, one-only room for washing and dressing. He supposed she had a similarly low opinion of the clothing laid out for him. Not for him to boast these were the finest, newest clothes he'd had against his skin for years.

He surveyed the result in the mirror. White pants, like the crew's, loose ankled over comfortable, slipperlike shoes. The pants were long enough, but he had to draw the waist fastener half around again to keep them in place. Good thing the ship's interior was so warm, since they couldn't find anything with sleeves to fit him. He'd been informed something was being made—*imagine that*—if he wouldn't mind wearing this yellow sleeveless vest. Malley thought it more likely this was Grant's way of preventing him from easily blending in with the crew. On a ship this size, on its first voyage, surely not everyone would be known on sight.

Malley pulled the knife and Earther weapon from their concealment in his old clothes and tucked them into a pocket and the waist respectively of his new ones. *So*, he told himself, *I'm to be trusted with these.* He'd already checked the weapon and found it contained a full load of ten trank doses. An interesting choice, if not particularly useful against things like locked doors. A knife was more—all purpose.

It said a great deal about the Earthers that they'd faced the mob with only tranks. *Stupid as well as brave*, Malley decided, but he was impressed in spite of himself. Whatever one could say about Gail Smith—and he could think of a lot—her soldiers played by civilized rules.

His stomach growled again. Malley ignored it, preferring to pay attention to his hands and arms, their cuts now glued into thin white lines. A permanent mend, he'd been told, that would be reabsorbed and disappear once the tissues beneath had healed. Beat the staples the doctor had punched through his upper thigh last year, after a fragment of steel had become a little too intimate. The bruising on his shoulders, something Malley rarely noticed, was fading as Aisha claimed it would. She'd applied a soothing cream to the skin before he showered. *Nice hands, as well as voice.*

His hair. Malley scowled, then dug his fingers into it again. The Earthers' lather hadn't changed its dull red—something he'd half expected—and its dense, at-attention style still seemed ready to resist anything but exceptionally sharp scissors. He found if he wet his fingers—a distracting luxury—he could pull the mass into something that looked planned.

*Ready for inspection*, as the saying went, although stationers normally used it to refer to things hidden that should be, with everything else out where expected. Kept Station Admin happy. Malley patted the pocket with his new, second knife, the long, thin one he'd borrowed from a table in the lab, and thought it appropriate.

"Still no change."

Malley gazed down at Aaron and saw at least one: they'd managed to wrap his friend's torso in a sort of gown. It trapped the little blue bubbles over its surface until it looked more like a layer of froth than fabric. Malley had hoped for something a little closer to real clothing. Now he'd have to scrounge something and keep it ready.

When—not if—Aaron woke up, he wanted them both set to move quickly.

*Out which door?* Malley had made sure to check the exits. There was no telling how long the reprieve would last. That's how it felt around here, with the formidable Gail Smith temporarily out of the way. He'd done her a favor, recognizing her imminent collapse from the boost, and was quite sure she wouldn't be grateful for it. Gail had that much in common with Aaron. *He hated being warned of weakness, too.*

"Do you see something wrong, Mr. Malley?" Philips had a quick, quiet voice, like someone used to talking in a room full of sleeping children. He was one of the several lab techs constantly hovering over the instruments connected to Aaron's strange boxlike bath. Right now, he was hovering at Malley's right elbow.

"Just Malley," the stationer said absently. He registered the question. "Nothing wrong—if you mean does he look the same. Are you getting good results from the pancreatic sampler?"

"What pancreatic sampler?" Philips replied innocently.

Malley hid a grim smile as he wandered over to the banks of equipment. "My mistake," he said, adding another dib to his mental balance sheet against Dr. Gail Smith.

There were three techs working at the moment, all of whom gave him a curious look then turned back to their readouts and valves. No scientists. *Ship's night*, Malley reminded himself. Convenient, having a set time when the bosses were asleep.

The lab itself, now that he'd had time to examine it, seemed intentionally temporary, something oddly comforting to the stationer. It was about three times the size of Sammie's, high-ceilinged with purposefully asymmetrical walls. The lighting was localized around working stations, such as the one near Aaron's tank. There were six others with collections of equipment and cluttered tables, as though experimenters had been forced to abandon their work with Aaron's arrival. The lights on those were diminished. Malley wondered if they'd protested or if Gail Smith's control of this place was absolute.

One thing was clear: this wasn't any sort of hospital or medical facility.

Most of the walls were as mobile as his bed or Aaron's tank. Marks on the floor revealed how the room had taken different configurations in the past—perhaps some larger than this. He had taken a close look, when no one had stopped his prowling about. Malley had a feeling Gail hadn't decided whether to call him a prisoner or a guest.

Grant had an opinion on that. Two of the five closed doors in the walls were guarded by his people, making those the only doors of interest to Malley. One was used by the techs and scientists coming and going, so they likely led to other sections of the science sphere—perhaps quarters as well. Malley noted, then firmly ignored the second guarded doorway, knowing it probably led somewhere he'd leave to Aaron.

Of the unguarded doors, one was the room with the shower Malley had enjoyed. Another was to a storage area. *The third?*

Someone had ordered a portable screen placed in front of it, similar to the two flanking his bed off to one side of Aaron's tank. *Her doing.* For Aaron's sake, Malley was willing to accept any help dealing with his personal demon, but this rankled. It was ridiculous to feel safer simply because from most of the room he couldn't see what was obviously an air lock. It was potentially very dangerous, given the source of his comfort.

Not an exit he planned to use, however, so Malley didn't bother looking toward it. Two of the—First Defense Unit, that was it—stood inside each of the guarded doors, their eyes never leaving him. Their scrutiny didn't bother Malley; he'd grown up within a crowd of people watching his every move. Wasn't easy for a kid who liked to play pranks, but he'd managed more times than not.

One of the best techniques was simply to be numbingly predictable. During the eight hours since Gail Smith had left, Malley had established his routine: he'd check on his unconscious friend, then watch the techs at work for a while. Following that, he'd take a few moments to stretch out on his bed, reading the literature Gail Smith had sent for him, nibbling from a tray of "safe for the novice" delicacies Aisha had arranged. Then a stretch and back to check on Aaron.

Malley was prepared to keep this up for days, if necessary. The food was great.

And he was learning. *Gail recognized his capabilities*, he gave her credit. What she'd supplied to him appeared to be summaries of her research on the Quill, including several unpublished papers with Titan U's bright red "official release only" stamps on every page. He dove into her work, reading voraciously.

Make that desperately, since the first thing Malley learned was how much Gail Smith and these Earthers knew about the Quill—and how appallingly little he or anyone else did. While no one could confirm what they looked like now, the original Quill had borne no resemblance to any rumor or so-called fact he'd grown up "knowing." No three-meter giants with googly eyes and long tentacles. No jellylike masses hiding in dark crawlways. The truth about them was . . . not threatening at all.

At first.

It had been deep-space explorers, Gail's work confirmed, who'd found the Quill—or found what became the Quill. They'd reported finding what looked like thin, long filaments of iridescent plastic on a distant world, a world with a thriving, alien ecosystem. Otherwise, S-9131 Sigma-D was another disappointment, cataloged and left. In those days, humanity had been looking for others, confident the universe had to be crowded with nonhuman intelligence. In those days, the search had enraptured everyone.

The explorers enjoyed a rare freedom in their search, but paid for it with extremes of isolation, boredom, and unending failure. Little wonder that they sought diversion wherever they could. The Quill were one such.

Who first discovered that the lovely filaments would cling to bare skin? It wasn't recorded. Nothing official ever was, since the explorers and their pilots weren't supposed to transport alien life, no matter how innocuous it appeared. No, all that existed were personal records and diaries. Gail had searched hundreds of these with a tenacity Malley found remarkable and others probably thought obsessed.

It was clear that filaments were taken off S-913 1 Sigma-D by someone. Why? They looked pretty. They were harmless. Some diaries claimed they weren't alive at all, since they ate nothing, changed nothing, and produced nothing. An organic oddity. A diversion.

The thought of their nemesis reduced to a diversion offended Malley—but it had inspired Gail Smith. *A digger, all right*, Malley thought with grudging approval, rereading the copy of a letter he couldn't believe she'd found—or that he could be holding in his own hands.

### Titan University Archives
### Excerpts from the personal recordings of Chief
### Terraform Engineer Susan Witts
### Access Restricted to Clearance AA2 or Higher

. . . You don't know me, young Jeremy. I've obeyed your father's wish and stayed out of your lives. Don't worry. I know he's gone. As usual, the news reached me a year too late. A lifetime late. At this point, I can't imagine it would do any good to suddenly reappear and be your grandmother.

But I hope you don't mind my writing to you. It comforts me, even though I'll never send these letters. You might read them one day—after I'm gone, too. I'd like to be remembered by my own flesh and blood. History no longer seems enough.

Things have been difficult. Does the news make it out to your freighter, or do you hear it in the stations where you dock? I keep track of you as best I can. It's Titan, Terra-Cor, and Earth. They can't make up their collective minds, if they have any. First, they want the project accelerated.

Seems they started the immigration drive too soon—or it was too successful. Now hundreds of thousands of people have left their jobs and packed to go.

We explain that we're rushing the plant growth as much as physically possible, but if they insist, well, early settlement will mean restricting people to the better-established areas. That's what they want, so we get ready. But suddenly Titan and the other universities are arguing with the Earth Research Council—some nonsense about *slowing* us down to allow another cycle of reviews and debates on genetic drift in the terraformed plants. Fine. We get ready to slow down again. I've no problem with caution.

But the ERC gets wind of this and what wisdom results? While one set of bureaucrats is talking delays, another authorizes TerraCor to start moving immigrants to the stations, even though they'll have to be packed in like sardines. Something about how they'd become a nuisance at the spaceports, filling up hotels and camping outside the fields. As if being first is going to matter so much.

Maybe it is, Jeremy. Not for why they rush to come—not to get the most or have the best. But because those first few to land will be the last to see these worlds as we do—as I do. Vast, open, waiting. Ready to become whatever the colonists decide. With sixteen different worlds, there's room for a lot of choices. Do they know they're an experiment? That humanity is tossing handfuls of itself outward and waiting to see what springs forth?

Some of the others are eager to greet the new tenants. I'm not. I'll leave well before then. Titan's rumbling about my heading the Department of Terraforming. I won't put up with it, Jeremy. The next set of worlds are ready and I'll be working out there, or I'll retire. I'm not sitting behind a desk. I'm not living under a dome.

I do have some good news, in case you think your grandmother does nothing but complain. A box arrived yesterday with an old spacer friend of mine. He snuck it through customs—said it was brandy. It wasn't. Somehow he'd come across a case of untouched Quill and wanted me to have it.

They'll probably be everywhere by the time you finally receive this letter, but right now, these lovely things are about as rare as sense in a funding committee. Spacers hoard them almost religiously. I've never had one of my own before. I tried to refuse or at least pay—he could probably have traded them for a ship—but he wouldn't hear of it. I assured him I'd share his gift with the other team leaders. They deserve them. And need them, too, the way things are right now.

Quill. I doubt anyone who hasn't worn one understands the name. But it's true. I have mine around my wrist now, Jeremy, and it gives me such a feeling of peace and calm. It's quite remarkable, as though the Quill can filter out the worst of any negative emotions and enhance the comfortable ones. See why the name's an inside joke with spacers? Instead of popping tranquilizers, you wear your 'quil.

I'd send you one, but I've only enough untouched Quill for my team. And I couldn't bear to be without mine—even if it would transfer to you. Not now.

I'll need mine, Jeremy. Very soon, everyone will expect me to smile and be gracious as I give away these beautiful worlds. They'll be watching to see I'm properly grateful for the plaques and memorials, for my page in the archives. They'll want me to show how happy and fulfilled I am at the end of my life's work, so they can take it from me with an easy conscience.

Is that how I'll feel? It doesn't matter. It's my final duty to grant them the illusion of success.


Malley reread the letter each time he sat on the bed, trying to imagine what it had been like before the Quill, each time angrier at how huge an accomplishment had been destroyed by so small, so human, a mistake.

There were other reports clipped to this letter. Gail, on a hunch or because she didn't appear capable of ignoring any detail, had correlated medical records and drug requests among deep-space pilots with diary entries mentioning the Quills. It was commonplace—though officially frowned upon—for pilots to rely on stress-relieving drugs. No one argued with what kept them sane and willing to fly.

Sure enough, pilots mentioning the Quill had the lowest drug use of all. In fact, they had superb records and, in many cases, accepted more and longer missions than average.

Malley couldn't blame them. Drug use, except for beer and boost, was almost unknown on Thromberg—not because people wouldn't have sold their souls for a chance to escape their reality, but because Sol System, Earth in particular, refused to allow any quantities of drugs to reach the station. 'Tastic? A local product with a limited clientele, since users didn't last long.

But what if the stationers and immies had something that could numb fear and make them happy, without causing them to space walk sans helmets?

*They'd all be on it, and fight to keep it.*

Gail Smith argued, persuasively, that the path of the Quill to the terraformed worlds led back to S-9131 Sigma-D. It was one of the red-stamped "eyes-only" papers, that stamp explaining why news of the discovery of the Quill homeworld had never reached the station.

Gail Smith argued, just as persuasively, that the deadly Quill Effect had to be connected with the organisms' known action on the human nervous system. There were no papers dealing with how, or why, the Quill had changed from soothing pets to a menace once they reached the terraformed worlds. Had they multiplied until their tranquilizing effect actually killed? Was the Quill filament the inanimate stage of a virulent plague, released once on a suitable planet? There had been literally hundreds of possible mechanisms and countermeasures proposed, but not one had ever been tested. There remained the central problem: no Quill filaments were safely in reach.

The science was fascinating, if occasionally obscure—not surprising, given Malley's own knowledge base was eclectic and self-taught, not comprehensive. He probably would have read it all at once, but, every so often, a turn of phrase would suddenly jump out as Gail Smith's. That was usually when Malley would toss the reader aside and check on Aaron.

Besides, Malley knew it really didn't matter whether the Quill were three-meter googly-eyed monsters or mind-bending organic jewelry—they'd stolen the terraformed worlds and that was that.

Watching the techs was more worthwhile. Malley asked vague questions, more to mislead than to get real answers. They soon stopped being concerned about his presence and talked freely among themselves. Most of their efforts involved assessing Aaron's present physical state. They were monitoring everything he'd ever heard of, as well as things he didn't know could be monitored. In each case so far, their results seemed to be falling within expected norms. There was a brief flurry of excitement when one of the analyses turned up an anomaly—then calibrations were checked and the interesting anomaly vanished.

Gail Smith's so-called "pancreatic sampler" remained a mystery. Malley presumed it was an attempt to somehow intercept whatever passed through the gold vessels under Aaron's skin. The techs were silent on that one. Since no one knew if there was anything inside—or if they were vessels at all and not simply an unusual coloration—Malley intended to have this particular testing end as soon as someone in authority woke up. Which should be soon.

*Patience wasn't his strong point*, Malley sighed to himself, staring down at Aaron's still form, watching the streams of fine bubbles rising up through the blue liquid.

"Philips? Get over here," another tech, a woman named Benton, called softly. *Funny how they whispered during their night*, Malley thought, *as though someone might be asleep in a nearby closet*. Even-cycle day should be so considerate. He could have slept easily through any sounds these people made.

Philips went to join Benton, both tipping their heads to examine a readout. Malley followed casually, keeping out of the way but making sure he moved close enough to overhear.

"I can't believe you only just ran this, Benton," Philips was saying in a fretful voice. "I thought Dr. Smith wanted it done immediately."

Benton shrugged. "Then she should have gone and pried the

equipment from Dr. Sazaad. You know what he's like . . . *middle of an experiment, oh, I'll lose all my data, oh, the universe will implode . . .*"

"I know. I know. Well, it's done now." Philips paused, then said in a heavier voice—perhaps forgetting Malley was near. "This is the second trial?"

Malley wasn't sure why his heart started hammering.

"There's no mistake," Benton said, pointing at a screen and tracing her finger along a flat, horizontal line. "See the base? I'm telling you, we should call this, Philips. He's gone."

With remarkable restraint, Malley took each of the smaller techs by a shoulder instead of a throat to swing them around to face him. "What are you talking about?" he asked.

Their mirrored looks of sympathy made him drop his hands. "What are you talking about?" he repeated, or thought he did. Nothing seemed to come out of his mouth.

They spoke quickly and at once: "Only preliminary findings—" "We should report to Dr. Smith—"

"Now!" he demanded.

Philips' shoulders slumped but his eyes met Malley's. "Benton ran a cog screen—a cognitive function assessment—on your friend. There's—the baseline's flat. There's nothing. I'm sorry, Malley."

"What do you mean—nothing?"

Benton spoke up when Philips didn't—or couldn't—answer. "It means that even though his body is still functioning, your friend, Mr. Pardell, is dead."

# Chapter 26

THERE were things that shattered sleep, rather than simply woke a person. Gail felt alert and fragile at the same time, as though she'd forgotten to collect all of herself before leaving her bed. But the summons had been more than urgent and left no time for fantasies.

*Pardell was dead.*

FD Picray had been on watch in the science sphere. He'd reported to the Second on duty, who'd reported to Grant—another rude awakening. Grant had wasted no time disobeying her orders not to be disturbed.

*Pardell couldn't be dead.*

They hadn't found his ship.

The commander had intercepted her at the door to the waist, still pulling his belt through its loops and thus relieving her of a long-standing suspicion, that he slept in uniform. Together and silently, they'd taken the walkway to the second locked door, and then rushed into the science sphere proper, Gail doing her best to keep herself centered and calm and failing miserably. This was the last straw, even though she'd suspected as much.

*Even Malley had said it—how could Pardell survive?*

Now, breathless moments later, Gail stood watching Malley rather than the body in the tank. Part of her mind was cold and detached, congratulating herself on having the foresight to arrange the genetic sampling when Pardell had first arrived, minimizing deterioration. The rest of her mind spiraled around useless things to say, meaningless words, nothing that could possibly comfort the stationer. As Chief Scientist and Project Leader on the *Seeker*, she'd never had so much power in her life before—and so little it could accomplish now.

"Malley?" Gail ventured. Malley was sitting as they'd found him, on his bed, her research papers strewn about. *So. He'd been reading them.* She didn't notice at first how he was clean and better dressed—it hardly mattered next to the lost look on his face, the limpness of his massive frame. His right hand rested loose and open on his knee, his left was clenched around the metal support at the head of the bed, knuckles white. The metal had bent.

"Malley. I'm—"

"Sorry?" his eyes flashed up to meet and hold hers.

Gail swallowed what she might have said. "I wish I'd known him," she told Malley instead. "You said he was a good man. I—"

"You're as bad as the rest of them. Stop talking about Aaron as if he's dead," Malley snapped. Gail sensed more than saw Grant easing to her side, as if he feared the stationer would try to take out his anger and pain on her.

Gail didn't think so. Suddenly, she wasn't sure what to think. Could Malley know something none of them did? Was it possible—or was it just her own hopes? *There was something about his eyes*, she decided. He was miserable and distraught, but not grieving—not yet. *Why?* "There are no measurable higher brain functions," she challenged the stationer. "That's the going definition, Mr. Malley. Lawyer approved."

Malley's head sank into his shoulders, like a bull about to charge. "So you think he's dead, too."

"A machine says he's dead," Gail corrected. "What do you say?"

The stationer unclenched his left hand, looking at the white ridges left on the palm from his grip with a puzzled expression, as if its actions hadn't been his, then stood. When he reached his full, towering height—prompting Grant to straighten even further—Malley said in a monotone: "I don't know. I hope not. Aaron told me once that his foster dad, Raner, had him wired to a machine like yours, that measured higher brain function, back when they were still trying different things and looking for a cure. He said the readings dropped to zero when he had one of his seizures. It scared his dad, but then Aaron woke right up again and the machine recorded him normal as could be. They decided it was a glitch in the machine—heaven knows where Raner got hold of one in the first place—but now I'm wondering. What if it can't follow where he goes?"

Malley didn't wait for her answer. Instead, he strode impatiently over to the racks of monitors. *He knew which one*, Gail thought as she followed, ignoring the rest of the devices to stop before the cog screen. "You've been hunting for ways Aaron might be different from other people," the stationer continued. "What if that includes something in the activity this machine measures? If his brain is somehow different, would this machine still pick it up? Can you be sure?"

"Philips, get Sazaad in here," Gail ordered without hesitation. "He's our neurologist," she explained to Malley. She didn't bother adding that Tabor Sazaad was the most difficult of several unique personalities Titan had allowed her to bring on the *Seeker*—Malley'd find out soon enough. The man had built the device presently damning Pardell; they needed his expertise if it was to do anything else. "What else can you tell me?" Gail asked instead. "Did Raner somehow make Pardell have a seizure in order to test him? Was it coincidence?"

"That's all I remember," Malley growled with obvious frustration. "We were kids. At the time, Aaron thought it was pretty funny, scaring his father like that."

"Never mind." Gail said absently, reaching out almost idly to shift the frequencies being scanned and displayed by the cog screen. Nothing. The flat line irritated her, a puzzle without clues.

"Aaron's body—is it maintaining itself, or have these—" a disparaging gesture at the whirring, blinking machinery to either side, "—taken over?"

The question might have sounded matter-of-fact. Gail sensed it was nothing of the kind. "The life support is connected as insurance," she said, glancing up at Malley. He seemed calm enough. "His autonomic functions appear unaffected, but we're keeping his systems under close watch in case something changes." Gail hoped he'd settle for the half truth, knowing full well what Malley was really asking: Would she order Pardell's body kept alive in case Malley might be right? Or for her own reasons?

She really didn't think he'd like her answer.

She did know, his promise to Rosalind notwithstanding, Malley would never be allowed to remove his friend's body from the *Seeker*. Not now that Reinsez had made his preliminary report back to Titan U. A dead Pardell was simply too valuable.

*A living Pardell?* He could have a few more choices.

Waiting for Sazaad to arrive took on the bizarre trappings of a social event. Gail asked for coffee, something Grant and Malley were quick to second, and soon all three found themselves perched on lab stools near the tank with Pardell floating inside, for all the world as though they'd arranged to meet for breakfast. Gail didn't bother checking the wall chrono to see how long it would be before the *Seeker*'s cooks began serving that meal. The expression "the dead of night" was pretty much on target.

Malley looked reasonably fresh—this would be early evening for him, Gail calculated, and he'd had some sleep courtesy of the tranks. She yawned and took her cup from Benton with a grateful nod. "What's keeping Sazaad?" she inquired, before the woman could retreat.

Benton, one of the older, more experienced lab techs, gave an eloquent shrug as if to suggest Gail should know better than to ask, but said: "He shouldn't be long. All you have to do is imply one of his gadgets isn't up to par and he's down here like an avalanche." Then she grinned, bright blue eyes twinkling. "If the twins aren't visiting, that is."

Gail wasn't amused, though she heard Grant choking on a mouthful of hot liquid. Sazaad had substantial appetites and it wasn't a secret he'd brought along a matched pair of assistants who shared at least one. If the young ladies in question had been anything less than superbly qualified electronics techs, Gail would have sent them packing. As it was, Sazaad appeared to be the envy of several on board.

*And if Sazaad's feminine distractions were keeping her waiting now, they'd be moving into the bowels of the command sphere to work on the* Seeker's *comm systems for Tobo.*

"Any word from Station Admin?"

Startled, Gail looked at Malley. He raised one eyebrow. "I

don't know. I've been asleep," she said without thinking, then found her face heating up with embarrassment. She wasn't sure if it was the connection to Sazaad's preoccupation or her own displeasure at being reminded how Malley had sent her to bed, like some errant child. *The stationer*, Gail decided, *was far too good at making her doubt her own reactions.*

Grant beckoned to one of his guards. Picray, Gail recalled. "Any updates from the bridge?" the commander asked quietly.

"One, sir. Aleksander came on an hour and a half ago to report there'd been a query about the state of the *Seeker*'s supply lines." Picray smiled wolfishly. "The station was offering to repair the damages and restore the connections. The First Officer politely declined, as per Captain Tobo's orders."

*Fast work*, Gail thought. But then, she'd never doubted the FD could take things apart, only that they'd wait to ask her permission.

Grant turned to their guest. "Were you expecting something in particular, Mr. Malley?"

"Malley. No Mister. Was I expecting something? Not really. Opposite cycle folks usually try to keep out of the messes they wake up to—it makes life simpler."

"So a closer watch when Forester's group is back in charge," Grant nodded affirmation of this to Picray, who went to the nearest comm panel to spread the word. "Thanks, Malley."

"Don't thank me," the stationer objected. "All I want is to get back into what's routine."

Gail nodded thoughtfully, not in promise but in understanding. To change the subject, she asked: "What do you think of the Quill now?"

"Having gone through your work?" Malley's eyes gleamed suddenly. "I'd like to read what you don't want me to know."

*At this rate*, Gail told herself dispassionately, *Grant was never going to get an intact swallow of his coffee.* "Ah," she said, sipping her own, inwardly pleased to have judged Malley so well.

"Ah?" he echoed, raising one eyebrow.

Without planning to, Gail found herself raising her own. "What do you think I left out, Malley?"

Instead of answering, Malley swiveled on his stool until he

was facing the far wall. Then he lifted one long arm and simply pointed.

Gail fought the urge to grin. Of all the work left abandoned here to deal with Pardell, somehow Malley had spotted what really mattered. She imagined Grant was probably ready to clap him in irons about now. She had a different idea. Gail hopped off her stool and motioned Malley to follow.

What had caught Malley's attention was a transparent case, taller than he was, holding nothing but a dark blue, one-piece jumpsuit, complete with feet. The fabric was suspended from a spiderweb of fine connectors frosting its surface. A nearby bench held smaller, but otherwise identical cases, some with gloves and one with a goggled headpiece. Gail hit the switch to turn up the task lighting. The fabric gathered the light and reflected it with diamondlike fire.

*Beautiful*, she thought admiringly, *in the way purposeful, dangerous things could be.*

Malley walked around the case. "When you talked about a Quill retrieval device," he said with wonder, "I thought you meant some type of remote probe, or robot."

"They've been tried. And failed." Gail continued sipping her coffee, gazing at her creation with a faintly impatient pride. "The Quill Effect remains the only way to confirm the Quill are present in a place. Until now, we couldn't use human investigators because they'd experience that effect . . ." She left it hanging.

"By dying," Malley finished, but thoughtfully. "So what's the principle here? Surely someone's tried making a protective suit before."

Before Gail could start to explain, the stationer rested one hand on the case and then looked over at Pardell's tank. "You said you're collecting genomes from selected human lines—why?" He nodded rapidly to himself twice; Gail watched him think it through with the anxious delight she felt when a promising student worried at a new concept. *Do you understand now, Grant?* she crowed to herself. *This was why they needed Malley.*

He'd gone on: "You're after the descendants of the terraformers. The ones Susan Witts gave Quill. You think the Quill on those worlds might somehow respond to their genome and not harm someone wearing—" Malley stared at the suit again, "—the right genetic disguise."

"Seems you had more than enough to read." This dry observation came from Grant.

"I didn't ask for the privilege. I preferred believing the Quill were three-meter googly-eyed alien monsters," Malley said. "If you wanted me kept ignorant, you should have consulted with your boss."

Gail felt the rising tension between the two men and said impatiently: "Ignorance is never preferable."

"Really?" Malley countered. "I'd prefer ignorance over knowing you, Gail Smith. But we can't always have what we want."

*An honest man.* Gail turned up the left corner of her mouth, quite aware this deepened the dimple on that side. *You use the weapons at hand.* "No," she agreed easily. "But I'm sure you're a man who plays the cards he's dealt, Malley. Especially when the stakes are this high—"

A call from the door. "Dr. Sazaad's coming, Dr. Smith." It somehow came across more as a warning than an announcement.

Gail sighed, watching the commotion as Sazaad made his entrance.

*Too short a night and, now, what promised to be a long day.*

# Chapter 27

WITH the exception of Sector Administrator Forester, the vastly annoying Todd brothers who'd lasted a scant quarter shift in the recycling depot with him, and now Gail Smith, Malley wasn't prone to automatically dislike someone. He prided himself on being a broad-minded, fair man. One who went on actions, not first impressions or by what others said.

In the case of Dr. Tabor Sazaad, Malley took one look and knew he'd probably kill the man if they spent any significant amount of time in the same room.

Not reassuring in the person who was supposed to prove your friend was alive.

It didn't help that Malley could see the identical response, insufficiently smoothed under a civilized veneer, from Commander Grant.

Gail Smith, on the other hand, had her civilized veneer very much in place, greeting her colleague with every appearance of apologetic charm for disturbing his sleep. Malley began to seriously doubt he'd ever seen an involuntary, open expression on her face—then he remembered the look of outraged shock when he'd stolen that kiss.

*Probably wouldn't work twice either.*

Sazaad was older, closer to station average, Malley judged, though he suspected the well-nourished Earthers appeared younger than they were. The scientist arrived, not in pajamas, as the unfortunate Temujin had earlier, but dressed in a tailored jacket and pants that were probably current fashion back in Sol System, dark hair immaculately in place. Obviously, he hadn't taken Gail's summons as overly urgent. *Or his pride required the clothing*, Malley speculated to himself.

No doubt about Earther arrogance here. Sazaad hadn't shut up since arriving, mainly delivering a diatribe about how techs panicked at the least irregularity and he needed his rest. Some of it had been interesting—Malley hadn't realized the cog screen was based on neural-speak technology, with living neurons within the device analyzing the voltages from cells in Aaron's brain. Sazaad's speech included numerous, and quite probably true, protestations of how his machine was beyond anything ever made before. Malley was prepared to be impressed by the technology, if not its creator.

The stationer disobeyed Grant's "suggestion" he stay out of the way and came to stand beside Gail Smith. She shot him a warning look, and he smiled. It didn't make her look happy, but little would, given she was taking the brunt of Sazaad's ire.

"My machine is perfect," Sazaad was saying, loudly and in a guttural accent new to Malley's ears. "I am incensed you've disturbed me—me!—to answer questions on its reliability, particularly for something as straightforward as this. Your own techs should have assured you there can be no doubt of such results. Bah!"

Give her credit, Gail Smith kept her voice calm and reasoned. "If I didn't need your expertise, Dr. Sazaad, be sure I wouldn't have had you brought down in the middle of the night. I wouldn't be here myself. We have reason to believe the patient may still have higher brain function—"

"The reading is obvious even to an idiot." Sazaad glanced at the tank and said, dismissively: "Your freak is dead."

*Tall.* They'd meet eye-to-eye if Sazaad bothered to look his way, Malley noticed, coldly and automatically assessing the man as a target. He moved like someone who didn't just keep in shape, but worshiped his body. Probably trained in some exotic martial art, like Grant and his people.

*Wouldn't matter.*

If Malley let himself touch the Earther, it would be once, with a knife in low to the rib cage and up.

Two cold-as-ice fingers rested lightly on his arm. Gail Smith didn't acknowledge him otherwise. *It wasn't to control him*, Malley realized abruptly, seeing how she looked at Grant at the same instant, almost imperceptibly shaking her head. It was a collecting of resources. At some point, she'd added him to her side of the equation.

"Then, Dr. Sazaad, it won't take you long to refute that finding," Gail told the scientist in a commanding tone that suddenly and completely belied the fact she had to crane her head back to look the other scientist in the eye, "—since I'm the idiot who knows our patient, Mr. Pardell, is alive and your precious machine is grossly in error."

Sazaad's face suffused to an alarming shade of red. Malley watched, less concerned than Grant seemed to be. The commander really should rely more on Gail's Machiavellian gift with people, he thought, and spend less time preparing to leap in her defense.

"Very well, Professor," with a bow, no less. Sazaad settled himself onto a stool and laid his long-fingered hands on the control panel of the cog screen with the same air of an artist preparing to perform that Malley had seen Sammie use when decanting his latest batch of beer. He hoped the results would be more remarkable.

Apparently, Sazaad also shared Sammie's ability to tune out observers. Gail turned her back on him after watching for a moment, putting a hand up to cover a yawn.

"I'll stay," offered Grant. "Any change, I'll call."

Gail shook her head and pushed some errant hair back behind her ears. "The minute I leave, Sazaad will find some excuse to wander off. Go while you can, Commander. I've got your people and Malley here if I need help. If all goes well, things may be—interesting—in the morning. I'll need you fresh."

The last came out as an order, whether she'd meant it to or not. Grant, Malley observed, didn't argue or even bother giving him one of those cautionary looks before he nodded and left. He did, Malley noticed, stop to talk briefly, and very quietly, to all four FDs before going out the door.

Malley followed Gail as she stepped up on the platform. Together, they stood looking down at Aaron. He might have been in suspended animation, but for the steady rise and fall of his chest.

"This guy's the best you've got?" Malley questioned very quietly.

Gail snorted. "In his field? Yes, when he's not thinking with his gonads."

"Pardon?"

She dipped her head so he couldn't see more than the curve of a cheek. It looked pinker than usual. "Let's just say the good doctor is a man who doesn't take interruption particularly well. Or rejection, for that matter."

*So.* While he could appreciate the attraction, Malley's estimation of the neurologist lowered, something he'd thought impossible. *On a project like this, with stakes like this?* Sazaad was six ways a fool if he thought he could annoy Gail Smith with unwelcome advances, and not pay—when she was ready. He could almost feel sorry for the man.

The lady in question ran one hand along the tank rim, as if the movement helped her make up her mind, then looked up. *Yes, both cheeks were pink.* "He mistook which of his qualifications I was interested in for this mission," she told him. "Why I'm telling you this, Malley, I don't know." This last was delivered with a slightly annoyed toss of her head.

He knew he had a good smile and used it deliberately, deepening his voice at the same time. "Because of *my* qualifications?"

Malley hadn't expected a flash of dimples—or that the now-warm fingers running along the rim would lightly brush over his own. He found himself trapped in a lingering, too-knowing look from bottomless blue eyes, and felt his breathing quicken involuntarily. "I admit it's—refreshing—to have someone to talk to who doesn't report everything I say to someone else," Gail said with a sincerity he suddenly wanted to believe.

*And dared not.* "Oh, if I had someone to report you to, I would, Earther," Malley said with deliberate harshness. "Bet on it."

She didn't look offended. "Circumstances are what they are, Malley," she told him. "I think, had we met otherwise, we might have been friends," suddenly deeper dimples, "or rivals. But we are neither of us fools. Unlike some," this with a seething glare to where Sazaad was now shouting at Benton for no apparent reason. "Excuse me."

Malley stared after Gail Smith, no longer wondering why rooms felt so much smaller when she left them.

# Chapter 28

"I LEFT the lab to read a message?" Gail glared at Manuel Reinsez and was ready to turn around and walk off the bridge, but Tobo beckoned her over. She continued glaring at Reinsez as she obeyed. Tobo's value to her was more than old friendship; she knew the measure of the man and depended on his calm, understated competence. Gail, who hated being a passenger at the best of times, had long ago paid Tobo the ultimate compliment of completely ignoring his ship. In return, Tobo did his very capable best to make sure she could.

So the captain's unusual call might have been low on specifics, but it was clear on the urgency. She'd hopefully been equally clear with Sazaad about his responsibilities. At least there should be no confusion about her instructions to the FDs: Sazaad wasn't to leave the lab unless Malley had broken his neck. They'd looked a little askance at the big stationer at that. *Fine. A little respect where it was owed.*

She'd owed Malley her attention to his friend, but Tobo had used those key words: *ship's security.* When she told him she had to go, Malley had simply picked up a stool in one hand and walked over to sit behind Sazaad, who'd looked around in shock at this intrusion.

Hopefully, they'd both be there when she'd cleared up Tobo's emergency. Even better, that Malley was right and she'd have a living Pardell to question about his ship.

"Looks like station business," she began, scanning the top of the message printout Tobo put in her hand. It had been sent to Station Admin, but copied to them. She read further and stopped protesting. Tobo had been right.

*Thromberg Station*
*The arrival of the Earther ship* Seeker *marks the renewal*
*of normal relations between Sol System and her people.*
*The time has come for our return home. You will release*
*control of station freighters* Journeyman II, Freda's Hope,
*and* Mississauga *to the crews waiting outside their ports.*
*The Earthers will not interfere. Failure to comply will re-*
*sult in escalating damage to the station. You have one*
*hour.*

"In case you haven't noticed, Dr. Smith, we are still partially
attached to the station these terrorists are proposing to damage," Dr. Reinsez said, wiping his forehead with a cloth. He
didn't usually venture on the bridge—or Tobo was usually
quicker to seal the door. Obviously, the situation had deterio-
rated while she was busy in the lab. "Call Commander Grant,"
Gail ordered. A nod from the grim-faced FD stationed beside
the comm operator.

There were three of Grant's people on the *Seeker*'s bridge, at
any time. One was his designated Second-in-command—this
shift, Tech Specialist Kelly Aleksander. The other two, presently
the Miller sibs, Matt and Jana, monitored FD equipment, as well
as comm chatter and the vid feeds from the public areas on the
ship, including the main lab in the science sphere. The less public areas were watched from another location, an illusion of privacy for the bridge crew. Aleksander stood within easy reach of
the control that would disengage or disconnect the science
sphere. No doubt all of the FDs had been thoroughly briefed on
the procedure. *They could probably*, she reminded herself, *operate the* Seeker *without her crew.*

"The commander's on his way up, Dr. Smith." Gail wasn't
surprised. Grant had probably been on alert since she'd left.

Gail nodded absently as she sank into Tobo's command
chair, rereading the terse message and trying to make sense out
of it. Malley had sounded confident the station was stable—at
least until yesterday's troublemakers were back in charge and
making their demands. She seriously doubted anyone on the sta-

tion would threaten their only home, no matter what they wanted.

Which left the Outsiders.

And Rosalind Fournier. *Damn.* Gail had assumed—wrongly, she now judged—that the woman had been at the *Seeker*'s air lock to check on Aaron Pardell, one of her own in the hands of Earthers. "Where are these ships?" Gail asked, handing the note back to Tobo.

His almond-shaped eyes crinkled in worry. "They're docked in sequence from us—there's a gap in between the *Seeker* and the first, the *Journeyman II*, but not more than two ships' worth."

"She was here to scout those ships—we were an excuse so Thromberg wouldn't suspect."

Reinsez dropped into the first officer's chair. "Who was here?" he demanded anxiously. "We had visitors and no one informed me? That's—"

With an effort, and most likely a frown, Gail focused her attention on Titan U's representative. "What are you doing up so early, Manuel?"

He attempted to look doleful and wound up simply more wrinkled than usual. "Couldn't sleep. Too worried. Too much risk and uncertainty. This isn't how you were supposed to run this mission, Gail. Not in the least—"

"You've been on the comm to Titan, haven't you?" she accused him abruptly, now having no problem whatsoever paying attention to her resident nuisance. She could have asked Aleksander for the confirmation she was bound, by the command chain, to give her, but didn't for good reason. The more autonomy Reinsez thought he had, the more he revealed to her.

At least he didn't bother denying it. "It's my duty to report—"

"It's your duty to report complete and accurate information, Dr. Reinsez. Since you haven't been briefed on last night's events, I'm going to assume you based your report on eavesdropping and guesswork."

A puffer fish couldn't assume that pompous, offended-dignity look any better. "Events were moving too quickly to leave for your convenience, Dr. Smith. We were facing life-threatening circumstances—"

Gail surged to her feet. Maybe it was exhaustion, or maybe Malley had infected her with something of his rebellious stationer attitude, but she'd had enough. "You haven't faced a life-threatening circumstance—until now, Dr. Reinsez. I suggest you voluntarily confine yourself to quarters and get the rest you need. I'm willing to keep you informed on a need-to-know basis. Or you can refuse to get out of my face—in which case I will have you escorted off this bridge and kept in isolation. Am I clear?"

"You don't have the authority—" he blustered.

Gail lifted her right hand and bent one finger slightly. Aleksander and another of the FDs came to her side, where they stood at attention, staring impassively at Dr. Reinsez. "Am I clear?" she repeated very softly.

He was clutching the arms of the chair, doubtless leaving sweaty palm prints Tobo's fastidious first officer would dislike intensely. "Titan will—"

"Go," Gail told him. "One way or the other."

Reinsez levered himself up, wrinkled lips pressed together in a thin white line, his eyes hard. But he knew better than to argue. Gail had half-hoped he would, but the spectacle of watching him dragged off the bridge was an indulgence she could ill afford. She did wave one of the FDs to follow the angry professor. No point giving Reinsez encouragement to reconsider his destination.

"Did you make a copy of whatever he sent out?" she asked Aleksander after the bridge was clear, feeling her heart pounding with frustration. *A frightened man and a petty one. What had he told Titan?* She'd have to send her own report chasing after his—and soon.

Grant's Second looked faintly insulted. "Dr. Smith," she protested.

Gail smiled an apology. "I shouldn't doubt you. I'll view it in my office please." She hesitated, then added: "And have the room swept again. I think Dr. Reinsez and whomever he has working with him among the crew may have been busy while we were otherwise occupied. Now. Captain Tobo."

"Oh, don't apologize to me, Dr. Smith," Tobo assured her. "You have my unending gratitude for removing that pestilent lump from my bridge. I'm surprised you didn't space him. There's a thought . . . it could be an accident." Tobo looked to be only partially joking. He must have been interceding on her behalf with Reinsez more than she'd realized. She'd already been relying on the Captain to handle all the dealings with Thromberg—as well as keep a watchful eye on reports from home.

Gail made a mental note to send a bottle of Tobo's favorite brandy to his quarters later. She'd brought a few in her luggage, knowing she'd be bending their friendship regularly during the mission.

"Space him?" Gail chuckled but shook her head. "I'll keep it in mind. I still need Dr. Reinsez, a happy and cooperative Reinsez, when we dock at Titan U, or my career options narrow to teaching first year biology in an asteroid dome." Gail took the first officer's chair, avoiding the damp armrests, and motioned to Tobo to join her. For a brief moment, they sat peacefully side by side, looking out over the heart of the *Seeker*.

For no particular reason, Gail found herself wondering what Rosalind Fournier would think of this bridge. A far cry from anything docked at Thromberg—or Earth, for that matter—but the 'sider would find familiar elements. Its design drew heavily on deep-space experience as well as more traditional starship models. *The result*, Gail thought, *was stunning as well as functional.* A bonus for her unusual level of responsibility on this mission.

The center point of the bridge was the display screen. Instead of being along a wall, or crammed into small screens per station, the *Seeker*'s screen filled one half of a broad, flattened column rising up from the lower level to just below the ceiling. The screen could be split into multiple readouts, or, as now, be set to a view outside the ship. Duty stations spiraled outward from it, command stations on a second, shoulder-high level allowing easy viewing of any point on the bridge.

It was an unusually large bridge for the size of ship, but that was to allow each station room for two sets of chairs, both to allow smooth changeover at shift's end, and a convenience permitting additional personnel to be present as observers. While the latter was intended so scientists could be involved in any ship's maneuvering that might affect particular experiments, the reality on *Seeker*'s first mission was something different. The extra seats allowed Grant's people to sit at key stations with the crew.

In a sense, Tobo's practical jokes on the military component of the ship had served them well. There'd been virtually no tension left on the bridge since the episode of the surprise null gravity drills. Gail suspected Grant of unusual tolerance in that regard for much the same reason. *Whatever got the job done,* she reminded herself.

When docked under normal conditions, only comm and ship systems were crewed this late into ship's night, *or early in ship's morning,* Gail corrected. It was a sign of the tension in and out of the ship that Tobo had a full crew in place and had chosen to stay here instead of relinquishing command to his very capable First Officer Frank Szpindel. *Capable,* Gail suddenly remembered, *but also one of those who'd been added to the crew on Titan's direct recommendation rather than hers.*

A sleepless night for many. *But not Pardell,* Gail thought, seeing his slack features and golden-veined skin in her mind's eye. *Could he really be alive? Or was Malley simply refusing to admit defeat?*

"You know who's behind this?" Tobo raised the note in one hand.

"There was a woman—ah, Grant," Gail paused in her explanation to greet the commander. "We have a new situation."

Grant took the message from Tobo and read it swiftly. His expression, when done, was about what Gail expected. She shook her head before he could open his mouth, saying firmly: "We aren't leaving the station."

"That's—" he began.

"An order. But redeploy some of those spy 'bots of yours, if it will make you happier. I doubt Station Admin will object under these circumstances."

"Krenshaw, see to it. Dr. Smith? I strongly recommend an exterior patrol as well."

Gail closed her eyes to better recall Rosalind Fournier. "No," she decided, opening them again. "If it's the Outsiders, your people would be at too great a disadvantage. We aren't risking any more lives unless absolutely necessary."

"A laudable intention," Tobo said. "But, not to parrot the departed Manuel, aren't you risking all of us already?"

"How much time is left on that ultimatum?" Gail asked instead of rising to the bait.

The comm tech answered, his voice sounding strained: "Thirty-seven minutes, Professor."

"Three 'bots deployed, sir," reported Krenshaw from his station at the far end of the bridge. "Aft, stern, and longitudinal sweep."

"Send one of them toward the other ships," Grant commanded. "And put the feed on screen."

"Has Thromberg responded?" Gail asked Tobo.

"Not a word over regular channels. Unless the good commander has heard otherwise?" Tobo was unshakably convinced Grant's experts could and did monitor every comm frequency shipside and out. Aware of how stretched the FDs were—especially after losing five of their own, Gail seriously doubted they were bothering with more than the emergency surveillance already in place.

Grant's lips twisted sardonically as he confirmed her thoughts. "Believe me, Captain, if we knew anything about this, I'd have told you both before now."

The 'bot's feed was already showing on the screen—Grant must have kept them ready to relaunch despite her earlier disapproval. The assorted sounds on the bridge subsided as everyone's attention was caught by the image.

Thromberg's curving side was presently black on black, punctuated by running lights marking the various docking ports and air locks. Most of these had gaps like missing teeth, as if replacing failed exterior lighting wasn't a priority. *Or*, Gail realized, *as if replacement parts were impossible to come by.*

The various docked ships splashed their own lights against the station, washing the darkness back in overlapping circles. Everything looked normal as the 'bot was taken closer in—

"There! Veer left." Krenshaw obeyed so quickly he must have already spotted what caught Grant's eye.

At first, all Gail saw was another work crew—there were several such. *Business as usual, even-cycle day*, Gail told herself. It was important to remember Thromberg never slept.

Krenshaw dropped the 'bot closer.

*Not a work crew.* They were looking down at a tight group of at least fifteen figures, in those patched suits Gail was beginning to find very familiar. They carried tools—tools that could be weapons.

"A boarding party," Tobo concluded unhappily, probably thinking of his own precious ship.

Two of the figures looked up and pointed, one raising what appeared to be a grappler to aim at the 'bot. Just as Grant said: "Back it off," Gail snapped: "Hold."

"Hold," Grant confirmed, glancing at her.

*She'd recognized one of the suits. She was sure of it.* Gail watched with the rest as the figure she thought might be Rosalind took a few steps away from the rest, staring up, then beckoned to the 'bot. *Down*, the gesture said.

"Drop it down," Grant said. "Slowly. We don't have a limitless supply of these things."

Krenshaw brought the 'bot to hang directly in front of the figure's helmet, but out of reach. The helmet, another museum piece but originally of higher quality than Pardell's, reflected the 'bot rather than revealed anything, then the figure must have switched on the interior lights.

The dim, blood-red glow shone over the cheekbones and brows of an unsmiling Rosalind Fournier. Gail released the breath she hadn't been aware of holding.

Rosalind mouthed some words, tapped her helmet, then pointed at the 'bot.

"Krenshaw, scan and capture the local signal. Pipe it through."

It was Gail's turn to look at the commander. *How did the 'sider know something about the capabilities of Grant's little spy satellites she didn't?*

"—welcome to my world, Dr. Smith." Slightly distorted, Rosalind's voice remained exactly as Gail remembered it from their first meeting—calm and utterly sure of itself. "I've been waiting for you."

# Chapter 29

MALLEY wasn't good at waiting. Most things in his life moved when he'd wanted them to—usually right away. Even the daily ration line was something Malley couldn't tolerate without a reader in his hand or a good argument underway. Aaron, always the more cautious, had long ago given up preaching the value of patience. But then Aaron would stand and count to a hundred and one just to be sure there wasn't anyone watching him go home. A count he'd cheerfully restart at zero if Malley interrupted—and would continue to restart as many times as Malley chose to be a nuisance.

Even Aaron's patience might have been tested by now. The neurologist, Sazaad, gave every appearance of being hard at work, adjusting controls, muttering to himself, leaping up dramatically every so often to pace back and forth—with more muttering. All a great show of getting something done.

*With nothing to show for it.*

The metal seat of the stool felt as though it was growing attached to Malley's behind, but he stayed in place. He wasn't going to be the one to interrupt and restart this so-called genius.

The only problem with sitting quietly was that it encouraged thoughts. Noisy, irritating, hard-to-ignore thoughts. Malley wasn't sure which ones bothered him more: not knowing what was happening in the rest of the ship and on the station, or thinking about being on a ship and not on the station.

He firmly quelled any tendency of his thoughts to wander into the dangerous territory guarded by dimples and deep blue eyes. Gail Smith might be many things, but a romantic fantasy she wasn't—not if he was going to save Aaron and—

Malley shifted on the hard metal. The "and" part was another path to steer away from, since it led inevitably to heart-pounding, mouth-drying panic. Aaron knew all about ships and the nasty, cold, black places surrounding them. Once they were ready to return to Thromberg, Malley would be content to shoot himself with a trank or two and let Aaron drag him around for a change.

Not the most helpful of plans, but it did make sitting and staring a hole into the back of Sazaad's head seem like progress.

# Chapter 30

*P*ROGRESS, *of a kind.* Gail rose to her feet without conscious plan, feeling as if Rosalind could see her and it was important to stand her ground. She'd wanted to talk to this 'sider again. Rosalind might be her only chance of finding Pardell's ship and records.

Facing off with an ultimatum between them hadn't been part of the plan.

"Rosalind Fournier," Gail said evenly, trusting Grant's people had set up the necessary comm links. "We've received your message. I'm not sure I understand what it has to do with us."

Being lit from below gave all the wrong shadows and impressions to a face. Still, Gail thought, the menace in Rosalind's slow smile was probably accurate. "Time's passing, Earther. Bring me on your ship and I'll explain."

Gail ignored Grant's silent but vehement "no."

"Agreed," she said.

Rosalind's helmet returned to being a reflection of the 'bot's lenses. She seemed to take Gail at her word, gesturing to the others, then beginning to walk with surprising speed. The 'bot followed, giving an unnecessary view of the *Seeker* ahead.

Grant growled something and the 'bot returned to watching the remaining 'siders. The screen split, giving two new views of Rosalind's approach as Krenshaw picked her up on the ship's exterior vids.

"May I ask why we are immersing ourselves deeper into Thromberg's woes?" Tobo asked with deceptive mildness. "When we could simply leave?"

"I have my reasons," Gail told him, hoping he'd take that as "*not here, with so many ears.*"

Grant was in full officer mode, standing at attention as if in mute reproach at her violation of what he doubtless viewed as minimal safety protocols. *Fine*, Gail thought, unrepentant. If safety was the important thing, they'd be back orbiting Titan by now. "Look after the details," she told him. "I'll be waiting in my office."

It wasn't neutral ground, but Gail wanted every advantage in an encounter with Rosalind.

Unfortunately, being seated behind an imposing wooden desk hadn't helped. Rosalind had taken one look, sniffed, and said: "Biogen maple. You'd think Titan would have sprung for the real thing," before taking her seat with the elegant confidence of a queen.

"The *Seeker* is a working ship, not a liner," Tobo replied, sounding offended. Gail silenced him with a look.

It was the three of them and the 'sider—Grant leaving his people outside the door this time, but keeping a portable comm link in one ear. Gail had thought, briefly, of including Malley. But his relationship with this woman was too unknown. They didn't need complications such as had arisen on Thromberg. She'd also considered getting Forester in here—in case this was what Tobo thought, a purely internal matter. But again, there was likely history there.

Gail was interested in the future.

So, it seemed, was the leader of the Outsiders. "I'll come straight to the point, Dr. Smith, Captain, Commander," Rosalind nodded graciously to each. "This ship is the signal from Sol System my people have been waiting for all these years. The time has come to leave our prison and reclaim our proper place." From her, the words weren't bombastic—they sounded like statements of fact.

"A signal of what?" Gail asked curiously. "That Earth is taking an active role in restoring the terraformed worlds to the colonists? I agree, but it's only—"

"Worlds?" Rosalind's lips twisted over the word as if it left a foul taste. "We are not interested in dirt, Dr. Smith. My people are spacers, have been and always will be. We were trapped here by mistake during the immigrants' uprising—tarred by the same brush and left to rot with them on this hunk of metal.

"But we were patient. We knew Sol would reopen deep-space exploration, that the universities would again look beyond Earth's petty interests in creating replicas of itself. This ship—your ship—is proof of that. And we are ready."

Gail recognized the rhetoric. She knew many former pilots and explorers who felt abandoned by Earth's turtlelike approach to expansion, as promoted by the Reductionist movement. It shouldn't have surprised her from Rosalind—but it did. She supposed it was because the survival of the 'siders and the station itself was so remarkable, she hadn't expected the older dream to survive as well. Then, as she looked into those cold, almost fanatical eyes, she knew her mistake.

*A dream could be a reason to survive.*

"You say you are ready," Gail said, careful of every word. "For what? To steal three freighters from Thromberg?"

Rosalind clicked the two wide paddles forming her right hand together. An irritated sound, Gail thought. "Theft? Merely a request for transportation. One Thromberg has agreed to—my people are replacing their crews as we speak. Feel free to ask the commander to check with one of your spy bots if you doubt me."

"So you no longer threaten the station," Tobo said in a relieved voice.

"Our deadline stands. It is your contribution on the line now."

Gail narrowed her eyes. "Ours? And what might that be, Outsider?"

"You will arrange for our ships to be welcomed at the Callisto Spaceport."

Callisto. Sol System's largest starship construction facility. *Of course*, Gail thought. For over a hundred years, eager young pilots and would-be explorers had marked its orbit around Jupiter, hoping to attend its schools—while retiring spacers who couldn't bear to be grounded drifted home to it and filled its bars and lounges with stories. If ever humanity surged outward again in earnest, Callisto would be its launching pad.

"Earth hasn't opened the blockade," Grant said bluntly. "No

person or ship originating from a station will be allowed into Sol System."

"Ah," Rosalind said, shaking her head at him. "Times change. Now we have a spokesperson to open that doorway. Do we not, Dr. Smith?"

Gail stiffened. "I have nothing to do with Earth policy, whatever you may imagine. I'm a scientist. This is a research vessel." She stole a look at the wall chrono. *Ten minutes left.* "You've threatened the station. How?"

The 'sider smiled thinly. "You look at our equipment, at our dead ships, and judge us harmless, don't you?"

"No," Gail said quite sincerely. "I don't consider you harmless in the least."

"Good," Rosalind replied. "Because the hearts of our ships still beat. And you should appreciate what power that puts in our hands." She lifted hers in emphasis, probably very aware of the contrast between their grotesque replacements and her long, graceful arms.

*The translight drives.* Gail didn't need Tobo's gasp or Grant's step forward to tell her the stakes had just risen. Even if their fuel cones were essentially spent, there would be enough power remaining in the initiation matrix of any of those derelicts to put a substantial hole in the station.

*If they all went at once*—Gail didn't need to do the math to know the resulting force would send Thromberg wobbling, jarring the station from its orbit. A choice of deaths: starvation if the station was pushed too far from the sun to collect sufficient energy to sustain it, or radiation poisoning, if the station moved too close. Both of those endings assumed the hull of the abused station remained intact—otherwise, a moot point, since everyone would already be dead.

*Evacuate?* Gail thought desperately. *Even if there were enough ships, where could they take the people?* No wonder Thromberg was silent. Their fate was in her hands. They had nothing left to bargain with and every reason to fear.

"You want the impossible. Thromberg may have given you ships," Gail said, "but I can't open the blockade to any ship—anyone—from a station. Sol System—Earth—fears the Quill."

"The Quill." Pure scorn. "That old, tired song."

*Had she found an opening?* Gail spoke cautiously: "Yes, the Quill. And if our mission is successful, which I believe it will be, it won't be much longer before the terraformed worlds are—"

"Show me a Quill," Rosalind interrupted coolly.

Gail blinked.

Rosalind leaned forward, eyes gleaming. "Go on. Show me one. You can't, can you? That's because they are all dead. You know the only thing dangerous about a Quill? What happens to anyone who owned one!"

"Fournier." Gail felt pieces dropping into place. "You're Stuart Fournier's daughter," she breathed in amazement, remembering the incident. "The deep-space explorer who—"

The 'sider sat erect again, knees together, shoulders back, and stared at Gail with cold, hard eyes. "Captain Fournier. The explorer thought missing, who brought his ship limping home after three long years. Only all hell had broken loose and he didn't know why. Do your records also tell you that when he arrived home, with his Quill around his wrist as always, he was burned alive by a crazed mob?

"You'd think we'd learn from the past," Rosalind continued. "But it's a human failing, isn't it? As is wasting time." The 'sider made a point of checking her wristchrono. "You have five minutes left, Dr. Smith, before my colleagues lift from Thromberg—safely, if the station has been diligent in undocking procedures. Fifteen minutes more we grant you, in which to guarantee their deserved welcome at our home port of Callisto." She paused, then added: "Don't think we'll hesitate, Dr. Smith. We are dying—two a month, five, soon it will be more. Our time has already run out, Dr. Smith. We are not prepared to be patient."

Gail tilted back her head and regarded Rosalind Fournier. Brilliant, angry, full of purpose. She *knew* this woman—not her personality or history, of course, but what drove her. They might have taken different paths to this place and time, but they were uncannily alike. Like Gail, what mattered to Rosalind wasn't power itself, it was achieving her goal. *By whatever means.*

Gail was familiar with that trait as well.

"I have a counterproposal, Rosalind," she said almost cheerfully. "May I call you Rosalind?"

# Chapter 31

"**M**R. MALLEY?"
        Malley started at the low voice in his ear. *Damn.* He'd dozed off on the stool, a useful skill when there wasn't much streaming down the recycling floor, but hardly what he'd planned to do here.

He looked around almost frantically. The voice was Benton's. The lab tech stood a little distance away, as if his jump awake had surprised her, too. Otherwise, nothing in the lab seemed to have changed. Sazaad—

*Where was Sazaad?*

"Mr. Malley?"

The stationer stood up and made himself stretch, leery of moving too quickly after being in one position for so long. "Yes, Benton. I'm awake," he told the tech, still scanning the room.

He should have looked at the tank first, instead of last. Sazaad was there, Philips at his side, busy with something at the far end. "What's he doing?" Malley demanded, not bothering to keep his voice down.

Benton raised her own voice. She sounded, and looked, angry. "Dr. Sazaad has taken it on himself to disconnect Mr. Pardell's life support."

Malley was across the intervening space, with his new knife across Sazaad's throat, before the Earther could do more than turn, wide-eyed. In the next instant, he'd wrapped his other arm under and around Sazaad's so he could press the man's head forward while pinning him against his chest.

The Earther wisely chose not to struggle, since the hold gave him the option of severing his own neck or feeling Malley snap it, but he sputtered indignantly: "Get this lunatic off me!

Guards! Guards!" The guards in question had moved closer, but showed no interest in interfering.

Malley put his lips to Sazaad's ear. "What are you doing to Aaron?"

"The man's dead. Dead! Dead! Dead! You are wasting my time—there's nothing on the cog—nothing! Let go! Guar—"

Malley flexed the arm providing leverage against Sazaad's spine. There was a most satisfying creak.

Philips was hurriedly reattaching tubes and cables to the exterior of the tank, Benton coming to help. *Sazaad must have been pulling them free at random.* "Is Aaron all right?" Malley asked the tech.

"How can you ask if a corpse is all right?" shrieked Sazaad.

"How can you keep talking if I cut your throat?" Malley thought it a reasonable question, but the man turned into a limp weight and slid bonelessly out of his grip. Getting the knife out of the way just in time, the stationer grabbed for a new hold, sure this was a trick, then realized the Earther had fainted. Malley let him drop.

"We've been trying to get orders, Mr. Malley," this quietly from one of the FDs. The techs both nodded. "But the brass has been tied up with some crisis—"

Malley hardly listened, too intent on looking for any sign Aaron had been harmed.

The bubbles restarted within the liquid as the techs continued restoring the systems. Nothing else seemed to have changed.

*Was Aaron's face more shadowed along the cheek and around his eyes, as if bruises were starting to show? He should have black eyes along with everything else*, Malley thought in helpless rage. There'd been a big enough pile of bodies on him—and hardly gentle treatment to get him here. Purple smudges on his arms and thighs marked where the remote handling arms had gripped to move him. His chest rose and fell—*was it as strongly as before?*

"Malley. Aisha's on her way to the lab. She'll check the life support and go over what Dr. Sazaad has done."

"He's fading," Malley heard himself say.

There was a sarcastic mutter from the floor: "Maybe Aisha could try a defib—but, oh, I forgot. He's dead."

*Defib?* Defibrillator. Malley had watched the doctors restart his Uncle Roy's failing heart, seen for himself the limp body arching up, falling back, then the triumphant announcement of a pulse. "Would it work?" he asked out loud. *Was it that simple?* he asked himself.

Benton answered, her voice gentle: "Your friend's heart is beating just fine, Malley. The shock from a defib wouldn't help."

*He didn't need courage*, Malley decided, nodding an acknowledgment even as he flexed the fingers of his right hand. *Not if he understood what went on inside Aaron at all.* What Malley needed was a completely calm state of mind.

That being unlikely any time soon, speed was the thing.

Without hesitation, the stationer plunged his bare hand through the warm gel until his fingertips touched—

*Fire!*

As Malley instantly yanked his arm away from the consuming pain, his legs collapsed beneath him. He tried to hold on to the side of the tank, but there was no strength left in his body. The room whirled into the darkness of his nightmares. . . .

As he passed out, Malley hoped he'd been right.

# Chapter 32

"THERE'S been an incident in the lab."

Grant's whisper tickled her ear, reminding Gail for no reason of Malley. Then she processed what he'd said and went cold to her core.

Somehow, she managed to keep her expression set to polite interest and her mind focused on her negotiations with Rosalind Fournier.

For they were negotiations, plain and simple. Gail had been right—given a tidier alternative, the Outsider leader was willing to listen. The ultimatum's deadline came and went. Whether the 'siders had ever been prepared to turn their ships into doomsday weapons, or if it was all a bluff . . . Gail didn't want to know. She did believe Rosalind perfectly capable of anything necessary. *A refreshingly straightforward attitude.*

*There's been an incident*—Gail gave a tight nod that sent Grant back to his seat, one hand cupped over his ear comm as though the report was still coming in. *Past tense*, she told herself. Whatever was done—whomever had died—was beyond changing now.

She wanted it otherwise. But her place was at this table, just as it was Rosalind's. Doubtless, the 'sider would have preferred the bridge of one of her extorted ships, over sipping oolong tea with Earthers.

"Bad news?" Rosalind asked.

Gail weighed several choices, then smiled. "An update. I like to keep posted."

"How is young Aaron?"

"No change—which is why I've made this offer."

Rosalind locked the appendages forming her left hand

around her cup and turned it, released and readjusted her grip, then gripped and turned the cup again. *A habit*, Gail thought, taking advantage of Rosalind's sudden preoccupation to ram half a biscuit into her mouth. She was going to have to start carrying snacks in her pockets at the rate she was missing meals.

The tray of tea and warm biscuits had relaxed tensions, as had rearranging the seating so they were comfortably spaced around the table. Courtesies were never meaningless—especially, Gail reminded herself, in places where the living was hard and people had to share to survive.

"Your offer." A hairless brow lifted. "What makes you so sure I have access to young Aaron's ship?"

Gail washed down her biscuit with tea before saying: "A hunch. If I'm wrong, I'm sure you know someone else who does."

"In order to look for clues to young Aaron's—predicament."

"Exactly."

"And in exchange for the *'Mate*'s location and entry codes, you offer to take a delegation of Outsiders with you to prove to us that the Quill exist, that Earth's paranoia has been valid all these years, and—lo!—you, Gail Smith, are about to save the day."

Gail poured herself more tea and offered Rosalind the same service. "Just so," she said pleasantly.

It gained her an honest laugh and a closer look from those challenging pale eyes. "Deep spacers know the Quill, Gail. Not by rumor and lies. Records, firsthand accounts passed down from generation to generation. All say the Quill are harmless, helpful things. Toys to make the translight passages easier to bear. You can understand why true spacers never bought into the Reductionist hysteria about murderous aliens." It was Rosalind's turn to sample a biscuit, the only sign she'd been living on station rations for twenty years being the slowness with which she chewed and swallowed. Then she said: "Mind you, that's not something for casual talk on Thromberg. You've noticed their tendency to scream first and check the tag later."

"If you're so sure about the Quill and Earth," Gail challenged her, "come with us. Prove it once and for all."

There were fine age lines etched at the corners of Rosalind's lips and eyes. They tightened now, as if she steeled herself against a quick response she'd regret—or as if, Gail hoped, she was considering the offer.

"Another option," Rosalind said finally. "You take myself and one other with you. You permit us to bring our own communication equipment, so we can reach our people here as necessary. And—one of our ships makes a goodwill trip to Callisto at the same time."

Gail opened one hand, palm up. "I'll put through a request for clearance—that's all I can do. If Sol refuses . . ." She left the obvious unsaid. The 'siders had tried the blockade once. It had most likely cost Rosalind her hands.

"Excuse me, Dr. Smith," Grant said quietly. "There's an incoming call for you."

The commander wouldn't interrupt for anything less than a major crisis—or Titan. *There's been an incident . . .* Gail fixed her smile a little more tightly in place and stood. "Please forgive me, Rosalind. Perhaps you'd care for a tour of the bridge with Captain Tobo?" She gave Tobo a look he returned with an imperceptible bow.

The 'sider's eyes shone with anticipation and she put her cup aside. "I would. Thank you."

"We'll resume our discussion back here in half an hour, then." Gail waited until Tobo had escorted the taller woman out the door before turning to Grant.

He'd hurried to her desk to key in the comm, but paused before finalizing the link. "Who first? Titan or Thromberg?"

"Both? Lucky me. Who sounds less hysterical?" Gail asked, walking by him and dropping into her chair. She glared at the pending call lights.

"Unfortunately, it's a tie."

Gail raised her hand to cue the comm, then stopped and looked up at Grant. "What's going on in the lab? Is it Pardell?"

He shrugged. "I'd left orders not to be disturbed, so Aleksander just passed along the highlights. No one's dead—although I'm told Sazaad came close and Malley was critical, but is now out of danger. Odds are, they tried to take each other apart. I'll send someone down to get the details."

"Go yourself."

"Dr. Smith—"

"Go," she insisted. "The science staff won't listen to anyone of lower rank—when they listen at all. And Malley knows you. We can't afford mistakes among our own. Deal with whatever mess is down there and get back here as fast as you can. Tobo should be able to keep our guest fascinated and out of mischief long enough."

A hint of a salute as Grant turned smartly and headed for the door. Just shy of it, he turned and stood looking back at her with an unfamiliar expression.

"Yes?" she suggested.

"Before we left Titan, I'd had—concerns—about the chain of command on this mission, Dr. Smith." Grant paused, then said. "I don't anymore."

Before she could react, he'd left.

Gail smiled to herself, then her smile faded as she prepared to take the calls waiting on her desk. Thromberg? She thought she could guess the content of that message. Now that she had the beginnings of an agreement with Rosalind and her forces, that call should be easily handled.

Titan? It all depended on what Reinsez had spewed forth in her absence. She thought it unlikely his opinion of her was as high as the commander's had been.

# Chapter 33

*M*ALLEY?
        His entire body had been asleep, the way a foot goes numb in one position then complains with ferocious pins and needles of sensation when moved.

There was nothing wrong with his head. *Malley had just been talking to him—where was he?*

Opening his eyes might help.

The concept of sight led to other interesting thoughts. His mind raced along, considering the sense of touch—*his didn't seem to be working*—hearing—*there were sounds, he just didn't understand them*—taste—*definitely old vomit, he knew that one*—smell—*flowers?*

There couldn't be flowers here. He recognized the smell because a woman—a woman with no hands—had held a tiny treasured vial to his nostrils and commanded he learn the word *lilac*.

Lilac? His thoughts traced botanical concepts, his imagination painted a world with browns, purples, and greens, under the arch of a turquoise-blue sky. *Malley wouldn't like it.*

*Malley.* The name intruded, disrupted, threatened. Other things floated upward with it, turning on their backs to reveal faces, lips drawn back in death, eyes protruding in accusation.

He had done something terrible.

Lilacs. The smell of lilacs. *The taste of vomit.*

"No!" A primal sound, like the howl of air from a blown air lock, sucking life outward until there was nothing but cold, dark metal. *Malley hated air locks.*

A splash, as if a container of water had spilled nearby. Another, closer. *He was splashing?*

Where was he? Thoughts of location, vectors, time, and

distance flipped past one another. Images of places resolved into one—a huge empty space, filled with people who turned to reveal their faces, lips drawn back in death, eyes protruding—

"No!"

This time he knew the scream was from his throat. The pain of it was a welcome anchor to what had to be reality. He groped for more, fearing visions.

*Light.* He was floating in light. No matter how wide he opened his eyes, the illusion remained.

He happened to narrow them. The world gained sides and edges. He looked down, finding a body with tubes protruding from it, floating in lilac blue bubbles.

*Malley?*

A hand appeared, dripping blue liquid, etched in gold and purple. An artificial hand. *A deadly hand.*

Faces turned with dead smiles and eyes—

"No!"

"Get the remotes—we need those cuffs back on—"

*More reality?* It seemed unlikely, since it wasn't Malley's voice. *Whose was it?*

A cold, steely grip fastened on him, somewhere, a leg. It was on his leg. *It was a dead hand.* He leaped upward, heaving free of the tubes with sudden, sharp twinges of pain, shedding water and illusion at the same time.

Aaron Pardell found himself naked, draped half over the side of a strange bathtub, and confronting a roomful of strangers.

He took a gasping breath and another, then asked the only question he could think of: "Anyone seen Hugh Malley?"

# Chapter 34

"NO, SIR."

Gail drew another small circle beside the larger one.

"Yes, sir," she said at the appropriate moment, then dragged a heavy thick line through both.

Not that the voice on the other end, Departmental Secretary Carlos Vincente, cared whether she agreed or disagreed. The point was to make a noise whenever Vincente paused for breath. It reassured the man she was paying attention. Gail added a series of squiggles to each end of the line. "Of course, sir."

"I don't think you're listening to me, Dr. Smith."

*Maybe she'd underestimated him.* "Of course I am, Secretary Vincente," Gail said, carefully coaching her voice into something approaching respect. "I've heard every word."

*Not that it had been pleasant hearing.* Gail stared down at the tip of her now-broken stylo. Reinsez had indeed contacted Titan University without her knowledge, consent, or even a reasonable briefing beforehand. As a result of his hysterical prattle, Titan U, in the persona of Secretary Vincente—the voice of power in the Department of Xenological Studies— wasn't pleased. *No*, Gail thought, tossing her stylo into the recycling bin, *not pleased at all.*

"I think we should continue this discussion face-to-face, Dr. Smith. How soon can you be back at Titan University?"

Gail closed her eyes and counted to three. "Secretary Vincente. There is everything to lose and nothing to be gained by interrupting our project before it has properly begun. I will forward a complete, updated report on our present situation— which is, I assure you, quite stable—"

"The esteemed Dr. Reinsez—"

*Can suck vacuum.* "My colleague and I were unfortunately out of communication before he chose to make his preliminary report, Secretary," she said out loud, priding herself on the smoothness of her voice. "Once he has been made aware of all the facts, I'm sure Dr. Reinsez will agree there is no need for concern."

"Your report—and a conversation with Dr. Reinsez— before I leave my office today. Both to be satisfactory, or the *Seeker* is recalled. Titan out."

*His* office. Translight comms allowed him to diminish her, to make it seem as though they were down a hall from one another when reality placed her at the limits of humanity's settled space. The silence in *her* office descended like a blanket. Gail took in one deep breath after another, surprised to find her hands shaking.

She hadn't anticipated Vincente's reaction. *Some face-saving whining about risk factors and being obsessively careful, yes.* But not this threat to her mission. There must be more opposition to her project back on Earth than she'd imagined, perhaps extending right into her own department at Titan. She'd bumped others from the waiting list for the *Seeker*. The Reductionists on the university council had voted against her budget requests—nothing new. They always tried to scuttle more deep-space spending . . .

The *why* didn't matter. What mattered now was cooperation. She had Tobo's—she needed Grant's as well. She was almost sure she would have it. Almost wasn't good enough.

Time was her enemy, speeding forward to when she either had to produce a willing Reinsez and a soothing report of all things nominal . . .

Or take the *Seeker* where Titan couldn't follow or interfere.

In stark contrast, Thromberg had been utterly reasonable. *No, make that utterly desperate,* Gail corrected herself, replaying the earlier conversation through her mind. Station Chief Nateba had tried to bluff—but only briefly. She'd tried to deny the existence of the Outsiders, talking instead about criminals and terrorists from Outward Five—even implying such were responsible for the attack on *Seeker* personnel.

When Gail mentioned Rosalind Fournier was aboard the *Seeker* and that they'd had surveillance 'bots recording the takeover of the station's freighters by 'sider crews, Nateba's bluster had collapsed. Station Admin, it seemed, had become completely, if belatedly, aware that Thromberg was vulnerable to a segment of its population hitherto completely disregarded.

They wanted her help to disarm the 'sider ships. In fact, they demanded Earther protection.

On general principle, Gail had thought it wiser not to remind Nateba that the *Seeker* was merely a research vessel, and her crew was hardly capable of locating and disarming who knew how many locked, guarded, and probably booby-trapped ships' engines before the 'siders could retaliate. Grant's FDs? Maybe they could deal with one ship, one threat. She sincerely doubted his solitary unit could make any difference to the end result, not that Thromberg could know how many troops she had.

So rather than promise protection they couldn't give, Gail had advised the station to take standard collision precautions, while she continued the negotiations interrupted by Nateba's call.

In other words, suit up their residents and close any airtight doors.

Gail chewed her bottom lip savagely. The moment the words had been out, she'd wished them unsaid. *Of course they didn't have enough suits,* she lashed at herself again. *How could they?* She'd done her best to cover the mistake, to head off any panic. The riot they'd witnessed on the docking ring would be nothing compared to what could happen—*what would happen*—if the stationers believed their air was at risk.

She'd promised—Titan U had better not find out how much she'd promised. *Among how many other things Titan shouldn't know?*

*When had things spiraled out of control like this?* Gail dug the heels of her hands into her eyes until she saw spots. *It was the damned station.* Nothing was normal here—nothing went as predicted.

*There's been an incident . . .* her thoughts kept flashing to the lab—the least of her worries and responsibilities. She'd sent Grant to deal with it. *He would.*

Gail stood up, brushing the creases from her tunic. *One problem at a time.* Rosalind Fournier was on the bridge.

Everyone—everything—else would have to wait in line.

# Chapter 35

*EVERYONE was waiting for him*, Pardell realized, taking another throat-searing breath. The air told him the truth immediately—he wasn't on the station or any 'sider ship. This had to be within the *Seeker*.

His eyes adjusted to the lighting; his bared skin ached with it, but he wasn't about to ask for any favors—not until he understood the cost.

Everyone was watching him. Pardell clung to the side of the tub, feeling more than slightly ridiculous. At least being embarrassed helped fight down the fear. He swallowed, pushing back the taste of bile.

Nearest were a matched pair of Earther troops—no, make that a set of four, as two more, identical uniformed figures pounded in through a doorway. No, not identical. One was a woman. Pardell heard an odd sound and looked down. A dark-haired man wearing some kind of fancy suit was propelling himself along the floor in a very undignified fashion. Away from the tank.

There was another sound. He pulled himself up farther and managed to turn to find its source.

Two white-clad figures were standing over a crumpled form. A very large and familiar form. "Get me out of this thing!" Pardell shouted, scrambling desperately. Water—or blue liquid—splashed everywhere as he tried to rise to his knees and climb out, but he couldn't gain purchase on the slippery floor of the tank and fell, cracking his chin painfully on the upper edge.

"Is it safe to handle him?" This plea from one of those near Malley hit Pardell even harder.

He drew himself up again, holding very still this time, as if that might calm those staring at him into making sense. "What's happened to Malley?"

"He touched you."

That was a little more sense than Pardell wanted. "You made him—!" he choked out angrily.

"No!" One of the white-clad figures, an older woman, stood and came close, but not too close, Pardell noted. "We thought you were dead. There was no higher brain function. Your friend said something about trying a defibrillator—then touched you."

*Malley, you idiot!* Pardell swallowed once, then tried to think. "Is he still breathing?" The question should have been impossible to ask, but he heard the words come out of his mouth with a hard clarity that sounded like someone else's voice.

"Yes."

"Irregular—but steady," from the one kneeling beside the stationer's left side.

Relief made the room spin, and Pardell gripped the tank edge until it stopped. He'd knocked Malley out before. The circumstances had been different—*God, they'd been playing around as kids*—but Malley had roused pretty quickly. Once, Raner had been nearby. Pardell struggled to remember what his foster father had done, besides give him the scolding of a lifetime. "Use just one finger," Pardell told them. "Touch any bit of bare skin quickly and lightly. If you don't feel anything like a static charge, you can handle him. Otherwise, you'll have to wait a few minutes."

"No, Philips—" the woman cautioned fearfully, but not in time to stop her partner from following Pardell's advice. With almost comical care, he reached out and just brushed Malley's bare arm with a fingertip, then gave it a firm poke before looking up expectantly.

"Nothing," Philips told Pardell. "We can move him now?"

Pardell nodded and sagged against the side of the tank. "If you have a crane handy," he said dryly, startling chuckles from a few.

*Better that*, he knew, *than letting them stay afraid of him.*

Even if they should be.

# Chapter 35

OF several scenarios Gail had built in her mind on the way to the bridge, she had to admit finding her Captain and the grim leader of the Outsider rebellion sitting in the command chairs, laughing together, hadn't been one of them. She paused in the doorway, making her FD shadows stop at her heels, and considered.

*All in one basket.*

The phrase dropped into her thoughts with the suddenness that marked most of her best, deepest insights. True, it warned against risking everything at once. But, far better, it meant having everything in her hand. *Soon*, Gail promised herself.

"I'm glad the Captain has kept you amused, Rosalind," she said, moving forward as if never having paused. "My apologies for the interruption."

Rosalind's pale cheeks were flushed and her eyes glittered, an animation sweeping years from her face. Gail noticed more than a few appreciative looks. "No apologies necessary, Gail," the 'sider told her with a pleased smile. "Tomoki has been spinning me tales—"

"Tales?" Tobo interjected. "Hardly tales. All true, my dear lady. All true!"

Rosalind arched a brow. "If so, you are remarkably well-preserved for so traveled a pilot, my dear Captain."

Before Tobo could cheerfully continue to protest his dubious innocence—having heard some of his wilder yarns before, Gail could only imagine which he'd decided to tell the 'sider—she said: "I've been contacted by Station Admin," and watched caution wipe away Rosalind's laughter and replace it with serious attention. "They are understandably anxious whether any of your ships remain poised to be detonated against Thromberg. I told them I would seek to obtain your reassurance."

Rosalind stood up, making the simple motion elegant and meaningful. "Did you also speak to your superiors at Titan University and request clearance codes for our ship?"

*Two could play grace.* Gail inclined her head then lifted it. "I requested. They refused. Adamantly. Until the *Seeker* returns with proof there is a way to detect and destroy the Quill, no vessel from outside Sol will be allowed to enter."

They might have been alone on the bridge. Gail waited, knowing Rosalind understood exactly what she was offering. And its price.

The 'sider looked around the bridge, her expression one of hunger, then locked her eyes on Gail's. "I have the codes for the *Merry Mate II*," she said simply.

Just as Gail felt the surge of triumph, an emotion she carefully kept to herself, FD Krenshaw approached from her right, holding out a message slip. "From the commander, Dr. Smith," he informed her as she took it in her hand. "He's waiting for a reply."

Gail read: *Pardell is not only alive, he's awake and appears quite rational. In my opinion, we shouldn't delay questioning him about his ship. Shall I proceed? Grant.*

Gail folded the paper neatly once, then again, and tucked it into her pocket. "Tell the commander to keep watching Mr. Pardell and to notify me immediately of any change in his condition," she told the waiting FD, not surprised when he didn't so much as blink. *Grant's people were good.* "Otherwise, he's to leave the situation as is."

"Young Aaron has not improved?" Rosalind's expression was unreadable.

Gail knew her own face looked properly sympathetic. *Sharing the anxiety of a family member.* It was one of the easier ones, since it masked guilt so well. "I'm told he's in no danger. There's full life support available if he does decline before we are able to revive him." She gazed steadily into Rosalind's icy blue eyes. "Would you like to see him before we go to the *'Mate?* Check over our hospital facilities?"

The 'sider's eyes shifted, as if she were uncomfortable, then came back to hers. She shook her head. "I'm sure your facilities are better than anything else available. If what might help him is on the *'Mate*, we shouldn't waste time obtaining it."

Rosalind paused, then went on with the brutal directness Gail was coming to expect from her. "I choose not to see young Aaron when he is—mindless. His father would care for him during such episodes. I could not."

From anyone else, this would have been a confession of weakness. From this woman, it was a statement of fact, a personal assessment she revealed not as an excuse, but to prevent further well-meaning attempts to put her into a situation where she wasn't qualified or willing to act. Gail's estimation of Rosalind rose, even as she felt for Pardell.

He wouldn't appreciate her pity. He wouldn't appreciate her stealing the family skeletons from his ship either. Gail hardened her heart. Pardell was a test subject . . . an opportunity. Besides, she was saving his life and potentially the lives of everyone on Thromberg. Surely, if he was the man Malley claimed, he'd understand that was more important than maintaining his right to privacy.

As Gail began ordering the preparations necessary to follow Rosalind's directions to Pardell's ship, she hoped he would understand why she hadn't dared wait for his approval.

*She couldn't take the chance he'd refuse.*

Not if Titan was ready to recall the *Seeker*.

# Chapter 37

"**N**O reply." The Earther commander dismissed the messenger, folding the page before putting it in a pocket.

Pardell took another sip of water. It tasted peculiar enough. He wasn't about to try the thick yellow liquid Malley was pouring down his throat. *Typical—Malley treated his body like a dump tank at the best of times.*

Some things stayed the same no matter where you were. But here and now? *Not routine,* rang in the back of Pardell's thoughts like an alarm klaxon.

Malley'd survived his own stupidity. Pardell's mind gratefully skittered away from any other option. He'd survived as well—very well, according to Dr. Lynn. *Not your typical physician*, he thought, still fascinated by the insect life decorating her lab coat and festooning her intricately braided and bound hair. He might have been alarmed, but for her gentleness with the remote handlers when she needed to touch him, and the pleasant sound of her voice.

And Malley seemed to like her.

Right now, the big stationer seemed fully recovered and in his element, performing introductions, pulling up chairs and stools so he and Pardell sat like honored guests, generally acting like someone who'd checked his brain at the door.

*Classic Malley*, Pardell decided, studying his friend without being obvious about it. The message was coming through loud and clear, passed through the subtle, almost unconscious signals they'd developed between them through years of mischief—as well as real peril. *We're in trouble, Aaron. Big trouble. This time it's your fault—I'm expecting you to get us out of it.*

There was more to read from his friend. Malley was

scratched and dented, even more than usual. They'd taken care of him—high-tech, state-of-the-art medicine—*altruism or was Malley worth more to Gail Smith than a means to find her freak 'sider?*

A shudder rocked him and Pardell quickly set down his drink to avoid spilling it. He'd made enough mess of the place getting out of the tank. The techs were still mopping it up.

"Cold?" Malley asked him doubtfully. The stationer was in bare sleeves and sweating.

Pardell, on the other hand, was fully dressed in new clothes, complete with soft gloves. It had been quite the scene, really, Pardell thought as he shook his head in answer. *No, not cold. Not his body anyway.* The Earthers had done exactly the right things to reassure him. They'd focused on Malley, several working together to gently lift the stationer to a portable bed, then bustling around with every move showing professional skill and personal concern. Only one had stayed near Pardell, and that one, Benton was her name, had quickly lowered a side of the tank so he, and quite a bit of liquid, could escape it. The liquid collected in drains on a platform. She'd brought him a stool and a blanket, putting both within reach and stepping back. Soon, there'd been a parade of others offering him a bewildering array of towels and clothing.

They'd mimed how he could bandage himself with flat sheets of plastic. Propped against the stool, Pardell had obeyed, shaking with despair at being naked in front of strangers who stared at his gold-veined body, his freak's skin. He discovered wounds—holes and tears—in inexplicable places, then realized he was repairing damage they'd done while experimenting with him.

He hadn't bothered with anger. For all he knew, they'd saved his life.

*Maybe they'd saved others, getting him off the station.* He refused the thought.

"You in there?"

Pardell glared at Malley. "I wasn't—distracted—if that's what you mean," he said defensively, needing all the dignity he could get. Malley in free-advice mode wasn't helping. "What did Smith have to say?" This to the Earther commander, Grant, who'd returned to his seat on the other side of the low, wheeled table, a table overloaded, in Pardell's opinion, with far too much food for the three of them. Grant and Malley reached for the same pastry simultaneously.

Malley won—or the Earther declined the race for reasons of his own. Pardell watched them both, abruptly close to losing his train of thought just as Malley had suspected. Grant's answer helped him focus down from the concepts of competition, dominance, and alliance. "Dr. Smith is still in conference."

*Not routine.* "I don't care what Dr. Smith is doing," Pardell said, quite impressed by the cold steadiness of his own voice. "Either she—or you—explain why you wanted me here badly enough to start a riot on the station, or Malley and I go back to Thromberg, now."

Grant had a way of looking at a person, the same assessing, careful way Raner had had when he planned to say something difficult but important. It made Pardell's palms sweat. "Mr. Pardell—what do you remember from the riot?"

*Faces, lips drawn back in death, eyes protruding, pulses of* HATE *and* FEAR *throughout his body . . .*

Pardell drew in a shuddering breath and raised his eyes to meet Grant's somber brown gaze. "I—" he started, then the words drifted loose again. "There was—" He couldn't think it, let alone say it.

"What the Earther's getting at, Aaron," Malley growled, his voice low, "is that Thromberg isn't the safest place at the moment. The riot's done—assuming they're telling us the truth. But folks working in the stern ring, well, they—" suddenly, Malley seemed at a loss for words, his face growing unusually flushed.

"Your friend is right, Mr. Pardell," Grant said, leaning forward, eyes intent. "Too many people saw what you can do. Too many are afraid. It wouldn't be safe for you to return to the station—not yet."

Pardell found himself on his feet. "Then give me my suit. I want to go home—to my ship. You can't keep me here."

Grant had stood at the same time. He reached out his hand as if to offer comfort, then curled up his fingers and let the arm drop. The look of sympathy—or was it pity?—on his face froze the blood in Pardell's veins. "Mr. Pardell. Aaron."

"What have you done to my ship?" Pardell said, stumbling away from them all, seeing heads turn as the others working in the lab heard his rising voice. Some began edging toward the doors and he stared at them, unable to fathom why. *Nobody feared him at home.*

"Fins down, Aaron," Malley cautioned, putting himself squarely in front of Pardell, not coincidentally keeping one broad shoulder in Grant's way. "These people don't know you."

"Don't know me?" Pardell shut his mouth over the betraying crack in his own voice. *Don't know me?* he railed to himself instead. *They stripped me and hooked me up to every machine known to medicine and you think they don't know me?*

Malley's haunted eyes told him the stationer understood well enough. "It's just another queue, Aaron," he said, making no sense whatsoever. Pardell blinked.

"You know how things work. We wait our turn for everything," Malley continued, his tone suggesting he explained the obvious. "So we can wait for Her Ladyship Smith. We can wait for things to calm down back home. We can wait—" to his credit, Malley said the next without flinching, "—to get back on your ship. No worse than waiting at Sammie's for a beer." He stretched out his long arm to show Pardell the glass of yellow liquid. "Better stuff, for sure."

"You can't understand," Pardell found himself saying, aware of a larger audience but unable to look beyond these two men. It didn't seem to matter that he'd known one all his life and the other for less than an hour. "If I try to remember—if I think—" Finally, the words shot out: "Did I hurt someone?"

Pardell saw Malley's throat work, as if the stationer tried to swallow. Then he looked at Grant, who nodded slowly.

*. . . eyes protruding . . . convulsions . . .*

"It was worse, wasn't it? I killed someone, didn't I?" Pardell whispered. Malley's face had always been easy to read, especially in the grip of strong emotion. Now it was like looking into a mirror as horror and guilt spread across it. "More than one?" he breathed, knowing the truth of it before the stationer's eyes closed briefly in acquiescence.

He fumbled his way back into the chair. "How many?"

Malley pleaded: "Aaron, no—"

"How many?"

"Eight," Grant told him. "The rest appeared to be stunned. They moved under their own steam after a few minutes."

"Who did I kill?"

"Aaron—"

"Who were they?"

Malley flung himself into a chair that protested such abuse. "Damn you, Aaron," he said in a strange, flat voice. "Fine. Want to torture yourself? Go ahead. They were Inward Four—dock workers, likely—I didn't recognize any faces, if that's what's in your head. They were trying to kill you—remember that part? And almost succeeded."

"I remember." Pardell looked down at his hands, willing them still, *willing them normal.* "I didn't know."

"Know what?" gently, from Grant.

"That I could kill."

"You still can't," Malley disagreed. "Look at you. You're beating yourself up because some fools died while trying to turn you into floor paste. That's about as reasonable as expecting the Quill to care that humans drop dead on their planets . . ." Suddenly, Malley stared at Pardell as if he'd never seen him before. "The Quill. . . ."

Pardell opened his mouth, but before he could argue, Malley leaped to his feet again and loped across the room. From Grant's frown, he wasn't expecting this either. They both started, and several techs shouted, when Malley picked up a clear box from one of the tables and brought it smashing down.

Before Grant could do more than leap to his feet and wave over his guards, Malley was back. *The stationer was wilder-looking than usual,* Pardell thought uneasily.

Malley's right hand now wore a glove studded with a network of fine wires and metal nodes. He thrust it at Pardell before the latter could avoid him.

*Excitement. Desperation.*

Freed of the painful blast of sensation the instant contact was broken, Pardell gasped for air. Spots swam in front of his eyes and his heart, not particularly peaceful to start with, hammered with sickening blows. He threw up what little he'd put in his stomach and hoped it landed on Malley's boots.

Maybe it did, but when Pardell looked up resentfully, he saw Malley busy examining the glove. *As though* nothing *had happened,* Pardell told himself, first in outrage, then in stunned disbelief. *Nothing.*

In fact, rather than any sign of pain, the stationer had that fiercely joyous look on his face—the one he always got when he'd solved some impossible equation or delivered the killing line in a debate.

"It works," the stationer was saying in a hushed voice. "It works."

"What do you mean, it works?" Grant demanded. Pardell thanked him silently, too busy rinsing out his mouth with water Aisha passed him, to do the same. "What's going on here, Malley?" The Earther looked from the stationer to Pardell and back again. "Are you saying what I think you're saying? It can't be—"

Malley seemed impervious, as if his mental gears were whirring out of control. "This was what she wanted with you, Aaron," he said triumphantly. "This—!" He waved the ridiculous-looking glove again.

"You'd better start making sense, Malley," Pardell finally ground out, his stomach still trying to express its displeasure.

Grant held up his hand for silence. His other hand was cupped over the comm in his ear. From the look on his face, the Earther didn't like what he was hearing, Pardell decided.

The stationer wasn't paying attention. "I should have seen it, Aaron—" Malley started to explain, only to stop as Grant backed his demand for silence with the weapon now magically out and in his hand.

"Unfortunately, now isn't the time, gentlemen."

# Chapter 38

*NOW wasn't the time*, Gail fumed. Protocol, regulations—when you were already breaking ninety percent of them, what possible difference could one more make? But Tobo could be incredibly stubborn, and he'd insisted on notifying Thromberg Station's docking controllers of their intention to move the *Seeker.* *Hazard to shipping*. Gail tapped her gloved fingers against the porthole. What shipping? In the wake of the Outsiders' demands, nothing was moving. Nothing dared.

*Where was Grant?*

It had to be done quickly. Rosalind had notified her supporters, but didn't claim to control the majority of those who clung to Thromberg's outer hull. She'd advised speed over caution, to take advantage of confusion and a lack of central authority.

Gail wondered what that said about the 'siders, but agreed. Fast suited her. Any long-range patrol ship from Sol System could outrun the *Seeker.* Her only hope of evading the righteous interference of Titan U was to put the *Seeker* off the map. Of course, her only hope of returning home again without being arrested was to succeed. A little something she didn't plan to share with Tobo, Grant, or the miserable Reinsez until absolutely necessary.

*Where was Grant?*

*There.* Pounding feet as the last of their boarding party climbed the shuttle's ramp, pulling on his suit as he came. Gail made herself relax and nod a greeting, before donning her helmet. Immediately, Grant's voice echoed around her ears—presumably on a private setting between the two of them. "What the hell's going on? And what are *you* doing here?"

Gail wanted to laugh. She'd finally gotten a rise out of the taciturn officer—unfortunately, not at a moment she could enjoy it. "We have an opportunity to retrieve the tapes and other records from the *Merry Mate II*, Commander Grant," she informed him, keeping her voice to "briefing" formality. "Given the instability of the situation out here, I deemed it essential to take that opportunity. Rosalind has been very cooperative—but she'll only work with me."

Silence. *He was probably grinding his teeth*, Gail thought cheerfully. She functioned best when things moved like this, when she rode a current of possibilities and had to pick the optimum course by instinct. It had smacked her into a few walls in the past—but, more often than not, it had taken her to success well before anyone else saw it coming.

They didn't have long to wait, She'd had Tobo relinquish the *Seeker*'s final holds on the station before letting him notify the station of their flight path. They'd suited up as the ship drifted free and began moving along Thromberg's axis with only the most delicate of maneuvering thrusters involved. Gail doubted anyone on the ship not watching the view screen or a monitor even realized the *Seeker* was in motion. It would take a fraction of the time it had taken Pardell to walk the same distance to reach his ship.

*He was alive and conscious.* Sazaad must have wet himself.

"Stand by." The announcement came from the shuttle pilot. There was a clang, and Gail kept hold of the nearest strap, anticipating the minor roughness as the shuttle coasted down its ramp and out of *Seeker*.

Gail checked her gauges, making sure her comm was set to wide open, knowing the others were doing the same. There were eight of them in the shuttle's freight air lock: herself, Grant, Rosalind Fournier, FD Tech Specialists Bennett, Wigg, Cornell, and Sensun, and Ops Specialist Allyn. Grant had chosen his team; Gail had insisted on meeting them and learning their names before entering the air lock. Allyn didn't look to have rested—how could he, given the loss of his entire ops group?—but he was the FDs' surviving expert on null-g operations. The others were new faces to her.

Grant likely considered her both nonessential and too valuable to risk. Gail hadn't allowed debate. She trusted no one else to recognize what she had to find on the 'sider derelict—what had to be there or she'd lost already. Being wrong about this would mean being wrong about many other things—her entire chain of reasoning would crumble.

*More of those details she didn't plan to share beyond Grant and Tobo.*

"In position." The air lock display winked through its paired sequence of reds, ambers, and greens; Grant and his people slipped open the tops of their holsters, the weapons within secured by both tether and mag clamp. Gail stepped to the back, willing to let the FDs do their job. As long as they didn't interfere with hers.

The air lock door slid into its holding position along the hull, revealing their destination.

Gail heard someone swear. She echoed the word to herself.

The vid recorded by the 'bot had lied. It hadn't shown her the reality of Outside.

It was the scale that overwhelmed the senses first. The curve of the station had definition now, its true size plotted against space by rank after rank of toy starships. Gail forced herself to look up and try to find the *'Mate*.

Leaving the *Seeker* a safer distance away, the shuttle floated under the Outsiders' city, a direction Gail's mind wanted to register as down, but her ears insisted was up as long as they were within the shuttle's gravity. The confusion was something she ignored with the ease of practice. After all, she'd spent months in orbit around Titan, watching Saturn loom overhead.

The station had turned this side to its sun, bathing everything in harsh, white light. In contrast, the air lock was suddenly flooded in soft yellow. The null-g warning sounded in their helmets. With the others, Gail reached down and activated the mag on her boots. Small ships—or expensive ones—could afford to run gravity induction systems tagged to their translight drives. Bigger space objects, such as Thromberg herself, relied on their spin to mimic the effect for inhabitants, accepting that only certain levels would have optimum gravity. Among the few early efforts Earth had made on behalf of the overcrowded stations was to provide inducers for those with abundant power sources. On Thromberg, such gifts had opened up the industrial levels to habitation. Outward Five, they'd called it.

Gail doubted those living there were grateful.

She swallowed, adjusting to the familiar sensation of falling in place.

Rosalind's cultured voice sang out in her ear: "The *'Mate*," she said, pointing one prosthetic hand outward. "Between those two large freighters and what's left of the *Aces Adrift* casino. They didn't build liners to last." This an aside, as if Rosalind took the failure of such ships personally. If she was like other engineers of Gail's acquaintance, she probably did.

Gail didn't bother trying to decipher the *'Mate*'s location from the mass of ships leaning this way and that. Others would take her there. She wasn't even to use her own propulsion system. Allyn would ferry them as a unit, including Rosalind—whose patchwork suit lacked the system anyway. She'd rejected an offer of one of their suits, but accepted replacement power packs. Gail wondered if Rosalind wanted to avoid looking like one of them. *Not the most confidence-inspiring notion.*

There was a short discussion about the cables draped like strands of seaweed, or fragments of net, between the ships. Allyn believed they wouldn't be a problem. Gail remembered watching Pardell slide along his cable and hunted for suited figures.

None in sight. That didn't mean there weren't dozens of 'siders lurking in the black shadows of their ships, or waiting inside air lock doors. For the first time, Gail appreciated how impossible a conflict it must have been. How could the stationers have imagined they could dislodge these people? It wasn't a question of having the high ground—it was having the technology and knowledge to survive with no ground at all.

She was startled from her thoughts by hands at her waist. Someone—Grant—was fastening lines to her belt. "Release your boots," rang in her ears. Rather than get out of her way, he bent and did that service for her. Before Gail could protest being treated like luggage, she was pulled from the air lock with the rest of them.

*They weren't dropping like rocks*, she reminded herself,

keeping her eyes open with an effort. Allyn was in the lead, having provided the initial push to get them out of the air lock and moving away from the shuttle. They were beads along a string attached to him; Gail found herself next-to-last. Doubtless, Tobo was watching them on the *Seeker*'s vids as well as the shuttle's.

She counted out the seconds. Five, and past the outermost cable. It glinted dangerously, like a trap set to capture animals much larger than they.

Six, and Allyn had reversed, using his movement away from the rapidly approaching ship hulls to slow them down. It was a fine balance, to dump velocity without dragging them outward. As she twisted helplessly on the string, Gail decided it was far too late to suggest they might have tried practicing this maneuver first. *Besides*, she assured herself, *she was probably the only one here who hadn't tried rocketing down into a maze of decayed starships.*

For a maze it was. The *Aces Adrift* was the only landmark Gail could keep in view, her gaudy exterior still attention-catching even here, decades after her former life transporting gamblers. How she came to be limpeted to Thromberg had to be a story in itself, one Gail doubted she'd ever hear. The ending was written in jagged cracks along every seam that made the *Aces* more like a child's sculpture of a broken egg rather than the proud starship she had once been. Had she shattered when her crew tried to follow the other ships into the station? Or was it, as Rosalind implied, simply that they didn't build longevity into things meant to amuse?

*Nine*, Gail counted to herself. They'd slowed—enough that Gail started to concede their landing might not involve a helmet-smashing thud or a rebound into nothing. They were between hulls now. Two of the FDs had disconnected from the string and were under their own propulsion. Gail could see them touch down and quickly lock their boots to the station plate, then move aside with weapons out.

Somehow, they only looked like targets themselves.

Then, Gail found herself drifting shoulder-first against Thromberg's comforting bulk. She cautiously but quickly released the fastening on her belt, to avoid being dragged into any of the others. Like them, her body began to slowly rise again until she switched on her mags. Her feet, as if they were hands, grabbed the surface and held.

They were encompassed by irregular shadows and irrational tubing. No wonder the cables were used to move any distance. Down at the surface, there was barely room to walk between the writhing mass of wiring and conduits, let alone to navigate the heaved and buckled plates they punctured. From the look of it, Gail suspected the 'siders simply made a new connection whenever an older one failed.

Considering what many of these connections carried to their ships, Gail sincerely hoped none would fail while she stood within reach.

"Follow me." Rosalind's voice was emotionless, as if she could care less about the reaction of Earthers to the reality of Outside. *And why should she?* Gail asked herself, walking with the others toward the smallest of three ships nearby. Earthers had known. The station knew. It hadn't made a difference before—*why would it now?*

The chair appalled Gail beyond all reason. She'd been expecting the interior of the *Merry Mate II* to be like her owner's suit: patched and repaired until nothing original showed, but with the integrity of her function intact.

The chair proved otherwise. Rosalind had claimed it, as the only thing to sit on within the *'Mate*'s bridge. It had been hand-made from scraps of plastic and fabrics, a giant bag without back or armrests, but with a broad lumpy seat that could fit three. *Or one curled up to sleep.* She pictured Aaron Pardell here, surrounded by dark monitors and scavenged panels. Did he pretend his ship could still fly? Was he, like Rosalind, consumed with a spacer's hopes—or was he of a newer generation, focused on surviving here?

One thing Grant's people could tell her after scouting through the *'Mate*: Aaron Pardell had lived here alone.

"Ah." Rosalind made a noncommittal sound. There were a pair of consoles with still-flickering lights: internal systems. She sat before one of those, cross-legged on the chair despite her suit. Grant's people were quietly and carefully checking the rest. Gail thought this very wise. They could end their mission just as easily by assuming a dark panel was a safely dead one. On a larger scale, the *'Mate*'s translight drive and initiation matrix was intact, if out of fuel. Rosalind made no effort to conceal the information that this was one of the ships her people had rigged to use against Thromberg. *Could still use, if she chose.* So they were standing inside a bomb. It didn't seem to make much difference.

They'd taken off their helmets. Grant's people excelled at deadpan, professional faces, but there'd been a few wrinkled noses. Gail had trouble not sneezing. The chill, thin air was breathable, if you spent most of your time in a poorly ventilated machine shop. She occasionally caught a whiff of mold, as though something was growing behind the metal bulkheads. It could have been the damp rags hanging on lines in the main corridor.

Gail stood beside the console, watching Rosalind use her more dexterous left hand on the controls, and tried to ignore the chair. "Are you in?" she asked impatiently, when the 'sider paused.

"I need only enter Raner's codes to access the *'Mate*'s data records," Rosalind replied, her eyes lifting to meet and hold Gail's. "Which I will do, once you tell me what you really want, Dr. Smith. And don't tell me it's anything to do with young Aaron's health—because I doubt you'd go to even half this trouble for one man, no matter how unusual."

*The trouble with extortion*, Gail reminded herself, *was how easily it became predictable.* She had expected something from Rosalind. Hoping it would be complete cooperation would have been naïve.

"I don't deny I'm here for more," Gail admitted without hesitation. "I need to find a planet. Specifically, the planet where Aaron Raner found this ship and the 'unusual' child inside it."

Rosalind's look sharpened, if that were possible. "This would be where you plan to take your ship and find the Quill," she stated, raising one brow sardonically. "What's wrong with all the other so-called contaminated worlds? Why this one?"

Gail felt Grant's attention but didn't acknowledge it. Once

they left Thromberg, she didn't care who knew. *It wouldn't matter.* "Because I have evidence this may be the first world contaminated by the Quill. And because I believe your unusual young man is the only person to have been on such a world and survived."

# Chapter 39

MALLEY stretched until his heels reached the end of the cot. He drew up his knees with a muttered complaint.

*Even* Earther *beds were too short.*

A minor inconvenience, taken in perspective. Aaron was alive. They were both better fed and clothed than either could remember. And they had these nice, private rooms.

*With locks.*

The cot creaked as Malley shifted his bulk around. The room wasn't quite dark—he shouldn't stumble into any of its fixtures if he got up to try pacing again—but it was too small for more than four strides in any one direction.

*Hardly satisfying.*

Neither was not knowing what had set Grant off and landed them in the next-best thing to cells. Had it been the incoming message in the commander's comm—something requiring his presence and so this rather drastic means of keeping things stable until he returned?

*Malley could understand that.*

Or had Gail Smith left orders to keep Aaron in the dark about her research and what it meant to him?

*Not while* he *was around.*

What he wanted most was to talk to Aaron about what had happened with the Earther glove. More precisely, what hadn't happened. Malley flexed the fingers of his right hand, still amazed there'd been no detectable sensation when he'd touched Aaron. His friend had definitely been affected—and furious. But Grant hadn't given him time to explain or apologize. Over Aisha's vehement protests, the FDs had rushed them both out through the doorway leading to the rest of the science sphere, hurrying them each into what appeared to be quarters. Already occupied quarters.

With locks.

Abandoning the social niceties of his odd-cycle upbringing, Malley had gone through everything he could find. Which wasn't much. He vaguely remembered annoying a tech named Cooper—the name was inscribed on several personal articles, as if the man was paranoid about losing things. Cupboards and drawers held clothing suitable for someone of conservative tastes and a smallish frame, along with a collection of vids. *Westerns.* Malley knew better than to watch fiction with big, open skies. Sunsets weren't bad. Starry nights made him queasy.

So when the lights dimmed, for want of anything to do—or break that wasn't Cooper's—he'd lain down and tried to rest.

Aaron was likely doing the same, lying in the dark, wondering what the Earthers were doing.

*Yeah. As if he believed that.* Malley stretched again without thinking and met the wall this time. No, Aaron would be wallowing in guilt. You could talk to him until you ran out of air, but nothing penetrated that thick skull once an idea took hold of it.

Ideas. The stationer winced to remember how he'd been so consumed by his own moment of revelation he hadn't particularly thought how Aaron might react. But it had been so—so amazing! Things were beginning to fit together with that wholeness he loved. The universe, Malley firmly believed, was prepared to be reasonable and make sense—if you knew the questions to ask it.

*Why hadn't the spacers shared their filaments?* They'd been rare as well as prized, but the records were clear: spacers knew you couldn't share or steal someone else's. First come, only served. It had to be because each Quill filament, once used, bonded irreversibly somehow to its host. This was the premise of Gail's protective suits and gloves—that the Quill recognized individual human beings, hypothetically, through that person's genetic makeup.

*What use was that recognition so many years later?* For some reason Gail hadn't shared, she was obviously assuming present-day Quill would also recognize, and be unable to harm, the same or very similar genetic makeup. Did she know something of their life cycle? Had she some evidence? Or was this another of Gail Smith's leaps into the unknown? Malley didn't begin to guess. He did appreciate the only way to find out—until today—had been to put someone in a suit and drop them on a planet of Quill. Which was the part of Gail's intentions he was quite sure Commander Grant knew and supported.

*Why was today different?* Malley put his hands behind his head and looked at the dim outlines of the ceiling. Today, he'd confirmed for himself what else Gail Smith knew—or at least suspected.

Somehow, the malady afflicting a young 'sider named Aaron Pardell had a great deal in common with the Quill.

There was no doubt in his mind. A suit to protect against the Quill had protected him from Aaron. Malley wouldn't be surprised at all to find it wasn't just any genetic disguise she'd installed on her protective suit—it was Aaron's.

*Knowledge that didn't help anything*, in Malley's estimation. The glove hadn't protected Aaron. Maybe the technology could be modified to do so, but helping his friend wasn't a priority for the Earthers. If anything, this gave them the perfect way to control him. The bare rumor of a connection between Aaron and the shadowy menace of the Quill had produced a lynch mob. If the Earther scientists confirmed that connection—well, there wouldn't be any safe place for Aaron, anywhere. And Gail Smith would use that weapon, if she had to . . . she'd do anything to keep Aaron.

*Because*, Malley told himself numbly, *now she had what humanity had been searching for, in vain, since the Quill stole their worlds.*

A test subject.

# Chapter 40

"HOW much longer?"

Gail looked up at Grant, startled out of her concentration on Rosalind's efforts by his low-voiced question. "However long it takes," she answered firmly.

Techs Bennett and Wigg had linked a portable data recorder to the *'Mate*'s antique console and were copying anything and everything Rosalind was coaxing from the ship's surviving computers. They would sort it on the *Seeker*, where they had the equipment to rapidly scan through the decades of entries. But, on the *'Mate*, the process could only move as fast as two things permitted: Rosalind's artificial hands and the levels of encryption within the data storage.

There was more than Gail had expected. The stationer who'd taken on the ship and the responsibility of raising its owner had not been a comp expert, but, according to Rosalind, he'd offered room and board to anyone who was—particularly in the early years, when Raner had been communicating with his uncle and other Earthers. He'd learned what he could, in order to protect his foster son's past.

And he hadn't been the only one. Suddenly, the console flashed red and Rosalind flinched back. "What's this?" she muttered, as if alone. "Another layer. Personal logs, family records. I've never seen . . . damn it." The 'sider turned to stare at Gail, for the first time looking amazed. "These need a gene key."

Gail nodded at Tech Specialist Sensun, who came over to the console, a handful of standard key chips in her hand. "Which one first, Dr. Smith?"

"Witts," Gail said, feeling a deep, expectant breath filling her lungs—despite the used taste of the air. "Susan Witts."

Sensun reached past a suddenly motionless Rosalind to drop the chip into its slot. *A perfect fit, as it should be.* Without explaining why, Gail had made sure Grant's people prepared a variety of gene keys, including those suited to an older ship like this one.

The console's red disappeared and its lights returned to their normal, about to fail, flickering. *Access granted*, Gail said to herself. She hadn't doubted it would be.

"Susan Witts." Rosalind shook her head wonderingly, then narrowed her eyes in speculation. "And you knew, all this time. Why didn't you tell me?" Her voice lowered to a whisper. "Why didn't Aaron?"

Somehow, Gail knew she referred to Raner, not Pardell. "He likely didn't even know, Rosalind. How could he?" As for the younger version—the ship would have accepted his gene key, as owner and descendant. But had Pardell ever had one made? Would he have known to bother?

Without conscious decision, Gail's mind flashed through a sequence of Pardell's face as she'd seen it for herself, as if searching for the answers. Curious and wary, in the bar; furious—at her—during the riot; slack and lifeless, in the lab.

*How much did he know of himself?*

# Chapter 41

*H*E *hadn't known himself.`*
 Pardell sat on the one chair this room offered and knew it was true.

*Freak* didn't begin to describe him.

He knew Malley would throw a pillow at him—more than one or something more substantial—while saying all the imminently practical, sensible things the stationer found defined his sense of right and wrong. Not that Malley was an amoral man. Far from it. But his conscience was definitely of the "what's done, is done" variety.

Pardell couldn't afford that comfort, though he'd have given anything to have Malley near, pillow-tossing or not. A sharp-edged sword needed a scabbard. *He had none*, he thought, gripping his knees with his hand. He was dangerous simply by being.

*He was deadly.*

Malley would doubtless remind him that he'd almost died, too. Irrelevant. A bomb also "died" as it killed. Did that make a bomb less a problem to have around? Less a threat to others? To friends?

He was ashamed to feel relief only strangers had died; the joy of ignorance, doomed to end the moment word spread that so-and-so in Outward Five, or this 'sider, had lost an aunt, or a cousin, or a lover during the riot, and did anyone know what had happened? It was a large station—not a limitless one. Eventually, the chain of who-knew-who would link itself from death's face to those with tears in their eyes and hate in their hearts as they looked at him.

The bridge of the *'Mate* wouldn't be far enough.

He'd hoped the *Seeker* would be his way to a better life. *Now*, Pardell told himself, *cooperating with this Dr. Smith was his only chance to survive.*

But it wasn't Malley's.

Funny how the universe continually bent itself into the most inconvenient shape possible for all concerned. Pardell knew he could walk off this ship now. *The locked door?* No barrier—not with what was in the room for him to use. *The guards?* Grab a suit, find an air lock, and he could vanish Outside before the Earthers strapped on their fancy boots. *His body?* The scientist/physician, Dr. Lynn, had insisted on an uncomfortably thorough physical—using remote handling arms—before letting him walk around. She'd found him in good health by any standard, let alone for someone who'd been brain-dead hours before.

Pardell could leave—but he had nowhere else to go.

Malley, on the other hand, had family, work, and friends waiting—every imaginable reason to leave the *Seeker* and none to stay. But Pardell was quite sure Gail Smith knew locked doors or guards weren't what imprisoned the stationer on her ship. Pardell himself still found it incredible that Malley'd made it through the air lock and into the *Seeker* on his own.

*Which didn't change things.* Malley had to get off this ship and back home. If the Earthers wouldn't help him—if Gail Smith wouldn't make it possible because she had plans for the stationer as well—then it was up to him.

Pardell had to smile at himself. Here he was, sitting in the near dark—once he'd found out the quarters belonged to someone, a woman named O'Shay, he'd been unable to bring himself to lie down on her bed—planning and plotting to outdo the Earthers with their uniforms and clean, shiny ship.

*No one could say he didn't dream big.*

# Chapter 42

HER dreams had always been big—Sol-wide, her dad used to say fondly. Gail knew herself fortunate her parents had seen nothing wrong in the breadth of her ambitions even as a child. Perhaps they knew some problems required those who dreamed on a grand scale. *Otherwise*, she reminded herself, *you failed to have the correct perspective.*

She judged Rosalind Fournier to be another such dreamer. The 'sider would hold Gail to her promise to either prove the existence of the Quill or provide safe passage for her companions' ships into Sol System. *Well enough.* Gail wanted both.

"We're almost done, Commander," Wigg announced. "Just a few more—what was that?"

"That" was a jolt along the floor of the bridge. They all grabbed their helmets and dogged them tight, an automatic response, then Grant called to the FDs he'd left guarding the air lock, not bothering to keep it to private mode: "Cornell. Allyn. What's going on down there?"

Wigg and Bennett had returned to retrieving the data, packing filled cubes into the pockets running down each side of their suits as quickly as the machine disgorged them. Tellingly, Rosalind was on her feet, her face, lit from below, clearly startled. *So this wasn't part of her plan*—a conclusion Grant must have reached on his own, since he had his back to the 'sider. The remaining FD, Sensun, pointedly did not.

Another jolt, this time accompanied by a fluctuation in the gravity. Any objects jarred loose gained a trajectory only to crash back on the nearest surface almost immediately. Gail did as the others and turned on her mags to reinforce her grip on the floor.

A voice in her ear made its report. "We're trapped, Commander. It was necessary to secure the air lock from within. There's a superior, organized force surrounding the ship."

Gail didn't like the sound of any of that. "Is there another functional air lock other than the one below?" she asked Rosalind. "A backup—or emergency pod?"

The 'sider had regained her composure and now seemed amused by Gail's question. "Just the one. As for backups? Pods? Dual systems? Around here, those are commodities, Earther. Raner scrapped anything removable long ago."

Grant had switched to private mode—doubtless obtaining specific information from the two in the air lock as well as communicating with the rest of his unit on the *Seeker*. The jolts didn't abate, but didn't seem to further affect the gravity or power systems. Yet.

*She hated being useless.*

"Everything's transferred, Dr. Smith," Bennett reported, shutting down the machine they'd brought.

"You're sure?" Gail asked. "There's nothing left in the system—nothing we could have missed."

Wigg's voice was confident. "We have it all. Guaranteed."

Gail motioned to the console. "Then make sure we're the only ones who do."

Wigg and Bennett began tearing the console apart, rapidly and methodically, collecting specific components in a pile on the floor. When they indicated they were done, Sensun pulled out a weapon that had nothing in common with the tranks the FD usually carried and fired at close range. The white-hot beam of energy melted the components into a glowing orelike lump.

Rosalind had stood to one side, watching all of this, her body easily adjusting to the jolts now shivering through the floor every few seconds. Seen through the helmet, her face was impassive, almost detached.

Gail could wear that expression at will and wasn't fooled. Rosalind was furious. *At the attack, or at what Gail had ordered?* After all, they hadn't just stolen Aaron Pardell's past—they'd destroyed part of it.

The gravity went again, long enough to make her stomach

lurch in response. Luckily, the white-hot slag had welded itself to the floor and wasn't going anywhere on its own.

"Dr. Smith." It was Grant, on private. Gail looked at the figure she assumed was him, getting a nod of confirmation. The suits restored the illusion that all the FDs were identical, especially as they'd switched off their interior lighting.

"What's our situation, Commander?"

"I liked the odds on the docking ring better."

*Impossible*, Gail thought numbly, *not now, when we're so close* . . . "Just as well I don't gamble," she told him, matching his cool tone. "Who's out there?"

"Who?" It wasn't possible to shrug and be seen in a suit, but Grant's voice managed to convey the same effect. "No way of telling—not by us. The stationers' equipment is only marginally better than what we've seen on our friends here." She knew he meant Rosalind. "Numbers? Uncertain or changing. Cornell estimated twenty-five swarming around and on the hull before he and Allyn ducked for cover. The three 'bots sent out by *Seeker* found another fifty to a hundred, then were destroyed. We're down to relying on the shuttle's vids until the shop preps more 'bots for vacuum. Tobo's rotating to bring the *Seeker*'s highest gain lenses our way, but he can't bring the ship any closer. Cornell did see a couple carrying homemade launchers. We don't want them throwing anything at the *Seeker*."

Gail chinned her comm to open. "You've rigged this ship as one of your bombs, Rosalind. Do we have to worry about it going off if they keep this up?" A timely jolt underscored her words.

Rosalind tapped her helmet. "Voice code activation. Mine or that of a colleague on—one—of our new ships. Otherwise, the matrix is harmless."

*While Rosalind was not.* Gail knew Grant got the message. She imagined his techs were already figuring out how to block such signals from reaching their destinations. Their job. There were more immediate problems.

"Have you tried contacting whoever's out there?" Grant's answer was lost in a scream of metal as the floor abruptly shifted several degrees off horizontal. The mags kept them from sliding along with Bennett's equipment and the appalling chair, but at the cost of having them all lurch off-balance. "What are they doing?" Gail demanded.

Rosalind answered, her voice ice-cold and calm. "What they have done in the past. They are trying to rip the *'Mate* loose from the station. First, they sever the holdfasts and cables. This is what we are feeling. Once those are gone, they will weld launchers to every reachable surface. Only then will they attempt to cut through the live umbilicals.

"That's when we usually lose most of the fools—and when we go out to defend ourselves."

*She was reliving their wars, for wars they must have been*, Gail realized, her heart thudding heavily in her chest. So it had been battle damage as well as decay marring these ships. Gail could replay all she had seen and understand it now. The *Aces Adrift* hadn't quietly succumbed to age or structural flaws—she'd been torn apart by stationers using launchers to try to pull her from the station.

"If it's Thromberg, we can talk to them. Grant, get a link through to Nateba—"

Rosalind's eyes had lost nothing of their power, shining fiercely in the reddish glow within her helmet. "You are dealing with Outward Five now," she told them. "Station Admin has no control over them."

Gail knew someone who did. "Get Malley on the comm," she ordered, managing to ignore the little voice in her head that knew how very much the stationer was going to enjoy this.

*Almost.*

# Chapter 43

IF Malley'd ever had a better start to his day, he couldn't remember when.

"So Gail wants to talk to me," he repeated. "Right now. Can't wait. Her Ladyship herself."

"Yes, Mr. Malley. It's urgent."

He leaned back against the pillows and contemplated the now-flushed face of the FD—Taggart, it was—holding out a handheld comm. "How urgent?"

"Very—"

There was a squawk from the comm he could almost decipher. "That urgent?" he surmised, smile widening.

"Their lives are threatened, Mr. Malley," Taggart said and practically threw the comm at Malley. "I'll ask you to cooperate now, sir, or you'll come with me to the bridge." The man's voice had developed a distinctly menacing edge.

Malley cupped the device in one hand. *The bridge?* Where they doubtless had some obscenely large view of space on display? Not to mention passing through that hellish tunnel? "I'll cooperate."

"Malley!"

No mistaking that voice, even through what sounded like an inferior signal transfer—*or* the stationer decided for no reason, *through some minimal attempts to jam the transmission.* "The one and only, Gail. Miss me?"

"Listen," she demanded. "We're on your friend's ship, the *Merry Mate II*. It's under attack."

*Been busy again, haven't you?* Malley rolled to sit up on the cot and stared at the tiny device. "Who took you there?" he demanded. "Did you make Aaron—?"

"No." Flat, definite, and convincing. Malley sagged in relief, then sat up in outrage again. *Rosalind!* She was the only one Aaron trusted with his codes. Several things became more than clear. Malley looked around for something to throw. Something large.

"You gave one of our comms to your friends, Malley," Gail had continued, her voice cool enough, but rapid-fire. "Rosalind thinks those attacking the ship—and us—might be from Outward Five. Is there anyone you can contact? Someone with authority there who can stop them?"

He didn't deny it. *Waste not, want not,* was prime stationer thinking. "I'll do my best—but why are they attacking at all? And what makes her think it's stationers?" Malley swallowed his pride and admitted: "A lot are like me—they don't like it Outside. And there aren't many intact suits left. The 'siders have been trading—or stealing—parts for years."

"Since you are in a better position to answer those questions than I, Mr. Malley," Gail responded with a more familiar bite, "I suggest you start calling. Before your 'friends' turn the *'Mate* and us into a debris field around the station."

"So glad you need me," he rumbled back at her before thumbing the link closed.

Once he had, Malley noticed Taggart waiting by the open door. "I'll need to talk to Aaron—the other one from the station—about this," he told the FD. "He'll know who might be involved. You heard the lady. It's urgent."

# Chapter 44

HOWEVER urgent the reason, it was good to be out of the dark room and back in the lab. The doors were just as locked, but the big, busy room didn't feel much like a brig. Aisha had been delighted to see them, although the Earther guard had kept away anyone else, keeping the two from Thromberg in a corner. *A shame*, thought Pardell, *the reason for their most recent liberation was the destruction of his home*.

He counted to one hundred and one under his breath, tapping a finger surreptitiously against one thigh. Malley hated it when he was compulsive, but right now, the old habit was all Pardell could claim as his own.

"Rosalind has the right to let the Earthers on board," he'd told the indignant Malley, along with other not-quites like: "I wasn't planning to go back to the 'Mate regardless," and "I don't care what happens to her." *The ship—or Rosalind? Or the Earther?* He was confused himself which *her* he meant.

Malley likely bought it all. Easy to convince him about disliking the 'Mate. He'd been on board only once, that horrific day he'd lost his mother and been forced Outside. Suffice it to say the 'Mate held no good memories for the stationer.

She held those and everything else for Pardell. Now the 'Mate was lost to him—*Danger, Damage, Thieves!*—Pardell's insides churned with grief. His ship was more than home and shelter. She'd been a companion and mother, confidant and playmate. If he imagined how the ship might feel in return, he grew almost paralyzed.

He understood the method of attack—better than Malley. They'd tear the 'Mate apart, if allowed. That's what the launchers did. There was no science or plan when attackers welded them on and set them off, no matter how they claimed to be trying to peacefully remove squatters. Ships cracked and their human insides spilled out, scrambling for shelter in other ships, or crawling into the station to beg for air.

He'd miss Raner's teaching vids the most—*who'd have thought it?* Dry things—a self-conscious man doing his best to provide an education for his son. And his readers. Probably the Earthers had the same titles and thousands more, but not the ones he'd held until his hands cramped, until his eyes throbbed, Until . . .

"Aaron. Stay in the here and now, if you please. We have a situation to deal with—remember?" Malley, seeming satisfied by Pardell's look upward that he had his attention, waved the comm device in the air. "I gave one of these to Syd. But we need to tell him who'd be in range of your ship. The nearest section, at least. It's the late end of odd-cycle night. Who are we likely dealing with?"

"In other words, who wants me dead?"

Malley's face tried to restructure itself into denial and failed. Instead, his friend's broad mouth turned down at the ends, and he gave a sigh like a bellows emptying. "Fine. Who wants you dead? Although I was hoping we could stick to guessing who'd want Her Ladyship cast adrift for a few days."

"Her Ladyship?"

"Gail. Gail Smith. The Earther behind all this mess? The woman who causes trouble just by breathing? The plague—?"

"Then why'd you kiss her?" Pardell asked.

*Wonders*, Malley actually blushed. "Who told you about that?"

Pardell's eyebrows shot up involuntarily. "You mean you did?"

"Listen," Malley started to say, then rubbed one hand over his face. "Forget it. What can we do from here to help them out? Who can we reach—?"

*Who cares?* Pardell thought, but didn't say it out loud. Regardless if something was or wasn't going on between Malley and Dr. Smith, past experience had taught him the pointlessness of expressing an opinion about any female Malley found enticing. *And there was always*, he remembered with unexpected amusement, *at least one.*

"The nearest access point to the *Merry Mate II*," he told his friend, "is E49."

Malley's expression was all he could have wished. "You're kidding."

"Would I joke at a time like this? About something so important?"

"That's the closest 'lock to Sammie's. You never use that one. All these years, you've made me hike a quarter spin around Outward Five with you. No matter how drunk or how late or how many were chasing us—and you lived right there!"

Pardell shrugged nonchalantly. "Makes sense, don't you think?"

"Only to a paranoid 'sider," Malley said with a growl. "Okay. So Sammie should know what's going on—if anyone does." He held up the comm as if to use it, then paused, glaring at Pardell. "Right there, huh? All this time."

Pardell gave his most innocent look.

The clarity of the voices, all of them, impressed Pardell—the present conversation didn't. He stood as close to Malley's shoulder as he dared, out of habit knowing to allow space for the bigger man to swing his arms when exasperated. Malley never had figured out how much useful air that took from a room.

The stationer had also failed to calculate just how drunk their friends might be at this hour. "Syd, just get to the bar and pass this over to Sammie, okay?"

"Hi, Malley!" Syd said happily, and for the third time, shouting to be heard over that dull, familiar, background roar. "How'sss tings—thhh-ings?"

It might have been funny, except that lives hung in the balance. The Earthers had set up a more powerful comm system on one of the lab benches, not wanting to risk a smaller unit being jammed. *Given the amount of attention the receiver of the signal was paying to its content*, Pardell thought almost hysterically, *the extra power hardly made any difference.*

"SAMMIE. NOW."

*Well, there was the bellow into the pickup grille approach.*
The Earther helping them, Taggart, winced with Pardell.

"You don't have to shout, Malley," Syd said with the abused dignity of the truly soused. There were some indeterminate sounds, including a curse or two and what might have been a chair breaking, then a new voice.

"Malley?"

"Tanya," a word spoken with complete relief "We're okay," Malley said quickly and urgently. "Aaron, too. But I need to talk to your grandfather."

A rustle overlaid the drone of voices and clink of mugs. Pardell could almost see Tanya turning from the crowd— waving an apology to those howling at being abandoned—then edging past the other bartenders until she was against the back wall. "He's not here tonight," breathless and low. "He and the older ones had a meeting. I don't know when he'll be back."

"Ask her. What was the meeting about?" Pardell whispered, feeling suddenly cold inside. "Was it about me?"

Malley made a shushing gesture with one hand. "Tanya. What were they talking about—do you know?"

"Where are you? On the Earther's ship—the way Syd's been saying?"

"Yes. Now about you—"

"Is Aaron there?"

When Pardell would have answered, Malley repeated his gesture to silence him. "He's on the ship, but not right here," Malley lied easily. "Should I get him?"

Then Pardell lost any urge to speak as Tanya said in a low, distressed voice: "No. Don't get him. But it's good he's on the ship with you. That's really good, Malley. You keep him there, okay? There's bad things running the halls about him—things people here, who grew up with Aaron, don't believe. You have to tell him that."

"I will," Malley said in a strangled voice. "But I need to know what kinds of things, Tanya. How serious is it? The man wants to get home eventually."

She didn't answer for so long, Pardell wondered if their link had been severed. He looked over at Taggart, who was monitoring the equipment. The Earther shrugged and nodded, as if to say everything was still okay.

"What are they saying, Tanya?" Malley repeated.

"That Aaron killed some stationers for the Earthers. That he's got some kind of power. Power like the—"

"Like what?"

"Like the Quill. It's foolish stuff. The kind that rattles around here when there's nothing better to talk about. No one believes it."

"Are Sammie and the older ones talking, Tanya? Or are they *doing* something?"

Pardell shaped the word *No* with his lips. *Don't ask*, he begged silently, too late. *I can't hear this.*

*Don't answer it.*

"Aaron's with you for sure, Malley? On the Earther ship?" Anxiety in her voice now. No denying it. "There was word he'd come back to his own—Outside. People started acting crazy, Malley."

"Aaron's sleeping in the next room," Malley told her in so calm, so friendly a voice, only the cords standing out on his neck betrayed the effort it took to keep it that way. "They're taking good care of us both. Prime stuff, all the way. Real orange juice."

"Thank God." That break in the words. She was crying now.

"So Sammie and the others—which others, Tanya?"

"All sorts. Immies. Stationers. Some 'siders. They needed a bigger place to meet—Sylvie grabbed her extra sweater. It's cold in the aft—" her voice faded.

"Docking ring," Malley said, words falling like rocks now. "They've gone after Aaron's ship, haven't they? That's why Syd's drunk himself stiff—he couldn't bear to think our own would turn on Aaron like that."

Sobbing now. Tanya never cried. *Heaven knew what the rest at the bar would think at the sight.* "Malley—I tried to stop them. They don't think Aaron's in control of it any more. They're—afraid."

"Listen to me, Tanya," Malley said "You get there—or send someone reliable. Those are Earthers on Aaron's ship right now. They've gone to get his stuff, hear me? If anything happens to them, you know Earth is going to send troops in—they'll want heads bagged and ready to go. You get the word to them that Aaron's here and staying here. Where he's safe from his friends." This last with a bitterness that made Pardell close his eyes briefly.

"I'll do it, Malley. But you're wrong about his friends. Tell Aaron," her voice choked, then went on: "Tell Aaron his friends stayed here. All of us. We know what he is—and it isn't what they say. Syd and the rest, they told us it wasn't Aaron's fault. Those out there—they're parents and parents' parents. They want to protect us. They've been doing it so long now, they don't know what to protect us from anymore. Tell Aaron that, Malley. Make him understand it, if you can. Please."

"I'm not sure I do, but I'll try. You keep the comm, Tanya," Malley said gruffly. "Damn Syd can't hold his beer at the best of times. I don't know when I'll be back your way. But I will."

At Malley's signal, Taggart switched off the unit and the sounds of Sammie's Tavern were gone.

Pardell listened to imaginary echoes; it was easy in the complete silence surrounding him. Without looking up, he turned and walked away.

He didn't know what his face showed.

He did know he didn't want anyone, even Malley, to see it.

# Chapter 45

"STATIONERS and immies with 'sider help. That's a new one," Rosalind pronounced, the curl of her lip and disdainful tone suggesting this wasn't a development she personally favored in the least. "You do have a talent for stirring the pot, don't you?"

"I'd say your spoon was in this one as well," Gail retorted.

They were still in the *Merry Mate II*, but Grant had moved them into the air lock—tight quarters, but the sturdiest available. Most likely, he also wanted them close to the only exit. They'd had a terse report from one of Grant's people. Malley had succeeded in contacting the station and identifying those outside. It remained to be proved if he'd accomplished more than that.

Still, the ship had been quiet for several minutes. When Gail had ventured this was a positive sign, Rosalind had reminded her about the launchers and how the stationers were likely welding the small rocket packs all over the hull. Quietly.

*Ironic*, Gail told herself. To come so far, with all the latest technology at her disposal, only to be stopped in her tracks by the very people her success would help most. She supposed it was her own hubris, not to have laid all her cards out in front of the station, to assume she could breeze through here, grab what she needed, and leave.

*A strategy that had always worked nicely in Sol System.*

The comm link activated. From the slight distortion, it was from *Seeker*.

"I want to talk to Dr. Smith, please."

The voice was male, but unfamiliar. She didn't know all of Grant's people. "This is Dr. Smith."

An odd pause, as if the other person was checking something, or hesitating. "Yes," Gail prompted. "What is it? Do you have any word on Malley yet? Was he able to talk some sense into these people?"

"Can Rosalind Fournier hear me, too?"

*Oh, no*, Gail thought, feeling the blood draining from her face and hands. *It's Aaron Pardell. Who'd authorized him—?*

"Yes. This is an open signal, young Aaron," Rosalind's voice came through Gail's helmet. She couldn't see her, or anyone but Grant and Bennett from her position, squeezed at the rear of the *'Mate*'s airlock. "I am pleased you are—back."

"You let them on my ship, Rosalind." His statement wasn't quite an accusation. There was a note of puzzlement, Gail decided, as if Pardell groped for understanding rather than condemned. "You gave them my codes."

"You were unconscious, young Aaron," Rosalind informed him, the truth as she knew it. Then her voice acquired a sharper note: "Or were you?"

"It doesn't matter," he said, to Gail's surprise.

"Can we open the air lock without being attacked?" Grant asked impatiently, obviously not caring who gave them the good news.

"I want my things."

"We have all of your ship's data, including personal logs," Gail said quickly. *He couldn't mean the rags hanging in the corridors.*

"What personal logs? Rosalind? What is she talking about?"

"A layer of encrypted records that predate Raner's, young Aaron. From your family. The Earthers knew it was here."

"We don't have time for this," Grant muttered. Louder: "Pardell. You can discuss anything you like with Dr. Smith once we're back on the *Seeker*. Is it safe to go outside or not?"

The calm, gentle voice seemed impervious to the commander's parade-ground snap. "Rosalind? Show them where to find the readers from my cabin. And Myriam's sketches. There are some things in my trunk. Just bring it all. And don't forget the *'Mate*'s certification. It should come off the wall pretty easily. I'd like to keep that."

Gail could see Grant's face inside his helmet and it looked apoplectic. "Mr. Pardell," she began, unsure if the 'sider was taking some bizarre revenge on her or had left some of his brains in the tank—but quite sure she was going to talk to Tobo about who'd let Pardell take over this comm link. *When she was back on board.* "This is Dr. Smith. We'd like to bring your things, but this is an emergency situation. There simply isn't time—"

"I'm not crazy, Dr. Smith, You see, that's my life you're going to pack up for me. I think it's only fair, considering you're the one who made it impossible for me to continue living it. And there's plenty of time." The gentle voice became even softer, but somehow Gail felt a chill running down her spine, as though each word was an icy finger. "Anyone can leave the *'Mate* without harm, as long as it isn't me. You've made sure of that, Dr. Smith. Those outside the ship—stationer, immie, 'sider— they're going to wait and see. They need to be absolutely sure Malley told them the truth, that I'm leaving with you.

"You wanted me, Dr. Smith," Pardell's voice continued. "By making sure no one else does—you've got me.

"And don't forget my socks. They should be dry by now."

A rough estimate? She'd been in the shower stall twenty minutes—about a quarter of the time it had taken to scour every conceivable personal belonging of Mr. Aaron Pardell out of its cupboard, box, and corner, everything tossed into bags or tied in bundles, then ferried through the ship's dank, dark corridors to the air lock. The seemingly-permanent, fifteen-degree list of the *'Mate* hadn't helped.

Gail wasn't going to begin to guess how many trips she'd made herself. She had blisters on both feet from her mag boots.

Rosalind hadn't touched anything, simply led the way through the dying ship, pointing the paddles of her right hand toward this or that. *Garbage, all of it.* Gail could have replaced everything with brand-new equivalents from the *Seeker*'s storeroom. *Especially the socks.*

She sat in the corner of the stall, water beating on her knees and the back of her head, unable to understand why she had blisters on her feet.

Her motives were always crystal clear. Gail prided herself on self-knowledge, of admitting to herself anything and everything that might affect her goals and how she went after them. Of all the tools at her fingertips, she valued her own mind and its honesty above all.

*So why hadn't she just lied to Pardell?* He wouldn't have known until they were back on the *Seeker*; too late then for more than a recrimination or two. She'd taken worse from people far closer and far more powerful and never . . .

. . . hidden in a bathroom.

*People hadn't died before.*

Gail lifted her face, closing her eyes and mouth as water pounded against them, breathing through her nose. She was tired, that was all. Add the relief of being underway—of leaving that hellhole . . .

*Where people had died because of choices she'd made.*

The glory of being the Salvation of Humanity, of being remembered as Gail Veronika Ashton Smith, Destroyer of the Quill, of showing Titan University and all its doubters she'd been right all along . . . none of it was worth the price. It wasn't worth those who'd died.

*It wasn't worth Pardell's rotten little ship.*

Oh, yes. They'd destroyed it. She hadn't watched, but the report came from the bridge. She'd known they would. After the last trip with Pardell's things, each time having someone peer into their lighted helmets and poke any body-sized package, suited figures had swarmed over the *Merry Mate II*, attaching their launchers, getting set to pluck the starship from Thromberg like a sliver from a festering wound.

Her bottom was getting sore. Not to mention her skin was becoming almost as swollen and wrinkled as Reinsez's. Gail couldn't make herself move, not when outside the bathroom waited the consequences of her actions.

*And those who had to face them with her.*

Was that it? Was she afraid if they knew the truth, there'd be a mutiny?

Once the shuttle was safely inside, Captain Tobo had sent the *Seeker* soaring away from Thromberg, then put First Officer Szpindel at the helm for the night shift. It was as if Tobo could finally believe things were back to normal and could relinquish command. Neither had questioned the sealed course she'd provided, based on information peeled effortlessly from the 'Mate's stolen records by the redoubtable Bennett and Wigg, information now locked in her office safe. Tobo because he would know what was inside—Szpindel because he didn't.

Grant hadn't said a word, beyond commands to his on-shift second, Tau, to have Rosalind Fournier settled comfortably and under constant surveillance. Gail had no doubts the commander immediately went to listen to all incoming and outgoing messages. Would he contact his superiors once he found out she was disobeying Secretary Vincente, or would the military's chain of command hold?

*How long a rope would Grant give her to hang herself?*

The rest of the ship? The crew obeyed orders and spent leisure time in the rec facilities; the science sphere bubbled with excitement that likely wouldn't be affected by her bending or even breaking Vincente's nose. She hadn't picked rule followers.

Her new guests? Rosalind had gone peacefully to her new quarters, although the *Seeker* didn't pick up her colleague as promised. Technically, their arrangement had been to transport Rosalind and one other 'sider. With Aaron Pardell conscious, that's just what they were doing.

Gail fumbled for the faucet and turned off the water, but didn't get up. Had anyone told Malley they'd left the station— that the *Seeker* had gone translight? Probably not. When they did—*when she did*—better have tranks at the ready. Would it matter to Malley that she was glad he was still on board? That they needed him?

Pardell.

*What was he?*

She had to tell him. What she knew . . . what she guessed . . . what she hoped.

What she knew—Gail pressed her forehead against the damp, chilled skin of her knees, squeezing her eyes shut. They'd had no trouble finding the coordinates of the planet—it even had a name, *Pardell's World*, one of those excruciating ironies the universe so enjoyed.

She knew too many names.

*Jer and Gabby.*

Oh, she'd worried about her reputation—fancied herself clever in how she'd save it, known herself in charge, congratulated herself on her secrets . . . until Gail had watched these two bring their child into the light of day and die doing it.

Gooseflesh spread up her arms as water evaporated. *What could she possibly say to their son?*

Gail staggered to her feet and out of the stall, not bothering to dry off. She had to go to Pardell. Whatever she told him . . .

*Destroying the Quill had better be worth the look in his eyes.*

# Chapter 46

$W$HATEVER the Earther wanted from him, it couldn't be worth this. Pardell wished he could be like Malley, and relieve his rage by throwing whatever was handiest into a wall. Instead, he smothered it and unpacked his things with exceptional care. He sorted the broken to one side of the bed for mending—they'd been careful, but many of his belongings were too old or fragile for much handling. Whatever remained whole he tucked into the array of closets and drawers he was now supposed to call his own.

*His own.* All he could call his was gone. Even his past. The Earther, Gail Smith, had not only taken it—she'd dared impose a schedule for its return, slotted a time between upcoming tests for him to view what his parents had left behind, like some contraband entertainment vid Sammie might run late in a cycle and charge admission to see.

Pardell stared at the shabby chess set in his trembling hand, made himself recognize it, remember the games he'd played with Raner—with himself. He found space for it in an upper drawer, behind his carefully rolled socks.

A soft knock on the door made him jump. The sounds were all unfamiliar here, on this new ship. Fewer echoes, longer vibrations. He was almost distracted into contemplations of architecture and interference zones, but the knock repeated, as softly, but insistent.

Probably a tech, come to get him ready for the Earther's experiments. *Odd, to come in the dead of ship's night.* Pardell shivered but went resolutely enough to open the door. He'd given his word—

Only it wasn't a tech at the door. It was Gail Smith.

*Come to see what she'd done?* Pardell glared down at her, speechless. At first, he was simply so choked with fury he couldn't begin to sort out which accusation to spew into her face, then, abruptly, he realized this was no ordinary visit. He couldn't imagine what to say to this apparition.

The Earther was alone. And wet. Her hair dripped water on the floor and over her bare feet, as though she'd just come from a tank, too. She wore some kind of robe over shapeless pink trousers. Her face bore the strangest expression—not really an expression at all, he decided, but a state, as if a soul-deep weariness bruised her eyes and hollowed her cheeks. *Perhaps*, Pardell conjectured to himself almost wildly, *she'd come to apologize.* If so, likely she'd planned the conversation as carefully as everything else she appeared to do. Even her disheveled appearance could be a ruse.

*Perhaps.*

Here and now, he couldn't bear to hear anything about the *'Mate*, least of all from her. "Dr. Smith," Pardell began. "I—I wanted to thank you for . . ." he groped vaguely at the cabin behind him, saying anything that came to mind, ". . . for saving my things. And for giving me—Malley and me—quarters on your ship. And the medical care. I appreciate all your staff did for me. For us." *Was she listening?* Her face didn't change—but Pardell felt more confident with each sentence, as though the courtesies built a protective wall between them.

"We aren't freeloaders," he went on, picking plain, clear words. "I know what you want from me—Malley's told me some of it. Dr. Lynn, too. I'll help you as I can, for what good it does. Whatever it takes to earn my keep and Malley's." Pardell didn't bother adding what they both knew: he'd be paying his way with what he was, not what he could do. *As if they'd need a 'sider's skills on a perfect ship like this*, he reminded himself bitterly.

Gail still didn't speak. Instead, she took a step forward, the toes of her small foot coming to rest on the softer, warm-colored flooring of his Earther quarters as if asking his permission to enter. Pardell stepped back in a reflex to put more space between them, inadvertently giving her room to come in another step.

"These are yours," she said at last, holding out a small bag he hadn't noticed until now. "There's a reader inside, or you can use the room's console." Her voice was low and feathered, as if she'd only just regained her breath.

Pardell took it, cautiously, in case her fingers moved unexpectedly and came too close to his, From the feel, it was full of data cubes and he didn't have to ask what they were. *Or whose.* The records from the *'Mate.* "A little schedule change, Professor?" he snapped, the flare of his anger so swift and sudden he shook with it. "I thought it wasn't my turn to see these until tomorrow."

"I've seen all I need to see, Mr. Pardell," she said quietly. "What I came to find—it was there, and I thank you. They're yours, now."

"Mine." *What was the matter with her?* Pardell studied her face, his anger not fading but now joined by growing suspicion. "What's on these?" he demanded. "Why are you giving them to me like this?"

"Do you want me to tell you?" she asked. "I will, if that's what you wish."

It was like having all the gauges on his suit flare red at once. "Was I—made?" he shot at her. "Am I a monster? Is that what's on these, Dr. Smith? Proof I'm a freak?"

He watched Gail put one hand on the doorframe, as if for support. "It shows your birth," she said evenly. "It shows how your parents were killed almost immediately afterward—by the Quill—but not before your father was able to save you. He put you into the *'Mate*'s shuttle, which I have to assume returned on auto and docked with the ship in orbit." Her voice stopped, then continued. "The rest . . . ? Family records, accounts, cargo logs, personal things. I didn't go through it all. And there are letters. From your great-grandmother."

At least his mind stayed put. Pardell wasn't sure if it was the shock of learning he'd had a family or the shock of how he'd lost them, but he was grateful to whatever let him keep his eyes fixed on hers and his back straight. He tossed the bag of secrets to his bed. *Later and alone,* he promised himself. "You could have sent these, Dr. Smith," he said coldly.

"There are many things I could have done differently," she replied, making no sense at all.

*Or too much*, Pardell decided, disturbed to feel a wave of compassion pushing aside his righteous anger. This troubled self-doubt hadn't been part of the woman who'd taken over Sammie's or caused a riot in the stern ring. Now, he judged her almost fragile, as though the wrong word could shatter whatever determination had brought her here, and strip away the dignity that let her face him. He pressed his lips together, then said, reluctantly, "Raner—the man who raised me—used to say there's no point regretting choices, only living with them the best you can."

"Living with them." *Did her eyes sparkle with tears before she lowered her head and hid them?* "That's harder, isn't it?"

"I suspect it is," Pardell answered, as much to himself as the Earther.

"Thank you, Mr. Pardell."

*They were still out of balance.* He looked around quickly, then opened the drawer he'd filled before she'd arrived, taking out his chess set. He held it for an instant, before turning to face her. "Dibs, for the *'Mate*'s records," the 'sider explained, feeling better as he passed her the small box. It didn't matter what she thought of the gift—what mattered was what it cost him to give it.

The Earther likely had no idea she'd put him in her debt. "Finders keepers" was the rule on-station, and no one begrudged the finder when, more often than not, the original owner was dead anyway. Returning the found was exceptional courtesy.

He'd underestimated Gail Smith's perception—or there was something about being here, both alone and vulnerable, that encouraged understanding. "Dibs. We're even, then," she acknowledged softly, holding the box in two hands, then bringing it close to her heart, as though precious. "Good night, Mr. Pardell."

Pardell stood in the doorway of his cabin, watching his enemy walk away down the deserted corridor, her bare feet silent on the flooring. Somehow, his rage dissolved and left at the same time, leaving only a peaceful sort of weariness behind.

"Thank you, Dr. Smith," Pardell said softly, when he was quite sure she wouldn't hear.

# Chapter 47

UNCARING who could hear—and there were dozens in the lab this eventful morning—Gail hummed tonelessly to herself. She kept her hands deep in her lab coat pockets, fingers pushing around the inevitable lint, and rocked back and forth on the balls of her feet in anticipation. The lab computer was digesting the latest test results. In the past three hours they'd already learned remarkable things about Aaron Pardell, including mapping the veining of his skin, taking base-line readings of several sorts, and proving conclusively only human touch caused the adverse reaction. Her scientists were lining up to examine his metabolism and nervous functions, let alone explore the gold writhing beneath his skin—spurred by Temujin's failure to find anything.

Between their requests and her own ideas, Gail was already busy planning the afternoon. If the results went as she thought likely, she'd simply move along to the next experiment in the sequence. If they differed—ah, that was the splendid part of science, to be faced by the unexpected turn of events.

Gail deliberately kept her mind on the work—on finally doing what she'd hoped to do all these years. It was infinitely preferable to dwelling on her guilt-driven visit to Pardell's quarters last night. Grant had found out, of course; inconvenient as well as embarrassing, since her door guards now had direct orders to disregard her commands when it came to moving around alone without Grant's approval. Dangerous, he'd called it. Among other, less polite terms.

*Nonsense*, Gail said to herself. The only danger she'd exposed herself to was being a fool in front of the 'sider.

Gail glanced involuntarily at the dark-haired man seemingly

asleep in a chair set close to the nearest bank of instruments, trying to make it appear that she was checking on the progress of Aisha's latest trial. Pardell had appeared with the techs first thing this morning, ready and, if not exactly eager, then willing to participate in whatever they had in mind. He'd greeted her no differently from the rest, with a polite smile and nothing at all to read in his hazel eyes.

Last night might never have happened.

Others would have exploited that moment of weakness, Gail knew, and should have been relieved. But, perversely, she found herself wanting to talk to Pardell. She wanted to ask what he'd thought of the records she'd brought—how many he'd seen, what he'd felt learning about his parents, about Susan Witts. His "nothing happened" attitude made that impossible; she couldn't doubt it was intentional.

So, instead, Gail turned back to her list of pending experiments.

"Starving you today, Aaron?" The just-arrived Malley didn't quite bellow the question, but he'd obviously meant the words to carry past his friend.

Pardell, who must have been startled, didn't so much as twitch—likely a relief to the techs assigned to check for any loosening of the abundant sensors stuck over the 'sider's head, as well as his bare arms, chest, and shoulders. It had taken longer than anticipated to apply the sensors using remote handling arms; they'd already found it was hopeless trying to use gloves of the thickness required to protect both Pardell and anyone touching him. The 'sider helped with what he could reach. Philips was becoming quite adept with tongs, if prone to nervous tremors while using them.

"We're doing some preliminary measurements on his metabolism. Mr. Pardell can eat when we're finished. Which should be soon," Gail said, fixing the unrepentant stationer with a warning glare, "provided you don't interrupt what's underway."

The man in question cracked open one eye. "You heard the professor, you big oaf. And I told you last night I wouldn't be joining you for breakfast."

Malley shrugged shoulders that would have made two Pardells and grabbed a stool to sit on, all the while passing a deceptively casual eye over the apparatus engulfing his friend. "Just routine, huh?"

"Routine, it is." Pardell's lips stretched into a grin. "You don't need to stick around, you know. It was nice and peaceful before you arrived."

Gail thought Malley would look taken aback at this, given how the stationer had been campaigning like some medieval champion on his friend's behalf. Instead, he appeared relieved, chuckling deep in his throat before saying: "And who'd keep an eye on these lovely ladies for you?"

"As if you need me for an excuse," Pardell replied.

They continued to exchange friendly banter, even drawing a blush from Benton, whom Gail didn't think could blush. Meanwhile, Gail accepted a sheet of results from one of the techs, making a show of reading it as she reconsidered the two from Thromberg. She'd obviously missed something important during that time when Malley was the force to be reckoned with and Pardell lay comatose in the tank. Malley, bold, bright, and daring, wasn't the leader here—not if she read his body language, the tones of his voice correctly. Instead, he deferred to his friend; he sought, consciously or not, reassurance about the state of his universe from Pardell, not the other way around.

*It had the weight of a revelation.* Malley's single-minded anxiety hadn't just been the caring of one friend for another—it had been the gallant desperation of a faithful knight for his fallen king, or perhaps more like the terror felt by a man who finds himself rudderless and adrift on a featureless ocean.

And now that Pardell was back on his feet, regardless of the situation, Malley was free to simply enjoy himself and leave agonizing over their situation and future to his friend.

*Pardell knew*, Gail decided, suddenly caught by a look from the 'sider as he glanced idly around the room—unable to deny she'd been staring. She recognized both assessment and challenge in his eyes. If they'd thought Malley was protective of Pardell . . . now, Gail knew, they'd have to deal with Pardell's sense of responsibility for the stationer.

And of the two, she thought Grant should worry more about now-homeless Pardell, with his knowledge of starships—and deadly touch.

*     *     *

Not that the stationer wasn't still capable of being a problem in and of himself. The very next day, while Pardell cleaned up between tests, Gail found herself facing off with Malley—again. "I'm not ready to test the suit's properties," she told him, well past exasperated and inclined to call over the FDs leaning in the lab's nearest doorway.

"I tried your fancy suit already," Malley said in an annoyingly superior tone. "It worked just fine. So if that's what you really want Aaron for, why not go ahead and try the thing? Then you can be done with all this—" he threw out his long arms as if to wipe away the entire lab.

Gail stood her ground, having become resigned to the fact that Malley would always take advantage of his height during arguments and that her neck muscles would pay for each and every one. "'This' is what's necessary to make sure we have solid results and Mr. Pardell is safe." She used the word deliberately, willing to guess exactly what had prompted Malley's new impatience.

*It was as though she'd pushed a button*, Gail decided, somewhat smugly. "Safe! Safe!" Malley's face suffused with red and his fists clenched. "Where were you when Stanley, over there, thought he should test Aaron's sensitivity to pain?"

"You know I was here, Mr. Malley," Gail reminded him, feeling her own face growing hot. They'd all been there, watching as the 'sider obediently gave quiet, utterly controlled rankings of how much he suffered at each new increment, all recorded and compared against the monitors. She'd been there, when Pardell's face had dropped its calm mask, suddenly turning into a rictus of unbearable suffering as the monitors screamed for him. "Dr. Temujin made sure the test kept within safety limits. Did you think it would all be easy? We don't know what to expect—that's the point of the tests—"

"Are you sure? Or is the point to find out how much he can take before—"

"That's enough." Neither of them had noticed Pardell's arrival—*the man moved like a cat*, Gail thought, even when forced to carry around the leads from a dozen or more sensor probes under his robe.

"Aaron—I was—"

Pardell shook his head and Malley closed his mouth, but the stationer's look at Gail was bleak and unforgiving. "What's next, Dr. Smith?" Pardell asked her.

Somehow Gail managed to ignore the glowering Malley and adjust her face to something neutrally pleasant. Before she answered, however, she took a moment to study Pardell. He looked relaxed as he stood and waited for her decision, but a glance down showed her his feet were planted slightly wider apart than usual. *Unsteady, but hiding it.*

Regardless of Malley's opinion, the pain trial had been important—telling her far more about Pardell than the numbers listing his tolerances and sensitivities. The 'sider was patently a man used to driving himself past his own limitations, paying the price later when his task or goal was done. She didn't need to hook Pardell up to the monitors to know he wasn't ready for more—not that he'd admit it even to himself.

"Lunch first, Mr. Pardell," she ordered calmly, keeping her face and voice free of anything more than light courtesy. "I want you to keep up your nutrient levels."

Unlike hers, and to some extent, Malley's, Pardell's expressions seemed totally unscripted and sincere. In fact, his face could change so quickly, Gail found him harder to read in a way than Grant, whose features might have been carved stone. At the mention of lunch, Pardell's face went from serious attention to delighted anticipation, lighting up like a child's. "In the dining lounge?" he asked her eagerly.

She winced inwardly, thinking of the time lost. But . . . *the walk out of the lab would do him as much good as the food.* "Certainly, if you'd like. Do you know the way?"

Malley's, "I know it," crossed Pardell's, "But you'll join us," so Gail wasn't sure she'd heard the 'sider correctly. But Pardell lifted one dark eyebrow and repeated his invitation. "You do eat lunch, don't you, Dr. Smith? Join us. Please."

*What did he want?* Gail had started to believe the 'sider wasn't planning to seek any further advantage from her about the *'Mate*'s records—or her ill-advised visit to his quarters. *Now?* She narrowed her eyes slightly, then saw Malley's face creasing in a scowl. Whatever Pardell wanted with this meeting, the stationer wasn't happy about it.

*Dissension among one's opponents was a bonus.* Gail nodded before she could change her mind.

"I'll meet you there," she promised.

# Chapter 48

"YOU want Gail Smith at our table?" The stationer had that stubborn, planning-to-lock-his-mags-to-the-deck look on his face. "You seriously want us to make peace with her, as if she'd understand it. Honestly, Aaron. Did that test unhinge something vital? Talking to that Earther's like hitting your head on a bulkhead."

*As if talking to Malley when his mind was made up on something was any more productive*, Pardell chuckled to himself. He fell in beside his friend as they walked down the corridor. He'd changed back in the lab—they had a washroom there set aside for his use. *Walking was about as active as he wanted to be.* The 'sider was quite sure the observant Earther had noticed. *Maybe food would help.* "You do know the way to the lounge?" he asked Malley.

"Sure." It wasn't quite a snarl. "And I suppose you'll be inviting Rosalind next and asking what she's up to—now that she's finished selling you out."

"Rosalind is meeting me for supper tonight. You know it's necessary, Malley," the 'sider said softly, pitching his voice to Malley's ears only. "It's the way things have to be."

Few people had the lung capacity to produce such a thoroughly opinionated sigh. "I need to drop by my quarters," the stationer said in no uncertain terms. "It'll just take a minute. If Her Ladyship arrives early, she can wait."

Pardell somehow doubted Dr. Smith would, but went along—the stationer wasn't close to listening to reason yet.

Making it unlikely this would be his opportunity to tell Malley what Gail Smith had brought him that night. *If he did.* Pardell wasn't sure how he felt about gaining so much past at once, not to mention being related to the infamous Susan Witts. *That wasn't going to be easy to talk about.* He hadn't made it through all of her letters yet, just enough to recognize something of a kindred spirit to Gail Smith. Did she feel it? Or was the Earther as focused on her quest as Witts had been on hers? Pardell sighed.

The FDs followed along without comment, as they did each time either he or Malley left the secured area of the lab. Adams and Baier, today. At least they were willing to wait outside while he and Malley went in to retrieve whatever the stationer was after.

Which Pardell was not surprised to find was simply privacy.

"Make whatever peace you want, Aaron," Malley growled the minute the door closed behind them. "But first, you tell me something. What was that crap this morning?" His face was pale and set into lines that made something implacable, something deadly. Sammie wouldn't have recognized the expression. Pardell was quite sure Gail Smith would.

Pardell sank down on the bed, just as glad to be off his feet. "They needed to quantify my reactions," he said. "It likely looked worse than it was. That last bit—I was surprised, that's all. You try getting a shock where it hurts and see what you do."

"So that's how it's going to be?" Malley asked, hands clenching into fists as he towered over the 'sider. "You're going to take whatever she feels like doing to you, no complaints, like a good little 'sider? Think this is going to make up for what happened on the station? That this is all some little bit of hell you deserve to be in?"

Pardell let the harsh words roll past, knowing there was truth in some of what Malley said, if not all. When the stationer paused for breath, he looked up. "Someone, somewhere, was going to hear about me and want to find out what makes me tick," he reminded Malley. "At least with these people, there's a reason—a good one. Isn't that enough for you? It is for me."

"Oh, I get it. You're buying her whole story, every bit, and letting them torture you because of blue eyes and a noble cause." Malley sank into the only chair, elbows on his knees as he leaned toward Pardell. He said in a tone of complete conviction: "I'm telling you, Aaron, you can't trust Gail Smith. You can't believe a thing she says. Look at what she's done!"

"Is it what *she's* done, Malley? Is it really one person's fault?"

Malley appeared incredulous. "Are you kidding me? You know Gail Smith started all this mess. Things were fine before she came!"

"Were they?" Pardell countered gloomily, shoulders sagging. "The Earther may have stirred things up—but all of this, the riot, the attacks, must have been ready to happen. If not now, then in another few months, a year. No. Things aren't fine at home, Malley. Thromberg is dying. Everyone there—stationer, immie, 'sider—knows it, deep inside, in that place where we hide desperate, unthinkable thoughts from ourselves, until they can't be hidden any longer. Once that happens," he paused, then said heavily, "then anyone becomes capable of doing the unspeakable."

Malley dropped his face into his hands for an instant, but didn't disagree. *How could he?* Pardell thought compassionately. The stationer was smart enough to see it all for himself. He just hadn't wanted to admit it. Gail and the Earthers—it was so much cleaner to put the blame on strangers than on the shoulders of people you considered family.

Finally, Malley lifted his head, his expression resolute, if troubled. "And you believe this project to find the Quill can save the station."

"They believe it," Pardell stated. "It doesn't matter if we do—there aren't any other options, Malley, in case you hadn't noticed."

"There's one." Malley leaned even closer, until Pardell could feel his breath. "You sabotage the ship. They'll have to turn back to Thromberg for repairs. We can escape—hide out in the aft ring. We can tell them what we know. Syd and Tanya can spread it around. Defuse the crisis, explain—"

Pardell held up a hand to silence the stationer, then started walking to the door, saying: "Time we headed to the lounge."

Malley's voice was almost quivering. "Didn't you hear me, Aaron?"

"Hear you?" Pardell whirled to glare at the stationer. "Of

course, I heard you. I'm sure everyone did," he said flatly, pointing up to the ceiling, watching Malley's eyes widen in shock. "What? Did you think they'd leave us unwatched—ever? Although it's hardly necessary—they could let me have the run of this ship, but doing any serious damage that didn't kill us all would take tools and expertise I don't have." The 'sider rubbed his gloved hands against his chest, finding sore spots where the last set of probes had left their marks. "Even if I did," he emphasized, trembling with rage, "I will not go back to Thromberg Station. Ever. Gail Smith didn't destroy my home and put me on this ship, Malley.

"My friends did."

# Chapter 49

GAIL knew where the dining lounge was—she just didn't use it. She took her meals on the run, in her office, or in the officers' mess in the command sphere, where she could conduct meetings with Tobo or Grant. Many of the seniormost science staff had the deplorable habit of taking meals at their workstations, but at least they ate. For some, it was a struggle to get their minds on anything but their research; Gail had assigned ship's stewards to the more muddleheaded of those.

The techs and crew of the science sphere were the ones who took their free time seriously, filling the semicircular dining lounge during meals and returning here for music or other recreation at night. The place was rarely empty, given there were two shifts of techs during the day and a skeleton one through the night. Gail had insisted on both the turnover and first-rate facilities to entertain those off-shift—knowing full well the burden her own research schedule could be on the most devoted and professional staff.

For the *Seeker*, she'd sought the best available, which also meant they were an unusually observant group. Gail wasn't at all surprised when her entrance temporarily stopped conversations within a radius of twenty tables, then inspired a veritable storm as the techs speculated enthusiastically about her presence. It didn't help that Grant had insisted her FD shadows accompany her even in here, standing at each shoulder.

Gail felt like a one-person event.

"Over there, Dr. Smith," one of her shadows offered helpfully. Gail wondered if the FD really believed anyone could miss Malley and his hair, even at this distance, but nodded she her thanks.

The two men had prepared for her arrival by having a glass of water matching theirs placed before the third seat. Pardell tilted his head interrogatively at the FDs following her. "They won't be joining us," Gail announced before he could ask. The FDs took the hint but moved no farther away than the next vacant table.

*This hadn't been part of her carefully planned schedule*, Gail thought as she took her seat, trying to analyze why she'd accepted Pardell's invitation. There were four days remaining—no one, least of all Gail, had time to waste. *They could have pumped her for information, doubtless the reason for this, back in the lab.* With a sense of things skewed from predicted, Gail lifted her glass to theirs in what seemed a customarily formal toast. Rosalind had done the same with her tea.

Before she could put down her glass, Malley said sarcastically: "Grant's clones tuck you in at night, too?"

Pardell merely watched her, his eyes curious. *So*, Gail thought. "Not quite," she answered. "They stand outside my door so I'm not disturbed. Most comforting."

"I'll keep that in mind," Malley said, but it wasn't banter. He was after details. Gail was willing, to a point, to supply them. *Questions could be more illuminating than answers.* The stationer continued: "I can see having security on Thromberg, but here? These people can't hate you that much."

Pardell coughed suddenly, a hand over his mouth as though to hide a grin. Gail didn't bother to hide her own. "Most of these people, Malley, have worked with me for years. Many are friends as well as colleagues. Grant's unit is assigned to protect the project, not me. But since I'm the head of the project, Grant has interpreted that protection as meaning having me followed everywhere. Even on the *Seeker*. Call it professional paranoia." Gail let her grin widen. "In case you haven't noticed yet, you two recently made Grant's Vital to the Project list."

"We've noticed," Pardell said, nodding toward the matched set of FDs at another table. "They wouldn't sit with us either."

"On duty," Gail explained. "Grant's a bit of a stickler for that sort of thing."

"And you are on duty, as well, Dr. Smith," Pardell said, rather than asked, lifting his glass and waiting.

"On duty?" Gail reached for her water again, thinking over the question. She didn't take anything from Pardell—or Malley—as idle conversation. Pardell sipped as she did. She wasn't surprised Malley didn't; she thought this an Outsider ritual. "Always," she said honestly. "Until we find a way to find, capture—and destroy—the Quill."

"Thank you for sparing the time to join us," he replied with unexpected seriousness. "We value your sharing a meal with us, on this shift, and on this ship."

Alerted by the changing nuance of Pardell's voice, the formality in his choice of words and how he said them, Gail paused. She met his eyes and saw nothing beyond polite interest. She looked at Malley and saw resignation, as if the stationer knew exactly what was going on and no longer disputed it.

Before Gail could speak, the steward arrived with three identical trays. Malley surveyed his with displeasure. "I thought in here I'd get to choose my own food," he complained to Gail.

"Dr. Lynn has explained the complexity of getting a full range of nutrients after relying on Thromberg's rations," Pardell said firmly. "This is from her approved list. If you had your way, we'd be living on spiked orange juice and candy."

The stationer roared with laughter and the tension at the table subsided, but only barely, Gail thought.

She reached for her fork, but Pardell and Malley did not. Instead, they gently pushed their trays inward, until they touched in the middle of the table. There was space left for hers.

Gail hesitated, then copied their action so all three trays were together. She looked to Pardell for some clue as to what was happening. He appeared to be studying the trays, comparing one to the other. Finally, he smiled and reached for her tray.

Before Gail could protest, Malley took Pardell's, then pushed his over to her. "Enjoy your lunch, Dr. Smith," he said. He appeared more relaxed, and began attacking his apple crisp with enthusiasm.

*What was all that about?* Gail wondered, accepting Malley's tray.

Pardell's eyes twinkled. "It's a Rule, a custom," he offered, unasked. "To accept anyone on board a ship—or in station quarters—that person must show and share food. It's more cer-

emony than substance, now that Thromberg has enough rations
to go around. But it was—necessary, once."

"My aunt shot a man for hiding a day's ration in his pants,"
Malley claimed, straightfaced. "You can imagine how she
found it."

Pardell shot a quelling look at his friend. "These days, it's the
thought that counts."

"I'm glad of that, Mr. Pardell," Gail replied demurely, "considering I've no intention of searching Malley's pants."

They both looked stunned, then burst out laughing—Malley
loud enough to attract attention from most of the lounge. Gail
shrugged mentally. *There were worse ways for the staff to notice
her.* "Thank you for explaining the ceremony, gentlemen," she
said, when they'd calmed to the point of wiping their eyes. "And
for including me in it."

"It means more than the sharing of resources, Dr. Smith,"
Pardell told her, his expression turning serious again. "After the
terrible battles and riots on the station, people needed a way to
return to normal, to think about survival instead of grudges and
revenge. Thromberg wouldn't be here, otherwise. The Rule is
that adversaries, old and new, must come together at the table,
show all they have, share all they have. As we've done."

"Making the best of what remains," Gail said, thinking back
to that night and Pardell's words with new understanding. "No
blame; no apologies. It could stop a lot of needless conflict if
more people ascribed to that philosophy, Mr. Pardell."

"Aaron."

"Aaron. I hope, like Malley, you'll start calling me Gail."

The stationer almost choked on a pierogi.

Pardell nodded easily. "Thank you."

From that moment, Pardell, and to some extent Malley, set
themselves up as her hosts, complete with an entertaining series
of stories which were about as believable as anything Tobo
might come out with after a few brandies. If Gail hadn't known
she was on her, own ship, she'd have thought they'd taken her
into their own homes on the station. She wasn't sure exactly
how they managed it—perhaps because the lounge was a
strange setting to her as well—but the fact remained she'd quite

literally lost any control of the situation or conversation from the moment she'd sat down.

*Something*, Gail told herself, still waiting for the reason they'd sought her company, *something Pardell could well have planned.*

That something was still unclear after they'd finished eating. Gail didn't need to look at her chrono to know she was overdue to be anywhere but sitting here, no matter how diverting, if unpredictable, her companions. *It would be nice*, she thought rather grimly, *to gain something other than food from all this, if only information.* "What do you think of the dining lounge, Aaron?" Gail asked, running her fingers down the stem of her glass. "I imagine it feels something like Thromberg—so many people together."

"This place?" Malley looked amused. "It's almost deserted."

Pardell had taken her question more seriously and turned in his chair as though to examine the entire room. He stayed like that for a moment. *A very long moment.* Gail was about to ask what fascinated him so, when Malley leaned back in his chair with a creaking sound and shook his head. "You shouldn't have set him off, Gail. Trust me."

"Set him off?" Gail looked at Pardell, whose head remained turned away from them, as though he could see something beyond the near bulkhead. He wasn't staring at anyone in particular—there wasn't an occupied table in that direction—but the 'sider seemed to be completely focused. Gail thought he was unaware of being talked about. "What's the matter with him?" she demanded in a whisper, trying not to alarm the nearby FDs.

Malley put his large hand over hers on the table, effectively capturing it unless she pulled it free with force. "Nothing to worry about," he said, leaning close and speaking just as quietly. "Aaron gets spacey at times. Tunes out the universe. He calls it thinking. I couldn't tell you if it is or isn't—he doesn't talk about what he thinks, that's for sure."

"How long does it last?"

"Never know," Malley replied with a slow smile, his fingers wrapping warmly around hers. "But look at it this way, Gail. We don't get much time alone. . . ."

Gail didn't bother fighting for her hand or smiling. "Do you want me to clear the room, Malley? Or is it enough to have everyone here see how helpless he is at the moment?"

"I'm only being friendly, Gail." Malley's lips twisted wryly and he released her fingers. "Hey, Aaron," he said, at his usually forthright volume. "You in there?"

Pardell shuddered and turned, as though Malley's voice had given him the ability to move again. When Gail saw his face, his eyes were at first dilated and startled, then returned to normal. At the same time, the high bones of his cheeks colored, as though the 'sider realized what had happened and was now thoroughly embarrassed.

*Another difference his friends ignore for him*, Gail concluded, feeling a mixture of curiosity and triumph. *It wasn't necessarily a favor.* She dropped her eyes to her glass and kept her voice casual. "What did you see, Aaron?"

"See?" The word faint, as though Pardell didn't believe the question. Or that she'd asked it.

She lifted her eyes to hold his gaze. "You saw something, didn't you?" Gail said, aware Malley was bristling beside her. "My question to you about the lounge—it made you see more than this room. What was it?"

"Leave him alone," Malley warned. Pardell raised his gloved hand to stop anything further.

"No, it's all right," the 'sider said, his expression flashing between puzzlement and something closer to relief "Seeing. Yes. That's what it's like. How did you know?"

"I—" *Fair was fair.* Gail pressed her lips together then admitted: "I didn't know. I guessed. I—" She took a hasty swallow before going on, afraid she was about to blush herself. "I lose myself sometimes . . . when ideas come at me faster than I can absorb them. It's like seeing the same, everyday things, but they appear strange—reconnected differently than before. While I'm like that, the world unfortunately tends to keep going without me, especially in meetings."

She might have grown antennae, to go by Pardell's expression. Then it softened into something closer to awe. "That's it. Exactly it. But I can't stop it," he told her in a low, intense voice, eyes sliding to Malley and back to her again. "I can't keep my mind on what's real sometimes. It's—it can be inconvenient."

*Inconvenient?* Gail suspected that wasn't the word Pardell wanted to use, but a lifetime spent trying to fit in with others couldn't have made it easy for him to confess either the depths of his differences or his feelings about them. "That's unusual," she told him honestly, "but not unheard of. We have a couple of cog function researchers on the *Seeker*. If you like, I can have them look into how you could gain more control."

"Aaron isn't nuts."

"I didn't say he was, Malley," Gail countered. "Everyone needs training to get the most from their abilities. Don't you agree?"

Gail wondered if it was the startling idea that his affliction might be an ability that drained the color from Pardell's face. He swallowed, his throat working. There was a nakedness to his face, a depth of hope surely beyond anything she'd implied. Gail had a moment's doubt—*what did he think she'd promised to do for him?*

Before they could pursue it, the steward reappeared to collect their trays. Hers was almost full, but Gail waved it away. It didn't matter what Pardell thought—what mattered was getting him back into the lab this afternoon, fit and ready for the next trials. *Definitely some new possibilities to consider—*

"That's all you're eating?" The sneer from Malley interrupted her thoughts. No more polite host—the stationer was back in full attack mode. Gail guessed he hadn't liked either her admission, or Pardell's reaction to it. Sure enough, he didn't stop there. "Oh. I forgot. You're probably riding another boost by now."

Gail folded her napkin and put it beside her bowl. *Coming here, allowing herself to interact on a social level with them? A mistake.* She stood. "I'll see you gentlemen back at the lab," she said tightly.

Pardell stood as well. "I'll walk with you."

"As you wish."

She didn't see whatever signal Pardell used, but Malley remained seated, glowering at them both, but silent at last.

They walked out side by side, Pardell keeping his distance

from her and those they passed. Three FDs followed, her two
and one for Pardell. Gail didn't bother arguing that one wasn't
enough to leave watching the big man with the temper.

"I want to apologize for Malley," Pardell said quietly as they
reached the relative privacy of the corridor.

"You'd need a few days," Gail snapped. She suited the pace
to her own impatience. The 'sider, whose legs weren't much
longer than hers, kept up easily, but she slowed after a minute,
contrite. She was supposed to be looking after his health, not
running him down before the next tests. "I've grown used to
your friend," she admitted reluctantly, "Don't let it trouble you."

"But it troubled you—what he said about the boost."

*Pardell tended to a bit too much honesty for comfort*, Gail
realized, then shrugged and matched it with her own. "I used it,
once, the day following the riot. A lot was going on that I
couldn't delegate. My own people didn't know, but Malley
picked up on it and, well, it was embarrassing at the time. I'm
not in the habit, no matter what he said back there."

"Malley used to be. That's how he recognized it in you."

Gail found her feet stopping at that. She faced Pardell. "Malley? An addict?"

"Years ago." The 'sider raised hands in a helpless gesture.
"When he lost his mother, he wouldn't—couldn't—live with
me on the *'Mate*. He had the choice of moving in with another
family, but he wanted to keep his quarters. Personal space costs
dibs. He was just a kid—not strong enough to earn much, not
back then. So he took extra shifts as often as he could get them.
The supervisor," the word came out of Pardell's expressive
mouth as though having a foul taste, "gave Malley boost to
keep him going. He was hooked in a week . . . eventually, he
couldn't move without a shot."

Gail tried and failed to imagine the giant stationer weak and
drug-ridden. But, looking up at Pardell's lean, passionate face,
she thought she knew what had happened. "You cleaned him
up," she said.

It was Pardell's turn to shrug. "I helped. Malley's too smart
to let something like boost own him for long. He's fine now—
but touchy on the subject. He wouldn't want you to know, but,

after what he said, I thought you should. He's a good person, Gail. For all his noise and protest to the contrary."

Gail raised a brow at this, but nodded graciously. She looked back at the FDs, standing at attention several paces behind them, and lowered her voice. "While we're exchanging confidences, what had you wanted to talk to me about? I know that's why you asked me to lunch."

The warmth of his smile surprised her. "Nothing, Gail. I thought it was time we shared rations, that's all. Make a fresh start. Get to know one another."

"Get to know one another?" she echoed, wondering if she was astonished or appalled. "My job is to take you apart, Aaron, and find out everything possible about you—hopefully without causing you harm and perhaps helping you, if I can. But the project doesn't require us to be friends. Frankly, it may be easier on both of us if we're not."

Pardell nodded. "I understand what you have to do to me, Gail. That's my job on the *Seeker*." His lips pressed together for an instant, as if to rein in some emotion. "What you did the other night—that wasn't part of your project. I want to thank you for giving me my past." He appeared suddenly almost shy, then smiled down at her in a way he hadn't before. "I won't tell Malley—but I believe you're a good person, too, Gail, no matter what face you need to show for your work. I'd be pleased to call you a friend." With that, he bowed and went back to the dining lounge, his FD shadow following behind.

Gail stared after Pardell, unable to think of anything for a moment except that her test subject had a remarkably charming smile.

*And wanted to be friends.*

Lunch had been a very bad idea.

# Chapter 50

*F*RIENDSHIP. Gail did her rounds of the night-dimmed lab, pondering the word with all its ramifications. *She had friends, here and on Earth.* She wasn't isolated by her position and ambition.

*That wasn't the point*, she admitted to herself, nodding to the bright-eyed techs at those workstations still operating. Anything nonessential or unrelated to the Quill was to be dismantled and stored—orders straight from Titan U. But there was room in this new configuration of the lab space for some interesting nonessentials. Besides, Gail knew it would take longer to persuade the physicists to pack up than it would to let their work run its course.

The point, Gail knew, was that until recently she had been sure of herself and her work. She'd made decisions, some difficult, without hesitation or doubt—when they dealt with numbers on a screen, or genetic samples. But now the subject of her investigation was lying on a slablike bed at the far side of the room, a vid player mounted so that he could see something other than ceiling.

*Now she had to deal with a charming smile, an intriguing personality, and worst of all, someone who wanted to be friends.*

She couldn't sleep anymore.

It took longer to walk around the lab tonight. They'd reconfigured the space to accommodate the rising pace of investigation, enlarging it threefold, adding a second floor over half that, not incidentally, provided a ceiling from which to suspend new equipment. *Malley'd been fascinated*, Gail remembered, smiling to herself.

Pardell had been too busy in his own corner of the lab to see much of the changes, but there'd been no breakthroughs yet. In spite of all the measurements she'd made over the last three days, she was no closer to understanding what Pardell experienced when someone touched him, beyond discomfort. *There was something more. There had to be.*

Gail watched Pardell when he didn't know she was there; she shamelessly reviewed lab vids made when she wasn't—shamelessly, because she was honest enough with herself to admit there was no scientific justification for invading what little privacy they'd left him. She couldn't seem to help it. It was as if the more she saw of Pardell, the more she heard his voice, saw him move, the more fascinated she became.

The 'sider might not have Malley's breezy friendliness, but he had something else, less definable. For safety's sake, they'd had to brief everyone on the *Seeker* about Pardell's condition, giving him a reputation that should have made people at least cautious of being near him.

But it hadn't turned out that way. Pardell did most of the work of avoiding contact himself. He moved among the mainly taller, heavier-built Earthers with an easy, unobtrusive grace, always keeping his distance, but with a quiet attentiveness that seemed to put others at ease. His face changed expression like mercury, often thoughtful, but at times amazed, delighted, and usually intensely curious.

*Intensely sad.* She'd caught that twice, when he hadn't known he could be seen.

Everyone liked Malley. Well, Sazaad couldn't stand being in the same room, so they'd moved his workstation to as remote a location as possible, but that only added to the stationer's popularity within the rest of the science sphere. *Aisha seemed particularly smitten*, taking Malley under her wing to help with the now-named anti-Quill suits.

*But everyone cared about Pardell.* That was the difference, Gail decided. It wasn't pity or curiosity. There was something about him that grabbed your eye and held it, that made you want to ask if he needed anything, if he was happy . . .

*If he thought about her.*

"Dr. Smith? What do you think?" Gail blinked, realizing she'd heard the woman's question once already.

"Sorry, Kai," she said contritely. "Must have been day-dreaming. Why don't you pull up a new sensor from stores—we aren't getting reliable calibration from this one anyway."

Kai O'Shay, a tech who'd been with Gail since both arrived at Titan U, grinned broadly. "Daydreaming? Maybe you should get some rest that isn't standing up, Dr. Smith. I replaced that sensor half an hour ago."

"My apologies," Gail said. "What's the question, then?"

"I was asking you about bringing Aaron something to drink when the next readings are complete. There's nothing from Dr. Lynn on the charts stipulating it."

"I'll look after it. Thanks, Kai."

Gail went over to where Pardell was supposedly sleeping, moving as quietly as possible. She stopped tiptoeing when she saw the glints of light reflecting from his open eyes. "Hello, Gail," he greeted her. "I thought this was ship's night."

"It is," she nodded, checking the leads to the various probes. "Having trouble falling asleep?"

Her eyes had adjusted enough to the dimmer light at this side of the lab to see he was smiling. "I've been asleep. Sound asleep. Now I'm awake. I'm afraid that's it for tonight."

Gail glanced at the datastream. "Three hours?"

"Full night for me," the 'sider asserted. "I don't need much rest. Can I get up now?"

"No. You'll have to stay put until morning, or Dr. M'Daiye will have my head on a platter. She wants a full night of readings."

"Then will you stay a while?" he asked. "I've been through all the vids they gave me. Twice. I could use some company."

Gail's lips twitched. She didn't care for being bored either—which was why she hadn't stayed in her quarters, staring into the dark and trying to sleep. As for why she couldn't sleep? It had nothing to do with knowing Pardell was trapped here by her orders, strapped to a bed and hooked to machinery. *Nothing at all.*

"A short while. Are you thirsty?"

"Yes, thanks."

Gail grabbed two drinking tubes from the nearest storage fridge. These looked to be Aisha's, but she read the labels and made sure the seals were intact. There'd been some interesting

additions to the supply after Tecka had left his party supplies
chilling in every cold storage in the lab.

"Here you go." Handing things to the 'sider made Gail
acutely aware of the placement of her own hands and his. People so rarely avoided physical contact to this extreme. Pardell
seemed to do it unconsciously, but Gail judged it a very conscious act indeed, well practiced and utterly necessary.

One of the ubiquitous stools was beside his tablelike bed.
She sat, then bent and twisted her head to see what was
presently on the vid screen. It was a view panning low over
wheat fields and forests, a type of travelogue for wide-open
spaces. "This doesn't bother you?" she asked, absently biting
the end from the tube and beginning to suck the juice from inside it.

Pardell chuckled. "I grew up without the boundary of an atmosphere. This just looks—cozy. And beautiful. I can't get
enough of the colors. Makes me want to be there, to see if it's
real."

"Interesting from a 'sider," Gail said curiously. "I didn't
think you would want to visit a ball of dirt."

"You've been talking to Rosalind, I take it."

Gail could see Pardell's face quite well now. He looked relaxed, so she went on. "She doesn't appear in favor of col[missing]iz-
ing planets."

"True. Tell me, Gail. Have you ever met anyone whose ideas
became locked down at one point in their lives?" he asked.

She grinned, thinking of Reinsez. "I've one on board
right now."

"Then you know what I mean. Rosalind and her disciples
keep waiting for their ship to dock and whisk them to deep
space. No, she wouldn't speak kindly of planet life. But I was
raised by Aaron Raner—he loved Earth. He'd show me images . . . tell me stories about his favorite places. He planned to
retire to a cottage on Lake St. Joseph, in Canada. Last I heard,
it was still in his family. A great-nephew owns it. If the Quill
hadn't come, that is." His mouth turned down at the ends.

"If the Quill hadn't come," Gail offered impulsively, "you
wouldn't have had him for your father. He seems to have been

a good one." Pardell went silent at this. "I'm sorry," she said. "I shouldn't have said that."

"No. You're right. I've had a good life, overall." His voice softened. "When I watched the tape of my father, Jer Pardell, I admired his courage . . . felt sorry for him. But it wasn't grief. It was just such a relief to know—" he stopped.

"To know you were undeniably human, born the way humans are born?" Gail finished for him.

"Exactly. You've no idea the things I'd imagined over the years." Pardell paused and managed to laugh. "Maybe you do, if you think like I do at times."

She smiled, then yawned in the middle of it.

"Speaking of sleep, Gail, why don't you get some?" Pardell suggested. "I'm fine. I'll read a bit."

Gail shook her head. "I'm not tired." But she stretched and found a more comfortable position, leaning one arm and shoulder along the edge of Pardell's bed. "I'm sure Malley would insist I stay and keep you company, as you asked."

"This isn't Malley's shift," he retorted. She thought he smiled. "Besides, he's hardly likely to approve of us spending time together—he'd be sure you were going to stick pins in me when I wasn't looking. You aren't, are you?"

"Not until tomorrow," Gail chuckled, then let out a long, slow breath and laid her cheek on her arm. "Aaron, how is Malley doing? Besides his unflattering opinion of me."

"He doesn't trust you," the 'sider corrected. "Otherwise, I think he rather likes you."

Gail rested her head a little more on her arm. Amazing how comfortable a stool could become after a while. "The feeling's mutual," she admitted candidly, finding herself drifting free of her usual protective bubble of strategy and hoarded secrets. *Being with Pardell was like that*, she thought in the unguarded moment. He was always himself, open, kind, and trusting. *She wanted to be those things—he reminded her how.* "I trust your giant," she told Pardell. "I trust him to look out for you first and damn anything I want. I respect that."

His voice seemed to come out of the darkness, low, even, soothing. Gail shut her eyes to listen more closely. "We've been together all our lives, you know," Pardell was explaining.

"Raner needed advice on how to raise me. There were so few babies, but Mrs. Malley—she was a wonderful mother. I'd watch her holding Malley when he was hurt or just tired. She'd take him into her lap and rock him until he fell asleep." A touch of amusement in his voice. "Until the time came when there was more Malley than lap and she had to put him beside her or be crushed."

Somehow, Gail could see the moment Pardell was remembering, only she saw the other child, the one standing at an uncrossable distance, imagining how it would feel to be cuddled, to be held and made safe. She shuddered involuntarily, filled with pity.

It was as if her lower arm had brushed against an open flame. She lurched away, hearing the stool clatter to the floor, the alarmed calls of startled techs and guards . . .

And over it all, Aaron Pardell's cry of pain.

# Chapter 51

HIS agony was gone. *A shame*, Pardell thought savagely, *since that was the easiest to bear.* Anything was easier than remembering the soft feel of her skin, the very instant they'd both . . .

PAIN.

Gail had fallen to the floor, huddling there with her right arm clutched to her chest. He remembered how tears had spilled from her eyes and her lower lip had trembled. But she hadn't blamed him.

*Why would she*, Pardell raged, *when she already felt such overwhelming pity?*

PITY. He'd seized upward, breaking most of the probe connections, before somehow leaning to the other side of the table before worse happened. She'd understood and left his care to the techs who'd rushed over, using the handling arms to help straighten him on the bed, cleaning the embarrassing remains.

It was quiet again. The techs had left him. Gail was long gone.

Pardell lay there, his arm over his eyes to make something closer to true dark, and tasted vomit. *What had made him think the Earther saw him as anything but a freak? What had made him reach out to her?*

Whatever it was, he wouldn't do it again.

# Chapter 52

H ER right arm and hand tingled suddenly. Gail clenched the fingers into a fist for a second. Nothing like the searing pain of that instant. *What remained was all in her head*, she reminded herself, having tested her arm quite thoroughly after—after she'd been a fool. Two days later, you'd think she'd be over it.

*What had she thought she was doing, half-dozing against Pardell's bed as though they were old friends, chatting the night away?* She should have gone to her own bed, or at least held the urge to talk to the man until ship's day, or chosen some neutral or interesting location, or had someone else there. *Been awake!* Anything would have been better than her carelessness just as Pardell was reaching out and trying to gain some control over his life. She'd never forget the horrified look in his eyes.

*Hazel, with green flecks.* She'd examined them often enough to know. Like his mother's, Gabrielle Lace Pardell.

The computer chimed, displaying its conclusions in a moving, three-dimensional array. Gail made herself attend to it. This early, the lab was relatively peaceful, but soon there'd be upward of twenty scientists and a seething multitude of techs milling around. She liked a head start, especially before others came bustling up with their own findings and questions.

She spun the data array to examine it from the opposite side.

"Something didn't work out?" *Malley should wear a bell*, Gail decided, mustering a smile of greeting. *Not to mention he had some kind of internal radar telling him when she least wanted to see him.*

"No, everything's fine. Did you get a good night's sleep?"

He yawned theatrically, then grinned down at her, eyes bright and challenging—as always. "A very good night, thanks. Not too much sleep. And you?"

Her cheeks felt suddenly warm. Innuendos in that deep, rich voice came out a great deal closer to invitation. *He knew it, too.* Gail reminded herself that the stationer was an outrageous flirt. Her reactions had nothing to do with taking his attention personally, but simply that no one else on board, including the chastised Sazaad, would dare talk to her this way.

Not that she couldn't feel the heat from his body through her lab coat. The man was a walking furnace. Little wonder he preferred the sleeveless vest over the coat the stewards had altered to fit. Someone less charitable might think it was so others could appreciate the muscles bulging from shoulder to wrist. That same someone might think Malley practiced bulging in front of a mirror.

"I slept very well," she told him blandly, then fell silent.

Pardell was coming their way. On seeing her beside Malley, he turned to talk with a couple of techs, the act of avoidance deliberate and quite unmistakable. Gail pretended not to notice, but the stationer wasn't fooled.

"So . . . what did you do, Gail?" he asked, his voice dripping with sarcasm. "Our Aaron's usually the forgiving sort. A natural gentleman. I've never seen him quite this—adverse—to meeting a lady."

Gail twisted her lips. "I don't know."

"Really." Her answer didn't please Malley. She could tell by the way his eyes hardened with speculation, looking to Pardell then back to her. "Something personal?"

*Perhaps there was a reason*, Gail realized, abruptly. *A reason they all needed to know*, little as she enjoyed the thought of talking about that night. Steeling herself, she took the stationer's arm. "Over here, Malley." He let her pull him closer to one wall of the lab, where temporary cubicles had been formed to house equipment sensitive to interference. "Whatever's bothering Aaron," she told him, "I think it started when he—and I—had that accident two nights ago."

Malley knew what she meant. Gail was reasonably sure the entire ship's complement had known before she'd even made it back to the privacy of her quarters—a privacy disturbed within minutes by a thoroughly outraged Grant who seemed to think it was her fault.

*Maybe it was. It didn't change anything.* "I wouldn't ask, except that it's important to the research, Malley," she said as earnestly as possible. "Is this normal? Does Aaron usually try to avoid anyone he's touched? He didn't with you."

"He's wallowing in something, that's for sure," Malley muttered, more to himself than to her. "If that's what it is . . . stay here a minute."

Gail watched the stationer stride through the milling techs, head and shoulders above most, until he caught up with Pardell. She could follow their conversation without being close enough to hear words—Malley wasn't being subtle. First he pointed at her, then threw both arms in the air as though making some point that required volume. Pardell shook his head almost continually. Then Malley shrugged and came back to her—alone.

Gail kept her expression set to neutral interest. Whatever the stationer had said about her, she knew it was likely to be embarrassing at best, especially with the audience nearby. But she had been honest: her feelings about the night of the accident were irrelevant—Pardell's were not.

"Well?" Gail demanded. Might as well get it over with—she had work to do, and now, thanks to the stationer's idea of a private conversation, far too many who'd be watching her every move for the rest of the day.

Malley's face was impossible to read. "Aaron says he apologizes for having misinterpreted your interest in his welfare. He says—" Malley seemed to gag on the next part, but struggled on as though he'd sworn to repeat what Pardell had told him word-for-word, "—that he appreciates your position on this ship and understands that you were only being professional." The stationer drew in a deep breath, then almost bellowed: "And what the hell is that supposed to mean?"

Gail bit her lower lip for a moment. "I don't know, Malley."

*After six days of Aaron Pardell*, Gail added to herself, *she only had more questions.*

# Chapter 53

"**Y**OU'D think after six days, I'd be able to win at this," Pardell complained cheerfully.

Grant laughed and used the back of his wrist to clear sweat from his forehead. The drops caught in the dark curls on his chest and lower arms glistened in the table's illumination, except where three broad and parallel scars traced what the Earther referred to only as "camping misadventure" from left shoulder to lower right rib. Those on Thromberg kept their scars because they had to. Pardell wondered, but never asked, why this Earther chose to cherish his. "You'd think after that long, you'd get tired of losing," Grant quipped. "Your serve."

*Win, lose. The game was more than its outcome*, Pardell thought, tossing up the small white ball and swinging the paddle. The complexity of directing and anticipating the ball's movement pleased that distractible part of his mind. He toyed with torque and rotation, while enjoying the effort of trying to match the Earther's grace and speed.

Perhaps Ping-Pong, though not a game played on Thromberg, was a favorite pastime of the Earther military. Grant was possibly good enough to play competitively—Pardell suspected the man had slowed his own game down, at least in the beginning, just so the newcomer could return the occasional volley.

Regardless, Pardell was grateful for more than the new skill and exercise. The *Seeker*'s enforced day/night cycle found him sitting up reading or wandering aimlessly through those areas he'd discovered were safely vacant while others slept. The aloneness was somewhat welcome. Not that he complained, but occasionally the press of enthusiastic, curious people in the lab grew uncomfortable. Malley knew the signs and could be all too blunt about getting others to back off.

On the other hand, Pardell soon found pacing the vacant halls was also numbingly boring, until he'd encountered Grant, who apparently didn't sleep much either—or kept very strange hours—and who professed to need a partner for his game.

*A watcher, beyond doubt.* But a surprisingly agreeable one. *It could be worse.*

"Aha!" He'd scored a point.

"Didn't see that one coming," Grant confessed proudly. "Much better, Aaron. At this rate, we should set up a doubles' match against Szpindel and his comm tech."

Pardell hesitated. One of the things he'd grown to like about these post-midnight games was that they played in shorts only, Grant claiming to need the change from his uniform. He'd known Pardell's sensitivity to light and had the regular lighting of the gym dimmed except for the table and wall surfaces. *Malley's deduction*, Pardell supposed, since he'd never told anyone how bright light made the veins under his exposed skin crawl unpleasantly; there were enough strange things about him.

Raner's advice: stick to friends, avoid strangers, and don't show what could stay hidden.

The first time Pardell had stripped down, he'd almost hoped Grant would stare or be uncomfortable, so he could be properly insulted. Instead, the Earther had ignored his gold-veined skin and taught him the rudiments of Ping-Pong—including how the ball felt driven into your cheekbone or rib cage at a high velocity.

*Have someone else here?* A stranger?

"On the other hand," Grant said as if he hadn't noticed Pardell's lack of reply, "maybe we should drag your lazy friend in for a game."

*Malley? With a Ping-Pong paddle?* Pardell laughed as he lunged to catch Grant's next serve. "He's quick. But I'm not sure how long your table would last. I'll ask him."

"How is he finding it, by the way? The ship—moving about."

Pardell just missed the ball and peered at Grant. *A real concern or probing for information about potential hazards?* From what he'd learned of this man, likely both. "Malley's fine. He's used to not thinking about space while inside a station. He'll get used to not thinking about space while inside a ship." Pardell loved knowing he was moving translight, sidestepping time and space the way the *Merry Mate II* had done, his atoms cushioned within the initiation matrix of the ship so they didn't really exist—but did. These were imaginings he didn't try to discuss with the stationer. "Dr. Lynn and the others are keeping him too busy to think about it much." If Pardell's return serve was a little skewed, Grant was gracious enough not to comment.

Malley'd settled right in, almost one of the crew, as if his intellect had been waiting for the science sphere and all its toys. Pardell had seen the stationer walking the daytime corridors trading jokes and knowing names, just as he would on the station. *Nights?*

He wasn't always in his quarters at night, just as on the station. Pardell studiously avoided finding out where the stationer went. It wasn't to exercise in the gym.

The next volley lasted longer than most. He found himself leaping from one side of the table to the other, smashing the little ball triumphantly, watching Grant mirror his movements. Again. Again. Then, suddenly, he had to lean too far forward to make a shot and scrambled back in time to hear Grant's return whistle past his ear.

"Game," Pardell said, saluting the Earther with the paddle.

"Barely," Grant admitted, grabbing two towels and tossing one at Pardell. "Let's head down to the crew lounge and see what's up for breakfast."

The crew lounge was in the command sphere, a section of the ship Pardell had visited only once, during an afternoon's tour with Grant.

*Not routine.*

Pardell gathered his clothes, but didn't immediately follow Grant to the showers. "That's where off-duty crew spend time. Am I allowed in there?"

When not on duty himself, Grant had an expressive face. Right now he looked torn between impatience and sympathy. "You're 'allowed' anywhere you want, Aaron, just not alone. Dr. Smith's orders were quite clear on that. You aren't under quarantine or arrest—although the hours she has you wired up in the lab probably feel like it. Make use of your freedom—the *Seeker*'s a remarkable ship."

Pardell had heard Gail's orders, all right. He hadn't believed them for an instant. *Maybe*, he thought, *it was time to test them for himself.* "So I could go to the bridge," he ventured.

"Get dressed, first," Grant suggested, with a distinctly challenging smile.

*Orders. Requests. Messages. Instructions.* As Pardell pulled on his clothes—still *his* clothes, not *Seeker* "hand-me-news"—he realized those had been the sum of his communications with Gail Smith since they'd touched in the lab. *His fault or hers?*

*His*, if he were honest.

"You almost ready, Aaron?" Grant called from the corridor.

"Coming," Pardell replied, pulling on his boots and trying to dismiss the memory. He'd deserved what he'd felt.

They'd not spoken a word to one another beyond the needs of her experiments since. He'd been too humiliated and angry at first, at everything, not just her.

*Later?*

Pardell had found himself studying Gail Smith even as she studied him, hour after hour, day after day. He'd seen the way her eyes clouded when she concentrated, then snapped into brightness with each new idea or approach. He'd seen—did the others?—how she drove herself harder than anyone around her, her seemingly boundless energy fueled by passion for her work. It couldn't have been sleep. Her face had grown thinner since he'd learned it, tired around the eyes, though it still possessed dimples.

He'd seen them in her smiles at Malley.

At some mysterious, otherwise unremarkable instant—had it been when he'd noticed how Gail stood close to ask him questions, unafraid, though she knew firsthand the pain of his touch? or maybe when she'd stopped an experiment because a tech had forgotten to strap him in for his own safety—his heart had started to pound and he'd lost himself in the way her hair caught light and transmuted it into gold.

So now, he still couldn't talk to her. *But it wasn't anger.*

"You fall asleep?" Grant rapped on the door impatiently. "We do have be on duty at some point today."

Pardell shook away any thought but anticipation. He'd never seen a working starship bridge. Grant was right—it was time he started enjoying his freedom.

*No point daydreaming about anything, or anyone, else.*

# Chapter 54

*I*T *might have been a dream, except for its importance.* Gail ran her fingers over her forearm again, fearing the impulse was on its way to becoming a habit, but using it to try and extract everything possible from the memory. Her arm had touched the edge of his thumb. There'd been pain, a burning that shot from that contact to her fingers and upward, to wrap from shoulder to throat.

Pardell had confessed to pain, less localized than hers, likely more intense. He'd been ill. That was all.

*It couldn't have been all.* Her every instinct insisted he'd lied, even though she had no idea why he would. Proof? Nothing Gail could take to her colleagues. But until that moment, there had been something growing between them. Gail might want it otherwise—*could there be a worse time to be attracted to someone, or a worse someone to choose?*—but she wasn't blind to her own feelings. She didn't think she'd misinterpreted his. Beyond reason, beyond sense, time they'd spent together had passed like nothing at all. Time apart . . . had become merely waiting.

Pardell's avoidance of her, his careful distancing and oh-so-businesslike conversation—*yes, Dr. Smith . . . of course, Dr. Smith*—when they had to work together, weren't helping. Unless she buried herself in her work, Gail found herself distracted. Sometimes, even then. *Irony come to roost*, she thought, in those moments of mental clarity when she could step away from herself and take a good look. What had put her in charge of this ship and its search for the Quill—her intensity, her judgment—conspired against her now. She was consumed by longings and judged herself a fool.

"Cooper?" Gail called to the tech. "I need corroboration on these results. Get something worked out with Dr. Temujin and don't let him go off on a tangent again. Remember, we've a great deal to accomplish in the next couple of days."

"Two days? What then?" Malley, never far, pulled over a stool.

Gail could look him in the eye once he'd sat and she did, treading with sudden care to say only: "We'll reach our destination." Malley had taken to being on the ship a little too well, according to the preliminary psych reports she had on her desk. He might be young, smart, and adaptable. Or he might simply be dumping the entire concept into someplace dark and scared that could ultimately explode from the strain.

No sign this bothered him at all. "What happens there?"

"We orbit," Dr. Temujin offered gleefully, stopping short of bouncing as he walked over to them. He'd learned very few of his colleagues were impressed by physical enthusiasm before their third coffee. "We orbit, we examine, and if all is as we hope, we begin implementation of Trial Number One! Two days, Dr. Smith. You must be so excited. The culmination of your work is at hand."

"And Trial Number One might be?" Malley raised his eyebrows quizzically, with no sign of any other reaction but curiosity. Gail was impressed.

She raised an eyebrow back. "What precedes Trials Two through Fifty, Malley. You're welcome to check the list of approved experiments." She pointed to the scrolling display board near the main exit, on one of the lab's two permanent walls. The D-board itself was becoming a crucial tool as the various research leaders posted last-minute requests and changes. "This isn't only about my mission to retrieve Quill tissue, you realize, although that's our central purpose. What made it easy to fill the *Seeker* with the brightest and best was the chance to do some deep-space science—"

"And put Titan University back where it should be, at the forefront of human exploration and understanding of the universe."

"Good morning, Dr. Reinsez," Gail said politely to the man

arriving with a trio of FDs. "You're up early." *Another one who always knew when she didn't want him around.*

Dr. Reinsez smiled benevolently. "The closer we get to your mystery planet, Dr. Smith, the less anyone seems to be sleeping on this ship. Why should I be any different? It's the air of discovery. The lure of the unknown—"

"The certainty that no matter the outcome," Gail said cuttingly, "you'll earn that Chair of Extrasolar Studies you've been after for fifteen years." They'd come to an understanding of sorts. If she failed, he had enough evidence to end her career and make his own. *If she succeeded?* Gail had willingly volunteered to share any fame and glory, going so far as to give Reinsez her written guarantee.

*Such things were irrelevant now.*

Reinsez, to whom such things were still everything, looked insufferably smug. "There's that. So what's up today? And where's your test subject?" The latter was said with an uneasy glance around, as if Reinsez feared Pardell might be sneaking up on him from behind.

*Where indeed?* Without being obvious about it, Gail looked around as well. Pardell typically came in with, or shortly after, his friend, waiting until the stationer rapped on his door before making an appearance. Grant had confirmed Pardell rarely slept more than three hours a ship night, so she assumed this practice was another deliberate attempt to avoid being alone with her.

*What had he felt from her touch?*

Cornell, one of the FDs who "happened" to arrive with Reinsez—Gail's orders being very specific in how little autonomy the man was to be allowed—spoke up, "Mr. Pardell is on the bridge, Dr. Smith."

Gail had overruled Tobo in granting her guests shipwide access. It had seemed only reasonable at the time, considering it could well be argued she'd kidnapped all three. With Grant's people assuming responsibility for monitoring their movements, she hadn't given it further thought. *Until now.*

"Where's Rosalind Fournier?" she asked. The two 'siders took their evening meals together, but as far as she'd been told or observed, Pardell didn't seek Rosalind out otherwise. The older 'ider spent most of her time, understandably, in the *Seeker's* engineering section.

FD Sensun answered. "In her assigned quarters, Dr. Smith."

*Aaron was on the bridge.* She wondered what Tobo was going to say about that.

Her heart gave a sickening lurch. Without a word, Gail almost flew out of the lab, dodging past sleepy incoming techs without apology, running flat out down the corridor to the waist connecting the science sphere to the rest of the ship.

She'd shown Tobo and Grant the recording uploaded from the returning shuttle and buried under layers of code all these years within the *'Mate.* She'd had to—it was too much to ask their blind cooperation in ignoring Titan's orders, when their heads would roll with hers. But only those two, besides herself and Aaron. And, as far as she knew, the 'sider hadn't shown Malley.

Perhaps Aaron wouldn't care that Tobo and Grant had seen his past.

Unfortunately, he was very likely to care about something Tobo and Grant knew that she hadn't found a way to tell him yet. That in two days they'd be in orbit around no mystery planet, but the world where he'd been bom. And his parents had died.

Gail could only hope Tobo knew when *not* to tell stories to a guest on his bridge.

# Chapter 55

PARDELL leaned forward in the first officer's chair. He hadn't felt so at home since leaving the *'Mate*. "And no one saw the ship again, Captain?" he prompted Tobo. Spacer tales were the folklore of his youth—he'd grown up sitting at the feet of those who'd either lived them, or embellished with gusto. Or both. The *Seeker*'s round-faced Captain was a master storyteller of the same ilk.

"Never again, Mr. Pardell. You can be sure the families of the lost crew searched, but to this day, not a trace, not a whisper of a signal or translight trail, has ever been found." Tobo's voice was suitably low and grim.

Pardell grinned with delight. Tobo took one look at him, tried to keep a straight, somber face, then burst into laughter, his dark eyes twinkling. "Well, if that didn't scare you, young man, have you heard the one about the star barge *Misery's Company* and her blackhearted captain?"

"No, and I'd love to, Captain," Pardell said sincerely, "but I can tell from Commander Grant's monotonous twitching I'm late for my duties in the science sphere. But thank you." He hesitated, then asked: "May I come again?"

Pardell had thought the *Seeker*'s bridge would make him homesick, but there'd been no points of comparison to draw him into memories of the *Merry Mate II*. This was a place of wonders, wonders he could comprehend, as opposed to those in the lab which Malley had to explain to him, usually more than once, or which involved being wired up like a console himself. When they'd arrived, Grant had introduced him to First Officer Szpindel, whose night shift boredom was patent in the speed with which he'd offered a tour. Afterward, Grant had suggested breakfast, but Pardell couldn't bear to leave. Not for something as ordinary as food. The commander had promised to be back to collect him.

Pardell was used to becoming unremarkable. It hadn't taken long before the bridge crew forgot about him, to all intents and purposes. He'd sat, drinking in the view of a passing nebula on the towering screen, for once content to let his surroundings expand and grow strange around him as his perceptions deepened and wandered, relaxed enough to permit his mind its hunt for connections, seeing the past in the curve of a man's spine and the curl of a nebula, the future in tones of language and tamed light, letting his thoughts expand and roam as they would.

He could well have sat there forever, but Captain Tobo had arrived, complete with tea service, and offered to tell him the real truths of space travel.

And now Commander Grant stood, ready to provide another official twitch if he didn't get moving, all trace of the cheerful Ping-Pong partner occluded by a uniform and a tough, professional bearing. *Well, not all.* Pardell had seen Grant holding in a smile of his own at the incredible finale to Tobo's story.

*Maybe,* Pardell admitted to himself, *just maybe, this wasn't such a bad place to be.*

At the same instant, the door to the bridge whooshed open and in ran, not walked, Gail Smith, followed by two of Grant's FDs. Grant straightened with a subvocal oath and Tobo surged to his feet.

Pardell stayed in his seat, hoping whatever sent Gail Smith chasing all the way to her ship's bridge had nothing to do with his being here.

*Even if part of him hoped it did.*

# Chapter 56

*T*HERE *really wasn't going to be a graceful, easy way out of this,* Gail told herself, coming to a breathless halt steps from Tobo and Pardell, Grant already in "full alert" mode and looking to her shadows for clues to the emergency.

She clawed loose hair from her eyes and couldn't tear her gaze away from Pardell's face. He looked normal, if a little wary. Not the look of someone who'd just learned how soon, and how directly, he was going to meet the dark truths of his past.

*There wasn't an easy way,* Gail knew suddenly. *There was only one way.*

"I came——" Her voice was still too shaky. Gail took two more deep breaths and smoothed down her lab coat by jamming her hands in the pockets. "I came to ask you to have breakfast with me, Aaron." She then took another breath and added reasonably: "If you have had breakfast, we could have coffee—or tea."

Now the hazel eyes were puzzled, but oddly off guard, as if she'd caught him relaxing at home. "I've had tea with your entertaining Captain, Dr. Smith." Then, perhaps because her face wasn't under any type of control and must have shown something of her desperation, Pardell clarified: "But I haven't had breakfast."

"Good. That's good. Someone call the steward's office and have breakfast for two sent to my office. You've had breakfast," she informed Grant, staving off any thoughts he might have of joining them.

*This was going to be hard enough without an audience.*

\*     \*     \*

Gail had fully expected to have to order Grant to allow her to
be alone with the 'sider. After all, to the FD commander,
Pardell was still an unknown quantity and proved lethal—a security risk by any definition. But Grant hadn't argued. In fact,
the flash of sympathy in the look he sent after Pardell was almost unnerving.

*Grant knew what she planned to do.*

Gail fervently wished she did as the door closed, leaving her
alone with Aaron Pardell. "This is my office," she heard herself
announce.

Aaron looked at her out the corner of one eye. He was prowling, something he seemed to do automatically in a new room, as
though checking the exits. Probably a 'sider habit—Gail had
seen Rosalind do it, too. "Not in the science sphere?" he
sounded surprised.

"It's a compromise. I'm close to the bridge if Captain Tobo
needs me. And I've meetings with representatives from the university here. That sort of thing."

"And breakfast."

"And breakfast," she agreed. Gail shoved her hands in her
pockets again, then realized that might appear defensive and
shrugged off her lab coat, tossing it over the back of her chair.
A rain of stylos, clips, and forceps hit the floor. She hurriedly
bent down to retrieve them, holding her hair out of her eyes with
one hand and wishing she'd remembered to tie it back.

"Here," a quiet voice said. She tilted her head and saw Aaron
balanced on his heels in front of her, with most of the escapees
from her lab coat in his glove. "Hold out your hands."

"Thank you," Gail said softly, in case her voice might startle
him back behind the wall he'd kept between them. She cupped
her hands and held them out, studying his face rather than looking down as the small objects dropped into her palms.

*His face.* She'd mapped it, surface and underlying tissue
both, and tested its skin's sensitivity with remotes and volunteers. If she were an artist, she could have drawn its clean, sharp
lines from memory. It haunted her dreams.

She'd never seen it, not like this, with his eyes traveling over
her face as if finding something lost, his lower lip slowly drawn
into his mouth and held between his teeth, then released with a

sigh that feathered warm against her skin. His eyes traced their way across her mouth, then her neck, then lower—not assessing, but memorizing. They stopped where she hadn't bothered fastening the top of her shirt this morning and she watched the blood rise along his cheekbones.

Her own were flaming. Gail felt an almost visceral shock as Pardell brought his eyes to hers at last and she saw the naked *wanting* in them.

She couldn't remember how to move.

"Your breakfast, Dr. Smith?"

Aaron leaped to his feet and Gail heard him talking to the steward. She took advantage of the distraction to fasten her shirt all the way to her throat, then collect the escaped contents of her pockets from the floor. She'd dropped them again. *When?* By the time she stood, Aaron and the steward had two places set at the meeting table in the corner.

*Keep the steward here*, part of her mind babbled, even as she nodded her thanks and realized the man had taken it for dismissal.

They were alone again.

"This was why you asked me here, Dr. Smith, wasn't it?" Pardell asked, his voice deliberately curious, nothing more.

"What?" Gail blinked, realizing she was still standing behind her desk while Aaron had taken a seat at the table.

"Breakfast?" his mouth deepened at the corners, as if he tried not to smile.

"Yes. Of course." Gail hurried to the other chair and tried to compose herself.

Aaron glanced up at her, his face oddly unreadable, then took two glasses and poured water into both. He put one glass in front of her, took the other in his hand, and waited.

*No blame; no apologies.* Gail's hand almost slipped from the glass as she recognized the ritual and suddenly realized what Aaron must be assuming. He had to believe she'd brought him here for this, to put aside whatever conflict lingered from that night. Since he accepted the gesture, she knew beyond doubt he'd abide by it. She lifted her glass and sipped once, when he did, then again. They put their glasses down in unison.

*How strange,* Gail thought. The small act didn't reduce the tension between them at all—merely changed its focus from the past to the present. "I have a—confession—to make, Aaron," she said. "When I said I was the only one to see the vid from the *'Mate*, the one with your parents—that was a lie. I'd shown Captain Tobo. Grant as well. I had a reason—"

Aaron didn't look surprised. He simply raised one eyebrow and waited.

"I knew about the *'Mate* before leaving Titan University. I came to Thromberg to find you—a direct descendant of Susan Witts—that part's true. I needed your genome for the suits. But I also came to find your ship and her records. I was looking for—"

"Pardell's World?" He raised both eyebrows. "That is where you're taking the *Seeker*, isn't it?"

*Damn.* Gail stared at him. "You knew? I didn't tell anyone but Tobo and Grant. The course is sealed even from the bridge crew. Who told you?" *So much for worrying about his reaction.* Now she had a major security leak to report to Grant—who wasn't going to be pleased. *At all.*

No mistaking Aaron's amusement now. "No one, Dr. Smith. Your secret destination is safe. But I do know something of starships and the section of space around Thromberg Station. If you'd wanted the nearest Quill-contaminated world, you had your choice of three in the time we've been translight. The only possible explanation I can see for bypassing those—opportunities—was that you wanted not just a world with Quill, but a specific world. The one where I was born."

"Have you told Malley any of this?"

"You'd know if I had." This time, he sounded less amused.

Gail blushed, not because the 'sider was right about being under surveillance, but because of the collection of those surveillance records she wasn't by any stretch of protocol supposed to have in the drawer of the desk. The desk she could see behind him, with the cup shard from the *'Mate* in plain sight. "Best we keep it to ourselves a bit longer," she managed to say. "We'll be in orbit in two days; then it won't matter who knows. I should have told you, Aaron."

"You couldn't know I'd respect a secret," he replied frankly. "I hope you do now."

"Yes." Gail took a deep breath and the universe seemed to settle itself, or she was simply light-headed. She wasn't taking bets on either. "Let's have this breakfast before it's cold. Coffee?"

"Please." He held out his cup and she poured, acutely aware of the distance between her fingers and his.

When Aaron was alone, he removed the gloves to eat. He didn't now—she caught herself wondering if it was for the same reason she'd fastened her shirt uncomfortably high. *As if it helped*, Gail told herself, feeling her skin burn beneath the clothing.

"Are those grapes?"

The table was set with a variety of dishes. Since all were to be shared, Gail hoped this satisfied the 'sider's sensibilities. She found the fruit plate and spotted the generous bunch draped over one end. "These? Yes. Would you like to try some?" Without thinking, Gail picked up the bunch and held them out, then realized Aaron might not know which parts to eat. She tugged one grape free and popped it into her mouth, then offered the rest to him. "Watch for seeds inside. They're not supposed to have any, but they might. You don't swallow those."

He looked fascinated and somewhat alarmed, but went to take one. Then he hesitated. Before she could ask what was wrong, he solemnly pulled off his gloves and folded them neatly on the table beside his plate. "You don't mind, do you?" he asked. "You've seen—"

"Of course not," Gail assured him quickly.

"Thank you." The 'sider pulled one of the grapes from the bunch in her hand, his gold-wrapped fingers close enough to hers that she imagined their warmth, but carefully no closer. He chewed then swallowed with a curious expression. "They didn't get them right, on the station," Aaron decided, taking two more. "The look, maybe, but not the flavor or texture."

The rest of the meal was like that. Aaron seemed to take it as a chance to experiment, perhaps feeling that way inclined in her company—more probably enjoying the freedom to choose outside Dr. Lynn's list. He liked the slips of ham but frowned after the egg. He'd already discovered salt wasn't a favorite, but pepper was, and used the mill to sprinkle the spice on almost everything.

They found themselves talking easily about food and its preparation. Gail traded no-longer embarrassing stories about her family's occasionally disastrous tradition of home cooking on Sundays for Pardell's anecdotes about the efforts of the station to add variety to the daily rations.

"They tried to make apple pie out of fungal proteins? Did that work?" she asked, frankly amazed.

Pardell grinned at her. "I wouldn't know. I've never had apple pie. But it tasted awful to me. Malley ate mine and Syd's—almost made himself sick."

Gail shook her head. "I confess—I had this image of life on a station as being a grim battle for survival, with people barely able to think about tomorrow, let alone share apple pie, real or not."

His face immediately closed up and she wished the words unsaid, but it was too late. "We don't want your pity," he said, his voice abruptly harsh. "I don't want it."

"I don't pity you," Gail protested. "I never have."

His eyes bored into hers. "That's a lie."

*Was it?* Gail made herself coldly analyze everything she'd felt about this man since she'd first learned of his existence. *Had she pitied him?* "Once," she said, sensing herself on the verge of something vastly important. "Only once. When you told me how you watched Malley with his mother. I thought of how you must have felt—how it would feel to be a child unable to be touched."

"Only then?" he challenged her, his face grown pale and stern, like a judge demanding an oath. "Am I supposed to believe that?" he demanded fiercely.

*Don't ask him why it matters*, Gail warned herself, *don't think about what this said about his actions since that night.* She wouldn't allow distraction now, when she was so close to understanding. *Did Aaron understand?* "You felt it," she said, slowly, carefully. "The emotion. *My* emotion. You felt it through my arm, through your hand. That's it, isn't it? When anyone touches you, you experience their emotions somehow. That's what we couldn't measure—"

"I get sick," Aaron rebutted angrily. *Too angrily*, she thought, considering how hard he'd been trying to make sense of himself during their experiments, of results showing only what he'd already told them—that the response was immediate and its intensity scaled geometrically upward depending on the interval between contacts, and the amount and duration of each. *But nothing of* what *he responded to*, what *he sent back out.*

"That's all," Aaron continued. "It hurts. You measured that just fine. That's all I feel."

"It can't be," Gail insisted. "You said I pitied you—I don't. The only way you'd think so is if you picked up that emotion *the only moment* I felt it. Maybe you don't recognize it as such; maybe you process emotions differently—"

"How much more of a freak do you want me to be, Dr. Smith?" Aaron interrupted, getting to his feet. "Isn't this good enough for you?" He thrust out his hands—their gold veins pulsed and writhed under the skin.

Gail made herself calm, controlled, the antithesis of his passion. She had to. "There's been a piece missing from the equation—my instincts knew it. I was waiting for the truth about what you feel from other people."

"Feel?" he almost shouted. "Pain. I feel pain. I feel sick. I feel nauseous. I feel my body exploding and about to die—"

"And what else?" Gail demanded, seeing his distress but refusing to react to it. "If you can't admit the truth to me, at least admit it to yourself."

She was making him shake. "How can it help? Tell me that, Gail. How can it help anything to know what a freak I really am?"

"You have to trust me," Gail said, coming to stand in front of the 'sider, where she could reach out and touch him, if she dared. "You do feel something else, something more. Tell me. You must."

Aaron wasn't as tall as Malley, but he still looked down to meet her eyes. His were haunted and she saw sweat on his forehead. "Pain, like daggers plunging into me," he said in a low, tortured voice. Hesitation. "But you're right. I can tell it's—theirs. It's what they feel when they touch me, when I hurt them. I feel anger at the pain. Their anger. Their fear. Fear's always part of it. Even from my friends. Even from you." He paused, then asked almost pleadingly: "How can knowing this help?"

"I want you to understand yourself," Gail said earnestly, desperately. *Believe me, Aaron*, she begged silently, knowing she had no proof, no way to convince him beyond her own belief. "I need you to understand. There has to be more than pain and fear involved. Those could simply be reactions to what they experience, what you experience."

"No."

*There was a way.* Even as the thought crossed her mind, Gail stretched out her hand, palm up. "Touch me now."

Pardell shied away, putting his hands back as if she'd tried to grab them. "No!"

She looked into his eyes, seeing and understanding the fear there. "Just for an instant. We've tried everything else—every tool, every device—and failed. This time, Aaron, I want you to test yourself. Touch my hand. Tell me what you feel. What *I* feel."

He didn't want to—and he did. The conflict raged across Pardell's face, expressions flickering faster than she could recall seeing before. Gail held herself aloof from amazement or curiosity. She was afraid of the pain and even more afraid of failure, but these were emotions she'd battled before. What was at first difficult, then all at once easier than breathing, was summoning the complex mix of caring and desire that had tormented her these past days. A relief, to let go the guard she'd kept on her heart.

"Touch me, Aaron," she urged softly.

He came closer, as if obeying in spite of himself, his hand rising to hover over hers. "Gail. This isn't necessary," he said almost desperately.

"Yes, it is," she said, lifting her hand to his before he could avoid it.

PAIN!

"Gail. Gail. Can you hear me? Please say you can hear me."

It was Aaron's voice. "I hear you." She rubbed a hand over her eyes, her left hand. The right still throbbed with remembered agony. It was an effort, but Gail looked up. She was sprawled on her office floor. *Most undignified.*

Aaron was kneeling as close to her as he dared, his face white with strain, eyes deep holes of worry. "Are you all right?"

"Are you?" Gail countered, getting to her knees and, when that wasn't too difficult, rising to her feet. She stayed upright long enough to reach a chair and sit. Her legs were still unsteady. "Aaron?"

He had one hand pressed to his head as if to hold it together. "You are—I don't know what you are," he said weakly, sitting down himself, but on the floor. "That was such a stupid idea, Gail."

"Was it?" she asked, willing him to answer.

Aaron gazed at her, as if seeing her for the first time, as if the sight of her gave him strength. "No," he said at last. A slow smile spread across his face, igniting something in his eyes that took her breath away. "No, it wasn't."

Gail collected her wits. "Then I was right—somehow emotions pass into you from others," she said, trying, and failing abysmally, to achieve a professional tone while he kept looking at her like that. "They affect you. And maybe," the flare of ideas cleared her mind, "maybe what you send back out is a result, a reflection. Only other people can't process that reflection and feel just the pain. But why . . . what function could it serve . . . ?"

"You're trying to find something useful in what I am— something to make sense of it." Aaron shook his head. "You're wrong. I'm a freak of nature."

"Anything Nature does is worthwhile—in the right place, at the right time, to the right organism."

"Organism?" His eyes widened with dismay. "What do you think I am?"

Gail made herself relentless. "Can you remember feeling any other emotions?" She watched him think, his pupils dilating, and scarcely dared breathe.

"Yes," he admitted, coming back to her a long moment later, his expression startled. "Malley's mother. She pushed us out of the way of weapons fire—saved us both. There was pain and fear—hers and mine. But there was something else."

"What?"

Pardell's eyes warmed, the unhappy line of his lips softened.

"She loved us. I'd never thought about it until then—kids don't—but I felt it as she touched me. Before I felt her die." This last so quietly Gail barely heard the words.

Then, forcefully, demanding her answer as his right: "So what possible use is this? What am I? Why am I?"

*No more secrets.* Gail clenched her hands into fists, but was proud her voice was steady as she began the explanation she knew might destroy the man she loved.

"First, Aaron, I have to tell you about the Quill Effect—"

# Chapter 57

*H*E *owed it all to the Quill.*

Pardell swung, watching the ball shatter as it hit. He reached into the pail, picked out another one, and methodically swung again. *Smash.*

Like everyone in or on Thromberg Station, he'd used the Quill to explain the way things were, to excuse or comprehend their banishment from the rest of humanity, to make sense of why families consisted of those alive now, and those already dead.

But now, it seemed, the Quill were also responsible for his existence.

*Smash.*

She'd known. *Gail.* Her name flooded his mind with unwelcome, irresistible thoughts. He understood everything, thanks to her. He now understood—better than anyone—how dangerous he was to those he—

*Smash.*

Cared about. *Admit it*, Pardell told himself ruthlessly. *It wasn't a secret, not after the way he'd stared at her.* Not after he'd had to fight the urge to ignore the silly grapes and explore the smoothness of her skin, even knowing the complete impossibility of it. Instead, he'd done everything he could during that wonder-filled breakfast to touch what she touched, where she'd touched, as if it were the same. Had she noticed? Did she know how the warmth lingering on a plate from her hand had made his heart pound?

Had the blood in her cheeks and the dark, drowning heat in her eyes really been meant for him? Had what he'd felt from her touch, beneath the pain, that intense warmth and longing—had it been real?

Or had his own feelings played a cruel trick on him?

*Smash.*

And now, he wasn't even fully human.

"How many of those things do you think they have?"

For all the sound Malley had made entering the dark gym and walking to stand beside him, they could have been Outside. Pardell didn't look around. *Smash.* "Go away," he said.

"That's not exactly easy, if you hadn't noticed."

*Smash.*

"Did they send you from the lab?" *Did she?* "Am I holding up some great and necessary test? Do they need their resident—" *Smash.* This time the paddle. "—murdering—" *Smash.* The pail. "—Quill?"

"Well, isn't this productive?"

"Productive?" Pardell turned at last, glaring up at Malley. "If you want productive, then tell them to practice destroying the Quill—they have one now, don't they? Isn't that the whole point of this? To save us all from things like me?"

The stationer ignored Pardell's outburst, hiking himself up to sit on the Ping-Pong table—which creaked—and pulling out two cups and a flask. "Civilized man, Grant," he said. "Knows the value of a good fermented beverage. Mind you," Malley cautioned, sniffing the top of the flask—having opened it and tossed the lid over one shoulder. "Mind you, I've no idea what was fermented to make this fine . . . whatever it is."

"Twenty years ago, my parents died so I could be born a citizen of a world I didn't know existed," Pardell said, the words pouring out so fast he could hardly breathe. "Oh, excuse me. That's not accurate, is it? My mother died. My father somehow resisted the mysterious Quill Effect long enough to crawl to their shuttle and put me inside. Did you see that recording, too? Did you see how my father set the emergency lift on a timer, then went back for my mother? Only he didn't make the return trip."

"Grant showed me—Gail's orders," Malley told him, his eyes paired glints in the dim light. "Have some. I hate drinking alone."

*Some people want to be alone*, Pardell thought, but took the glass and swallowed hastily. Then he choked as something aromatic and bitter burned its way down the back of his throat, etched his esophagus, and landed with a minor explosion in his stomach. "You're sure this is safe to drink?" he sputtered.

"Grant said it was single-something Scotch. Claimed it was expensive on Earth," Malley's voice was dubious. "I don't think you're supposed to gulp it like that."

"Makes Sammie's stuff taste good."

Malley shook the flask gently. "Should be enough in here to get used to it."

"You could leave me alone," Pardell wished out loud, coming to sit on the table beside his friend. The thing held—gave a little, maybe. He held up his glass.

"We've a day and a half before we reach your planet," Malley said blithely, pouring into both. "By then, we need to be ready for the bad guys."

"Like me," Pardell muttered, taking his next dose of fermentation with a little more caution. Once he knew what was coming, it wasn't quite as bad. There was a welcome kick to it anyway.

"You don't look like a thin, iridescent filament with no pretensions of life. Well, you are scrawny." Malley gave a huge sigh, challenging the table again. "I was so hoping for something we could strangle or shoot. Like a three-meter googly-eyed monster. You ever talk to Grant or his folks about monsters?"

"Can't say the subject came up," Pardell admitted, holding his glass out again.

"They have an entirely different viewpoint than you or I."

"Different how?"

Malley's voice deepened, as though this was serious. "The First Defense thing? Aisha's told me it's not one-way. Sure, they protect people, no doubts there, but what's their definition of people? That's another thing altogether. In fact, the whole point of the FD is to prove it is."

"And how much of Grant's Scotch did you try before coming?" Pardell inquired politely.

"No, no. None. Hear me out on this, Aaron." Malley poured

again. "We're alone in the universe. Just people, dirt, balls of burning gases, and the odd alien rodent. Right? Well, so far."

"So far." Pardell repeated.

"Right. Remember reading about how things were before the Quill? Earth had an entire arm of its military devoted to First Contact, stuffed full of dreamers who wanted to be the first to shake a tentacle or hug a blob. Where are all those dreamers now?"

Pardell sighed. *Malley on a roll was impossible to deflect.* "I'm sure you're going to tell me."

"Think about it. Highly trained, motivated people seeing their budgets threatened when Earth begins pulling out of deep-space exploration to focus on terraforming. People out of jobs, unless they find something else, something socially palatable to offer the taxpaying public. So the military quietly scraps First Contact and loudly unveils its First Defense Units to protect humanity against the unknown, which became so much easier to justify when along comes a bona fide unknown menace—the Quill."

"Which is why Grant's unit is on the *Seeker*. This isn't news, Malley."

"No. Well, yes. But that's not the only reason. Remember, the FDs are people who've kept some older ideas and goals. The FD mandate isn't just to protect humanity from the alien. Oh, no. It's also to protect any alien intelligence we might encounter *from* humanity. Grant and his people are experts in communication and weapon tech—they don't mention training in negotiation psychology and xenobiology, do they?

"What we have with us, Aaron, my friend, are a bunch of diplomats with two chamber pulse cannons, ready to make sure we all behave at that inaugural meeting and play nice. Or whatever we're supposed to do with whatever we meet. Whenever we meet, whomever they are." Malley seemed fascinated by his own eloquence.

Pardell no longer doubted that flask had been full before his friend offered to share its contents. "And you are telling me this because . . . ?"

Malley's teeth gleamed. "I thought you might like to know the FDs would doubtless step in to protect you from Dr. Smith and her cronies. You'd have to put up with their tendency to use tranks instead of real weapons. But they'll talk up a storm for you, I'm sure. You just have that one small problem of convincing them you are a googly-eyed monster and not one hundred percent human."

"So you don't think I'm a—Quill."

"Why should I?" Malley said in his best "must I explain it again" voice. "You're a man born on a planet where the evidence suggests there were Quill. There's no proof—your parents might have died from some disease—but even if the Quill killed them, your parents were there to give you a better life, and died trying to keep you safe." He peered down at Pardell. "I'd feel pretty good about that, if I were you."

Pardell sipped thoughtfully. "Something there changed me into—this. I'm not stupid. It fits too many pieces . . . makes too much sense to ignore." *Just because the idea made him want to rip off his own skin . . .*

"Okay," Malley agreed. "So I think Her Ladyship's right. There were Quill there. By Gail's interpretation, your father survived longer than your mother because he was a descendant of Susan Witts—and the Quill somehow have her genetic information filed away. You might have survived for the same reason. Or because, as a newborn, you couldn't be affected by whatever the Quill Effect does to harm people. Or because, as a newborn, that weapon altered you instead." He paused, then said in a voice that brooked no argument, "You aren't a Quill. But you look to be the best chance we've got to learn how to get rid of them and help people we care about—and that's something you should be proud of, my friend. I am."

*It was probably Grant's liquor*, Pardell told himself, but some of the black despair seemed to lift from his shoulders. When Gail had told him what she believed, what she knew of the Quill Effect and how inherently similar his abilities seemed to be to those of a Quill—he'd wanted to put on a suit and push off from the *Seeker*. That simple. That final. That clean.

But he'd seen her lower lip trembling, the fingers on the hand he couldn't hold clenching into a small, tight fist as she told him what she knew of the Quill, of how she thought he'd been changed by them. Gail had sounded the dispassionate, determined scientist she was—and every movement betrayed her.

So Pardell had done his best to be dispassionate and brave himself, and wound up here, to destroy harmless Ping-Pong balls instead of himself.

"I don't know how I'm going to help," he wondered out loud. "Gail thinks my—ability—is similar to what the Quill do. Maybe that's—"

"Oh. So now it's back to 'Gail'?"

*Trust Malley to leap off the topic, no matter how important.* "You call her Gail," Pardell said defensively.

"That's because I've kissed the lady . . ." Malley's bantering voice died away. "Aaron . . . I didn't mean . . ."

"I'm rusty on Earther manners, but I didn't think that was a requirement before using someone's first name. Is it?" Pardell joked, before Malley's slightly drunk but thoroughly agile mind started wandering where it shouldn't.

*Where* he *couldn't.*

# Chapter 58

"PETRA'S good at this—relax, Aaron. Breathe evenly and as deeply as you find comfortable."

*She'd better be good at it*, Gail reminded herself, listening to Aisha briefing the 'sider. Aaron wasn't easy about this particular experiment, knowing its significance. Gail had done her best to find the ideal candidate: scouring the ship's personnel records to find anyone who practiced deep meditation. Small numbers to start with, then she'd interviewed to narrow the list to anyone who wasn't too afraid of Aaron's—peculiarity—to be effective.

Most, including Sazaad, didn't pass.

Grant had been a surprise possibility and she'd almost asked him. He'd formed a friendship with the 'sider that might have helped. But at this point in her research, there wasn't sufficient justification to risk the commander of the FD in any way.

Petra Sanders was the best they had. Gail watched Aisha preparing the hookups to the chair monitoring Petra's vitals and cog functions. Like most equipment here, the chair had been made on the *Seeker*, as needed. In its twin, Aaron was already strung with his by-now-familiar assortment of cables and disks. *Tied down like his ship had been*, she thought.

Aaron didn't usually squirm as he was doing now—Gail suspected he viewed being comfortable as secondary to what they did here. Then again, until now, they'd been testing his response to various physical stimuli, as well as taking advantage of his reactions to further enhance the construction of the anti-Quill suit. Now?

Now Gail was out to test her hypothesis: that Aaron Pardell was actually reacting to the emotional states of others, not the physical sensation of touch at all. Meaning that Aaron's ability had something in common with the reports of the Quill.

*One of those tests where a positive outcome wouldn't help him sleep nights.*

"Ready?" Aisha asked.

Petra nodded, her almost white hair slipping over one eye as she did. Her skin, even over her lips, was so generously freckled it resembled a mosaic of warm brown and beige. Her lashes were almost invisible, but she'd drawn delicate eyebrows over each eye. She was the assistant ship's engineer, a bright, cheerful young woman who practiced martial arts as well as meditation. Apparently she also played a wicked saxophone. Gail had enjoyed their interview, finding Petra a no-nonsense, kind person who grasped what they needed in very few words.

*There was no doubt of her courage.*

"Aaron?"

Instead of answering Aisha, Aaron crooked a finger at Gail. She walked over to his side and leaned close. "I don't want to scare her," he whispered, looking troubled. "But someone has to be ready to pull us apart if this doesn't work. I can't—and if she's in a trance, she might not be able to. But no one else can touch her while she's in contact with me. I should have thought of it before now."

"We did, Aaron. Don't worry. The chairs are on wheels. One boot and you're sailing to the other side of the room."

He visibly relaxed, one corner of his generous mouth turning up. "Let me guess. Malley volunteered for that."

"Insisted," she told him, smiling. "Are you ready? I need you to concentrate." Without thinking, Gail leaned a little too close and the ends of her hair slid along Aaron's cheek, catching where the skin was roughened by faintly visible stubble. Harmless, since the reaction required living cells in contact—except that it was a caress. They both knew it. "Sorry," she said quickly, standing up straight.

"We're ready here," she told Aisha briskly. Gail pretended not to see how Aaron's eyes followed her. *You want him to concentrate on the experiment*, she lashed at herself.

Preoccupied, Gail backed into Malley, doing his self-

appointed task of hovering over any and all of the tests involving his friend. It was like walking into an oak tree. Her
apology died unsaid when she glanced up and saw the stationer deliberately looking from his friend to her and back,
with a scowl.

"What now, Malley?" Gail asked under her breath. Petra's
eyes were closed and she was already breathing slowly, entering her meditative state. For the experiment, the entire lab had
been cleared but for the participants, Malley, herself, and
Aisha's six techs, presently monitoring the banks of devices to
take base measurements. The lights were dimmed. Everything
was peaceful, with the exception of the huge man scowling his
disapproval at her.

*He was really quite good at it.* Gail felt guilty without
knowing why she should.

Malley never let one wait in suspense. He bent down and
put his lips to her ear. "Flirting with Aaron, Dr. Smith?" he
rumbled softly. "If you feel the need that badly, you know
where to find me."

*Why that arrogant . . .* Gail imagined kicking Malley in the
shin, or higher, but spoke to Aisha instead. "You've double-
checked the glove?" They'd start with Petra's hand in one of
the anti-Quill gloves, so she would be insulated from the effect
of touching Aaron while he should still feel something from
her. But only a glove coated with the 'sider's own genetic
markers—or those of his grandmother, Susan Witts—would
insulate the wearer from the backlash of contact. It had been
one of the first, and most fundamentally significant, observations they'd made, thanks to Aaron. Clear support for Gail's
hypothesis that each Quill population could be descended
from one original Quill, genetically able to identify its human
host.

More proof the Quill had indeed left a legacy in the newborn Aaron Pardell.

Gail took several steps away from Malley, feeling this a
more-than-adequate response to his suggestion, given she
couldn't imagine what to say to him that wouldn't involve
shouting. Unfortunately, she knew the stationer well enough

by now to realize he'd assume she was wisely clearing his path to Aaron should he need to separate the two.

*Feel the need.* Gail didn't know whether it made her want to laugh or cry.

Aisha used a remote handling arm to gently lift Petra's limp arm. The woman was completely relaxed. Gail glanced at the console measuring her heart rate. Fifty beats per minute. Deep trance. *Quite impressive.* Maybe she'd look into the technique herself one day.

Aaron looked grim, but prepared. Aisha lowered Petra's arm so her hand rested on the small table positioned between the chairs. Aaron put his gold-veined hand beside Petra's gloved one, exhaled slowly, then touched the tips of his fingers to hers.

He closed his eyes immediately, his face going oddly slack. There were sensors to measure precise changes in Aaron's expression, but Gail preferred to watch the man rather than the readouts. One second. Two. He snatched his hand away, eyes flying open, his slim body arching up as if to escape the chair, then dropping flat again before anyone could react.

"Ouch," Aaron said unhelpfully, grabbing the cold compress Aisha offered him to press over his face.

Petra roused at the word, turning her head without opening her eyes. "Are you all right?" she asked, her voice low and slurred. "I didn't feel anything."

"I'm fine. Nothing that won't fix itself in a moment," Aaron mumbled graciously, his expression concealed under the compress. Gail noticed his free hand was clenching the arm of the chair.

"Tell me when you're ready for the next experiment," she said. He nodded.

"We were going to wait an hour," Aisha said in a neutral voice.

Gail looked up. Aisha's dark eyes didn't look this fierce very often—just every time the other scientist decided Gail was pushing too hard or too fast. They'd worked together long enough for Gail to appreciate Aisha's judgment, if not for her to automatically accept it. "I have my reasons," she countered.

*Among them that they'd reach their destination by ship's night tomorrow.*

Aaron removed the compress. He looked tired, but there was something new in his eyes when they met hers. Triumph. "Happiness," he said. "No. I'd say it was closer to bliss."

*It had worked,* Gail realized, almost numb. *He'd felt something from Petra, some emotion other than fear or pain.* "I'm ready, Dr. Smith."

Petra nodded as well. The next step was to repeat the experiment without the protection of the glove. She hadn't come very far out of her trance, so Aisha, after one more unhappy look at Gail, prepared to take another base line set of measurements from both.

*"Dr. Smith."* She hadn't seen Aaron since this morning. He'd needed time alone to digest what she'd told him. *Who wouldn't?* But he'd taken it better than she'd hoped—better than she had, in fact. It had been pure agony to explain the facts as she knew them, the suppositions and inferences as she'd made them. To tell Aaron Pardell he wasn't what he'd thought all these years.

*Was that the reason for the "Dr. Smith" now?* Gail supposed she was imagining more punishment for herself, the always-courteous 'sider was probably respecting her position among the others here. Something Malley never did.

Malley, who had warned her away from his friend in unmistakable terms. *Flirting?* Gail thought wildly, inclined to laugh. What she felt near Aaron Pardell, what she saw reflected in his eyes, had nothing in common with anything so harmless. *Did Malley know?* She thought too much of him to suppose for an instant he was jealous. She did believe Malley understood perfectly how dangerous—

*Enough!* Gail brought herself back to the lab with a shake of her head. Petra's hand, now covered only by its dusting of freckles, rested on the table, her arm held gently but firmly by the remote Aisha controlled from beside her chair. To all appearances she was unconscious, but her brain activity topped the scale in some areas. The key ones, Gail hoped—ones they could actually measure. She knew Sazaad was riveted to his remote monitors, cynical as always.

Aaron didn't hesitate. At her gesture, he reached for Petra's hand again—her bare hand.

They were all braced, even the techs at their stations, Malley already gripping Aaron's chair to pull him away from Petra if necessary.

Every test until now had shown a virtually instantaneous reaction, implying that whatever Aaron drew from contact with another reflected back, as if from a mirror.

The momentary stillness fooled them all. *Or had they unwittingly focused on Petra?* Gail wondered later. It took the shrilling of the monitoring alarms to startle everyone into motion, including Malley, who yanked Aaron's chair from Petra's so quickly instruments went flying and the chair itself would have tipped if he hadn't kept hold.

A perilous hold. Once contact was broken, Aaron began convulsing violently, his eyes rolled up so only the whites showed, a foam appearing at the corners of his lips. Malley strained to keep the chair upright while avoiding the gold-veined hands flailing in every direction. The strapping restraining the 'sider stretched but didn't break, At wrist and ankle, it dug into his flesh tightly enough to guarantee bruises.

Then, as abruptly, Aaron was still, except for the slow rise and fall of his chest. Malley let go, one hand at a time, sending an urgent glance at the now-silent machinery. One of the techs—Benton—gave a shaky thumbs-up.

"How's Petra?" Gail said into the ominous quiet.

"Give me a second," Aisha snapped.

Gail walked over, carefully not looking at Aaron. She understood Rosalind all too well now. The more time she spent with him, the less she could bear seeing him reduced to this.

"Well?" Gail asked, looking down at what appeared to be a woman peacefully asleep. More than peaceful—Petra's face looked almost esctatic. "Anything?"

"Some peaks on Sazaad's cog screen," Aisha said, consulting a notepad handed her by another tech. "We'll have to analyze those, but everything else appears to measure nominal. I'm surprised she didn't come out on her own when the alarms went off—must be pretty deeply under."

"Can you bring her out of it?"

Aisha scrutinized her patient. As she did, her fingers absently stroked the spider brooch on her lapel, a tiny thing most people didn't spot on the intensely colorful coat—a favorite, Gail remembered. "I'll assume you've reasons for that, too?" Aisha asked, her usually expressive voice toneless.

"I do."

Aisha released Petra's arm from the remote, then took the woman's limp hand in both of hers and began to rub it gently. "Petra," she called. "Petra . . ."

*Aaron was still out.*

Petra's eyes flickered under their lids and she smiled.

"Petra . . ."

Her eyes opened, revealing dilated pupils that quickly shrank to normal size. "Yes, Dr. Lynn? Aren't we doing the experiment?" Petra blushed and struggled to sit up. "Oh, dear, did I fall asleep on you? That happens to me all the time."

"The experiment went—" Gail deliberately didn't look at Aaron, "—very well, thanks, Petra. How do you feel right now?"

The blush deepened. "Well, I—feel pretty wonderful, Dr. Smith." The woman giggled, tried to stop herself, then giggled again. Aisha's lips twitched, even as she and Gail traded glances.

"Is this how you usually feel waking up?" Aisha asked.

Her green eyes were sparkling. "I'm always happy and relaxed during the trance—that carries through when I come out of it." Another infectious giggle. Petra put her hand over her lips as if to stop herself "I don't remember ever feeling *this* happy before. It's quite amazing."

"Thank you, Petra," Gail told her. "Dr. Lynn will take more details from you, if you don't mind."

From the contented look on the assistant engineer's face, Aisha could take all the details she wanted.

"Care to explain?"

Gail whirled, saying: "Aaron!" perhaps a little too enthusiastically for the moment. *Maybe everyone was too busy watching Petra giggle and coo.* No such luck. Aaron looked like he'd been run over by a freight trolley, but he smiled up at her with a warmth that said he'd heard the emotion in her voice.

Malley wasn't smiling at all. *In fact*, Gail thought with disgust, *the stationer was beginning to look downright grim.*

*Did he think she was a fool? They were going to have to talk*—she wasn't looking forward to it.

Gail firmly controlled her visible reactions as she went to Aaron's side. "First, tell me what you experienced," she requested, keeping it professional.

The way his eyes lingered on her mouth didn't help a bit.

# Chapter 59

*F*IFTEEN *hours*. Didn't sound like much, if you were talking a shift and a half to cover someone late, or how long that someone, usually Syd Denery, could sleep after too much partying.

It wasn't much, when you were talking about time spent screaming through the darkness, aiming at a tiny ball of dirt somewhere out there.

*Even less*, Malley thought, *when the end result would be standing on that ball of dirt, without walls or a roof to be seen.* Just standing, a column of atmosphere, taller than Thromberg was long, pressing on your shoulders, your feet glued to the floor—the *ground*—by gravity that had nothing to do with the capable maintenance guys in Outward Five.

"You seem a little unsettled tonight," Aisha observed, her hand poised over Malley's forehead. "Want to talk about it first?"

The stationer shook his head. "There isn't time. I'll only get one more shot at this before we—arrive."

He closed his eyes as his companion's fingers traced his eyebrows, then pressed gently into each temple, rubbing slowly at the tension there. *She'd put up with a lot, these past six nights.* "Sorry, Aisha. It was rough, today, with Aaron. That's all."

"Yes, it was. But worthwhile, don't you think? Your friend did. He's very brave."

"And stupid," Malley growled.

Her fingers lifted, and he opened his eyes. Aisha's head was tilted, her expression puzzled as she studied him. The light from the candles she'd placed around her room drew sparks from the tiny gold-and-crystal insects in her hair. This late, she wore layers of a silky fabric, its waves of red, yellow, and orange lapping at her midnight skin. It resembled nothing Malley was used to calling clothing.

*He'd grown quite fond of having Aisha surprise him.*

"Why is Aaron stupid?" she asked.

Malley took a deep breath and blew it out with a laugh. "Just kidding. I'm always teasing him—keeps him from being too serious about life. Can we get started?"

Aisha turned and went to her cabinet, then returned with the headset and goggles. "Lie down, if you're in such a hurry not to talk to me."

She had the oddest bedside manner. "Is this part of the therapy, Dr. Lynn?" he asked her, using his best smile. Malley stayed sitting on the edge of her bed.

"Maybe." Aisha had a pretty heart-starting smile of her own. "Or it could be part of being a friend, Hugh Malley."

"Friends, huh?" Malley nodded, thinking of the reaction if he brought this exotic version of the Earther into Sammie's. *Knowing Aisha*, he reminded himself, *she'd fit right in*—after making most of his friends faint with envy.

*Sammie?*

Malley felt confused whenever he thought of the man, of what Sammie and the others had done to the *Merry Mate II*. Of what they might have done to Aaron, if he'd been on his ship.

*Not routine*, Malley thought, suddenly homesick. Nothing was anymore.

"Friends talk to one another," Aisha ventured, taking her time untangling part of the headset. "About what makes them happy—or troubles them—"

"I don't want to talk—about today or Aaron."

"Ah," she said, standing so her thighs touched his knees, reaching to place the headset on his head. "I see. Who else don't you want to talk about?"

Malley loved Aisha's voice, if not her perception. He rested his hands on the roundness of her hips, and her smile broadened. Encouraged, he used this light hold to pull her into his lap. As he'd suspected, she fit quite nicely, one arm trailing cool silk as it went around his neck.

"And this is to distract me from finding out who you want to talk about—or don't want to talk about?" Aisha said with a laugh. "It might work—but then there's your session to consider." She calmly finished adjusting the headset, seemingly oblivious to his interested exploration of the warm territory under the silks.

"Could do more good," Malley mumbled, quite charmed by what he was finding, and by now thoroughly distracted himself. He dipped his head, aiming for her neck and anticipating sweet smells and softness, only to have Aisha slip the goggles over his eyes before his lips touched anything but air.

"Be good and take your medicine," she said. "You've come a long way this week and we mustn't lose momentum."

He felt the light brush of her mouth against his, as if in regret, then his lap was cold and empty. Malley sighed and blew a kiss in her direction, before lying back on the pillows and swinging his legs up and around. "You know what they say about all work and no play, Doctor," he grinned, unrepentant. "Look what's it's done to Her Ladyship."

"Gail."

The word wasn't quite ice-edged, but close. Malley pulled the goggles from his eyes and peered at her. "I didn't mean it as an insult—your 'Gail' doesn't seem to be the playful sort. That's all."

"Because she hasn't returned your advances?" Aisha asked, the lilt in her voice accentuated by a hint of scorn.

"Whoa," Malley said, sitting up and deciding he was insulted. "What advances?" *Anyway, if he'd made any serious ones, they'd have been returned.* Gail Smith wasn't immune—*until lately*, he added to himself.

"You're going to tell me you haven't displayed interest."

Malley felt his face starting to burn. "I'm always—interested," he said truthfully enough. "But unless it's mutual, I don't bother—you know, this really isn't any of your business, Aisha."

"It could be, if it is upsetting you—or affects Gail."

"Trust me. Gail Smith isn't being affected by me. In any regard."

"Ah," Aisha stretched out the syllable until Malley felt she'd expressed just about every possible reaction, including disbelief. Then she knelt in front of him, silks spreading over the floor, her hands on his knees. "But then there's your friend," she said, eyes serious. "The one who *is* affecting Gail."

"Aaron? What do you know about him and—" Malley rubbed one hand over his face, then dropped it into his lap and gazed at her fondly, if with some exasperation. "You set me up." He sighed heavily. "Look, I wasn't going to talk about it. I didn't think anyone else had noticed. Maybe it's nothing—"

Aisha smiled back at him, but sadly, as though they shared some grief. "Nothing? A polite and friendly man—whose eyes can't leave her for more than an instant. A reasonable, sensible man who doesn't just endure uncomfortable and dangerous tests. No, he conquers them for her, like some knight on a hopeless quest."

"Hopeless is right. Aaron's playing the fool to fantasize about her," Malley surprising himself by the bitter note in his voice. "Not that I blame him. A pretty face can be a powerful distraction. And, with what he's lost—the pressures he's under to help with the Quill—the doubt about himself? Wonder is he's stable at all." He paused, then growled, "Which means your Gail should know better than to encourage him." Without intending to, Malley remembered how her hair had drifted against Aaron's cheek—and the startled, then lost look on his friend's face. *Potent weapons, the woman had*, he thought bitterly, wishing he'd snapped her neck when he'd had the chance.

"Know better?" Aisha repeated thoughtfully. "We'd all like to know better, Malley—to pick the object of our affections using our heads, not our hearts."

"You think Dr. Gail Smith, Earther, scientist—bloody ruler of this ship—feels anything for Aaron?" Malley tried to laugh, but her expression made him stop. He went on almost angrily. "Aaron's her ticket to glory. If a few smiles make him work harder, risk more—why not? She manipulates people better than anyone I've met. I've seen it for myself."

"Then you've been looking in a mirror, Malley," Aisha accused. "You are so much the same there's hardly air for the rest of us to breathe when you're both in the lab."

"We're the same?" Malley curled his left arm and smacked

his right hand against the bicep. "Think I grew this studying at Titan University or being pampered on Earth?"

"I think you excelled at anything you did, the same way Gail Smith excelled. Not because anyone expected you to, but because you couldn't do anything less. You are both driven, passionate about your causes, single-minded to the point of obsession, and frustrated by anyone who can't follow your intellectual leaps. You both flip from obnoxious to charming at will. I only put up with either of you because you want the truth—and you care about what that truth means to others."

Malley realized his mouth was open and closed it firmly.

Aisha wasn't finished. "Gail's capable of many things—but not of seducing your friend into harming himself. Even if she was, she doesn't need to—Aaron wants to see the terraformed worlds restored to the colonists from the stations as much as any of us. You know that."

"I know Gail's not staying clear of him either," Malley said, choosing to disregard Aisha's comparisons as uncomfortably apt and not particularly the view of himself he preferred. "You could run the tests. There are a dozen others in the science sphere qualified." He threw his hands up in exasperation. "I could do some!"

"Gail doesn't delegate crucial work. Maybe that's the problem—" Her voice trailed off suggestively. "She always lives her work, her ambition—but I've never seen her wearing down, day by day, like this. What happened at the station troubles her. But this? It's like she's fighting demons."

"I'm not interested in Gail Smith's conscience or her health," Malley said bluntly. "Only Aaron's. And she must see how he's reacting to her. It's worse every day. She must know any—fantasy—is going to hurt him. How impossible . . . they can't . . . damn it, Aisha, you know what I'm trying to say."

"Ah," another of the wise, soft sounds. Aisha leaned her cheek on his knee and didn't look at him as she spoke. Her fingers found the palm of his hand, then intertwined themselves with his. "That no matter how much they want *this*, there's no having it? Perhaps. There is more to love—"

Malley traced one of the intricate braids along Aisha's scalp with a finger, staring out at the candles on her dresser. Another of her surprises for him—unregulated combustion wasn't permitted on Thromberg. "Tell that to Aaron," the stationer said heavily. "It's cut at him for years: the way he is, the things he can't do—but at least he didn't have strong feelings for anyone else to complicate it. And he's proud, Aisha. Proud to the point of blind and stupid. He's my best friend, but I've seen it. If this goes wrong—he can't run and hide on his ship anymore. She's left him without an escape route for the first time in his life. It will break him."

"All I can tell you is to try trusting Gail. If she cares about your friend, she won't let things go that far," Aisha looked up at Malley, dark eyes intent. "She knows the risks—she'll be careful."

"Careful?" Malley considered the idea, then shook his head. "That'll be the day. Your Gail likes the edge, in case you hadn't noticed. Ask Grant sometime about her concept of 'acceptable risk' and what that's cost already." He suddenly saw it all—*too clearly.* "If she's using Aaron's feelings to control him . . . well, that's a dangerous game. He'd better find out before something happens he's going to regret all his life—" *Or before a certain neck does get broken*, Malley added to himself. "But no matter how unhappy it makes Aaron, I hope that's all it is for her—a game."

"Why?"

"Because if Gail Smith cares for Aaron, the way you think, it's not a game anymore. And she's more than likely to throw caution out the 'lock and Aaron's life with it." *Not if he had any say in it*, Malley promised himself grimly, drawing his fingers from Aisha's. *Not if he had any say at all.*

"Either way," Aisha responded in a low voice, "you make it sound as though your friend must lose."

"Warned you I didn't want to talk about him," Malley said, making his tone almost flippant. "Depressing, isn't it? Never you mind, Aisha, m'love. Let me get a few beers under Mr. Lovesick's belt and I'll set him straight about women's wiles." He captured the hand she'd left on his knee, bringing it up to his lips.

"Really?" he asked. "And should I set Gail straight about the wiles of stationers?" Her generous mouth curved up.

His almost smile faded. "If you want to warn her I'm watching—that's fine."

"Oh, is that what you call hovering behind her, looking like the grim reaper? You have half the scientists and most of the techs looking over their shoulders now. Maybe you should ease off, Malley," Aisha suggested. "See how things go in the next day. There's going to be too much happening when we arrive anyway."

"Which means we shouldn't waste any more time," Malley put the goggles back on and lay down. "Can we get on with the session, please?" he gritted between his teeth.

"With you tense as a piece of steel?" Before Malley could think of anything to say, he felt the mattress shift as she joined him on it. "Roll over," she ordered.

He thought of objecting, but turned on his side instead. She tucked him into the curve of her body, one arm over his chest, one leg over his. "Now," a soft whisper in his ear, "see if you can calm yourself, Malley. Take a moment and think about being very calm, very rested. The day, the place, even your friend—you need to let it go."

Malley let out the breath he'd held, at the same time letting himself relax into her familiar warmth. When Aisha had offered to help him with his phobia, he hadn't expected that help to be so—personal. She'd said it was this, or being strapped down. He vastly preferred the option of her silk-covered limbs, even though until tonight there'd been no hint she might welcome a closer entanglement.

"Mmmph." He wasn't sure if that was approval a few breaths later, or Aisha getting comfortable. He was—

The headset activated as if cued to his physical state. If he hadn't known this was virtual and not real, Malley would have sworn he was now standing in a corridor similar to those he'd known all his life.

"Take your time. There's nothing gained by rushing." Aisha's voice now sounded as though she was right behind him. He still felt her, comforting and real, despite the illusion presented by the goggles.

There were doors along the corridor. Malley knew how the device worked—his eye movements were tracked by the goggles, bringing closer whichever door he focused on, opening that door if he blinked. Closing his eyes brought him back to the safety of the corridor. Knowing wasn't the same as believing. The flow was dreamlike, incredibly real and vivid, with the exception that he was in control at all times.

Malley ignored the first few doors. He "looked" down the hall and chose one farther along, watching it rush toward him.

An air lock. He shuddered once, feeling Aisha's arm tighten immediately to remind him he wasn't really alone, that this was a waking dream.

Every door would become an air lock. He was used to that now. He'd made it through fifteen, in six nights. One the first night. The hardest night.

Malley made himself concentrate. There were words he was to say to himself, techniques Aisha was teaching him to help control the response of his heart and nerves. When he was ready, he'd go through this air lock and experience what was on the other side, whether the dark of space or planet night.

It didn't get easier. He knew that by now.

It got done.

# Chapter 60

"IT'S done, Dr. Smith."

Gail started, so thoroughly captivated by the image on the screen she'd missed hearing Grant's approach.

"Thank you." She knew he referred to the robotic probes she'd ordered launched, some into orbit to survey the planet below them, more to drop into the atmosphere and relay information back to the *Seeker*'s environmental experts in the science sphere, and two—

Two had coordinates to follow: one based on the *'Mate*'s shuttle log, and the other on the records of Susan Witts. Those were on the same landmass, although separated by thousands of kilometers. Gail wanted to see both, before committing to a location for her trials.

No one, least of all her, expected any of the probes to return with signs of the Quill. It wasn't going to be that easy.

*Pardell's World*, Gail named it to herself, eyes never leaving the planet showing its daylight side on the huge column. Clouds made of water droplets, atmosphere a deep blue by virtue of the right blend of gases in its mix, liquid water restless with the tides from two small moons, with more locked into polar caps. The land masses, with their telltale splotches of green, were too regular and in the wrong place, as if this was a child's first rendering of Earth, but the whole was familiar enough to be a beacon to those evolved on that other world, a siren's call to sailors in a black, empty sea.

*As deadly*, Gail thought coldly. She preferred her worlds teeming with civilization, with proof of their welcome in bright lights and buildings, even if those were domes floating in Europa's frozen ocean. This place was a lie. A trap.

*An opportunity.* "I want to be ready to drop at one hour's notice, Commander, Captain," Gail ordered, tearing her gaze away. "Make sure your people are ready. I'll wait for no one."

Gail prepared for what could be the most significant moment of her scientific career by tidying her room. She did it on occasion—such as packing up to move quarters. This time, she wasn't quite sure why she was shoveling paper into piles and surprising herself with clothes she'd forgotten she'd brought with her this trip.

*Liar.*

Standing from her crouch, Gail pushed back a sweat-soaked lock of hair and put her hands on her hips. "Enough already," she told the room, and pulled out some data records to read on her bed. After only a few minutes, the numbers swam in front of her eyes. She rubbed her neck, trying to focus.

*Liar.*

"Fine," Gail grumbled and tossed the pages into the freshly cleared section of floor, throwing herself back on her pillows. "So you've got the jitters." She stared at the bag-hung ceiling. "It's not helping." *A suggestion her body was ignoring.*

Gail didn't need to analyze herself. The combination of gut-wrenching excitement and mouth-drying anxiety was natural. There was no need to listen to any of the other false alarms from her body, including the ones to either run to the kitchen or the washroom. They'd all pass, once she had the comm signal that the probes had uploaded their findings and it was time to prepare to drop.

Today, she was going to find out if she was right—or wrong.

*Today,* a voice inside her head said maliciously, *you get to find out the price of being wrong—you get to know who Grant has picked for the first trial run of the suit.* He'd reserved the right to chose from his unit—they'd all volunteered, of course. Gail hadn't the slightest intention of interfering, beyond being the one to give her first guinea pig his or her briefing.

She might have argued it was her place to go, but knew better—as did Grant. They both knew better. Later, after the trials proved the suits, after she was sure. . . .

Then, maybe Aaron Pardell could go down.

*There was another issue altogether.* Gail knew Temujin and most of the others—including Aaron, himself—thought the 'sider should go down in the first trial, not one of the FDs. Why bother testing a suit when they had a chance to test a living, breathing genetic match?

The exercise, Gail had reminded them all, was to find a way to put anyone on a Quill-infested world and retrieve a sample organism, not to see if Aaron Pardell could claim his birthright.

She could still see the betrayed look on his face after she'd said it, the hazel of his eyes closer to green in the briefing room fighting.

Worse, Gail knew why she'd disagreed. Cloak it in babble about controllable experiments and scientific reproducibility, but she'd refused to risk him. *She couldn't,* whispered a voice inside her head, the one that had nothing to do with rational thought and everything to do with how her body melted each time his look consumed her.

Aaron claimed she didn't trust him.

She could appreciate the irony, hardly able to stand up in a meeting of all interested parties, Reinsez included, and announce that Aaron Pardell, 'sider and probable part-Quill, was the only person on the *Seeker* she did trust, without reservation, without hesitation.

A knock. Gail didn't move, but peered suspiciously at the door. *No one knocked on her door.* That was why she had a comm panel in her room and two FDs, today Loran and a newer face, Neil Johnson, outside. She put her arm back over her eyes and tried to rest.

Another knock, this time louder. *Either her guards had abandoned their post, or it was Grant.*

On opening the door, Gail discovered both surmises were incorrect.

Aaron Pardell stood there, Loran and Johnson to either side, carefully distant and looking a little out of their depth. "I have to talk to you, 'the sider insisted, his face pale and set. Then he looked past her and paused, red spots appearing on both cheeks. "Is there somewhere else we could go?"

Gail pushed her hand through her hair, using the movement

to cover her own surprise. "You can come with me back to the lab—we can talk on the way," she suggested. "Wait here."

He—and the guards—looked relieved.

Gail took her time, gathering what she wanted to have with her while they monitored the trial, hesitating before sticking a boost needle in her pocket in case things dragged late into ship's night. When she was ready, she went to the mirror and studied her reflection.

"Oh, great." Her cheeks were every bit as flushed as Aaron's had been. *At this rate*, Gail told herself, *they might as well waltz around wearing signs: look at us—we're fools.* She was losing any ability to push thoughts of him away, no matter how much she understood the danger.

*The danger.* The part of her still able to be analytical cruelly suspected it only added spice to a powerful attraction. The emotional charge, however it was conveyed into Aaron's body from someone else, grew with the intensity of the emotion. They'd proved that with Petra's experiment, when the focused emotional load of her meditation had given Aaron convulsions.

With each look, each word—what was between them could rapidly grow beyond the bounds of sense or safety.

*Thinking about running your fingers through his thick, dark hair?* she asked her image. *Be ready to hear his scream—and your own.*

*Thinking about lying next to him, of holding each other, of just one kiss?*

*Ready to die?* Gail stared into her own eyes, heart pounding, abruptly afraid to know the answer.

"This is far enough. Holding," Gail warned Aaron as she twisted her hand on the bar to pause the walkway, feeling an odd sense of déjà vu. Midway, as before. Safe from eavesdroppers. Only the man with her had changed. She studied him when she thought he wasn't looking. The 'sider looked healthier—the diet on the *Seeker* agreed with him. He still chose to wear the clothes she'd brought from the *Merry Mate II.* They were clean, if well-patched. The faded blue suited him—not that Gail thought Aaron paid attention to appearances. He just wanted to be himself.

"Why is it called the waist?" he asked, looking up in wonder at the view of the planet hanging overhead.

"The ship resembles an insect found on Earth—a wasp. There's a similar elongation between its body parts. Same name."

"I see." If Aaron thought this a strange way to designate components of a starship, he was polite enough not to mention it.

"We don't have much time here," Gail said after a few seconds spent watching Aaron gaze at his planet—wary of the pleasure of seeing him enjoying himself.

"You don't have surveillance in here, do you?" he asked, looking back at her.

*One of those casual, bombshell questions Aaron excelled at,* Gail reminded herself. He knew to ask. Who from Thromberg would? "No. The interior is scoured after each passage. As a rule, there are vids in every public place."

"On the bridge?"

Gail smiled thinly. "The bridge—several. Protects the Captain and crew from accusations of misconduct; keeps records of what's happened on board."

"Your office?"

She gave him a sharp look, but the expression on his face appeared to be mere curiosity. "Grant's people remove them as quickly as they find them. I have to believe him when he tells me the FD don't plant their own. Why?"

"I can tell when you think you're being watched."

"I'm watched most of the time, Aaron," Gail shrugged. "It's a luxury to have space where I'm not." She paused. "But this isn't what you wanted to talk to me about—so urgently you tracked me to my bedroom."

"I knew where it was."

*Oh, dear.* Gail found the toe of her boot suddenly fascinating. "Aaron—" she started to say.

"Don't," he ordered. Gail looked up and saw his face had grown stern, as if he'd aged years in front of her. "Let me say what I need to say, Gail."

She nodded, her grip on the hold bar tightening.

Aaron pointed upward. "You have to let me go on the first drop."

Gail blinked, then regained her composure. *Of course this was what he wanted to say*, she chastised herself. She shouldn't have believed he'd give it up because she'd made an announcement in a meeting. This was the man who'd walked most of the station—outside—to find his friend. "I have my reasons," she told him, having no intention of giving way on this.

"Do you trust me or not?"

"Trust is not the issue here—"

"It's the only issue. You tell me I'm affected by the Quill—that I might be part-Quill for all we know. How can you risk anyone else?"

*How can I risk you, of anyone?* Gail froze, fearing she'd said that out loud. Fortunately, he was still waiting for her answer. Not angry, not yet, but with that stubborn pride she'd seen before. "You did enough by helping test the suits," she explained. "We've trained personnel ready to use them. I don't even know if a suit could protect you, Aaron."

"I wouldn't wear one."

"Wonderful plan," she retorted, furious. "Why don't you just walk out the air lock?"

"You don't know the Quill Effect would harm me. It didn't before."

She took a deep, reasoning breath. "You were a newborn baby. And who said you weren't harmed." Horrified by what she'd said, Gail added quickly: "Aaron, I'm sorry."

"If I've paid the price," Aaron told her, his eyes implacable, "I want something to show for it."

"What?"

"You heard me." They'd been standing a couple of meters apart. He stepped closer. "The Quill made me like this—I want to be the one to find them, to bring the sample back, so we can kill them." Suddenly, Aaron was standing so close she could feel the warmth radiating from him. "There has to be something more to me—to my life—than this, Gail," he said urgently, searching her face. "Don't you see? If I can't—" His hand hovered in midair, as if cupping her cheek. "Let me go down. Please."

"You want to be a hero," Gail said coldly, deliberately.

"I want to be human and hold you," Aaron countered. "But

you can't make that happen, Gail. Nothing on this ship or back on Earth can do that. Let me go down." He paused.

"All right." Gail closed her eyes, feeling moisture escape them to make prickly trails down her cheeks. "Go," she whispered.

"Gail—?" he sounded startled. *By what*, she wondered wildly, *her giving in or the tears?*

"Hold on. We're moving again." She opened her eyes but didn't look at him as the walkway slipped into motion, speeding them both along to the end of the waist. "There isn't much time—I'm planning to decide on a site within the next three hours—and there are conditions. You'll wear a suit. Allyn will brief you on it. And you'll follow the procedures for Trial Number One. No creativity . . . in and out."

"Thank you. I'll—"

Gail turned so that she could see him. "And you'll come back." She didn't care anymore what he saw in her face or heard in her voice. "I'm serious, Aaron. Go if you must. But you come back to me—or I'll be down on the next drop to find you."

# Chapter 61

**Titan University Archives**
**Excerpts from the personal recordings of Chief**
**Terraform Engineer Susan Witts**
**Access Restricted to Clearance AA2 or Higher**

. . . Pardell's World, Jeremy. I named it, and your father, after your grandfather. Extravagant gifts for a man I barely knew? It didn't seem so at the time, when the two of us were alone here, making love for hours on empty hilltops, sleeping by barren rivers—as if this world ached to hear new life and we were its instruments. We had to answer that need, however irrational it sounds now. Your grandfather? He went back to his ship when it made its next stop. Don't be surprised. We enjoyed one another. That's all it was, except your father was born of it. I loved him from the moment they put him in my arms, Jeremy. I always will, no matter what happened between us.

Now this world sings with life, Jeremy. It's as ready for settlement as any of the sixteen, but Pardell's World—your legacy—is still hidden, untouched. Our secret. You have the coordinates; I sent them to your father, years ago. If you haven't found them before receiving this letter, look for them now. His gene key or yours, as well as mine, will unlock the data. Do with this world as you wish.

This may be my final visit to this place. Oh, it's not my health. In fact, I've been approved for rejuv. No, I'm heading out to the next set of worlds, to oversee Stage Three.

Titan came to its senses. I haven't told them when I'm leaving—but you can be sure it will be before all the pomp, circumstance, and outright pandemonium of opening the finished worlds to immigration. They can keep all that.

Unfortunately, I can't keep my Quill. The ERC is insisting anyone working on the new projects run through a genetic screen—to be sure we don't bring unsanctioned material. As if that would pick up a Quill. But it was my recommendation, after all. I don't trust the modern terraformers. They seem to think everything's by the book now, that there's no risk. I bet half of them would bring the family pet. Life's always a risk, I tell them. Living things can't be predicted. But they don't listen. We probably did our job too well, made it look too easy.

I can't bring myself to destroy my Quill, not after what it's done for me, the comfort of wearing it through those difficult times. I've left it at the base of the tree I planted for your father. Unfortunately, it will be gone to dust long before you come here. It can't survive for long away from me, and we never found a way to make them reproduce—and believe me, spacers have been trying. One day, someone will track down their homeworld and learn what we need to know.

Someone else. I've new worlds to build. I hope you'll be proud of me, Jeremy. Perhaps, one day, I'll have the courage to call and introduce myself. But if I don't, you'll read this and know I care.

Be well, grandson.

"What's that, young Aaron?"

Pardell folded the sheet and tucked it carefully in a pocket. "You know Malley, Rosalind," he replied evasively. "He's forever coming up with new schemes." He took another drink, aware his face had likely showed a confusion of emotions, but determined to keep Susan Witts' letters to himself.

There weren't many that referred so clearly to the planet they orbited—his rationale for rereading them. *Not that he could re-*

*sist*, Pardell admitted, knowing himself fascinated by the drama in the simple words, the appalling consequences of his grandmother's decisions—*someone who meant so well.*

"He seems in his element," Rosalind agreed. She'd left their table to talk briefly with some of the *Seeker*'s crew. Like Malley, she had her way of fitting in. "So, young Aaron. Where were we? Ah. Camouflage."

Pardell took another bite of his supper, an animal protein he usually enjoyed, but tonight found completely tasteless. "Yes, Rosalind. Camouflage."

"This is what all the experiments in the lab and Dr. Smith's work have proved, young Aaron?" Rosalind questioned, sipping on the tea she enjoyed and Captain Tobo personally ensured was always supplied to their table. Her lips quirked. "Is that not how an animal hides from attention? I hardly see the Quill going unnoticed."

"But that's the point, Rosalind," Pardell explained. "They can't be found on any of the terraformed worlds. This morning's probes sent to the planet surface didn't find any trace of foreign organisms either."

"Is not everything on this world of yours foreign to it, young Aaron?"

He was surprised into a laugh and conceded: "I suppose it is. The probes only detected the founding mixture of Terran plants and their partner microorganisms, as described in Witts' notes. Not species-by-species the same mix as used on the other projects . . . a simpler group, less likely to need intervention. This world—"

"Your world," she reminded him gently.

*It hardly seemed credible*, Pardell thought again, once more caught by the vision of orbiting the world where his grandfather had been born—where he'd been born. *Of stepping on it.* "We share the name, Rosalind," he said, fishing on his plate for another of the green vegetables called peas. "Grant says, as sole citizen I could vote myself president if I wanted—or appoint myself king. Which would last about as long as it takes TerraCor and the rest who financed Witts' exploration and research to get out here and laugh."

"And how will they get here, young Aaron?" Rosalind had

dropped her voice. *An unnecessary precaution*, he thought, given there was no one else close by. Their usual table was in a corner, where they had quick access to two doorways from the science sphere dining lounge—'sider habit. Of course, from what Pardell and Malley had learned of the Earther habit to have surveillance in every public place, whispers likely wouldn't help anyway. He hadn't bothered sharing that paranoia with Rosalind.

*She had enough, it seemed, of her own.* "What do you mean, how?" the 'sider asked, willing to believe Rosalind might also have her own sources of information on the *Seeker*. She spent all of her free time in engineering and, if the *Seeker*'s crew contained individuals anything like other spacers of Pardell's acquaintance, there would be plenty of gossip to while away the translight hours. "They'll be sending more ships from Titan University to support this one—supplies, more equipment," he told her. "Aisha was talking about it. If this is the right place to work on the Quill problem, they might even detach the science sphere and leave it in orbit."

Rosalind had that look, the one where she was about to tell him something he didn't want to know. "They are sending more ships," Pardell repeated, but almost as a question.

"The course bringing us here was sealed, young Aaron, and remains so. First Officer Szpindel was quite definite on that. He was curious if I had any knowledge why that might be. A significant breach of protocol, it seems. Unsafe was a word he used. I do believe he thought I might know where we are." She dabbed her lips with a napkin. "Which I don't, of course."

"Gail must have a good reason." Saying her name brought it all back. Pardell swallowed hard. *How much he'd wanted to wipe the tears from her cheeks. How he hated his own hands, that couldn't. He belonged on that planet, with those monsters.*

The wistful thought that underlay all others: *but she'd made him promise to come back. She wanted him back.*

"Oh, I'm sure she has a reason. Whether it's for our good— or hers—remains to be seen."

*Always suspicious.* Pardell poured himself some of the tea, glad of Rosalind's familiar company if not of her tendency to schism the universe into enemy or 'sider. He knew about her extortion of ships and the threat she'd held over the station. It hadn't surprised him—Pardell was quite sure Rosalind still controlled the spacer faction of the 'siders from here, if only in the sense they'd be paralyzed without her leadership.

The last Ration Riot had taken a disproportionate number of moderate-thinking 'siders, especially those with strong ties to Thromberg. Including Aaron Raner, a loss Pardell hadn't known until seeing Malley back to safety, a loss that emptied his universe, too. Had Raner and those like him missed the signs, or simply trusted a moment too long? More likely, the true 'siders had never trusted at all. Regardless, a lot had changed Outside since. *Anyone's guess*, Pardell told himself, *how many of those changes were the result of this woman's grief and rage.*

"We were talking about camouflage," he said, firmly changing the topic and reaching for his dessert. "The basic idea is simple enough—even if the biologists are tearing out their hair trying to figure out the mechanism. Imagine this napkin is a plant." He picked up a second napkin and put it together with the first. "And this Quill is living on it, carefully mimicking its genome—presumably to fool any Quill-hunting predators, maybe even to help it coexist with the plant." Pardell folded the two into a rectangle and laid them both over his fork. "May I?" he said, reaching over and taking Rosalind's fork. "Now, this is a plant-eating organism. An alien cow, if you will."

"It's a fork, young Aaron."

Pardell didn't answer that, recognizing the gleam in the 'sider's eye. "A cow," he repeated. "Walking around, munching away, eating anything it finds." He danced the fork over the table, then mimed it "discovering" the napkin. "And it finds the plant with a Quill—but is it a plant?" Pardell's other hand turned over the napkin, revealing the other fork. He laid this on top of the napkin.

"That's a fork, too," Rosalind observed dryly.

"Exactly. The perfect camouflage—a mirror."

"So now the Quill change shape?" She sounded disgusted. "They're filling your head with nonsense—"

He smiled and held up the napkin. "It hasn't changed shape at all, dear Rosalind. But, when touched—" Pardell chimed the forks together, "—the Quill reflects something of the 'cow,' its emotional state or something else related to its consciousness. Making it obvious that this," he waved the napkin, "is not supper after all. All you need is an instant's confusion to deflect danger away, to move a mouth so it bites something else instead of you. The cow moves along."

Rosalind clicked the paddle tips on her right hand together twice. *Applause.* "Brilliant. This is the sum of the vital research they've been doing with you?"

Pardell tossed the napkin on his plate. He made himself say very evenly: "I do the same thing, don't I? A little less pleasant—but it keeps me safe from being touched." *Safe.* He loathed the word.

Rosalind considered this, her pale eyes sharp on his. "And now we have Smith's magic suits to keep us safe. So how do they work? Why would the Quill on this planet recognize your—or anyone's—genetic makeup?"

"Gail—Dr. Smith—figured that out," Pardell said, keeping a rather possessive pride from his voice with difficulty. "It would be a waste of energy to send out this reflected emotional energy every time something touched you. So she thinks the Quill identify each other—and other harmless organisms—by incorporating copies of that genetic material into their bodies. Maybe a coating, maybe just something like an antibody. Some kind of storage to allow them to compare something new to what they've encountered before. If it's safe, no reaction. If it's strange or dangerous, then react."

Her eyebrow rose. "Economical."

"Living things tend to be, I'm told." Pardell went on: "When humans found the Quill and touched them, a different kind of interaction took place. The Quill preferentially absorbed calm, peaceful emotions from their hosts and reflected those back. It could be that's something they do to one another, or to attract symbionts—other species they coexist with . . . so much of this is guesswork. If we could go to their world, we could learn all this and more."

"Something Earth isn't interested in funding, young man, even though Titan University stands ready. Good day, Rosalind. Aaron."

"Dr. Reinsez," Pardell greeted the new arrival at their table, less than pleased to have his conversation with Rosalind interrupted by the Earther, but accustomed to it. The scientist usually showed up around the time he and Rosalind were finishing their meal.

*Gail had asked him why.* Pardell hadn't been able to answer, beyond guessing that the wrinkled old man might find something in common with someone closer to his age. Rosalind seemed to welcome his company.

Sure enough, her "Hello, Manuel," was warmer than usual. As the Earther took his seat, Rosalind added: "Surely success here will open the doors to more deep-space work."

"One step at a time," Reinsez said, helping himself to tea. "We need these terraform projects up and running again, Rosalind, before anyone in Sol System will be willing to look outward."

"You know my opinion of dirt," Rosalind said, but without sting. "Young Aaron has been entertaining me with the latest speculations about the Quill."

"We've been studying them 'round the clock," Reinsez boasted. Pardell had finally grown convinced the man sincerely believed he was contributing by stalking through the lab and peering at what was going on. "Did you tell this fine lady about our success with the anti-Quill suits?"

"Oh, do tell me, young Aaron," Rosalind said, her eyes unusually fierce. "This was the supposed purpose for you and me to be taking this—diverting—cruise."

Pardell decided not to sigh, tempting as it was. "The deep-space explorers who kept Quill on their wrists weren't harming them, nor were the terraform engineers. If we're right about the Quill, they should 'remember' those genomes. That's the premise of putting the genome from the terraform team leaders on the suits, matching each to their planet—Susan Witts' for this world, using mine to confirm what they'd reconstructed. The suits should work, as long as they can be identified as harmless by the Quill on the planet's surface."

"The team leaders." Rosalind leaned back, her eyes with that uncomfortable gleam Pardell associated with questions about missing rations. "Such a vital piece to this puzzle. Do you know what happened to them, young Aaron? Has Dr. Smith enlightened you or did Raner insist you learn your Earther history?"

"Of course I know," Pardell said grimly. "They'd been recalled to Titan, along with Susan Witts herself. Some ceremony—Gail said it was business, too, so they could start assembling their teams for the next set of worlds. Do you think they were glad to be in Sol System when the news broke, when they knew it had been their Quill? Witts' wasn't the only suicide. At least the rest weren't persecuted. She took the blame—everyone knew the Quill had come from her, after all. She'd sent them under her name to the terraform leaders."

"So, young Aaron. Not one of them died on their worlds, did they? Or survived the Quill Effect. How—inconvenient—for Dr. Smith. To have no proof of this theory of hers. To build this entire scaffold of conjecture on nothing at all." A click of her prosthesis silenced his protest. "Oh, no doubt Commander Grant has people willing to risk their lives on this—premise. They'll go down to the dirt, expecting to be protected, and die— if there really are Quill."

Pardell kept his mind focused, despite the temptation to let it slip away to consequences and what ifs . . . *Rosalind prided herself on skepticism*, he recalled. *As potentially blinding a faith as any.*

He had support from an unexpected source. Reinsez harrumphed noisily before saying: "Ah, dear Rosalind. You have too many doubts. The suits have been tested. They protect others from our young friend here. Surely you accept that evidence."

"Evidence? Only if you assume young Aaron's condition has anything to do with your fantastic ideas about the Quill." Rosalind gave Reinsez an inscrutable look before reaching out her left hand to take Pardell's. "I wouldn't trust my life to that."

Pardell stared down at the mechanical fingers holding his, no longer part of the conversation as the Earther and 'sider continued to argue. His mind spiraled in sickening loops and whorls, but not outward.

*Inward.*

He imagined the fingers were Gail's; that she'd amputated her hand so she could hold his.

"Excuse me," Pardell heard himself saying, his voice strained to his own ears. "I have to go. Thank you for supper, Rosalind. Until tomorrow night."

"You'd better hurry," Reinsez said around a mouthful of dessert. "They're loading up the drop pod, and Gail's not one to wait." His eyes gleamed within their multifolded lids. "That's why I came in, just now. To tell you it's time to go home, Aaron Pardell."

# Chapter 62

*T*HEY'D all be watching Pardell's trip home. There were pickups in several locations within the science sphere, of course, including a massive one now hanging from the temporary ceiling in the main lab. Apparently they'd brought in chairs from the lounge and quarters so as many as possible could be part of the historic moment.

Gail wondered what Malley thought of that.

She knew what he thought of Pardell going down. There'd been an instant, meeting his eyes, when she'd fully expected the big stationer to explode into violence. That he'd held himself back, silent except for that searing glare, had nothing to do with Grant's watchful presence. It had been a promise.

*No doubts who'd be blamed if Pardell didn't come back.* As if it would matter then.

"*Athena* comm. . . . Landing in three minutes. All systems nominal."

Gail rubbed her thumb into the yielding material covering the armrest. As senior scientist and project leader, she'd had the choice of watching the landing and subsequent events in the lab—or here, on the bridge. She'd picked here. Let them believe it was to be close to the comm and control center of the mission.

*Easier to stay detached and professional around crew, rather than colleagues and friends*, Gail admitted freely to herself.

Grant and Tobo were on duty, of course, but much too busy with their own concerns to notice if hers strayed from mission parameters. Tobo stayed close to the *Seeker*'s pilot as she operated the remote controls on the drop pod—it could be flown independently, but for this trial they wouldn't risk it. Grant wore a comm headset and was in constant communication with

Catherine Dafoe, the FD ops specialist he'd chosen for Trial Number One. She'd christened the pod *Athena*, after the goddess of intellect who bore arms to defend civilization. Dafoe had been fitted with one of the anti-Quill suits.

Pardell wore one as well.

"*Athena* comm . . . site looks clear. Do we have final clearance from Dr. Smith?"

Everyone looked at her. Gail gave a confident nod—*what else could she do?*—and stared, with everyone else, at the screen showing the vid feed from the little ship.

A low, broad-shouldered hill, like many in the area-coated with grasses, taller and more lush where reflection marked an intermittent stream, but still more green than gold. By coincidence, the site Gail had selected was experiencing early summer. By plan, the pod was landing at midday, under a blue, cloudless sky.

Gail spared an instant to hope Aisha's sessions with Malley had been successful, at least enough so the stationer could bear to watch. Aisha had reported his phobia was most pronounced when he was confronted by the starry dark of space, or a clear planet night. She'd also reported significant progress—impressed with the stationer's efforts to overcome his weakness. The interventions had been Gail's idea, knowing full well Malley would never accept any help from her or through the medical staff. Aisha, on the other hand, could charm a broken leg into a cast.

The tasseled heads of the grass tossed wildly in the downdraft of the pod's descent. The vid angle shifted to scan the immediate surroundings, halting at the only structure still standing on the entire planet—a small, concrete bunker almost engulfed in two-meter-high stands of rushes.

On the other terraformed worlds, humans had left more substantial prints on the land. Gail had studied the vids—it was easy enough to "look," given the amount of remote monitoring in place, just not to land. There were huge, craterlike depressions left on every continent, the original landing sites for the self-propelled terrain modifiers. When done with their work, the mammoth machines had lifted themselves back into space and to the next world. Stage Three? Theirs was meant to be a more practical record. They left clusters of buildings, ready and waiting to serve: first as the center point of new settlements, then for whatever purpose the colonists chose. The largest of these had its own monument, erected in advance of that planet being opened to immigration. The standing joke was that the terraformers hadn't trusted anyone else to spell their names correctly.

For most, that monument was now a memorial. The onset of the Quill Effect had been marked by sudden, horrifyingly simultaneous death. Any bodies in the open were retrieved by remotes. Their families demanded it. After the autopsies revealed nothing, those bodies had been destroyed in a fear-filled decision that left Gail and other researchers nothing at all.

Pardell's World was different. No bodies. There wasn't any sign that Aaron's parents had ever been there, only lush fields. Susan Witts hadn't died from the Quill, and she'd mentioned no one else living on this world. No monuments, unless you counted the pair of wind-gnarled trees. Gail supposed they were the sterile oaks Witts had planted for her son and grandson.

They'd seen schematics of Witts' original terraforming headquarters, a sprawling complex of low buildings, with a landing site for visiting starships protected by the slightly higher ridge just to the west. The view from the living quarters would have been spectacular, overlooking a series of progressively lower prominences leading down to the start of a broad, river-carved plain. The living quarters, and everything else here, had been dismantled, the materials wrapped and left in a low mound behind the bunker. *Gifts for her grandson*, Gail thought with a rush of melancholy.

*Such as the Quill.*

"*Athena* comm . . . we've landed on Pardell's World."

No one seemed to be breathing on the bridge. Dafoe's voice rang out clear and strong through the silence: "No alarms on any monitors. No symptoms of the Quill Effect. Proceeding with Trial Number One on your mark, Dr. Smith."

The *Athena* was packed to tolerance with every measuring device the *Seeker*'s scientists could imagine—and some Gail knew they'd made up on the way here. All were feeding their measurements and readings directly to stations in the science sphere.

"Proceed, Specialist Dafoe. Mr. Pardell."

They didn't see the *Athena*'s outer doors drop open. Instead, the screen showed a dizzying blur of movement as Deployment Specialist Krenshaw switched the feed to his station as he sent out a 'bot and spun it to face the little ship. The image stabilized.

Gail gripped the armrests with both hands.

Two figures stepped out onto the ramp, both in dark blue suits catching sparks from the sunlight as they left the shadow of the *Athena*'s hull. Gail knew the shorter individual would be Aaron. Otherwise, they were identical, even to the thick umbilicals connecting them to the interior of the pod. The umbilicals were more than conduits of information on the condition of the two test subjects—they could be forcibly retracted by remote from the *Seeker*.

*Allowing recovery of the bodies*, Gail reminded herself. The equipment was hers—designed when she'd planned for every contingency but caring about the body being recovered.

"Dafoe reporting . . . no sign of the Quill Effect." The woman's voice was steady, solid—Grant had picked well. Gail slid a look his way. The commander's face was impassive, totally focused on the task at hand.

*As she should be.* "Aaron?" Gail asked. "Are you sensing anything unusual?"

He might have been standing beside her, his voice was so instantly and distinctly there. "The air's pushing at me," he said with wonder. "Wind, right?"

"Wind," Gail confirmed. "Anything else?"

He looked up at the 'bot and shook his head. The headgear was clear, but the coating made it one-way. Gail could only see the reflection of the 'bot where Aaron's face should be. *First design flaw.*

"Dafoe. . . . I can see Quill. They're— My God, they're everywhere."

Grant surged to his feet, but his tone stayed calm. "Krenshaw, switch to Dafoe's vid."

The screen changed to show Dafoe's line of sight. At first, Gail didn't see what the FD was talking about—she was apparently looking at the nearest grass, bent flat by the edge of the pod's ramp. Then Krenshaw stepped up the magnification slightly.

The grass itself was subtly iridescent. The play of color stopped halfway up the plant, as though each of its stalks had been dipped in a fine oil. Even as they watched, the color detached itself, first from one stalk and then several, falling like thin ribbons through the tangle of crushed grass.

"Dafoe's heart rate's up to 130, Commander."

Before Grant could reply to this advisement, Dafoe's voice came through the comm: "As if yours wouldn't be, Sensun."

"Keep it professional, people," Grant ordered dryly, but the break in tension was palpable.

"Did you expect so many, Dr. Smith?" Aaron asked. Without being told, Krenshaw changed to the 'bot's perspective, so they once again saw both figures and the *Athena*.

*Sitting in her field of Quill*, Gail told herself, stunned as she tried to estimate how many Quill there could be, if every blade of grass hid a filament, and grass covered this world.

"We wanted to find them," she said out loud. "Congratulations, everyone. Proceed with Trial Number One when ready." Gail saw Grant stiffening slightly and changed her mind. "Wait. Before you do, let's see if you can catch some filaments from on the ramp."

"Copy that, Dr. Smith. Setting up to retrieve filaments."

While Aaron waited on the ramp, as if entranced by the view, Dafoe went back inside the *Athena*, returning shortly with a stasis box she passed to the 'sider, and a portable remote handling arm. They watched as she used the arm to gently grasp some of the grass that was still coated in Quill, then pull.

The Quill slipped off and disappeared. Not just the filaments Dafoe tried to grab, but the telltale iridescence vanished in the blink of an eye from every blade in sight.

"You said they couldn't move," Aaron commented.

"They dropped to the ground," Dafoe argued. "That's not moving. Sorry, Dr. Smith. I may have knocked them loose. I'll try scooping up some of the underlying soil and roots."

"Bring samples of the plants, too," Gail ordered. "There may well be changes in the biota we should examine at the same time."

This task took a few more minutes. The root mass was thick and healthy, matted beneath decades of old growth. They'd known what type of vegetative cover to expect, since all terra-formers started with self-pollinating perennial grasses to develop soil layers. The *Athena* contained tools to slice through the sod. It still took time for Dafoe and Aaron to obtain the samples. During the process, they stayed on the ramp and used the remote arm, the 'sider being careful, as always, to avoid touching his companion.

Gail had Krenshaw move the 'bot outward, slowly. Now that they knew what to look for, they could see the area of Quill-free grass made a perfect circle around the *Athena*, approximately ten paces in radius. Gail made notes to herself on a pad. *Was this how Jer and Gabby Pardell had been able to land safely and move about at first? Had the Quill been temporarily driven underground by the arrival of their shuttle?*

"These suits could use some air conditioning, Dr. Smith," their son observed.

"Take it up with the complaints department," Gail retorted, but made a note. *Second design flaw.* There'd better not be any more.

"My own suit's worse," he replied with a short laugh. "I'll start with that one when I'm back."

"Dafoe. . . . Samples collected and sealed, Dr. Smith. What next?"

*What indeed?* Gail asked herself She was almost certain there'd be no Quill tissue in the samples—she'd ordered them because she wanted every scrap of information possible.

"Proceed with Trial Number One, Specialist Dafoe, Aaron," Gail said, keeping her reluctance from her voice. "Just take your time. At the first hint of any—trouble—I want you back in the *Athena*. Understood?"

"Dafoe. . . . Copy that."

"No arguments from me, boss," from Aaron.

Gail stood involuntarily as the screen showed the two figures walking slowly and carefully down the ramp, umbilicals trailing behind. She held her breath as they stepped off, boots landing on the neatly folded grass in unison.

"Dafoe. . . . Nominal."

*Ludicrous*, Gail decided, forcing herself back into her seat, aware she of all people couldn't show tension now, not with everything riding on these footsteps. At this moment, she couldn't want to be right—she had to be.

"Any reaction from the Quill?" Gail asked.

There were three on the bridge, including Grant's Krenshaw, whose sole duty was to watch all the available incoming vids. "The perimeter is unchanged, Dr. Smith," one offered. Choi, Gail remembered. Eric Choi—the best of his graduating class on Callisto in remote sensing interpretation. One of the assets she'd insisted on having with her. "Thank you, Choi. Krenshaw, widen the field, please," she said quietly.

The screen's towering image shifted until they were looking at Aaron and Dafoe, but backed enough so that the abandoned monitoring station and the *Athena* were both in view. "I believe I can enhance to show the extent of the Quill, Dr. Smith," Choi offered.

"Do so."

All of the grass, with the exception of the circle encompassing the two humans, became stained with red. Gail controlled a shudder. "Very helpful," she said dryly. "Commander Grant? A word."

Grant moved quickly, coming to stand beside Gail so he could keep his eye on the screen. "Yes, Dr. Smith."

Gail lowered her voice. "There has to be physical contact for Trial Number One."

His dark eyes met hers. "At your command, Dr. Smith." Calmly, confidently, as if they discussed plans for dinner rather than lives.

"Have them move outward, slowly, until they reach the Quill. At no time are they to exceed the limits of their umbilicals. Make it clear to Dafoe—no unnecessary risk. Understood?"

Grant nodded, and returned to his station. Gail listened to him relay the order. Heard Dafoe's curt acknowledgment. Aaron was uncharacteristically silent. *Perhaps*, she thought, *he was busy experiencing his first encounter with plant life*. Or first footsteps on his homeworld.

A few more steps, and they'd reached the unflattened grass.

Here, on the top of the hill, it rose well over their waists, but fortunately no higher. Closer to the creek, Gail estimated the occasional clumps of bluegrass would top Pardell's head for sure, possibly Dafoe's. No animal life hid among the stalks—unless Witts' meticulous records lied about that detail. There was no reason to suspect there would be. The mix of species used to kickstart a terraforming project began with botanicals and their microbial partners; other life—including human—was to be added later.

*Was.* But had never been, thanks to the Quill. So Dafoe and Aaron were making the first-ever trails in the grass of Pardell's World, their feet cracking stalks down no matter how cautiously they stepped.

"We've movement from the Quill."

*I thought you said they couldn't move*, flashed through Gail's mind. "Show me."

The 'bot's viewpoint pulled them down to the area directly in the path of Dafoe and Aaron. The red stain was slowly moving closer to them. Krenshaw upped the magnification, reestablishing normal color ranges so they could see how filaments were slipping up more and more stalks.

"Dafoe, Aaron—stay where you are," Gail ordered immediately.

On one level, Gail was fascinated. Rather than climbing back up on the grass they'd abandoned moments before, shrinking the entire circle around the humans and their ship, the area being reclaimed by the Quill was small and coordinated, the result like the tip of some giant's tongue slowly reaching out for a taste.

Grant returned to her side. "Dr. Smith, shall I have them withdraw?" he asked quietly, covering the pickup on his headset with one hand.

"No."

"This could be an attack—Trial Number One was to be a passive encounter."

"They stay," Gail bit off the words, not bothering to look at him. "If it's an attack, Commander, then it's the best possible test of the suits, wouldn't you say?"

"In which case, you're authorizing a jump to Trial Number Three."

Now she did look at him. "They stay, Commander Grant. My authorization. There's no predicting biological systems to the nth degree—we have an opportunity here and I don't intend to back away from it."

"Da–Dafoe here. . . . We have contact, Dr. Smith."

Gail and Grant turned to the screen. Against the dark blue fabric of the suits, the Quill filaments showed clearly, slipping up each leg, halting just below the thigh, as if the humans were merely thicker stalks of grass.

The Quill were beautiful in the sunlight, like rainbows made real.

The voice coming through the speakers startled them all. "Dafoe here . . . repeating . . . we have contact, Dr. Smith. No negative effects. The suits are working."

"Congratulations, Gail," Tobo said heartily, rushing up to shake her hand. Suddenly, Gail was surrounded by well-wishers from the crew, some pounding her back, others standing nearby and smiling widely. Most stayed at their stations, but cheered. She looked for Grant.

The commander had gone to the station monitoring the pair's life signs. *Perhaps, like her, he believed celebrating might be premature.* Gail pushed her way to his side, smiling and nodding politely. "How are they?" she demanded, keeping her voice down.

"Dafoe's vitals are a little shaky. Pardell's rock solid. You'd think he stepped out on a planet every day."

*No surprise.* "He has a way of taking the extraordinary in stride," she commented. "Let's have Dafoe get one or more filaments into a stasis box."

Grant relayed the request. On the screen, they could see Dafoe nod even as she said aloud: "Copy that, Cornmander. Dr. Smith, do you want each filament in a separate box?"

"That's ideal, Specialist Dafoe, but if you have any difficulty, together is better than none at all."

Another nod. "Let's get these back to the pod, Pardell," they heard her say.

Aaron didn't respond.

Gail froze, staring at the screen. *What was he doing?* As far as they could see, the 'sider was looking down at the Quill on his legs. His hands were limp at his sides. She remembered the dining lounge—she'd seen for herself how Aaron's mind could fade from reality. *Damn, this was no time for him to become disconnected.*

"Pardell," Dafoe repeated. "Are you all right?" Detectable uneasiness in her voice now. *Did she fear the 'sider was succumbing to some attack?*

*Or*, Gail thought suddenly, *did Dafoe fear Pardell was about to become the enemy?*

# Chapter 63

*T*HIS *was the enemy?*

Pardell gazed down at the slime on Gail's brand-new suit and fought the urge to simply wipe it off with his glove. *Malley had it right*, he thought with disgust. *People shouldn't have died—shouldn't have had to live as they did—because of something you couldn't grapple with, that you couldn't rip apart with your hands.*

Despite his rage, Pardell was helpless to hold his mind to the here and now. As his thoughts detached, expanded, grew distant, he could hear Dafoe's voice and sensed the change in it from caution to alarm, but it was as if the words became air, air that pushed and grabbed him as if it had fingers.

His awareness encompassed this world, *his world*, a planet coated in Quill. There wasn't one, or a nest, or a favored place— they were the world, contaminating everything that lived, even he and Dafoe. His thoughts spun outward, helpless to resist perception and analysis, toying with concepts like ecosystems and dependencies, balance and evolution—finding nothing to encompass this obscenity.

Just like this . . . that filaments must have slithered over his newborn flesh, found entry points, contaminated him as well as this planet. *They were under his skin even now.*

*Hopeless . . . hopeless . . . how to destroy the Quill without destroying all else?* Pardell understood, finally, the danger should the Quill reach the warm, living world that birthed humanity. The blockade, the deaths, the struggle to exist—all faded against the absolute imperative of species survival.

*How to destroy the Quill inside him?* He wanted to live, too.

"Hey, Aaron! Not the time, friend." Malley's deep and unexpected rumble jarred Pardell back into synchrony with the moment.

"So when did they let you have a comm?" Pardell asked, tearing his eyes from the Quill riding his suit and straightening.

"I'm not sure 'let' is the right word—these Earthers get kinda tense about their toys." The laugh filling his helmet was close to normal, if not quite. *Malley was watching this*, Pardell reminded himself, wondering at the cost to his friend of facing an open sky. "You okay? Not very considerate of your date, Aaron, going spacey like that. Cathy's going to think you don't care."

*Cathy?* Was there anyone on the *Seeker* Malley didn't know on a first-name basis after a week? Pardell turned to look for Dafoe. She was standing, as he was, in the Quill-grass. He had another complaint about the suits—it would have been much better if they could see one another's faces, instead of reflections of themselves in the headgear.

"Specialist Dafoe—my apologies. I was distracted. I'm not suffering any effects or sensations out of the ordinary—"

Malley snorted rudely in his ear.

"Thank you, Malley." Gail's voice. All business. *It had to be*, Pardell knew.

"Glad you're all right, Pardell," Dafoe told him, relief plain and sharp. "Dr. Smith wants us to put our 'friends' into a box to bring back up to the ship. I'll go first."

Pardell nodded his understanding. He watched closely as Dafoe walked back to the ramp. The Quill stayed on her legs, one on the outside of each calf. "I'd keep them separated, Dafoe," he called out.

"Why?" Gail again.

Pardell kept forgetting this was an open comm—something no 'sider would ever risk. "Only one climbed up each leg," he ventured, "even though there's room for more. Maybe they can't tolerate physical contact with one another. A guess." *Albeit an educated one*, Pardell thought somewhat wildly.

"One per box, it is," Gail responded. "Thank you."

Her voice lingered in his ears. *Not like music*, Pardell decided. *Something more intimate than sound alone, filled with the past, present, and—future.* He'd promised her he'd come back.

Pardell looked out at the horizon, tracing the lines of distant mountains with his eyes. *Were they real if he couldn't touch them?* Another breeze shoved against his back. *Was it air, if he didn't breathe it?*

"It's not going to work."

He whirled to see Dafoe rubbing her blue-only legs. "Dr. Smith. The things slipped through my fingers when I tried to handle them," she said. "Pardell? Any suggestions?"

"Toss me a box," he said. "I'll try from here."

The stasis boxes were small but heavy, a consequence of the technology meant to contain a biohazard of unknown potency. Pardell made the catch easily enough, but put the box down on the grass. He resisted the temptation to run his gloved fingers along the stalks and investigate their strange, living textures.

"Gail?" Pardell said lightly, steeling himself

"I'm here."

"This should work—but if it doesn't, I want you to know—I need to—" Pardell swallowed. "I'm glad you came to Thromberg. Okay? It's all been worth it."

"Wait!" nothing businesslike or calm in her sudden cry in his ears. "Aaron! Dafoe—stop him!"

Before Dafoe could do more than turn his way, Pardell had pulled off his headgear. He smiled, he hoped reassuringly, at the FD specialist, before stripping the gloves from his hands. He put the gear down, carefully, on a flattened patch of grass. *Old habits, new place.*

The first thing Pardell noticed was the way the air whistled and roared past his ears, even as it tossed hair to tickle his forehead. Then he felt the sun—warm and soothing on his face, overbright until his eyes adjusted, a prickling irritation on his gold-veined hands. "I think they stay on the lower parts of the grass to avoid the direct sunlight," he said, knowing every word would be recorded. The comm was built into the neck of the suit, not the headgear. Pardell drew a long, deep breath in through his nostrils. There was so much flavor to this air, it was like taking a drink of some exotic wine. If he'd ever had doubts this was a world built by humans, for humans, they were erased by the way his lungs welcomed this blend of gases, his blood soaked up its oxygen. *Pardell's World.*

Complete with a threat.

Pardell swallowed again, hard, then reached down and gently, but firmly, grasped the filament clinging to his right leg.

*. . . Recognition.*

He let go immediately, feeling himself shake.

"Aaron—what is it? Your vitals went off the scale."

"I don't know. Nothing." *Nothing*, Pardell reassured himself, not needing the suit's monitors to feel how his heart still pounded. *Nothing.* Just the unexpectedness of the filament's dry, almost powdery surface under his fingers. The thing looked like slime.

"You aren't feeling anything from the Quill—there's no effect at all?" *Was the relief in her voice for him—or the experiment?*

"All systems nominal," he quipped, winking at Dafoe. "I'll see if I can get this thing into the box." Cautiously, Pardell bent over and reached for the filament again.

"Pardell!" Dafoe warned. "Look!"

The 'sider followed the direction of Dafoe's pointing—and shaking—hand. All around them, the grass was vibrating, as if each stalk was being moved independently of the others. "The wind?" he asked hopefully.

"Get back in the *Athena* before I haul you in!" Gail ordered. "Hurry!"

"We came for the sample," Pardell objected. "Just give me a minute more." He moved quickly, in case the filament released and dropped to the ground, but it stayed in place until his fingers pulled it free.

*. . . Welcome.*

Pardell almost threw the slender filament into the stasis box, slamming closed the lid. The one on his other leg dropped and disappeared into the ground.

"Hurry up!"

"Done," he told Dafoe, picking up the box as well as his gloves and headgear, clutching the pile to his chest. "Let's go."

Almost running, Pardell made it to the ramp only to have Dafoe hold up her arm to stop him. He halted with barely enough room to avoid her touch. "What's—that?" Her voice was almost a whisper. She was looking behind him. Pardell turned and stared.

*That* . . . a spot marked by the end of the trail they'd stamped into the grass. *That* . . . place where the grass was coming free from its roots, whirling in a column that reached more than head high.

"Wind can do that," Pardell heard himself say. He might have believed it, if the air against his face wasn't perfectly still.

"It doesn't do *that* . . ." Dafoe replied, as the column began to condense into a shape.

Before Pardell could do more than gasp, the shape became something more, something they knew.

Human. A woman, woven from grass and Quill filaments, standing in what was now a circle of disturbed, black earth.

Disturbingly vague in detail, but the figure had two outstretched arms, holding what could have been a baby. Holding it out toward them.

Pardell dropped what he was carrying. He bent and began collecting the gloves, box, and headgear by feel, never taking his eyes from the statue.

Dafoe's voice came sharp, hard, and clear: "Dafoe here . . . Commander Grant. Code Alpha Prime. One, Niner, Niner. Do you copy, *Seeker*? I repeat . . . Alpha Prime. One, Niner, Niner.

"We have a First Contact situation."

# Chapter 64

GAIL had thought she understood the Quill—well enough to find them, and destroy them when she did.

She'd thought she was in charge of this ship and its mission—that all aboard, with the notable exception of the Titan-serving Reinsez and his few cohorts, obeyed her commands.

*What else would she be wrong about today?* Gail wondered, shaking her head wearily.

At least Pardell and Dafoe were safe. She had to trust they were. She hadn't seen or talked to either since the FD specialist delivered her code.

*Alpha Prime. One, Niner, Niner. First Contact.* Words setting a blur of events in motion with the smoothness of extensive planning and complete determination. Gail had barely time to be stunned by the words and their implications before Grant had commandeered the intership comm, rattling off a string of equally incomprehensible codes that echoed throughout the *Seeker*.

*He now ruled her ship.*

*Oh, Grant had had help*, she reminded herself. The First Defense Unit had come on board twenty-five strong. Twenty-five in blindingly obvious uniforms; twenty-five men and women so physically similar no one—especially herself—had thought to look for anyone else.

Of the *Seeker*'s crew complement, it now appeared that three-quarters were also FDs. Of the *Seeker*'s scientific population, a depressingly significant number of techs and even a few of the scientists had responded immediately to Grant's coded instructions.

*As a mutiny*, Gail decided, *it likely held a record for the most willing participants.*

"What's going to happen?"

Startled out of her thoughts, Gail looked up at Captain Tobo. Both of them had been evicted—courteously—from the bridge. It was no consolation that Szpindel had been among those barred from the command sphere. She shrugged. "I've no idea, my esteemed Captain. At least Titan U and Vincente are unlikely to worry about my little transgression in light of all this." Gail waved around the room.

Tobo's eyes twinkled. "There's that," he agreed, taking a seat at her table. They'd been herded into the science sphere's dining lounge two hours ago, Tobo spending much of that time in huddled conversation with others of his crew. Gail had decided she might as well take a late supper, if she was going to be here any longer. "Although I've heard three patrol ships are en route. On the behest of a concerned Titan University," he mimicked a worried parent, "following those alarming reports from their esteemed representative."

Gail took her time cutting, stabbing, and chewing her next mouthful. "Three, huh?" she mumbled thoughtfully after a moment, then swallowed. "That's all?"

Tobo helped himself to a roll from the basket between them. "Well, Vincente may have realized it was somewhat unlikely you'd single-handedly hijacked this ship, despite Reinsez's hysteria. He knows you. Three might seem to him accountably frugal, while sufficient to escort back one unsuccessful project leader . . . if you were wrong."

"I wasn't," Gail said with sudden, fierce delight. "I wasn't wrong about the Quill. They are here. The suits work. And, best of all, we have a living sample."

"All true. So Vincente and Titan will doubtless take the position you acted on their authority to achieve these marvelous things," Tobo said with cheerful irony. "You will be famous, of course. As you always wanted."

"Maybe in another lifetime, Tomoki." Gail lost her appetite and sat back, gazing at her old friend. "Or maybe it was another me . . . someone who cared about a reputation, about arriving on Earth to bands and parades. Gail Smith—the Salvation of Humanity."

There was no judgment on his gentle, round face—only understanding. "Whether you still seek fame or not, you've earned it," he assured her. "Defeating the Quill will mean everything to those people back on the stations. You will have saved them."

"Will I?" Gail shook her head. "Are you sure I haven't doomed them?" She drew little circles on the table with one finger. "I've read how strong the First Contact movement was on Earth, before the disaster of the Quill shifted power to the Reductionists. Now? We've caught the stations between those who want Earth to look outward and those who'd make translight taboo—if they could figure out the right incantation."

She paused, then tapped the tabletop in emphasis. "Think about it. If the Quill are intelligent—where does that put our mission? We were supposed to find a way to destroy the things, not talk to them! The stations? What do we tell them? And it could get worse, much worse." Gail steadied her voice. "What position will Earth take, if the first alien intelligence we meet turns out to have already conquered every human-inhabited planet outside of Sol System? Can the Quill be proved murderers? People will start taking sides, Tomoki. The riots on Thromberg might only be a taste."

Tobo shook his head. "It doesn't have to come to that. You have the people and expertise on this ship to determine if the Quill are intelligent. If they aren't . . . nothing's changed. If they are? Then we ask them to stop killing us."

Gail laughed bitterly. "Right. The last time I thanked your wife for supper, Ayo thought I was asking for a second helping. And that's between two biologically similar individuals who knew the precise context of the conversation, as well as understanding several words in each other's language. Who both have a language! I don't care how many linguists and comm techs Grant's tucked on this ship—they aren't experts in communicating with anything as alien as the Quill."

"Your young man might be."

*No doubt the same thoughts were going through Grant's*

*head*, Gail told herself. No matter her reasoned arguments for Tobo, her calm exterior, she knew herself so angry her very blood felt like ice—knew herself so deeply betrayed she had no trouble keeping her fury contained.

Until she had a target.

# Chapter 65

MALLEY knew the signs, all right.

Aisha and the rest of the science staff who'd gathered in the lab were milling around, a dozen conversations underway at once as they tried to make sense out of what was happening. They were surprised by Gail Smith's sudden absence from the comm and her "replacement" by Commander Grant and his second, Tau—but not alarmed. Of more concern, it seemed, was the time it was taking the FD to deliver the long-awaited sample of Quill tissue to their hands. The hint of an alien intelligence at work had them buzzing with excitement. Still, they'd been told to wait here and be ready; most seemed prepared to wait as long as that took, as long as they would be involved in this momentous discovery.

*Like 'tastic junkies, every one.* Malley doubted any had noticed the FDs' reaction to the mysterious codes Grant had snapped out over the comm, or seen how those assigned to the lab had quietly stepped outside, then closed and locked the doors behind themselves.

He was quite sure no one else had seen how about a quarter of those gathered in here to watch the landing on Pardell's World had exchanged startled, excited looks, then, gradually, moved together to form a quiet, cohesive group—separate from the others, but not obviously, nothing so blatant . . .

*He knew the signs.*

This was how it had always started on Thromberg, whenever Station Admin had had enough of Outward Five's independent ways and scanty record keeping, and planned a cleanup visit. From one minute to the next, there would be new voices on the public comms, new faces at the ration distribution points and checkpoints. As suddenly, there would be a wordless sorting out among those in groups—lines drawn between those prepared to support, or at least tolerate, Admin when it arrived in numbers, and those bloody-minded enough to want to scrap about it first.

*Martial law or mutiny.* It depended on your starting point.

Grant's was obvious. The military, obeying its older mandate to find and protect alien intelligence, had taken control of the *Seeker* from Gail Smith and, so, Titan University. *That,* Malley told himself grimly, *could be an improvement.* Grant had brought Aaron back to the ship. Point in his favor.

*Aaron hadn't been seen since.* Point against.

Gail must have been locked away—Malley grinned. Definite point in Grant's favor.

He was locked in here. While Malley wasn't happy about it, it was better than being locked up elsewhere—or being searched. One of his first tasks had been to double-check his small arsenal. Two knives and the trank. *Well, a little more than that now,* Malley admitted to himself: three knives, the trank, the comm he'd somehow forgotten to return to Taggart, and a set of tools most on Thromberg would consider very useful indeed. And a roll of remarkably strong string he knew Aaron would like.

*Handy pockets Earthers put into their clothing.*

The statue, or whatever it was, still dominated the room. At some point, everyone in the lab—including Malley, though he found the backdrop of sky and irregular ground somewhat unsettling—had stared, transfixed by the final image left on the screen. *Grant's idea,* he had no doubt. Make sure the first and only sign of purposeful action by the Quill stayed in their faces at all times, lest any in here doubt it or, Malley growled to himself, *lest anyone think the First Defense Unit was off its collective rocker taking over the ship for a planetful of slime.*

The Earther scientists seemed well on their way to group insanity, some excited to tears.

The stationer couldn't deny the slime had indeed constructed a compelling image—what troubled him wasn't the fact, but the intent. The figure of a woman and baby was a message for one human in particular, Aaron Pardell. Given Aaron's tendency to drift from reality under ordinary conditions, Malley wasn't at all comfortable with where his friend's mind might be wandering after this.

*It would help if he knew where his friend was, period.*

# Chapter 66

*WHERE was Pardell?* There'd been no word, nothing. He would have contacted her—Gail knew it—if he could.

Gail had expected better of Grant. What would it hurt his rebellion to keep her posted on the *Athena*'s return? He'd been friends with Aaron—he knew she'd want to know the 'sider was safe.

At the very least, Grant knew she'd spent most of her life—and risked what remained of it—trying to find the Quill. *Where was her sample?*

Gail sipped her tea and smiled quite menacingly at the figure rushing to her table.

"You have to do something, Dr. Smith! This situation—it's intolerable! Simply intolerable!"

Considering the unmistakable aroma of sherry accompanying these emphatic statements, Gail was quite impressed Reinsez was tackling any word more challenging than her name. "What do you expect me to do, Manuel," she asked, bored enough to be curious. "Call up the good commander and ask for my ship back?"

"You could call in the patrol ships—" Even this inebriated, Reinsez realized when he'd let something major slip. His normally gloomy face assumed an almost deathlike pallor. "You could call Titan and have them send patrol ships," he said hastily.

Gail arched one eyebrow. "Let me have your translight comm and I'll shout as loud as you'd like."

Reinsez's eyes scanned the dining lounge as though looking for help, stopping a moment where Rosalind Fournier was deep in conversation with First Officer Szpindel. "What makes you think I'd have such a thing?" he blustered.

"Clever," Gail acknowledged, her voice silky smooth. "Forming an alliance with the leader of the 'siders? I wouldn't have thought you capable, dear Manuel. Still, even the formidable Rosalind can't access equipment that isn't here, can she?" Gail leaned her elbows on the table, resting her chin in her hands. "What was your bargain with her?" She shook her head. "No, don't tell me. Let's see if I can guess. With Szpindel's help, she could get you our destination easily—after all, Rosalind could open the records from the *Merry Mate II* and retrieve her course data; you'd only need to get her into my office safe to access my copies. How did you contact Titan after Grant and I took away your comm privileges? You had your own—and where better to hide it than with—Rosalind! Did you promise her entry codes to Sol System in return for her help against me?"

Gail made as if to stand. "Should I go over to Rosalind and mention—just casually, you realize—that you knew full well you'd never be able to obtain such codes? What might we expect from the woman who's already risked her own life and that of several hundred thousand other people?"

"No. Sit down. Please, Gail." Reinsez licked his lips, then blurted out: "I don't want to die out here. I want to go home."

*The truth at last*, she judged it, whether brought out by the sherry or the honest dread of an old and frightened man.

Gail settled back into her seat, doing her best to appear calm and confident. "Then, Manuel," she informed Titan's spy, "you'd better be ready to back any play I choose to make, because your safety and comfort aren't even on our good commander's list."

More than that, she didn't bother saying. The man was drunk and scared enough to be careless—if he was even capable of remembering their conversation. *No*, Gail thought, gazing around the room at a truly pitiful collection of potential allies—other than Tobo, whom Grant would be watching like a hawk—*she wouldn't be relying on Reinsez or his cronies for backup any time soon—except one.*

Gail got up and walked over to Rosalind Fournier's table, noting the poorly hidden looks of dismay from several individuals she passed. Reinsez's lot, drawing their own conclusions about her conversation with their "leader" and her actions now. *Fools.*

"Tell me, Dr. Smith," Rosalind said, not bothering with a greeting and using a shooing gesture to remove her companions from the table. "Did you have any notion Earth planned to take away your precious ship?"

"Complete surprise, Rosalind," Gail admitted freely. "May I join you?"

"Oh, please do. The conversation was quite dull. You'd think these people had never experienced a disruption of the chain of command before."

"It's not particularly common, where we come from," Gail reminded her.

Rosalind smiled. "One forgets," she said.

*Unlikely*, Gail thought, but smiled herself "I must apologize for the inconvenience. If you like, I'll talk to Commander Grant about your situation. He must realize you are a—disinterested third party."

The 'sider's eyes glinted. "Must he?"

"Of course," Gail said smoothly, capturing the basket of rolls from the center of the table. "Why should you care who is in command of the *Seeker*, as long as you believe—" she stressed the word, "—that you'll ultimately get what you want." As she spoke, Gail divided the rolls between two plates. Three each. She pushed both plates into the middle of the table and waited. They were being observed, without doubt. *But would the observer understand this?* Gail sincerely doubted it.

Rosalind steepled her fingers, examining the offering but not moving to touch either plate.

Gail poured two glasses of water and put one within reach of the 'sider. She lifted hers almost to her lips before saying: "This assumes the present situation—remains stable. Are you a gambler, Rosalind?"

Rosalind tilted her lean head, as if the angle gave her a better view of Gail's face. "I don't take unnecessary risks, Dr. Smith."

"Neither do I," Gail said immediately. "But I do take the necessary ones."

The glass was in Rosalind's hand. Gail waited.

"This action by the Quill," the 'sider said, staring at her glass. "It has made the situation on this ship—unstable. One hardly knows what to expect next. Alliances, promises. These now appear less than reliable." An eyebrow rose. "I'm tempted to lock myself in my quarters until you Earthers settle things. But I doubt you'll do so to my—satisfaction."

"That's the obvious interpretation," Gail agreed, keeping her hand and voice steady. Rosalind had to know what she offered—a personal alliance with her, not Reinsez. Not Grant. Not Earth. "It may not be entirely accurate."

Rosalind flashed her an enigmatic look before raising her glass and swallowing. *No blame, no apologies—only what promoted survival for another day.* Gail echoed the gesture with a mixture of relief and caution, aware exactly how temporary this alliance could be.

The 'sider chose one of the plates, Gail the other. "I wait what develops with great interest, Dr. Smith," Rosalind told her, a careful choice of words. Reinsez must have made her aware of the Earthers' lack of respect for privacy.

"As do I."

"And young Aaron? Surely he has gained significant value in the eyes of your Commander Grant."

Gail looked at Rosalind sharply, stung by the implication that Aaron was another bargaining chip, not surprised by it either. She might have been tempted to talk to the older woman about Aaron, to learn more about his life, his past. But Gail was quite sure Rosalind would put a price to every answer, every revelation. This wasn't a mother, concerned for her son. This was a leader, ready to spend whatever lives she felt necessary.

"Quite significant," Gail nodded agreeably, grimly aware she knew exactly where they stood—and the coin Rosalind would understand. "Thank you for sharing your table," she added, standing. "I'm sure we'll be in touch."

Rosalind's eyes gleamed with anticipation. "I look forward to it, Dr. Smith."

Gail felt some anticipation of her own as she walked away from the table. She'd made a start. Now it was time to do more.

*How very thoughtful of Grant to confine her to the science sphere.*

It was time he learned why. Having excused herself from Rosalind, their business as complete as circumstances allowed, Gail went to the door. The FD on guard there, Cornell, had the grace to look uncomfortable at her approach, but stayed at attention. "Yes, Dr. Smith?" he asked.

"I'm exhausted, Specialist Cornell," she told him. "Am I to be allowed back into my quarters for the night?" It didn't take much to yawn, Gail discovered. *Nothing wrong with some truth in a cover story.*

"Sorry, Doctor. Orders are to keep everyone out of the command sphere."

"Fine. Assign me quarters here, then. Any bed will do." When he looked uncertain, Gail gave him her second-best smile, leaning wearily against the wall beside the closed door. "Look, Cornell. I can't believe your commander wants me to sleep on a chair in the dining lounge—especially if he needs me up and thinking tomorrow. And he will, you know. Those are my suits that protected Dafoe and Pardell on the planet. If you people want to accomplish anything more down there, it'll be my suits that make it possible. Call Grant, if you must. I'll wait."

"That's not necessary, Dr. Smith," Cornell decided. "I can't see any security risk to your getting some sleep. As for those suits—they're amazing things. I admit some of us doubted they'd work."

"Yet you all volunteered to test them."

Cornell looked mildly amused by the question. "Of course, Dr. Smith. Wait here a minute. I'll call someone to escort you to quarters."

"Thank you."

Gail took a seat nearby, chin in her hand, as though her head was too heavy to keep up. *Not hard.*

It wasn't long before FD Loran appeared, one of the science sphere stewards in tow. The steward, a mousy little man she vaguely recalled was named Bates, looked a little too nervous to be one of the FDs' plants among the crew. He looked immediately flustered when Gail smiled at him a little more warmly than he'd expected.

*A better-than-standard issue bed.* Gail made herself stretch out between the cold satin sheets, ignoring the tendency of her skin to crawl. Sazaad liked his luxury.

It hadn't been hard to arrange for this room—his room—of those available while the FD confined the science staff to the lab. Gail had merely given Bates the number of the room next to it, knowing it was vacant. Sazaad's nocturnal habits didn't induce popularity with neighbors. With commendable, if predictable, suspicion, Loran had refused to put Gail in the room of her own choosing, insisting on Sazaad's instead. Everyone knew, of course, there was nothing but animosity between Drs. Smith and Sazaad. It probably seemed a safe bet there would be nothing Gail could have hidden in there, no hidden motive for wanting Sazaad's room over any other.

*Unless you knew the man*, Gail thought coolly, lying in the dark. Any senior scientist's quarters would have sufficed, but Sazaad's had a singular advantage. He was completely paranoid about surveillance—he probably had to be, if he maintained a similarly prolific lifestyle back on Titan. She could be reasonably sure Grant hadn't planted any vids in here, or, if he had, they'd been neutralized. Sazaad was quite the genius, in his way.

That didn't mean Gail felt comfortable between his sheets. She lay down in case someone came in to see if she'd really intended to grab an hour or so of sleep, making sure to thoroughly crease the bedding and leave an imprint in the pillow. Unfortunately, this also had the effect of leaving proof for Sazaad that she'd been in his bed. He'd be impossible for weeks. *Maybe*, Gail thought more cheerfully, *she could find a way to have Malley threaten to sever Sazaad's head again.*

Not that Malley had done so with any notion of protecting her. But he had thoroughly cowed Sazaad for the time being.

She didn't put on the light—no need, all the quarters were similar and Sazaad's was incredibly neat compared to hers. Two steps and turn, hands out. *There.*

Gail used her fingers to hunt for the desk pad, ruthlessly

shoving anything else out of her way. She didn't bother with the internal comm system or waste time searching through Sazaad's doubtless revolting drawers for any illicit portable devices.

*Ah.* Pulling up the chair, found by the simple expedient of bumping one hip into it, she sat and began keying in the general access code every scientist on the *Seeker* used to send their routine updates and changes to the D-board in the lab.

Then, she began keying in something else.

*This was*, Gail told herself grimly, her *ship*.

# Chapter 67

*T*HE Seeker *wasn't Gail's anymore.*

Pardell had known something was wrong the instant Dafoe spouted code into the comm. There could only be one reason for it—the FD wanted to communicate to her commander, not Gail Smith.

He'd kept quiet, listening to Grant's voice—not Gail's—directing their return to the ship, sitting at a safe distance from Dafoe as the *Athena* bumped and jostled her way upward, the ride smoothing like magic once they'd cleared the impediment of atmosphere.

He'd kept hold of the box.

Dafoe hadn't argued. She hadn't said a word to him beyond notifying him of their position relative to the ship and when it was time to disembark. *As if he couldn't tell for himself.* The *'Mate* wasn't all that much more complex than the pod; Pardell had grown up playing with her control panels. There'd been teaching sims, too. He'd flown as many times as he'd been allowed, until Raner had had to trade them for dibs.

So he'd been ready when the *Athena* sighed to her rest, doors opening on the welcoming committee in the *Seeker's* hangar: Grant himself, Allyn, and two others from the *Seeker's* crew waiting in a line.

*Ready and angry.* And more than a little afraid,

"What have you done with Dr. Smith?" he'd challenged, staring right at Grant, and keeping hold of the box.

*There'd probably been smarter ways to play it*, Pardell told himself glumly. Malley would have bluffed, pretended to notice nothing odd or out of the ordinary, likely carried it off.

He'd only managed to end up here, in what appeared to be a

containment area for incoming shipments to the science sphere. A brig, by any other name.

Pardell sighed and leaned his head back against the metal wall. The box was heavy and cold on his lap. It didn't matter. He wasn't letting go of it.

*The monster in the box was Gail's.*

The monster outside the box? Pardell shuddered as he remembered, not the living sculpture, but the sensations he'd experienced when he touched the Quill filament. Compared to what he felt from other human beings, it was as if he'd somehow taken a glove and wiped the condensation from the outside of a frozen helmet—that sudden a clarity.

*Recognition . . .*

A surprise, but one Gail had tried to prepare him to face. After all, the entire premise of the suits as protection assumed the Quill either preserved or passed down some means of recognizing individual humans. She'd been right.

Pardell closed his eyes, trying to imagine the look on Gail's face when she'd first known for sure. Her lips would have parted, *so*. Her eyes? Their blue would have darkened, intensified— perhaps shone with tears. *None would have fallen.* She should have looked triumphant, proud—not just relieved. He hoped she'd had time to feel all she'd deserved, before the Quill and Grant betrayed her.

*Welcome . . .*

That impression had shocked him to his core. Pardell opened his eyes to stare at his hands, folded innocently on top of the box, their markings as sure a brand of inhumanity as the Quill's greeting for him and him alone.

*Intelligence?* He hadn't needed the structure they—it— whatever—had wrought to know there was purpose on that world. He'd felt it coursing up through his fingers, flowing along his arms, invading every part of him. What did it want? What could it have to do with him?

What was he?

*Had he been changed again?*

Questions no one should have to ask themselves.

*'Course, there was no one else to ask*, Pardell reminded himself with a laugh too close to a sob for comfort.

# Chapter 68

"I KNOW you're awake."

Gail found herself sitting up and squinting at the figure silhouetted in the bright arc of light from the corridor. "Well," she said, not having planned to sleep in the first place, "I am now."

Commander Grant took a step to the side and closed the door behind him, turning on the room light as he did so.

*A man chased by demons*, Gail decided without sympathy, looking at the commander's haggard face. His pulse was visible under the small, puckered scar on his temple. His dark eyes were hollow and strained, as if he'd spent too many hours staring into a sun.

Still, Grant's mouth twitched into an unexpected smile. "Wish I had a camera," he said. "Imagine what Sazaad would pay to see this?"

"Forgive me if I don't find my present situation as amusing, Commander," Gail snapped. She tossed the sheet to one side and got out as if Grant wasn't standing there, watching, making it obvious she'd slept in her clothes. Her fury at having him invade her privacy was as good as a boost shot, not that she planned to thank him for it. "Where's Aaron?" she snapped. "How is he?"

"The holding chamber," Grant told her. "He's fine. A little shaken up. A lot confused."

"That describes most of us," Gail shot back. "Dafoe? What were the test results?"

"There hasn't been time to run any."

Gail shrugged on one of Sazaad's lab coats. By the way it fit, it wasn't his, but belonged to one of his techs. *The results had better be worth finding out all too much about this man's life*, Gail told herself.

"Those tests should have been run immediately. You're risking everything we came here for—" Gail stopped deliberately, and glared up at him. "Everything Mitchener, Peitsch, Sasha, Joseph, Helios, Giardi, and Adams died for—"

The commander had himself under iron control. Even so, the muscles along his jaw worked before he said: "We'll run anything necessary once the situation on the ship has stabilized."

"Stabilized?" she repeated, not particularly caring that her voice cracked over the word. "What's not stable, Commander? Got a mutiny on your hands now? My scientists about to leap on your armed combat troops? Of course, if you've kept them locked up in the lab all this time, you'd better worry about some serious forms in triplicate heading to your superiors."

"Everything will be back to normal shortly—we had to make sure key systems were under FD control before any further action was taken. This is a critical moment in our species' history—"

Gail stepped up to Grant and shoved him in the chest with both hands. "What the hell did you think I'd do?" she all but shouted. "What were you afraid of? What could I possibly have done that would be worse than what you've already accomplished? Minimum, Grant," she accused with another push, "minimum damage—you've thoroughly betrayed everyone on this ship, starting with me. Just when we need to work together most, for everyone's sake."

She hadn't budged him, of course, not physically, but there was something close to shame in his eyes. "Do you think this was my idea, Gail? We're under orders—strict, highly specific orders no one imagined would apply to us, to this ship." He ran his hand through his hair, now collar-length. "You've got to understand—this was the first deep-space mission in twenty years—how could we miss any chance to look for intelligence out here? But no one thought this would happen. First contact? I never dreamed it would happen in my lifetime, let alone yesterday." He paused, then added heavily. "I didn't betray you. The protocols, our assuming control of the ship, it has nothing to do with you."

"Nothing?" Gail took a slow breath. "Let's put aside, for the moment, that I'm the only expert humanity has on the Quill. Let's even put aside, for the moment, that I'm the one who brought you here. Your superiors didn't send you without giving you the ability to make your own decisions. You could have ignored the protocols. You could have handled it differently." She reached for him again, this time grabbing handfuls of his uniform so he was forced to meet her eyes. "Do you think you're the only ones who've looked outward and dreamed of finally being in the company of Others? What do you think filled this ship with the brightest minds Earth produced? Altruism?"

*Others.* Before becoming old enough to know about surveillance and appearances, about careers and the unwhimsical nature of those who opened doors, Gail had walked outside every night before bed—dew-soaked grass of summer or snow of winter, didn't matter—simply to stretch up her arms to the starry sky and wish, wish with all her heart, to find someone *different* reaching back. To know humanity wasn't alone.

*They all had.* She knew that about her people, as Grant knew it about his.

"I follow orders, Gail," Grant insisted, almost leadenly. "Orders meant to ensure our first meeting with nonhuman intelligence isn't the mutual disaster it could well be. I had no other choice but to put my people in charge immediately." But one of his hands covered hers, pressing them firmly against his chest as if he tried to convey more.

*Had no other choice*, Gail repeated to herself, feeling her eyes widening. What was he trying to tell her? Then, she mouthed the words: another ship.

Grant nodded very slightly, then, slowly, almost reluctantly, touched one finger to the small, faded scar on his temple, then traced another oval in the whole skin—lower and closer to his ear.

*An implant.* Positional data at least—probably, from the care he was using talking to her, audio as well. It would depend on how closely they were being shadowed.

*She had to give Earth credit; this time, bureaucratic paranoia had paid off.*

No wonder Grant looked like a man being eaten from inside.

Gail leaned forward until her cheek rested against the back of his hand, the one holding hers. "If you expect the full cooperation of the science staff, Commander Grant," she said calmly, and not for his ears alone, "I suggest you start by letting me back into my lab."

She felt something feather-soft on the top of her head. Grant's chin on her hair, or perhaps a kiss. *Acknowledgment and relief, definitely.* But his voice remained as businesslike and unyielding as before. "That's actually why I'm here, Dr. Smith.

"There's been another incident."

Gail smiled.

# Chapter 69

"WE don't want any more trouble, Malley."
Considering the man expressing this desire was dripping blood from both nostrils, with one eye disappearing under a rapidly swelling lid, Malley thought this quite reasonable. *From the FDs' viewpoint.*

The stationer grinned. "Then you'll open the door," he concluded helpfully, crouching with hands at the ready.

The four men still facing him, which included a surprisingly tough and determined Philips, looked grim. And more than a little dismayed at the prospect of another round. Malley wasn't—this was the most fun he'd had since coming on the *Seeker. With no dibs to pay for breaking furniture,* he reminded himself contentedly. The three groaning on the floor probably didn't agree.

Aisha, standing behind them, gave him the thumbs-up signal. She was done. "Fine," Malley said, straightening up and holding out his open palms. "No more trouble from me."

They didn't look comforted, searching him with unusual diligence and a remarkable lack of success. Philips kept watch; Malley kept smiling. Since he was already locked up and under guard, there wasn't much more they could do with him.

*Just like old times,* the stationer thought, even though some of the Earthers were no longer very happy being crowded together in the lab. He couldn't see why: there were enough chairs or cots for everyone to sit at the same time—and an abundance of food and drink for the asking. All they needed was some music and beer—even that gut-rotting liquor of Grant's would do—and this place would be perfect.

*No accounting for taste.*

"Hey!" Malley objected, suddenly noticing one of the FDs

returning with a fistful of binding cord. "I said I was done—you don't need to do that!" Bad enough Philips was grimly determined—the FD with the cords was Mike Barber, a man who usually had a wicked sense of humor. He didn't look to be joking now.

"Excuse us if we don't take your word for it," Philips said dryly. "Have a seat, Malley."

Aisha and Temujin stepped forward, a couple of the other Earthers joining them. "We'll take responsibility for him," Aisha offered. "Malley just—panicked. It's got to be hard on the man when he doesn't know what's going on or what to expect."

Malley began tensing his muscles, in case the scientists weren't persuasive enough. It might buy him some slack—assuming they didn't notice and also assuming they conveniently wrapped the cord around his bulging biceps and not his wrists. He'd have more confidence in the vid-fantasy trick if he'd tried it before, but being tied up wasn't one of those things that had happened in his life. Yet. Still, *nothing ventured.*

Johnson, the FD with the bloody nose, wiped his face with a cloth and eyed the scientists. "Panicked, Dr. Lynn?" he questioned skeptically. "If this is how your friend here reacts to temporary overcrowding, maybe we should trank him instead."

Before Malley could laugh at this, a new voice intruded, saying: "I'll watch him." Sazaad came to loom over Aisha, gazing eye to eye with Malley, his expression unreadable. "There won't be any more outbursts from this lunatic."

Maybe Johnson read Malley's tension as preparation for a renewal of their one-sided struggle. Or, given how little Sazaad had endeared himself to the techs, maybe the FD looked forward to watching the scientist forced to make good on his promise. Regardless, the man lifted his hands in a gesture of surrender. "Then he's all yours, Dr. Sazaad, Dr. Lynn. Just keep him away from us, please?"

"Of course," Aisha agreed, hurrying over to Malley as the FDs moved off to consult with their group, Philips turning to keep watch. Malley tossed him a casual salute.

Once safely surrounded by Aisha and her companions, Malley bent his head and asked softly: "Was I right? Was it a message?"

Sazaad smiled broadly, showing his too even, too white teeth. "Sent from my quarters, you notice."

Aisha rolled her eyes theatrically. "Sent from wherever she could. Quick thinking, Malley."

The stationer didn't bother pointing out he'd likely been the only one thinking in the lab at the time. "Made sense Gail would try to get news to us if she could—and she'd need a way that Grant's people wouldn't be monitoring."

*Luck had played a role*, Malley admitted to himself, glancing over their heads at the D-board and its ever-changing list of materials and procedures. He'd been near it when the display had flashed to Sazaad's sequence of experiments, a red flashing bar indicating new changes being added. Since Sazaad himself had been standing in the middle of the lab, complaining about something or other, and so obviously not entering any information to the system, Malley had quietly attracted Aisha's attention.

He'd then very noisily attracted the attention of the FDs by trying to break out the door. *That had been the fun part.*

"What did she say?"

"Here," Temujin said, passing what looked to be a sequence of mathematical notations to Sazaad. "These were for you."

Sazaad went from puffed pride to puzzled as he read. He muttered something in another language under his breath, then simply walked away from them.

"Any idea what that's about?" Malley asked.

Aisha's eyes sparkled. "I'd say it's a challenge. The rest was for all of us. The situation's as you thought, Malley. Grant's taken control of the entire ship, locking up Gail and the Captain as well as those crew not part of his unit. Those not in here are confined to the dining lounge in the science sphere. Don't ask me how Gail got into quarters."

Malley shook his head. "Doesn't matter. Did she say anything about Aaron?"

"Somewhere in the science sphere. She believes Grant's isolated his potential problems away from the command sphere—including Aaron."

The stationer's voice dropped an octave. "Where?"

"Any problems?" Philips asked, appearing behind Sazaad.

Malley gave him the smile that usually made Sammie bring

out his antique baseball bat for insurance. "These fine people are explaining everything to me," he told the former tech. "It's vastly reassuring. How are the ribs?" he asked solicitously, quite sure a couple had bent, if not cracked, when Philips had gotten in his way.

"Sore," the smaller man said bluntly, then grinned. "But still in one piece. What did you hit me with anyway?"

Malley lifted his left hand and made a loose fist. It was nearly as big as Philips' head, and that worthy's eyes grew round as he looked at it. "Let's not do that again, okay?"

"Absolutely," Malley promised. Philips gave him a very sharp look but decided not to pursue it.

Once Philips was out of earshot again, Malley asked Aisha: "So, where's Aaron?"

"Gail didn't know. But wherever he is, he's safe," she said flatly. "The FD aren't here to harm anyone—if Aaron needed medical care, they'd bring him here. We have to concentrate on what Gail's asked us to do."

The stationer frowned. "Which is?" he growled suspiciously.

"Apparently we have some allies nearby," Temujin broke in excitedly, a state he'd been in since the moment the Quill had presented their statue. "Gail wants us to contact them."

"From here? While we're watched?"

Temujin smiled like a child given permission to draw on the walls of his room. "Malley, you've no idea what we can do from in here," he boasted, gazing around the lab with pride. "And neither does Commander Grant."

# Chapter 70

*S*O. *Commander Grant was caught as firmly as the rest of them.*

Gail found this a peculiar comfort, as if she needed to know her original estimation of the man had been right all along. Had almost dying together forged some bond between them? *More likely*, she reminded herself, *it was her stubborn pride, insisting on trusting her own judgment of others despite evidence to the contrary.*

Whichever it was, Gail walked beside Grant—preceded and followed by guards who'd only yesterday answered to her as science staff—and felt as though the universe was back in balance. *Cockeyed as usual, but balanced.*

Maybe it was as simple as knowing the right target.

"You don't seem surprised we've had some problems in the lab," Grant said as they approached the main door.

"You left Malley in there, didn't you?" she said matter-of-factly. "Did you really think he wouldn't have an—opinion—to express about matters?"

A corner of Grant's mouth rose. "There's that. Taggart, what's the situation?" he asked the FD standing outside the door.

Taggart gave Gail one of those "sorry, ma'am" looks she was growing accustomed to receiving from just about all of Grant's people—as mutineers, they were strangely apologetic types—and replied: "Nominal, sir. Everyone's getting a bit impatient, but they're being civil about it. There was a small fracas involving the big guy . . . Malley . . . but the others have calmed him down."

"Any injuries?" Gail asked expectantly. She was far from ready to forgive the FDs.

Taggart blushed, but stayed at attention. "Philips has three broken ribs, Dr. Smith. Johnson thinks his nose might be as well, but . . . the commander knows how sensitive Johnson is about his nose."

"Thank you, Taggart," Grant growled. "Open up." Gail managed not to smile.

But she couldn't help it when facing what amounted to a hero's welcome in the lab. The sixty-odd people waiting for her hadn't had a chance to celebrate what had happened on the planet's surface: the success of the suits, the discovery of the Quill—let alone the astonishing development that the Quill might be sentient. All this, plus the suspense of being bottled up in the lab for hours had most of her staff as giddy as if they'd been drinking all night.

There was shouting and laughter as well as the odd tear—not to mention a considerable number of bad jokes at the expense of the First Defense Unit and its commander, who stood watching from the doorway with an indefinable expression. Gail found herself hugged and kissed by people who'd never so much as started a conversation with her before.

*Where was Malley?*

She had her answer as unmistakably massive arms swept her right off her feet and she found herself suspended in midair. From the look on his face, the stationer was in no mood to celebrate—in fact, he looked as though he was debating with himself whether to toss her against the nearest wall or simply snap her in half.

Gail didn't give him time to make up his mind. She wrapped her arms around Malley's broad neck and kissed him soundly on the mouth. Then, before he could put her—or, more likely, throw her—down, she buried her face on his shoulder, as if succumbing to emotion.

It put her lips near his ear. "Aaron's all right, Malley," she whispered urgently. "He's in the holding area, but we'll have him out in a few minutes. Don't put me down yet, you idiot—" this a hiss as Malley's grip loosened. Obediently, he hugged her to his chest. Gail wheezed and he let go slightly. She slipped a piece of paper into his pocket.

"The military has a ship trailing us. Grant's got an implant: a tracer, audio as well," she hurried, knowing there wasn't much time. "Grant had no choice but to follow FD protocol—but he'll help us as he can. Did you get my message?"

"Yes, of course I missed you, Cupcake," Malley said heartily, lifting her up again as if she was some prized hunk of metal he'd found. Before she could more than wince—*Cupcake?*—Gail found herself on the receiving end of an enthusiastic kiss.

*A little too enthusiastic.* Gail squirmed her way out of it, only to see the warning in Malley's eyes. She glanced left. Loran was approaching. "Cupcake?" she spat under her breath. "Put me down." This louder.

Malley looked unrepentant as he deposited Gail gently to the floor. "You kissed me first," he said mildly.

Gail collected herself enough to glare at him. "I kissed everyone," she told him. "Spirit of the moment. I'm over it."

"Whatever you say, Dr. Smith," Malley returned with that lazy smile, his voice rumbling at its more devastating depth. The flirting wasn't for her benefit—Gail could read a completely different message in the tension of his shoulders and the fresh cuts on his hands. Malley'd fought once today and was hoping for more.

Gail preferred a more civilized, less messy approach. "Where's Sazaad?" He'd been conspicuously absent from the greeting throng, a relief in a way, but worrisome in others.

"He's at his workstation, Dr. Smith," someone offered helpfully. The little byplay with Malley had hardly caused a ripple among the boisterous group. Gail started trying to move through them to get to Sazaad, without much success, only to have Malley use his smile and shoulder to clear her path.

"Handy," she said.

"Practice," he replied as they reached the side wall and could see Sazaad.

Gail didn't waste any time. Grant would have to check on her soon or arouse suspicion. "Dr. Sazaad?"

He grunted something unintelligible, busy keying instructions into his device, then he seemed to hear her voice and turned his head only enough to squint at her. "Dr. Smith. This is a remarkable concept. But quite impossible, you know. I mean, if I had a year . . ."

Gail stepped closer, Malley standing so he blocked them from the rest of the room. "If it can be done, you can do it. And we don't have a year—we have hours, if we're lucky. Whatever you need, whoever you need. This is priority one. My authority. Got it?"

"Nice to have you back," Sazaad said. His black eyes gleamed. "Hours?" Abruptly, he leaped from his stool and headed for the party still underway. Gail watched the eccentric scientist long enough to be sure he was conscripting help and not joining in before turning back to face Malley.

"Aisha?"

"She and others are up there," Malley used his eyes to indicate the second floor of the lab. "Temujin is especially happy right now."

Gail grimaced. "That's going to mean some repair bills. But he'll get the job done." Grant was heading their way. "Listen to me, Malley," she said quickly, keeping her voice under the background noise of the crowd. "Aaron is the key to the Quill, whatever they are. The FD will want him—so will Titan. And as long as he's in reach, there's nothing we can do to stop them."

Malley's eyes were like ice. "Tell me what I don't know."

Gail licked her lips. "I've an idea. A way to get some breathing space, maybe a solution. I don't know. But I need your help. I put a list in your pocket. Get everything that's on it—I don't care how—but don't tell anyone else, even Aisha." Gail hesitated, looking deep into his eyes. "Once you have it all, Malley, I need you to put it in the lab air lock."

Grant was trying to give them more time, but suddenly another FD noticed their private conversation. She intercepted her commander, pointing in their direction.

"Say I do, what next?" Malley asked.

"No one goes through that air lock but me, Aaron, or you. No one. Understood? I don't care what it takes. They'll try."

He looked suddenly satisfied. "Fine by me."

"Dr. Smith, Malley," Grant said in greeting. "I trust you are beginning to get things back in order?"

Malley reached into his pocket, and Gail froze involuntarily. *Her list.* More than enough to damn her in the eyes of the FD or Titan. Enough to cost her the trust of her staff and friends. She'd counted on Malley as the only one who shared her priority: Pardell's freedom. *Was she wrong?*

The stationer's hand came out with one of the candies Benton had brought with her from Mars, sour things no one else would eat. *He'd probably done it to make her sweat,* Gail thought with disgust. "Everything's fine," he said to Grant, after unwrapping the treat and popping it into his mouth with what appeared to be relish. "Sorry about bending some of your men like that. Fragile types, aren't they?"

Grant's eyes narrowed. "Only when ordered to be careful, Malley. I recommend you don't try us again."

"I'll keep that in mind, Commander," Malley said, so cheerfully Gail could almost see the hackles rising on Grant's neck.

*Her allies.* Gail kept her smile to herself. They were so transparently honest—capable of crossing her, of course, but only if she foolishly put them into conflict with their own moral priorities. Otherwise, as predictable and reliable as sunlight. She'd managed with much worse on Titan as well as Earth, where every smile hid its own agenda and alliances involved finding those whose goals were closest—or at least not directly opposed—to your own at any given moment. Trust and loyalty weren't factors Gail usually had to consider. Or had ever relied on, until now. . . .

*Not true.* She shivered suddenly, remembering the station and the howl of the mob.

Trust and loyalty?

She mustn't forget how they also got people killed.

# Chapter 71

*H*E was the alien—*the killer in the box.*

Pardell rocked back and forth, trying to keep his imagination under rein. The hours alone didn't mean the Earthers had abandoned him. The ship outside this small, bare metal room wasn't empty or filled with the dead. The Quill inside the stasis box couldn't harm him or anyone else.

*He wouldn't harm anyone.*

They knew that. Malley and Rosalind. Grant.

Gail did.

*He had killed.* They knew that, too.

For the hundredth time, Pardell's hand strayed to the lid of the box, then clenched and dropped away. Curiosity and dread, in equal proportions.

Without warning, the door swung open, slowly, as if the person on the other side feared to wake him—*or feared him*, Pardell added bitterly. "I'm awake," he called out, deliberately assuming the better possibility.

And it was better. The face peering around the heavy door was Gail's—careworn, to his worried eyes, but smiling. "Then you'd probably like breakfast," she said.

Pardell couldn't smile. All he could manage was to stand, holding the box. He'd forgotten how to let go of it by now. "I kept it safe for you," he told her, knowing the Quill mattered most. "Grant's people wanted it, but they didn't argue. I don't think they wanted to risk touching me. So they quarantined us together. I've kept it safe."

"What matters is that you're safe," she replied, confounding his sense of priorities. "But bring the sample. There are a lot of people, including me, anxious to see what we're dealing with at last. You're sure you're all right?" Gail stepped into the room, studying his face and then looking around. There wasn't much to see, beyond the cot, blankets, and a shelf cleared of boxes so trays of untouched food could be stacked there. He hadn't been interested. "They didn't mistreat you—"

"Of course not," Pardell answered quickly, though warmed by the sudden outrage in her voice. "I'm sure the commander would have given me better quarters if I'd been willing to leave the Quill here. But—"

Gail held out her hands.

Pardell immediately gave her the box, not letting go until he was sure she felt the weight of it and was ready—holding a second or two longer than necessary because it gave him a harmless connection to her. She knew. *A man could drown himself in her eyes when they looked like that*, Pardell decided, *and consider it a worthy death*. He could almost hear Malley's voice adding: especially a fool light-headed from lack of sleep and food.

"Breakfast," she said again, as if hearing Malley's sensible voice as well.

*Malley had quite a bit more to say*, Pardell knew the moment he laid eyes on his friend again, but nothing he planned to come out with in present company. Gail had brought him directly to the lab; technically, he'd been brought by Gail and four FDs who seemed confused as to whether they were guards or escorts. Gail's tendency to lead the way at a brisk walk, while completely ignoring them, probably didn't help. Pardell kept his amusement to himself.

Judging by a few new scrapes on his knuckles, Malley'd been fighting, which usually had the effect of relaxing the big stationer for a couple of days at least. Unfortunately, Pardell judged, he either hadn't fought the right person or for the right reason. As a result, Malley's broad forehead was creased in what looked to be a permanent scowl, an intimidating expression that lightened the moment he'd seen Pardell and returned as the stationer had looked over at Gail.

Pardell bit into the sweet roll someone had offered him. *They were going to have to talk.*

Something that would be impossible, while the level of excitement in the lab stayed this high. Their arrival, or more precisely, the arrival of the Quill filament, had stirred everyone into action. Gail had told him she'd arranged with Grant to permit the science staff back into their quarters, vouching for them personally. From the look of things, no one had chosen to leave. Scientists and techs, most appearing to have slept in their clothes, scrambled to set up equipment and recorders. There were too many for the room, until Gail, with a look of exasperation, ordered a further expansion of the lab itself. Two walls were now inching their way deeper into the ship, with impatient researchers lining up their mobile benches to be first to fill the new space.

"They could have done this without me," Gail grumbled as she came back to where Pardell sat watching all the action. "This many brains in one room? There's a guarantee no one thinks."

He'd tucked himself on a stool behind one of the few empty workbenches, wary of the number of people and their busyness. In Sammie's, everyone would have watched out for him. Malley was, of course—a mountain of aggravated comfort. Pardell had seen Malley giving him one of those "how are you" looks, but this group still wasn't large or tight enough to bother him. The Earthers didn't know how to make a crowd.

Gail hopped up to sit on the top of the bench, looking out over what Pardell hoped was a more organized confusion than it appeared.

As if she'd read his thoughts, Gail observed: "We've been ready for this for years, Aaron. The stakes are just a little higher than any of us knew."

Malley hadn't gone far—*in full hover mode*, Pardell thought glumly, and unlikely to grant them even an instant alone. Gail didn't appear worried. She'd only spoken to Malley once, a cryptic: "Any problems?" and receiving a curt: "Nothing I couldn't handle," in return.

Now Malley surveyed the room from his naturally higher vantage point and asked: "Who gets first crack? Your people or Grant's?" The stasis box containing the Quill had been placed inside a larger, clear version. They'd already determined the safety of the single filament and this technology by the simple expedient of having Dafoe remove her protective suit once the *Athena* was in orbit.

Pardell wouldn't forget the frightened but determined look on the FD's pale face any time soon. *There was courage.* It was also, in his opinion, completely irresponsible to risk a life simply to test the stasis box—although he knew Dafoe would argue she'd already risked it to test the suit.

At least in this case, they had records indicating that no one had been harmed by a single Quill filament. Yet.

They'd used remote arms to open the box and pull out the filament. It now hung over a horizontal support like some bizarre decoration or forgotten scarf, its colors glowing in the muted illumination. Gail hadn't forgotten his comment about daylight.

"So that's a Quill," Malley announced, not for the first time, and in a tone of complete disappointment.

"No," Gail said suddenly, her eyes fixed on the case. "Calling it a Quill, or a filament—that may be misleading." She had the look Pardell had often seen on Malley's face—of grappling with an idea from a new direction and following where that went. "What if it's a fragment?"

Malley recognized it, too. Pardell could see that in the way his friend slowly stopped frowning and glanced at the Quill. "Part of a whole," Malley said after a moment. "Any proof of that?"

"Aisha's techs are running the biochemical analysis now."

"It acted—" Pardell couldn't finish. He wasn't ready to tell anyone—especially Gail—what had happened on the planet. *Not when he didn't know what it meant.*

Luckily Gail continued for him. "—It acted, the part we observed, as a unit. There was definite coordination between the fragments. How? The questions multiply as quickly as these creatures must have done." She sounded almost happy about it, as if having new questions was more satisfying than answering the old ones.

"You know the priority here, Dr. Smith," Grant didn't offer a greeting beyond this bald statement as he approached.

*Just a little closer, Betrayer,* Pardell decided, coldly calculating the number of steps Grant had left to take. *Then they'd see how deadly his hands could be.* The destruction of the *'Mate* by his friends—that Pardell could understand. *What Grant had done . . . ?*

"Aaron." Malley's growl was low—pitched to his ears only. Pardell lost his focus on the Earther, coming back to himself with a start. "Remember old Logan?"

"Mats? Of course, I remember . . ." Pardell stared at Malley, then looked back at Grant, hoping he'd kept his face under some control. Mats Logan was the next best thing to a folk hero in Outward Five—a high-up in station security who'd contrived to send out warnings of coming inspections and lockdowns for years, until he'd been killed by rioters. Typical of Thromberg, Logan's killers had been from Outward Five themselves, seeing only the target offered by authority and not the man, until it was too late. The name "logan" had become station slang for anyone who pretended to be what they weren't, to others' benefit.

*Grant?* Pardell flicked his fingers at Malley, code for understanding. *Did Gail know?* he wondered, then answered his own question. She had to, or he wouldn't be here. One thing he was sure about: Gail Smith would never cooperate under duress. She'd see the *Seeker* aimed at this system's sun first.

Rosalind liked that about her. *He feared it.*

"You agreed to let me proceed in my own way, Commander Grant," Gail was saying, in that calm voice that nonetheless had steel beneath. "It will make a profound difference to our approach—and yours—if this is a fragment."

"How?"

"If, as I now suspect, we have a fragment of an organism here, rather than one organism from an collective, this implies something about the genesis of the intelligence that may exist on this world. That intelligence, I don't need to remind you, has not been confirmed."

"It's damn well likely," Malley tossed in, unperturbed by an immediate glare from Gail.

Grant nodded. "Fair enough. But if we confirm we're dealing with intelligence—alien intelligence—what's the difference between a collection of Quill together forming that intelligence and one Quill made of seemingly identical, individual parts? We still need to talk to it."

Still perched on the bench, Gail drew up her knees and hugged them to her chest, as if she brought a puzzle closer to examine. "One Quill. That's the crux, don't you see? Are there any other intelligent Quill—or just the one beneath our orbit?"

Pardell hardly breathed, knowing Malley sent him a worried look, but not acknowledging it—too intent on what Gail was building with each word.

"If the Quill are a collective intelligence," she pondered aloud, "and that collective becomes deadly to us when it has enough members—let's not forget that for an instant—then any group of Quill of the right size should be intelligent. There could be more than one intelligent entity on Pardell's World. And every planet seeded with Quill should have one or more Quill entities." Gail rested her chin on her knees, still staring at the Quill hanging limply in the case. "If, however, we have a situation where one fragment of Quill multiplies, becoming a whole that is intelligent as well as dangerous at a certain minimum biomass, then each planet seeded with a different fragment should have one, unique Quill entity. But there's the third possibility—"

Malley whistled. "That the Quill on this world only shows signs of intelligence because of its interaction with Aaron as a baby." Then he smacked himself on the forehead. "It might not be intelligence at all—what if it's simply reflecting something from Aaron? The image we saw could be some kind of memory, an echo . . ."

"Exactly," Gail said, as if Malley's insight mirrored her own. "Leaving us to ask if what happened here was unique. We certainly have evidence to suggest that."

Pardell found himself on his feet, backing up until his back hit the wall. "I'm not evidence," he said furiously. "I'm— I'm . . ." Words failed him, and he stared at the three looking at him. *Had they all forgotten?* "We came here to destroy those— things." The words came out low and hard. "I lost my ship— everything—so we could destroy them."

Grant looked suddenly much older and sadder. "If they are intelligent, Aaron, we can't."

# Chapter 72

"WE can't."

Gail watched the words hit Aaron like blows. She closed her eyes for a moment, arms tight around her knees, refusing to feel what he was feeling, refusing to allow anything but clear, analytical thought. *There wasn't time*, she assured herself. *He'd forgive her—maybe.*

"There's a way to know," she announced.

"The other Quill," Malley breathed.

*Fast as well as smart.* Gail almost smiled. "The other Quill," she confirmed. "We send expeditions protected by the suits to, say, four of the terraformed worlds contaminated—" she saw Grant's frown and changed her wording, "—inhabited—by Quill. If there are signs of intelligence, that will immediately answer the question of whether the species as a whole is intelligent. Pardell's World won't be unique. First contact confirmed, Commander Grant."

"If there are no signs?" Grant countered. "What if the Quill on other worlds hide from us? There's no guarantee—"

"Ah," Gail exclaimed, letting go of her legs and swinging around to better face them all. "Yes, there is. The expeditions will each return to the *Seeker* with a fragment for analysis. We can rig a remote arm to be fast enough to capture them, now that we know how they move. If those fragments are biochemically similar to this one, we can assume any intelligence found here should be a function of any Quill, anywhere. You can send in your specialists, wait for the aliens to make the next move, whatever procedure you like.

"But," she continued, "if the fragments from the other worlds are similar to each other, but not to this one—" Gail pointed at the case, "—then we have every reason to suppose what happened yesterday is an anomaly, either because the influence of humans on this Quill somehow produced intelligence, or because something else is going on. I imagine the debate on whether that constitutes first contact could rage for years."

"Anomaly. In other words, Dr. Smith," Aaron said in a strangled voice. "This Quill could be a freak, just like me."

About to say something soothing, *a lie*, Gail met Aaron's anguished eyes and remembered this was the man who'd forced her to let him face his destiny. He might be hurt by the truth—he wasn't afraid of it. "Yes, Aaron," she agreed. "One of a kind. Like you. An accident of—birth."

There was something grateful in his look back to her.

Grant was frowning thoughtfully, like a man considering his future. "Dr. Smith. I presume you have something in mind when you specified four expeditions?"

Gail hopped off the bench, waving to the pair she'd had waiting nearby. "In fact, Commander Grant, I do. I believe you know Dr. Quinn and Tech Stadler?" Grant nodded a curt greeting. "Despite certain—interruptions—they've continued with their own project, which was to prepare anti-Quill suits for the terraformed projects nearest us."

"So we could be ready to kill them all—in case we found a way, that is," Stadler offered with her usual enthusiastic absence of tact.

Gail gritted her teeth. "And these suits are ready?" she made herself ask in a normal voice.

Quinn nodded soberly. "Yes, Dr. Smith. A pair for each of the four worlds closest to this one. As the suits used by FD Dafoe and Mr. Pardell, these are covered with a genome signature, but, rather than Susan Witts', each of these suits bears the signature of the specific terraformer who brought a Quill with him or her." Quinn coughed and Gail glowered at him, knowing this was her colleague's way of reminding her she was ultimately responsible for making that identification. Not that anyone disputed her findings; no one leaped forward to confirm them either. "It is our estimation they will provide similarly effective protection from Quill, as long as they are used on the appropriate planet."

Quinn added this last in a tone suggesting anyone foolish enough to mix up the suits deserved what they got.

"Thank you. Would you make sure the suits are packed and labeled—very clearly?"

After the pair left, Gail smiled at Grant. "Now all we need are eight volunteers who know how to use the suits."

He raised one eyebrow. "Unless you are suggesting we leave orbit—which isn't likely, Dr. Smith—there is the small detail of starships to transport them."

Gail looked up to where Temujin stood at the railing of the lab's second floor. He gave her a quick nod.

"It just so happens that I can supply three, Commander," she told Grant briskly. "Leaving you to come up with the fourth?"

"Really." Both eyebrows went up, and he almost smiled. "There might be a possibility of another ship—for such an important expedition, Dr. Smith. I believe the FD cruiser *Payette* might be on training exercises in this region."

*Training exercises?* Gail almost shook her head, but simply said: "Good. Let's get to it, then."

Gail thought she'd done it—she went so far as to congratulate herself just a little—when Grant looked at Aaron and said point-blank: "I'd like Aaron to come with me to the command sphere."

Her emphatic "No" came at the same instant as Aaron's "Of course." Both men gazed at her with comically identical expressions of surprise. "No," Gail repeated in a more normal tone of voice. "Not until I've run some tests to see how visiting the planet's surface may have affected him. Tests, I might add, that should have been run yesterday rather than leaving Aaron sitting in a hold."

Grant had the grace to look discomfited at this—how much for her benefit and how much for those FDs nearby, she couldn't be sure—then nodded once. "All right. In the meantime, I'll sort out the volunteers and see what I can do about another ship. I'm assuming your three are the patrol ships sent by Titan?"

Before she could answer, he shook his head ruefully. "They quite properly announced their presence a while ago, Dr. Smith—but if you've somehow talked them into cooperating with us instead of tossing regulations and jurisdictional writs across the comms, I'm delighted. I don't suppose you've still got the system you used to contact those ships . . ." Gail shrugged. " . . . I thought not. We will have to look for it, you realize."

"Be my guest, Commander," she said, quite sure Temujin had immediately disassembled to innocuous spare parts whatever he and Aisha had used to send her message to Vincente. She'd been equally sure Titan U would want to protect its leading role in any discovery about the Quill—and that each patrol ship carried its representative to ensure just that. By trying to usurp that role, the First Defense Unit had neatly delivered those representatives—and their enthusiastic support—to her.

His gesture sent two FDs fading back into the activity of the lab to start their search, although from Grant's expression, he wasn't hoping for much either way. "I trust I can expect a more forthcoming attitude about prepping the *Athena* for her return drop."

*Did he guess?* Gail carefully set her voice to exasperated. It wasn't hard. "She'd be ready by now, if you hadn't interfered with our procedures, Commander," she informed him. "As it is, you're asking my staff to work without proper rest—I'm assuming you intend to stop this ridiculous lockdown and give them normal access?"

He didn't quite give a direct answer. "We'll work with your experts, Dr. Smith. As long as there are no further incidents, they can come and go to the command sphere and hangar. With escort. I appreciate that there is specialized equipment to maintain and likely more to be installed." The noise level in the lab increased momentarily. Gail kept her curiosity firmly in check. "As long as they're quick," Grant added with rare impatience. "Every minute counts."

"I won't approve the suits for reuse until I've run my tests on Dafoe and Aaron."

"A diligence I find most reassuring, believe me. Just don't delay."

Aaron, who'd been silent, said abruptly: "You plan to go down yourself."

Gail stared at Grant. "Are you?"

"Two hours, Dr. Smith," Grant said instead of answering. "Then we'll be back for Aaron." He turned and left, almost marching. Gail watched him until he reached the door.

"Oh, he'll be back," Malley said, his voice plunged to its angriest depth. "He wants you, Aaron. The miracle man. The legendary Survivor. They all do—so why, Dr. Smith, did you just give Grant first crack by sending everyone else off on this wild Quill chase? What if Aaron prefers to play the market and get his best offer? Who are you to decide which faction gets hooks in him first?"

"No one is 'getting' Aaron." Gail held up one hand to hold the stationer from any more questions—there were upwards of ten people within earshot at any given moment—and turned to face the 'sider. He was leaning against the wall, a posture no longer tense but far from relaxed. "This isn't what any of us wanted, Aaron," she admitted. She'd been controlling her expression so long, it took conscious effort to relax and reveal anything. But she tried, hoping he could see her determination as well as hope. "But there's no ill will here. Do you understand that?"

His face, on the other hand, was so carefully unemotional she wanted to shake him. "What I understand, Dr. Smith, is that because the Quill can pull up plants and build a statue, thousands of people stay trapped on the stations. That is what all this means, isn't it?"

*The truth with him, always*, Gail had promised herself. She hadn't known it would be so hard. "It could mean that," she agreed, putting her hands on the table and leaning toward him, Malley looming beside her. It was the only privacy they had. She didn't fool herself they weren't being overheard. "I prefer not to work from that premise. There are other possibilities—"

"What other possibilities?" Aaron snapped, the strain in his face reflected in his voice. "These people—Grant's people— you know they exist to find alien intelligence, to protect what they find from human 'aggression.' Think they'll sit by and let you develop a weapon to destroy the Quill? To get our worlds back?" His voice dropped to a whisper. "To get my world back?"

"They'll study the Quill until everyone's grown old and died back home," Malley chimed in, like angry thunder. "Then it won't matter, will it?"

Gail smacked her hand down. "How dare you think you're the only ones who care about those people!" she said fiercely, glaring at them both. "Of course, it's unacceptable to leave the stations as they are—no one here wants that." Her vision shimmered suddenly, and she wiped her eyes furiously before tears betrayed more than she was prepared to show. "I said there are other possibilities and I meant it. You are going to have to trust me." She made that low and intense. *They had to believe.*

Aaron's throat worked as he swallowed, his face suddenly defenseless. Malley looked at his friend, then back to her. "Aaron already trusts you too much," he told her, voice pure threat. Before she could avoid his hand, he took her chin between finger and thumb, bringing his face so close to hers Gail inhaled warmed air from his mouth. "So I won't. Keeps things nicely balanced, don't you think?"

Before Gail could reply, the unthinkable happened. Aaron lunged forward, the hand that reached for Malley's arm stopping just short. "Let her go!" the 'sider demanded, something quite desperate in his eyes. "Don't you ever touch her!"

"It's all right, Aaron," Gail said quickly as Malley released her, the stationer staring at his friend with almost comical shock. *Almost.* "Malley and I understand each other."

"Do we have a problem here?"

*There was an understatement*, Gail thought, turning to face the pair of FDs standing a careful few paces back from her and Malley. They both had their hands on the weapons at their sides—presumably warned by Philips to avoid challenging the big stationer otherwise.

"Not in the least," Gail said, her mouth so dry the words came out sounding calm and composed. "Don't you have something better to do than interrupt my work?" When they didn't budge, she snapped: "Or do you want to explain to your commander why his suit wasn't checked before he risks his life in it?"

They exchanged looks, then glanced dubiously up at Malley. Gail could understand their concern; the stationer didn't look particularly stable at the moment. In fact, he looked as though he wanted to break something, most likely her.

"Aaron," Gail said without looking at the 'sider. *She couldn't.* "Please find Aisha and ask her to hook you up for testing. She's probably finished connecting Specialist Dafoe by now. Gentlemen? I suggest you do something more useful than jumping every time Mr. Malley sneezes. For one thing, you can make sure there are enough escorts to keep things moving to the hangar. And, Malley?

"You come with me."

# Chapter 73

MALLEY followed the Earther up the ramp to the second floor of the lab, feeling the metal shake slightly underfoot. The opposite walls were still creeping away from the rest, constantly changing perspectives.

He followed her small figure without saying a word, without argument, without another look at Aaron.

*Don't ever touch her.*

It was worse than he'd imagined. Poor Aaron had fallen completely—no judgment, no self-restraint left. It was her fault. *Don't touch her?*

He'd love to pitch Dr. Gail Smith over the railing.

Unfortunately, she led the way to a back corner, dismissing the lab-coated individuals from their work without apology. They were, for the moment, essentially alone. Sitting on one stool, she motioned him to take the other.

Malley remained standing.

No sign of dimples in the face turned up to look at him—in fact, he thought uncharitably, this was likely the face she'd find staring back from a mirror in another twenty years or so: lines traced the corners of her eyes, there were deeper creases where her lips compressed. "Satisfied?" she asked abruptly. "Did you get the reaction you wanted?"

"I wanted?" he felt his eyebrows lift.

Those blue eyes could become glacial, "Don't lie to me, Malley," she warned him. "You deliberately provoked him."

The stationer grabbed the other stool, placing it so when he sat, he boxed her into the corner. "You think I wanted to hurt Aaron?" he ground out. "That's something, coming from you. You're the one pulling his strings, not me."

"You wanted to see what he'd do."

*Why not admit it?* Malley threw up his hands in mock surrender. "Okay. Say I did. So maybe now Aaron will remember who he is and who his real friends are. Maybe he'll realize—" Suddenly, he couldn't say it.

Gail's voice was harsh and unforgiving: "What, Malley? That you—his *friend*—can touch me and he can't? You think he doesn't know?"

"Knowing and believing? Two different things," he pronounced, almost convinced himself. "Anyway. He'll get over it. Aaron's been mad at me before. This was for his own good."

"His good." Her expression changed all at once, as if she'd had a revelation. Her skin went from pale to flushed. "You're really believe—?"

"Believe? What I know, Dr. Smith, is that you've taken everything that mattered to him—everything, from his ship to his humanity. Wasn't that enough? Did you have to own him as well, to control him like some lab animal?"

"Control," she repeated, as though the word had extra meaning, looking down at her hands. "I've always been in control, Malley. Until now." She lifted her eyes to his again—they weren't cold anymore. They shone with unshed tears.

"Oh, you're good," he told her. "I'll give you that. But I won't let you twist Aaron around—"

"I know," Gail interrupted impatiently. "I know," she repeated more gently. "Any minute someone's going to check on us, Malley, and I have to convince you—" She broke off and stared at him, a hopeless look on her face. "I can't imagine how. They're just words, aren't they? And you won't believe them."

"What are just words?" He laughed, making it harsh and merciless. "Let me guess. You're going to tell me you're madly in love with Aaron—that he's the most important thing in the universe to you—your 'sider Prince Charming, who, although he's not quite human, does come complete with a space suit older than he is. Oh, yes. And I should trust you to do what's best for him, so you can live happily ever after on old Mother Earth, together always."

A queen might look like this, small and straight-backed,

all dignity and pride. "I can understand your thinking so little of me," Gail said quietly. "But not your thinking so little of him."

Before Malley could do more than open his mouth, she stood and walked away.

# Chapter 74

"OTHER than some stress markers, there have been no discernible changes."

"That's for both?"

Aisha nodded, her keen look at Gail filled with questions she knew better than to ask while they were surrounded by this combination of obvious and less than obvious observers. Gossip or straight feed to the bridge. Either would be disastrous.

As had been her attempt to reason with Malley. *Oh, she'd handled that like a pro*, Gail railed at herself, not for the first time. She should have left well enough alone—or hit him over the head. *Preferably the latter.*

Still, he'd been right that Aaron didn't seem to stay angry for long. *Probably from a lifetime of experience with the stationer's well-intentioned, if less-than-delicate approach.* The two were at the other end of this workstation, grabbing a bite to eat together from one of the omnipresent trays of sandwiches. She avoided looking their way, leery of giving Malley any further excuse to interfere.

Gail had already sent a note to Tobo, suggesting commendations for the stewards as well as other staff. She didn't want to forget anything.

*It was almost time.*

The tests had been negative—no surprise. No apparent change in Aaron's physiology, although she was reasonably certain something had happened to him down there. Something he'd yet to tell her. Since they weren't quite talking at the moment, that would have to wait.

Gail glanced at the wall chrono. Grant should be on his way to get Aaron at any minute. They'd already docked, in sequence, with the strikingly cooperative Earth Patrol ships, Dart Pursuit Class, and one, hitherto unnoticed, FD cruiser, the *Payette*. Tobo must be having fits, but Gail was grateful Grant had put the Captain back on his bridge to oversee the tricky maneuvering.

The volunteers, boxes, and suits had been safely offloaded, and the small fleet dispersed translight. No one outwardly disputed the urgency of settling what they were dealing with—first contact or fluke. The cruiser, being fastest over distance, would travel to the most distant of the four terraformed worlds. The starships, and their Quill, should be back within two and a half days, all going well.

Titan University's representatives on the patrol ships had relinquished—or more precisely postponed—their verbal and legal battle for the only human who could safely handle the Quill the moment they realized the FD ship would be leaving, too. After all, they had Gail and Reinsez on the *Seeker*. Grant had been very careful to imply she was still in charge of the scientific aspects of the mission, including Aaron. It hadn't hurt credibility, Gail knew, that each ship received a pair of anti-Quill suits complete with volunteers.

"Gail." She looked up, startled by Aaron's voice. He was standing in front of her, ramrod straight, his gloved hands behind his back—oddly formal, in a room crammed with people shouting and rushing from place to place.

"Yes?"

"Grant's coming, isn't he? I don't want to leave you like this . . ." His too-quiet voice disappeared beneath a sudden increase in volume—a group of three techs calling for room to move a trolley. Aaron leaned forward. "We have to say goodbye, Gail."

The words locked around her heart, like icy, clutching fingers. "No, we don't," she tried to reassure him, or herself. "This isn't our last chance—"

"What if it is?" He spoke so softly, she might have been reading his lips.

*What if it is?* Gail repeated to herself. She hated contemplating failure, as if acknowledging the possibility guaranteed defeat. *There wasn't time for this*, Gail told herself desperately. *What if it is . . . ?*

She pushed her notepad into someone's hands, saying something, she wasn't sure what.

"It will be quieter in the storeroom," she told Aaron.

The storeroom, usually a well-organized set of aisles and shelving, had become a tangle of boxes and leaning metalwork due to the changing configuration of the lab itself, as well as raids by techs in a hurry for supplies.

Gail didn't bother turning on the overhead lighting; the standby lights were enough to see their path to the back. She did make sure the door was closed. Aaron's footsteps matched hers. He didn't say a word.

She couldn't.

It only took a few steps to reach the farthest part of the room from the doorway. Gail stopped, putting her hand out to touch the wall. *No way out*, she thought, then turned and put her back against it. "I don't believe in good-byes, Aaron Pardell," she began bravely enough. "Even if you end up going with— anyone else—it's going to be temporary, I promise. I have contacts on Earth—wealth if it takes bribes. I won't let—"

"Shssh."

At first, Gail thought the 'sider had heard someone else entering the room, and she froze, holding her breath. *Nothing*. She looked her question at Aaron.

"Whatever happens, Gail," he said gently, his eyes warm as they explored her face. "Wherever I go after this, it doesn't matter now, does it? We have a little time. Let's use it for us, not the future."

Gail leaned against the wall. "A very little time, Aaron," she sighed, "Someone could come in any time—a tech, or someone looking for either of us—"

"We'd hear," he said. For all its quiet, his voice seemed deeper, more resonant. Gail opened her mouth to speak. "Shssh," he repeated, gently.

Without another sound, Aaron stepped closer. Gail looked into his eyes and couldn't look away. There was something almost pleading in them, as though he tried to say everything with a look, as though words couldn't be of use.

*He means it. This is good-bye*, she realized. In all her

schemes, she hadn't planned for this. *She should have.* Because schemes and plans were only hopes—and this moment might be all they would have to remember if they failed.

Aaron took off his gloves, then reached his hands to her face, Gail stood still, in perfect trust.

With two fingers, he collected a lock of her hair, running it across the back of his other hand, then, to his lips. As he held it there, his eyes sparkled, as though filling with tears. Gail lifted her hand, pressing two fingers against her parted lips in echo.

"You are so incredibly beautiful," he whispered unsteadily, putting his hands alongside her face; she felt the warmth from his palms on her cheeks. She stayed as still as her quickening breathing allowed. Slowly, carefully, Aaron moved his hands as if to cup her jaw, her throat. He brushed his fingertips along the upstanding collar of her lab coat, his eyes traveling downward.

Suddenly, he pressed both hands flat against the wall on either side of her head and bent his face into his own arm so she could no longer see his expression.

"Aaron," Gail whispered. "Look at me."

"I can't—"

"I can," she said with sudden understanding. "Look at me."

He straightened, keeping one hand on the wall over her shoulder as if needing its support. His face was pale and unhappy. "You don't—" he faltered. "I want—"

"I know," Gail reassured him. The same need burned deep in her own body. Without hesitation, she reached up to the fastening of her coat and began undoing the buttons, one at a time. She couldn't smile when his breath caught—it was too powerful a feeling for that.

The coat fell to the floor.

Gail gazed into her love's eyes and what she saw there made her fingers tremble even as they slipped open the fastening of her blouse. Aaron's free hand captured some of the loose fabric, pulling it gently off her shoulder. His eyes wandered caressingly over her face, her neck, lower still, and she watched the blood rising over his cheekbones. She felt the cold air on her breasts, gooseflesh tightening, then a sudden heat. Surprised, she glanced down and saw his golden hands were hovering over her skin, learning her shape from a distance, loving her as only he could.

Nothing had prepared her for the sheer sensuousness of it. Gail moaned deep in her throat and only the wall kept her standing—the wall and a rapidly diminishing sense of danger. His eyes leaped to hers, as though the sound had startled him and he had to be sure it was of pleasure. She had to fight the instinct to arch her back and press herself against him—

The distant rattle of metal against metal was shocking, like the scream of air out a ruptured hull.

Aaron reacted first, turning so his body blocked hers from view as he stared into the darkness. The noise had come from the next aisle.

Gail took a steadying breath and stood away from the wall. "Someone's working in here. That's all," she said, fighting to firm her voice. "We have to go. You have to go. First, or Malley will think I've locked you away somewhere."

He swung around, a look of sheer desperation on his face, his hands rising as though to gather her in, then dropping to his sides. "But—"

"Go," she urged and found a smile. "No matter what anyone says—whatever happens—this wasn't good-bye, my love. I promise." She wasn't sure if Aaron believed her or wanted her to believe it, but he nodded slowly.

"I'll hold you to that, Earther," he told her. "Are you sure you don't want me to wait?"

Somehow, Gail grinned at him. "You're too distracting," she accused and had the joy of seeing him blush. "Now go! I need to pull myself together."

She waited, frozen in place, until Aaron disappeared at the opposite end of the storeroom and a brief, distant brightness marked where he'd opened and closed the door to the lab.

A tall figure formed itself from the shadows. Gail didn't look at Grant. She pulled up her blouse and began fastening it—her hands shaking, this time with fury. Tears tracked the fabric. "You couldn't give us even a moment alone?" she asked, hearing her voice as though it belonged to someone else. "Not even that much?"

She didn't think he'd dare answer her, but he did, with

impeccable, despicable calm: "My duty is still to protect you, Dr, Smith."

"What did you think was going to happen?" Gail cried, throwing up her head. Whatever else she might have said was silenced by the depth of compassion in his eyes, the grim downturn of his mouth. Instead, she looked for her lab coat, cold to her bones, abruptly too cold to move.

Grant bent and retrieved it, holding it open for her to insert her arms, then did up the buttons, as though she was a child. Gail shivered, then found herself held tightly.

He didn't speak or move as the first anguished sobs tore themselves from her throat.

Only years of practice let Gail walk out of the dark storeroom and back into the people-filled lab, her head high and her face, if not smiling, then at least normal enough so no one seem to notice.

*It wasn't good-bye.* But it could be. She wasn't a blind optimist. Grant couldn't hold off much longer—he'd probably come very close to rousing the suspicions of his listeners as it was. Malley, and likely others, would willingly fight to keep Aaron here, but the 'sider would never permit it.

*So it was up to her*, Gail told herself firmly. *Aaron would have a say in his own destiny, and the varied self-interests of the universe be damned.*

*Almost time.* Just as well Grant had—interrupted them. Gail wormed her way through the throng, hurrying to her workstation. Aisha was there and nodded a greeting, busy sorting instruments and humming to herself. Without intending to, Gail found herself capturing her friend's warm fingers in her hand. "What is it?" Aisha asked, frowning slightly as she searched Gail's face.

Gail stretched her lips into a smile and let go. "Know how much you hate my mental leaps?" she asked lightly.

The other scientist frowned a bit more. "Why do you ask?"

"Just remember how often they've been right, that's all," Gail said.

*Time.*

What Aisha might have replied was interrupted by a dull

thud, as if a workbench had overturned, then a sudden, loud snap. As everyone started looking for the sounds, the lab lighting turned garish orange and alarms began to shrill.

*Crack!* A long, jagged rupture flowed down the side of the case holding the Quill fragment, joining one already climbing from the bottom.

"Everyone out," Gail ordered, hearing the order repeated throughout the room as people headed for the doors. "Leave that!" she called to a tech snatching up pieces of equipment.

No panic, but plenty of confusion and raised voices. Gail eased back, one step at a time. They'd practiced evacuating the lab on the way to Thromberg—for whatever good it did when everyone considered the alarm a break from routine and the ultimate danger being a scathing memo. The doors were open; a steady stream of people moved out through each. The FDs were proving useful at something other than guard duty.

A hail from somewhere. "Gail?"

"On my way," she called out, for once glad to be a head shorter than most. Instead of a door, Gail's target was the nearest biohazard panel, one being located every few meters along the permanent walls. Gail keyed in a specific sequence, then waited for confirmation.

"Gail—" Aaron appeared at her side, Malley right behind. "You have to get out, too."

"I think it's too late to make it to the door," Gail said calmly, although there were at least a dozen people still moving toward the exits. "Right, Malley?"

It was the first time she'd spoken to him since their argument about Aaron. Malley's face was being lit by a flashing orange light. He stood there, looking for all the world like some stone gargoyle illuminated by lightning. "Go with her, Aaron," he said abruptly, his eyes not leaving Gail's. "The halls aren't safe for you with this crowd rushing about. Get."

Pardell looked surprised but not suspicious. He nodded. "Where?"

Malley pointed. "Be good," he growled, before moving away with that unexpected speed of his—incidentally sweeping up three straggling techs in his big arms and hustling them toward the door. Gail heard him shouting to the room in general, not particularly helpfully: "She's gone out the other door!"

The 'sider hesitated, looking back at the now-completely fractured case and its colorful, motionless occupant. "The Quill isn't going to hurt anyone, Gail. If you want, I can put it into another box for you."

"Leave it. Come with me, Aaron," Gail said quietly.

"What's this all about?" he asked, with the beginnings of a frown.

Gail grinned as the floor shuddered once beneath them.

"How much I hate good-byes."

# Chapter 75

PARDELL had been raised where ship's alarms were taken very seriously. *Danger, damage, thieves!* It didn't feel right ignoring this one, if that's what Gail was doing.

Not that he had much choice. Malley seemed to be single-handedly preventing anyone from coming back in, while Gail hurried them both behind a screen.

Which hid an air lock.

"We're taking shelter in there?" he asked. Which explained why Malley went for the door option, if nothing else.

"Not exactly. Help me with this." This was the set of three inner locks. They came open with the smoothness Pardell had come to expect from the *Seeker*'s equipment. It still astonished him at times.

Pardell was equally astonished by what was inside the air lock. "Hurry, Aaron," Gail said, giving him no time to do more than follow her inside. She started closing the door immediately.

"Gail?"

She seemed unable to stop long enough to look at him, as though momentum was all that kept her going. "I don't want it opening from the inside," she explained as she started wrapping a length of wire around one of the inner locks.

"That won't be enough," he said knowingly, glancing involuntarily at the suits hanging to his left. Three. One extra large. One small enough for Gail. *And his.* "Do you want something permanent?" It pained him to suggest damaging the immaculate ship.

"Not if we don't have to."

There was an emergency tool kit mounted on one wall. For

the first time in Pardell's experience, there were tools in it. "Give me a couple of seconds, then," he assured her and found a couple of multigrips with handles the right size to jam into the lock mechanisms. *A shame to treat tools or doors that way.* "Done."

"Good. Thanks." She was busy pulling on the smallest suit. "Gail."

"Get dressed, Aaron," she said, not looking at him. "Please."

*The piece of Quill wasn't a threat—if anyone knew that, Gail did.* Something was up. Equally obviously, she wasn't prepared to stop and explain. Muttering under his breath, Pardell went over to his suit. He wondered which would impress her more—his ability with tape or that his suit held air—then really looked at what hung on the wall.

"What have you done?" he breathed, all questions and impatience forgotten.

"They tested everything; it's vacuum-ready. You don't mind, do you?" A pause. "I didn't think you'd want one of the *Seeker's.*"

He hardly heard, busy running his gloved fingers over what had been his suit and was now this beautiful thing. Someone with far more skill than any spacer or engineer Pardell knew had not just repaired it, but restored the suit to its original condition. Better, probably, since what working ship's crew bothered with polish and perfect stitching? There were a few additions—he turned it over and saw new power couplings, a propulsion pack he hardly recognized—but nothing that took away from this being his. Even the hooks for sliding cable were on the belt, cleaned and gleaming.

"Tobo's chief engineer, Michael Gilbert, took it as a personal challenge—he's a collector as well as an artist. I hadn't known before I asked him to take a look at it. It is all right, Aaron, isn't it?"

Pardell nodded. "I'll want to thank him."

"Prove it works," she suggested.

*Anxious.* He heard it in her voice. Much as he would have liked to linger over each invisible repair and flawless new part, Pardell suited up faster than ever before. It was certainly an improvement not to have to tape up seams or coax a reluctant conditioning system to work. He did pause before pulling on the boots. "They fit," he said out loud, dismayed beyond reason to find the mags no longer protruded past heel and toe.

"Gilbert said the ones you had were the best part of the suit and worth saving. He didn't replace them—only trimmed them to your size."

*A profound change*, Pardell thought, but forced himself to stop hesitating. When he had his helmet on and clamped, he switched on the interior light so she could see his face. The homemade gauges hadn't been changed—safety, he decided, inclined to believe the mysterious repairman had known Pardell might not have time to learn a new system.

Gail reached for the control to evacuate the air, but Pardell tapped her on the shoulder. "Tie up first," he said through the comm, making sure it was private. She nodded, following his lead in snapping one end of their belt tethers—another marvel: his was brand-new cable—to the ring beside the exterior door. He set the controls and watched the indicators tracking the decreasing pressure. Fast and smooth.

Pressure against his chest. Pardell looked down but couldn't see what it was. Then Gail moved to stand facing him, and he realized it had to be her gloved hands.

She'd noticed he'd safely touched her shoulder. *Or*, he reminded himself, *she knew from her own experiments that this double layer of metal-laced fabric was enough to protect the two of them, if not against the Quill, then from his skin.*

A second, better surprise. Gail put her arms around him, as far as they could go in the bulky suits, and leaned her helmet against his. He couldn't see inside from this angle, but the sound of her breathing carried through the comm system, clear, soft, and not quite regular.

Careful of tubing and seals, Pardell wrapped his arms around her in turn, awed by the sensation of enfolding her smaller self and the powerful protective feeling it aroused. "Now that you've got me where you want me," he said, keeping it casual and cheerful, the way Malley would, "want to tell me what's happening?"

"Trial Number Six," she said, just as the indicator light

flashed green and the outer air lock door swung obediently open.

She must have known what he would see; she didn't let go and turn, but simply added:

"Assuming you can get us across that."

# Chapter 76

THEY'D break through the inner door. Her air supply would run out. The sun would stop shining. All this and more would happen before Gail felt like leaving the first embrace of her life that sang to her soul.

"Gail."

The voice of reason, accompanied by a firm push to set her at a distance. She gave herself a mental shake before looking up. Aaron stared past her, outward, then bent his head down so she could see his half-smile. "You've been busy," he commented.

"Level three biohazard," Gail said absently. "Automatic sphere quarantine." She didn't say any more, having a healthy respect for the FDs' abilities when it came to invading private comm links.

Level three—the waist alarm would have sounded, its walkway accelerating to remove—more or less intact—any person with unfortunate timing. Then, evacuation to hard vacuum as the accordion walls stretched, thinner and thinner, until waist became tether and the *Seeker* became two.

The FDs could have kept them imprisoned simply by locking the access doors to the waist. *This*, Gail hoped, *gave them another option.*

*Mind you, she hadn't realized how far the tether could stretch between the two spheres of the ship.* Or that it would look so insubstantial against the night side of Pardell's World. The command sphere was so distant, she couldn't make out any detail beyond its round glow.

She tried to imagine it looked welcoming.

"We're going to take over the ship?" Aaron asked, paying her

the compliment of not making that sound as silly as it could
have. "We could use Malley."

Gail looked at the stationer's suit, hanging on the wall. He'd
made it into the 'lock with their gear—something she hadn't
dared doubt. "Nothing that dramatic. This is a kidnapping."

"Which of us is the kidnapper?" he asked, logically enough.

"Both. Neither. Can you do it?" Gail was feeling less sure of
this plan every second they stood looking out.

Instead of a reassuring answer, Aaron bent down and
switched on his mags before unclipping himself from the door
ring. "Wait here," he said, then walked out and over the edge of
the air lock.

Gail held on to the ring with one hand as well as the tether,
feeling as though she'd fall out if she didn't despite the gravity
of the air lock floor. After what seemed too long, Aaron's gloved
hands overlapped the door's edge and he flipped himself back
inside, catching the door ring with one hand. "No problem."

*No problem*, Gail repeated to herself.

Aaron unclipped her tether from the door ring and attached it
to his own belt, then pulled out the clamps he used for sliding
and leaned out, as if judging distance. When she went to switch
on her mags in order to walk on the outer hull, he stopped her.
"You won't need those." He hit the automatic lock, and the air
lock's outer door began closing.

"I won't?" Before Gail could more than ask, Aaron pulled
them both out into space, pushing off with an unusual twist to
his body that belied the awkward mass of the suit, sending them
flying.

*Snick.*

Gail gasped and fought against vertigo as their momentum
changed in an instant and they began whirling around a center
point.

"Look at me. Not the cable. Gail! Look at me."

She forced open her eyes, finding herself helmet to helmet
with Aaron. His face, lit from below, was concerned but calm,
as if her reaction mattered more than this lazy spiraling into the
void. "We're going to die," she said firmly, in case he'd missed
the point.

"Not at the moment," he countered. "Relax and enjoy the ride—it's not going to be long. This cable's pretty taut."

*Ride?* She cautiously looked away from him, at where they were going.

True, they were spinning around, but centered around the clamp in Aaron's right hand, that clamp wrapped around a wrist-thick cable—all that remained of the waist. She was looking where they'd been, the science sphere glowing in its own lights.

They'd jumped to bypass the waist's conveyer system, she realized, seeing the folded mass retracted against the smooth hull. She looked back at his face. "Nice catch," she said, pleased her voice didn't break over the words.

Hard to tell through the helmet, but she thought Aaron looked sheepish. "You said time was an issue. Climbing over the collar—it would have taken a while."

"And it was more fun leaping out into space."

"There's that." His smile was pure, heart-stopping mischief. "You sound like a 'sider."

"I don't spend all my time in the lab," she responded. Perhaps it was the sensation of spinning, holding on to one another, that made everything else fall away, leaving them in this comforting intimacy. It was as real as it was temporary. "How do we land?"

"Stay with me," he said, sounding supremely confident.

*That's the plan*, Gail said to herself.

She'd find out soon enough what Aaron thought of it.

# Chapter 77

WHEN Malley didn't know what to think about something— or someone—he took the ambivalence as a personal affront. He liked things clear, logical, and slotted into categories. *Probably why he'd lasted so long on the recycling floor.*

Gail Smith stubbornly refused to fit.

Each time he had her figured out, she'd change. *The only thing consistent about the damned woman.*

"Stationer."

Malley rolled his eyes up. He'd noticed Sazaad easing in his direction through the small groups dotting the dining lounge. Until the all-clear came from the lab, there wasn't much for anyone but the biohaz team to do. Most of the science staff had succumbed to exhaustion and gone to their quarters, but there were always those who had to talk their way past an emergency. Some, like Malley, were more interested in a meal that wasn't prewrapped.

He wasn't interested in the obnoxious Earther. "I'm busy."

Sazaad smiled as if he'd expected nothing better, but prudently lowered himself to the end of the curved bench farthest from Malley. "Obviously. But if you could fit me into your schedule, it would be of advantage to your friend."

"The dead one," Malley said.

Sazaad raised an elegant brow. "I stand by my findings of the time. However, if I'd pursued the course suggested by our delectable Dr. Smith sooner, my machine would have doubtless confirmed what you—believed." His lips curled over the last word, as if it was something Sazaad found reprehensible.

Malley leaned back, pushing aside the table so he could bring one foot up on the bench between them, resting his forearm on the knee. He stared at Sazaad across this barrier. The man looked insufferably proud of himself. *More insufferably proud than usual.*

"Do you have anything to say I'm going to care about, Earther?" he asked, keeping it polite—marginally.

"I am, of course, limited to what you can comprehend and I can say in a public place," the other said with an equal effort. Malley was quite sure the man remembered—and didn't forgive—being manhandled in the lab. He was also sure the failure of the cog screen device rankled even more.

"That should make it nice and short," Malley returned, reaching for his glass. They didn't—or wouldn't—serve alcohol in this lounge, but he'd found Scotch dissolved invisibly in orange juice. It didn't taste any worse than Sammie's brew. Which wasn't saying much.

"Here." Sazaad produced a silvered flask from an inside pocket. "We can be enemies tomorrow, Malley." He took a swallow from the flask, then passed it to the stationer. Malley waited long enough for Sazaad's face to grow clouded, then put down his glass and took the flask.

The mouthful was cold, sweet, and thick—with a promising burn down the throat. Malley passed it back. "Fine. Enemies tomorrow. So what advantage are you talking about?"

"Your friend will want to hear this. Where is he?" the Earther asked slyly. "And our good Doctor Smith?"

"Catching up on some sleep or working on the Quill—how should I know? Grant's people don't exactly keep me briefed, you may have noticed."

"I don't doubt you know more than the rest of us, Stationer," Sazaad laughed, offering the flask again. Malley refused. "Keep your secrets, then. What I have to tell you—" he took another, deeper drag on the flask, "—you don't want anyone else to learn first."

Malley took a casual look around. They were tucked into one of several alcoves within the lounge. The room seemed designed to encourage quiet conversations, although from what Aisha had told him, those conversations weren't to be considered private.

*The Earthers allowed an obscene amount of interference in their lives*, Malley decided.

"Let's take a walk."

Sazaad had been right. This wasn't something Malley wanted anyone else to know—not before Aaron, at least. Unfortunately, thanks to Gail, he didn't know where they were. He assumed they hadn't stayed inside the air lock, but that didn't worry him. Outside was Aaron's turf.

Sazaad's machine's failure—might as well call it a personal failure, because that was how the man had taken it—had driven him to work nonstop on the problem Gail had posed to him. He wouldn't say if she'd given him the blueprint or simply shown him a possible direction, but it didn't matter.

Their walk had taken them to Sazaad's own quarters—a choice Malley approved when he discovered they did have something in common: a loathing of being watched. While Sazaad swept the room for what he called "Grant's toys," Malley had amused himself by going through the man's vid collection. No surprises, there. Gail's estimation of the scientist's personal preoccupation was accurate.

Her estimation of his genius was equally so. Sazaad had literally rebuilt his apparatus to do something totally new, testing it by running through data obtained from the week of testing on Aaron. It no longer measured cognitive function through the electrical activity of various parts of the brain.

Now it measured something much less tangible. Emotion.

Back in his own quarters, Malley looked at his hand, examining the network of blood vessels where it slipped close to the skin to bypass barriers of ligament and bone. According to Sazaad, Aaron's skin wore a network of detectors, similar to those now in his machine, that picked up and amplified the emotions of anyone who touched him. The amplification went in all directions, a clue to why Aaron reacted at the same instant as the person touching him.

The Quill Effect. Muted, limited by being woven into human flesh.

*Still deadly.*

Sazaad's new machine couldn't detect which emotion was being transferred. He planned to test it on Petra, the woman whose meditation technique had somehow controlled the emotional feedback from her contact with Aaron, if not helping Aaron at all. The Earther was full of ideas, from using his new gadget to monitor the Quill to predictably bizarre commercial applications.

Around that point, Malley had stopped listening and left, Sazaad looking astonished—pesumably that anyone wouldn't be interested in all he had to say.

The stationer tensed his hand into a fist, watching how bone bleached the skin over each scabbed and scarred knuckle, how the veins between stayed blue.

*So.* Aaron *knew* things about others—things people weren't supposed to know about one another.

He spied on feelings the way the Earthers spied on one another.

An unkind comparison. Worse, a dangerous one. But Malley couldn't avoid it. He had a lot of questions piling up for his absent friend . . . starting with why Aaron hadn't told him.

And definitely including what Aaron had felt on the planet's surface.

# Chapter 78

FEELINGS. Trust. *Nebulous figments of imagination.* Until Gail had come to Thromberg Station, she'd relied on her skill and wits, confident no one else could—or would—help her succeed without coercion, self-interest, or a common goal.

She stood on the faintly scarred curve of a starship, held from drifting into her own fatal orbit around the planet below by the grip of two boots and a slip of string, depending on feelings and trust alone.

*Not hard at all.* She stood there, listening to the soothing background sounds of her suit as it fought the sun's radiation to keep her cool, gazing at the tiny craters pebbling the hull of the command sphere. No sign of a 'bot yet—if Grant wanted to deploy his remote spies, someone would have to walk to one of the hangared drop pods, pull out a 'bot, then change its housing to space capable. It could be done fairly quickly if ordered; she trusted—that word again—Grant to not act in haste.

There were vids on the hull, but clustered to view critical areas. Most near the waist should be fixed on the retracted collar, so the crew could ensure it was whole and ready to reattach. That process would require both time and several experienced crew working outside. If Grant wanted access to the science sphere, he'd have crew already in the air locks. If he preferred to keep the *Seeker*'s command sphere ready to fly independently—

*Well, that was something else she had to trust him not to do.* Where would he go anyway? The command sphere was atmosphere-capable. That didn't mean they could land on Pardell's World. Only the suits—so far—had proved any protection from the Quill Effect.

Trust aside, Gail knew they had no time of their own to waste. Aaron had gone to locate the air lock into the hangar. When he'd heard who was waiting to admit them—the *Seeker* being a ship whose ports stayed safely locked unless authorized personnel were outside—he'd laughed and said he'd know the code to use. Gail, at that moment, hadn't been in any shape to go along, mutely grateful to feel something solid grabbed by her boots. Aaron's notion of how best to dismount from the ship's tether had been a little more exciting than she'd anticipated.

*He'd probably find skydiving dull, given the certainty of a landing.*

A gloved thumb appeared in front of her helmet, the agreed signal. It was too risky to use their comms here. Her companion reattached the cable from her belt to his. Gail was somewhat amused by this sign that Aaron, who'd recently and casually risked both their lives, didn't take avoidable chances.

She followed the 'sider around to the side of the *Seeker* facing the planet, resolutely avoiding the temptation to look up and lose herself in the beautiful distraction of the coming sunrise. The hangar wasn't far—the smaller inset door of its air lock was already open, a black pit in the side of the ship.

Now for the unavoidable chance she'd taken, with Rosalind Fournier.

The rebel 'sider looked pleased with herself. *No doubt*, Gail decided, *it had something to do with putting her at a disadvantage.*

"I admit, I'd wondered how you planned to get here when Grant's troops had the waist locked tight," Rosalind had said in lieu of a greeting. "Neat trick, splitting the ship in half."

"Glad you liked it," Gail replied, more concerned with Aaron's reaction to where they were but doing her best not to show it. He was taking off his suit with care, stealing glances around as if he couldn't quite believe they had the *Seeker*'s hangar bay to themselves.

Themselves and three drop pods. The first, *Athena*, sat with her entry ramp down. Gail nodded at the two back in line. "They're temporarily out of service," Rosalind said rather smugly. "Nothing that can't be repaired—on Callisto."

Gail wasn't at all surprised. Who better to sabotage engines than someone who repaired them? "*Athena*?" she asked.

"Prepped and ready to fly. Your people had conveniently finished her when the biohazard alert sent everyone into a frenzy. The place was sealed tight like that," Rosalind clicked her paddles together sharply. "Good thing I was ready for it."

"So you knew," Aaron stopped pretending to be preoccupied with his suit, looking from Rosalind to Gail. "It wasn't an accident at all."

Before Gail could say a word, Rosalind laughed once. "Young Aaron. When will you learn there are no accidents—only momentum applied to events? Still, I'd have thought the Earther would have explained by now why you had to fly through vacuum."

"You'd better have sealed the door from the inside, Rosalind," Gail informed her coolly, then pointed at the ceiling above the stubby pods. "Unless you've disabled the vids."

Rosalind smiled, unperturbed. She'd taken to wearing crew coveralls and probably blended more easily into that group than Grant's people would have liked. It hadn't been difficult at all to convince her to slip into the hangar in the confusion—or to have Reinsez's own plants among the crew and staff help "prepare" the pods. *Nothing was difficult—for a price.* Predictably, Rosalind's very next words were: "What I care to learn, Gail Smith, is whether you can deliver on your promises."

"Promises?"

"Oh, yes, young Aaron. Your patron here has been profligate with them lately—to me, to the sadly worried Dr. Reinsez, to the station itself. What has she promised you lately?"

Gail picked up the bundle of her suit and boots. "You and your ships will get to Callisto, Rosalind," she said calmly. "Compared to what else I have to deliver? That's the easy part. Aaron? Let's go before Grant's folks start burning through the door. And they will—the FDs won't worry about Titan's property."

Her words and tone were light. Gail feared her expression was anything but as she looked at the 'sider, hoping the troubled look in his hazel eyes meant he was thinking it through—not preparing to balk. The FD might not be watching for trouble in the hangar. Tobo might distract them from the vids. Gail wasn't prepared to bet on either.

Aaron nodded. Without another glance toward Rosalind, or her, he picked up his suit and walked up the ramp into the *Athena.*

Before Gail could follow, Rosalind reached out and held her by the elbow, robotic fingers biting deeply into the flesh. "When it comes to the end of this, Earther," the 'sider said evenly, each word quiet and sincere, "remember that young Aaron and I are family. You've given me your word this is the only way to keep him safe from the schemes of Titan and the Earth military— he'd better be safe from yours as well."

Gail stared down at Rosalind's hand until the 'sider released her grip, then she looked up again. "No one's safe, 'Sider," she replied steadily. "This?" A wave at the pod. "A chance. If there was another option, believe me, I'd take it."

"Luck slide your cable, then," Rosalind told her, something genuine in the odd wish.

"Luck?" Gail repeated, then shook her head decisively. "I prefer to make my own."

# Chapter 79

PARDELL didn't like having others make decisions for him—not Malley, and certainly not Rosalind.

*Gail?*

Different and the same. He trusted her judgment in situations where he didn't have all the pieces. Malley doubtless believed it was because he couldn't see reason—*thinking with hormones,* he'd heard Malley mutter when one of their drinking buddies acted as if dazed by a pretty face.

Malley was wrong. Pardell might not know as much as his friend about relations between men and women, but he understood very well what it meant when someone risked death for you. That was when caring went deeper than infatuation or any of the other things casually labeled as love; that was when you became absolutely essential to one another.

That you could die because of one another was just a cruel trick fate played on occasion.

So Pardell walked into the now-familiar hold of the Earther's little pod, put his suit by the seat where he'd strap in before take off, and turned to wait for Gail. *This wasn't her decision to make.*

Gail hurried up the ramp, tossing her suit ahead, intent on reaching the door controls. Pardell gently put his hand over them first. "You aren't going," he told her.

She didn't look surprised, merely reached into a pocket and pulled out a pair of the blue anti-Quill gloves. "This will hurt you more than me, Aaron," she warned, putting them on, her blue eyes quite serious. "Move out of my way now. They could stop us at any moment."

*Despite her diminutive size*, Pardell decided, *Gail could give*

*Malley lessons on intimidation.* "I'll go back down," he offered, keeping a close watch on her hands. "You can tell me what to do, what trials to conduct. They won't stop you once I'm gone—"

"Trials?" Her eyes widened. Suddenly, a dimple appeared on each cheek. "Aaron my sweet, we're eloping, not conducting research. You can't do that by yourself." She waved impatiently at the control panel and he moved back, too stunned to do anything else.

Gail closed and locked the outer door, then headed for the pilot's seat. It had been vacant during his and Dafoe's earlier flight.

"Eloping." The word alone threatened to split his thoughts into a hundred directions at once; worse, it flared back into life those longings he thought he'd safely buried since those dangerous, stolen moments together. The memory of her—sight, warmth, *sound*—all began interfering with his breathing, as it had then. Pardell began to sweat with the strain of keeping his focus. "Eloping," he repeated.

She peered over her shoulder at him, taking off the gloves at the same time. "You do know the word?" she asked with a faintly worried air.

"Of course I know the word—"

"You don't mind, do you?"

"Mind?" *There was something wrong with the air in the cabin. That was it. Carbon dioxide poisoning.* But the alarms should have gone off by now.

Gail swiveled her seat around to look right at him. "We can keep talking and be stopped any minute—or we can get moving and talk later, Mr. Pardell. Your decision."

Aaron searched her face. For all her outward spirit and confidence, there was something uncertain, something almost wistful around her eyes and mouth. He coughed lightly, none too sure of his own expression or voice. "Talk later, Mrs. Pardell," he said, as if leaping to a cable, and was rewarded by a sudden, brilliant smile.

# Chapter 80

"Is this like Earth? Exactly?"

Gail turned, the headgear of her suit suffering from a significant lack of peripheral vision. *Proving there was no substitute for checking everything herself no matter who was on the design team.* Aaron was standing on the end of the ramp, his dark hair tumbled over one eye by the ever-present wind. He hadn't bothered with a suit, but wore his own gloves as protection from the rising sun.

As promised, they'd talked on the trip down, but more about what was waiting here than anything of the future. *Protection of another sort*, Gail thought.

"It's very close," she assured him. "You'd hear birds and insects as they woke up and started moving around. There'd be more smells in the air—wildflowers, possibly livestock in the distance. The stream over there—it would likely have a band of trees alongside it. The wind would make different sounds through their leaves than it does over the grass." Suddenly, the headgear and suit were a prison, keeping her from savoring this world, from being truly outside for the first time in—*when had she last been on Earth, actually taken the time to step outside a university building or hotel?*

"But those who were born on Earth—they'd feel at home here?"

*Ah.* Gail took a step closer to him, careful to stay on the ramp. She hadn't bothered with the umbilical—they could send a remote for her body, if it came to that. She'd hardly care, then.

They hadn't seen Quill yet, although the *Athena* had repeated her flight path precisely. A shapeless mound of torn grass marked the end of the path Aaron and Dafoe had made. The statue was gone—collapsed, perhaps, as the grass dried. Or deserted by the Quill. "Yes. Right at home. That was the point of terraforming, to produce an environment suited to our form of life. No domes, no pressure suits. Sky and fresh air."

"I told you Raner was from Earth. Sammie. Most of the older ones—the immies. The rest of us—" Aaron paused, as if transfixed by the light beginning to slip down the shoulders of the distant mountaintops. "We listened to their stories; I don't think we believed them."

"I have to be honest, Aaron," Gail told him soberly. "If we can make these worlds safe for people again, not everyone from the stations will be able to stand being outside like this. Look at Malley. He might—I think he'd try, if only to prove he could— but it would be a battle."

"For Malley, that would be the point," Aaron observed. He paused. "How do you feel?"

Gail, about to go back into the pod for more equipment, stopped at his sudden question. "Fine. Why?"

"She's back."

Fighting back excitement, and a healthy dose of fear, Gail looked down the path. Aaron was right. The now-drying grass stalks were aswarm with Quill fragments, together pulling the loose mass into cohesive, literate form. A woman, human, with a child—this time held to the torso by one arm, the other outstretched toward them.

Gail studied it. The legs were incomplete, more stumps than limbs. The face, though. There was a surprising amount of detail to the face, but the shadow-rich lighting of early morning didn't help. Given the Quill sensitivity to light, she hesitated to shine one of the pod's spots on them. Moving steadily and slowly, she brought out one of the portable vids and used its lens to enhance what she could see.

"Aaron," she said, then realized his name had dried on her lips. "Aaron. Look at this."

He came immediately, concern on his face. Gail held out the vid and pointed it at the figure. "What do you see?" she asked, watching as more Quill fragments shimmered up the grass stalks surrounding the *Athena*.

*This was why she was here*, Gail told herself sternly, forestalling any urge to run back into the pod—or simply stand and shake.

A shame she knew so much more about the Quill Effect than she did about communicating with aliens.

"More to the face than before . . ." his voice trailed away.

Gail rephrased her question, staring at the statue. "Whose face? Who do you see?"

"Who?" Aaron dropped the vid from his eyes to look at her.

"Go on. Forget what that is . . . where we are. Who do you see?"

He raised the vid again, holding it still, looking toward the grass and Quill sculpture. "It's not Gabrielle Pardell—my mother," he concluded, sounding almost disappointed. "There's no similarity."

Gail reached for the vid. She took it almost reverently, refocusing on that face. "I wasn't sure if you'd see it—you've only seen a few images of her. But I've been haunted by this woman most of my adult life—I know her face very well indeed."

She put down the vid and made an extravagant wave toward the statue. "Aaron Pardell, meet Susan Witts, your paternal great grandmother."

*What did it mean?*

Undoubtedly they weren't the only ones puzzling over the Quill's representation of the infamous terraformer. Gail had chosen, for the time being, to permit live feed from the *Athena's* outward-pointing vids to play up on the *Seeker.* One-way. She wasn't interested in hearing endless arguments or complaints, however deserved. The feed seemed the least she could do, given she'd effectively stolen most of the research opportunities from her staff—as well as Grant's main hope of finding out more about the Quill.

Not that Aaron seemed to mind being stolen. They'd turned the *Athena* into a makeshift camp, putting up a tentlike shade over the ramp surface to give some relief from the unrelenting sunshine of the day, and shared their first meal outdoors.

*A meal she'd never forget.* It didn't matter that the menu consisted of tasteless nutrient paste and tepid water. *The two of them, alone on a brand-new world.* It didn't matter that her portion came via a straw, that straw leading to a bag in a doubled pocket lined in anti-Quill fabric. They'd toasted each other with ration tubes, laughing and talking like friends who hadn't met in years. She'd surprised him with the chess set he'd given her and found, to her delight, that the 'sider was her equal or better at the game.

Then, after a sudden, solemn silence, they'd exchanged the simplest of vows:

*Always yours.*

*Were they fools?* Gail really didn't care. She'd never felt happier and Aaron acted like a man in a dream. He'd turn to her every few minutes, devouring her with his eyes as if making sure this was real.

It was real—but so was everything else, including the Quill. Aaron wouldn't let her step off the ramp, not yet. Gail wasn't in a hurry to push their luck herself.

"We have two days, likely less, before the other ships come back," she reminded him now, as they watched the Quill. As the Quill were presently doing nothing more interesting than swaying hypnotically with the grass in the wind, this watching was pretty much taking a rest themselves.

"Then we hide?" Aaron said in a deceptively casual tone. He was stretched out on his back, seemingly enchanted by the way the wind played with the translucent material of their shelter.

Gail bounced a chess piece on his stomach. "Then we'd better have answers to the main questions, Aaron." *So they won't need you*, she added, but only to herself.

"Such as why *her* face?"

Gail nodded, caught up in the mystery again. "This isn't the same representation they made for you the first time. Something happened between that moment and now." She lay back, careful of the suit. They didn't know if a person had to be fully covered to be protected, but it was a reasonable guess. Gail didn't plan to find out for sure.

*The suit . . . there was a problem she hadn't shared.* The suit was designed for extended wear, just as a space suit would be, but much lighter since it didn't have to provide life support. In theory, it should be easy to keep it on for another forty-eight standard hours.

Gail wasn't sure she'd last another three in the hot, itchy thing, but she kept that doubt to herself. Aaron had enough on his mind.

After a moment, the 'sider rolled over on one elbow to face her. "Are you smiling?" he asked curiously, eyes green with reflected sunlight as he tried to see inside the headgear.

Gail stuck out her tongue.

"Why do I think you just made a rude face at me?" he said.

"Because I did," she confessed, scrutinizing every plane and angle of his face, memorizing features she already knew by heart. His expressions flickered from one emotion to another like the play of shadow and sunlight in the moving grass. Curiosity, interest, exasperation, affection . . .

"What are you planning now?" Pardell asked.

Gail braced herself "I'm not planning. I'm hoping." She reached up and switched her comm so only Aaron should hear her voice. The feed from the pod itself was visual only, with audio recorded but not transmitted. They had that much privacy. "Aaron, what did the Quill say to you?"

A flicker of fear—not of her, of the question. "There wasn't a conversation. Just the statue."

"No one else can hear what you tell me." Gail propped herself up and faced him.

Almost sullen. "I don't care what *they* hear."

Gail smiled to herself "An impression? An emotion? You might as well tell me exactly what it was. In the best tradition of brides, I'll find out anyway." She could make him smile like this at whim, it seemed. It was very distracting—both the smile and the power he granted her.

"Then I'd best be honest," Aaron said, as if surrendering. "Emotion? More than that—almost concepts. I'm not sure what to call it. But the first time I touched that fragment, I was *recognized*."

"Go on," Gail said quietly, looking over the rippling waves of grass. *And Quill.*

"The second time, when I picked up the fragment, it was more than recognition. There was a conclusion—some decision made. I knew I was . . . *welcomed*." At this, his face tightened into hard, unhappy lines. "It sounded crazy to me then, Gail, and still does. I could have imagined all of it. It was nothing like I've—sensed—from people."

"Perhaps," Gail agreed thoughtfully. "But I doubt it. When people touch you, any message is confused with the experience. The Quill . . . they evolved this way—it stands to reason they'd be better at it."

Aaron stood up and walked to the edge of the ramp, looking out at the waving grass. "You think I could—talk—to them?"

Gail rose and followed, fighting the impulse to pull him back. "I think you could be able to listen. I don't know what it would take to be understood in turn. This all supposes there really is something out there to talk to, of course. Are you willing to try?" The question was forced past the gorge rising in her throat. *If there was to be an* always, she scolded herself, *it had to begin with the Quill.*

"Why not . . ." he said almost as though she wasn't there, then stepped off the ramp.

# Chapter 81

MALLEY held his breath as Aaron stepped off the ramp, hearing faint echoes as those around him did the same. The lab was still quarantined—according to the FDs, anyway—but the techs had rigged up displays in several rooms, the largest and best attended in this lounge. He'd heard the crew was busy reconnecting the waist, along with unpleasant details such as how soon it would be ready for those in suits to slide through the corridor. Everyone else was glued to a display.

The stationer assumed he was the only one watching who was struck by how the moving air . . . wind . . . pressed the 'sider's worn stationer clothing against his legs and back, creating new folds and wrinkles that changed as he walked. *What did it feel like, to be* inside *air that moved when and how it chose?*

"We've got vitals for Dr. Smith only," a voice said from behind. "She's showing some stress—normal levels."

*Trust the Earther to make herself part of the experiment.* "What's Aaron doing?" he asked out loud, reasonably sure someone among those gathered to watch would have an informed opinion.

"Not a clue," Aisha said, from beside him. "They don't have a box ready, so he's not after a sample. . . . Okay, there. He's trying to touch one."

That much Malley could see for himself. Aaron's hands came up empty, the Quill fragments nearest him slipping from the stalks. He looked back toward the pod, toward the small blue-suited figure that was Gail, and shrugged. She pointed at the new statue. She wasn't the only one.

The Quill hadn't simply vanished from Aaron's reach—they'd left a clear path to their construction. *An invitation.*

"He wouldn't," someone said. Malley realized it was him and closed his mouth. Of course, Aaron started walking over the bent grass. *Damn fool.* This wasn't Thromberg, where warnings came with convenient red-and-amber markings. The stationer's fists curled as if around a throat, but there was nothing he could do but watch.

"Dr. Smith's vitals are up."

Malley growled under his breath.

Aaron reached the statue. With him nearby for comparison, it was easier to see the figure was too wide and short, the arms overly long for the body. The face was the amazing part. Several here had called out in startled recognition when Gail initially brought the features close with her handvid.

*So that was Susan Witts.* Malley hadn't seen the face before himself, but the Quill had done a remarkable job of portraying a high forehead, distinctive cheekbones, and firm jaw. It was so lifelike, except for the shimmer of Quill amid the brown stalks, Malley wondered if Aaron saw the resemblance. Did it reassure the 'sider to see his unusual bone structure repeated here? *Probably not*, Malley thought grimly.

Aaron seemed to be waiting. Then his head turned. They could see his face and watch his lips move as he said something to Gail.

"I don't like the look of that," the stationer said to Aisha very quietly.

"Why?" she asked. "Your friend looks calm—unafraid. Determined, I'd say."

Malley grunted disapproval. "Exactly. That's how he looks before starting a brawl at Sammie's. You haven't seen anything like our Aaron when he's ready to make things happen." Before she uttered the obvious, Malley explained: "Chairs. Bottles. He's a mean shot with a boot, too. Can't trust those shy, introverted types."

"As if you're the angel," she said, but absently, intent on the screen.

Aaron looked to be arguing with Gail—probably about what he proposed to do. *If she didn't like it*, Malley realized with a chill, *he certainly didn't.* "Anyone here lip-read?"

"Malley." Grant appeared out of nowhere, tapping the stationer on the shoulder to draw his attention. He was wearing a comm link in his ear. "Come with me."

The stationer shot an anxious look at the screen, but followed Grant away from the crowd standing immediately in front, Malley could see over everyone's head anyway.

The commander had been conspicuously absent since the latest incident in the lab. Until the feed from Pardell's World had started appearing on everyone's screens, courtesy of Gail Smith, no doubt, Malley had presumed the Earther was busy with the Quill.

"It's a nice change—not having my people lined up at the infirmary after an encounter with you, Malley," Grant said.

Malley felt something being pushed into his hand; he slid it into a pocket without looking. "I'm making an effort," he played along.

Grant tilted his head downward, his eyes gleaming. "What did you know about all this?" he asked. "About Dr. Smith and your friend—"

*A question from Grant himself, or something aimed at those "listening" to his conversations?* Malley decided it didn't matter. Aaron's business was his own. "A surprise to me," he shrugged. "But the woman tends to jump where you least expect—I take it you weren't consulted either."

Grant's frown was real enough. "There was an explosive device rigged to the Quill's stasis chamber. We've talked to Dr. Temujin about its origins—he claims, naturally, to know nothing about it. Doesn't matter. The whole thing was an excuse to allow Dr. Smith to invoke her override on the *Seeker*'s waist controls. It looks as though she and Aaron planned this very well. But why?"

Malley nodded at the screen. "That much seems obvious. You got in her way—blocked how she wanted things done. She couldn't remove you, so she removed herself. As I said, the woman tends to jump."

"Maybe—" Grant looked suddenly alarmed, his head swinging to face the screen just as there were cries from everyone in the room.

Malley pushed forward, staring, like the rest, at Aaron Pardell as the 'sider stepped into the statue's embrace . . .

And was consumed by Quill.

# Chapter 82

STATUES didn't move. Gail stood like one, watching in horror as the Quill's version unfolded itself with blinding, inescapable speed, wrapping around Aaron Pardell until there was nothing to see . . .

But another statue . . . this one man-sized, slender, better proportioned, and unmoving.

"Aaron!" Gail heard herself screaming his name and closed her mouth. Her paralysis broke and she ran to him as quickly as the suit and uneven terrain allowed, only to be forced to a staggering halt—confronting a barrier that built itself before she was close enough to tear the Quill from his body and head.

Grass writhed into a chest-high wall, reinforced with streaks of shiny alien tissue. The wall formed a circle with one opening—gate to the path behind her, safe passage to the ramp, the pod, and—presumably—off Pardell's World. "Not without him," she promised, as if anything could hear.

*Talk to the Quill?* A flamethrower—or even a scythe—either would suit her mood at the moment. A shame there wasn't anything remotely dangerous on the *Athena.*

A glint of light from the wrong direction forced her to look up. A 'bot hovered an arm's length beyond the wall, nearer to where Aaron stood imprisoned. "I thought we disabled that," Gail said numbly, at this evidence they obviously hadn't.

"Get back in the pod, Gail. Before they attack you, too." Grant's voice filled her ears, picked up by the exterior mikes on her headgear, not the comm. It must be coming from the 'bot.

*If ever there was a moment to rise above fear,* Gail knew, *this was hers.* "No," she said, talking to herself as much as to those she couldn't see. "We don't know this is an attack. Aaron—

Aaron thought they'd have to touch him before there'd be a chance to communicate. I was—am—alarmed. But he was determined. Maybe he sensed this would be necessary." Somehow she mustered a lighter note to her voice, reassurance. *For whom?* "First contact, Grant. None of us knows what to expect from it. Maybe this is it."

"And maybe this is what the Quill Effect looks like in person. There's nothing here suggesting intelligence—a spider can build an elaborate trap! I want you back up here—"

"A mindless trap? Then why *her* face, Commander?" Gail countered. "Why Susan Witts, a woman he'd never seen? It could have shown him his own face—or his mother's." Experimentally, Gail moved toward the wall, her gloved hand outstretched. The wall immediately grew higher. She backed away slightly and the wall stopped growing. Finally, she sat, very slowly, on the yielding softness of bent grass. The wall sank down with her, until it was barely more than a lump.

"I take it you saw all that," she told the 'bot dryly.

"Copy that." Grant's response sounded as though blurted out on automatic, as if the man himself were stupefied.

She felt much the same way. Reaction to stimuli was one thing. Purposeful response was quite another.

Gail no longer doubted they were dealing with an intelligence here. Grant had been right. She reserved judgment on whether he was also right that this was an elaborate trap and she might be the next prey.

Folding her hands neatly in her lap, eyes never leaving the iridescent tower that was all she could see of Aaron, Gail prepared to wait and see.

# Chapter 83

HE couldn't see, but understood vision was irrelevant—at best, an interaction with the stimulating poison of solar radiation, at worst considerable threat.

He couldn't hear, but valued the intimacy of resonance and vibration—indicators of movement—always a warning of danger.

He couldn't speak, yet knew and expressed. Concepts flowed over and through him, as they always had, but instead of being a distraction from the world, they were sharp, purposeful, as if guided. Or as if this was the proper way to construct meaning, to see the whole before examining the parts, to look to the ending, before the beginning is contemplated.

On some level, there remained a human named Aaron Pardell, a man who gibbered in stark, utter terror at the imminent loss of his humanity, revolted by the way his skin crawled inside and out in gentle reacquaintance with others.

*Other.*

The concept of one was comfortable, normal. There was only One.

*No*, he thought desperately. *He was something else—something different.* There were more. Gail . . . Malley . . . many upon many . . .

*Others?*

The concept of multiple intelligences, cooperating as a species, rocked the universe. It was absorbed, tasted, ultimately accepted as a premise.

Pardell suddenly found himself able to think again, if still disturbingly unaware of his body or location.

*Recognition . . . Welcome.*

Not those words, but those meanings—couched in what his mind read as emotion, but he knew was far more complex.

A sense of waiting . . . *expectation.*

The Earthers probably had university degrees in what to say to a nonhuman intelligence. It was, of course, too late to return to the *Seeker* and ask for a crash course. Pardell groped for a way to respond, then fastened on the recognition and turned it back, trying to ask: *Identity?*

*Surprise* . . . as if he should be aware. A tinge of *disappointment* . . . as if he'd failed, somehow.

Pardell struggled to control what he felt, knowing it was the medium they used and quite sure he was failing miserably to make any sense. Finally, he gave up and discovered himself simply . . . *afraid.* For himself. For Gail. For Thromberg.

*Reassurance* . . . but tangled in complex strands of *confusion.* A repeat of *recognition* and *welcome.* Then, slowly, a building pressure, as though the Other sought to push one concept, one framework, into Pardell's being, but his very humanness was an obstacle.

He hadn't been aware of breathing until now, when breathing became impossible.

*Terror!*

The pressure didn't stop, but abruptly shifted focus, as if an opening had been detected. Pardell gasped for air as *certainty* lanced through him.

There was . . . *identity.*

More . . . a name.

However the information became part of him, as his lungs refilled, Pardell knew beyond question that the Quill on this planet, every fragment and piece, comprised one—person.

*Susan Witts.*

His great-grandmother, who'd encased him in her alien flesh, now sent waves of *approval* and *love* crashing through his body.

He hoped he'd survive her joy at being known.

# Chapter 84

GAIL might not have Petra's training in meditation, but several hours spent sitting on a grassy hilltop—in a sealed, dark blue suit at the sun's zenith, no less—pretty much guaranteed she'd nod off no matter what the situation.

"I know you're awake. We've got your vitals right here on the board."

Grant could be annoyingly persistent in person—as a disembodied nag he was unendurable. Had Gail had something to throw at the 'bot, she would have done so long before now. "Fine. I'm awake," she admitted. "Nothing's changed, has it?"

She'd already looked longingly at Aaron; he was still entombed in strips of Quill. She didn't dare think of what might be happening to him. *He hadn't fallen.* Cold comfort, but better than the nightmares she was trying her best to forget. Either the Quill supported him, or he'd remained standing on his own. *Both implied he lived.*

"No, except the *Payette* is on her return run—successfully, I might add."

All Gail wanted in her life right now was the ability to rub the sleep out of her eyes. She settled for sitting up straight. "What did they find?"

"Quill. From the vids, identical to these. And you'll like this—once they'd grabbed a sample, they saw a statue as well."

"Susan Witts?"

"No. The statue was of a man. No baby. No outreaching arms." Grant paused, as if for effect—*or maybe*, Gail thought, *because he found what he had to say too incredible.* We've made a match to the face from your data—"

Gail went through the list of names and ship destinations in her mind. "Josh McNab."

"The terraformer whose genome was on the suits," Grant agreed. "Witts' second-in-command on the projects and definitely one of those who received her gift of a Quill fragment. If not for your recent encounter, we might have assumed this representation was simply the Quill's response to the suits. A reflex—not communication."

Gail stared at the innocent mound of Quill-laced grass demarking her permitted incursion on this world in no uncertain terms.

"Let me know anything further the *Payette* has to say about the Quill," Gail ordered without thinking, then she winced. "Please."

"Dr. Smith. Gail. I've every intention of sharing any findings with you. That's not the issue. I want you to use the pod and come back to the *Seeker!*" Grant sounded a little harried.

Gail sympathized, but said adamantly: "Not without Aaron. And short of growing wings, I've no idea how to get past them." She waved all around her.

"The *Payette* has functioning drop pods on board," Grant's voice was implacable. "And even if your distinguished staff refuses to recoat any of the anti-Quill suits to match this world, you did leave us one suit, you know."

Gail squeezed her eyelids shut for a moment. The headgear might be torture, but on the plus side she no longer had to govern her every expression. Tears eased the itching in her eyes, but made new, maddening trails down her cheeks. *Sooner or later, she'd take the damn thing off if only to rub her face.* She knew it. "I didn't leave you the suit," she informed Grant, not caring if her voice was huskier than normal. "Aaron insisted." A safety line—*old habit*, he'd told her.

"Wise man. I'm not asking your permission or cooperation, Dr. Smith. When the *Payette* achieves orbit, I'm coming down for both of you as soon as we can get a pod ready. Understood?"

"Copy that," Gail said wearily. "Keep an eye on Aaron while I freshen up, Commander."

She stood and went back to the *Athena*, ignoring the Quill, walking by the blankets where she and Aaron had done their earnest best to marry one another, their hearts touching, if not their hands.

Gail was inclined to be practical. If it took cooperating with the FDs to free Aaron from the Quill, she was ready to consider it.

If Grant thought she'd leave this world without Aaron, well, she planned to be ready for that eventuality, too.

# Chapter 85

"THEY *eloped*, young Hugh?"

Malley shrugged. "You can listen for yourself, if you wish." He looked down at what was in his hand. A portable comm link, similar to the one Grant wore in one ear except that this was slightly larger and came with a small disk attached. He'd seen the like before—the techs used them to listen to procedural instructions, play background music, or spread around jokes they'd rather not be caught saying out loud.

This one contained something quite different: recordings of Aaron and Gail's conversations from the *Athena* . . . and Rosalind's voice, which was why Malley had sought out the older 'sider.

He put his back against one of the privacy columns that formed a visual barrier between the front and back halves of the lounge, keeping his eyes on the screen. Nothing had changed in the past hours: Aaron remained entombed; Gail sat on the grass as close to him as the Quill would let her, when she wasn't getting supplies from the pod.

As far as he could tell, Rosalind hadn't looked at it once.

She took the offered recording from his hand, using her dexterous left fingers; they felt cold and hard against his palm. "So, young Hugh," Rosalind said, seeming amused. "Dr. Smith's assumption that she controls what reaches this ship is, let's say, naïve."

Malley nodded. "The commander could hear them on the planet, even before deploying his 'bot." He remembered the comm link Grant wore and how quickly the Earther had reacted to Aaron's encounter with the Quill. *Secrets within secrets.* This one had been discarded the moment the 'bot activated—the FDs piping through audio as well as vid. *If you counted their vows to each other as binding*—he'd no doubt Aaron did—the newly-weds' sliver of privacy was long gone.

Not that Malley had told anyone but Rosalind about the recordings made earlier—but Grant couldn't help but spread the information to those listening.

"Aaron—if he survives—will take this eloping business seriously," Rosalind said, confirming Malley's own thoughts, then surprised him by adding: "as will the Earther." She regarded the silent stationer with a wry twist to her lips. "What, young Hugh? You doubt her veracity? You think this merely a ruse to keep control of an impressionable man? I hadn't thought you such a cynic."

"I doubt everything about her." But Malley didn't put much conviction behind the words. How could he, having watched Gail's vigil on that blue-ceilinged hill? "She put him in danger . . ." He hesitated.

"And you wonder why I helped?" Rosalind finished perceptively. She took a seat at the nearest table, motioning him to do the same. Malley obeyed reluctantly. His entire body quivered with the need to do something active—an opportunity unlikely to arrive anytime soon.

"Frankly, yes."

She steepled her hands, fingers and paddles touching only at their tips. The paddles were stronger and cruder in motion; Malley remembered she was always careful when using them together—spare parts being impossible to find. "Gail Smith bought my cooperation initially by promising to prove to me that the Quill were the real reason we've been barred from the terraformed worlds—she also promised to show me how she planned to destroy these pests."

"Initially," Malley echoed. "There's been another bargain since?"

"Oh, yes," Rosalind said contentedly. "In return for my help reaching the planet, the good doctor has promised to arrange for my partners and me to return to Callisto, where we belong. It might take several months—but we've waited long enough. You and young Aaron would be welcome with us," she added. "Your skills are not inconsiderable."

"You helped her take Aaron—*there*—in order to buy a ticket home?" Malley heard his voice drop into full threat and didn't care. This was exactly why the station had unspoken rules against private deals with Earthers. Rosalind was worse than a traitor to Thromberg—she'd sold out her own for personal gain.

The 'sider was unperturbed—perhaps, having faced so many battles in her lifetime, one angry stationer, however large, couldn't disturb her calm. "You do want to go home, don't you?" she asked. "If not Callisto, then to your station?"

"I can't go home, can I?" Malley rejoined fiercely. "Ironic, isn't it? They think I've done what you have—sold out to the Earthers. I might as well kill myself and save my friends the trouble, as go back."

Rosalind snicked her fingers together. "Such passion, young Hugh. Really—you should learn to pay close attention to your elders. We might just know more than you do about life and its risks."

Malley closed his lips to stop his instant, hot-headed response. Instead, he found himself considering what Rosalind was—not just what she'd done. This woman had absolute control over the extreme fringe of the 'sider population, those spacers who'd never believed in integration with the station or forgiven the past. There'd been rumors she'd somehow blackmailed Thromberg and the Earthers in order to join this mission—no details. It was clear she'd bargained away Aaron's ship without a second thought; she'd done the same, now, with Aaron himself. "What do you know that I don't, Rosalind?" he asked, making the effort to bring his voice to something resembling level and polite.

"For one thing, you will be most welcome back on Thromberg—a hero's welcome, in fact—now that we have proof the Quill are as harmless as we've always said."

"Harmless?" Malley thrust his arm toward the screen. "You call that harmless?"

"What do you see there?" she countered. "What do you *think* you see? I'll tell you what's really there: young Aaron, frozen in one of his usual fits. The Earther, unharmed after hours spent with the Quill—"

"She's wearing a protective suit—" the stationer spat.

Rosalind laughed. "A protection the Earthers can't even explain to themselves? Smoke and mirrors, young Hugh. Nonsense to delay and confuse us so they could bring in their ships to blockade this system. I thought you were bright—don't you see it? Gail Smith is a genius, no doubt. She's tracked down the only world the Earthers missed keeping from us. But why? To seal this system before our people learn the truth. To keep it for Earth."

"The Quill are deadly," Malley ground through his teeth.

"Are they?" Rosalind's eyes gleamed and suddenly she pulled up the sleeve on her right arm, showing the metal cuff replacing her wrist, binding her robotic hand to the remaining flesh. "Before the accident on my ship, young Hugh, what do you think rode here most of my adult life?"

He stared at her, feeling as uneasy as if he stared into the dark maw of an air lock. "No . . ."

"Yes. My father may have been killed, but not before our family saved his beloved Quill. It would wrap around no one's arm but mine. My beloved Quill," her voice shook with emotion, then firmed. "Where's the proof, young Hugh? They brought Quill on this ship. Was anyone killed? Have you seen anyone die? Are there skeletons in the grass at Aaron's feet?"

*The worst thing was, she made sense of a kind.* Rosalind must have read something of his doubt; she went on, each word like a hammer: "This is economics, not science. They want to harvest the Quill for themselves—and keep this world from your people. Of course I helped Gail Smith. Her hopeless love for young Aaron gave me exactly what I was waiting for. What you and I have been waiting for . . ."

"And that is?"

"A demonstration. She's proof that people can survive on this world—and she very conveniently sent the blockade ships away on a fool's errand."

Malley felt the blood drain from his face as he looked at Rosalind and saw the triumph of a fanatic. "What have you done?" he almost whispered.

"I think everyone is about to find out." The 'sider gestured toward the entrance. Malley turned his head to see Grant, flanked by four FDs with their weapons out, a passage splitting through the stunned crowd as they came directly to his and Rosalind's table.

"You will thank me, young Hugh," Rosalind was saying confidently. *As if he was listening.* "You will be a hero."

Malley surged to his feet in time to meet Grant. "What's wrong?" he demanded. "What did she do?"

Grant's eyes were flint hard, his face a forbidding mask. He looked past Malley at Rosalind, then back to Malley. "We have upward of fifty starships on approach to this system—a system on no charts or records," the Earther stated, his voice edged with fury. "They claim to have been invited."

Rosalind continued to smile, her pale eyes shining with anticipation. "And so they were, Commander. Did you never think to ask how Dr. Smith calmed the panic on Thromberg? How she managed to talk Station Admin into patience? Quite simply, if bold even for her. She promised them this planet for a home."

"Once it was free of Quill," Grant bit off each word. "We don't know yet if we can remove them from a planet—let alone if we're dealing with another sentience! There are people on those ships, 'sider."

"Oh, yes," Rosalind answered, as cool as Grant was furious. "I daresay those ships are crowded to the point of risking life-support failure. Some will be tows and barges, barely capable of reliably harvesting ice and transporting cargo, let alone moving families. I seriously doubt there's an experienced crew on any—since 'siders have no interest in dirt. But you can't stop a migration, Commander, just by making the journey hazardous."

"Migration?" Forgetting her age and rank, forgetting everything but the faces of those he'd left—he'd thought *safely*—behind, Malley grabbed Rosalind's shoulders and yanked the 'sider up to face him. "Why now? Why didn't they wait until it was safe?"

"How did they know where to come?" Grant added, standing by Malley's shoulder as if he'd like to be the one holding her. "Dr. Smith wouldn't have told them—"

"Because," Rosalind said, her voice faintly surprised, as though they should have guessed. "When Dr. Reinsez had me find the coordinates for his patrol ships to come and blockade the system, I sent them to my people on Thromberg as well. And when Dr. Smith so conveniently cleared that blockade, I informed them the time to approach was now—or never."

Malley opened his hands, as if they might be contaminated by touching her. "You can't let them land," he said to Grant, looking past to the screen where fields of Quill rippled in moving air. "You have to stop them."

"With what?" Grant said savagely. "This ship? We're hours from full reconnection—and even if I leave the science sphere in orbit, what could the *Seeker* do on her own? This is a research vessel, Malley, not a warship."

*Warship?* Malley heard a small noise of satisfaction from Rosalind and, for a soul-shattering instant, he knew exactly what she was thinking—and couldn't help but think the same. The Earthers would do it again if they could . . . destroy any ship coming from the station, no matter who was on board. Only this time, the enemy had faces: Grant, Benton, Aisha . . .

And this time, those who would die weren't strangers from the past.

# Chapter 86

"REPEAT that?" Gail asked numbly, then said immediately: "No, don't bother. It sounded ridiculous enough the first time."

"Ridiculous or not, Dr. Smith, I'm looking at a tactical display showing me fifty-seven ships, most of which I wouldn't trust to haul waste from Deimos to Phobos. Two didn't even make it out of translight. They are incoming and very hard of hearing. I've talked to them. Your stationer's talked to them. Hell, I had Reinsez pretending to be the Chancellor of Titan U, and it didn't make any difference."

*Rosalind Fournier.* On some level, Gail approved—the move was worthy of herself. The 'sider had backed her into the ultimate corner: deliver on all promises at once . . .

*Or prove the Quill are deadly.*

Gail understood it was nothing personal. The 'sider was powered by her conviction that the menace was pretense. She believed all the cards were hers to play.

*In that,* Gail knew, *Rosalind was mistaken.*

Grant's voice rang in her ears. "Maybe you can talk sense into these people—at least have them hold at a distance—" It had to be her imagination putting the words: *We all volunteered* beneath his.

"Good idea," Gail said, her eyes never leaving Aaron. "Make sure you pipe me through as vid as well as audio. I want them all to see this."

"Of course," *Grant knew,* she realized, hearing acceptance heavy in his voice. "Let me know when you're ready, Dr. Smith."

A moment passed in silence. The wind pressed against her

side, ran off to chase grassy leaves around Aaron's waist, twirled once, then dashed away to wherever winds went. Gail had done her best not to move, suspecting the Quill were sensitive to any vibration traveling through the ground or air. Now, she stood, wincing at the burn in both feet—and all the way up her right leg—as nerves protested and circulation resumed. Flexing her toes in her boots helped, even though she couldn't feel them yet.

"Swing the 'bot to the other side of Aaron," she ordered. The 'bot moved as if her voice controlled it, stopping on the opposite side as if staring at Aaron's face.

Gail could only see his back, still coated in Quill. As the sun's rays had intensified during the course of the day, they'd grown darker, less colorful—perhaps injured by the light; perhaps protecting themselves from it. They hadn't moved either.

"We're relaying vid and audio to all of the ships—some might not have the equipment to receive both."

*The 'bot should have her in view.* Gail lifted her hand experimentally.

"Copy that," assured another voice—probably one of the deployment specialists, used to testing equipment.

"Good," Gail said. Now that all was ready, she found herself delaying to take a quick sip of body-warm water from the straw by her lips. *Pointless?* Perhaps. But she needed her best public voice—the one with total confidence and that hint of compassionate power. She'd practiced it enough.

"Greetings from Pardell's World," she began. "My name is Dr. Gail Veronika Ashton Smith—Pardell. I'm the senior scientist on this mission, in command of the Earth Research Council's Deep-Space Vessel *Seeker*." She doubted Grant would leap on the comm to argue the point. "You are invited to observe Trial Number Six A of our project to determine the safety of this world for human life."

With that, Gail disconnected the clasps holding the headgear of her suit to the neck ring and lifted it free of her head.

Her first thought, as she squinted in the direct sunlight, was how incredible it felt to have warm, fresh air playing against her cheeks. Her hair, sweat-soaked, began to dry at its ends almost immediately.

There wasn't a word from the comm, either from the 'bot's speakers or from those embedded in the suit. A measure of the man, that Grant didn't diminish this act with meaningless protest, that he left everything to her. She was grateful.

Unfortunately, Gail didn't want to die. She realized it with her next breath. *Stay calm, emotionless, cool as ice.*

It wasn't humanly possible, but she tried. And failed. She looked toward Aaron, as if he could help.

LOVE.

Gail began to sob helplessly. Hopeless, desperate, her completion, their loss—she moaned and dropped to her knees, feeling as if she was being torn apart. The headgear had dropped out of reach. *Was this what Aaron went through?* How had he endured . . . she pressed her hands against her skull, trying to keep it out . . .

LOVE surged again and crushed her into oblivion.

# Chapter 87

*L*OVE . . . ?

   A passing reflection. A dimpling of consciousness. Nothing more.

*DESPAIR!*

That which was Aaron Pardell writhed with the echo.

*Surprise* . . . as if he should be safe, unharmed. *Concern* . . .

Pardell found himself abruptly aware of his body, bound and motionless, every nerve ending on fire. He still couldn't see, but the impact of emotion was gone. *No. It wasn't gone.* He fought back the physical sensations and could feel something—someone—but the impression was fading . . .

*Gail?*

Something seemed to snap loose inside him. He lashed out with *terror . . . fury . . . dread . . .*

*LOVE . . . longing, hope, peace . . .* drove him back.

*LOVE.* It wasn't his. It belonged to Susan Witts. He shook free of confusion. Not his great-grandmother. Not *human*. It belonged to the Susan-Quill.

Suddenly, it was his. For an instant, he *was* the Susan-Quill, spread over rolling hills, in shadow and sun, near ocean and limits of desert—not the entire world. There were endings, places where he/she was not, but had been, or would be. At the same time, he/she *was* Susan Witts, mother of this world, nurturer and protector.

His partner in this union, his other self, was confused by his reaction to the natural way of things. He should detect the strange—the not-belonging. He should fear those who moved—those who ate.

And why did he not know safety lay within the barrier—the barrier that drove the strange away?

*Away?* Pardell lurched free. *Madness and death!* He sent the feelings as many ways as he could. Gail was almost gone. *DENIAL!*

*Confusion . . . doubt . . .*

He reached into depths he didn't know he possessed for the strength to make one last effort to communicate. He couldn't stop the Quill Effect. Only *she* had that power.

*Identity . . . Susan-Quill . . .* he sent, infusing the concept with singularity, uniqueness, the need to survive.

*Identitiy . . . Gail . . .* he sent, overlapping the two until they grew inseparable to his mind. As he weakened, despairing it had worked at all, or in time, all Pardell had left to send was LOVE . . .

And he feared it would kill Gail. . . .

# Chapter 88

**N**OT dead. Yet. *How very strange.*

"Dr. Smith. Can you hear me? Gail!"

*I hear you.* Funny how the words were there, just not coming out of her mouth. Bad words. Disobedient, contrary things. She laughed, and heard that sound.

*How very strange.*

"Gail. We're trying to get down there. Hold on. There's a chance we can get one of the station ships. Try not to move."

*Not moving.* That meant something. Gail rolled her head to one side, wincing as her skull wanted to come loose from her spine, and found herself staring at a maze of brown stems covered in oil. She sneezed at the musty smell. The grass? She'd been in this suit for over a day now. *Must be her.*

Gail laughed again, quite impressed by her reasoning ability. *Musty Gail. That's what happened in universities when your career was going nowhere. You went musty after a few years—like Manuel. Musty Manuel. They were a team.*

"Gail," the voice was growing rather distraught. *Not very professional*, Gail thought scornfully. *There were standards to uphold.* "Dr. Lynn wants me to tell you . . ." a pause, as though the voice consulted a list, ". . . your vitals indicate a conscious state, but you're in shock. Blood pressure's too low. Your pulse is thready. . . . Are you sure I should . . ." This in a different tone, as if the voice spoke to someone else.

The someone else spoke next, to her, a lilting, lovely voice, like raindrops collecting on lilacs. *Raindrops. She could use a bath.* "Gail. I want you to follow the seam down your right side until you feel the waist seam cross it. Do that for me, please."

*Why not?* Gail walked her fingers around and down, stopping at the raised area where the two seams overlapped.

"When you find the junction, Gail, press it as firmly as you can. Press it now, Gail. Now!"

*Why not?* Gail pressed, only to flinch as something stabbed her in the side. She must have made a sound of protest, for the voice said soothingly: "It's okay, Gail. It's a boost shot. It should get your metabolism closer to normal. Just relax. You gave us a scare, but you're going to be fine."

*What about the ships. Ships?* More bad words, hiding from her mouth. "Ships?" came out suddenly, surprising her. *Ships. Ships. Musty ships.*

The first voice came back: "Holding, Gail. You stopped them from trying to land. Let's hope long enough."

It made no sense, but every sense. Gail watched the oil near her face shimmer and move, then closed her eyes, disinterested.

*And so tired.*

# Chapter 89

"I'M just saying it would have been more convincing if she'd died." Malley wasn't in the habit of soft-pedaling the truth.

"You saw the monitors, Malley," Aisha protested. "She came close enough. I don't know what kept her alive, but it wasn't anything I'd trust my life to—would you?"

"As if I'd go down there." The stationer's neck muscles tightened in a defensive reflex. "Lucky for me, you don't have a suit big enough," he reminded the scientist, smugly pushing away any further thought of stepping on that ball of dirt—even if they had practiced it all week.

"And we don't have a ship to use—yet," reminded Grant, who settled his long body into the corner seat as though someone had melted his spine. He rubbed the heels of his hands into his eyes. "I'm not getting any cooperation from our new arrivals. No surprise."

Malley studied the Earther, then made a sound of disgust. "I thought Gail was the only one on boost," he accused. "You're not going to be good for much in a while."

Grant blinked bleary, red-rimmed eyes, but chuckled. "Your concern is noted, Stationer, but believe me—military issue is considerably more effective and reliable—"

"Not to mention costs your body more," Aisha said clinically, but not with disapproval. She showed no signs of fatigue, despite being up for over a day as well. When Malley had commented, she'd smiled at him and told him it was clean living. But she had to be wearing thin—they all were. Even the stationer could feel the acid building up in his muscles and aching through his bones.

What kept him from sleep was the sure knowledge that Gail and Aaron were going through worse.

Grant must have thought along the same lines, saying: "Anyway, I'm functional—let's hope the same for Dr. Smith."

They watched—it was all anyone could do for the pair on the planet until the arrival of the *Payette* or the patrol ships. None of Thromberg's adventurers had agreed to dock with the *Seeker* and offload passengers, so Grant could commandeer their ship. *To say the stationers viewed the mere suggestion as a trick was to put it mildly.* Like Grant, Malley hadn't been surprised.

What had been a surprise, and an unpleasant one, was how many he knew on those ships. They'd stripped Thromberg Station of anything remotely spaceworthy, crewed them with sympathetic stationers and 'siders—despite Rosalind's assertion, there'd been more than enough—and loaded up with first rounders and their families. Malley had forgotten the designation until hearing it again: First Round, the most cherished distinction among the stranded immies, those selected and trained to prepare their new home for the rest. Tough, smart, survival-oriented folks—few had died in the Ration Riots; rumor said they'd started the first, most deadly one. Time had been their true enemy, the oldest among them now so frail they had a special corner table at Sammie's, where they waited, gnarled hands curled around mugs, pale sunken eyes still challenging the future.

Amy Denery's father was a first rounder, so Syd and Amy could be out there. *Of course they were*, Malley thought despairingly. Amy'd never given up her dreams of a home, her hopes for a family. He tried not to think of other names, fearing the darkness now held pretty well everyone he knew or cared about—ready to snuff out their lives.

He tried not to think of his best friend, wrapped in Quill, or the small woman lying crumpled in the grass, helpless and totally alone.

"We do have some good news," Grant offered, as if his thoughts had been heavy as well. "The remaining expeditions succeeded in obtaining Quill fragments—no loss of life, no problems."

"Did they see statues, too?"

The commander slid down until his head rested on the back of the seat, eyes slitted as though he didn't dare close them completely or he might pass out—or miss something. "One each, just like here and just like the *Payette*. Strangest thing . . ." Before Malley could ask, Grant continued ". . . in every case, the Quill statue was a duplicate of the individual used to make the suit."

"Or a statue of the terraformer who brought the first Quill," Malley thought out loud. "More than recognition . . . worship of a founder or creator?"

Grant sighed. "The brains on the *Payette* and back on Earth can muddle through that knot. I'd rather not leap to any conclusions. We don't even know if the Quill think—yet. There's still the possibility all we've seen is an alien life-form's reaction to the information on the suits themselves. A reflex. Maybe if we used a suit with another genome—"

"Empty, I hope," Aisha said quickly. "What Gail went through—that's enough."

*Enough?* Malley repeated, but to himself. Everyone watching had realized what the Earther was doing the horrifying instant she'd removed her headgear: sacrificing herself to demonstrate the Quill Effect. She'd hoped her death live and on screen would turn back those from the station.

Gail Smith might be difficult, opinionated, self-centered, and several other things Malley didn't like—but he finally understood what Aaron had seen in her. *That didn't mean he was going to apologize*, Malley vowed to himself, hoping he'd get the chance to make that clear.

His mind replayed what Grant had just said, turned it over, examined it from another direction. "That experiment's done, Aisha," Malley concluded, feeling the snick of at least one piece of the puzzle. "If it was a reflex, we should have seen the Quill weaving statues of Aaron—or Gail, once her genome was revealed. But the Quill on this world keeps making Susan Witts. It's as though that identity matters to this Quill—why is another issue—" he said when Grant's eyes opened and the man prepared to argue.

"Let me talk it through," Malley urged, sensing he was on the track of something important. "What if the Quill on this world and the others somehow incorporated a human—template."

"What kind of template?" Aisha asked. "Physical appearance?"

"No, no. Not only appearance—what if the Quill intelligence has a human pattern to it—provided by the person who wore the fragment before it escaped and multiplied."

"So you're saying the Quill on this world *thinks* it's Susan Witts, the terraformer." Grant's lips twisted. "And you complained Dr. Smith's mind leaps around."

Malley refused to be distracted. "No. I'm saying we have a species which has never shown intelligence before—but now it does. How? Why? It didn't evolve that trait overnight. Maybe Gail's idea of a critical biomass or number of fragments is involved, but that doesn't take us from nonthinking to comprehensible, purposeful thought.

"We know they are biochemical mimics. What if they copy more? What if each Quill somehow copied a template for intelligence from the person who wore it? Then, regardless what on these worlds let them multiply, the result was an immense number of fragments that also incorporated that template." Malley found himself on his feet and sat down somewhat sheepishly. *Aaron was always after him for getting physical about his ideas.* "First contact, Commander Grant? What if it's multiple first contacts—a unique Quill entity on each of over a hundred worlds? They'd have thought processes as different from one another's as any two humans could be—while being as different from human as anyone could imagine."

"If that's true, if the Quill are becoming intelligent based on individual human models. . . . Oh, my God. Not McNab . . ." Aisha stopped, her voice shaking. Her dark eyes were wide, as if she'd seen a ghost.

Malley felt suddenly cold, all the fire of his ideas quenched. "One of the terraformers. What about him?"

"If McNab was the pattern for the intelligence of that Quill, what might we be dealing with?" Aisha said slowly. "Gail's research on McNab's descendants turned up an inheritable mental disorder. He didn't show symptoms, or he wouldn't have been put in charge of such a project, but three of his four sons required treatment for dementia—one found not guilty of the murder of his own children by virtue of insanity."

"Monsters in our own image? It wasn't bad enough for you that the Quill were deadly simply by existing? Listen, you two. All I wanted," Grant claimed, heels of his hands pressing into his eyes again, and sounding completely frustrated, "all I ever wanted, was to someday find another civilization—a civilization with people in it I could recognize, talk to—"

"Take out for a beer?" Malley suggested.

"Take out for a beer," Grant agreed, then smiled wistfully. "Sounds like a dream, doesn't it?"

Aisha covered Grant's hand with hers. "You aren't the only dreamer, Commander."

"In the meantime," Malley said, "look on the bright side—if I'm right, it could mean the Quill think like we do. That's the first step in being able to communicate with one another, right? And they don't drink, which saves you money."

Grant's appreciative chuckle died as one of his FDs came running up to their corner. "Commander," the woman said urgently. "Something's happening on the planet."

# Chapter 90

"GAIL . . . Gail."

*At the rate her name was being abused*, Gail grumbled to herself, *she should have it changed*. This couldn't be morning. She'd barely fallen asleep. The nagging someone could just go away. There were more than ten in the science sphere alone who could handle any minor emergencies, and likely major ones. *Wake them up.*

*Start with Sazaad.*

"Gail! Something's happening to Pardell."

*Aaron?*

Gail wasn't sure which came first: the flood of memory—*she'd almost died*—or the burst of energy driving her to her knees and then to a shaky stand.

*Aaron!* He was as she'd last seen him—or couldn't see him. A man-shaped statue of Quill and grass, gripped by another, facing the distant mountains.

*No . . . wait.* Nearly imperceptibly at first, then more quickly, Quill fragments were slipping from his head, neck, and shoulders, exposing the black of his hair, the faded, almost-gray of his stationer tunic. As they left, they dislodged others below, until the whole mass appeared to flow down his body.

"We can see his face, Gail," this in Tobo's excited voice. "His eyes are—closed. No. They're open. Looks like he's unconscious, but breathing. Do you hear me? He's alive!"

*Of course he was alive*, Gail thought, knowing she hadn't dared doubt it.

In the blink of an eye, the shimmer of movement was over. Aaron's head and shoulders had been freed, nothing more.

*Why?*

Once she was convinced the Quill had finished whatever they—or it—was doing, Gail took a cautious step forward, then waited for the wall to rebuild to block her way.

The grass stayed quiescent.

She took another step, feeling exposed without her headgear and fragile without the full protection of the suit. *Survived thus far,* she reminded herself.

*No reaction.* She lifted her left foot to avoid stepping directly on the mound of Quill-coated grass marking where the wall had been. Her heart began pounding—her next step had to be on Quill, unless they conveniently moved out of her way.

They didn't. She gingerly put down her foot, and a fragment climbed her leg.

"Gail—are you all right? Should you be moving?"

"Hello, Commander," she said, more or less normally. "As you can see, we're making some progress." Another step, another Quill hitchhiker. She continued, walking slowly and more-or-less steadily toward Aaron, carrying her pair of Quill with her. There wasn't any detectable sensation to having them on her legs, just as Dafoe and Aaron had reported. But her heart wouldn't settle down. She knew what to expect now. The Quill Effect.

Who'd ever sung that love could kill—they'd been right.

*So why wasn't she dead?*

She kept moving until she was directly behind the Quill's original statue, finding the head low enough that she could see over it to Aaron's face. Gail sagged with relief. *He wasn't dead.*

Then she realized she couldn't tell if what he was—was alive.

His features weren't slack and expressionless, as they'd been during his coma on the *Seeker.* Now, they were in constant motion, eyes blinking, lips working, as if every muscle of his face was contracting at random. A trail of saliva meandered from the right corner of his mouth to his chin. The marks of dried tears coursed over each cheek. He'd bitten through his lower lip more than once. The blood had dried.

*It was the face of madness.*

Gail didn't hesitate. She charged through the Quill's version of Susan Witts, scattering it to the ground in her frantic drive to reach Aaron, to tear the Quill from his body and free him. But Aaron's body spasmed at her first touch, his mouth opening into a soundless howl of pain. She staggered back, horrified, her gloved hands out as if he could see that plea for forgiveness.

*How could she have forgotten?*

The 'bot gained a voice. "Gail. There are remote handling arms in the pod."

She didn't bother answering, already hurrying back toward the tiny ship. Suddenly, the Quill wall rose to block her path, completely encircling her, this time within a space including Aaron.

"To keep me here?" she wondered out loud, fighting to stay calm, to think. "Is that it? Did you think I was going to leave? I wouldn't leave him."

The wall settled back to a mound of disturbed grass.

*Communication . . . or coincidence?* "This is ridiculous," Gail muttered once more, taking a few, ragged breaths, trying to calm herself She walked back to Aaron, this time keeping her distance. Trying not to let his ever-moving face disturb her, she said gently but urgently: "Aaron. Can you hear me? I need to know if you are . . . if you are in there. If you are still with me." *Or if I'm alone*, she wailed to herself. "Can you talk to me?" Her voice began to shake; she couldn't steady it. "Please, Aaron. Try to say something to me—anything! Tell me I was a fool to bring us here. Tell me I was wrong."

The flickering of his eyelids slowed. Gail held her breath as his eyes stopped dancing in their sockets to look outward—at her. There was abrupt sense to their gaze, as if a switch had been thrown inside his head. Muscles continued to twitch along his jaw, forehead, and cheeks, but his tongue—scored a savage red with bites—recovered the saliva from the corner of his mouth as it closed. "That's it, Aaron," she urged, guessing this was a battle being fought, that he was struggling to regain control of his own body. *From whom?* "Please. Come back to me. Talk to me. I have to hear your voice. Please. Husband."

His head lolled to one side then the other. Suddenly, it was up straight again and Aaron's eyes burned into hers. "Why—why did you—?"

His voice, thick and blurred as it was, weakened her knees.

Gail heaved a sigh of relief, even though she knew what he asked. "There wasn't a choice. We have visitors, Aaron. From Thromberg. They wouldn't believe it was dangerous—they were going to land—I—" Gail couldn't make herself finish. The memory was too terrifying. She could see some of that terror in his face, in the way his throat worked as if trying to swallow bile. *Had he felt what she'd felt?*

"The ships are safe, for now. Something saved me—you?" she wondered instead, using one hand to keep a freshening wind from tossing her hair into her eyes. "What's happening here, Aaron? What are the Quill doing to you? Are you all right?"

". . . drink."

Gail fumbled in her suit's pocket, pulling free the water container she'd tucked in there an eternity ago. She gave it a quick shake, hoping there was something left. About a third.

She approached him very carefully this time, having to climb what was now almost a ramp. The Quill had made themselves and the grass into a base that tapered down and out from Aaron's chest and arms. *A support*, she suddenly realized, faintly reassured they'd done this much for his comfort. Of course, it was also an effective means of imprisonment. Gail's hands wanted to tremble as she held the straw to his lips. She didn't permit it.

From his expression, the tepid liquid was pure elixir, but Aaron didn't waste time enjoying it. After two swallows, he demanded, in a much clearer voice: "Who's on the ships?"

*Not, "what do they want,"* Gail noticed. Aaron knew his people, well enough. "*Seeker*," she said slightly louder, her eyes never leaving his. She didn't bother telling him it had been Grant's move to establish contact, not hers. At this point, it hardly mattered. "Any word on who we're dealing with out there?"

"Malley said they're 'first rounders' and their families," came an immediate response. Aaron looked grim, but unsurprised. "How are you, Aaron?" Grant continued. "Had us worried."

Wonder of wonders, Aaron's damaged mouth assayed a grin. "A little stuck, at the moment."

"I can get the remote—" Gail began, only to watch the Quill reweave their wall. "Aaron—do they understand what I'm saying?" she asked incredulously.

"Not exactly," he said and shook his head gingerly, as if testing the control he'd regained over his neck and shoulders. "I understand you and our—hostess—is aware of what I understand. She doesn't get it all." Aaron winced and Gail made an involuntary sound of protest. He smiled faintly at her in reassurance. "Susan's efforts to comprehend aren't very comfortable."

"Susan?" It was Grant, sounding numb even though broadcast. "The Quill uses a name? Or did you name it?"

Aaron gave another wince, deeper, more pained.

"Commander," Gail said quickly. "No questions."

"I see it. Sorry, Aaron. Tell us what you can."

Aaron looked grateful. "I'll do my best, Gail, Commander. There aren't words—she doesn't speak to me, as such—but there are . . . let's say areas of convergence, where our reactions to things are similar. The rest I can't begin to comprehend." Gail nodded encouragement, sinking down in the grass in front of him to listen, ignoring the shimmer of Quill on her legs. She drank in every word, hoping for some clue how to help him.

It was easier than ignoring how Aaron remained locked in place, wounded, and beyond her reach—for now.

"There is one entity here, on this world," he began, every word a struggle. "One Quill, comprised of all the fragments. Including me," he said with what looked like the memory of some horror, "—that's why I couldn't talk to you before—for the first while, she collected me into the whole and I couldn't break free or make her understand. What's in my skin . . . that was the link . . . I've Quill growing through my skin . . ." He stopped.

"It's okay," Gail said, seeing the wildness in his eyes. "I'm here, Aaron. Go on."

"Yes. Of course." Aaron steadied himself "She had—trouble—comprehending me as something separate. I think . . . no, I'm sure she's grasped the concept now. It gave her joy, to learn she wasn't solitary."

"Joy?" Surprised by the word, Gail looked around at the wind-ruffled grass being ridden by Quill.

"What we exchange with one another is in the forms of feelings," Aaron explained. "I realize there's no way to tell if any of our emotions mean the same to the Quill. Likely they don't . . . but I have no other frame of reference. It felt to me like joy." He looked weary, all of a sudden. "I think, if I'd had more time, I might have been able to get across the idea that there were more like me, not Quill, not dangerous. But she didn't realize that before you took off the headgear, Gail. I'm so sorry."

Gail said with what she thought commendable calm under the circumstances: "It's not your fault she tried to kill me."

Aaron winced again. When he went on, his voice was strained—as if he fought to keep using it. "I know. You were right about the Quill Effect. Susan, the Quill—she has a fear of organisms who move . . . a fear so deep and potent it's more instinct than thought. When she couldn't recognize you, she reacted to defend herself. We had a little—disagreement about that."

"You saved my life," Gail acknowledged softly. "I know that."

Unsmiling, he shook his head. "She saved your life. The best I could do was try to explain what you were—that you were an entity like me—that you were—important. I don't know if any of it got through. It seemed to make the greatest difference when I told her you'd die."

"She didn't know? That the Quill Effect—" now Gail had to force words out but continued, "—that it kills people?"

"No. Her intention was defense. She isn't hostile. She wanted to drive you away, to remove the threat of your attention, not you. I'm not sure of everything—it was a confusion of dark feelings, as if even the Quill didn't have a framework to understand her reaction. But she had difficulty believing me when I said you were . . . dying. That she was a killer. She was unhappy." He stopped, as though gathering his strength. "I don't know how much control she has over the reflex." The words were a warning. *He knew they were being overheard*, Gail thought with approval. "For now, for you, she's made the effort to accept your—identity."

"If she's so benign," Gail told him, "have her let you go. You need medical treatment—you must be starving."

Aaron seemed to look inward. "I'm not hungry," he assured her, sounding perplexed. "I should be, shouldn't I? My mouth was dry, before. But I'm not thirsty. I think she's caring for me somehow, through my skin."

Gail studied the Quill surrounding Aaron with scientific detachment. *Easier, now that she could hear his voice, see his face.* They were most dense around those areas where his skin bore the strange, gold veins. "That's good to hear," she said neutrally, while her mind fought against terrible possibilities, while she tried not to envision new Quill penetrating his human tissues, meeting up with their alien kin, forming new and perhaps irrevocable links through Aaron's flesh.

"Don't be afraid," he said. She met his eyes, saw understanding in them. And a hint of his own fear.

"Reading my emotions?" she asked archly. "Doesn't seem fair, husband."

The word brought down the corners of his mouth, turned the look in his eyes into something desperate. "About our vows—"

"Don't even think it, Aaron Pardell," Gail said sternly, wagging a finger at him. *Words weren't enough.* She looked at the glove on her hand and took it off impatiently, tossing it to the ground. The other followed. Then, deliberately, she laid her bare hands on the bent grass by her legs. "I've no intention of letting you off the hook."

A Quill poured itself up her left wrist, wrapping around like a bracelet. *Gorgeous color*, Gail thought, licking her lips, *if a bit gaudy for regular wear.* The fragment had no detectable weight. She touched it with a finger. Dry—powdery, almost. *How very odd.* She felt *something*. A . . . tranquillity, as if some of her anxiety and stress was *leaving*—no, as if whatever self-control she had left was being reinforced somehow. Gail took a deep, almost relaxed breath, understanding a great deal more now.

"What do you think you're doing?" The first words out of Grant after all this time were predictably harsh.

"What I'm here to do, Commander," Gail informed him calmly. "Experiment. Aaron? Did anything change?"

"Great-grandmother approves," he said in a funny tone. *Distracted*, she decided. There must be something going on within the Quill.

*Great-grandmother?* Gail didn't like the sound of that. *The letters. Had giving them to Aaron been a mistake? Was he confusing the voice from the past with the present?* She stood, staring into his puzzled, almost-green eyes, and said firmly. "Susan

Witts died before you were born, Aaron. Don't let the Quill confuse you."

Aaron's cut lips tightened, and he nodded. "It's hard," he admitted. "I'm at fault, not Susan—the Quill. It's not as though she's trying to be a specific person. It's as if she uses that sense of identity as a paradigm. It lets her interact with me—maybe even to organize her thoughts into ways I can comprehend. When she's happy with me," his face softened, "I can't help but feel it's real, that she cares."

"Sorry to interrupt, Aaron," Grant's voice intruded. "Dr. Smith, the ships with the other Quill fragments are now in-system. The first will dock with *Seeker* within the hour. How do you want us to proceed?"

"As planned. We still need to do the analysis—to know if this Quill—if *Susan*—is a unique phenomenon. Get me the results as soon as possible."

"How do you want the results?"

Gail understood what Grant didn't want Aaron, and Susan, to overhear—did she want him to rush down in the *Payette*'s pod? No doubt as to Grant's preference—or that of his superiors. He was treading a fine line, trying to give her as much control as possible. She turned to look at the 'bot, and shook her head very slightly. "That's going to depend on preliminary findings, Commander," she cautioned. "We don't want to disrupt the progress being made down here. Keep me posted, please."

"Copy that."

"So, husband," Gail said, turning back to face him, trying not to see his living prison. "What should we do next?"

# Chapter 91

*N*EXT? *He wanted to be free!*

Pardell fought himself, as well as the surge of *unhappiness* from the Susan-Quill. Gail's fear was all too accurate. He didn't need to look down to see the blurring of any physical distinction between Aaron Pardell the Human and the organized mass of Susan's fragments. Gail had tried to pull him loose. Even with the handling arms that would allow her to touch him, it wasn't going to be that easy.

If it could be done at all.

*Maybe it was for the best*, the young 'sider tried to convince himself, gazing helplessly into her worn, beautiful face, past the calm demeanor of a scientist to her anguish at seeing him like this. He didn't doubt Gail's devotion—her love. It mirrored his own, as if they were two halves of what should be one. But if he was truly trapped within the Quill forever, well, she'd have to move on. . . .

*Gail Smith? Be sensible and abandon him?* Pardell stopped and gave himself a mental shake, feeling an easing of the despondency he'd felt—and inadvertently sent through to the Susan-Quill. He could hear Malley now . . . 'Aaron, my friend, there's so much you don't know about women.' *He knew enough about this one.*

"We need to get rid of this barrier," he said out loud, gaining a relieved flash of blue eyes. *They were meant to be seen in sunlight*, Pardell decided possessively, as was her golden hair. "Walk to the pod and tell me what you plan to do. I'll see if I can—translate."

Gail nodded, announcing in a clear, ringing voice: "I'm going to the *Athena* for some supplies. You need a hat and more water, for starters. I'd like to change." This with a familiar exasperation, as if Gail disliked justifying herself even in these circumstances. She retrieved her gloves and the headgear as she walked toward the pod with determined, quick strides.

*So much courage.* Pardell's thoughts flashed to the stationers watching through the *Seeker*'s vid feed. *Utter fools*, he raged inwardly. *They'd better believe what Gail had tried to prove to them—with her life.* Like Malley, he could name most of those likely to be there, if not all. None of the first rounders had been stranded to live Outside—Raner had said it was because they'd never lost hope and tried to run home with the rest. *If so*, Pardell thought with a sudden chill, *they'd be all the more willing to die to set foot here.*

They didn't have much time.

*Dread* . . . slithered up his spine and along every nerve—an ominous darkness. It wasn't based on his thoughts, so Pardell could only guess at why. Did the Susan-Quill dread the presence of more humans? As a threat—or because she feared causing more death?

Or was he completely wrong? Could she dread the concept of time itself? That it had limits within his conception, and now hers? He couldn't be sure and didn't dare interact more deeply to find out. He was learning not to become absorbed in the Susan-Quill's reactions, but it was agonizingly difficult. Merely noticing them threatened his sense of self. *Having Gail here, with him*, he told himself, *was like a tether holding him from that void.*

She'd walked out of his sight, but he could hear the reassuring sound of her voice as she called out: "Aaron, she's not letting me pass."

"Grant," he said. "Can you move the 'bot in front of me? Thanks. A bit left. Up. There." With a sense of déjà vu, Pardell found himself staring into the gleaming lenses of the dark little hoverbot. This time, he used their reflective surfaces to see over his own shoulder, to where Gail stood, more-or-less patiently, in front of a stubborn wall of grass. "Wait," he told her.

*Need* . . . Pardell concentrated on the dryness of his mouth, pushing his swollen, aching tongue against lips that were cracking where they weren't already cut. *Trust* . . . he projected as he looked at the image of Gail's small form in the 'bot's surface.

A fragment slithered inside his mouth before he could close it. Pardell struggled not to gag as it filled the back of his throat, fought not to scream at the thought of the Quill penetrating the inside of his body through that opening. Before fear overwhelmed him, the fragment slid out again, as if finished exploring.

"It's okay now, Aaron!"

"Oh, good," he said weakly, witnessing the collapse of the Quill wall in the reflection.

Then Pardell closed his lips firmly—in case great-grandmother became curious again.

# Chapter 92

CURIOSITY warred with worry. Gail pushed both aside as she hurried to take advantage of Aaron's apparent truce with his—friend? *What was the relationship?* she wondered, stripping out of the foul suit as quickly as possible, beyond caring who saw her skin or witnessed the indignity of unplumbing herself.

*What did the Quill gain from infusing itself with a human? What impulse had sent fragments into Aaron as a newborn?*

It wasn't instinct. The Quill riding her legs had dropped off before she'd set foot on the ramp. The one on her wrist had showed no sign of wanting to burrow under her skin. She'd experimented: she could unwrap and hold it. The fragment simply rewound itself over her arm the moment she released it. Despite feeling a new reluctance to give up its comfort, Gail had no difficulty coaxing it to leave her for the grass.

*What was different about Aaron?*

She was missing something—something fundamental about the Quill and its environment. The Quill was alien here, yet it must be reacting to them and to this world as it would to its home. The clues were here.

After the briefest—and utterly blissful—effort to clean herself, Gail pulled on a plain pair of coveralls and stuffed the pockets with ration tubes and water containers. She yanked out the sled and dumped the monitoring equipment from it without apology to anyone spying. It was the work of a few minutes to load it with all the blankets and protective gear she could find. It might be early summer, but at this altitude and with no shelter from the wind, it could be a cold night.

*And a dark one.* On that thought, Gail went back and found

as many portable light sources as she could, adding them to her pile.

When Gail was satisfied she'd scoured everything useful, she dropped into the pilot's chair and reactivated the remote control system. The *Athena* could now be operated from the *Seeker*—allowing its eventual retrieval, if no one was left to fly it.

Or a very quick retrieval, if she was dragging Aaron inside on the sled.

She was about to leave, when a small flashing light on the comm board caught her attention.

*Message waiting . . .*

"Another drink?"

"Maybe in a while, thanks," Aaron responded. The hat—technically a piece of blanket material Gail had cut into a triangle—drooped on either side of his head as he spoke. He'd appreciated it—especially as the sun dropped low on the horizon and the air immediately took a chill. They were both used to a more regulated climate.

Gail wished he could turn around and see his first sunset. The last rays were torching the river below the hills and igniting the clouds spired to the south. The lighting had also turned the grass pink, rather than green/brown. A temporary change, as the dimming encouraged the Quill to slip farther up each stalk, adding their purples, reds, and golds to the landscape.

The hat, and drinks she suspected Aaron accepted more to make her feel better than because he needed them, were the only comforts she'd been able to offer. He claimed to be warm enough. The woven grass would be insulating, although Gail had concerns about his circulation.

"You sure you want to sleep there?"

Gail chuckled, busy creating a layer of blankets for herself "Did I ever tell you I used to camp every summer as a kid? This is great. A little hard," she thumped the dried soil beneath her with one foot, "but that's good for the back."

A whirlwind of activity began a few meters away. Gail stared as grass bent and broke, then seemed to drag itself like a beast of straw toward her. Before she could do more than say, "Oh . . ." the mass settled into a pile beside her blankets. The

Quill in the mass slithered into the soil and away. "Thank you," Gail said as calmly as possible.

The Susan-Quill, as Aaron referred to it/her, was becoming capable of acting appropriately—even generously—on some understandings. Frustratingly, these usually involved needs or wants—as if its intelligence favored those ideas over others. Aaron assumed this was due to the template of Susan Witts, his great-grandmother.

Gail wasn't so sure. She was beginning to grasp when they were up against something more alien. To her, this was one of those somethings. She accepted the gift of the bedding material, but she reserved judgment on the reason.

She curled up inside the blankets, not needing to feign exhaustion—the boost shot was taking its toll as well as all else. "I'll be here, Aaron," she promised, finding the comfort of lying down almost painful. "Call if you need me, or if anything changes. Grant will have people monitoring us through 'Bob,' there." Gail had nicknamed the 'bot; only fitting—it represented a visitor, in a sense. Aaron hadn't questioned her choice of "Bob" beyond a raised brow. She hadn't bothered to explain, but it made the exposed hillside seem friendlier, less alien-infested, to name the sophisticated machine after the smelly, grouchy old uncle whose stories had kept her entertained so long ago.

"Good night, wife," Aaron said softly. She felt tears come to her eyes and didn't let him see—just blew a theatrical kiss toward his silhouette before tucking herself under the top blanket.

Once there, she didn't waste any time bringing out the disk containing whatever message had waited for her inside the *Athena*, slipping it into a small reader whose light Gail hoped wouldn't show beyond the blanket. It wasn't Aaron's attention she avoided, but the unknown watchers represented by "Bob."

She read quickly. Then again, more slowly.

It was from Aisha. Temujin had performed his customary sleight-of-hand to get it to her without going through the FDs. Her scientists might be trusting sorts, but recent events were doubtless making even them uneasy.

Once the Quill fragment had been safely contained—by having Dafoe use the protective suit to simply walk into the lab and put their "guest" into another container, the teams had gone straight back to work. *There was a lot to be said for the inertia of research*, Gail told herself with a smile. Through everything else, they'd kept to their list of analyses and experiments.

And results were already pouring in—

First, and as predicted, biochemical analysis of the exterior of Quill produced results consistent with bluegrass, not only in its DNA, but other molecules as well. Ideal camouflage, if you were hiding from sensors—or something that searched by taste. The interior was alien enough to completely confound their machines.

Sazaad's report—typically self-congratulatory—was a little late to be useful. Thanks to Aaron, Gail had already confirmed her suspicions that the Quill interacted on a level which tapped into what humans experienced as emotion. She moved past his list of suggested commercial applications to the next report.

*Aisha's.* Opposite to Sazaad in approach and assumption, the biologist had included the raw data as well as her conclusions. Gail didn't bother with the former, not when the latter made such sense to her. The missing *something*.

The wind picked up, finding a tiny opening by her feet. Gail used her toes to fold over the blanket, less worried about the cold than a curious Quill fragment. Aaron had told her how the Susan-Quill wasn't always aware of the impact of her intrusions.

Curiosity. *How much of that was the original Quill and how much the human?*

Among Aisha's findings: the Quill lived on the grass because they had to—they were symbionts, taking a share of the abundant energy harvested from sunlight by the plant's chloroplasts, in return—well, Aisha hadn't been sure what benefit the grass experienced, but she felt there had to be one or more. Wherever the grass on Pardell's World was exceptionally lush and healthy, it contained Quill. In Terran ecosystems, a symbiont might have antibacterial properties, perhaps grant protection from fungi. In the case of the Quill? Difficult to determine the partnership's parameters, when one of the symbionts had evolved . . . elsewhere. For all they knew, on the Quill's homeworld plants competed to attract Quill of their own. Gail examined the premise thoughtfully.

More significantly, Aisha had had some growth models run by her team's population dynamics expert. It looked as though the terraformers' very choice of seed species had been their downfall.

Gail closed her eyes and tried to imagine what it had been like—the rain of seeds from the shuttles landing on the vast, waiting expanse of prepared soil, bouncing, lodging in every crevice. The terraformer, perhaps almost forgetting the Quill on his or her wrist—beyond enjoying its soothing effect—walking out to inspect the first sprouts of green after the obedient rains.

The Quill fragment, sensing the first appropriate partner since being taken from its homeworld, flows from wrist to soil before the human can stop it.

Did the terraformer even hunt for it? Futile. And how many did as Susan Witts and simply discard their Quill, confident the organisms would die?

*Instead, how quickly did the fragment multiply and spread?* The loss of all human life on the terraformed worlds had come before the grasses had set their first seeds. Aisha's modeler had a chilling conclusion. The fragment was morphically uniform, simple at the macro level. It likely reproduced by multiple fission—its strength was in numbers, after all. Given an entire planet that was basically a monoculture of a suitable partner? The Quill had virtually exploded over their new homes. How many had been needed before the Quill Effect had been deadly? The calculation was there—less than she'd expected. It didn't matter now.

*What had been created that day?* Gail asked herself sleepily. Something unintended and of dreadful consequence—but was it evil? Something alien and new—but was it merely the stranger's face before being introduced?

She fell into dreams of coexistence that faded into night-mares of being imprisoned by stalks of dying grass.

*A whistle?* Gail dug her way free of blankets and straw, not sure what she'd heard but recognizing a summons. "Aaron!" she called immediately.

"You were snoring," he said with reassuring levity. Gail climbed to her feet, pulling what she hoped were blades of grass and not Quill bits from her hair. "And I missed you. How many hours of sleep do you need? It's almost dawn."

*Almost being the word.* She walked over to him, stretching as she went, peering at the glow behind the mountains—its light insufficient to reveal color, although one of the paired moons helped. "Implying you didn't sleep at all," she mock-scolded.

"I don't need much," Aaron reminded her. His hat had fallen or been blown off. Gail went in search of it; the exposure to yesterday's sun had already burned his nose and forehead. "Here," she said, taking her time close to him, letting herself bask in the warmth of his smile.

"I watched the stars. They jiggled."

"Twinkled," Gail corrected.

"Explaining much about a certain rhyme which always puzzled me," the 'sider said with a laugh, then grew serious. "Susan and I had—well, I think it was a conversation. She's quick to learn. Quicker than I am."

"What did you talk about?" Gail asked, waving cheerfully at Bob as she grabbed a ration tube out of the pack on the sled. *Amazing what even a partial night of sleep—despite the dreams—could do.* She patted the gear. It might be lonely on Pardell's World, but camping out was easier without flies or mice.

He accepted a squirt from the tube with a nod of thanks. The Quill might be sustaining him, but the idea wasn't comforting either of them. "I was trying to convey how we—humans—are independent beings, but work together in a society. The concept of identity, of oneness." He hesitated. "It seemed a place to start talking about living together. Coexisting."

Gail swallowed her own share thoughtfully. *Coexisting?* This from the 'sider who'd wanted the Quill eradicated from his people's worlds—who was, at the very least, being forced into the role of diplomat by both sides. *Perhaps*, she thought, *this was more 'sider philosophy: share and move on, survive together or not at all.*

"How frank can I be, Aaron?" she asked bluntly. "Will it hurt you if Susan objects to something I say?"

"She's become quite good at sparing me the worst of her reaction." Calm words, but Aaron looked unhappy, as if he'd whistled her awake because he'd made some kind of wonderful discovery or pact—and now doubted she'd be pleased.

Gail pretended she hadn't noticed. "So, did Susan grasp this idea? It must have been difficult to express."

"I found it difficult—she didn't. There's a similar concept in her nature . . . an awareness of multiplicity. I couldn't make sense of it until I began thinking of music."

"Music?" Gail glanced at the Quill now rising up the stalks on all sides. They must spend the hours of true darkness in the soil. "Does she hear?"

"No. Her fragments sense vibrations and movement, but not sound as we do. But that's not what I meant—her conceptualization reminded me of music. It contains an awareness that existence can consist of different parts in combination. Like the way a group of singers can sing different keys but together produce one unique note."

"Harmony."

"Or not. Right now, she feels great loneliness, as though she is only one, from one, like a single string being plucked over and over. There aren't other 'sounds' in her consciousness. I think that's why she felt such joy to learn I was something separate—but it hasn't worked, Gail. I'm not distinct enough to 'sing' with her, maybe because I'm—part of her."

"What about me?"

"You aren't Quill. She longs for—needs—more Quill, but somehow I don't believe she means more of her own fragments. So I thought, maybe there's more than one 'sound' of Quill—or more than one entity—on her homeworld." Aaron nodded his head in enthusiasm. "It made it easier to help her understand there can be more than one intelligence in a place, and those intelligences can work to a common goal. A good start, don't you think?"

Gail stared into the distance, her gaze caught by a beam of sunlight as it broke over the mountains, streaking living green down the hillsides.

"Gail?" Aaron sounded a little hurt, as though she should have responded to his accomplishment.

*He was right*—but she held up her hand for patience; she

dared not disturb the thought slipping into her mind like that beam of light.

What was thought . . . how did it move through a mind, a consciousness? What made it possible for an organism like Susan-Quill to think, but not the grass? *What if* . . . Gail's lips parted . . . *what if different Quill fragments produced their defensive Effect at slightly different 'frequencies?'* What if those frequencies normally interfered with one another, dampening the Effect, reducing it in strength and distance? It would be reasonable, possibly essential, in order for the different Quill to react to local situations. But then, the Quill Effect couldn't be a carrier of thought—it would be like a jumble of white noise.

She looked out at one Quill, all its parts operating at one unique frequency, all its parts able to produce the same Effect at the same time. *Thought?* Nothing would stop it traveling around the planet and back—nothing would interfere with it. Given a conceptual model, such as a human host—perhaps Quill intelligence had been—inevitable.

*As was something else*, Gail realized with a shock. "Aaron, from what you're saying . . . I believe Susan is able to think for the same reason her natural defense has turned deadly," Gail whispered. "It's being the only Quill of her type here. It's not normal for her kind. On some level, she knows it."

"Gail, you're frightening her."

She turned to look at Aaron. His face was troubled, flashing between fear and determination. *Was she witnessing a conversation based in emotional parameters?* "I'm sorry, Susan," she said quietly. "I am, like Aaron, trying to understand you. Part of that understanding is how you came to be."

His face subsided into something more like melancholy. Gail decided it was probably a shared feeling. Could Aaron see the deeper possibilities in what she'd said? He'd confessed he wasn't as good as Susan in keeping his reactions to himself

Gail didn't know if Aaron or Susan saw the full consequences. With Bob hovering nearby, she wasn't about to ask. They were the only two humans on this planet, but had never been less alone. Hundreds, millions, could be listening to every word—possibly as far away as Sol System and Titan. For all she knew, they could be on the evening news.

First contact? Who was she kidding? *They'd be the* only *news.*

And of all of those listening—would any hesitate if they reached the same conclusion she had?

Gail's mind felt as though it was on fire. If there were other Quill here, different Quill, there would no longer be a single Quill entity—*and no deadly Quill Effect.*

The flip side of the coin?

There would no longer be a Quill entity capable of thought. *The Susan-Quill would die.*

"What the hell is that?"

Gail, shaken from her dark thoughts by that shout, looked at Aaron in time to see the alarmed expression on his face turn to dread. He swung his head as far around as he could to follow a blaze of light across the dawn sky. She watched with him, as the light turned in midair to become a focused cone directed downward.

"Dr. Smith! Dr. Smith!" From the 'bot, Grant's voice yelled, full volume and desperate. "We have an unauthorized landing. A station ship, the *Mississauga*, slipped past the patrol—they claim to be out of fuel. Can Aaron protect them from the Quill?"

"I don't know!" that worthy said before closing his eyes, his face screwing into a tight knot of concentration.

Gail walked away, numb, knowing there wasn't anything she could do but avoid being a distraction. She could see the *Mississauga*, already fin-down on the flat plain, midway between the base of this hill and the distant river. She couldn't make out much detail from here, except that it had burned a landing pad for itself as well as starting a series of small grass fires in every direction.

*That wasn't going to help.*

"Aaron's doing his best," she said to anyone listening, but mostly to Aaron himself, in case he could still hear. Gail hugged herself, trying to keep her emotions from adding to whatever milieu the Quill tapped into, trying to observe. It was hard to keep calm. On the thought, she bent over and offered her wrist to the Quill around her feet; it didn't seem a good sign when they slithered deeper into the soil rather than approach.

"We're sending the 'bot over there, Gail," Grant informed

her. "Before I do, and we lose voice contact, I wanted you to know the *Payette*'s pod has docked with the *Seeker*. We're going to load her up for a drop. *Seeker* out."

"Copy that," Gail said, but to herself and posterity, watching Bob zoom toward the distant starship, like a hummingbird to a flower garden. *Funny*, she missed the little thing immediately. The hilltop felt barren and desolate, no sound but the rising wind in the grass.

Then Aaron screamed.

# Chapter 93

*L*IKE old times.

Mind you, Malley reminded himself, the slug corner on the recycling floor didn't have chairs like this, or any lighting that stayed on consistently, but there was the same comforting sense of being out of authority's sight, doing something authority wouldn't want you to do.

*The Earthers had their hidden virtues.*

"Okay. I've got the 'bot's feed back up." Stan Temujin tended to cower and whisper a bit too much for a proper coconspirator, but Malley was prepared to be tolerant. The man had the toys.

So he, Aisha, and Temujin huddled over an impressive, if homemade, screen and comm system. The three of them were tucked inside what Aisha referred to as a parts closet and the stationer considered big enough for quarters, even though their knees were usually in the way of his.

*Close quarters and comfort.* He admitted he needed both, if only to himself. Those weren't strangers squatting on the dirtball below—*they might be idiots whose necks he'd cheerfully wring*—but they weren't strangers.

They were friends and family.

The image on the small screen plunged down, then stopped as the 'bot came to rest over the *Mississauga*'s ramp. Someone in the command sphere modified the settings so the usually inconspicuous Quill leaped into view like a sea of red, lapping at an island of scorched earth, inhabited by a lone ship. Malley didn't think it was particularly helpful, unless anyone doubted it was a hopeless situation.

"What's happening?" he growled impatiently. Aisha laid her

hand on his knee. Malley turned to glare, only to find her face crumbling as she tried to say something and failed. He managed to get his arm around her shoulders despite the tight space and pull her close. *Too many hours of giving strength to everyone else—including him.*

"They're coming out."

Malley could see that for himself. The oldest led, of course, the ones who'd been born under a sun. Made sense, of a sort. They'd find the conditions easier. *Sense be damned*, he thought. They wanted it most—dragging their families with them in the crazy belief nightmares could just disappear. *Poof.*

*Damn Rosalind.* It was becoming a habit.

"Oh no. Frasier . . ." He'd hoped not to recognize the very first to ease her feet over the ramp's ridges. Bethany Frasier—one of the less cranky old women, the type who could transform rations into sweets as easily as she repaired electrical systems or anything else broken. She used a cane but didn't have it with her—relying instead on the strong arm of her son, Gregory. Gullible Greggie: brunt of a dozen Malley-special practical jokes, the latest the night before the Earthers had arrived on-station.

Malley refused to close his eyes. Someone who knew them had to watch.

He didn't close his eyes, but he buried his face against Aisha's hair when the figures on the ramp started to scream and collapse.

*Let it keep the rest away*, Malley prayed silently.

"Wait. Malley. Aisha. Look!"

She moved first at Temujin's urging, so he had to lift his head and stare at the screen.

They were sitting up—all of them—some rubbing hips or elbows, perhaps bumped when they fell—but no one was unconscious or worse. Several, particularly the younger ones, were heaving up their stomachs' contents at the opposite side of the ramp. Reaction to the Quill Effect, or merely to being under a sky?

*It didn't matter.* "No one's dead!" the stationer roared in amazement, hugging the two Earthers until a faint squeak reminded him others tended to break if squeezed too hard. "Aaron did it!"

"Switch to the *Athena*'s vid," Aisha said when she could breathe again. "We can try and see how Aaron's doing." Temujin's hand flew to his makeshift console.

Before he'd succeeded, there was a loud crackle as Gail's voice blasted into the storeroom. "Grant! Temujin? Malley? Anyone!"

Temujin frantically lowered the volume, muttering something about amateurs and ship comms, while Malley answered quickly, his mouth dry: "We're here. How's Aaron?"

"Malley? Aaron's stung, but okay now." The words tumbled out, too fast—*not*, Malley thought, *as if out of control, but as if Gail feared being stopped before saying what she wanted to say.* "Unharmed—as far as I can tell. But what about the people in the ship? Aaron's saying something, but it's confusing—and I can't see them from here."

"They seem okay now, Gail," Aisha said over his shoulder. "Thank Aaron—"

Another crackle, then: "Susan—the Quill—when she knew they were people, she stopped herself. But it was too close, Aisha. The damage to the grass, to the Quill in the grass—I think it hurt her somehow. Aaron told me I have to tell you—you have to tell Grant—there can't be any more landings. Not for a while. Susan isn't stable. Do you understand me? She's doing her best not to defend herself, but if more ships come down before Aaron can help her—she might not be able to stop fast enough. Do you hear me, Malley?"

*Why him?* The stationer frowned at the woman he couldn't see. "I hear you— Why?"

"The entire solar system's hearing you, Gail," Temujin broke in. "I trust you know that."

"Good. Anyone hearing me—stay off this planet. You won't be safe. Just give us time. Please." The comm was dead a moment, then her voice came back. "Reality confirms the data, Malley," Gail said cryptically. "Smith out."

"Gail—?"

"She's signed off, Aisha." Temujin said regretfully. "But sounds like she got our stuff."

Malley tapped one finger on the screen, lightly but firmly. "What stuff? You did notice she was talking to me . . ."

The Earthers exchanged looks, then Aisha pulled a disk from the pocket of her lab coat. "Here. Obviously she wants you to have this."

"And this is?"

"Everything we've found out about the Quill so far. We wanted Gail to see it first—before the FDs took it and who knows what might happen to the truth."

Malley tucked the disk into the same pocket as his favorite knife. "Gotta go," he said, surging to his feet but careful of their toes.

"Where?"

He looked down at Aisha. "They didn't listen to her before—they won't listen now. It's the message from that ship they'll care about—Bethany telling her friends, 'It was a bumpy landing, dears, but we're fine now. Come on down.' That's what's going on right now—guaranteed."

Temujin frowned, but he didn't disagree. "What can you do?"

"Start by talking to Grant. He'd better have a plan for this—before all hell breaks loose out there. Or Tobo. Whoever can stop this."

Malley left them, feeling his guts still half-jelly from what might have happened.

*They'll never listen.* He dreaded what might be to come.

# Chapter 94

GAIL shut down the comm, watching her hands shake as though they belonged to someone else, feeling as though her entire body echoed with dread.

*They wouldn't listen.*

Nothing could have done more damage than the survival of that one shipload of would-be colonists. She knew it and accepted it with a familiar, cold detachment.

She'd told Malley that Aaron was fine. *What else could she say?* The stationer couldn't be here; there was nothing anyone could do to help. Aaron's screams of pain still rang in her ears. *Aaron's or the Quill's.* It didn't seem to matter which anymore, Gail told herself wearily. They'd both suffered. They'd both saved those people. *Those fools!*

Given the cost, she seriously doubted they could do it again.

She walked back outside, paying no attention to the beautiful sky or mountain vista, looking ahead to Aaron. When a Quill slipped up her leg and body, then down her arm to wrap around her wrist, Gail hardly noticed, until she felt the soothing calm pushing back the worst of her fears and anxieties. The relief brought tears to her eyes. "Thank you, Susan," she said, unsure if Aaron could hear.

There were subtle changes taking place around him. The stalks the Quill had originally used had turned brown and dry. The Quill kept insinuating fresh green ones between the old, as if it was important to keep living material next to his skin—or next to themselves. As a result, the mass around him was thickening, until from a certain angle he might have been a statue of Neptune, rising on a wave of shimmering green and brown. From any other, he looked like a man buried up to his shoulders in straw, the flesh on his face melting away by the hour as if something was taking place under the straw neither of them could bear to know about.

"I talked to Malley, Aaron," Gail said, making herself see only the fine, brave eyes of the man she loved and nothing else. "He knows—everyone's fine on the ship. No one was hurt. They asked how you were." She lightened her voice. "Mind you—the big oaf was his usual self. You're going to have to talk to him when we get back."

A by now familiar whirl of stalks and Quill took shape in front of Aaron, settling into what Gail was astonished to recognize as a chair. The mass was oddly proportioned and the back didn't go all the way along, but there was no mistaking its function.

"Thank you," she said faintly, and sat. The grass was remarkably dense and the result quite comfortable.

"Susan's—grateful," Aaron said suddenly, as if he'd lost, then found, his voice. "She's aware you're trying to prevent more landings."

"Trying, being the word," Gail said despondently, rubbing her fingers over the Quill on her wrist, finding comfort from the alien. How incredibly far they'd come since—*was it only yesterday?* "Aaron . . ."

"Yes, dear?"

She glanced up, feeling herself smile in spite of everything. He had that power over her, even like this. His eyes and smile alone melted her resolve until she couldn't help it: "Aaron. Will Susan let you go? Can she?"

Aaron pressed his lips together, as if preventing an impulsive answer. They were healing, but still swollen. Gail knew there was salve on the pod that might help, but the remote arms weren't that fine. She caught herself wishing passionately for Rosalind's hands, not her useless ones.

"I'm sorry, Aaron," she said before he could form an answer. "Forget I asked. I know what you've told me—that this connection between you is outside her conscious control. I just can't help but . . . hope."

"We aren't alone, Gail," he said earnestly. "Remember that. And here's the proof. Hi, Bob!"

Gail's lips twitched as she imagined one of Grant's dignified deployment specialists having to endure the name. No doubt Tobo and his crew would make the best of it—even through this.

The 'bot's return included Grant's voice. *He must be living on the bridge.* "Dr. Smith. Aaron. Our sincere thanks to you— and Susan."

"The best thanks will be preventing another potential disaster before it enters the atmosphere, Commander," Gail said bitingly, knowing his superiors were listening. *Always.*

"We're doing our best. But there's been another development you should know about."

Gail and Aaron exchanged worried looks. "And why do I doubt it's good news, Commander?" she asked wryly.

"Because it isn't. We've more guests on the way. While some of those are reinforcements from Sol System—I'm afraid the early arrivals will be from Hamble and Osari."

Gail hadn't dreamed Aaron could look worse. They stared at one another—and all she could do was imagine holding him tightly.

Grant misinterpreted their silence. "You do know those are the—"

"—the two nearer stations to Thromberg?" Gail finished. "Yes, Commander. We're well aware. Same intentions—same first-class transport?"

"As far as we know. And the ships from Thromberg are claiming they've passed their return fuel reserves. Between us, I doubt they brought enough fuel to go back in the first place."

Aaron spoke up bitterly: "Why would they, Commander? These are first rounders—they've waited most of their lives to die out here. Why should they make any plan to return?"

"They'd assume we'd never abandon them," Gail countered. "And we won't. What's the condition of the ships, besides crowded?"

"They range from barely-holding-orbit to ready-to-crash— into each other if not the planet," Grant said grimly. "Desperate people, Dr. Smith. We're running out of time here."

"The *Seeker* can take some—what about the other Earth ships? Surely they'd be willing—"

"Of course, but we don't have sufficient space for those already here, let alone the numbers coming from Hamble and Osari. Besides, we can't transfer them against their will—"

"Even if they wanted to, they couldn't transfer to your ships," Aaron reminded them, his eyes lifted to the sky as if to see for himself. "No suits—and I'd bet half don't have functioning ship-to-ship air locks."

Gail began considering options. There was gear in the fabrications storeroom; perhaps they could rig up some kind of airtight tubing. "Grant, I want you to—"

"Wait."

The silence beat against her ears. Gail found herself digging her fingers into the Quill-chair and fought the inane urge to apologize. If this was how she felt with the Quill on her wrist, she'd likely be having a tantrum without it.

A furious string of swear words rent the air. Gail stared up at Bob in shock. "What's going on up there?" she cried, rising to her feet. "Grant? Tobo! Someone!"

"Dr. Smith. This is Tau. The commander is on the other comm, attempting to handle a—situation. If you would wait—"

"I will not." Gail looked at Aaron. "What situation—tell us!"

Grant's voice—sudden and hasty: "Gail—some of the ships are making a run for the planet. Warn Aaron and Susan! The *Payette* is moving to intercept . . . she's got orders to protect the Quill entity."

"What does that mean?" Aaron asked in a hoarse voice.

"The *Payette* is preparing to fire."

# Chapter 95

*PREPARING to fire!*

Pardell heard the words, part of him trying to translate the folly of humanity for the Susan-Quill, part of him reeling helplessly into images and battles past . . . imagining too well what could be happening . . .

. . . ships scattering to run from the cruiser like fish startled from a school . . . klaxons screaming—those still functional—*Danger! Damage! Thieves!* Each ship has one choice to be made in haste: one possible trajectory in the time given.

Some will choose wrong.

A fuel-heavy cruiser or nimble patrol dart can pick a prey. They can run it down, then perform a stop and turn with their perfectly functioning grav units—a maneuver that would kill everyone belowdecks on any other ship—in order to chase another. Theirs the luxury of cheating physics.

Some prey choose to pull closer to perceived neutrality, getting warn offs from the nervous Captain of the research ship, but risking collision to hide from threat. Proximity alarms sound in unison, the *Seeker*'s perhaps louder: *Danger! Damage! Thieves!*

Others hear a familiar, horrifying song. The line of Earth ships is one they've seen before and barely escaped. They turn and run, leap into translight too close to one another and the planet. Skill and the luck of fools prevents collisions. Nothing prevents the failure of overworked engines. Three ships go adrift, life support on emergency, their inhabitants helpless to do more than cling together and try not to breathe too often.

Seven run for the planet. Why that choice? The odds are better—they outnumber the blockade. Perhaps their captains are too young to have seen this before—perhaps they believe no human ship would fire on them to protect a lie.

Do their ships appreciate irony?

Incoming transmission: *Turn back. Pardell's World is under quarantine to protect the Quill Entity from human interference. No one will be permitted to land until this ban is lifted.*

*Turn back or be destroyed.*

Do ships know fear and uncertainty? Humans do. Three ships slow and obey, pick up a patrol dart as escort, limp back into higher orbit.

Four press their luck.

The *Payette* waits at the upper edge of atmosphere, huge, dark, unable to imagine a challenge from a garbage barge, two antique freighters, and one rental tow ship. She arms weapons. *Intimidation.*

They won't stop, not with a verdant, living world so close. *They can't.*

The *Payette* is struck by a garbage barge unable to make a final course correction to avoid her. As she shakes off the blow, the barge tumbles and burns its way into the atmosphere, only melted droplets reaching the soil.

Perceiving attack, the *Payette's* autodefenses fire, obliterating the rental tow ship and one of the freighters.

The last ship survives, triumphantly riding its flame to the surface, passengers suddenly left to hope they were right and this flight would be to safety and a new life . . . and not death.

*They were wrong.*

. . . Pardell groped his way free from thoughts of ships, vacuum, and disaster. He fought to sort reality from his daydream, realizing he'd been processing information as it was being relayed from *Seeker.*

Realizing it was real. There was a ship on its way to the surface. Aaron fought to calm the Susan-Quill, fighting back *fear* and *revulsion* . . .

Countering with his *grief* . . .

# Chapter 96

G AIL had retreated to the *Athena* again. She had full comm
capability there.

*And it distanced her from Aaron's pain.*

Not that she didn't want to comfort him—had that been remotely possible. Not that she didn't think he might need help
communicating with Susan through the morass of emotions
everywhere, including hers.

But Gail knew she was the only person who could end this.

Susan hadn't killed all of the occupants of the second ship to
violate her world. A small mercy there. Some older ones had
survived. Gail knew exactly how they were feeling at the moment. *A fascinating topic for future study*, she thought furiously.
The relationship between emotional capacity and an increased
risk of death due to abject stupidity.

*Not that she would do the study herself.*

Now that she was in position and knew what to do, Gail
found herself unable to do more than run her fingers along the
comm controls.

*Grief.* If Aaron's had been terrible to see, Susan's had been
worse. The Quill had snapped every blade of grass at the base,
until the hillside was bare of anything taller than Gail, Aaron,
and the drop pod. Waves of similar destruction had spread down
the hillside like clawing fingers, stopping short of the two is-
lands of scorched earth and silent ships.

Aaron had tried to find words for her reaction, but was almost incoherent between his own emotion and the Quill's. The
Susan-Quill, he'd told her, perceived herself as harmless, inconspicuous, a benefit to the world. What was happening—was unacceptable.

*As it had been to Susan Witts*, Gail thought. She rubbed her eyes, remembering.

She'd ordered away the 'bot, saying it upset Susan-Quill to be watched. Then she'd used all her skills to lead the way. Perhaps Aaron hadn't seen where she wanted to go; perhaps Malley would have. Regardless, with more care and deliberation than Gail had ever used to bring a difficult committee around to her way of thinking, into making the key decision for her—as if they'd had a choice once she'd decided—she walked the Susan-Quill down the path she had already seen.

The last step couldn't be hers. Gail had talked herself hoarse, Aaron had worn himself to the point where he'd pass out every so often, until Gail woke him. They'd forced their way around and through concepts until Gail wasn't sure whether she always used words or sometimes simply *felt* things for Aaron to translate.

And now, Gail sat in front of the comm with a message to be written. Eyes only. She knew who to send it to—and what had to be done. It wasn't going to be easy.

But, in the end, it had been Susan-Quill who had taken that final step into understanding. And decided.

*Anguish.* She could no longer bear to kill. She would not.

*Longing.* She could no longer bear to be alone.

And would not.


"Done?"

"Done," Gail affirmed, wrapping herself in a blanket and working her body into the chair. With the grass flattened, the wind had nothing to slow it down. Now it bit any exposed flesh. "It's up to them, now," she sighed. No sign of Bob yet—the FDs must still be checking on the other ship.

Another mercy, after all. The first rounders had come prepared. Gail had watched in astonishment as the *Mississauga* offloaded a cargo of prefab shelters and even earth-moving equipment, the would-be colonists moving with sure speed to produce what by now amounted to a real, if tiny, settlement. When she'd questioned how they'd kept these supplies from being used by the station, Aaron had simply remarked that he'd heard Station Admin had tried—only once—to expropriate the colonists' equipment from the storage bays. Besides, how useful would any of it have been?

Until now. Now, it not only offered the passengers of the *Mississauga* essential shelter and the real potential for survival, but they'd gone to their new neighbor, the *Clarkson*, and brought the survivors back to join them.

Gail was glad she couldn't see the line of fresh graves.

"How is Susan?" she asked.

"Frightened. Determined. She's asking me about . . ." his voice failed and she looked up at him.

"What does she want to know, Aaron?"

He shook his head in wonder. "Everything. The more time I'm like this—part of her—the easier it becomes to transfer ideas and information. She wants to learn whatever she can. More than I can teach her. Even though she knows it won't last. . . ."

"You've been a good friend," she offered softly. Aaron stood there, as he'd stood all this time, hardly seeming real anymore unless she was the target of his eyes. *Then*, she thought, *he was everything, and the only thing, real.* "I don't know what kind of music you like," Gail said, oddly alarmed. She sat upright again. "What do you like to read? What do you—" she stopped, feeling silly.

He smiled down at her. "I like anything played with heart and joy. I read everything I can find—which isn't much, I'm afraid."

Gail smiled back, suddenly shy. "I have a library at home—on Earth, not Titan. It's filled with books. My family's. My own."

"Books—as in paper?" His eyes widened. "I didn't think they still existed."

"Yes. Convenient on Earth, where paper can be grown—it's the transport cost that made them a problem for spacers. I would think the new worlds . . ." She couldn't say anymore.

Aaron finished for her: ". . . the new worlds will probably have their own books, soon enough."

"Soon enough." Gail looked into his eyes and felt her own filling with tears. "Aaron—of everything—I don't regret us," she said fiercely. "You know that, don't you? Not for an instant."

His voice was like his face, expressive, changing in flashes. Now it was richer than usual, more resonant. She could feel it. "I know," he said. "And I won't deny I'm glad you're here, instead of safely up on your fancy new ship. Selfish of me, isn't it?"

"Safe?" She made a rude noise. "If I'd wanted safe, I'd have stayed in the library."

Aaron nodded slowly, as if he knew what she couldn't bring herself to say—*not and be able to endure this*. Gail didn't doubt he was braver—braver than anyone she'd known or could imagine.

"Think you could stay awake and watch the stars with me tonight, wife?" he asked.

"You need your rest," she told him.

"Perhaps," he drew in a long breath, tilting his head back to scan the sky, then looked down at her, eyes aglow. "But every minute with you is—it's like the first minute of my being alive and not just waiting for life. I don't want to miss even one."

Gail pressed her fingers to her lips for a long moment, then lifted the kiss to him. "Then you won't, husband," she promised.

She refused to calculate how many minutes they had left.

# Chapter 97

MALLEY smiled. *This should only take a minute.*

He could see his own reflection in the glossy door between the two FDs. *Definitely the smile that made Sammie nervous and Aaron pick up the nearest blunt object.*

"Evening, gentlemen," he said happily. The pair looked at one another, then back at Malley. Doubtless they knew he wasn't supposed to be here; likely they knew he was incapable of entering the now fully-reconnected waist.

*A shame they didn't know the most important thing about Mrs. Malley's youngest,* the stationer chuckled to himself, as the FDs gave him identical surprised looks and slid to the floor. He pulled the trank from what remained of his pocket.

*He didn't fight fair.*

It was ship's night—combined with the continued restriction of the science staff to quarters, it made for conveniently empty halls. Of course, this critical entryway would be on vid. Malley smiled congenially at the likely corners of the ceiling. But he should have time at this end. The other? Well, he'd deal with that problem once through the waist.

And he'd deal with the waist, once he made his way through the door. *All of which*, he thought morosely, *would have been unnecessary if Grant was answering the comm.*

The impregnable door. Malley wondered if Gail appreciated the level of enthusiastic anarchy among her science staff. *Then again*, he thought with a grin, *she'd picked them.* Suffice it to say he'd had his choice of methods to deal with the locking mechanism—most involving loud noise and significant releases of energy.

The stationer helped himself to the FDs' weapons—*finally,*

*something a bit more motivating than the tranks*—then pulled
their unconscious bodies down the corridor, arranging them so
they'd form an obstacle to anyone trying to charge him. But, just
as he began fastening his favorite destructive device to the side
of the door, the lights began flashing to indicate it was being
opened from the other side.

*Why do the dirty work when someone else will do it for you?*
Malley's grin turned wolfish. He crouched out of the direct line
of sight, but well in range, trank in one hand, what looked to be
a very new energy-projectile pistol in the other.

The door opened, but no one stepped through.

"Malley?" A hiss, not a demand. Grant's voice.

Malley made sure both weapons were ready to fire, and
waited.

"Damn it, Malley, I've no time for this!" A more typical snap,
but again, very quietly.

"Then come through the door, Earther," Malley suggested
cheerfully.

Ready as he was, Grant's rolling dive through the door almost surprised him—almost, because if it had, Malley would
have shot the man. But he had time as they froze, weapons
aimed at one another, to see that Grant was not only out of uniform, he was wearing one of the blue anti-Quill suits.

Grant, lying on the floor, lowered his weapon first. He held
out his hand for a lift.

Malley took it, heaving the Earther to his feet in one motion.
"I take it this isn't quite official," he said.

Grant put a finger over his lips, then turned to close the door
behind him before coming back to stand in front of Malley.

Then Grant tapped the side of his head, once, very lightly.
There was a world of meaning in his dark eyes.

Smile turning to a baring of teeth, Malley took out one of his
knives, the small, sharp one from the science lab. It wasn't sterile, but he figured infection was tomorrow's problem.

Obviously Grant, like he, knew they had other things to
worry about.

When it was done, Grant smashed the tiny, blood-soaked device
under his heel. The wound had already soaked through the

makeshift bandage they'd wrapped around his head, with a runnel of blood starting its way down his cheek, but Malley judged
it would stop soon. Slices on the face tended to make a short-
lived mess.

Malley didn't comment on the existing scar on Grant's
face—obviously the man had his own issues with authority.

"Thanks. Buys some time from the *Payette*," Grant said
shortly as he led the way to the lab at a trot. "We're still monitored by the *Seeker*'s vids." He'd passed his unconscious guards
with a look of complete disapproval—at them, the stationer noticed, not him. "But my people—the ones who understand the
situation—they'll turn a blind eye. So will Captain Tobo and his
crew. Our problem will come when we get to the *Payette*'s pod.
She's got crew who won't appreciate what we're doing."

"Which is?"

A dark glance. "Less said is still better."

Malley could make a reasonable guess involving illegalities
and taking matters into one's own hands—things of which he
approved in general terms. He wouldn't have minded details, especially given the suit Grant was wearing. The Earther likely
had the headgear and gloves in the bag strapped to his back.
"There's only one of those," he ventured, keeping up the pace
easily.

Grant grunted. "That's all I need."

Malley hoped his relief wasn't obvious. He was managing—
barely—not to shake with the aftermath of having steeled himself to enter the waist, with its horrifying exposure to space.

They turned the corner to reach the main entrance to the lab.
Two FDs Malley knew quite well, Cornell and Loran, stood at
attention to either side. As he and Grant approached, Loran
swiveled without speaking to open the lab door. A sled came
wheeling out, the hands that pushed it letting go as the FD took
the near end, as though the person within tried to avoid being
caught on the hall vids.

Grant didn't hesitate, walking boldly past as though there
was nothing unusual in his appearance or Malley being armed
with FD issue. He motioned to Malley to take the sled.

Cornell and Loran didn't react at all, staring straight ahead as
though their commander and his companion were invisible.

Once out of earshot, Malley observed dryly: "Handy, that."

"Best scenario," Grant said in a bitterly proud voice, "we'll all be retiring a little sooner than expected. If things go badly—and they probably will—court-martial . . . treason . . . The reaction of our superiors will depend on the public mood of the moment."

"Then why risk it?"

Malley thought Grant looked faintly insulted by the question. "We've been on Thromberg," he answered, as if that should be enough.

*Perhaps it was*, the stationer decided, finding another of his preconceptions about Earthers—and this man—falling short of the truth.

Grant led the way down a corridor Malley hadn't explored yet, knowing it only led to the freight air locks and other places too close to the dark of space for his comfort. There was access to the freight area from the science lab, but he didn't need to ask to know Grant wanted to stay well away from innocent bystanders.

The sled was heavy, despite carrying only a box Malley could wrap his arms around easily. Box? He'd given it one quick look. It was a version of the stasis boxes used to transport the Quill. From the lights on the side, it was in operation.

Even if he'd had questions for Grant, they reached the door to the freight hold before he could ask them. Unguarded, Malley noticed. Surely it should have been—he suspected Grant's people had conveniently forgotten to appear for duty.

"Put the hardware away," Grant ordered, stopping just short to study the big stationer. "We'll go in as though I've apprehended you trying to break through the door. You were planning to steal the pod and run off with that—" A nod to the box. "Should get their attention."

"Why don't I really break through the door?" Malley offered reasonably. "Add some authenticity."

The commander snorted. "They'd shoot you before I could. We do it my way. And Malley—just tranks."

"You promising they'll play by the same rules?" the stationer complained, but tucked his weapons into their hiding places. He'd like to have kept his hand on at least one, but Grant shook his head.

"Hands on the sled, in plain sight. You're scary enough, without giving them an excuse. As for the tranks—these are FD troops," Grant said, taking hold of Malley's shoulder and starting to push him toward the door. "It's tranks only around civilians."

The stationer was aggrieved. "That's not what the two at the waist had."

Grant chuckled low in his throat. "Oh, they were supposed to guard against you, Malley."

*Compliment or threat?* As Grant hit the door controls and propelled him forward into the cavernous freight hold, Malley decided it was likely both.

"What—?" "Commander Grant—" Words overlapped as the guards inside leaped to their feet. They'd been sitting around a table covered in food trays—no coincidence, Malley thought admiringly.

"Who's in charge of this detail?" Grant's snap made Malley's back want to straighten. He resisted, doing his best to look contrite, embarrassed, and, above all, harmless—not being at all happy to see Grant had been wrong and these four had the lethal-variety handarm at their sides. That didn't appear to perturb Grant, who was giving a very credible impression of an officer looking to assign blame. *And lots of it.*

"Ops Specialist Pimm, sir." This from the nearest woman, with a nervous glance toward the back of the hold where an air lock door gaped open. All four, two men and two women, stood at attention. They wore the same uniform as the *Seeker*'s unit, and, like them, were physically matched to uncanny perfection. There, any similarity ended. The *Payette*'s FDs were extremely pale-skinned, with almost white hair, shorter by almost a hand's width than Grant and more heavily built. All had light blue eyes.

Light blue and very suspicious eyes that appeared to find him particularly alarming. Malley smiled peacefully, while tensing every muscle to leap out of range. Did Grant notice? *This wasn't going to work for long.*

It worked for exactly one more heartbeat. Then, before the

stationer could do more than start to flinch, Grant had shot two of the FDs with tranks, sending the others scrambling for cover. "Move it!" he shouted to Malley as he dashed for the air lock.

*No guesses why he was along*, Malley thought, ducking down to use the sled and box for cover while pushing it after Grant as quickly as he could.

He took quick peeks over the top to see what was happening. Grant had his back to the open air lock, facing toward him, waving him on. The Earther shot again and Malley heard a thump as a third FD went down somewhere behind him.

*Almost there.*

A snap-whip of a sound. A scorch mark appeared on the wall beside Grant—warning shot, Malley judged it and drove his legs even faster. The sled smashed into the side of the pod and he turned, weapon in hand, to face what might be coming at them.

"No." Grant fired again. "Get the box inside. Hurry!"

Malley hesitated, trying to see where the remaining guard was hiding among the piles of packing crates and sleds.

"Now!"

The stationer growled something about the stupidity of Earthers, then shoved his weapon into its pocket before whirling to grab the box. He grunted at the weight of the thing, but quickly readjusted his grip and heaved it up against his chest. The effort kept his mind from the air lock, which resembled a giant version of those from his nightmares. Two steps, up the ramp, over the sill—with every move, Malley expected a shot in the back. When none came, he presumed the box was more valuable than he was.

*It had better not be fragile, then*, he thought grimly as he hurled it at the figure emerging from the interior of the *Payette*'s drop pod. The man gave an "oof" as the box connected with his chest, both dropping to the deck with a nicely solid thud.

Another snap-whip from outside, this time punctuated by a wordless cry of pain. Malley spun around, weapons in both hands and headed for the freight hold.

He dared a quick look out the air lock door. Grant was down, motionless, to his left. He could smell burned flesh. Malley dodged back inside . . .

. . . feeling smaller, all of a sudden—*being* smaller as his mind played its ultimate trick, trying to make him see another air lock than this, look out to see a different burned body. Only this time, Aaron didn't block him, wasn't closing the door, wasn't sobbing at him: "You can't help! She's dead already! I have to save you! I promised!"

. . . Malley shuddered free of the past, then crouched down as low as he could before looking out again.

A snap-whip as the hidden FD took a shot at him, a brief flash of light marking his location. Malley leaped, firing both weapons as he ran forward, shouting at the top of his lungs.

*Give him a barroom brawl any day*, he thought a second later, looking down at the lifeless form. *At least, then, you finished up buying one another beer.*

"Malley . . ."

The stationer hurried to the voice. "Thought you were cooked, Grant," he said roughly, going down on one knee by the commander.

The Earther's eyes were open and he'd rolled to his side. "A little toasted," he quipped, then coughed painfully. His upper left arm and shoulder were blackened and leaking blood. Another streak of burning arched across his upper chest. "Damn suit's ruined," he said with astonishing clarity.

Malley picked him up carefully. He'd seen burns before— they weren't things to fool with. "I'm getting you to the meds—" he began, only to have Grant shake his head vigorously.

"No time—get us into the pod. Hurry!"

The stationer stared at the man in his arms. "Why?"

Grant's dark eyes were watering with pain, but they still conveyed utter determination. "Because Gail needs what's in that box. Hear me? Or more people are going to die. There's no time—it's up to us."

"Wonderful," Malley muttered to himself, but started moving again. Even from the planet, Gail Smith was capable of getting him into trouble.

\* \* \*

"Did you remove Specialist Pimm?"

Malley dropped into the seat next to Grant. "Yes, although I don't see why I couldn't leave him under the box. He wasn't moving anytime soon."

"The more—the more people are on the pod, the harder it's going to be for Aaron to protect any of us."

The stationer made a noncommittal noise, more immediately concerned with Grant's ability to pilot the pod. The man should, by rights, be unconscious or dead already. "You're bleeding on the deck," he observed callously. *All over the deck*, since Grant had, with Malley's help, insisted on locating and disabling all of the FDs' own spies within the pod. "How long can you keep that up?"

"The pod has emergency medical supplies," Grant answered, as if he could read Malley's doubts. He patted the broad arm of the pilot's seat. "Boost, stims, painkillers. I'll be fine as long as it takes. What about you? Planning to go nuts on me?"

Malley managed to get the straps over his shoulders, but they wouldn't stretch across his broader-than-Earther-issue chest. He shoved them aside with a resigned sigh. "Sounds fair. I'll worry about your running us into the dirt and you can worry about my running around screaming if you don't."

"Fine. In the meantime, be useful and operate the comm," the Earther said. Given the breathless gasping he was presently using as a voice, Malley thought that the most rational idea he'd heard in some time. "Notify the *Seeker* we're ready to drop. You closed the air lock?"

"Sealed up tight." It had been oddly reassuring to be the one locking the nightmares out. *Perhaps he should have tried that before.*

"Let's go, then."

Malley keyed the comm and sent out a message bound to stir up more trouble, then sat back and studied Grant. He soon realized, as they lurched free of the science sphere with a clang of grapples against the pod's hull, that he had as much chance of taking over the pod if the gravely wounded man passed out, as he had of walking around space without a suit. Grant's uninjured arm and hand moved ceaselessly between a dozen controls and he didn't appear to have anything automated.

*Sense of a sort*—automated meant someone else could take over and bring the pod back to the *Payette* and numerous nasty consequences. The stationer got up and hunted for more medical supplies to keep his pilot conscious.

A bizarrely familiar voice suddenly boomed through the tiny cabin. "Hey you—! You in the shuttle."

Grant waved his hand to summon Malley, who dropped back into his seat and keyed to reply. "It's not a shuttle, moron, it's an FD drop pod," he explained considerately. "Which shows how much you know about starships."

"Malley—my God—it's Malley!"

Malley shrugged apologetically at Grant, before saying to the comm: "Of course it's me, Syd," he growled. "You'd better be taking good care of Amy and her family. Damn fool stunt— I thought you'd all been killed."

"Enough have been. We're on the *Wombat*, snugged under the belly of your Earther friends—safe, until your 'FD drop pod' almost rammed us just now. What's going on, Malley? What's this about Aaron being the Survivor from the stories? Can he really save us from the Quill? Do we land? What should we do?" This last with a definite note of panic. *Typical Denery*, Malley thought. *Always did leap into things without any idea how to get out again.*

Still, the relief he felt knowing at least some of their friends had survived the carnage of the past day was reward enough. "Hang on," he said, then muted the pickup on the comm. "Well, Grant? Any suggestions for this lot?"

Grant was crouched over the controls, favoring his damaged side. The face he turned to Malley was deathly pale but alert. "If they've got the fuel and guts for it, we could use some interference. We have to get to the surface . . . once they figure out why, the *Payette* will try to shoot us down. The patrol ships aren't—aren't—they aren't . . ."

"Grant?" Malley reached out with his long arm, taking Grant gently by his uninjured shoulder. "What about the patrol?"

"The patrol." The Earther took a carefully shallow breath.

"The patrol ships aren't a factor. They answer to Titan—to Titan and those interests who want these worlds for humans— under any circumstances. They won't interfere—"

*With what?* Malley looked at the stasis box, strapped in its corner of the pod. "Those are fragments," he guessed. "The Quill fragments from the other planets."

Grant's lips pulled back from his teeth. It wasn't a smile. "No time to discuss—We're on approach, Malley. 'Scope shows the *Payette*'s moving—notice they haven't called us?"

"You want me to ask my friends to get between this pod and your warship?" Malley shook his head. "Taking our chance is one thing, Earther, but these aren't combat pilots. These are families in rundown, inadequate ships."

Grant coughed, then spat out furiously: "Don't you get it, Malley? Most of them, maybe all, are going to die unless they can land and soon! And more are coming—too many for us to help, in ships unequipped to remain in orbit, out of fuel to return. It will be a riot—you understand the concept—but out here. They'll have to run for the only safety in reach—they'll head for this world the way the Outsiders headed for your station—but this time each and every one will be killed by the Quill Effect, unless we help Gail prevent it."

*It was like entering an air lock*, Malley realized, *a similarly inevitable moment of transition, with death one of the likeliest things waiting on the other side.*

Without another word to Grant, the stationer turned to the comm. "Hi, Syd. You know, we could use a bit of help at that." Malley closed his eyes, deliberately keeping his voice light as he gave what might be a death sentence to his friends. "Remember the time you and most of Outward Five kept Sammie off our tails so that Aaron and I could liberate that excess furniture?"

"Which time, Malley? Seems we're always covering for you." Despite the words, Syd sounded scared. Malley didn't blame him.

"I know it," he said softly. "Do what you can—but make sure you listen to Amy. She's smarter than both of us. And don't land till you hear from me—me and no one else. Okay?"

A pause, then: "Sure. We'll be careful—you, too. See you and Aaron later, Malley."

The stationer looked over to where Grant leaned against the controls. Blood and fluid oozed from so many tiny blisters, there hadn't seemed a point trying to stop it. "I certainly hope so," the stationer told Syd, but it wasn't a bet he'd take himself.

*A bright, blue, star-free sky would be nice*, Malley added to his list of hope-so's.

It seemed somewhat late to worry about such things now, but he'd never made it through one of Aisha's planet night simulations.

# Chapter 98

*A SHORT night to be so rich in time.*
  Gail sat, still and content, in a peaceful silence new to her, her throat sore with words, her ears ringing with Aaron's voice. It was as though they'd said a lifetime's worth of silly, solemn things to one another—finding more and more to say until they'd stopped and fallen silent at the same moment, knowing suddenly there was no reason to speak, and every reason to simply feel.

*Perhaps it was Susan*, Gail thought, keeping her back to the mountains and the coming dawn, her face to Aaron's silhouette. Could the Quill have created this sense of connection between them even at a distance? Or had they, in this so short night, reached the point old well-married couples do, when words are shortcuts to what is understood and loved?

*If it was Susan*, Gail told herself, *fitting they should share this night and these feelings with the Quill*. A being who hadn't asked to exist, but did. Who hadn't wanted to be alone, but was. Who'd never wanted to kill, but couldn't help herself.

*Her last night, if they succeeded*. Susan's decision, not theirs.

A willing sacrifice or needful change? Altruism or some instinct inexplicably tied to the Quill's survival? Susan couldn't tell them—Gail couldn't begin to guess. But it seemed only right not to leave her alone.

Suddenly, they weren't alone either. Bob zoomed up at them. Instead of producing a voice, the little 'bot bounced up and down, its dark surface reflecting the remaining moonlight.

"Malfunction?" Aaron whispered, as though his voice was hoarse, too.

"Message," Gail said reluctantly. She stood and stretched,

arching her neck back to better survey the sky. The mountains were more than starless shadows now, they'd transformed into doom-sharp peaks edged by light. *Dawn was always in a hurry,* she thought to herself. "Grant must be on his way. I'd better go to the *Athena* and see if there's any word."

"Why don't I wait here?" Aaron said with what might have been a laugh. Gail wasn't altogether sure—but if he wanted to play it light and cheery, so could she.

"Good idea," she replied, straight-faced. "I'll be right back. Keep an eye out for company."

As she went to the pod, she gazed down the hillside of ruined grass to the little community below. Voices couldn't carry this far, but the light of several small fires could. *What did it feel like,* she wondered, *to be outside after so long?* Did they celebrate a victory or huddle wearily together, relieved the worst was over? How did the younger ones feel—or would they sleep inside the ship until it was scrapped for materials, forcing them to come to terms with their new home?

The Quill fragment on her wrist dropped free as Gail stepped on the ramp—perhaps Susan consolidated herself, or perhaps she worried about losing another piece if Gail suddenly powered up the ship and left. Gail missed the subtle calming effect, but not as much as she'd thought. The peace of her night with Aaron stayed with her—for now.

Suddenly, a spectacular fireball streaked almost from horizon to horizon before it fractured and dissipated into light. More gouts of flame from above—a battle was raging!

*Or a massacre was taking place.*

Gail rushed into the pod. The comm light was already blinking, and she hurried to sit in front of the panel and key the control. A blast of overlapping sounds fired back at her, as though a dozen frantic voices tried to be heard at once.

She wasn't surprised. *So much for stealth, Grant,* Gail grumbled to herself, listening for anything sensible from the mess.

*Deliberate confusion,* Gail decided a moment later, both relieved and concerned. Anything deliberate probably involved Grant, which was a hopeful sign. Unfortunately, she couldn't imagine any reasonable explanation for how the commander had apparently enlisted the help of those from the station in his quest.

"He didn't," she whispered out loud. *Malley*. Despite being inside the pod, Gail looked up, as if she could somehow see what was happening at the limit of atmosphere, trying not to think of the ship that had already lost the battle and plunged to the ground.

Gail hurried back to Aaron, not bothering to add her voice to the cacophony. Of all the players in what was well beyond tragedy, she knew her mark on the stage.

"You think Malley's coming down here?" Aaron's voice went from hope to horror as he thought it through. "He can't be."

"I don't know for sure, Aaron," Gail cautioned. "Just—be ready, that's all. I hope it's only Grant in the pod—" they could see landing lights overhead, "—and he should be in the suit, so Susan won't react. But your friend has a way of surprising me on a regular basis."

There was sufficient glow from the horizon to show his nod. "That's Malley, all right."

They waited, together. There was nothing else to do but watch the lights approach. It seemed too slow, but Gail reminded herself the pods were designed to drift down on antigravs, a gentler and less destructive—if more expensive—landing than riding the flames of a starship's jets.

Gail used Aaron's face as her barometer for trouble. If the pod now landing mere footsteps away was filled with FD troops or other fools, she'd soon see him struggle to restrain Susan-Quill's instincts, try to help her identify each one as quickly as possible as not-enemy. Some would die. It couldn't be helped.

If, as it should, the pod contained Grant, alone and protected by his suit, Aaron's face wouldn't change at all, beyond perhaps a nod to let her know.

It took only twenty-five heartbeats for the pod to settle on its stubby legs and drop its ramp. Gail looked from Aaron to the ramp and back again, then her attention was distracted upward.

Something else was falling out of the sky—a ship. Under control and not another fireball, at least. *Damn!*

"Gail!"

The sound of a new human voice startled her back to the here and now. "Malley?" Gail whirled. The gigantic stationer stepped out of the pod with a stasis box in his arms, the combined weight rattling the ramp with each step. "Stay there," she warned. "He's got to tell her who you are before it's safe."

*Safe?* Somehow she doubted the Quill Effect was Malley's biggest worry at the moment. He was covered in blood, hopefully not his own, muscles trembling to keep hold of the heavy box, and his eyes were fixed on her with the kind of desperate look a drowning man might give a rope just out of reach.

The sky. Stars still showed—dimly now, to her night-accustomed eyes, but likely more than enough to remind Malley of his greatest fear. "Aaron," Gail called softly. "Can Susan help Malley?"

It was a strange idea, but she thought if the Quill could selectively collect and retransmit emotion, perhaps the Quill could ease some of Malley's terror.

*Not that Malley was doing badly.* He was aware and in control—so far. "Grant's here with me," he was shouting. "He's hurt."

"Go," Aaron told her. Just the one word, as though most of his focus had to stay elsewhere.

Gail ran to the other pod and up its ramp. "You can put it down here, Malley," she said right away. When he'd done so, and stood there looking down at her, Gail held herself from collapsing into his arms and sobbing by the single greatest act of will of her life.

"Show me Grant first," she asked.

"What about Aaron?" the stationer demanded, his eyes wild. "Look at him—we can't leave him like that—"

"Be glad he's like that, Malley," Gail said, hoping her voice was getting through. "If he wasn't—you'd already be dead." She didn't bother telling him that it would be another minute or so before she could be sure Aaron had convinced Susan to spare these newest arrivals. *Why have more people worrying than need be?*

She led the way back into the pod, only to stop and stare, aghast, at the body lying on the floor as if it had just fallen from the pilot's seat. The now-useless suit was the least of it. The body's head rolled around so a pair of familiar dark eyes could see her. "You look like hell, Dr. Smith," Commander Grant said in a wisp of his former voice.

"You should talk," Gail retorted, going to her knees beside him to assess the damage. *Force projectile, narrow spread, close range.* The images she'd been forced to endure in that forensics course many years ago were finally useful. "Do I want to ask questions?"

"Let's just say we won and leave it at that."

*Won.* Gail thought of the box outside and wondered if she'd ever use that word.

As she hesitated, Grant reached up with his good hand and gave her a push away. "I'm not going anywhere," he said urgently. "You've got to hurry—ask Malley. We could have dozens of station ships landing any minute. They ran interference for us—one took fire—but the rest may be running too low on fuel to stay up any longer."

Gail bent down and whispered: "I know what it took for you to do this, Commander. I won't forget." She pressed her lips against his sweat-cold forehead, then stood, quickly, before her resolve could waver, and walked out of the pod without looking back.

Malley made a soundless protest but followed her. When Gail realized it, she stopped and put her hand on his chest to stop him. too. "Listen, Malley. I don't know if you should—"

He looked worn yet patient, like some mountain that had stood for millennia and wasn't shifting any time soon. "I've come all this way, Gail," he said with unexpected calm, his low voice vibrating through her hand to her arm. "I want to talk to Aaron."

*As if she could stop him*, Gail told herself, but somehow knew Malley wouldn't go against her wishes this time. She sighed. "He's—he's not just Aaron any more. Can you handle that?"

"I've watched. I've tried to understand." His straight brows drew together thoughtfully. "I think I can sort it out, if Aaron can."

Gail was reminded of the fierce brilliance under that shock of standup hair and felt less alone. "Let's go, then. Bring the box. And don't worry about where you step. The Quill will get out of the way."

He looked a little startled by that, but Gail had no more time to coach him. *Who knew what was still happening above?*

# Chapter 99

*WINGS... a new concept... something to let he/she soar up and away... something that would let them see what was happening in the air above...*

"Aaron."

*... he played with designs and tested them in his mind's eye, trying for the ultimate simplicity...*

"Aaron."

*Recognition... Love...*

Pardell pulled himself inward again, tightening his awareness until Susan-Quill retreated to one side, quiescent, patient, while he interacted with *those that moved*. As he became more himself again, Pardell gently rejected the label, careful to keep to those which belonged to his human self.

*His love...*

*His friend?*

"Malley!" Pardell looked at the stationer. Even after a double shift, a brawl, and a night definitely not spent recovering, he hadn't seen this much wear and tear on the man before. And blood? "You're hurt!"

Malley brushed self-consciously at the stains. "No. Grant bled all over me. He's going to be okay. Tough guy."

Pardell had wondered when the two big men would come to blows. He winced. "You didn't—"

The stationer's sudden grin transformed what had been a very grim face until now back into something Pardell recognized. "Wasn't me—more's the pity. There's been another mini-revolution upstairs. Earthers can't seem to make up their minds about anything without a scrap of some kind."

"Sounds familiar," Pardell said dryly, drinking in the sight of his friend like that first cold one at Sammie's. "Now that you're here, what do you think of my planet?"

Malley gave a theatrical shrug and peered over his shoulder at the light coming over the mountains. "That's—interesting," he decided in a very noncommittal voice. "The ground doesn't seem to slide around, which is a relief. I wanted to see some growing things, but they're all gone."

*Regret . . .*

"Aaron? You with me here?"

Pardell nodded. "Yes, I'm with you. Susan—the Quill—understood what you said about seeing the plants. She's—sorry—so many were destroyed here. They'll grow back in a few weeks."

Malley examined the brown stalks all around him with what appeared to be greater interest. "Really," he said, *and probably would have happily gone off on this tangent,* Pardell decided, if Gail hadn't rested her hand on the box sitting beside her on the ground and said:

"It's time."

*Time.* The human concept had beginning, duration, and end. Pardell swallowed, abruptly unsure of all of it, feeling Susan-Quill's *determination* but having none of his own.

"There has to be another way," he heard himself say. "We can try harder—I can try harder. We didn't harm Grant or Malley—there were survivors on the ships . . ."

Her voice was gentle but implacable. "Can Susan protect hundreds at once? Thousands? Because that's what's coming." Gail's small hand rose upward and stabbed at the sky.

"What's going on, Aaron?" This from Malley.

*An ally!* "Releasing the other Quill will destroy Susan—her intelligence," Pardell explained quickly.

"And stop the Quill Effect," Gail said mercilessly. "Something Susan herself has asked us to do—Aaron. What's happening? Has she changed her mind? Is she afraid?"

*Peace . . . resignation . . . inevitability . . .* like a soft blanket sliding over his mind.

"Yes," Pardell almost shouted, trying to drown out the Other. "She's changed her mind! She wants to live! I want her to live!"

"Why?" Malley growled, stepping closer. His eyes were

blazing and hard to meet. "Why? Have you looked down at yourself lately, my friend? You're glued into a pile of fermentables, in case you haven't noticed. And this alien, begging her pardon, has killed a substantial number of our friends—and your parents. Seems to me, any chance to end this is worth taking."

"I understand . . . Aaron." Grant's voice was punctuated with pain-filled gasps for air. Pardell couldn't believe the man was standing, let alone had walked from the pod to stand here. "Because . . . we are . . . we . . ."

Grant slumped to the ground. As Gail and Malley hurried to him, Pardell felt Susan reflecting his *concern. Sympathy.* "Wait!" he called out. The others froze in place, then they all watched as dozens of Quill fragments slithered up Grant's legs and body, sliding over his wounded arm, coating the blackened flesh. Malley made a move to approach. "Wait," Pardell said again, more gently. "She's trying to help."

"Help?" the faint echo was from Grant as his eyes flickered open. The commander pushed himself up with his good arm, looking down at his now iridescent torso. "What—?" he began, then stopped. "It doesn't hurt," he told them, a look of astonishment crossing his face. The Earther trembled, not in pain, but with feelings Pardell couldn't help but share through the Quill. *Fulfillment. Satisfaction.*

*Joy.*

"First contact," Gail said softly. "Commander Grant, meet Susan-Quill."

A mass of straw rolled itself together beside Grant, and he sank into it with a bemused smile—the image of a man achieving his life's dream.

But his very next words weren't the support Pardell had expected—had hoped—to hear. "Thank her, Aaron," Grant said quietly. "I'll never forget this. And tell her how sorry I am."

Pardell didn't want to pass along the concept, but Susan-Quill was ahead of him. He lost himself in her *loneliness . . .* her *despair . . .* the *longing* for the touch of others of her kind. This wasn't how she was meant to live.

"This isn't how I was meant to live." Pardell heard the words coming from his mouth and couldn't honestly say which of them, *or was it both?* had spoken.

"Then I suggest we hurry, Aaron my friend," ·Malley said roughly. "Because those lights in the sky aren't stars, are they? And you know who's in them? Syd and Amy Denery, for starters."

"Gail," Pardell tasted her name, devoured her with his eyes. "You do it, please."

She seemed paralyzed. "Aaron—what's going to happen to you? What if . . ."

Susan-Quill's calm was all that let him say: "No regrets, then. That's what you said."

Gail pressed her lips together in a firm line, then nodded. The sun was sending beams over the mountains now, picking gold from her hair. Without another word, she reached down and unlocked the box in four locations.

There appeared to be a pool of dark oil in each section of the box. Gail plunged her hands deeply into two, bringing them up to show a Quill wrapped around each of her wrists, its color showing as the sunlight began to refract from its shimmering surface. As she stepped forward, arms outstretched in offering, Pardell saw Malley make a face before mirroring her actions. The stationer shuddered as the Quill touched his skin, but he didn't pull away.

When both of them were close enough, the Quill dropped from their wrists and squirmed into the mass around Pardell's legs.

*Welcome . . .*

"She's greeting them," he told the others, blinking away tears. He couldn't find words for the sudden rush of joy coursing through every part of him/her/them.

Pardell sensed a change almost instantly. The One, the Other . . . she was absorbing what was different from her, what was unique to each, from the new Quill. It was like a chord being struck, not just here, but across the entire plain, the entire planet—some rising harmony, a never-before-heard note of such surpassing beauty and passion the human in him began to attenuate, striving for a point of coherence, anything to become part of that new whole.

*Rejection* . . . he was blocked, kept away, isolated like a sore from the wonder of it. Pardell had never felt such grief, such aloneness. He begged, he pleaded. *Include me!*

A ghostly pressure, as though the mind behind the concept was expanding into something other than thought. *Remember* . . . came a whisper. *Love* . . .

Then silence.

"Aaron? Is anything happening yet? The first ship is landing."

Opening his eyes was a foreign act; the requisite movement of fine muscles the accomplishment of a stranger. Pardell looked outward and saw nothing, his mind filled with alien music, his thoughts unable to form anything but emptiness.

"Aaron!"

"Out of my way, Gail," a deeper voice ordered.

"Malley—No! Wait!"

Then PAIN. . . .

# Chapter 100

"MALLEY! Stop!" Gail's efforts to drag the huge stationer away were about as effective as the hilltop breeze at moving the drop pods, but she tried her best, encircling his arm with both of hers and digging her heels into the brown turf. He didn't appear to notice, merely pulling her along as his next swipe ripped loose more and more of the grass and Quill around Aaron's body.

Aaron's mouth gaped open, as if he screamed without sound. "Malley—stop!" she shouted for him. "You're hurting him."

A hand on her shoulder. "No—Gail—look at the Quill!" Grant used his hold to keep standing, but his grip was reassuringly strong. The Quill had dropped from his skin.

*The Quill.* They were leaving the mound, their dispersal into the surrounding soil melting away the structure almost as quickly as Malley was destroying it. The final layer of vegetation fell away from Aaron's upper body and they all took a step back.

"Dear God," someone said.

Below what the Quill had left exposed, Aaron's clothing was transparent, the fabric's weave remaining but most of the threads gone, as if dissolved. There were rents in various places, as though the Quill had needed larger openings to reach his skin.

Now, those rents were boiling with Quill, tumbling out to flow down and away from Aaron. His skin seemed to bubble before her eyes. *The pain on his face wasn't being caused by Malley,* Gail realized with horror, it was the Quill as they deserted their former host.

"We've ships landing—no reported injuries, Dr. Smith." The

disembodied voice from Bob made her jump. She didn't bother to reply.

Wounds were appearing: thin, bloodless lines lengthening as they watched, as though Aaron's skin cracked like some egg to free the imprisoned Quill. Similar fractures raced along his arms as they came clear of the straw; his hands shook with them, bits of Quill flying loose like drops of water.

Suddenly, there were no more Quill.

Aaron sank to his knees—a man again. The fractures closed, becoming a tracery of white where there had been gold.

The wind played with the dead grass, tossing hair into Gail's eyes until she pushed it behind her ear impatiently. "Aaron?" she said hesitantly.

Her voice—or the wind—made him shiver. "I'm . . . here." The words were faint and trembled, but wonderful. She started to move closer, hardly daring to believe it might be over and that he might be . . .

Grant's hand tightened on her shoulder. She'd forgotten he was there. "Careful, Gail," he rasped. "We've got remote handling gear on the pod—"

"The hell with that," Malley said, shaking himself like some bear coming out of hibernation. The stationer reached his hand down to Aaron. "Let's get out of here," he said with deliberate casualness.

Gail scarcely breathed. The 'sider stared at his friend's hand as if he'd never seen it before—the strangest expression on his face, as though he had to think through the ramifications first.

"You in there, Aaron?" Malley teased gently, and pushed his hand a little closer.

Aaron lifted his right hand, ever so slowly. The stationer reached past it without hesitation, wrapping his fingers around Aaron's wrist. Aaron's fingers closed to echo the hold, at first lightly, then digging in so that his knuckles whitened and his fingertips pressed hard into Malley's skin.

The two men stayed like that, as if frozen, then Gail saw the most incredible smile spread across Aaron's face. A cue for Malley, who heaved his friend up and out of the straw with a suddenness that could well have popped Aaron's shoulder from its socket—but he didn't seem to mind. Instead, he raised his other hand and held it out.

*To her.*

Grant gave her a little push.

Gail didn't know if she moved of her own will or if the look in Aaron's eyes had the power to simply eliminate the steps between them. But, suddenly, she was *there*, collected in a confusion of hands, arms, and tears—one set of arms strong enough to save them all from falling.

Much as she didn't want to stop the celebration—and much as the wondering way Aaron's fingers lingered on any flesh in reach endeared him to her even more—Gail knew it wasn't quite over.

Malley helped Grant into the *Athena*. As he did, she stood beside Aaron, watching the sunlight paint the plain below in yellows, browns, and green. Ships were coming down as they watched; Gail spared a moment to hope they were careful where they landed—there were signs of bustling activity around the three already findown.

Aaron was weak, but seemed so happy to simply lean against her that she couldn't bear to rush the moment. Besides, she had a question. Before she could ask it, he said quietly: "She's gone—Susan. My great-grandmother. The Quill Entity. Whatever name was right."

"There are Quill," Gail offered. While they now seemed shy—and, so far, no longer climbed legs or rode wrists—if she looked carefully, the telltale iridescence shone at the base of any intact stalk of grass.

"She's gone," he repeated.

"Did we do the right thing?" she asked then.

His lips twitched. "From whose point of view?" he asked with deliberate irony.

"From hers."

"Ah," Aaron was silent a moment, then recited from memory:

> . . . It will not matter that it was a mistake. It will not
> matter that the Quill are blameless. In the end, it is the

consequence, not the intention, by which we must judge ourselves. By which we decide our fate. And a heart can only take so much pain.

Goodbye, Grandson. May humanity recover its dreams.

Gail remembered the words and sighed heavily. "Susan Witts. Her last letter."

"How much of Susan-Quill was human?" Aaron asked, then continued: "Enough to feel as Susan Witts did at the end? To be unable to live with the death of others on her conscience? I don't know. I do know it wasn't enough for her to live alone, without her kind. So, yes. From her point of view, maybe it was the only thing to do."

He paused. "From my point of view? I'll miss her. I never thought I would. She's still out there, you know, tending her grass, humming emotion to distract anyone, anything, who might want to eat it. But that's all."

Malley came up beside them. "Nice lighting effect," he commented, seeming more relaxed without the presence of ominous stars overhead. Still, Gail decided, he'd done better than well. Aaron reached out his hand for his friend's, as if still astonished he could.

The stationer's eyes softened, but he used the grip to tug Aaron toward the pod. "You need to get dressed in more than a blanket, my friend," he suggested with a wink at her. "No matter what Her Ladyship thinks."

Aaron actually blushed under his sunburn. Gail was afraid her face mirrored his.

"And Grant's moaning and groaning," Malley continued cheerfully, as if he hadn't noticed. "Babbling nonstop."

"Fever?" Gail began to hurry her steps.

"No—court-martial. Seems he's the only one not expecting a hero's welcome."

Aaron stopped in his tracks to look at Malley. "A hero's welcome?"

Malley grinned. "Comm says there are more ships on their way here—and hundreds heading to the other terraformed worlds. Each and every one carrying people who owe their futures to us. Grant's just grumbling."

Gail looked at Bob, still hovering in earshot, and *knew*. "The Patrol ships," she said numbly. "They must have exchanged fragments and headed to the other worlds as soon as the *Seeker* passed along word we'd—eliminated the Quill Effect."

"By eliminating Susan. So they've gone to kill the other Quill Entities?" Aaron shut his mouth tightly, then nodded. "That was the plan all along. Your plan." He took his hand from hers; her palm felt cold and barren.

"I didn't plan this, Aaron. But—" *She had to be honest and, if he hated her now*, Gail knew, *she'd paid the highest possible price*. She stood up straight. "But I would have recommended it when we got back to the *Seeker*. The Quill on those worlds will, as Susan, be restored to their natural state. Ending the experiment is the best we can do—for that's what has happened here, make no mistake: an experiment with the Quill's evolution."

"You could have left them intelligent—we might have found ways to communicate—"

She cut him off. "Susan was only able to communicate through you, Aaron, and you were as unique as she was. The others? What if we could never talk to them . . . what if some were insane? Would you have them be alone? Susan told you how dreadful that was for her, how unnatural." Gail searched his face. *You know how that feels*, she added to herself. "Aaron, what matters more is . . . why. Why should we force the Quill into this state? So we don't feel alone in the universe? How is that fair to the Quill? As a species, we know they have the potential for thought—but don't you see, that has to be Quill-thought, Quill-intelligence—not something patterned after our minds. A Quill Entity, not Susan Witts as a Quill."

"I know," Aaron said. "I understand what you're saying. But I can't help wishing it had been different—that we could have done something more. That we could have saved her."

Gail pressed her hands over her eyes and cheeks, then said with the exasperation of the truly exhausted: "The colonists are safe, the stations will thrive, and I'm sure I can salvage everyone's career—hopefully including mine—based on those facts alone. Don't you think that's enough for one day, husband?"

There was a choked noise, as if Malley had something to add to that—*no doubt*—but restrained himself. Then Gail felt her hands pulled gently away from her face and found herself looking into a warm pair of hazel-green eyes.

"As long as you teach me how to kiss you before it ends," Aaron Pardell said in the wise way of newlyweds.

# Epilogue

"The science sphere reports all systems functional and all data has been uploaded from both the underground and orbital monitors, Dr. Malley."

"Just Malley. No 'Dr.' Damn techs," the big man in the lab coat grumbled, but failed to be convincing about it. The tech gave him a mystified look, then went back to her station.

First Officer Daniel Grant grinned, the movement emphasizing the crooked scars on his temple. "Tell them you never went to school—that ought to help."

Malley grinned back. "I'll try that next time." He dropped into the seat beside Grant, Captain Tobo being off-shift. "You ready to get us out of here?"

Both men gazed at the huge columnar screen, showing a world patterned in alien purple and golds. Third visit in as many years—the biologists loved the place, even though restricted to remote observation. Malley was always glad to leave. *The Quill Homeworld sent shivers down his spine.* He, for one, wasn't anxious to find a Quill doing anything more remarkable than hugging its chosen plant.

"First contact," Grant said instead of answering. "Whether it really happened, or was just a fluke, we made a mess of it."

Malley stretched out his long legs, stopping short of kicking the duty station in front of him. "Human nature," he replied. "Isn't that the usual answer?"

"Not good enough, Malley," Grant answered fiercely, a frown over the dark eyes. "We're alone in the universe—maybe we deserve to be."

"Now you sound like Aaron. As if anyone is as good at wallowing in might-have-beens." Their eyes met in perfect understanding. It had taken time—and several bottles of Scotch—for Pardell to finally turn his regrets to hopes for the future. That, and happiness.

The former stationer shrugged his massive shoulders. "According to Gail and various other brains on board, the Quill could be telling us stories sooner than we think. Hence our diligence in supplying this world with the latest spy technology. You realize, don't you, that you Earthers take an obscene interest in other people's business. There'd better not be any vids in my quarters." Malley paused, consideringly. "Or Aisha's. Or Petra's—"

"Spare me your list," Grant said, but with a laugh. "Fine. So the Quill will have the smarts to join our little club in a few thousand years, give or take a million. You and I aren't exactly going to be around for that, Malley."

Malley keyed a change in the view screen and stared up at the swirling mass of stars it portrayed without flinching. *Much.* "And that, my friend, is why the *Seeker* is living up to her name. You aren't the only one a little curious about who else might be out there." He chuckled deep in his throat. "Anyway, if Her Ladyship wants to find them, who are we to say they won't be found? So—when can we get going?"

Grant leaned back in his chair like a lazy cat. "It's going to take a while. They're at it again."

*Of all the times.* Malley started to get up to send a comm signal, then sat back with a sigh. "You had to authorize the extra cables," he complained to Grant, but couldn't help but smile.

*They could wait.*

. . . Outside, bathed in the reflected light of a world and its sun, a pair of space-suited daredevils raced each other from sphere to sphere, leaping and whirling through the void for the pure joy of each other's company.

As they would, always.

# Roll Call

## Thromberg Station and Vicinity

| | |
|---|---|
| Anzetti, Joe | Immie; Outward Five |
| Cohn, Jase | Outsider |
| Denery, Amy | Immie; Outward Five |
| Denery, Syd | Immie; Outward Five |
| Forester, Sector Administrator Garfield | Stationer; senior bureaucrat within Outward Five |
| Fournier, Rosalind | Outsider |
| Frasier, Bethany | Immie; Outward Five |
| Frasier, Gregory (Greggie) | Immie; Outward Five |
| Lang, Tommy | Stationer; Outward Five |
| Leland, Samuel (Sammie) | Stationer; Outward Five; bartender and owner of Sammie's Tavern |
| Leland, Silvie | Stationer; Outward Five; Sammie's daughter; Tanya's mother |
| Leland, Tanya | Stationer; Outward Five; bartender at Sammie's; Sammie's granddaughter |
| Logan, Mats | Stationer; former security officer |
| Malley, Hugh | Stationer; Outward Five |
| Malley, Roy | Stationer; Outward Five; Hugh's uncle |
| McNab, Josh | Earther; terraformer working with Susan Witts |
| McTavish, Yves | Immie; Outward Five |
| Pardell, Aaron Luis | Outsider; owner of the *Merry Mate II* |

| | |
|---|---|
| Pardell, Gabrielle (Gabby) Lace | Immie; former co-owner of the *Merry Mate II*, wife of Jer |
| Pardell, Jeremy (Jer) | Immie; captain and former co-owner of the *Merry Mate II*, husband of Gabby |
| Pardell-Witts, Raymond | Earther; original owner of the *Merry Mate II* |
| Raner, Aaron | Stationer; foster father to Aaron Pardell |
| Nateba, Chief Administrator Leah | Stationer; seniormost bureaucrat on Thromberg Station |
| Wilheim, Fy | Immie; Outward Five |
| Witts, Susan P. | Earther; former Chief Terraform Engineer, Titan U |

**Earth Research Council Deep Space Vessel *Seeker*** (All Earthers)

| | |
|---|---|
| Benton, Marsha | Science Sphere; Tech |
| Choi, Eric | Crew; Remote sensing specialist |
| Cooper, Jeremy | Science Sphere; Tech |
| Gilbert, Michael | Crew; Chief Engineer |
| M'Daiye, Dr. Ute | Science Sphere; Senior Biologist |
| Lynn, Dr. Aisha | Science Sphere; Senior Biologist |
| O'Shay, Kai | Science Sphere; Tech |
| Philips, Paul | Science Sphere; Tech |
| Reinsez, Dr. Manuel | Xenopathologist; Titan University's representative on the *Seeker* |
| Sanders, Petra | Crew; Assistant ship's engineer |
| Sazaad, Dr. Tabor | Science Sphere; Senior Biophysicist |
| Smith, Dr. Gail Veronika Ashton | Chief Scientist, Project Leader on the *Seeker* |
| Szpindel, First Officer Frank | Crew; second-in-command |
| Temujin, Dr. Stanley | Science Sphere; Senior Bioengineer |
| Tobo, Captain Tomoki | Captain of the *Seeker* |

| | |
|---|---|
| Vincente, Secretary Mario | Titan University; Departmental Secretary, Xenological Studies (on Titan) |

**First Defense Unit Assigned to the ERC *Seeker*** (All Earthers)

| | |
|---|---|
| Adams, FD Yvonne | Combat Specialist |
| Aleksander, FD Kelly | Tech Specialist; second-in-command |
| Allyn, FD Matt | Operations Specialist |
| Baier, FD Les | Combat Specialist |
| Barber, FD Mike | Operations Specialist |
| Bennett, FD Clarisse | Tech Specialist |
| Bob | 'bot, deployed on Pardell's World |
| Cornell, FD Wayne | Tech Specialist |
| Dafoe, FD Catherine | Operations Specialist |
| Giardi, FD Romeo | Operations Specialist |
| Grant, FD Commander Daniel R. | Seniormost FD assigned to *Seeker* |
| Helios, FD Amy | Operations Specialist |
| Janssen, FD Lara | Comm and Code Specialist |
| Johnson, FD Neil | Combat Specialist |
| Krenshaw, FD Carl | Deployment Specialist |
| Loran, FD Natasha | Combat Specialist |
| Miller, FD Jana | Tech Specialist |
| Miller, FD Matt | Tech Specialist |
| Mitchener, FD Art | Combat Specialist |
| Peitsch, FD Dianne | Deployment Specialist |
| Picray, FD Michael | Weapons and Code Specialist |
| Sasha, FD Morgan | Combat Specialist |
| Sensun, FD Liu | Tech Specialist |
| Taggart, FD Chris | Tech Specialist |
| Tau, FD George | Comm Specialist; second-in-command |
| Wigg, FD Trish | Tech Specialist |

# TANYA HUFF
## *VALOR'S CHOICE*

"Readers who enjoy military SF will love Tanya Huff's
VALOR'S CHOICE. Howlingly funny and very
suspenseful. I enjoyed every word."
—*scifi.com*

Staff Sergeant Torin Kerr was a battle-hardened professional.
So when she and those in her platoon who'd survived the last
deadly encounter with the Others were yanked from a well-
deserved leave for what was supposed to be "easy" duty as
the honor guard for a diplomatic mission to the non-Confedera-
tion world of the Silsviss, she was ready for anything. Sure,
there'd been rumors of the Others being spotted in this sector
of space. But there were always rumors. Everything seemed
to be going perfectly. Maybe too perfectly. . . .

0-88677-896-4 $6.99

Prices slightly higher in Canada **DAW: 149**